BUTTERFLY RIVER

LUC VAN HUISZEN

ISBN 978-1-7377691-0-1 Paperback
ISBN 978-1-7377691-1-8 Ebook

PROLOGUE

The Renegade Brigade

"A band of brothers, we are,
A rough and rowdy bunch,
We eat nails and shit stones,
Bust heads and break bones,
We ride the wind and surf the sky
The fuckin' Taliban are gonna die
You're gonna die, motherfuckers,
You're all gonna die!"
—Pvt. Calvin Jones

The night had turned dark and wet with the rain beating down on the hapless men of the reconnaissance team led by Robbie Olsen. They called themselves the Renegade Brigade, a tough bunch of battle hardened vets along with a few inexperienced POGs. They split into two groups - one flanked the outer fringes of the hill where the Taliban were thought to be and the other took the more direct route up towards the ridge. The silhouette of peaks and valleys that spanned across the horizon lent credence to the rugged, mountainous terrain that the team had to negotiate. And to add to their misery, the rain had intensified turning the ground into a slushy, slippery hell.

They were halfway up the incline when gunfire from above erupted catching them by surprise and then the night lit up in a fiery hailstorm of bullets, blazing arrowheads with flickering yellow tails, streaking towards them from all sides. It was an ambush.

"Get down! Get the fuck down!" Robbie barked hitting the dirt behind a large rock.

The return fire from his men was sporadic and wild, shooting at invisible enemies, wraiths melting into the darkness. He heard screams and grunts of pain and in the ensuing chaos, a voice yelling, "We gotta get outta here!" and someone else muttering, "Fuck! I've been hit!"

He saw bodies falling, rolling down the hillside disappearing into the thick abyss of night. The enemy had them pinned in their crossfire and unless he did something soon they would all be dead.

He got up and ran towards the top firing blindly at spectral shadows that blended into the rock face until he came to a plateau in front of a tunnel. He stopped and looked around, muscles aching and gasping for breath, but there was no one there only wispy threads of smoke spiraling upwards accompanied by the acrid smell of gunfire. He stood motionless confused by the deafening silence. And then, just as suddenly, he was surrounded by a swarming mob of Taliban fighters. They had materialized, almost magically, from behind the curtain of a rolling, diaphanous mist that had replaced the rain.

They were silent, staring at him with their piercing, unforgiving eyes. Tall rangy men hardened by war, driven by hate, their turbans and beards making them seem identical, one indistinguishable from the other. They parted as he walked towards the tunnel. He could hear the murmur of 'Allahu Akbar' building until it reached a thunderous rumble. He had to get away and pushing past the men, he ran into the gaping mouth of the tunnel.

Once inside, he stood still waiting for his eyes to adjust to darkness and when it did, he had to stifle the urge to scream. The place was teeming with the bodies of dead Afghani children and women, their sightless eyes boring into him, filling him with guilt and horror.

"This can't be. Where am I?" he said to himself stepping over the arms and legs of corpses and stumbling towards the light at the other end.

When he got there he saw more bodies but these were riddled with bullets and had been decapitated. And as he approached the gruesome pile, he saw the heads stacked high and realized that these were his men. He looked around and the Taliban fighters had surrounded him again. They were smiling, their knives drawn...

He woke up covered in a cold sweat.

A SOLDIER'S STORY

The rain from the previous night had left the hill dangerously slippery and this coupled with the unpredictable gusts of wind had slowed his descent to a crawl.

"Is that a body?" Robbie Olsen mused, squinting to get a better look. His view was partially obscured by the trees that lined the riverbank, "You're seeing things, Olsen, it's got to be garbage bag or a pile of trash," he muttered to himself.

He had been trekking in a remote part of the Appalachian Mountains, past the town of Monson, miles off the trailhead leading to the Hundred Mile Wilderness and except for his dog, Ronin, and a rather nosy black bear, he hadn't seen or passed a living soul. Not in the last three days.

This was rough, unexplored terrain and reminded him of the Continental Divide Trail that he had trekked a few years back. There was a small path near the tip of the Triple Divide Peak that was similar to this one, a bit steeper in places but just as rugged. The one major difference was the lack of a clear trail. Here, he was cutting a virgin path, trekking through uncharted territory.

He had stopped on a large rocky ledge about halfway down the mountain. It provided both respite and an opportunity to soak in the panoramic scenery. The sight of the mountain tops poking through the blankets of white, fluffy clouds and the early descant of nature's awakening never failed to lift his spirits. His muscles burned and twitched from the exertion and his breathing was heavy and labored. This was both torture and therapy. The trek had been a lot more strenuous than he had anticipated but it had been worth it. It represented a revival of sorts for him - a rekindling of his faith and the resurrection of hope; both requisite salve for a troubled soul.

He took a sip from his water-bottle and looked again at the strange form that seemed so incongruous with the rest of the surroundings.

"It must be a garbage bag. Those jerks have no respect for nature," he said to no one in particular. He was referring to the weekend tourists he had run into a few nights back.

The only reply he got was the chirring sound of the leaves as the breeze swirled through the ubiquitous Sugar Maple, Birch and Oak. The shifting shadows created an origami of capricious, molting shapes that came alive at one moment only to die and remain still the next.

His mind wandered back to that night at Fat Joe's where the altercation with the out-of-towners had occurred. They were a raucous bunch who were seated in the corner of the small restaurant talking smack, laughing a bit too loudly and were making a general nuisance of themselves. As he stood on the ledge basking in the splendor of the morning sunshine, the events of that evening came rushing back in vivid color and he grimaced at the memory.

He was familiar with the type; he had run into them before. Not this bunch but they were all the same – weekend hikers and thrill seekers with their BMWs and Gucci bags who hired guides so they could experience danger without really putting themselves at risk. What a bunch of pussy-assed crap! Their shrouded agenda revealed itself on Monday mornings at the weekly meetings or around coffee machines, sharing photographs and tweets only to impress their followers on Instagram, Facebook, Twitter and the like. Robbie resented the deceit and the obtuse, privileged lifestyle they embodied. He knew he was being judgmental but they were just the types to donate to wildlife and environmental conservatories while their personal lifestyles were almost always lived to the contrary.

"A bunch of assholes!" he hissed and looked down at Ronin and shook off the memory.

The dog cocked his massive head as if understanding exactly what was being said. Ronin was a Caucasian Mountain Dog, sometimes referred to as the Caucasian Ovcharka or the Russian Bear Dog. He was huge standing almost thirty four inches at the withers, the high point of his shoulders, and weighing over two hundred pounds. His thick, reddish tan coat, floppy ears and obsidian eyes gave him a bearlike appearance. This ancient breed was primarily used to protect sheep and had a well-deserved reputation for fighting off predatory wolves and bears.

Robbie ran his finger through the dog's thick fur taking comfort in his presence. Ronin was not just a companion dog but had been his emotional support during those early years after Afghanistan. The alcohol, weed and opiates had done nothing to help him deal with the PTSD except to leave him indifferent and numb. He kept sinking deeper and deeper into a depressive morass unable to stave off the revenant memories of his dying and dead comrades until one night, after killing half a bottle of the tequila, he sat in the darkness,

Glock in hand, contemplating the exit strategy that so many of his brothers had taken. It wasn't the first time the thought had crossed his mind but at that precise moment, the phone rang, shaking him back from his suicidal stupor.

"Robbie?" The soft feminine voice asked.

"Yeah, it's me. Who ..." He stuttered, "What ... what do you want?"

"Robbie, this is Rachael, pull yourself together! Listen to me - Derek and I are coming to see you. We'll be there tomorrow afternoon. Robbie? Robbie, did you hear me? We'll be there tomorrow afternoon. I've got a surprise for you, soldier, so get yourself together!"

Rachael was his younger sister and Derek was her husband. He had tried to dissuade her with drunken gibberish and nonsensical excuses but Rachael was as stubborn as the mules on their father's farm. She was coming and he had better get ready.

That was four years ago and the surprise, an ungainly little puppy, was the reason that Robbie was able to crawl out of his "dark place" and get back to being functional again. The responsibility and constant attention it took to deal with a puppy had given him a new purpose. He slowly weaned himself off the pills, weed and alcohol and got himself back into shape. The helpless little fur-ball had grown into a formidable animal, a dependable and loyal friend. The bond between them was stronger than any other, even those he shared with his brothers in the Rangers. And that was saying something.

Just then a gust of wind kicked up around the riverbank and he caught a glimpse of a fluttering ribbon, flashes of gold and maroon, and realized immediately that he had been wrong - it was a body and not a trash bag.

"Come on, big dog, let's go!" Robbie said and they headed down.

The trail had narrowed, snaking precipitously down through the foothills to the base of the mountain. They made a cautious descent, glissading in choreographed synchrony, zigzagging through the trees, brush and rocks like dancers in a complex ballet. A wrong step could mean a twisted ankle or a broken leg or worse and there would be no help in this remote place.

For Ronin, it was in his DNA. His ancestors had roamed the Caucasian mountains from Armenia into Southern Russia and those bloodlines gave him the uncanny ability to avoid loose rocks, crevices and other scree common in the Eastern Appalachian trails. His balance and agility would have made a mountain goat proud.

Robbie, on the other hand, had discovered his natural propensity for climbing and hiking during the Mountain Phase of the Ranger Assessment and Selection Process appropriately termed RASP. It was at Camp Merrill located in the remote mountains near Dahlonega in Georgia that he had excelled reveling in the intensity and challenges of the course but now, he indulged in his passion as a way to heal, to clear his mind and to come to terms with his past.

He would spend days researching the most remote locations, then make detailed plans and disappear for weeks or months on end. Together, they had hiked and trekked most of the notable trails from California to Maine which included several sections of the Appalachian Mountain Range but this region in Northeast made for some of the most beautiful and dangerous trekking. In their many expeditions, the two of them had encountered Grizzlies, Elk and Moose, Black Bears and even Mountain Lions but never a dead body. This was a first.

They cut a path through a small field covered in brush before crossing a dirt road and down a shallow gully to the river's edge. The dead girl lay face up and mostly on the riverbank with the water lapping gently at her feet.

He leaned over the corpse to get a closer look.

"Damn!" He muttered under his breath.

She was a pretty girl no more than sixteen or seventeen. The ribbon he had seen had been woven into her fulvous hair in a type of Halo Braid with a bow on top of her head. Her face had the ashen hue that often accompanies death. Her dress was ripped and torn in several places and she had only one shoe on, a pink and white sneaker with laces undone. The small tattoo of a blue butterfly above her left ankle contrasted starkly against her pale skin but what made it unusual were the emblematic words in French, *'L'amant des Papillons'* – The Butterfly Lover. It was done in French script and formed a semicircular sickle under it. There were telltale bruises on her neck and arms; indications that there had been a struggle but it was the bullet hole in the center of her forehead that had ended her young life. The speckled stippling under where the bullet had entered was a clear indication that she had been shot at close range.

He dragged her further up onto the embankment to keep her from sliding into the river. The killer or killers could still be around and warning signals shot through his brain like an express train. Years of training and combat had ingrained in him a healthy paranoia. He straightened up and looked around, scanning the trees and bushes; listening for telltale sounds that might be an indication of danger but there was nothing, just the cacophony of birds and the gentle babble of the river. He waited, standing still for what seemed like an eternity before fumbling through his rucksack to retrieve his cellphone. A few snapshots would capture the situation in far more detail than any description he could muster. Walking away would have saved him a lot of trouble but that wasn't in him and this girl deserved better. What if this had been Rachael? He was determined to make sure that at the very least her family got some form of closure.

He scrolled through the pictures taking time to study each shot carefully. The unusual tattoo of the butterfly, with its intricate detail, would certainly help in the identification.

Satisfied that he had what he needed, he checked again for a signal.

"No luck, buddy!" he muttered looking at Ronin.

He moved around hoping that the cell tower gods would smile favorably on him but gave up after a few attempts. He recalled a statement regarding insanity. It was quote attributed to Albert Einstein that defined insanity as doing the same thing over and over again and expecting a different result. That would certainly characterize his actions. He decided to walk to a more open space away from the shadow of the mountain. Ronin meanwhile was sniffing the body with the natural curiosity peculiar to dogs. This was the first dead body that the dog had encountered.

"Stay" he commanded, "I'll be back soon. You stay here," and with that Robbie dropped his backpack and walked up the grassy slope and onto the dirt road.

The big dog growled in protest and then lay down near the dead girl's head. He wasn't happy being left behind but his innate protective nature took over and if it came to it, he would defend the corpse with his life.

There was a spattering of cottages and trailer homes that Robbie had seen when he first arrived here. It was customary for him to spend a day or two scouting the surroundings before undertaking the actual trek or climb. He would do a thorough reconnaissance, familiarizing himself with the back roads and hidden trails so in case of an emergency he could get help. It was an old habit learned through experience and honed over time so now it had become a part of his routine. He made detailed notes and sketches on the small pad he carried with him and would refer to them often until they were indelibly etched in memory. He knew exactly where he had seen the homes and headed towards them.

He hadn't gone but a short distance, around a sharp bend in the road, when he spotted a man walking a hundred yards or so in front of him. He broke into an easy trot to catch up and called out, "Hey mister! Hey, wait up … do you have a phone?"

The stranger turned towards Robbie. His movements were slow and deliberate. He was in his early fifties, tall and lean, with a receding hairline. His face was gaunt and his eyes were red and swollen as though he had been drinking or crying or both. He was hunched over, with his arms crossed tightly across his chest bracing against the elements.

"Do you have a phone? There's a dead girl back there by the river," Robbie repeated while motioning towards the body, "and I don't have a signal." He paused then added, "I need to call this in."

The man studied Robbie; jaws clenched and his face a sullen mask. There was an awkward silence before he replied, "It would serve you well to mind your own business. This doesn't concern you." His voice was deep with the hint of a peculiar drawl.

"Wait a minute! 'You know about the girl?" Robbie was incredulous. When he got no answer, he continued, "She was just a kid! It should concern all of us. Now, if you have a phone let me have it or I'll be on my way." He didn't try to hide his irritation.

The man uncrossed his arms, looked around furtively, his eyes darting left and right, before speaking again. "It's pretty obvious you're not from here. You know nothing of what goes on around here. We take care of our own." He paused then added as an afterthought, "You seem like a nice young fella so I will say it again, mind your own business and go back to wherever it was you come from. This is no place for you." There was a noticeable change in the man's tone, a steely edge that was hard to miss, "She's gone and nothing will bring her back!"

With that, he turned away and continued walking, stooped over, hugging himself. Robbie was about to follow but the man abruptly changed course. He shuffled down the shallow causeway and hurried across a grassy knoll before disappearing into a cluster of trees.

The warning wasn't lost on Robbie. He had half a mind to chase the stranger down and take his phone by force, a citizen's mugging of sorts, something that could be easily justified if he needed to but decided against it and instead kept walking down the road in the direction of the houses.

It was a good twenty minutes before he caught sight of the nearest dwelling, a small log cabin. It was nondescript except for the corrugated metal roof which was painted a bright red. The side of the cabin facing him was windowless and overrun with honeysuckle vines that reached up to the top of the wall, some encroaching past the roofline. The yard was covered in underbrush and weeds that spilled over onto gravel driveway. A black pickup truck, a Nissan Frontier, with floodlights mounted on its roof was parked a few feet from the stone steps that led up to a narrow wooden porch. There was a woodpile of logs scattered unceremoniously by the stoop and a pair of lantern lights, tarnished and cruddy, flanked the front door. The place was in obvious disrepair.

"Oh boy, this doesn't look promising!" Robbie thought. He looked around but the closest house, a trailer home sitting high up on a slope, did not engender much confidence either.

He checked his phone for the hundredth time but there was still no signal so despite his apprehension he walked quickly past the truck, up the steps and knocked on the door. There was no response. He knocked again, harder this time, and heard the shuffling of feet followed by a terse, "Hold on to your horses! I'm coming."

A few seconds later the door swung open without the preliminary caution. The man was short and squat. His black hair, thick and unruly, matched an untrimmed mustache and beard. The large horn-rimmed glasses seemed oddly out of place on his square, angular face and gave him a nerdy look which was misleading. The handgun strapped to the man's waist was warning enough to set right any misconception.

He gave Robbie a swift once over and abjuring any pleasantry asked, "What can I do for you?"

"I need a phone. I don't have any reception," Robbie answered, holding his cell phone in plain view, "there's a dead girl a few miles back."

There was an immediate change in the man's expression.

"A dead girl you say?" the man asked, cocking his head and furrowing his brow.

"Yes, with tawny-blond hair and wearing a pink dress. She's been shot …" he paused then added, "She has a tattoo of a butterfly above her ankle."

At the mention of the tattoo, the man's expression changed to shock. Robbie pulled up the photographs he had taken earlier and handed his phone over to the man.

It took a few minutes for the shorter man to study the images before he handed the phone back to Robbie. The pain was clearly etched on his face, "Who'd want to do that? She was a sweet little gal who wouldn't hurt a fly and I mean literally!"

"So, you know her?"

"Yes, that's Marisa. Marisa Gorecki, that's her name. She's been missing for a week now." He responded, shaking his head in disbelief, "I knew her. She loved butterflies and this place is filled with them. It's the trumpet honeysuckles." He made a motion towards the side wall. "They swarm here in spring and summer for the nectar. She'd come by to catch a few for her collection."

The man glanced past Robbie scanning the driveway, "How did you get here? Did you walk?"

"Yeah, I had to. My car is back at the motel, the Sleepy Crest … the one off 15."

"That's a shithole if ever there was one!" was the man's blunt response.

"I wouldn't disagree," Robbie replied, "but it suits my needs - cheap and conveniently located."

"And full of vermin!" the man added.

He looked Robbie over again before stepping back, "Come on in, I'll take you to the Sherriff's office, it's on my way to work." He waited a few seconds lost in thought, "Marisa dead? I can't fuckin' believe it! We were all hoping that she would turn up somewhere, unharmed. A lot of kids run away for home especially here." He stood dejected, looking distracted.

Robbie hesitated. "Listen, I don't want to intrude. I can call if you have a phone … save you some trouble."

"I don't have any reception either. We're in the fuckin' boonies if you hadn't noticed. Don't believe the bullshit they give you when they sell you the service. You know that shit about 99.9 percent coverage … more like 10 percent here. And I don't have a landline." He paused then continued, "It's no trouble. Sit down and make yourself comfortable. I'll be ready in a few minutes." He took a few steps toward the bedroom but stopped and turned back, "Sorry, I didn't get your name?"

"Robbie Olsen."

The man walked back and shook Robbie's hand, "Anthony VanArcen. Just call me Tony. Sit," he said again waving towards a worn out, rumpled sofa, "give me a couple of minutes and we'll be on our way."

Robbie wasn't sure which was the more painful – the drive to the Sherriff's office or the thought of dealing with the local authorities. On the drive there, VanArcen chattered incessantly. It was non-stop palaver about his job working for the North Eastern Park Services as their Forest Maintenance and Regulatory Officer. The desultory ranting included his meager pay, his boss who had to be the world's biggest asshole, the inbred locals and the dangers associated with his assignments.

"You wouldn't believe the number of times I've been accosted by some dumbass hillbilly with a gun and told to bugger off!" His eyes widened with the retrograde memory then continued, "These fuckers think they own it all. What they own is a shitty little plot of land hardly big enough to piss on but they assume that the State property is theirs. They cut down trees, build sheds, outhouses and stills … fuckin' moonshine stills all over the place. You can't spit without hitting one!" He turned onto a main road that was paved and continued, "I've been shot at a few times just checking on some dead trees - dead trees, for chrissake! Can you believe that shit? One time the bullet whizzed right by my ear, scared the bloody piss out of me!" He glanced over at Olsen, patting his holstered gun, "This here, it ain't for show brother, it's for fuckin' survival! I should be getting hazard pay."

"Why not get another job or go someplace else?" Robbie asked and regretted it the moment the words left his mouth.

"Because my gramps was from here and I'll be damned if I let these inbred assholes chase me off. We used to call him 'Pappy' as kids and it just stuck. Everyone called him Pappy even his friends. Pappy VanArcen was a stubborn and tough old coot but always had time for us kids … took us fishing, hunting, taught us to fight, stuff that little boys should know. My father left as soon as he could but Uncle Danny, Dad's younger brother, he stayed back. He died a few years back and left me the cabin … needs some work but it was Pappy's before him so I'm going to keep it."

VanArcen was quiet, lost in thought for a moment before resuming, "You've heard of Daniel VanArcen, haven't you?"

"No, can't say I have."

"Damn boy! He was the best bareknuckle fighter this side of the Mississippi … maybe in the whole fuckin' country! Everyone knew Danny VanArcen, he was a legend!" It was more of a protest.

"Sorry, never heard of him and honestly, I'm not interested in bareknuckle fighting or any fighting for that matter."

"Ah, you're one of those liberal pacifists, eh?"

Robbie glanced at the man but remained silent.

"That's strange. You have that look, you know, that 'don't mess with me, man' look."

"Hmm, I've never heard that before."

"No, you do. It's the first thing I noticed about you, Olsen … that Charlie Bronson, tough guy aura."

Robbie had to suppress a smile, "Charlie Bronson? You're dating yourself."

"Okay, the Rock then … whatever! You know what I mean."

"Nope."

You're a regular chatterbox, aren't you?" Tony retorted, trying to get Robbie to engage.

"Can you go a little faster? I need to get back. My dog's with the body."

"Sorry, I know, I know. I talk too much. Liz tells me that all the time. Liz is my gal. Pretty as a picture! Never could figure out what she sees in me. I mean, she could be a fuckin' model." He paused to catch his breath, "Big tits, nice ass and as sweet as can be but once the lights go down, Mama Mia! Watch out, she's a damn hellcat!" He had a big smile on his face, winked and added, "I'm not complaining, mind you, but some days that little gal plumb wears me out!"

Robbie had to smile, "You're a lucky man but that's a little more than I need to know. Now if you could just speed up a bit …"

"Oops, here I go again! Damnit all! I'm trying not to think of Marisa. I can't wrap my head around that shit, you know, it's like …fuck!" he exclaimed loudly slamming the steering wheel with the heel of his palm, "Fuck! Fuck! Fuck! I saw her just the other day, smiling and laughing, hanging out with her friends…"

He continued, a little more deliberately, "She wanted to be a Lepi …" he stuttered, struggling with the word, "Lepidopterist."

He peeked over at Robbie and paused for effect, "That's a person who collects and studies butterflies."

"Yeah, I know."

"Well, I *didn't* know. It's a big fuckin' word and I got to be honest; I had no idea what it meant. She had to explain it to me and now …dammit!" his voice trailed off and he fell quiet. He drove lost in thought until they arrived at their destination.

The Sherriff's Office, which served as the local law enforcement authority, was a small, flat-roof stone and wood structure with large windows and an arching entranceway and had both the American and State flags flying high above the rooftop. There were three cars parked in the parking lot. A full-size 1973 Jeep Cherokee that said 'Cherokee Chief' on the back, a beat-up old Toyota Corolla of questionable vintage and a relatively new GM Suburban. The sides of the Jeep and the Suburban were emblazoned with 'Sheriff's Office' and under that, 'Chase River County'.

"Listen, a bit of advice," VanArcen looked around then continued, "Hank Carlson owns this shithole town. He owns Dolan, the sheriff, and maybe the deputy and everyone else here. Nothing happens without his knowledge and more importantly, his approval. Just so you know."

"Okay. I have no idea who that is but what does that have to do with the girl?"

"I don't know, maybe nothing and then again, maybe everything." He paused then added dejectedly, "I'd better go before my mouth gets me into a wagonload of trouble. Poor Marisa! Old man Gorecki will be devastated."

They shook hands before Robbie exited the vehicle. He closed the door and leaned in through the open window, "Listen, thanks for the ride."

"Hey, do me a favor," VanArcen requested, "leave me out of this … I really don't need the hassle."

Robbie slapped the top of the truck lightly, noncommittal, "You take care!"

The inside of the Sherriff's Office was nondescript, consisting of one large room with three desks, a row of file cabinets, a coffee station and a vending machine in one corner. A wide corridor led to the rear where he assumed the cells were located. The two desks in the back of the room sat side by side with a narrow aisle between them and the third desk, where the receptionist sat, was in the front a few feet from the entrance.

She was a heavyset woman with long fingernails, fake eyelashes and dyed blond hair worn in a ponytail; a middle-aged sleeper with garish makeup and way too much lipstick. Her top was an embroidered number a few sizes too small and her perfume was cheap and overpowering. It was all he could do to keep from turning away.

"Well, hello there!" She cooed as he walked up to the desk.

"I'd like to report a dead body … a young girl."

"A dead girl you say?"

"Yes, a young girl … she'd been shot."

"Joe!" She screeched, turning back towards the man seated behind her, "Joe, you'd better get your ass here. I think we've found Marisa!" She looked up smiling coyly and asked, "You're not from around here, are you, handsome?" And when he didn't answer, she continued, "Where did you find her?"

But before he could respond the man was by her side. He was tall, a good three to four inches taller than Robbie, with sandy hair, pale gray-blue eyes and a strong jawline. He had a no-nonsense air about him.

Robbie handed him his phone, "I took some pictures."

While the man was scrolling through the shots, the woman peered over his arms, tiptoeing to get a better look, pressing her ample breasts against the officer, "God, she's really dead! The poor girl!" she exclaimed, genuinely distraught, the photographs driving home the reality.

"That's Marisa alright," he confirmed, his voice emotionless, "she's been missing for a week."

The woman turned to Robbie, moving closer, "Was she assaulted, you know, raped?"

"There were bruises on her arms and neck and her dress was torn, other than that I couldn't tell. The forensic pathologist will have to determine that."

"The forensic pathologist?" she blurted out loud with a sarcastic laugh and grabbing onto Robbie's arm, "That's a riot! We've got Gilbert Dorsey and that's all the forensics we're gonna get! Unless you take the body to Abbot or Guilford."

The commingled fragrance of lavender and jasmine permeated the entire room and proved to be too much for Robbie. He inched backwards, as discreetly as possible, an involuntary response to the osmatic assault.

The man smiled, commiserating, "You get used to it. Sally loves her essential oils and because of it, I've gone nose-blind. My wife insists that I can't smell a damn thing anymore!"

"What's wrong with it?" the receptionist protested, "Lavender helps you relax and gets rid of anxiety and jasmine –"

"I'm Deputy Joe Bradley," he cut her off; "and you are?"

"Robbie Olsen."

"And Jasmine improves your mood! God knows the mood here needs improving!" she snapped and plopped back into her chair.

The deputy shook his head in resignation and then to Robbie, "Alright Olsen, I need to make a phone call and then we'll head out."

He looked at the pictures again before handing the phone back, "Where did you find her?"

"About a mile or so past the railroad tracks towards Devil's Ridge. You have to go past the houses on Mulberry and hang a right onto Depot Road."

"Before or after the bend"

"After the bend, about four or five hundred yards," Robbie answered.

"I think I know where that is but I'll follow you."

Robbie hesitated and thought about what VanArcen had cautioned and decided to leave him out of it. "I don't have a car; I walked here."

"That's a long walk." He studied Robbie for a minute, eyebrows raised, before adding, "Alright, let's get going."

He turned to Sally and instructed, "Call Gil and tell him to look for my car on Depot towards Devil's Ridge. He needs to get there as soon as he can. Then call Chief Dolan and let him know that we've found her. He can talk to the family. If he doesn't want to do it, I'll call on them later, once I secured the site."

"Okay, will do." She looked at Robbie and smiled, "You be careful, handsome, the gals here are desperate … like the Desperate Housewives. They will eat you up!"

"I'll risk it," was the nonchalant reply.

Echoes of her cackling laughter and the intoxicating redolence of lavender and jasmine followed them out to the parking lot.

The drive to the body gave the deputy the opportunity to question Robbie: *'When did you get here, where are you staying; what were you doing on the mountain; how did you come across the body,'* all seemingly relevant and harmless enough but then it took a turn.

"Why did you lie about walking to the station?" he asked looking over at Robbie, "I saw you getting out of Tony VanArcen's truck."

Robbie studied the cop for a few seconds, "Then why did you ask?"

"Curiosity I guess. In my line of work you try and figure people out. I wasn't sure what you and VanArcen were doing together."

Bradley answered which begged the obvious question.

"You're not implying that we are suspects, are you?"

"Everyone is a suspect until we catch the bad guy or bad guys. But do I think you and Tony were involved? No! I knew Tony's grandfather, Pappy VanArcen and his uncle, Danny. They were tough, hard men but salt of the earth folk. His father, Peter, left this place when I was a kid." He stopped, rolled the window down and spat. "Damn, I can taste the jasmine … Sally will be the death of me!"

He waited then resumed his declamatory monologue, "Where was I? Oh yes, Tony's dad, Peter … he was the odd one. He left Chase River Town when he was seventeen or eighteen. I don't know Tony that well but what I do know of him tells me that he is a decent guy. Now you, Olsen, you are a different kettle of fish. You didn't kill the girl but there's something about you that worries me … I need to figure that out."

"There's nothing to figure out. I didn't mention VanArcen as a courtesy to him. I don't know the man and had never met him before today. He was nice enough to give me a ride but made it clear that he really didn't want to be involved. That's it."

Bradley shot him a quick look, "Tony's a yapper so I'm sure there's more to it but things have a way of coming around. You keep poking and prodding and stirring the pot and sooner or later things begin to shake loose. People start saying stuff and then one thing leads to another. I guess old habits die hard … I'm suspicious by nature. That's what makes me a good cop."

"Then why weren't you out looking for her?" Robbie questioned, recalling VanArcen's line about everyone being owned by Carlson.

Bradley's expression changed, his lips pursed in a thin, hard line, "We looked for her. The whole town looked for her. Three days, twelve to fourteen hours a day. Do you have any idea how large of an area there is to cover? Mountains, caves, rivers, forests … it would take years to find someone if they didn't want to be found. And, kids run away especially from here. We've had several teens run off – some of them call from New York or Boston or wherever and some, well they just disappear." He paused, jaws clenched, "After three days there were only two outcomes, she had run off and didn't want to be found or she was dead."

"She could have been alive in someone's basement or attic being held against her will? That's happened before." Robbie offered.

"That's a possibility but I know this place and I know the people. I grew up here. She had run off or was dead. I was pretty sure of that."

He waited but when Robbie didn't respond, he continued, "I may be a lousy husband, Olsen, and I doubt I'll ever win 'Father of the Year' but I'm a good cop. So don't go taking the high road on me. And, I'm not sure what Tony said to you but no one owns me, no one!" He stressed the last part with a passion that surprised Robbie.

When Robbie didn't react, the deputy said nothing more. They drove in silence until Robbie motioned for him to stop.

"Here, pull up here," he pointed to the clearing where he had left Ronin guarding the dead girl.

"Stay in the car," Robbie instructed getting out of the vehicle.

"What? What do you mean?" the deputy was surprised.

"Stay in the car. I need to get my dog – he's not very friendly."

As soon as Ronin saw Robbie walking down the declivity towards the river, he bounded over and jumped on him, knocking him down. They play-wrestled, rolling around on the grass until the big dog had him pinned, licking his face and growling playfully.

After a few minutes, Robbie squirmed out from under and got up brushing the grass and dirt off his clothes, "You missed me, didn't you boy?" He ruffled the dog's fur behind his ears, something that Ronin liked.

The dog wagged his tail and nudged Robbie almost knocking him down again. When Bradley finally opened the door, Ronin growled and moved towards him; the playfulness was gone and the innoxious demeanor had turned menacing in an instant.

"Easy boy, easy now … it's okay, come with me, come on," Robbie commanded, grabbing his collar. He stroked the top of Ronin's massive head reassuring the dog and led him to a grassy patch away from the body. "Here, stay here."

When Ronin lay down, Robbie called out, "You can come down now."

"That is a serious fuckin' dog! What is he?" Bradley inquired, walking cautiously towards them.

"He's a Russian Mountain Dog, also called an Ovcharka."

"What is that, a cross between a Saint Bernard and Godzilla? Hey, you're sure it's safe?" He hesitated when he got closer, hearing the low guttural, growls coming from where Ronin lay.

"You're safe, don't worry." Robbie assured him.

"I guess *nobody* likes cops, not even man's best friend!"

"It's not you, Bradley, trust me, he doesn't like strangers but he'll stay put."

By the look on the deputy's face it was evident that he wasn't fully convinced but he went over to the body and did a quick preliminary examination without touching it. He scribbled some notes on his pad and then went back to the car and returned with yellow, crime-scene tape and proceeded to cordon off the area.

"Did you handle the body?" he asked, looking over at Robbie.

"I did. I moved her higher onto the embankment away from the water. I didn't want her slipping into the river." Robbie replied and then delineated, "I held her by the shoulders, her upper arms really, and tried to be as careful as possible."

Bradley pulled his notepad out and was jotting down the additional information when a white van pulled up. It had a large decal on the side that read: "Gilbert Dorsey & Son" under which, in smaller letters, "Funeral Home & Mortuary Services".

Two men got out of the van; an older man in a dark jacket and corduroys and a boy, about eighteen or nineteen, in blue dungarees with a sweat shirt. The older man was the same person he had seen earlier walking away from the body, the odd Rasputin who warned him to mind his own business. He nodded when he saw Robbie but other than that gave no indication of their prior meeting.

The boy was a strapping lad; big arms and barrel chested and a vacant look on his face. He walked past Robbie but stopped when he saw Ronin.

"Nice dog. Big doggie …" he said with a silly, fatuous grin.

The warning growl, deep and angry, didn't seem to faze him. He edged closer towards Ronin with his right arm extended, "Good boy. You're a good boy."

The big dog growled and with fangs exposed, began to get up.

"Hey, stop right there. Stop, you're going to get hurt!" Robbie cautioned loudly, stepping quickly in between the boy and the dog. "Down, boy, it's okay. It's okay."

"Nice dog. I like him." The boy seemed oblivious of the danger.

"He's not friendly, kid, and if you are not careful, you're liable to get hurt … seriously hurt." Robbie cautioned gently pushing the boy back.

"Junior! What are you doing? I told you to get the camera." The older man yelled at his son, "Leave the dog alone and go on, go now, get the camera and take pictures of Marisa."

He waited until the boy had made his way back to the van before turning to Robbie, "Sorry mister, my boy is simple minded. He doesn't know any better. He happens to like your dog, that's all."

"It's alright. We just need to be careful," Robbie replied.

The boy came back with a camera and once his father had checked it, they went over to the body. Dorsey stood by giving his son instructions regarding the various angles and perspectives that were needed while the young man crouched over the body and began snapping a series of photographs. It was obvious that Junior had done this before and was familiar with the protocol.

Officer Bradley walked over to Robbie and said, "Sorry about that. I should have warned you about Junior. It didn't occur to me."

"No sweat; I'm glad he didn't get hurt."

"He's a good lad, dimwitted but has a good heart."

Robbie was silent watching the father and son take pictures of the body and the surrounding area.

"He wasn't always like this. He was a perfectly normal kid. About five years back, he went swimming with a bunch of his friends and nearly drowned. He was blue when we fished him out of the water. I performed the CPR and rushed him to the emergency ward. He was never the same. The damage to the brain was irreversible."

"That's too bad."

"He's all that Dorsey has. The boy's mother died of cancer the year before the accident and his daughter moved out right after. She's living with some guy on the other side of town. Gil is a good man. Life just dealt him some bum cards."

Robbie didn't say anything.

"In some odd way, I feel responsible for the kid." Bradley confessed, "Like saving his life has left me with an additional responsibility, if you know what I mean."

"You did what you could. You can't be expected to watch his every move. That's responsibility belongs to his father."

"Sure, that's logical but I can't help how I feel." Bradley countered.

Before Robbie could reply, Dorsey came back to where they were standing.

The man shook his head and said, "A damn shame."

"I can't say I'm surprised. After a few days the chances of finding the victim alive are almost zero. She was a sweet gal … she didn't deserve this." Bradley declared.

"No one deserves this but it hurts when it's someone you've watched grow up … she's like my kid, Joe, I don't know what I'd do if something happened to Marylou." The man replied with the hints of the soft southern twang.

"Marylou and Marisa were good friends, weren't they?"

"They knew each other. Not really good friends, a passing hello and such." Dorsey corrected.

"I'll want to speak to her at some point. Is she still at Carlson's Mill?"

"Yes, but I'm not sure of her shifts anymore. She's living with that bum, Greg Humphry. He sits on his ass playing video games and smoking weed while she busts her ass."

"Kids, what are you going do?" Bradley commiserated. "A few more years and I'll have some of the same problems. Annie's ten and she already got pictures of some baby-faced kid pasted on her wall … not looking forward to the next few years."

The two of men stood by the body talking quietly to each other. There was the comfort of familiarity between them that had worn well over time. Robbie wondered if the mortician would mention their earlier meeting but decided to let Bradley deal with it. Anything that he'd say would only lead to more questions and add to the time he needed to be there and that is the last thing he wanted.

He waited a few minutes before deciding that his presence was redundant, "If you don't need me … I'll be heading back."

The men stopped in mid-conversation. Bradley, looked over, "Thanks for your help, Olsen. I may have a few questions later so stick around, okay?"

"You have my phone number and you know where to find me," Robbie replied and gathered his backpack, "Let's go, boy."

"Do you need a ride?" Bradley asked, then looking at Ronin, "On second thoughts, I take that back; I don't fancy being that dog's lunch!"

"Hey mister, can I pet the dog?" the boy called out.

"Not just yet, maybe later if you get to know him better, okay?" Robbie answered.

"What kind of dog is that?" Dorsey asked, his curiosity getting the better of him.

"The nasty kind," was the reply and as though on cue, Ronin growled his displeasure.

THE SLEEPY CREST MOTEL

y the time they got back to the motel it was late afternoon. The Sleepy Crest Motel on Route 15 was a rundown, ramshackle, roadside dive catering to truckers, transients and whores but it did offer some advantages – it was walking distance to most of the hiking trails and suited his budget. He stopped by the front desk while Ronin waited outside.

"My keys, room 216," Robbie said brusquely, his eyes adjusting to dim lighting in the dingy room.

The man behind counter was engrossed in a girlie magazine. He was shaved bald and heavily muscled, no neck, hairy arms, beady eyes and a lined, craggy face that told the story of a life lived between sleazy dumps and the slammer. He was wearing a sleeveless singlet that revealed tattoos of snakes, wrapping around his neck and torso. He gave Robbie a quick look, put the magazine down and then got up to retrieve the old-fashioned brass key tag hanging on a pegboard behind him.

"You the guy with the big dog?" he questioned, obviously unfriendly.

"Yeah."

"Keep him on a leash. He's scaring my girls."

Robbie reached for the keys but the man held on to them, his grip tightening around the key tag, his face a hard mask, "You hear me, bubba? I won't ask again."

The threat was obvious and Robbie's first impulse was to confront the lawless buzzard but it wasn't worth the trouble, instead he shrugged, "Not a problem." his tone was conciliatory, "I'm tired and it's been a long day, okay?"

The man tossed the keys onto the counter and went back to naked pin-up that he had been ogling. *'Friendly bastard'* Robbie thought as he walked out.

Room 216 was on the second floor at the end of the walkway. It had a small balcony that overlooked the parking lot and was adjacent to a stairwell that wound directly down to an open field. Robbie had specifically requested that room. It made things convenient for Ronin and since it was the furthermost away from the front office, he would be assured of some peace and quiet. The pavement skanks usually conducted their trade near the front driveway of the building often calling out to the truckers and night crawlers looking for drugs and sex. The stairway on the side also offered a quick exit in case of trouble. He recalled what Bradley had said, *'old habits die hard'* and smiled, *'They do, they surely do'*.

Most of the weekend hikers and tourists chose places in the larger towns staying at hotels that offered WiFi, room service and other creature comforts and for that, Robbie was thankful. The last thing he needed was a bunch of wannabes playing the fictional Jeremiah Johnson during the day and partying late into the night, proclivities that invariably led to trouble and trouble was the one thing he avoided.

After a long and much needed shower he drew the shades, lay back on the bed and promptly fell asleep. It wouldn't take long for the events of Kunduz to filter through his subconscious and reemerge to seek retribution. Sleep was a time to pay the proverbial piper; there could be no refuge for his mea culpa.

Kunduz, Afghanistan

THE YEAR 2015,
EARLY AUTUMN

It was an October evening about thirty miles outside the city of Kunduz. There had been rumors that the Taliban were preparing for yet another push to take the city. Robbie and his team were part of the US-led NATO force sent there to train the ANA, the Afghan National Army, and assist them in their efforts to drive out and hopefully, destroy the Taliban.

The training proved to be a slow and tedious process. Most of the recruits in the ANA were civilians, young men with no past military experience and to make matters worse, many of them were sympathetic to the Taliban. These disaffected men usually joined the ANA to learn about weaponry and study military tactics but with a hidden agenda. It wasn't uncommon to see soldiers that the Americans and NATO forces had trained defect to join the enemy or some other extremist faction like the ISIS. The Afghan Army needed recruits but there was no way of determining the motive behind the soldiers who enlisted. This was a poor country and men needed to feed their families, it was also a fractured country with influences from several foreign groups - this was a conundrum that had no real solution.

The day had started like any other in autumn, sunny and warm with blue skies kissed by feathery white cirrus clouds scattered high like stringy cotton candy. But towards the afternoon, with little warning, dark undulant thunderclouds rolled in blotting out the sun. It had rained off and on late into the evening and the men had retired to their tents, some, including Robbie, were engaged in a game of Blackjack when Captain Harris poked his head in and said, "Olsen, get your men ready and secure the periphery. There's word of enemy activity. Maybe nothing but let's make sure."

Yes sir!" Robbie responded standing up and tossing his cards down. Captain Harris was one of the few officers that Robbie respected. He was a no-nonsense battle-hardened veteran who engendered loyalty from his men.

"Fuck! I was sitting on Ace Ten!" was a dejected groan from one of the soldiers as the game came to an abrupt end.

"The T-man's in his cave smokin' a fuckin' hookah," interjected another, "he ain't coming out in this shit!" It was an oblique reference to the Taliban.

"You heard the man." Olsen turned to two of his men, "Frankie, Juan ... find Jabroot and the kids and get ready. We leave in ten minutes."

The "kids" that Robbie referred to were a pair of 21-year-olds, Calvin Jones and Jaimie Cranston. You would be hard pressed to find two more disparate men. Calvin was a black kid from Detroit, street-tough and wise beyond his years. Jaimie, on the other hand, was a redhead from Aurora, a small town in Nebraska. He was a naïve and friendly farm boy. From the moment they met the two men had hit it off and were inseparable partly because they were the least experienced and were considered POGs by the rest of the men but mainly because the inherent chemistry between them transcended race, cultural bias and social strata. *(A POG is a derogatory term for a soldier who lacked combat experience and stands for Person Other than Grunt).*

The two were huddled just inside the tent taking shelter from the downpour waiting for the rest of the team. Jaimie pulled a photograph out of his pocket and was studying it when Calvin grabbed it from him. It was a laminated picture of Cranston's wife and ten-month-old son. They had often talked about their families and their lives back home but had never shared pictures.

"Wow! She is beautiful … fuckin' gorgeous!" Calvin blurted out, staring at the dark haired girl in the photograph.

"That's not a she, dumbass, that's my son!" Jaimie corrected.

"I meant the woman, birdbrain, she is fuckin' gorgeous. Tell me that's not your wife!"

"I knew exactly what you meant. I was giving you a way out of it. You don't drool over your friend's wife! That's not done. Now, give it back."

"Sorry, man, but it was a compliment. She *is* beautiful. When you told me you had a pretty wife, I thought *'yeah sure! A fat-ass, huckleberry farm girl'*, but she is really beautiful. I'm sorry, didn't mean no disrespect." He looked at the picture again and added, "You're one lucky hombre!"

Jaimie snatched the photograph back, "Apology accepted. Abby *is* beautiful. Now what do you think of my son, Aaron James Cranston?"

"He's a kid! What do you want me to say? He's cute. You had better hope that he takes after your wife because it would be a life of hard fuckin' labor if he looked like you!"

Jaimie laughed, "I don't disagree! Look at him," he said, staring proudly at the photograph, "have you ever seen anything cuter?"

Cal shook his head and asked, "Hey, your wife, does she have a sister?"

"Yup! And, she's single."

"That is sweet. When we get back you've got to hook me up, brother!"

"We'll have to go to Japan."

"She's in Japan?" Cal was incredulous.

"Yeah, she's a Sumo wrestler; you know, one of those fat-ass, huckleberry farm gals," Jaimie quipped back.

"Oh, fuck you, Red!" he retorted, elbowing Jaimie in the ribs.

"A huckleberry farm girl, where do you come up with this shit, Cal?

They laughed and then Cranston got serious, the change was not lost on his friend. He looked over, curious, "What's on your mind?"

Jaimie hesitated then said, "I want you to promise me something."

"Relax, I won't hit on your wife, I promise, at least not when you're around," he replied, tongue in cheek and eyes dancing with mischief.

"Stop the bullshit for a minute; I'm serious. You need to promise me something, Cal, it's important, and if it is too much of an imposition, just say so and I'll understand."

"Okay, okay … what's up?" His curiosity piqued unsure where this was heading.

"If something happens to me, if I don't make it back, you promise you'll go see my mom and dad and Abby," he hesitated again, wondering if he was asking too much from someone he had befriended recently, but they had forged a unique friendship and this felt right. "Go see them and tell them that I died fighting for my country and that they were always in my heart and thoughts. Always! Promise me that."

For a second Cal was about to respond with an offhanded quip but the look on Jaimie's face changed his mind, his smile disappeared and he replied, "I promise. But nothing's gonna happen to you, okay, *nothing*! Trust me Red; we'll go get a drink and laugh about all this when this shit is done."

"You do it in person, Cal" Jaimie was earnest, "no phone calls, text messages or emails … you go see them."

Cal nodded, "I'll go see them, I give you my word. Now quit … you're giving me the fuckin' creeps!"

Cranston looked at the picture again before slipping it back into his pocket, "I've told them all about you, Cal; told them you were the brother I never had."

Cal didn't say anything. This unexpected admission caught him by surprise; it was baffling and tugged at his emotions. He felt overwhelmed and looked down at the ground, then without a word he turned and grabbed the redhead in bear hug.

"Nothing' gonna happen, you big lug! We're the Renegade Brigade, remember?" his voice choking up with emotion.

"Yeah, I know… eating nails and shitting stones!" Jaimie answered, "Thanks, Cal, I feel better now. Okay, you can let me go, people are gonna talk."

Just then Robbie Olsen, Frank Bocelli, Juan Guerrero along with the Afghan, Jabroot Durrani, walked up, their slickers dripping wet and glistening in the rain.

"What's going on? You ladies look like you're in love," Frank Bocelli quipped.

"Nothing's going on! I was just telling Red that he's better not bend over when our pal is around," Cal nodded towards the big Afghan, "he would love nothing better than to drill a pale, freckled red-ass!"

Jabroot spoke fluent English and understood the implication

being made but he chose to ignore it. He stood expressionless waiting for instructions.

"We just saw you dry-humping little gingerbread boy here!" Guerrero interjected, "so if I were Jaimie, I'd worry about you!"

"Okay, cut the shit," Robbie said. "Let's get our heads on right. Jabroot, you take point. Cal, Jaimie the two of you stay close to him and focus."

The Afghan knew the terrain like the back of his hand and was a valuable interpreter. He didn't really care for the Americans but his hatred of the Taliban far outweighed any resentment he harbored towards the US troops. The Taliban was responsible for the deaths of several members of his family and he was determined to see them destroyed. *If Allah wanted him to use the Americans to achieve that goal then so be it.*

He nodded at Olsen and gave Cal and Jaimie a precursory glance before moving out, "Come on, you follow me."

Frank looked at the two young soldiers, "You assholes quit the jabbering and focus. Do you understand? Cal, get your shit together or the only sky you'll be surfing is up in heaven."

"Yes sir!" was the immediate response.

"Can we get Jake?" Robbie turned to Juan.

Jake was a fearless German Shepherd trained to sniff out explosives. This war-dog would charge into the heat of battle without hesitation and as far as the men were concerned, he was one of them.

"No sir. The Czech team has him. They are patrolling the north side."

"Shit! There's nothing on the north side and we could've used him tonight," Robbie muttered, the added with resignation, "It is what it is, let's go."

When they had gone a few yards Frank turned to Robbie, "Maybe I should take point with Jabroot?"

"It's alright. At some point these POGs have to learn … trial by fire."

"Then let's bring Calvin back here." Frank persisted, "He can be a real pain in the ass. One of these days that Arab is going to gut him."

"He's not an Arab, he's an Afghan." Robbie corrected making the obvious distinction.

"They're all fuckin' ragheads!" Frank spat back.

"Cut it out Frank, sometimes I wonder about you." Robbie admonished, "And nothing's going to happen. Jabroot is not going to gut anyone. Cal has potential, a bit of discipline and he has what it takes to be Special Forces, maybe even the Rangers."

"No way," Juan opined, "those fuckin' Meat Eaters ain't gonna want no oxygen thief … he jabbers too much." The men in the Special Forces were often referred to as 'Meat Eaters'.

"You're forgetting what you were like, Guerrero. The kids will be okay so the two of you ladies just relax."

"I hope you're right," Frank conceded reluctantly, "I have this shitty feeling …"

"You need to get laid," Juan added, "I know, I have the same feeling. I've had a freakin' hard-on going on three days now!"

"And here I thought you were just happy to see me, Juanita!" Frank needled.

"I can't believe I have to listen to this shit all night," Robbie hissed as they marched out.

The main encampment sat on a small butte. It provided the advantage of high-ground which made it easier to secure and defend but the darkness coupled with the rainfall made the walk down from the ridge slow and arduous. The rain came down like sheets of silver daggers, stabbing at their faces, swirling about them with the changes in the wind, heavy one moment only to let up the next. The soldiers were having a difficult time of it; eyes blinking constantly, straining to keep sight of the man in front while navigating the rocky terrain. The big Afghan had stumbled a few times but was able to right himself. Once they reached open ground the patrol eased into a steady cadence and the men relaxed.

Calvin Jones and Jabroot Durrani didn't care much for each other. Sometimes when people meet there is an intuitive and inexplicable dislike but in this case the root of their discord could be traced back to what the young American said when he greeted the Afghan.

"Hi there, Osama," Cal joked, "Hey, once this shit is done, you can go to Hollywood and play that motherfucking terrorist. You must have had the same fucking father!"

That didn't sit well with the Pashtun and from that day on, they had been at odds. Cal now had a target and took every opportunity to harass the big man.

"Hey Rooty Fruity," he called out over the drumming of the rain. No response. "Hey man … come on, don't be like that. Let's talk, keep this gig interesting."

"Leave him alone, Cal," Jaimie attempted to deflect the teasing.

"Come on, just having some fun, brother!"

When Jabroot didn't respond, Cal continued, "Hey Osama, do you have one of those Bacha Bazi dancing boys?"

It was common knowledge that many Pashtuns engaged in the reprehensible practice of "Bacha Bazi" where older men dressed up attractive young boys as dancing girls and used them for sex. It was a practice punishable by death but the law was seldom if ever enforced.

The Afghan did not respond and Cal persisted, "Come on, you like fucking little boys, don't you? Hey, it's better than fucking goats!"

Remarkably, Jabroot held his tongue but that only seemed to encourage Cal, "Hey, King Kong, does your mama know you have a little boy hidden somewhere? Or maybe he's at home dressed up as a bitch … helping mama cook dinner, eh?"

That did it. The mention of his mother got to Jabroot. He slowed down so Cal and Jaimie were closer, right behind him. "You do not speak of my mother. Show some respect. And why you call me names? My name is Jabroot not Osama or Rooty or Fruity," he was obviously irritated.

"Pay him no mind Jabroot; he's just pulling your string, having some fun." Jaimie interjected trying to mollify the angry man.

"This is not fun. And, it is not Jab-Root. It is said like J'brood."

"Jebrut?" Jaimie tried.

"Better. J'brood," he repeated.

"Fuck that!" Cal interjected, "You didn't answer me, boy, where's your Bacha Bazi?"

The Afghan's roughhewn features contorted in anger, "What are talking about, man? That is against Islam and I do not do shit like that!"

"Sure you do. I know all about you Pashtuns … fucking little boys and goats are what you guys do!"

"You better be careful, pretty boy, or I will fuck you!" The tall Afghan growled.

"I'm sure you'd like that you sick bastard! But I ain't dressed up like some dancing Bazi-bitch!"

"Hey, ease-up Cal, give him a break. Okay?" Jaimie tried to calm things down. He could sense the Afghan reaching his breaking point but it was pointless, the two antagonists were locked in.

"You will die here soon, you bastard, you and the rest of you foreign devils!" Jabroot Durrani bristled; his face in a dark rage. He had stopped and was now facing Cal and Jaimie.

"Go fuck a goat!" Cal shot back, bleating loudly, "Baa! Baa!"

Without warning, the big man lunged and pushed Calvin with

such force that it sent him sprawling to the ground, "I will teach you, you bastard, I will …"

Calvin Jones was not a small man but he was caught off guard and was surprised by the suddenness coupled with the force of the assault. He responded, "You fuckin' Hajji …" his words were cut-off by the shattering flash that lit up the night sky.

When the bomb exploded, Robbie and the others were still several yards behind the commotion up front. They were oblivious to the scuffle between Jabroot and Jones. The inclement conditions compounded by the darkness had created the perfect foil. The bright flash followed by a deafening roar dramatically altered their status quo and the night exploded in a slushy concoction of rocks, muck and dirt. It was like a scene from a movie except the hero didn't get up, dust himself off and run to save his men. The ringing in their ears caused by the concussive forces of the bomb blast shuttered out all other sounds and they instinctively dove, facedown, taking whatever cover they could find. It was several minutes before any of them could hear or think clearly.

"Is everyone okay?" Robbie called out as he began to regain his senses. His first reaction was concern for his men.

"I'm okay. My fuckin' ears!" Frank responded, trying to suppress the pain, then added, "Juan's alright, I think … "

He got the thumbs up from Guerrero and added, "We're both good."

Robbie had managed to get behind the remnants of a derelict, old, mud and brick wall. His mind was still reeling from the effects of the blast. His vision was unfocused, creating a jumbled collage of real and imaginary shapes that floated in some nascent, alternate reality. The terrifying spectrum of the carnage was made worse by the opaque dimension of night.

"Jaimie!" he tried again, "Calvin?" There was no response,

"Jabroot? Are you guys okay?" Robbie's voice echoed strangely, the reverberations in his ears modulated by the continued ringing.

An eerie silence ensued in the aftermath and except for the steady beat of the rain the night was inexplicably quiet again.

Jaimie was dazed. He knew he was hurt badly but he wasn't sure where he was or why he felt this way. He managed to get up on all fours before rocking back onto his haunches. He looked around in confusion, his fingers wiping the blood and dirt from his eyes with Cal's rap doggerel playing in his ears.

"A band of brothers, we are,
A rough and rowdy bunch,
We eat nails and shit stones…

Or is it, we eat stones and shit nails… his mind was exploding with a million disconnected thoughts.

We bust heads and bury bones,
We ride the wind and surf…

He fumbled for his rifle while a chimaera of images and thoughts flashed through his addled brain. *"Mom, Dad, Abby …God, Abby, where are you? I have to get back… get back home to Abby and my baby. I'm coming home, son. Abby! God I miss you so much. Cal, hey buddy, are you okay? Abby, Aaron … I'm coming home! We ride the wind and surf the sky…"*

His sight seriously compromised, he staggered to his feet, rocking unsteadily from one foot to the other. He let out a soft groan as the pain racked his shrapnel riddled body and he stumbled forward, lurching blindly into the darkness.

"Get down. Jaimie, get down!" Robbie shouted as loudly as he could but it was obvious that Cranston couldn't hear him. He scrambled to his feet and was about to run towards the wounded man when he was pulled back down, forcefully.

"Are you fuckin' nuts?" Frank Bocelli snarled.

"Let me go, damn you, let me go!" Robbie barked and tugged free.

A sudden burst of gunfire from their left flank split the night. The golden stilettoes raced across the darkness towards where the Jaimie stood staring blindly into the night. For a moment the quantum of time and space was bridged and he stood still. He saw the flashes in slow motion, fireflies darting towards him. His body jerked spasmodically as the bullets tore through him. There was no pain, the mind had shut down, and he fell in a crumpled heap his fingers clutching tightly to the photograph of his wife and son. The blood streamed from his lifeless body in angry rivulets and was washed away by the unforgiving rain.

Cal was luckier, by virtue of being thrown to the ground by Jabroot, he had avoided being hit by the fragmented projectiles but his proximity to the bomb blast had left him far more susceptible to the shock from the concussive forces radiating out from the core of the explosion. It almost knocked him unconscious. A strident, high pitched siren emanated from the back of his skull and tore through the center of his forehead crippling him at least temporarily. He fought desperately to cling to his senses, to shake loose from the red haze pressing down on his brain but it was to no avail. The piercing hum continued on and on and on building to an unbearable crescendo. He covered his ears rolling from side to side seeking reprieve but it refused to let up, strangling his rationale and severing the ties that bound him to his very consciousness.

After a few minutes though, almost miraculously, through the din, pain and confusion, he felt the noise lessening, diminishing in its intensity, gradually subsiding until traces of clarity returned. And while he grappled with the vicissitude of his circumstance, he thought he heard a groan just a few feet from him. He could see the body of the Afghan lying next to him, unrecognizable, his head and body blown apart from the direct hit. There was another groan, softer this time.

"Jaimie? Hey, Jaimie, are you okay? Say something, brother," but there was no answer. Then as he was about to get up, the staccato sound of machine gun fire filled the night and he saw his friend convulsing in an uncoordinated dance, stumbling and falling lifeless to the ground.

Cal cried out in disbelief, "No! Jaimie, no … no, no, no …"

He crawled, hands desperately clawing at the slush riddled dirt to get to his friend, "Speak to me, Red, speak to me!"

He shook him violently, unable to reconcile his compromised perception with the reality before him. "Wake up, bro, come on, please wake up …" he kept shaking the body hoping that this was a bad dream until finally reality registered. He laid his forehead on his friend's chest and sobbed, deep heaving sobs that wracked his entire body.

"I promised I'd take care of you…" he muttered, between sobs, "… you dumb huckleberry farm-boy!"

Rationale and reason are often deterrents to courage and uncompromising courage defies logic. His reasoning was long gone. Cal got up to his feet and rushed towards the enemy screaming like some demented banshee, a fearless warrior seeking revenge. There was no thought of safety or the ramifications of what he was about to do, just anger; anger and an unyielding rage.

"Die you motherfuckers, die, die …" and hell's fury returned.

> *We ride the wind and surf the sky,*
> *You motherfuckers are gonna die…*

There were muffled screams and groans of pain from within the dark trenches of the enemy lines followed by a disjointed eruption of commands before gunfire from all sides rained down on him while he continued to rush towards the killers of his friend.

I'm coming home, Ma, your boy is coming home.

There was no scripted escape, alone and outnumbered, the odds were against him. With his life draining out he dropped to his knees, looked skyward in a final act of defiance and fell, gun in hand and eyes wide open.

It was over just as quickly as it had begun. The spirit of Calvin Jones had moved on. The rain came down in silvery sheets, drawing the curtain on another stanza of this dark Cyprian charade; in a case of life imitating art, the intrepid soldiers lay still in death bathed in Aphrodite's tears. The joyous chants of "Allahu Akbar" filled the night.

"Cover me!" Robbie yelled and ran staying low to the ground, ducking, dodging, left and then right while Frank and Juan provided protective fire, squeezing round after round without break.

He ran past Jabroot Durrani's mangled body to where Jaimie and Cal lay. His intent was to carry them back but another explosion knocked him off of his feet and backwards and the last thing he heard was the sound of Captain Harris's rumbling voice, "Get those shit-eating bastards!" and the rat-a-tat-tat echo of machinegun fire.

Autumn 2019, Appalachian Mountains, Maine

SLEEPY CREST MOTEL OFF RT. 15

The rhythmic banging on the wall mercifully jolted him from his nightmare. Robbie rolled out of bed, covered in sweat, grabbing for his Glock, a model 20. He sat, heart pounding, listening to the lascivious sounds coming from the adjacent room. There was a moment of sensory disconnect; an irrational coalescing of the repetitive banging and the staccato gunfire from his somnolent nightmares that bridged the schism between violence and sex.

"Fuck me, Daddy, fuck your baby girl … yes, yes … harder, Daddy, harder!" The fake little-girl voice could be heard clearly through the flimsy walls. The whore's phony moans and mewling cries were accompanied by the loud grunts of the trucker.

"You like your daddy's fat cock, don't you, you little slut?" His voice was hoarse and desperate.

"Oh yes, yes, yes … oh, yes daddy!" Her sensual parody aimed at getting the man off as quickly as possible so she could reenact the salacious farce with another John. Time was money and for her and an access to drugs.

Robbie got up and shook his head, *"Whatever rocks your boat, amigo,"* he thought as he slowly made his way to the bathroom.

The sounds of passion were a painful reminder of his self-imposed abstinence; a result of the acrimonious break-up with his girlfriend two years ago. *"It's been too long, Olsen, way too long …"* he thought trying to shut out the frenzied banging and cries of pleasure as the man approached the final act of their sordid play.

He washed his face, wet and slicked back his hair and studied his refection in the mirror. It was a sensitive face – high cheekbones, large wideset eyes, a prominent nose, full mouth and a strong chin. There were lines and scars that he wore as badges of honor – some earned in battle and others that marked his thirty-four years on this earth. Women had always found him attractive but what *he* saw, and the only thing he saw, was the pain and sadness in his eyes. The nightmares were less frequent but the discovery of the body and the death of a young girl returned him to the battlegrounds of Kunduz. The threads of grief and pain had tied him to Marisa Gorecki in ways that he wasn't prepared for. It revealed the minuscule cracks in his psyche and the vulnerability of his emotional state.

He threw on a Polo shirt over his blue jeans before stepping out onto the balcony – it was dark outside. The night was cool and breezy. It had been over fifteen hours since his last meal and his stomach growled in protest. He had fed Ronin when they returned but the meat was gone so all he had was dry food. He had to get some more meat for him this evening.

"You stay here." He said to the dog, "Be a good boy, Ronin, I'll come back soon."

The dog growled in protest but moved back from the door and reconciled to his fate, lay down.

The parking lot had several light poles but only two of them were functional, illuminating the space immediately under them. The rest of the lot was in varying degrees of darkness. Robbie had parked his car under one of the working lampposts, the one that was nearest to his room. His SUV, a 2010 Ford Expedition EL, had a modified interior to accommodate Ronin and a completely rebuilt engine which boasted over a hundred and thirty thousand miles. The big V-8 still purred like a kitten.

The extended cargo space in the back allowed him to incorporate a small ice box and still leave enough room for Ronin's dry food, Robbie's gear and other accessories that were essential for their long trips. The luggage space was augmented by a beat-up old Thule cargo box that attached to his roof-rack. Ronin's food took up a lot of the space and he had to install secret compartments under the floorboard for his rifle and handguns. His weapons of choice were the Beretta M9 and the Glock 20. He almost always had one of them on his person.

Robbie was close to the SUV and about to open the door when he heard a high-pitched squeal. He couldn't quite make where it was coming from but it was obvious that the person was in distress. He walked slowly towards the sound, his hand on the Glock tucked into the waistband at the back of his jeans.

A slight waif of a girl was backing away from a hulking man who was partially concealed by shadows. He had her by the front of her tank top.

"Please, Al, please don't hit me ..." the girl pleaded, "I don't know what you are talking about! I swear! I was never on Facebook or Twitter ... I don't even have a computer."

The man smacked her on the side of the head and snarled, "You lying cunt, what did you see? Who did you talk to? Who is 'Taxi Girl'? I'll carve that pretty little face up … then no one's gonna want to fuck you, do you want that?"

"No, I swear, you can ask Angela, I don't know anything about that!" She pleaded in terror, "I would never do that …"

He was about to hit her again when Robbie saw them and cut in, calling out to the man. "Hey, stop … let her go. Let her go, now!"

The man spun around towards him and stepped out from the shadows. It was the thug with the snake tattoos. His bald head and muscle beach look created a menacing sight.

"You better beat it chump, before I break both your fuckin' legs!" was the snarling response. He kept his grasp on the girl but was facing Robbie, assessing the threat.

They were about ten yards apart and except for the three of them, the parking lot was deserted. Robbie began walking towards them, his voice hard with a steely edge, "You let her go."

"This ain't your concern, motherfucker. You leave now and you'll save yourself some serious pain!"

"You don't listen, do you asshole? Let her go!"

That did it. The man gave the girl a rough shove and closed in quickly, "You're dead, motherfucker. I'm going to rip your fuckin' heart out and feed it to your dog!"

The pimp came in low and fast throwing a wild, looping haymaker aimed at Robbie's head. The instinctive reaction would be to pull straight back but that would have been a mistake; he would have left himself open to a follow-up left hook. Instead, Robbie stepped in, deftly blocked the punch with his left forearm and in one fluid motion, threw a short arcing elbow aimed at the bridge of the man's nose. There was sickening crunch of bone and cartilage accompanied by an anguished cry. The man grabbed at his face with both hands; a reaction to the pain that exploded in lights and spread through his brain. He staggered blindly, his eyes tearing and he felt the salty metallic taste of blood trickling down the back of his throat - it made him want to throw up. He didn't see the knee that drove his nuts upwards into his abdominal cavity. He gasped, doubled over and dropped like the proverbial sack of potatoes.

"Are you alright?" Robbie turned his attention to the girl who had moved closer to them during the short melee.

"Oh God, oh God ..." worry and concern etched on her face, "You are in trouble, mister! You better leave. Getaway now and go as far as you can from here," she mumbled, then continued, "They are gonna kill you," a pause, then terrified, "... and me! They are gonna kill us both!"

Robbie could sense the mounting fear in the girl, she was petrified. She inched closer, staring at the tattooed bum lying in a fetal position curled up, whimpering like a spanked child.

Robbie could see her clearly now; she was just a kid, no more that thirteen or fourteen.

"Don't worry about me. Are you okay? Did he hurt you?"

"No, he just ... it's nothing. Are you a cop?"

"No, I'm not a cop." He answered, exasperated. "Come closer, I'm not going to hurt you." The young girl moved closer, "Let me get a look at you. How old are you?"

He lifted her face up to the light by the chin. She was petite, no more than five feet two or three, and the gaudy makeup looked ridiculously inappropriate on her young face. The bruises on either side of her cheeks told the sad story of abuse.

"How old are you?" He repeated.

"I'm fifteen," she hesitated, "I'm going to be fifteen."

"You're not fifteen!" He shot back, incredulous, trying to figure out what to do with her, debating whether to call Deputy Bradley or not. "Listen, I don't believe…"

"Jodie, are you okay?" A woman called out to them from the shadows. She emerged from around the corner of the building, walking quickly in their direction.

The young girl ran towards her and pointed to the man still curled up on the ground. "Angela, look!"

The woman was tall and slim, a light-skinned black woman wearing a blond wig. Her painted face and tight revealing clothes were the uncompromising advertisements for her trade. She looked at the man and then at Robbie, "You'd better get out of here, mister, this ain't going to end well for you. That there is Hank Carlson's man."

"Hank Carlson, here it was, that name again," Robbie thought, ignoring the warning, "That girl is a child. She doesn't belong here. Who are you? "

"You worry about yourself. I'll take care of her. I've been trying to get her to go home."

Her reply was interrupted by the groan from the asphalt. The thug was sitting up, still holding his nose, "You bitches get outta here! Go on, get back to work." His voice strangled, sounding oddly congested and nasal. Then he looked over at Robbie, "You're a fuckin' ghost. You're dead … so fuckin' dead!"

"Then I have nothing to lose," Robbie replied. He leaned over the man and in one quick motion, pulled his hands down, away from his face, and punched him on the point of his chin. He put his shoulder behind the short right, pivoting to generate maximum force. The man's head bounced of the concrete, his eyes rolled back and his body stiffened - the impact jarred his brain and rendered him unconscious. When Robbie looked up the women were gone, swallowed up by the shadows.

Madison 'Maddie' Wilkins

THE CLAIRVOYANT

He needed to gas-up the SUV and had two choices – a large, modern Shell station with all the amenities located on Main Street or a smaller Mobil rest stop that was off of Willow Street at the intersection of SR-15 and Route 6. He decided on the smaller one. There was a large oak tree with branches overhanging an antiquated wooden signboard at the entrance that read 'Madison Wilkins Mobile Mart' under which, in smaller letters: Since 1948.

The old, bi-level stone structure was made of Gritstone and Turbidite. It had two pumps in the front that offered both petrol and diesel. On the right side of the building was a propane filling station with tanks of varying sizes stacked neatly on steel shelving and on the left, towards the front, was a coin-activated air compressor for tires. The pumps were brightly illuminated and the frontage was free from litter and debris. The manicured lawns and clean, neatly clipped stepping-stone sidewalks augmented the archaic but appealing appearance.

After fueling up, Robbie went into the convenience store to stock up on some bottled water. There was no one behind the counter but down an aisle at the far end of the store was an old woman, thin and bent, dressed in a long floral dress reminiscent of the late forties and fifties. She was preoccupied with rearranging items on a wall-mounted shelf and didn't seem to notice him come in.

He rang the call bell that was on the counter and waited studying the sundry impulse-buy items, primarily chocolates and other candy. He grabbed a bag M&M's and placed it alongside the water bottles.

"Hi, how's it going?" he said when she got to the register.

"It's going," was the short reply.

She was old, really old like in ancient with skin that was deeply wrinkled. The speckled brown age spots and hatched over lines gave her complexion a distressed, leathery mien. Her blue eyes were cloudy behind granny glasses and her once small nose had turned haggish with age. Her hair was white, the color of virgin marble, and was done in a classic bun. He got a whiff of an antiseptic, a comforting aroma that reminded him of his grandmother.

She pursed her lips and made a clucking sound while peering at the barcodes on each item, almost like she was memorizing them, before scanning it with a handheld scanner. It took her a few tries to focus the laser but eventually she managed to ring the items up.

Robbie stood by patiently, resisting the urge to help. He could tell that she was a proud woman and any offer of assistance would have been summarily rebuffed.

"That will be five dollars and twenty seven cents," she said in a raspy but soft voice.

She took a long look at the twenty that that Robbie gave her, holding it up against the light and turning it one way then the other before stashing it away in the cash register. She counted the dollars and the loose change carefully before handing it to him. "You'd better check that; I don't see that good anymore."

"Thanks. It's all there, Nana, you did just fine," he replied with a smile.

"I ain't your Nana," she scolded, "You can call me Maddie or Crazy Maddie … most people here call me Crazy Maddie and that's fine, 'cause that ain't far from the truth!" She let out a soft chuckle.

"I'm sorry Maddie, didn't mean to offend you. You reminded me of my Grandma, that's all."

"Then you ain't all bad," she shot back. She pinned him with a steady gaze and quizzed, "You a soldier?"

"I was … a long time ago." It was a topic of contention and one he wasn't quite ready to visit. He deflected the topic with a question, "Any good places around here where I can grab a bite?"

"A long time you say? You're but a whippersnapper yourself, long time indeed!" She quipped, studying him and noticing the sadness in his eyes, "Let them that died, rest in peace. You get on with your life, you hear?"

Robbie was quiet, wondering what this strange woman could glean from his demeanor. She peered up at him over her granny glasses, her intuitive perception making him uncomfortable.

"Now, Bucky Johnston's Diner has the best burgers around. The trout ain't bad but that Lamb Stew is something I could eat every day of the week. They serve it on Tuesdays and Thursdays so you're out of luck today." She continued staring at him, unwavering, "The place is owned by Hank Carlson and therein lies the rub but the folk working there are good people so I don't pay him no mind."

"I've been here only a few days and hear his name a lot," Robbie observed, nonchalantly, hoping to elicit a bit more about the man. After all, Tony VanArcen and the hooker in the parking lot had cautioned him about Carlson.

"Hank Carlson is a slimy, slithering, dung-eating snake! He's been trying to shut me down or buy me out going on twenty years now. But that ain't happening. I was running this place when he was still sucking on his mama's teats. His father, Hank Senior, was a malevolent old coot; evil as the serpent in Eden. He spawned a nest of vipers, he did. And the king of all them snakes is Hank Carlson. You be careful around him, boy, real careful and when the opportunity shows itself, step on his head and crush him like a bug! You will be ridding this world of the worst kind of evil there is." Her face twisted by anger and rage.

The intense vitriol from this frail, old woman had caught him off guard, "Much obliged, ma'am, but I'll be heading out soon … going back home to Montana."

She gave him a long, hard look that bore into his soul.

"You know nothing, soldier, your story and our story are tied together. Avenging angels are sent in different forms and there's a reckoning to be had for those who did to Marisa Gorecki what they did. And she ain't the first, no, she certainly ain't." She was speaking faster now, her voice trembling, spitting ambiguous innuendos without real context, "It was no coincidence that you found her. She will come to you for justice – you wait and see, yes, just you wait and see. You ain't going home. You ain't going nowhere, boy."

He was more than uncomfortable now but the old termagant held a mysterious fascination and kept him rooted and silent. He watched her closely wondering whether this was just an old woman's rant or if she was a clairvoyant and somehow able to see into his future. He had often wondered about predestination and karmic atonement.

Sensing his ambivalence, she asked, "Do you know about the Four Horsemen of the Apocalypse and the one that rides the pale horse?" And before he could answer, she proceeded to quote from the Bible: *"So I looked, and behold, a pale horse. And the name of him who sat on it was Death, and Hades followed with him."*

Her quivering voice lent an eerie overtone to the passage and when the old woman saw the expression on Robbie's face, she laughed, a loud high pitched chortle, "Don't mind me, boy, I get crazy now and then!" this was followed by more cackling laughter.

"I know the story of the four horsemen … from the book of Revelations. My grandmother was a gentle, Christian lady and tried to instill the teachings of the good book in us." Robbie offered, his uneasiness growing by the moment. There was something strange about this woman – she was part grandmother and part witch.

"Yes, Revelations 6:8," she confirmed then questioned "And what of your father or grandfather, were they good Christian men?"

"I didn't know my grandpa; he died when I was a kid. My Pa, he tried but he had his demons, mainly those that lived in a bottle."

"Ah, there you have it. Women are called the weaker sex but we are indeed the stronger. We take care of our children, we take care of our men and we take care of our house. My Thomas, bless his soul, was as hard and tough as they come but his demons tormented him until his heart gave out when his was but seventy. I turn ninety-eight in a few months… been taking care of this business by myself for over thirty years now! Weaker sex? Nonsense!"

"They certainly don't make them like you anymore!" He said with a broad smile, eyes crinkling, impressed by her strong will and perspicuity despite her age.

"And thank your stars for that, Robbie Olsen! You couldn't handle me even on your best day!" She laughed again, a shallow cackle, "Now go on with you and your sweet talk. Get the Bucky's Supreme – it's a burger worth dying for."

He was genuinely surprised, "How did you know my name?"

"That is for me to know and for you to figure out. But know this, you are among mountain folk, child, there are very few secrets here. You assume that everyone knows everything and don't you forget that!"

Hank Carlson and
Seppo Heikkinen

SNAKES DEN

Hank Carlson sat behind a large oak desk staring at the four men sitting in front of him. Carlson was a tall man, lean but with a budding tummy, a testament to his taste for expensive wines, fried foods and an abhorrence of physical exercise. His face was drawn lean and unremarkable except for his eyes, they were dark and penetrating. The office was in the back of the restaurant, located at the end of the hallway from the main dining room. The men seated in front of him were some of his key employees, the ones he depended on to keep things running smoothly. Alvin 'Snake' Goddard, the pimp who got worked over by Olsen, was seated on the far right. His face was swollen and the telltale blueish red bruising had begun to spread around his eyes and cheeks. He had a handkerchief pressed against the underside of his nostrils, dabbing at the blood that was still trickling down from his broken nose.

"So you say he coldcocked you?" Carlson questioned the pimp.

"Yeah, got me from behind when I wasn't looking," the man nodded to confirm his version, then added, "I was dealing with that little bitch, Jodie, she's a lying whore! That's when he came up from behind me … got me good."

Carlson didn't respond but instead kept staring at Goddard, the unwavering glare making the thug uncomfortable. He squirmed in his chair still dabbing at his nose.

"That's not what I hear, Snake," Hank Carlson rebutted, "I heard that you threw the first punch, then got your nose crushed and was laid out with a knee to you balls! That's what I heard. Your memory of the events is a bit skewed and that is understandable because it looks like you got your noggin rattled a bit, wouldn't you say?" His voice had a smooth, silky quality, a baritone timbre that would have made Sinatra envious.

When the goon didn't answer, Carlson continued, "I can have Seppo check on your nuts to establish the truth; what do you say?"

The bald man felt his toes curl and the hair on the back of his neck stand on edge. He squirmed, desperately trying to decide on a course of action that wouldn't include Carlson's recommendation. Though he considered Seppo a friend, no one in their right mind would want Seppo Heikkinen conducting a physical, especially one that involved the scrotal area. He was a sadistic, unfeeling bastard that scared the shit out of the toughest thugs from New York to Montreal.

"I don't remember clearly," Goddard replied, sheepishly acknowledging the truth, "You may be right."

"I am right, you stupid asshole!" Carlson snarled, "I am always right! I got the story from three different girls who were watching every move from the shadows. You think I don't keep my eyes on you?" He waited before asking, "And speaking of Jodie, where *is* she?"

No one answered. Carlson drilled them with his eyes – unwavering, going from one man to the next. "I don't give a shit about you getting your ass kicked but I don't aim to lose my business or end up in the cooler because of that little bitch, you hear? I got wind of something that makes me uneasy so someone better find her. Where is she?"

But before Goddard could reply, the door to the office swung open and a very large man, hair in a frosted blond Mohawk, came in, leaned over and whispered in Carlson's ear. Seppo Heikkinen was Carlson's 'go to' man – his enforcer.

"Well, well, well, guess who is sitting at the bar? Yes, the very same Robbie Olsen in person."

"You want me to take care of him?" The man asking the question was a large, portly fellow with ruddy complexion and round jowly face seated next to Alvin Goddard.

"So you can get your nuts crushed too?" Carlson snapped, "You idiots sit here; I'll have Seppo take care of this." And with that he motioned to the big man, "Take it outside, you hear, do it discretely!"

"Got it," acknowledged Heikkinen, turning to go.

"Outside!" Carlson repeated so there could be no misunderstanding, "See if he knows about Jodie and make sure he's gone; back to wherever he came from. If the word gets out that some asshole came up here and did whatever he fucking well wanted, what do you think is going to happen? You'll have every two-bit wannabe tough guy wandering in here and creating havoc. People will think that I've gone soft. That ain't going to happen! You take him outside and make a fuckin' example out of him!"

Heikkinen, his face a granite mask, nodded before walking out.

Seppo Heikkinen was a Finn with a checkered past. He was a huge man, a professional wrestler before deciding that there was more money to be made in the Bodyguard and Bouncer business. Rumor had it that he fled his hometown of Vantaa in Finland after killing a fellow bouncer in an argument over drugs. A single blow to

repeated snapping him out of his reverie.

"Oh sorry, a beer … do you have any local beers?"

"We carry a stout beer brewed by Cinnamon Alley. They're a small brewery outside Scarborough," then added with a laugh, "Not really local but local enough for us locals!"

He smiled at her play on words and took a seat at the end of the bar away from the other two men. *'Now there's a cool drink of water if there ever was one,'* he thought to himself and said, "I'll try that, thanks."

She flashed him a big smile that lit up the room, "Coming right up."

There is something about mutual attraction that is titillating; the instant chemistry that draws two people to each other that is both indescribable and inexplicable. She brought the frosted beer mug over to him. The dark, reddish golden ale capped with a frothy head would have at any other time warranted his undivided attention, but now it was the woman that intrigued him.

"Here you go." She said, placing the beer and a bowl of peanuts in front of him.

"Thanks."

She stood watching while he took a long gulp of the fermented drink. He wiped the foamy mustache off with the back of his hand and smiled.

"Well?" she inquired.

"Pretty good … that certainly hit the spot!"

"I'm glad you like it," she said and extending her hand, "I'm Meghan Hollier."

She had the uncanny manner of looking straight into the eyes when speaking to people. For some, it was disconcerting but not for him. Standing there holding her hand, he could sense the attraction mounting, the sparks of energy that breached the traditional norms of 'getting to know you' and for the moment the drink, hunger pangs and surroundings were forgotten.

"Robbie Olsen," he answered, introducing himself.

Her handshake was warm and firm, "I know who you are, Robbie Olsen. You're making quiet a name for yourself!"

"I am?" He was surprised despite crazy Maddie's warning about strangers and Chase River Town.

"Oh yes, you are! We don't get too many outsiders wandering through our mountains tilting at windmills," she explained, her green eyes sparkling with a hint of mischief.

"Not sure what that means," he answered truthfully.

"Don Quixote?" She cocked her head, "Fighting with windmills … his imaginary enemies?" She added with the implication that it was or should be common knowledge.

"I must have skipped that class," Robbie replied nonchalantly.

They were quiet for a moment, awkwardly studying each other, before she turned serious, "How did you find her? Marisa, I mean?"

"I had gone trekking with my dog and was coming down the approach near Devil's Ridge …" he stopped when he noticed her expression change, "… are you okay?"

"Poor Marisa, none of us can believe it. She was a lovely girl … a sweet, sweet soul who wouldn't hurt a living thing."

He watched her, not saying anything. He recalled that Tony VanArcen had said the very same thing.

"She used to babysit for me occasionally." She said, her eyes misting up. She wavered, trying to stifle the emotions that Marisa's name rekindled.

"I'm sorry," he said and waited for her to compose herself then asked, "How old are you kids?"

"Kid." She corrected, "My son is four now."

He didn't understand the solicitous feelings that coursed

through him. Apprehension, disappointment and dejection seemed to swell in one massive wave crashing down on the excitement he had felt just moments before – *if she had a son, she must be married or have a boyfriend; someone this pretty couldn't possibly be unattached.*

"And your husband, what does he do?" He asked unable to restrain his curiosity or hide his disappointment. *'Damn! What's the matter with you?'* The rhetorical question flashed through his mind.

"There is no husband, Olsen; we *are* living in the twenty first century! I know that is hard for you strong, silent types to accept but single mothers rule!" She teased.

"Strong, silent types? I've been packaged and pegged…and we just met!" The remark was said with a smile masking his relief.

"Yes, the troglodyte that clubs his women and drags them off to his cave!" She laughed; a vivacious and infectious laugh and he found himself laughing with her.

"Well, you happen to be right. I *am* the last of a dying breed, though clubbing women hasn't been working of late," he joked, smiling wryly at the self-deprecation. It had been a while since he had experienced anything close to this and he felt his controlled demeanor deteriorating by each passing second.

"I doubt that. I think there'd be plenty of women willing to come to *your* cave and I know under that cold, hard exterior is a sensitive heart. It's in your eyes – the windows to your soul, laddie." She said being conciliatory. She reached over and ran her fingers over the tattoo on his forearm, "Is that a special regiment or something?"

The tattoo was a depiction of a knife with the words 'Death Before Dishonor' wrapped around it and under that was scripted, '75th Ranger Regiment' over the American Flag.

"Army Rangers. It was an impulsive thing. A buddy and I decided on it one night after getting wasted. We thought it would be cool, a memento for completing the course … three months of hell."

She traced the tattoo running her finger gently, almost sensually, over it, still looking into his eyes. The mood shifted; they remained silent neither wanting to break the spell of the moment until finally he balked, his heart, a jackhammer pounding in his chest. *'What the heck is wrong with me? I feel like a bloody sixteen year-old out with the Prom Queen.'*

He cleared his throat and asked, "I'm starving. Do you serve food at the bar or do I have to go over there? He motioned to the dining area and then added with a smile, "Or maybe I'll just have to get my club and chase down a Tyrannosaurus".

She laughed grabbing a menu from under the bar, "Touché! No clubs needed. We do serve food here and I recommend the T-Rex steak."

"I'll pass on the T-Rex and get the Supreme, the Bucky's Supreme Burger."

"Okay, who have you been talking to?" Her eyes widened in mock astonishment.

"No one, I swear it. Bucky's Supreme Burger is famous all the way to Montana!"

She slapped his hand playfully, "Go on … who?"

"Okay, okay, I confess! It was Maddie Wilkins at the gas station. I'm deeply enamored by her."

She let out a laugh, a loud, throaty laugh that surprised the men at the bar.

"Crazy Maddie! How can you not love her? She's a doll but sometimes I do think she's a bit batty."

"It's remarkable that she's still working and taking care of that place – that's no easy job."

"There's more to that story but let me get your order in – the Supreme is half a pound of prime Black Angus beef topped with bacon, sautéed mushrooms, red onions, tomatoes and lettuce all doused in the chef's special cheese sauce. It comes with fries but you can swap that for mashed potatoes or coleslaw," she rattled off the description with practiced efficacy.

"That's impressive. Do you know all the items on the menu by heart?"

"Only the ones I like. What'll it be, fries, mashed potatoes or slaw?"

"I'll take the slaw."

"Good choice. It's fresh, made daily and is a favorite. How do you like you burger cooked?"

"Medium rare."

"Okay, give me a few minutes and I'll be right back. Don't you go anywhere, Robbie Olsen!" She flashed him one of her high-wattage smiles and disappeared through the swinging doors into the kitchen.

He watched her leave, his eyes involuntarily following her tight, callipygian behind, the gentle sway of the hips as she walked knowing fully well that he was checking her out. He tried to contain the excitement he felt – who'd have guessed that in this remote place he'd find the woman of his dreams. *Woah! Slowdown cowboy!* But the thought persisted – this was karma.

His mind raced back to the old lady and her augury that he wouldn't be going back home. Was it the dead girl, Marisa, or this beautiful bartender that would keep him here? Or, were the two women tied together by some metaphysical thread? And what did the old clairvoyant mean by the Pale Horse and Death? He had experienced enough death to last him a lifetime but it seemed to follow him. He stared blankly at the TV screen wondering if Maddie Wilkins was right after all. Myriad thoughts ricocheted in a tangled morass of the past and the present – whispered thoughts of life and death and a ray of hope in the form of this beautiful woman, Meghan Hollier.

His preoccupation had made him careless. He had let his guard down and was so lost in thought that he didn't notice the presence of the Finn until an enormous hand, the size of a catcher's mitt, appeared on the bar next to his drink.

Seppo Heikkinen was leaning over him, one hand on the counter and the other on Robbie's shoulder, whispering in his ear, "Let's step outside, Olsen, we need to sort some things out."

He looked up, taken off guard by the looming presence. "Do I know you?"

"In a few minutes you are going to know all about me. Let's go." His voice was high-pitched. In vocal pedagogy, it would be considered a tenor and was certainly incommensurate with his immense size.

Robbie couldn't believe this turn of events. *What's with this place? All I want is a peaceful meal!* This was the second time in a couple of hours that a man the size of Godzilla wanted to kick his head in.

"Listen, mister, I'm hungry and whatever it is that is bothering you can wait. I'm going to sit here and enjoy my meal and if you still want to pursue this, we can do it after I'm done eating." His voice was steady and without emotion.

The Finn leaned closer, his face almost touching Robbie's, "Don't make me drag you outside like a little bitch so cut the crap and let's go." He gave Robbie's shoulder a hard squeeze. The soft tone and odd European accent had a peculiarly ominous effect.

"Get your hands off me! You're crowding me, man… back off!" Robbie warned, feeling the man's breath, humid and warm, against his ear.

The Finn tightened his grip, "I usually hurt people as part of my job, just business. But you, Olsen," he paused looking at Robbie in the eyes, "you I'm going to enjoy hurting. You shouldn't have fucked with my friend; that was a big mistake."

Robbie shrugged the giant's hand off his shoulder, "You friend shouldn't be hitting little girls. Maybe you need to get yourself some new friends. And don't ever put your hands on me again."

The big man straightened up and stepped back allowing Robbie to stand up which negated his initial advantage. Seated, he was much less of a threat. They were about the same height but the man had him by over a hundred pounds, all of it muscle. Robbie for his part took quick stock of situation – the big man was confident, maybe overconfident and had his hands by his side; a serious mistake, giving Robbie the advantage. Deception and surprise were the real keys in any confrontation. It was the Chinese General, Sun Tzu, who said 'warfare is based on deception', well, that principle worked in street fights too. Robbie knew this and had his first strike lined up. The man's thick, long neck presented an exposed trachea and a clean shot to the throat would end the fight irrespective of size.

"Enough fucking talk! I'm not going to ask again, let's take this outside," Heikkinen said his eyes cold, his face expressionless. He was used to intimidating people by virtue of his colossal presence and this was new for him – here was a man who didn't seem perturbed at all and that was irritating.

Maybe the gods of peace had decided that love needed a break and that warriors like Robbie Olsen had paid the price and earned every reprieve, yes, every second chance. The timing of Meghan's interruption was impeccable.

She placed the plates on the counter and was totally oblivious of the confrontation that was escalating. "Here you go. The plate's hot so be careful. I'll get you another beer."

Only then did she notice Heikkinen. It took her a second to comprehend the situation. "You leave him alone, Seppo! He's here to have dinner. Hank's rules – no fighting in the bar or restaurant. You know that."

"This is straight from the boss. He's got to go, one way or the other and you stay out of this," His tone turned ominous.

Deception! Robbie thought, it was time to set him up.

"Listen, you're a scary dude, man, and I'd be crazy to start any trouble. I'm just looking to enjoy a quiet meal."

Robbie was getting ready to strike; he had angled his position, eyes unblinking, muscles relaxed in anticipation, when a voice from behind the Finn interrupted, "Seppo, you heard the man? That's not too much to ask. He wants to have a quiet, peaceful meal."

The newcomer had materialized from nowhere. He was of average height, slender build, with blue eyes, blond hair, a full mouth and a sultry face; the pretty boy looks that women fawned over.

"Hank wants him out now," was the intransigent response from the Finn.

"Well, Hank is going to have to wait. The soldier boy is going to have his dinner and that's that," the newcomer asserted.

The smaller man moved closer, gliding in to the side to form the third leg of their tripod. In the bright fluorescent light Robbie could see a scar running from the side of the man's forehead down his cheek and into the hairline at the back of his neck. Time had faded the hypertrophic malady but it only added to the intrigue.

"What the fuck is going on here?" It was Hank Carlson. He looked at Robbie and then directed his attention to the newcomer, "Luke, what do you think you are doing?"

"I'm making sure no one fights in the restaurant – your rules, brother!"

Hank Carlson didn't respond. He stood motionless, assessing the situation when his brother laughed and said, "Looks like we have a Mexican standoff... come on, let the man enjoy his meal. We owe him that," then added as an afterthought, "I'd pay to see these two go at it but not today. I've got to go win me some money at Frank's."

The playful tone diffused the tenseness closing the window on any unpleasantness. The moment had passed and for Robbie and Meghan it wasn't a moment too soon.

"Army Rangers or is it the Green Beret?" Carlson asked, noticing the tattoo on Robbie's forearm.

"Rangers," Robbie replied absently, his focus still on Heikkinen.

"Where did you serve?"

"Afghanistan."

"I have nothing but respect for the men and women who serve this country. We owe you a debt, Olsen." He sounded sincere, his smooth voice taking on a respectful tone. "Enjoy the dinner; this one's on the house and there will be no trouble, not tonight." Then turning to his enforcer, "Let him be. Let's go. Luke I need to speak to you."

With that he turned and walked away, back to his office in the rear.

"This isn't over, so Hyvää Ruokahalua! That's bon appetite, soldier, enjoy this meal because I'll be seeing you soon," the big man said before following his boss. The obvious threat wasn't lost on Robbie.

Meghan was the first to speak breathing a sigh of relief, "I'm glad that's over. You better eat you burger while it's still warm."

"I guess I should be thanking you." Robbie said to the younger Carlson who was standing there studying them both.

"No thanks needed, Olsen, and I'm not too sure… I might have just done Seppo a favor," he replied with a charming smile, "Army Rangers! Yeah, coming to think of it you have that look. Go on enjoy the meal and the company. I'm sure we'll be meeting up again."

Then with a departing nod and a smile he retreated down the corridor. His movements had a dancer's quality to it, graceful and effortless.

"They're brothers?" Robbie asked, incredulous, watching the smaller man disappear.

"Yes they are. Luke takes after his mother." Meghan answered, then shivered and added, "That man frightens me."

"You mean Hank Carlson?"

"No, his goon, Seppo Heikkinen… he's a nightmare," she replied.

"You don't worry about him."

"He gives me the creeps," she looked at the food on the counter, "Do you want me to warm that up or if you don't mind waiting a bit, I can get you another one?"

He took a big bite and after washing it down with a swig of beer, "No, it's still warm and damn, this is a good burger! It's huge; do you want me to cut you half?"

"The magic is in the cheese sauce and if you're a good boy, I'll share the recipe with you," she said tongue in cheek, "I'll take a bite if that's okay? All this excitement has made me hungry."

"Of course," holding the burger towards her. She held onto his hand and took a small, dainty bite but managed to smudge some of the sauce onto the side of her mouth.

He dabbed her chin and mouth with a napkin, "Damn girl, you ate half the burger!" he said playfully, faking alarm.

"Stop that! I didn't." She said smiling, then hesitantly, "Would you like to come home for a cup of coffee? I'm almost done here."

"I'd love to if it's not too late for you," he felt the nerd with the Prom Queen thing again and had to control his excitement.

"No it's not. I'm off tomorrow. But I do have to pick my son up from my parents place. It's all walking distance from here."

They sat making small talk, enjoying the excitement and discovery that accompanies all new relationships. It had been a long time since either of them had felt like this. For Robbie, it heralded the chance at a normal life and his past seemed to fade into irrelevance, at least for the moment.

THE CARLSONS

Back in his office, Hank Carlson perfunctorily dismissed his men except for Heikkinen and his brother. Luke for his part was leaning back against the back wall.

"Get out of here, all of you! Not you Seppo, you stay and you too Luke. I need to speak to you both," then to the men who were leaving, "Find Jodie, you hear, I need that bitch back and soon. If she talks …" he left the rest unsaid; the warning clear as day.

When the men had departed, Luke asked, "What do you want, Hank? The boys are waiting for me at Frankie's, it is poker night!"

"This isn't going to take long. Frank can wait."

Hank Carlson sat back in the large leather chair, placed his feet up on the desk and addressed his brother, "You shouldn't have done that, Luke, I don't appreciate your interfering in my business. You put me in an awkward position and you made Seppo look bad. You had better figure out where your loyalties lie."

"Fuck loyalties! I know exactly where my heart is. I don't like men who beat on women … especially little girls. Al Goddard is a pig and got exactly what he deserves," he waited for a response then added, "and, you know what? I like Olsen. He seems like a stand-up guy."

"First, Snake was doing his job and second: stand-up guys who interfere in things they know nothing about get themselves and others killed. This ain't the place or time to play hero. Jodie is a commodity. These women are commodities and we are in the business of selling the services of these commodities. But that is not the reason I'm concerned; it seems Jodie has an account on Facebook or Instagram – Taxi Girl Jodie or some shit like that. I have no idea what she posted because she took the post down but there is no telling what she will post in the future. Do you know what happens when rich, powerful men are threatened? Chris Donnelly, the Lieutenant Governor of Boston was at one of those *special* parties."

"I could care less. Nikolai Zakirov and his buddies don't scare me – up here it is a different kind of jungle, my kind of jungle," Luke countered.

"They're not coming here! They know better. All they have to do is choke the supply – no drugs, no booze, no business!" Hank spat back.

"There are plenty of suppliers. We can get the stuff from someone else."

"And that means going into their jungle! Let me handle the business. You take care of the fights. This whole thing with Marisa, and now Jodie, needs to get shut down and quick!"

"Speaking of Marisa, was she a commodity, Hank?" Luke asked, angry, "I'm hoping you had nothing to do with that because that crosses the line."

"And what line is that?" Hank shot back, eyebrows raised, "We deal in drugs, prostitution and the fight game. All of which appeals to man's baser instincts. So exactly what line am I crossing?"

"Quite being a jerk. Marisa was an innocent girl who had nothing to do with any of this shit and we do not kill the innocents especially children and those who are not involved in our business."

"I had nothing to do with that!" Carlson spat back vehemently, his tone defensive, "I'm going to find out who did and they will pay, oh, trust me, they will pay. But get this through your thick skull, there are no innocents. Marisa, Jodie, Kelly … none! You know nothing about Marisa so don't go acting like you care. Jodie is business, nothing more."

"She's a kid! The girls keep getting younger and younger … what is she, twelve? Thirteen?"

"She's fifteen and I'm a businessman. The demand is for younger girls. I'm not forcing anyone to do anything. She came to us. No one coerced her or bullied her … she came of her own accord. She was giving blowjobs in parking lots long before she ever came around here."

"And how would you know that?" Luke questioned.

"Because she sucked my cock better than any of the cock-sucking whores I've auditioned! I always try the merchandise first before offering them to the public - that's just good business practice."

"You're sick!" His brother summarized.

"Really, I'm sick? Aren't you forgetting something, little brother?" The older Carlson was beginning to enjoy this.

His brother's expression changed, "What do you mean?" Luke stepped closer to the desk, "It had better not be what I'm thinking, Hank. Don't push it."

The big Finn got up from his chair in the corner of the office, surprisingly quick for a man of his size, ready to neutralize any threat to his boss but was waved back. "That's okay Seppo. You wait outside and I'll buzz you if I need you. Go on, it's time for us to settle some family business."

Heikkinen gave Luke a long hard look before leaving the office, closing the door softly behind him.

"I don't need a lecture from you," Luke said.

Hank Carlson waited until the big man had left before speaking, "Apparently you do. You seem to forget where we come from, the family we come from and who we really are. Do you remember when we were kids, all of us sharing that big room in the attic? The girls on one side on that huge, king sized bed and you and me on the other side, cramped on that double bed – do you remember?"

"Yeah, I remember. It used to get really cold at night until Uncle Jack put that wood stove in."

"What do you think Pops was doing in our room in the middle of the night? Cuddling with Emma and Pauline to keep them warm?" Referring to their older sisters, "No, little brother, the strange noises you heard, you know, the grunting, the moaning, the bed creaking … do you remember because I do. It was him fucking them! Emma was fifteen and Pauline was fourteen. I was only eleven but I knew what was going on."

Luke's eyes widened, "Stop! I don't want to hear this. Pops is gone …"

"Pops is gone because I made him gone." Carlson interrupted, snarling, "He didn't fall off the roof; I pushed the sick bastard off the fucking roof! He was a crazy old coot and was ruining the business," he paused, taking his feet off the desk and leaning forward, "but it had nothing to do with his fucking Emma or Pauline; it had to do with business. People were ripping us off and taking advantage of Pops and he had no clue and wouldn't listen to anyone. He had to go."

He waited a few moments, his forehead furrowed, lost in thought, then went on, "One morning I asked Emma if Pops was hurting her and do you know what she said? She said no, she loved the old man and enjoyed playing the Lovey Games … that's what Pops called it. He told her that those were the games that men and women play!"

Luke sank slowly into one of the chairs, slouched over, silent.

"Do you think he built that house on top of the hill because Emma wanted to live there? And didn't you think it was strange that on the nights Emma and Pauline would be gone, Pops would be missing too? He was fucking his daughters, you idiot, and everyone knew it but you. I think deep down you knew but you were in denial. It was always 'poor little Luke, or 'beautiful Luke', that's all I ever heard but no one gave a shit about me! I used to lie there, night after night, listening to the old man grunting and rutting like some wild boar! Fuck! I hated him. I couldn't tell anyone not even Mom."

"Why didn't you? Mom would have done something."

"Yeah, right!"

"What do you mean? She would have!" Luke protested.

"It's called being complicit. She knew exactly what was going on but she made a choice and decided that fucking her brother every chance she got was more important. They were most probably fucking each other long before she got married… Pops knew that but as long as he could hump his daughters, he didn't give a shit."

He waited, a part of him wanting to spare his brother, but he was driven by a deeper need, and continued, "Has it ever occurred to you why Allison and you look so different from the rest of us? Both of you blond and with those blue eyes? Do you ever wonder about that? Of course not! Because you've got your head up your ass! You are so fucking naïve! Uncle Jack and Mom weren't playing checkers up in his room!"

"You're lying!"

Carlson laughed, "Why would I lie? I love Mom and Uncle Jack was always nice to me so what do I have to gain? You never wanted to face any of this. You ran off every chance you got, wandering around in the woods and playing Davy Crocket while the rest of our deviant family fucked each other. All except me; I'm the *only* one who wasn't into that incestuous bullshit!"

He waited for a reaction but there was none so he continued, "On my sixteenth birthday when I was in the backyard trying out the new rifle that Uncle Jack gave me, Emma and Pauline came over and wanted to give me a 'special' gift. Do you know what that was? No, not a cake or a sweater or a penknife but a blowjob! Yeah, a fuckin' blowjob! My sisters wanted to suck my cock. Before you even think of asking the question, I told them to fuck off!"

They sat silently for a while; Hank staring at his brother, boring through him with those dark brooding eyes. Luke was miserable, looking down at his feet, dejected. He knew that most of what his brother was telling him was true. He had avoided dealing with the dark secrets of the family, secrets that filled him with remorse and suffocated him.

The older Carlson waited but seeing that Luke wasn't going to respond, he continued, "Girls learn about life a lot sooner than you think especially up here in the mountains. But I'm pretty certain it's the same all over the fucking world."

He paused, poured himself a drink, then continued with his pontification, "Fathers, brothers, uncles, cousins, friends … they're all looking to get their cocks into a tight, young pussy. And that explains why most of the folk around here are a bunch of inbred yokels."

"That's not true!" His brother protested.

"Connect the fuckin' dots, Luke. What do you think happens in those one room trailers? All those teenagers sleeping together, brothers, sisters, cousins; their hormones raging out of control, cuddling through the winter cold – I know exactly what happens, not for sure, but an educated guess. Here's the one thing I do know for sure, I'm not humping any of my sisters. All I did was get my knob polished by some little slut and that makes me the sicko?" He let out a chuckle, "Do me a favor, little brother, cut out the sanctimonious crap and let's talk about pretty, little Allison, why don't we, huh? The only reason she was spared was because she was too young even for Pops but she wasn't too …"

At mention of their younger sister, Luke leaped out the chair seething; he leaned over the table brandishing a Bowie knife, eyes blazing, "Be careful, Hank, 'less you forget who you are dealing with," he hissed, the sinister twelve inch blade gleaming in the muted light, "and if you think that big gorilla out there scares me, you'd better think again. I'll slice him up and skin him like a pig. And as for you, brother, blood only counts for so much … you leave Allison out of your morbid little world. Now, I'm late for a game so you take care and watch yourself."

And with that he slid out of the back, closing the door behind him.

Hank waited trying to regain his composure. On some deep, primal level, Luke scared him. He would never admit this to anyone but the fact remained that his younger brother frightened him and made him nervous. For one, he couldn't be controlled and two, he lacked any fear. He recalled an incident when Luke was only fifteen. They had gone hunting in the Adirondacks with their older cousin, Brad, when they inadvertently surprised a large Black bear. Before any of them could react, the animal charged. Brad and he took off running as fast as they could but not Luke, he stood his ground and killed that bear with the same pearl handled Bowie knife. No gun, just the knife. He had been mauled badly but that didn't stop him from skinning the animal and taking the pelt home. It was an amazing thing to witness and he knew right then that Luke was different – a very scary different.

Carlson sat watching the images from the security cameras on two large flat-screen monitors mounted high on the wall across from his desk. He couldn't hear the conversation between Meghan and Robbie but they were huddled close and seemed to be getting on well, pretty cozy to say the least. They looked good together – a beautiful couple and Meghan deserved that. He felt a jealous tug at his heart; *why couldn't he find someone suitable? Nothing ever seemed to work out for him.*

He watched them for a while before getting up and walking over to a large oil painting hanging on the back wall behind his desk. It was a re-creation of the Joe Luis-Max Schmeling rematch where the Brown Bomber knocked out the German. It was the only painting he had kept when he acquired Bucky Johnston's Diner. He took the painting down exposing a wall-mounted vault. He punched in the six-digit code while placing his left thumb on the biometric pad – this vault allowed only two tries before it went into 'lockdown' mode. He opened the vault door slowly, peeking involuntarily over his shoulder, a paranoid reflex he couldn't control. There was a small handgun hidden from view, a Beretta 21A, behind which were stacks of currency in hundred dollar bills, gold bars and American Eagles arranged neatly in plastic containers. And all the way in the back, his most prized possession, a blue velvet bag full of two. three and four carat, grade D, ideal cut diamonds. This was his "if-everything-goes-to-hell" stash.

He took the bag out and dribbled a few of the sparkling gems into his hand and studied them with fawning adoration. *My beauties!* He thought as he picked one up and looked at it carefully. *Perfection!* He put them back and then counted out five thousand in cash and shut the vault, hung the large painting back and sat back down at his desk. He hit the buzzer and waited for the Finn to come in.

"Is everything okay?" Seppo asked, noticing that Luke was gone.

"Yeah, it's too bad that you don't get to choose your family. Listen, you stay away from Luke for a few days, okay?"

"Sure. What about Olsen?"

Hank didn't respond, he used the remote to click on the display bringing a close-up of Robbie and Meghan sitting at the bar. The image filled the screen.

"What do you think?" Carlson asked.

The big man studied the screen stoically before replying, "I think he's going to get lucky tonight unless you want me to break his legs."

"Leave him alone. We can turn this into an advantage if we have to."

He handed the Finn and envelope, "This is a bonus. Now, go find Jodie - I think she rooms with Angela. Talk to Monique and Kelly first, they were the last to see her."

Seppo Heikkinen pocketed the envelope, "Thanks. I'll find her, don't worry."

And with that the big Finn left the office.

THE BROTHERS CARLSON

After leaving Bucky Johnston's Diner, Luke Carlson didn't go to the card game at Frank's. His somber mood was certain to throw a damper on the lewd jokes, ribald stories and drunken laughter that invariably accompanied these poker sessions. He felt shame and guilt gnawing at his conscience, monsters that manifested in a hard knot at the pit of his belly. He needed to be alone and the mountains and forest were his sanctuary. Nestled in the deep woods, away from others, he felt most at ease.

His brother had a way of pressing his buttons, even when he was a kid, except this time he had gone a bit too far. The dark rage that consumed him had shut out any sane thought pushing him as close to the brink as he had ever come. Fratricide! Only the unadulterated look of fear on Hank's face had snapped him back to his senses. He took a deep breath and looked up at the stars through the tunnels of Aspen and Pine and felt his calm return.

For as long as Luke could remember, their relationship was anything but conventional. The sanguinary ties that bound the siblings were rife with contradictions – one that blew hot and cold and ran the entire spectrum of love to indifference to hate. Hank himself was a contradiction though there were those rare occasions when he could be warm and caring. Like the time when Luke had just finished building his cabin on top of Moose Head Point, a small hill that merged with Katahdin to its south. Except for his sleeping bag, he had nothing in it – no chairs, sofas, beds, stoves, heating, water nothing. Hank had sent a bunch of his men with furniture, kitchen appliances, generator, water pump and everything else that was required to make the place habitable, in fact more than habitable, he made sure it was comfortable. And when it was all done, Hank even made the tedious hundred yard trek up from the parking platform at the foothills to assess the cabin. He wanted to make sure that the place lacked for nothing. Luke was overwhelmed by the gesture and when he thanked Hank, his brother looked at him and said: "No thanks needed. That's what brothers do and I know you would have done the same for me."

Luke had spent the following years trying to repay his brother, not with money but in kind and slowly but surely he had been drawn deeper and deeper into Hank's many schemes until he became an integral part of the family's many enterprises that included the hospitality business, construction, restaurants, prostitution, drugs, alcohol, gambling, loansharking and bareknuckle fighting. The restaurants and construction businesses provided a front for the illegal side of Hank's enterprise giving him the ability to launder his ill-gotten gains.

Luke was mainly involved in the management of the gambling and bareknuckle fighting – things he had shown a natural propensity for. It now occurred to him that Hank's earlier kindness may have been a plan, a well thought out ploy, to snare him and keep him within the folds of the Carlson empire.

Hank was an astute businessman with a ruthless streak and a mind for numbers. Fear was the key that kept his men inline and the small rewards he periodically doled out kept them loyal. He had the uncanny ability to assess a person's character, their needs and their weaknesses that led to their vulnerability so that he could exploit and profit from it. Whether it was women, liquor, drugs or money he identified the weakness and was ready to oblige, but sooner or later, the favor would come calling and always with interest. He had photographs and videos of some of the most powerful men from New York to Maine, caught in the most compromising and bizarre of situations. The sexually explicit footage were neatly categorized and stored in a safe place to be revisited if and when necessary. This was the Ace in the Hole that had kept him out of prison on several occasions.

But despite his reputation, Hank Carlson disliked physical confrontation. Luke couldn't tell whether it was fear or just indifference that made Hank shirk away from fights, especially fistfights. He had never gotten into one – not a single fistfight. And that was strange for a boy growing up in these mountains. The gauntlet of high school was something Hank manipulated like a marionette. His friends did all the dirty work and Hank benefitted, whether it was girls, booze or money. Hank led and the others followed – all except Luke and that had been a thorn in Hank's side.

Luke was a free spirit and did pretty much what he liked when he liked. He was the diametrical opposite of Hank. Where Hank liked to be among men, Luke chose to be alone. Where Hank used others to settle his scores, Luke settled his own and had earned a much deserved reputation as one not to be messed with. The pretty face belied an indomitable spirit and it was many a man who learned that painful lesson the hard way. Luke Carlson's apodictic toughness was well chronicled in local folklore.

LUKE AND ALLISON CARLSON

After his brush-up with Hank, Luke wandered around aimlessly for hours going from rock to river's edge and back. The mountain air and the physical exertion had a way of clearing his mind putting him at ease. He had hunted, fished and camped every inch of this mountain and there wasn't a man alive that knew the cobbled cracks and crevices of this vast boscage like he did. The murmur of the trees and the sweet fragrance of the grass had a way of settling the restlessness that he was born with. This place was his; no one, not Hank or anyone else, could ever challenge that. He was lord and master and held sway over the vast forests that covered his side of the mountain.

Deep within his heart he knew that from any normal perspective Hank's aversion to their family's irredeemable history was understandable. The indecorous liaisons between Pops, Emma and Pauline and that of his mother with Uncle Jack were undeniable. He knew there were laws prohibiting incest but that isn't to say that it did not occur – from the whispered gossip of his sisters and convivial teasing of friends he knew that several of them had experimented with their siblings. Then why was it that he felt this way? When it came to Pops and his sisters or his mother and Uncle Jack, the question of right and wrong had never crossed his mind. They were willing participants and the morality of their actions was irrelevant to him. But when Hank brought up Allison it hit a nerve, a raw and sensitive nerve that he kept bandaged.

The thought of his sister stirred him like nothing else in this world. For as long as he could recall this thing, undefined and aberrant, existed between them. They were both much younger than their other siblings - Luke was ten years younger than Hank and Allison, who was the youngest, was a year younger than him. The phylogenetic schism between them and their older siblings only widened when Luke and Allison hit puberty.

Emma had moved into the house Pops built for her and Pauline had gotten married and moved across the street from the family house. Hank had moved out a year before Luke's fifteenth birthday leaving Allison and Luke pretty much to themselves.

He thought about the first time they had made love and though it was a long time ago, he felt the same thrill shoot through him like it was just yesterday. They had gone swimming in a small lake hidden in the woods, a place that others seldom visited. He closed his eyes and let the visage of his sister, naked and wet, wash over him drawing him back to that moment when they looked at each other's naked bodies and willingly crossed the traditional boundaries of filial love. The intense emotions that he felt were pure and without guile and he refused to let Hank or anyone else sully it.

He needed to get back to Allison, to possess her and to reclaim that part of him that Hank had dirtied with his recriminations and innuendos. Nothing else mattered. With Allison it felt intrinsically right, absolute in its normalcy and the hell with them all - fuck tradition and fuck all societal norms and most of all, fuck Hank. They had no right to adjudicate on the morality of their consanguineous relationship. What did they know?

When he walked into the cabin, he found her sleeping on the couch, curled up next to fireplace, her hair tossed about her in a tousled, yellow shroud. The thin woolen shawl covering her did little to hide the curves of her enticing form. And in the soft under-glow of the night lamp, she looked radiant like some ethereal Viking goddess. He stood silently studying her, hypnotized by her aura, basking in the fact that this sensual creature was his and his alone. She was beautiful, a fairytale princess, and it made no difference to him that she was his sister.

He gently brushed back her hair trying not to wake her and ran his fingers lightly along the slope of her cheeks, tracing the curve of her lips. He couldn't help himself, she evoked in him the obduracy of lust, a seemingly limitless desire, and no matter how many times he possessed her, he wanted her even more. She consumed him – body, mind and soul.

Her lips parted slightly allowing him to push his thumb gently into her mouth and titillated by the warmth of her breath and soft-ness of her tongue, he drew back the shawl so he could see more of her. He felt her stir, eyes blinking open, languidly feline, waking from the transcendence of sleep, lost in that phantasmal state of hypersexual awareness.

Without a word she clamped her lips around his thumb, sugges-tively sucking it in and out of her mouth, nibbling on it, while staring deeply into his eyes. She was now fully awake.

She rolled off the couch and stood in front of him wearing only a translucent, sleeveless chemise and except for her tiny panties he could see that she was naked under her nightie. He pulled her to him and kissed her hard, their tongues wrestling and swirling in quiet desperation as their need to possess the other slowly intensified.

He felt her moan and gasp into his mouth as he toyed with her breasts, rolling her nipples between his forefinger and thumb, pulling and pinching and squeezing, thrilling in the spongy fullness of her.

She pulled away, breaking their embrace, "I know just what you need, darling brother," she murmured, her voice husky and strangled by her growing excitement.

She dropped slowly to her knees and with practiced skill, unzipped his jeans pulling it down and setting him free. Then without hesitation, she engulfed him, welcoming his hardness into the warmth of her soft, wet mouth. The flames of her passion were being stoked by her own wants and needs, the many cravings that were manifested in her overt sexuality. And by this symbiotic gesture, she knew she could control and possess him in the most intimate of ways.

He threw his head back, a captive to her oral skills, lost in the intense sensations shooting through him and waited with anticipation for that inevitable velvet thrill that would consume him and send him tumbling, freefalling mindlessly through the tortured depths of nothingness.

Hank was wrong, so wrong, because if this was wrong then nothing in his life was right.

Robbie and Meghan

A KNIGHT IN WHITE ARMOR

"We can take the car if you don't mind a bit of dog hair," Robbie said when they were in the parking lot of Bucky Johnston's Diner.

The night had turned cool and Meghan braced herself, buttoning up her cardigan.

"That's not a problem. I love animals, especially dogs. I've heard about your dog – a Woolly Mammoth or close to one." Meghan said.

"Boy, word travels fast here. He's big alright, a Russian Shepherd Dog … about two hundred pounds."

"My God, that *is* big! Joe, Deputy Bradley, had stopped by earlier for a drink. He told us about Marisa and also mentioned your dog." She hesitated and then added, "Oh, he did warn us about you … mysterious and charming but a health hazard especially for the females of the species!"

"Bradley's full of shit!"

She laughed, "I made that up. Though Sally was quite taken by you."

"Sally needs to ease up on the perfume or whatever it is she uses … I was close to passing out!"

She laughed again, "Sally's harmless. If you ever want gossip, she's it. If you want the truth about something, talk to Joe. He said you were very helpful and that your dog was bigger than a house."

"That part may be true."

She stood patiently while Robbie adjusted the front passenger's seat for her. The backrest had to be raised from the fully horizontal position and relocked into place. He had modified the ratchet mechanism which controlled the backrest so Ronin could fit comfortably in the SUV.

"We're not far at all. Make a right out of the parking lot and take the third right onto Hollow Creek Road. My parents live in the first house," she said belting herself in.

"That's easy."

"Yes, it's just a few blocks. I usually walk. What's your dog's name?"

"Ronin, I named him after the samurai. Warriors without masters … you know, the movie, Forty-Severn Ronin."

"I've read the book. I'd like to meet him. I work with Dr. Susan Boswell, she's the local vet. That's my real job. The bartending is to make some extra money and I'm there only three nights, Monday, Thursday and Saturday."

"You're a busy gal."

"Busy is right. We deal with dogs, cats, raccoons, cows, goats, chicken … we have it all." She responded then glanced over at him while they drove, "My dad's not too well. He has fibromyalgia and suffers from Parkinson's but he loves having Ryan over, it helps him stay busy."

"That must be hard on your mom."

"My mother is a don't-complain, get-it-done woman. She's been one of those people God blessed with a happy heart and her glass is always half-full! Here, you can park right here. "

They arrived at the house, a small brightly lit cottage reminiscent of the old English country homes. The house had Gable windows on one side with large, arched skylights in the front. A stone verandah overlooked a woodland garden with clusters of daisies, purple violets and morning glories wrapped around the natural rock formations. A small stream snaked through these floral citadels cascading down a narrow stone-face waterfall before splashing softly into a shimmering aquamarine pool. The gentle gurgle created a soothing backdrop for the noisy, whirring of the pervasive cicada.

There was an unmistakable potpourri of fragrances, flowery and baroque, that clung to the air as they walked down the pea-gravel pathway leading to the house.

"It smells nice," Robbie remarked.

"It's my Mom's passion – her garden."

He saw the curtain part and caught the glimpse of a fleeting shadow before the door opened. There was no mistaking who the woman was. It was obvious from her appearance that she was Meghan's mother. Except for the fact that Meghan was younger and taller, they were almost identical.

"Hi Ma, this is Robbie Olsen," Meghan said, giving her mom a quick hug.

"Oh, the young man with the big dog." She replied stepping back and smiling at Robbie, "Hi, I'm Elizabeth Hollier, Meghan's mother. You can call me Beth."

"Nice to meet you, ma'am," He replied shaking her hand. She had the same firm handshake as her daughter.

"Beth. Call me Beth. Come on in."

Robbie smiled, "It's easy to tell where Meghan gets her looks from. You could be sisters."

Beth Hollier laughed and turned to her daughter, "I like him already. Your father's asleep and so is Ryan. Do you want me to get him?"

"No, Ma, I can handle it. You sit and talk to Robbie."

"How about some coffee?" her mother asked.

Meghan declined, "No, it's late and you need to get to bed. I'll come by tomorrow to see dad."

A few minutes later she returned carrying a small boy. He was fast asleep with his head resting on her shoulder. A halo of blond curls accentuated his cherubic face and a ragged teddy bear hung loosely from his little hand.

"Would you like me to carry him?" Robbie asked, picking up the stuffed bear that had escaped the boy's grip and noticing Meghan struggling with her son.

"Yes, if you don't mind; he's getting too heavy for me."

There was an awkward exchange and the little boy stirred, mumbling, and for a moment stared wide-eyed at Robbie.

"It's okay, baby," his grandmother cooed, and handed him the teddy bear, 'Here's Boo, go to sleep now."

The boy lay his head on Robbie's shoulder and went back to sleep, clinging tightly to his bear in one hand and the other wrapped around Robbie neck.

"Thanks, Ma, I'll talk to you later."

"Just a minute, don't go yet. I baked some chocolate cake and cookies for him," Beth Hollier said and dashed off into the kitchen.

They said their goodbyes and made the short ride to Meghan's place which was also on Hollow Creek Road but on the other side of Main Street. Meghan had been right; it was all within walking distance.

Her home was a small two-bedroom log cabin with a tiny garden and a short, flagstone walkway. There was a beat-up old Chevy truck parked just outside the front picket-fence gate.

Meghan opened the front door and turned on the lights. "Sit anywhere. Just move the books and toys over. I'm sorry it's such a mess but Ryan is a handful and I'm …" she stopped and looked at him, "just sit anywhere you want."

She disappeared down a corridor carrying the little boy and had to maneuver by a bulky hallway dresser that pinched her access. Robbie picked up a thick book lying on a sofa and sat down. The pillow-back and seat cushions were plump and comfortable with a faint scent of laundry detergent. The sofa was an old Chesterfield with a mahogany frame that was nicked and scratched, the vestiges of skirmishes with a four-year-old. The edges of the armrest were frayed and worn and the seat cushions were patched by way of repair. The book was 'An Introduction to Veterinary Anatomy and Physiology'. There were other books and magazines scattered nearby and toys, a bushel full of them from Hess Trucks to a remote controlled helicopter. Robbie smiled, *this kid has it all!*

The sofa sat across from a stone fireplace with a rustic oak mantel and next to the fireplace was a repurposed metal bookcase used to stack logs, timber and kindling. There were several picture frames with family photographs, mainly of Ryan and his grandparents, and a vase full of artificial lilies seated on top of the mantel.

Meghan returned after a few minutes and stood by the doorway, arms akimbo, "Okay, now for that cup of coffee."

"He's asleep?" Robbie asked.

"Finally! He was curious about you, wanting to know if you were a superhero!"

"I hate to disappoint him but I'm as far from a superhero as you can get."

"You don't have kids so you don't know this but little boys look at men and want them to be heroes, to be perfect so they can be like them." She replied and moved towards the kitchen.

The cabin's open floorplan allowed for easy access to the small kitchen that was adjacent to the living-room. He could hear the tick-tock of an old grandfather's clock that was mounted on the side wall. On the far end, against the cabin's rear wall, was a pretty blueish-gray soapstone counter with a sink and a window that overlooked the backyard. The upper and lower cabinets were all in natural redwood with brass fittings which were tarnished and antique with age.

"I have regular Colombian or Hazelnut flavored coffee. What would you like?" She asked.

"Regular is fine for me."

"I keep the Hazelnut for Dad; he loves his coffee with heavy cream and a bit too much sugar. I keep reminding him that sugar is not good for him, especially with his Parkinson's, but he's so stubborn and refuses to change anything."

"What's your father's name?" Robbie inquired.

"Mark Edward Hollier. Everyone calls him Mayor or Mayor Mark. He was the mayor of Chase River. There was no real election; he took the job because no one else wanted it. Then there's Dr. Boswell's husband who is also named Mark so when people refer to him it's just Mark or Marine Mark and Dad is still 'Mayor Mark' even though he retired several years back."

She added the water to the coffee machine and turned to Robbie, "How about your parents? Where do they live?"

"We're from Montana. My dad's passed. My sister and her husband have the farm now."

"And your mother, does she live with them?"

He looked away, waited a bit before replying, "She left a long time ago."

Embarrassed she quickly said, "Oh, I'm so sorry. I didn't mean to pry."

He was quiet. This was a part of his life that was painful and tied in with his military service. "It's a long story and one I had buried. Maybe someday I'll dig it up for you."

"You don't have to. I was only curious … you seem so together and I have these doubts about Ryan and bringing him up as a single mother. Boys need their fathers to show them things that mothers can't. I know that's not politically correct, but it's true."

"Don't do that. Don't sell yourself short. In an ideal world, boys and girls would grow up with both parents and they would be loving and kind. They need each parent in ways that are pretty unique. But having both parents is no guarantee … we don't always get to choose and we have to make the best of what we are dealt with. You seem to be doing just fine."

"I'm not always sure, I mean with what I'm doing, but I guess you're right, we do the best we can."

She poured the coffee into mugs and brought them on an in-laid wooden tray along with a carton of cream and a small bowl of sugar. She placed the tray on the coffee table and sat next to him on the couch.

"Cream, sugar?" she asked.

"No thanks. Black is fine."

They were quiet for a while enjoying the warmth and richness of the coffee, comfortable with the silence and each other's company. She kept glancing sideways at him, attracted to his looks and the silent confidence that he exuded. He had 'military' written all over him.

He spoke softly, so softly at first that she had to strain to hear him, "My father was a quiet man. Never said much; he kept all his emotions locked up inside him. You never knew if he was happy or sad or pissed off … it was his way of dealing with the world. Shut them out so they can't hurt you."

He paused but she didn't say anything, allowing him to talk at his own pace.

"My mom was just the opposite - vivacious and vibrant. She needed to talk and laugh and fight and make-up. You can't fight with a rock and you certainly cannot breakdown impenetrable walls and despite her easy smile there was sadness in her eyes that she couldn't hide. My father sensed it but he had no idea how to deal with it. She was beautiful, extroverted and loving but what she needed he couldn't give her."

He looked at her wondering if he was saying too much but she was listening, eagerly with rapt attention.

He continued, "Farm life is tough but for a small farmer it is even tougher. We lived month to month, season to season, year to year. No frills, no vacations – nothing. My father got up at the crack of dawn and worked until dinner and then he fell asleep in front of the TV, exhausted. At some point he took to drinking … when I was fifteen, I found him lying passed out on the living-room carpet. I remember helping him up the stairs to the guest bedroom and undoing his shoes. The socks were torn with holes in them and his feet were badly calloused and cracked. I'm not sure exactly when it was but my parents had taken to sleeping in separate bedrooms. I think that drove him to drink."

He took a sip of his coffee, seemingly lost in thought. She could sense him struggling but said nothing.

"My sister, Rachael, and I learned at an early age exactly what it takes to survive in that environment but I think the sacrifices and the daily grind were killing Mom. Add to that my dad's bouts of drunkenness and it became too much for her. Anyway, a few days after Rachel got married, Mom left. Rachel was twenty and I was twenty two. I guess she figured she had done her job. There was a handwritten note on the dining table that simply read, *'I love you all but I need to find some happiness in the life I have left.'* And that was it. We never heard from her again. I was my mother's son and a week later, I left, I enlisted and that was that."

She took his hand in hers, feeling for him and wanting to comfort him in the worst way. The tough exterior had hidden the many cracks and peeking in through them she saw a little boy who was lost. His vulnerability and willingness to share his past only made him more desirable to her.

"For years I blamed my dad but I have come to realize that there was no one to blame. He did the best he could and he didn't run off looking for happiness. He stayed and there's something to be said for that. I don't blame my mom either; everyone has a right to find happiness and sometimes kids are just collateral damage. There was no Yellow Brick Road for us. Ours was a road cracked and riddled with potholes and Oz ended the day Mom left. But, Rachael stayed… I left, running away like my mother."

He sighed, staring down at the abstract patterns on the tray that was on the coffee table. He was caught up in the moment of catharsis and abject memory, "You thought that I had it together, well, I don't. I have my demons and I'm also a lot like my father but I don't want to end up like him."

The last part was almost a plea. "You won't," she reassured him, squeezing his hand.

"How do you know?" He asked, needing her reassurance.

"I just do." She said then standing up she leaned over him and kissed him gently on the lips.

It was a quick, soft kiss, an impulsive act, acquiescing to the lubricious attraction she felt for him. She looked deeply into his eyes, their faces inches apart, her breath, warm and sweet, lips parted slightly, her eyes bright with desire and in that moment she was the most beautiful thing he had ever seen. He could see the reflection of his hunger dancing in the shadows of her eyes and reaching up, he pulled her to him, kissing her hard and deep and felt her gasp with surprise and desire.

She had to straddle his lap, her hair falling in a silky veil about them. She probed his mouth with her tongue, tentatively running the tip along the inner contour of his lips but then lost in the fervor of her excitement, she pressed her mouth against his, venturing deeper, allowing him to draw her in, their tongues swirling and twisting, teasing each other – a prelude to the exigency of their primal needs.

He thrilled in the softness of her mouth, the sweet taste of her, and felt his body respond. She could feel his hardness throbbing against her mound and began to rock back and forth, imperceptibly at first and then as their kisses lingered longer and deeper, she squirmed, her hips gyrating with mounting urgency. He cupped her ass in his hands, squeezing and caressing her cheeks, while she slid back and forth, the frottage sending jolts of pleasure through them.

She felt him gently nibbling on her earlobes, tracing the curve of her neck with his tongue, working slowly downwards. He had unbuttoned the top of her blouse and was kissing the cleft of her breasts, kneading them in his hands.

She moaned and sighed, "Oh, God …"

They were so lost in their passion that they didn't hear the shuffling of tiny feet.

"Mommy, I'm scared," the boy cried, walking unsteadily, dragging the bedraggled little bear behind him.

She broke away, startled, scrambling off his lap and went over to her child. "It's okay, baby, you just had a bad dream."

She knelt down hugging him, murmuring softly, comforting him like only mothers can do, then turning to Robbie, "Give me a minute. And don't you go anywhere, Robbie Olsen, we have things to finish."

She led the boy by his hand down the corridor and after a few minutes, Robbie could hear soft strains of her singing a lullaby. He got off the sofa, his erection pressing uncomfortably against his trousers, and walked over to the fireplace mantel. He was studying the photographs when he heard the grandfather's clock strike one.

He checked his watch and kicked himself, muttering, "Ronin! Shit, I have to get back."

He was perched on the backrest of the sofa when she returned.

"He's asleep," she said and noticing the change in his demeanor, realized their moment had passed, "I'm sorry ..."

He pulled her to him and kissed her, a gentle peck, "I have to go. Ronin will tear the place up if I don't get back soon. You have a way of making me forget everything."

"Is that good?" she teased.

"I don't know but what I do know is that I want to see you again. You said you were off tomorrow - can we have lunch?"

She smiled and put her arms around his neck, "I'd like that very much but on my days off I take Ryan to the park. It's not really a park but a small playground. He loves the monkey bars and he gets to play with the other kids. Would you like to join us and then maybe we can go for lunch?"

"Sure. What time?"

"Anytime, it doesn't matter as long as it is after nine. I get up late on my days off." She ran her fingers gently over his jawline and chin, wanting him to stay.

"Sounds like a plan." He said, then as an afterthought, "You wouldn't have a steak in your freezer, would you? Ronin hasn't had meat in four days and I forgot all about it."

"I always keep a few steaks handy; it's the surefire way to attract a caveman!" She retorted before going into the kitchen.

He smiled watching the wiggle of that perfect behind, "You don't need steaks, girl."

She was smiling to herself when she wrapped the meat in a brown paper bag. She walked him to the door her arm around his waist.

They kissed again by the doorway.

"I wish you could stay." She said holding on to him.

"I do too but I'll see you tomorrow and I'm not going anywhere," he said before leaving with a large sirloin and a raging boner.

Tony VanArcen

PARTNERS IN CRIME

The knocking on the door and the low-pitched growling and barking woke him up. Robbie sat up slowly, squeezed his eyes shut and waited, hoping the person would go away but whoever it was, knocked again, this time much louder. He took a quick look at his watch, 6:38 AM. He didn't get to bed until it was after 2:00 AM, 2:04 AM to be exact. He had planned to sleep in late before meeting with Meghan. This had better be important, he thought, trudging reluctantly to the door.

"Back-up, boy, it's okay." He said to Ronin who was by the door, growling at the interloper.

He opened the door a crack, squinted against the bright sunshine, surprised at seeing Tony VanArcen.

"Wake-up, cowboy! It's almost 7:00 and we've got work to do." VanArcen said enthusiastically.

"Oh no, not today; I had a late night…" Robbie protested.

"Ah, a date with the lovely Miss. Hollier and you got lucky. Damn boy! Every red-blooded, hard-drinking renegade in the greater Piscataquis County has been trying to wiggle down those knickers but with no luck. You breeze in, like some fuckin' White Knight on a wild stallion and jump right into her panties!" VanArcen shook his head in disbelief, and giving Ronin a quick glance, "Okay, so not a wild stallion but a huge, ugly-assed dog."

Ronin growled in response and Robbie had to nudge him back with his leg.

"What? How the… oh, screw it. You're giving me a freakin' headache, VanArcen, what do you want?" Robbie bristled. He wasn't sure how Tony VanArcen could have known about Meghan but at that moment he didn't care.

"I want you tell me how you do it. It must be that Charlie Bronson, cool as ice look. It's got to be! Either that or you've got an enormous dick!"

Robbie shook his head in exasperation.

"Not now, okay, I'm not up for company … maybe later. And your fascination with 'Charlie Bronson' and my 'dick' as you put it, is beginning to worry me."

"Hey, hey don't be casting aspersions! But jokes aside, I need to show you something. You're the only one I can trust. I know, sad but true," the smaller man replied, looking past Robbie at Ronin. The dog was standing motionless eyeing him suspiciously.

Robbie studied him quizzically, clearing his sleep addled brain. He ran his fingers through his hair wanting to get back into bed.

"I'll fill you in, trust me, it's important. We'll grab a quick bite to eat and then we'll take a ride to Calico Bluff," the smaller man implored, then noticing the tattoo and the deep scars on Robbie's body, "Were you in Iraq?"

"Afghanistan. Let's drop it, okay?"

"Hey, no worries man… trust me, this is important," VanArcen reiterated, in all seriousness.

Robbie thought about it before answering, "I have to be back by 10. No later.”

"Deal! You’ve got it, bro," VanArcen assured him with a broad smile, "Another tryst with the beautiful Miss. Hollier, I presume?"

"Go to hell!"

"Oh, come on! I’m envious and I’m fuckin’ impressed. No, really I am," was his comical reply and then his expression changed and he got serious, "No bull, you’ve got to see this. I’ll get you back in time, you have my word."

"Okay. It’s going to take around twenty to thirty minutes. I have to shower and feed Ronin and then let him out to take care of his business. Do you want to come in and wait?"

"That will be a *no*! I’ll sit in my truck and chew on my toenails if I have to but I’m not waiting in any room with that thing!"

"Suit yourself," Robbie said and closed the door.

Roughly 30 minutes later, they drove with Ronin in the back of VanArcen’s pick-up truck. He pretty much took up the entire bed of the pick-up. The first stop was at VanArcen’s cabin to drop the big dog off.

"It’s a fenced in backyard. I’ll leave the kitchen door open so he can go in and out of the house. We’ll pick him up on the way back," Tony said trying to assuage Robbie’s apprehension.

"How high is the fence?"

"It’s a eight foot fence made to keep the bears out. It has barbed wire on the outside. Uncle Danny built it and trust me, you’ll need a bulldozer to break it down. You can check it when we get home."

That seemed to satisfy Robbie. After dropping Ronin off, they made their way to the second stop to grab a bite to eat. It was off the main road and down a serpentine dirt pathway that led to an open yard with a converted trailer sitting on cinderblocks. There was a weather-beaten picnic table in front jammed full of people and several pick-ups randomly parked, windows down and doors open, with men leaning against their vehicles, enjoying their meals. There wasn't a lot of talk, just the clatter of pots and pans and the strains of some classic, old Blue Grass.

The enticing aroma accompanied by the sizzle of bacon, sausage and eggs being fried wafted into the pick-up as they pulled up.

"Sit tight and leave this to me," VanArcen said, jumping out and going to the open window.

After a few minutes he came back with two large discolored and dented metal plates, "Here you go. You can thank me later. I'll be back with the coffee. How do you take it?"

"Black," was the reply.

This was the only time that VanArcen was quiet. He was busy chowing down the fried eggs and sausages, dipping the thick, flaky biscuits in the bacon fat and runny egg yolks.

"Well, what's the verdict?" he smacked his lips, turned and asked Robbie when he was done.

"A heart attack waiting to happen," was the curt reply.

"That's a pretty clean plate for a heart attack." VanArcen countered, nodding towards Robbie's plate.

"I didn't say it wasn't tasty … just unhealthy," Robbie clarified.

"You're wrong, Bronson, animal fat and eggs are the best for you! Come on, man, join the twenty-first century. It's called the Paleo diet."

"Saturated fat and animal protein are good in context of a balanced diet and what that means is including healthy servings of vegetables and fruits and limiting simple carbs, like sugar and these biscuits," Robbie corrected, taking a sip of the hot coffee.

"You have to have the last word, don't you? Now you're making me feel lousy about the meal," he lamented, then nodding to the table, "You see that big dude, the one in the plaid shirt? That's Ed Carlson, Hank's nephew. He's bad news, stay away from him. The monkey sitting next to him, with the long hair and biker jacket, is Jericho Reinhardt. He was a member of the Hells Angels somewhere in northern California and is said to have iced a few people including a cop. He grew up with Ed and Ray and they are thick as thieves. Ray is Ed's brother. He's the tall dude in the red shirt with his back to us. He's another deviant that you want to avoid."

Robbie gave the table a cursory look and took note of the individuals that VanArcen was referring to. Ed Carlson was tall and lean with a long, gaunt face, bushy eyebrows and dark hair cropped short. His beak of a nose and thin lips gave him a predatory look. Jericho Reinhardt was almost the opposite. He had a round chubby face and was of average height. He was stocky with big arms and a barrel chest with Gothic style tattoos decorating his arms and body but the distinguishing feature was his long hair that fell below his shoulder blades.

"Everyone here seems to be bad news. Is there anyone that isn't bad news?" Robbie remarked.

"Yeah, Meghan Hollier and from the looks of it, you've done more than meet her!" VanArcen shot back smiling and they took off, driving towards Calico Bluff.

"I wasn't kidding about Edmund Carlson," VanArcen said while they were driving, "Ed and Ray are Emma Carlson's boys. There are all kinds of rumors about their paternal lineage but I won't go there. The two of them along with Jericho run Hank Carlson's Wood Mill and that in itself should keep you away from them. But the real problem is that they are not the smartest pencils in the box – dumb guys in positions of power or strength are the most dangerous. They don't think things thru'; they react and that's never a good thing."

"Okay now I know," Robbie said, "unless it's Meghan or you, I'll run for cover. And in your case, your fascination with Charles Bronson and my dick is worrisome."

"You're something else, man, I'm trying to help you ..." VanArcen protested.

"You wake me up at the crack of dawn, feed me enough cholesterol to keel over a Grizzly and take me on a wild goose chase and all this is to help me?"

"It's not a wild goose chase. Here look at this," VanArcen replied.

He fished out a torn piece of diaphanous material from his top pocket and handed it to Robbie. It was a strip of cloth, pink and white, about eight inches long that had obviously been ripped from a dress or a blouse.

"Marisa?" Robbie questioned.

"Yeah, I had seen her in that dress before. She usually wore jeans but every now and then she would wear this pink and white dress that looked really nice on her. I would tell her that she should wear more dresses. But I guess cheap jeans from Walmart were the best old Jacob could do."

"Where did you get this? And why aren't you talking to Bradley?"

"I'm taking you to the place where I found it and as for Deputy Bradley, I'm not sure about him. He could be on Carlson's payroll. I'm not saying he is, just that I'm not sure."

After roughly forty minutes of driving, they pulled off the paved roadway and onto a dirt track. VanArcen followed the dusty path for half a mile or so, winding through trees and bushes, before stopping and parking the car behind a thick covey of elderberry and arrowhead bushes. This cluster was spread wide standing over six feet in height.

"You can never be too careful," he said, glancing around before locking the truck. He checked his gun, a Smith and Wesson 1006, "Are you packing?"

Robbie nodded and said, "Yes. Keep the safety on, I don't plan to get shot by you."

"Hey, I'm not an idiot, okay?" was the defensive response.

They trudged slowly up the mountain side, their progress hindered by the heavy undergrowth, thick with thorny bushes and overgrown weeds, until a small hunter's cabin came into view. The box-style wooden structure was built on an incline mounted on four pilings. The two in the front were about three feet in height and the ones in the rear, about a foot. The roof had weathered wooden shingles and a makeshift chimney. There were spikes and nails around the base of the cabin walls, an attempt to discourage the more curious of bears. Strewn carelessly under the cabin were empty cans, beer bottles, plastic bags and some old rags.

VanArcen was breathing heavily, panting with the effort, "Fuck, I need to get into shape. No more pancakes or cookies! You're not human, Bronson, you're not even breathing!"

"You need to take better care of yourself," Olsen quipped back.

"No kidding, Einstein," was the sarcastic response before elaborating, "This cabin was built by Gil Dorsey many years back. He doesn't hunt much these days so everyone around here uses it. Gil doesn't seem to mind."

The front stairway was a crude construction made of two logs and some roughhewn four by fours. The planks were nailed into the matching L-shaped wedges that had been whittled out of the logs to form the treads, that is, the actual steps. The lack of support risers made the stairs unstable but it was good enough to serve the purpose. There were cigarette butts scattered on the sides and under the stairs.

"Marlboro's and Camels," Robbie observed, shifting through the cigarette butts.

"Everyone around here smokes either Marlboro's or Camels so that doesn't narrow it down," VanArcen replied, "but they weren't here a few weeks ago when I was surveying the boundaries of

Dorsey's property. And neither were these footprints."

"That doesn't mean anything. A bunch of guys could have come up here to do some hunting. I've gone hunting with friends, in fact, I rarely go hunting alone."

"Yeah, sure, except here is where I found the strip that was ripped from Marisa's dress. Follow me."

He walked to the side of the cabin and down an uneven gradient; the area was bound peripherally by a divide with a bubbling stream that drained noisily into a watershed. There, next to the small pool, was a grassy mesa that served as an oasis for wildlife. The location of the cabin was perfect from a hunter's perspective.

"Look at these footprints, they are smaller," he pointed to sets of prints left on the soft ground around the water. "Come on, we have to go further down a bit, on the other side." VanArcen said, leading the way past the pool and down from the edge.

He stopped about ten feet from the brow, "Here, I found it here under this … shit!" he swore, his forearm raked by the thorns as he reached under a bush. "See the footprints, smaller and scattered. Whoever it was, brought her here. She most probably tried to run off but they caught her and dragged her back. Look at the way the footprints merge with the drag marks and then they disappear. Someone must have carried her into the cabin."

He wiped the trickle of blood from his arm, "I would never have seen it if I hadn't gone down to the demarcation corner of Gil's property line. You couldn't see it from up there." He pointed to the edge of the mesa.

Robbie didn't say anything. He studied the prints and took some photographs using his cell phone before climbing back up to the ledge. There were footprints around the pond, several of them, but only a few of the smaller ones that were distinct. The others had been trampled over and were indiscernible.

He snapped a few more pictures and looked up at the cabin, "You may be right. Let's take a look inside."

When they opened the door, they were greeted by the musky odor of mildew and cigarettes. The window was closed and it was dark inside. Robbie turned on his cellphone flashlight and left the door open so they could examine the interior. There was a sleeping bag on the floor with some old pillows scattered nearby. A kerosene lamp sat on a makeshift counter along with a woodstove for heat and cooking. There were several stains on the cabin floor. The crusted food stains were obvious but there were others that were less distinct and could have been blood or semen.

Robbie got his Glock 20 out and used the muzzle to smooth out the wrinkles and creases of the bedsheet that lay partially tucked into the sleeping bag.

"See if you can find any hair or ..." he began when he was interrupted by the loud crack of a gunshot.

The bullet whizzed by his head, struck the lamp sending it caroming against the back wall before falling to the floor. The strong and distinctive smell of kerosene permeated the air.

His military training kicked in instinctively.

"Get down!" Robbie yelled and took cover behind the door, "Get down!"

VanArcen crouched low against the side wall, edging away from the doorway, when a second bullet hit the lamp. There was a flash and the place burst into flames.

"Stay low. We need to get out." Robbie said as the flames began to spread. The spilled kerosene and the dry planks of the flooring and walls created the perfect tinder for the flames.

They crept out, slithering down the make shift stairs when a third shot kicked up dirt close to Robbie's face. He fired back, squeezing off three quick rounds in the direction of where the shots came from. He saw the bushes rustle and fired two more shots, the loud booming of the 10 mm from the Glock echoing through the mountainside.

Minutes went by while they waited, neither moving. "Are you okay?" Robbie asked standing up.

"I'm fine. Pissed my fuckin' pants but other than that, I'm okay," VanArcen replied.

"He's gone. We'd better get going. We're exposed out here, like sitting ducks."

They moved back as the fire crackled and engulfed the cabin. The flames shot higher as the roof began disintegrating, falling into itself, sending plumes of smoke and ash up and in every direction.

"Now do you believe me?" VanArcen asked, "Why would they try and kill us unless they are trying to hide something?"

"Let's go before he decides to circle around and finish the job."

"Wait, I dropped my gun! My fuckin' hands are shaking," VanArcen said, down on his haunches searching for his weapon.

"There it is," Robbie said, spotting the handgun lying a few feet behind VanArcen, "come on, we better scoot."

The descent getting back down was easier than the way up to the cabin but when they arrived at VanArcen's pick-up, all four tires had been slashed.

"What the heck! Goddamn motherfuckers!" VanArcen swore.

Robbie made a quick assessment. There was no point in waiting around and there was no way to drive the pick-up. "Let's get back to the main road, there's a better chance of hitching a ride."

VanArcen looked dejected, "This is a problem. I'll have to get four tires and come back here. You'll be with the beautiful Meghan Hollier getting your jollies off and I'll be target practice for the asshole trying to waste my sorry ass."

"Stop being a crybaby. It doesn't suit your image."

"Listen Bronson, unlike you, I'm not Delta Force trained to kill or be killed. I happen to like my life, shitty as it is!"

"I was in the Army Rangers," Robbie corrected, "and if it will make you feel any better I'll come back with you to get the tires changed. Just stop the whining."

"Delta Force, Army Rangers, who the fuck cares? You assholes eat bullets and shit nails or something like that! Not me, brother, I just want to check on trees, preferably dead ones, drink some beer and make love to my gal. Is that too much to ask?"

"Oh boy, here we go."

"You'll really come back with me?"

"Yeah, anything just stop yakking!"

"You know, I think we are brothers. From very different mothers but brothers …"

And with that they began the long walk back towards town with VanArcen chattering on about life in this remote Appalachian town and Robbie wondering where this would lead him.

LUKE CARLSON AND MADDIE WILKINS

Luke Carlson walked into Maddie Wilkins' gas station smiling and eager to spend a few minutes with the old lady. He had a brought a ceramic container with him which he cradled like a baby. And though the doorbell chimed, it had no effect on her. She was nodding off to sleep behind the register.

"Hey Maddie, wake up! It's your favorite son!" He said, leaning over and bussing her forehead.

The old woman snapped out of her slumber, a look of confusion on her face, blinked her eyes rapidly, and then, recognition followed by chastisement. "Luke! You didn't come to see me last week, boy!"

"Sorry mama, just a lot of crazy stuff that's been going on." He hugged her and gave her another kiss on her forehead. "You still look as lovely as ever."

"Oh, you… go on with you! You and that Olsen boy! You make a pair."

"So you've met the mysterious man," he responded, brushing back strands of her silver white hair.

"That I have and a man he is. You and he can make this place clean again… rid it of all the evil."

"Now, now, mama, Hank is my brother and he's not evil, just

misguided. He wasn't always like this, you know."

"There are brothers bonded by blood and there are those who are by spirit." She cackled, "True brothers are bonded by both but it is your brother in spirit who will lead this war, this Armageddon!"

Luke threw back his head and laughed, "Armageddon! Maddie, Maddie, Maddie… whatever am I going to do with you?"

"You laugh at me, boy? Do not forget who it was that brought you into this world; that wiped you down and placed you on your mama's breast. And when she took ill, who was it that fed and cared for you and that beautiful angel, Allison? Do you not remember?"

"How can I forget, Maddie, you know that I love you almost as much as I love my mother. You have always watched out for me… and for Allison. And, you were the only one who did not judge us. If anyone and that includes Hank, means you any harm they will have to come through me." His tone turned serious and cold.

"Ah, there is a reckoning to be had. It is coming and you will be called on to choose." She said in a voice thin and shaky.

Luke studied her wrinkled face affectionately. He had always shared a bond with this strange, old woman, a mystic who had been his mother's midwife for his birth and Allison's. She was like a second mother to him.

"Tell me more. What is it that I have to choose? And what does Olsen have to do with all this? Can you see that?"

"That I do not know. What I know is that you will be tested and you will have to choose – good over evil. It will be yours to pick and there is one who rides a pale horse who is yet to come here but he will and there will be a reckoning."

He gave her another hug and placed the ceramic container on the counter, "Your favorite. Lamb Stew, made fresh and I got you the best pieces of meat, picked them out myself."

She pinched his cheek with bent bony fingers, smiling, "Go on now, and when the time comes you pick good over evil. And, don't pay them no mind when they talk about Allison and you. You two are meant to be together. There are those whose lives are joined by karmic destiny and some, like Olsen, preordained to intersect, however brief."

"You call me if you need anything. I'll be by next week and I promise, I won't forget."

When Luke left the old woman, he was feeling a lot better. He always felt batter after visiting with Maddie. She was a strange one, mystical and odd, but he knew that she loved him like a son. And, he believed every word she said even the bit about the pale horse.

ROBBIE OLSEN AND TONY VANARCEN

Robbie and VanArcen were lucky; they managed to hitch a ride with a truck coming in to pick-up a load of quarter-sawn planks from Hank Carlson's Lumber Yard. The loquacious trucker was almost as talkative as VanArcen. Robbie sat quietly while the two men debated politics, food, sports and women. The trucker was a diehard Democrat; voted Blue his whole life and VanArcen, a staunch Republican who thought the best thing to happen to America was Ronald Reagan. The trucker was a Yankee fan while VanArcen lived and died with the Red Sox. VanArcen swore by the Italian restaurants in Boston while, according to the driver, New York boasted the best of all cuisines. The only topic they could agree on was women. Their consensus - all shapes, sizes, colors and temperaments were beautiful. *Amen to that*, was the thought that crossed Robbie's mind.

The trucker pulled up at the brightly lit Shell station on Main Street and jumped out, "This is where we part company, fellas. It was pleasure Tony, and if you ever come down to New York, you look me up. We'll do some barhopping and I'll take you to a place that has the best pasta in the whole damn world and that includes Boston!"

He couldn't resist the parting jibe.

"You've got it, Fred, but I'll be the judge. I have your number and I'll give you call and we can set something up. I'll be bringing my girl with me, if that's okay?"

"Sure! I'll bring the missus and we'll make it a foursome."

And with that, they shook hands and began walking towards Bucky Johnston's Diner when Robbie's cell phone rang. It was Meghan.

"Are you alright?" she asked without preamble.

"I'm really sorry. I tried calling several times but had no reception. I am with Tony VanArcen." He paused before continuing, "We were at Calico Bluff when we had a flat tire. Right now, we're heading towards Bucky Johnston's Diner. I am really sorry, Meghan … the plan was to get to your place by ten."

He turned and gave VanArcen a dirty look.

"Give me the phone," VanArcen demanded, reaching for it, "let me talk to her."

"Hold a second; he wants to talk to you." Robbie said, handing the phone to the smaller man, curious to hear what he had to say.

"Hi Meghan, I just want to make sure that mister-cool-as-ice didn't downplay the story. We didn't *'have a flat tire'*, we were shot at and damn if I wasn't lucky to make it out alive! I'm not Charlie Bronson; bullets fly by his head and he doesn't blink. He's humming 'Mary has a little lamb' when flames are scorching our asses! Then if that wasn't enough, some asshole slashed all four of my tires. Not one, not two, not three but all four! Fuckin' lowlife bastards! Pardon my French."

"Tony, you're not making this up, are you?" Meghan questioned. She wasn't convinced, "You remember the time you said you were attacked by a pack of wolves and we later found out it was Dennis' two dogs?"

"I swear on my mother, what I just told you is the truth. And

Dennis McCarthy's dogs look like wolves … they're freakin' huge. Not as big as Bronson's here but then Dennis ain't mister-cool-as ice!"

"Let me speak to mister-cool-as-ice," she replied tongue in cheek but concerned about what she had just heard.

"Did you really get shot at?" She asked when Robbie got the phone back.

"I'll tell you all about it. Are you at the playground?"

"No. We're still at home. I was worried about you, Robbie Olsen, and it seems I had good reason to be." She replied then with her voice getting softer she confided, "I thought I may have frightened you off … you know, last night." She paused a bit then added, "I haven't stopped thinking about you."

He didn't say anything. He liked the fact that she was worried and was thinking about him but he wasn't sure what his response should be. Sharing feelings wasn't part of his make-up.

"You better say something before I die of embarrassment!" She said when he was silent.

He moved away from VanArcen and replied as softly as he could, "When I'm with you, the rest of the world disappears, it falls away and I haven't felt like that – in a long time. I'm not sure what else I can say but if you are willing to be patient I can learn, I'll do my best to learn; to say what I feel."

"Oh-My-God! Charlie Bronson's in love! *To say what I feel*? I love you, honey, I love you soooo much!" VanArcen teased loud enough for Meghan to hear.

"Piss off, VanArcen! You're a freakin' juvenile! Show some respect for my privacy… you've heard of that, haven't you?" Robbie reprimanded.

Meghan laughed, "Just ignore him. That was sweet and you are fine just the way you are. Do you want me to pick you up?"

"No, it's okay; you don't have to pick us up. I need to get Ronin. You go ahead to the playground and ..." Robbie started when VanArcen grabbed the phone from him.

"Please pick us up! My feet are killing me. I'm not mister-cool-as-ice and I eat too much pasta. I don't work out and my legs are too short. I'm in pain, girl, serious pain. If you have a grain of kindness in your heart, a bit of sympathy for this chunky, little boy, please, I implore you, don't listen to him. He's not human ... he's ... he's Delta Force on steroids!"

Meghan laughed, "You crack me up, Tony. Wait there, we're on our way."

VanArcen tossed the phone back to Robbie, "What's the matter with you? When they offer to do something for you, you let them! They are not like us - when we do something for others, it' a pain in the ass or a favor. When they do something for us, it's sharing, bonding, nurturing or whatever bullshit emotion of the day it is but they do it because they want to."

"They?"

"Yeah, women, females, the fairer sex; that 'they'! We are different, men and women, and I know it's not the right thing to say these days but we are as different as night and day!"

"What are you, Dr. Phil?"

"Listen, Bronson, guys like you have never had to figure women out. All your lives they've thrown themselves at you. Let me guess, Quarterback in high school, the frat house for jocks in college ... how many women? A hundred? Two hundred? Maybe a thousand?"

"I played linebacker in high school and it was Lacrosse in college because I was too slow to play football. I was never part of any fraternity and no, I wasn't a serial womanizer!"

"Okay, I may be a bit off in my numbers but you get the drift. You've never had trouble getting a chick. On the other hand, guys like me deal with something you've never heard of, it's called rejection! I've been rejected more times and by more women than there are fleas on a feral dog. And I don't mind admitting it. One thing I'm not is a quitter. I'm fucking persistent and that's how I got Liz. I had to figure them out and then kept at it 'til I got what I wanted!"

"You never cease to amaze me and it's only been a day!" Robbie said shaking his head, his remark laced with sarcasm.

"Listen up, pal, and learn something. One plus one for us is two every day of the week, every week of the month and every month of the year. One and one for them can be two or three or four or five hundred depending on whether it's the first week, second week, third week, fourth week … and I'm not talking about the fuckin' calendar month; I'm referring to their menstrual cycles! Hormones, bro, it's the bloody hormones. It gives them that glow, makes you want to hug and love them like there was no tomorrow!"

"I have a sister and I've dated a few women so I'm not a total idiot," Robbie snapped back.

"Then stop acting like a Neanderthal and open up that emotion chakra."

"What? What in bleeping heck is that? Speak English, VanArcen," Robbie shot back, bewildered.

"It's left brain, right brain stuff. Men are more left brain and women, right brain. Logic versus intuition. Do I have to explain everything? Have you even heard about the book 'Men are from Mars and Women are from Venus'? Let me put it in a way you'll understand - when you go fishing, what do you do? You think like a fish and when you go hunting, you think like a fuckin' deer so when it comes to women, you have to think like them. Throw logic and linear thinking out the window and say hello to feelings and sensitive talk, lots of talk, brother, lots of talk and emotional sharing. And that means you, Bronson, need to open up that emotion chakra and stop being so anally retentive!"

And that's how it went until Meghan arrived in her beat-up, red Chevy C/K 1500. This model pick-up had an extended Cab with a Big Block V8-engine that sounded like a F-14 fighter-jet ready for take-off. The front bumper was dented and the paint on the hood had faded and peeled. In contrast to the exterior, the interior of Meghan's truck was surprisingly well maintained. The cotton seat covers were like-new and dashboard was spotless and shining. There was a faint, lingering scent of perfume reminiscent of Jasmine and Rose petals.

"No wisecracks about my truck," Meghan told the two men when they got in.

"Where's Ryan?" Robbie asked.

"He's at my mom's." She answered, "I wasn't sure what the plan was so I thought it best to leave him there."

"I'm sorry about this, Meghan, the plan wasn't this at all." Robbie regretted putting her out on her day off.

"It's fine, it really is," she reached over and touched his arm, "I'm just happy you didn't get hurt." Meghan replied and checking her rearview mirror, "Tony, are you okay in the back?"

"What? What did you say?" VanArcen asked over the rattling of the chassis and the low rumble of the engine. The extended Cab seated four but the backseat was cramped, "I always get the shitty seat because I have short legs!" he complained.

"Would you rather walk?" Meghan asked.

"No, but I'd rather sit in the front," he shot back.

"Well, that's not happening unless you want to sit on Robbie's lap. He's too tall to fit back there." She said looking in the rearview mirror and smiling.

"I'll pass. In my next life, I'm coming back as you, Bronson, yeah, that's right. I want to ride up front for a change. And have women swooning over me. It must be nice."

Robbie shook his head, "I've had to deal with this all morning."

Meghan smiled, commiserating, and asked, "What's the plan?"

"We can drop Tony off and I can get Ronin. And if it's not too much trouble, drop us off at the motel. Tony and I can get his pick-up and then meet up with you and Ryan at the playground."

"No, no, no." VanArcen interjected, "No can do! You drop me off and introduce me to that monster you call a dog and don't worry about the truck; we can take care of it later. It ain't going nowhere. You two go enjoy the afternoon. There's no need for all of us to suffer!"

"Are you sure, Tony? You didn't do too well with Dennis' dogs," Meghan questioned.

"That was then, before I began hanging out with Bronson here. Now, I eat bullets and shit nails! Just call me Tony 'Colder-than-Ice' VanArcen. Has a ring to it, don't it?"

Meghan laughed, "It does," then turning to Robbie, "What do you think? I really don't mind driving you to the motel and waiting."

"Hey, you two lovebirds listen to Uncle Tony and do as I say. All this excitement has made me hungry and there's a juicy Ribeye in the fridge that has my name written all over it so don't argue. Let's roll!" He waited and then added, "I've always wanted to say that! Damn! I *am* turning into Tony 'Colder-than-Ice' VanArcen!"

Meghan wasn't convinced and questioned Robbie, "You think it's safe, I mean Tony with Ronin?"

"We'll see how it goes and take things from there," Robbie answered, "Ronin is actually a big teddy bear once you get to know him so Tony may have a new friend especially if he shares his steak."

"That ain't happening so don't even go there," came the prompt response.

"You may not have a choice so I suggest you cut a small portion for him and when you get ready to chow-down, give him his share on a plate. He'll take it raw."

"Damn! I always end up getting screwed! Now I have to share my steak with a monster dog. Just remember, Bronson, you owe me a dinner."

"That I do. Anywhere you'd like to go, it's on me and you can bring that lovely gal of yours."

"Really?" he asked Robbie, suddenly serious.

"Yeah, really, any place you choose." Robbie confirmed, "Just stop with the bellyaching."

VanArcen turned to Meghan, "Do you see what I mean? I'm doing him a favor and he treats me like dirt!"

She laughed, "Tony, I'm not getting in the middle of this."

The introduction at VanArcen's cabin went off better than Robbie had anticipated. After some initial trepidation and coaxing, Ronin allowed Tony to pet him and that was the clincher; he knocked the smaller man down, pinning him with his front paws and under his huge body and began licking his face. No matter how hard he tried, wriggling and squirming, VanArcen couldn't free himself. Ronin had him trapped until Robbie, mercifully, pulled him off.

"I guess you have a new friend," Robbie said helping Tony up.

VanArcen had to wipe his face and his glasses clean. "Damn! That was a near-death experience. I swear I saw my life flash in front of my eyes but what did I tell you? It's the new me. Now go on, get out of here and have some fun," he said with a satisfied look on his face.

"If you run into any trouble, you just say 'bad' and he'll stop whatever it is he's doing. And if you say 'back-up', he'll move back. Got it?"

"Yeah, yeah, got it. 'Bad' and 'back-up' ... that's what I'll be saying when I'm cooking that steak!"

Robbie looked at his dog and scratched him behind his ears,

"You be a good boy, you hear?"

Ronin growled and then barked wanting Robbie to stay but stood beside VanArcen and watched with his head cocked as Meghan and Robbie left.

On the way to Meghan's parent's place, Robbie showed her the piece ripped from Marisa's dress and the pictures of the footprints. He was convinced that Marisa had been abducted and brought to the cabin especially after what had occurred. The shooting was no accident and the cabin burning down seemed too much of a coincidence.

"Oh God, that's awful!" she said when he had finished, "What happens now? If the cabin burned down, is there any other evidence?"

"I don't know," Robbie answered, tucking the piece of cloth back into his pocket, "Any traces of DNA would have been destroyed. I wanted to bring Deputy Bradley in but Tony wasn't so sure. He thinks Bradley may be on Carlson's payroll."

"I personally don't think Joe is a dirty cop. He has confronted Hank on some issues before but you never know, almost everyone in town is on the Carlson payroll one way or the other."

"Maddie Wilkins said some things, weird stuff but some of it is beginning to come true."

"Maddie is the local soothsayer but I wouldn't pay too much attention to her premonitions," Meghan said then added, "Do you want to come in?"

"I'll wait here. I need to think this through and decide on a course of action."

Robbie sat in the car while Meghan ran in to fetch Ryan. He felt torn. There was a part of him that wanted to focus on Meghan and Ryan and not have to worry about Marisa Gorecki but he couldn't. She was in the back of his mind, her ashen face reminding him that she had been murdered and deserved justice and that he was her one last hope.

ALLISON CARLSON

By the time Allison woke up and tumbled out of bed, Luke was gone. They had made love long into the night. She could never get enough of him. She picked up his shirt, which was lying next to her on the bed, and inhaled deeply delighting in the scent of him. She closed her eyes, reliving the memory of the previous night, the fragrance, the taste, the feel of his sinewy muscles; the softness of his tongue when he pleased her - she basked in it all. She loved the piquancy that lingered in her mouth, the sweet, salty succulent taste of his ejaculate that she savored. From the very beginning she had enjoyed the act of fellatio and relished sucking his cock knowing that it excited him to watch her go down on him. It gave her control over him and she basked in that feeling. But most of all she loved the feel of him inside her, his cock buried deep in her. She felt the familiar tingling at her core and wished he was with her. She lay back with his shirt pressed against her nose and her fingers between her thighs.

It was almost noon when she reached her mother's house. She split her time between Luke's cabin and their mother's place and though a lot of her things were still here, she thought of Luke's cabin as home.

"Hi Ma, I'm back," she called dancing through the large front door.

"I'm in the kitchen, dear," her mother replied.

Lisa Carlson's house was the largest in Chase River Town. Hank had renovated the old cabin for his mother soon after he took over the family business. He made sure that she had everything she had ever wanted. He had installed a new furnace that burned propane with central heating so she didn't have to live with the smell of oil or the hassles of burning firewood. He later added an air conditioning unit despite the fact that it rarely ever got hot enough to use. The renovated place was a modern stone and wood house with cathedral ceilings, large glass windows that provided spectacular views of the surroundings. It sat high on the mountain side a little lower than Emma's cabin and was a far cry from Pops' original place.

"Hank!" Allison let out a gleeful cry when she saw him sitting at the kitchen table. She ran over and hugged him and catching the hint of cigarettes on him said, "I thought you promised to give up smoking?"

"I am almost done. I'm down to one or two a day now and soon it will be goodbye Camels!"

She stepped back and complained, "You don't come to see us anymore!"

"Work, baby girl, work takes up a lot of my time, but I have missed you." He said sincerely. Allison had always held a soft spot in his heart. "You get more beautiful every day and I'm not just saying that, you belong in the moves, doll-face!"

She beamed at the compliment, "I know you have to work but you need to come over for dinner like you used to. I know you go to Emma's," she remonstrated, pouting like a little girl.

"He prefers Emma's cooking," Lisa Carlson chimed in, giving her son a reproaching look.

"Don't say that, Ma, you know Emma's having problems with Ed," Hank protested though it was common knowledge in the family that Emma was a fabulous cook.

"I know dear, but it has been a while since we saw you or Pauline. I have no idea what is going on with that girl. And, Edmund is a grown man. A mother can only do so much," his mother responded.

"Don't worry, I'll look in on Pauline and make sure she's okay," Hank reassured her, then turned to Allison, "Where's Luke?"

"I'm not sure. He left early. I know he wanted to get everything in order for fight night. He told me that there were some real good fighters coming over on Wednesday. One of them actually fought in the UFC," Allison commented.

"The UFC is for pussies!" Hank declared vehemently, "Three five-minute rounds? Are you kidding me? And with breaks! We have no rounds and we have no gloves and no weight classes. It's a twenty by twenty foot pit and that gives the little guy enough room to nullify the size advantage of the bigger fighters. The best damn fighter I've ever saw was Daniel VanArcen and he was only five-feet-ten and weighed all of a hundred and seventy pounds."

"I remember Danny," Lisa Carlson said, "he ended up punch-drunk and silly. This fighting is not a good thing for young men."

"Ma, you're not with the times. There are many women who fight now," Allison responded.

"Well, it's not good for them either."

"If we didn't give these men and women a platform to make a living doing what they are good at, they'd starve or resort to crime. We are offering them a way to earn a decent wage while entertaining people," Hank defended his business.

"I don't know about that. All I know is Danny VanArcen ended up unable to speak or take care of himself and he was only sixty. I knew Danny from school. He was a smart kid and nice looking too. That was before he decided to do this fighting thing."

"And that is why I kept Luke out of it. He wanted to fight and could have been one of the great ones but I didn't want him to end up like VanArcen."

"And we thank you for that. He is too beautiful to be fighting anyway," their mother said settling the issue.

"And speaking about VanArcen, he was up at Calico Bluff with that stranger and the word is they burned down Gil Dorsey's hunting cabin. That's what I wanted to ask Luke about ... whether he knew anything about that." Hank probed. "He should have been able to see the smoke from his cabin."

Allison had seen the smoke from the porch but assumed that someone was burning dead trees and shrubs. Though the family knew about Luke and Allison it was a subject that no one brought up.

"Why would Luke be involved with that stranger?" His mother asked, "And I heard his dog is bigger than the two wolves Dennis Mitchel has."

"Ma, they are not wolves. They are giant Shepherds ... Giant German Shepherds." Allison corrected.

The conversation was getting circular and pretty soon they'd be talking about the weather in Alaska and Hank wanted to bring it back to Luke.

"Ma, you know what Luke is like. Remember how he'd drag home every stray he'd come across? And that time when he got bitten by that mangy hound? He didn't say anything until it smelled so bad, Uncle Jack had to rush him to Monson, to the hospital there. Luke has a soft corner for anything he thinks needs help."

"And that's why he's special," his mother quipped back.

Hank rolled his eyes and got up and gave his mother a hug, "I have to go but I'll come by more often. Do you need anything?"

"No, hon, I'm good. The steaks and roast you sent over are still in the fridge. You need to take care of your health, Hank. You are looking thin. Are you eating regularly?" She scolded.

"I'm fine, Ma, look at this belly? Does it look like I'm missing meals?" Then he tuned and kissed Allison on her forehead, "You let me know if you need anything. And tell Luke to come see me, can you do that?"

"I will. I'll call him when I get into town. Hank, please stay out of trouble. I don't know what I'd do something happened to you."

He looked at her for a while, "There are things I do because I have to, that's just life. But how I feel about Mom and you, that is real. I love you both dearly and I will take care of you as long as I can. You remember that," he pinched her chin and repeated, "and, don't forget to talk to Luke."

Allison watched him drive away and felt a melancholic tug at her heart. There was a sadness in Hank that he tried to hide but she could see through that. She was very fond of her eldest brother. Not in the same way as she loved Luke but in the more conventional sense. She had never understood the side of Luke that was cold and indifferent to Hank. They were brothers, well half-brothers, and they should be kinder to one another. She knew that Hank had often tried to get close to Luke but Luke was unreachable when he decided to shut you out and that was the one thing about him that concerned Allison.

Unlike Luke, Allison had no issues dealing with her mother's abnormal relationship with Uncle Jack. She couldn't. She shared the same relationship with her brother and was very comfortable with it. On the other hand, Luke never thought of Uncle Jack as his father. When he referred to his Dad, it was Pops he was talking about. Uncle Jack was always an Uncle to him.

She smiled to herself because Luke was such a peculiar anomaly but she loved him and that's all that mattered to her.

"Ma, I'm going into town," she said, "can I take your car? I like driving it."

"Sure, hon. Stop by Bucky's and pick up the stew and greens that Jake is keeping aside for us."

"Okay, I'll do it on the way back."

And with that, she grabbed the keys to the new SUV, a BMW X5 50i, that Hank had bought for their Mom. The car handled beautifully, a lot better than her Toyota Tacoma, and offered a far more comfortable ride.

Meghan and Robbie

THE MEETING WITH THE GOLDEN TIGRESS

Allison was driving past the playground when she spotted Meghan and Robbie. They were seated on a grassy knoll, huddled close together, watching the children cavorting on the monkey bars. She pulled over onto an unpaved curb and parked. She looked around and waved at some of the parents she knew before walking towards where the children were playing.

As soon as he saw her, Ryan came dashing over and ran into Allison's arms. She hugged him lifting him up and showering his plump little face with kisses.

"That's Allison Carlson, Luke's sister," Meghan said for Robbie's benefit.

"The resemblance *is* uncanny. They don't look anything like Hank Carlson. Are you sure they are related?"

"That's the official word. There are rumors that I don't pay attention to. She's very sweet and is crazy about Ryan."

After tolerating Allison's fussing for a few moments, Ryan went back to the slide where his friends were playing and the young woman strolled over to join Meghan and Robbie. There was a certain 'je ne sais quoi' about her that set her apart. Unlike the fake, exaggerated catwalk struts, she exuded a natural sensuality that is innate in some women. Her perfectly proportioned body was crowned by a mane of long, golden tresses that shimmered in the sunlight cascading around her pretty face giving her an ethereal quality. Her cute nose, full mouth, pixie chin and cornflower blue eyes completed the picture of the proverbial fairytale princess.

"Hi there!" she greeted with an open smile and confidence that most beautiful women possess.

Meghan got up and the two women hugged, then, still holding Meghan's hand, Allison turned and addressed Robbie, "You must be Robbie Olsen, the stranger with the big dog."

"Guilty on both accounts," he replied, "It's nice to meet you Allison."

"You're making quite a name for yourself," she stated extending her hand. Her handshake was soft and gentle very unlike Meghan's firm grip.

"Don't believe everything they say," Robbie quipped back.

"Oh, it's not all bad, some of it but not all," she teased and laughed. She had a soft, infectious laugh that made Robbie smile. She reminded him of a character straight out from a Hollywood movie.

She sat across from them, studying Robbie, "Where's your dog? I've heard so much about him."

"I left him with Tony VanArcen," Robbie answered.

"Oh! Is that safe? The word around town is that he's not very friendly and he's bigger than a Grizzly."

"He's big alright but a Grizzly? That's an exaggeration. And, knowing Tony, he'll talk Ronin into cleaning the cabin!"

They laughed, and she asked, "Are you going to stay long? I mean in Chase River?"

"I'm not planning on leaving anytime soon," he glanced at Meghan but she was distracted, looking over where the children were playing.

She got up, "I'd better check on Ryan. He just took a tumble."

They watched her as she walked towards the slide and Allison remarked, "She's so beautiful and strong. I admire her. I don't know if I could raise a child by myself."

"I don't think you need to worry, you're as pretty as they come" he complimented, "and I'm sure you'll do just fine as a mother."

"You think so? You think I'm pretty?" she questioned with a coquettish smile, looking into his eyes.

"I think you are well aware of your looks, Miss. Carlson," he responded, returning her smile.

"And you; are you aware of the effect you have on women?"

"Are you flirting with me, Allison?" He questioned playfully.

"I might be," she said laughing, a melodic ring to her laughter. "You remind me of a handsome teddy bear."

"Well, I am truly flattered but I have been smitten by Miss. Hollier and in life, timing is everything." He came back with a broad smile. He found himself drawn to this sensual creature and had to cling to his feelings for Meghan.

"What are the two of you laughing about?" Meghan asked rejoining them.

"I was trying to steal him away from you," Allison declared, "but he's too far gone. He's trapped in your web, Miss. Hollier! It seems we have the same taste in men."

Meghan blushed crimson and glanced at Robbie before answering, "You had better stay away from him, Allison. He's taken."

"Hmmm, we'll see." And she got up, "I would love to stay and chat but I have to get some shopping done. It was nice meeting you Robbie and don't be stranger," then giving Meghan a hug, she complained, "I rarely get to see you anymore and I do miss Ryan. Please stop by – Mom complains that she hasn't seen either of you in a while."

"Tell her I'll bring Ryan over soon," Meghan promised.

Allison smiled at Robbie and said, "Bye, Teddy Bear," and then added for Meghan's benefit, "If you want to keep him, you'd better not let him out of your sight! There's plenty of honey around here," and with a concluding wave she headed for her car.

They watched her walk back to the SUV, graceful and effortless, and like she owned the place.

"Nice car," Robbie observed.

But Meghan ignored the remark and instead asked, "Do you think she's beautiful?"

He hesitated, "Is that a trick question?"

She took his hand in hers, "No! I just want to know if you think she's beautiful."

He wasn't sure if he should be honest or take the safe route so he took the middle ground instead. "She is striking; like some airbrushed photograph. But it's almost not real. I think *you* are beautiful, and in ways that are real not like a Barbie doll."

She smiled and squeezed his hand.

"You're not jealous, are you?" he asked, surprised.

"Women are insecure beings, at least I am," she said honestly, "and Allison is exceptionally beautiful and when I saw the two of you laughing together, I had this feeling..." she paused then finished lamely, "I wouldn't blame you."

"You don't have to worry. I'm not interested in her," he replied reassuringly but the truth was that Allison had touched a part of him, a curious but very sexual part.

Meghan was quiet, holding his hand and tracing lazy patterns on his arm.

"What's going on in that pretty little head of yours?" Robbie inquired, noticing her preoccupation.

"I had better tell you a bit about myself so we don't get too far ahead of ourselves," she began and then stopped, gazing blindly at the kids playing.

"This sound serious. What's going on? Please tell me this has nothing to do with Allison!"

She took a deep breath, "No, no it doesn't. This is about me and about Ryan. When I was eighteen, like many of the kids here I left Chase River and headed for the big city. In my case it was New York City. A friend of mine, a girl that I grew up with, was living there and she would call going on about how fabulous life was in the city. The nightlife, the sophisticated men, the glamor and excitement … all the things an eighteen-year-old would miss here."

She paused and looked at him, "I don't know if anyone can understand how mundane and boring life here is, and as a teenager, I was easily influenced. I longed for the excitement of what was being portrayed on TV shows and the movies … it was irresistible. The final nail in the coffin was when Betty told me that I could model and make a lot of money and travel to all these exotic places. She would call almost every week trying to get me to come there."

"I'm from a small town in Montana – I get it. It's like cabin fever … there's a need to explore what is on the other side of the mountain; to see what you're missing." Robbie empathized.

She studied his face, encouraged by his empathy, "My parents were dead set against my going but when they saw that I was determined to leave, they relented. My father was heartbroken. I am an only child and was his baby and he was worried sick about me. I had no real perspective; no understanding of what this was doing to them. I just wanted to get away. Looking back, I was such a spoiled, ungrateful little brat."

He remained quiet, studying her face and the emotions she was struggling with. Meghan continued, "Anyhow, they drove me to Bangor so I could catch a flight to Newark Airport and from there I took a train to Penn Station. You've got to understand just what a big step that was – I had never been out of Chase River. It was frightening and exciting all at the same time. Long story short, the four years of city life got old and there was no modeling contract. The sophisticated men turned out to be shallow creeps looking to get their jollies off and pretty girls were a dime a dozen. Most of them get used and tossed aside like soiled tissue and I wasn't about to go that route. I was never the party girl so I swallowed my pride and decided to get back home. The only good thing to come out of my stay in New York was bartending. I had learned to be a pretty decent bartender."

He reached over and gently pushed her hair back to the side so he could see her clearly.

"When I got back, things had changed here and believe me I had my share of doubts and misgivings. I was lonely and there was no social life to speak of and that's when I ran into Luke Carlson again. We had gone to school together but he had grown and had changed from the shy boy to a self-assured, handsome man."

He could see her struggle and wanted to spare her. "You really don't have to get into this. It's the past and now I get it … Ryan. Ryan is Luke's son, right?" Robbie asked.

"Yes. We had a short and intense affair. I mean really short-lived but I got pregnant. He wanted me to get rid of 'it' but when I refused; he told me that he would never be a father to the child. In all fairness to him, he did warn me and he was true to his word. Luke has shown no interest in Ryan; none whatsoever. When he does see us together, he ignores him completely. I feel bad for Ryan but it is what it is."

"I cannot judge the man without knowing him and Luke seems very different from Hank. I don't get his reasons for reneging on his parental responsibility as a father but the decision is his and he has to live with it." Robbie offered, trying to see both sides.

They both fell silent lost in their own thoughts. Ryan being Luke's son would mean that he would be tied to the Carlson's in perpetuity and Meghan wondered how her son's lineage would affect how this man felt about her and about Ryan. *Why would a handsome, single man settle for a woman with a child?*

Finally she stood up and pulled him to his feet, "I will understand if you don't want any part of this. Ryan needs a father and I need a man. It's been years since I have been intimate with someone and I miss that. Not just the sex but waking up in a man's arms and feeling that sense of security … that completeness."

She paused and when he didn't respond, continued, "I'm twenty eight going on forty. That's what raising a little boy by yourself will do to you. I'm not very good at playing the coy maiden or any of the other games that women play. The moment I saw you walk into Bucky's; I felt the promise of my dreams. And now that I know you a little better, you are more than I had ever expected or wanted. And if that comes across as being aggressive or desperate, then so be it. I'm a woman who knows what she wants and I don't have the time or energy to pretend otherwise."

He was looking into her eyes, admiring her courage in verbalizing emotions that most women wouldn't have.

He said truthfully, "I don't know if I am that man. God knows I wasn't looking for a readymade family but it was the same for me. From the first moment I saw you, I felt something I had never felt before. And though there's a lot we have to learn about each other, I can't wait to begin that journey with you. I find myself thinking about you all the time and that too is a first."

She smiled and tiptoed to kiss him gently on his lips, "I'm going to drop Ryan off at Mom's tonight. We are going to have a romantic dinner, Robbie Olsen, and I'm going to find out what is behind that mister-cool-as ice exterior!"

He hugged her then held her at arms-length, "Mister-cool-as-ice? Really, you too?"

She laughed, took his arm and they walked to the slide where Ryan was playing.

It was late afternoon by the time they finished lunch at Bucky Johnston's Diner. Ryan had wanted a Junior Burger and it was conveniently located, just walking distance from the playground. It also gave Robbie a chance to try the much vaunted Lamb Stew that proved to be everything Maddie Wilkins had said it was and more.

When they got to VanArcen's cabin there was a note pinned to the front door. He had gone with a neighbor, Fat Paddy Haskell, to fetch his pick-up and had left the door unlocked. It also said that Ronin had eaten most of the steak, a can of spam and everything else that was in the fridge. When Robbie and Meghan walked in, they found the big dog asleep on the couch. The living room was in total disarray. The side tables and a footstool had been knocked over and the frayed, old rug was rumpled and shoved unceremoniously into one corner. Robbie could only imagine the total chaos that must have taken place – Ronin chasing Tony and bullying him until he got the rest of the steak.

After the usual roughhousing that threatened to hurt Meghan, Robbie managed to calm Ronin down. He then rummaged through the kitchen cabinet drawers looking for a pad or some paper and found an old notebook. The book was a journal filled with neatly written notes giving instructions on how to prime the pump, service the tractor, patch the roof and other necessities related to the cabin. Robbie tore a clean page out and scribbled a thankyou note before they left for the Sleepy Crest Motel.

During the fifteen minute ride to the motel, Ryan sat on Robbie's lap and had a barrage of questions that stemmed from the curiosity of a four-year-old but the one that made them laugh was when Ryan asked Robbie whether he was a Ninja. It was Meghan who saved him, "Ryan, he is more than a Ninja, Robbie fought for America!"

"You mean like Captain America?" the boy asked, eyes wide with amazement, leaning back resting his head on Robbie's shoulder and looking up at his new hero.

"Yes, baby, like Captain America!" she said and laughed. Robbie could only roll his eyes and was grateful when Ryan noticed his tattoo and began with a new set of questions.

When Meghan pulled up in the rear of the motel, the parking lot was deserted. Afternoons were usually quiet. "This place is a dump! One of Hank's seedy holdings. Are you sure you want to stay here?"

"It's fine for now," Robbie assured her, then turning to Ryan, "Hey little man, it was fun, huh?"

He tousled the boy's hair and said, "I'll be there at 7:00 pm give or take but you don't have to cook anything fancy. I am pretty stuffed."

"Leave it to me. You job is to get there without beating up the local thugs and getting shot at!" she teased.

He leaned in and gave her a quick kiss on the lips and was about leave when she stopped him, "Hey, I almost forgot. Here, this is for Ronin," she handed him a brownbag, "Steaks stolen from Hank's freezer!"

He smiled and took the package, "You shouldn't have, but

thanks. I never pegged you for a thief and never thought I be indebted to Carlson."

"You're not! You are indebted to me and don't you forget that! And steaks are not the only things I steal, watch your heart, Robbie Olsen," came the sharp reply.

He placed his hand over his heart, "I'll make it up to you, I promise."

"You had better," she said then turning to Ryan, "Don't you want to say goodbye to Ronin and Captain America? Say goodbye, we're going to Grandma's."

"Bye, Ronin … bye, Robbie, bye!" the little boy shouted through the window as the pick-up drove off.

ANGELA MERCIER &
JODIE GRASSHOFF

It was close to 3:00 pm when Robbie got back to his room giving him sufficient time for a much needed nap. He shucked the T-shirt and jeans and crawled into bed and was asleep as soon as his head hit the pillow. He woke up two and a half hours later and had finished showering when he heard a soft tap on the window, the one facing the balcony. At first he thought that it was the rattle of the wind but the following thumps had Ronin growling.

He quickly got his trousers on, grabbed the Glock and drew a crack in the curtain to check on who it might be before opening the side door. It was the girl, Jodie, and the tall woman she had left with after his run-in with Al Goddard.

"Back boy, get back." Robbie commanded, "It's alright. Go lie down."

They came in quickly and shut the door behind them. Ronin was on alert and growled but another stern command from Robbie and he lay down by his master.

"I'm Angela," the woman said in a low, smoky voice, "Angela Mercier. And, this here is Jodie."

Neither Angela nor Jodie had much makeup on and without the added maquillage the young girl looked even younger, like she was ten or twelve. For her part, Angela appeared more like a suburban housewife than the hooker he had seen the day before. The blond wig was gone and in its place was a speckled head kerchief, tied like a military bandana, covering her short wavy hair. She was dressed in a loose fitting blue, cotton blouse and a baggy pair of gray trousers with summer sandals on her feet and a leather purse in her hand. Definitely middle class cool instead of garish night-crawler.

Robbie nodded and said, "This is a surprise. What can I do for you?"

"Hank's thugs have been looking for Jodie but I managed to keep her away from them," she said sitting down at the end of the bed, "Sooner or later they will find her, especially Seppo. I heard he's been asking about her … about her whereabouts."

"Why don't you go to the police? Agent Bradley seems…" he started to say but was interrupted by the woman.

"There ain't no police here! And the Sheriff's Office is bought and owned by Hank Carlson. You can't trust no one. I've been trying to reach her family for months and finally got hold of her brother. He has a small farm in upstate New York, near Elizabeth Town. When Jodie first went missing, he had tried to find her but she got rid of her phone, so he had no way to reach her."

"I didn't get rid of it; someone stole it at bus station when I sleeping," the young girl protested.

"Whatever. Go on," Robbie encouraged.

"Jim Grasshoff, her brother, wanted to come here to pick her up but I told him no … it was a bad idea. If they see his car they will follow him back to his farm and God knows what they'd do. He has a wife and three little kids. I told him that someone would drop her off at a meeting spot that was convenient. They are watching me, so…" Angela left the sentence hanging. There was no need to complete it. The implication was clear.

There was a long pause before anyone spoke. The woman had a plan but that involved Robbie's assistance and it meant asking for help which was something she wasn't accustomed to doing but she cared enough for the young girl to reach out.

"And so you decided that 'the someone' was me," Robbie smiled. He seemed to be the default choice for everyone. First it was VanArcen and now, this woman.

"Listen Mr. Olsen, all you have to do is call him and pick a place one hour or two from here. He'll meet you there. Two or three hours of your time, that's all I'm asking. If they find her now, they will surely hurt her; maybe even get rid her especially after today," she couldn't get herself to say 'murder' or 'kill'; it was obvious that Jodie meant too much to her.

"What do you mean, *'after today'*? I don't get it," Robbie was puzzled.

"Jodie was on Facebook, Instagram, Tumblr and who knows what!" Angela answered, "These kids live on these sites. She's deleted her profile now but we think Monique saw what Jodie posted. I don't use social media too much so it is better she explain." The woman turned to Jodie, "Go on, girl, tell him ... tell him everything."

The young girl hesitated, "Marisa made me promise that I wouldn't tell anyone but I guess now it's okay to tell you. She told me that if something were to happen to her, I was to post the videos one at a time and gave me the names to tag," Jodie paused, looked towards Angela for encouragement and then went on, "Marisa was my friend. We talked a lot, she was like an older sister and she never judged me. She was always there for me."

She stopped, trying to formulate her words, not wanting to say too much or betray her friend.

"Go on. Did you talk in person or over the phone?" Robbie asked. He was fully attentive now.

"Both. She didn't like the Sleepy Crest so I would meet her by the river, she called it Butterfly River. There were hundreds of butterflies, maybe thousands, different colors and all so beautiful. She loved them, especially a blue one called the Bog Copper. I remember the name because I thought it was the Big Chopper but she corrected me. And, there was another one, a very rare one that she pointed out but the name... I always forget it. Crow something..."

"They are called Crowberry Blue," the older woman prompted.

"Yes, the Crowberry Blue, that's the name! She told me that I was like the Crowberry Blue, rare and beautiful. Marisa knew all the names, what kind they were and how long they lived. She was so smart."

"Where is this river? Is it the same one where I found her?" Robbie asked impatiently, he didn't want to rush the girl but he was intrigued by what she said about posting videos.

"Yes but you have to go past Devil's Ridge. It's a ten or fifteen minute walk through the forest. The trees open up and there's a rock in the middle of the river, it's a big rock called the Big Boulder, but the water is not very deep there so you can climb up and watch the butterflies and listen to the water flowing. It's so peaceful. Marisa told me that it was the place where she could get away from everything and jot down her feelings in her diary and one day she would write a very interesting book, a bestseller."

"Where is the diary now?" He couldn't hide his curiosity.

"She hid it by the railroad tracks and only I know where it is," Jodie answered but she was getting defensive not wanting to say too much.

"That's okay, you don't have to say anything if you don't want to. How did you post the videos?" Robbie was a bit confused.

"I used her laptop – she has the videos on her laptop. She also gave me copies of the photographs and a memory stick with the videos on it. She told me to keep them hidden separately so if someone were to find one, I would always have the other. She also told me to write a note for Tony explaining where everything was and leave it with Angela. Marisa thought of everything. I first thought she was being paranoid but now I know she was right. They killed her because she knew too much."

"Who's they and what did she know? Where are you hiding the laptop and the photographs?"

"I can't tell. No one knows about the laptop … only Angela. I keep it hidden with Marisa's diary in her secret place. I hid the photographs and the memory card in another place that no one will find."

"Listen, Jodie, if you want me to help you, you're going to have to trust me. I need to know what was in those videos, who the people were and where you hid all this. Only with proof and hard evidence can you get people arrested," Robbie wanted to win her over. *She's young and people had mistreated her so why would she trust anyone?*

Jodie looked over at Angela, she felt helpless and was about to say something when they heard footsteps walking along the corridor. Her eyes widened and she moved closer to Angela, grabbing her arm. The tall woman stood up, her face etched with concern.

Robbie put a finger to his lips, "Quiet."

Ronin was on full alert, growling deep in his chest. A few seconds later there was a knock on the door and a sonorous, deep voice said, "Olsen? Robbie Olsen? We need to talk."

Ronin moved towards the door, hackles raised with the growls getting louder.

Robbie pointed to the bathroom and whispered, "Be quiet."

There was another knock that set Ronin off, rumbling growls followed by deafening barks. "Go, now … quickly," He whispered softly to the women and then yelled at the door, "I'm coming. Let me get the dog settled. Stop knocking on the door."

Robbie walked over next to Ronin and waited for the women to disappear into the bathroom. He stalled for a few seconds before saying loudly enough, "Back boy, back-up. It's okay, come on, back, back!"

He cracked open the door just wide enough so they could get a glimpse of the big dog.

There were three of them; all hard cases. Robbie recognized the man standing to the left. He had seen him at Bucky Johnston's. The man had a distinguishing scar that ran down the length of his face from forehead to his lower jaw narrowly missing his left eye. He was average height, lean with a tough, hard look about him. The man in the middle was heavy set and tall, about the same height as Robbie, with small beady eyes, a weak chin and a thick-lipped mouth. The third was a little man, a Mexican or Italian, black hair, olive skin, with random tats on his prominently veined arms. He had a boyish, handsome face with a perpetual smile. The gold chains around his neck, the expensive loafers and silk-blend trousers were incongruous with the roughnecks he was with. But he was the one Robbie was going to watch; it was almost always the little guy that was dangerous.

"What's up?" Robbie asked.

The fat man in the middle, appropriately named 'Fats', did the speaking, his voice terse, "Have you seen Jodie?"

"Who?" Robbie asked, forehead furrowed.

Scarface cut in, "Stop fucking around. Jodie, Snake's bitch … you remember that little whore don't you, wise guy?"

Ronin growled, fangs flashing, saliva frothing at the mouth, pushing against Robbie's thigh to get at the man. The big dog sensed danger and was in protective mode.

Robbie held Ronin in check blocking him with his leg, "You mean the little girl and I'd watch that mouth. My dog's not very happy and that's not good."

"Fuck your dog! I'll gut him like a pig!" the man with the scar spat back.

The fat man tried to diffuse the situation and said to Scarface, "Hey, Jake, calm down. No need for that." Then he addressed Robbie, "Hank wanted to know if you had seen her or if she had contacted you? That's all. We think she's in danger and Hank wants to make sure nothing happens to her. My friend here has a short fuse and a foul mouth… he don't mean nothing by it. Right, Jake?"

Robbie did something totally unexpected and took all three by surprise. He pushed Ronin back, stepped into the walkway and closed the door behind him. He moved to his left, closing the distance between him and Jake and said, "No, she didn't contact me and no, I haven't seen her."

The fat man responded in a conciliatory tone, "Then you wouldn't mind if we looked in your room, would you? Just get the dog out and we'll take a quick peek. How about that? Take us a minute, that's all. And, it will make my boss real happy. "

Robbie's faced hardened. "Are you calling me a liar, mister?"

"Yeah, asshole, I'm calling you a fuckin' …" Scarface started when Robbie struck; a right that landed on the point of the man's chin. It was short, straight and delivered with the explosiveness of a boxer's 'snap'. The man's eyes rolled back as he fell and before the others could react, Robbie pulled the Glock that was tucked in the back of his trousers.

"Unh-ha, I wouldn't do that." He said to the small, dark-skinned man seeing his hand move. The dark haired man froze.

"Why'd you go and do that?" Fats asked in total bewilderment.

"He has a big mouth and I don't like people threatening my dog!" Robbie looked directly at the smaller man, "Now listen up, I don't want to get involved in this shit. I'm late for a date and if I see you again, I'll assume that you're not coming over to play chess and I won't ask any questions, I will kill you. You get that?"

"Hank is not going ..." the fat man started.

"Zip it, fatso! I'm not talking to you," Robbie cut him off and addressed the small man, "Do you understand?"

The man nodded, "Si, si ... I understand." He spoke with a heavy Italian accent and with a voice that was strangely feminine. His fingers played with a pendant on one of the many chains around his neck. It was a subconscious habit.

"Okay, get going and take your garbage with you," Robbie instructed motioning in the direction of Scarface Jake.

"La prossima volta sarà diverso," the small man said as he walked toward Scarface Jake, "It will be different, the next time we meet."

"Yeah sure, remember what I said. Now get going," was the terse reply.

Jake was still disoriented when his friends tried to get him up. His eyes were glazed and he was unsteady on his feet. They started down the corridor half carrying and half dragging the still disoriented man.

"Hank ain't gonna to like this, no, not one bit," the fat man said in parting, laboring under the weight and awkwardness of shouldering a shorter man.

"You tell Hank to come and see me," Robbie shot back and slipped silently into his room.

He waited a few minutes, peeked through the curtain and watched as the men got into a dusty red pick-up and drove off.

"Okay, you can come out," Robbie said walking towards the bathroom.

There was a look of relief on both their faces. Angela was the first to speak, "God Almighty! That was close. I recognized the voices of Fats and Jake. Was there anyone else?"

Robbie described the smaller, dark-haired man with the accent.

"That's Cat, everyone calls him Cat but his real name is Cataldo Cascone and he's as dangerous as they come. Hank only uses him if he thinks there's going to be trouble." She paused before asking, "What happened? I could hear noises and I thought for sure they were coming in."

"It was nothing," Robbie brushed it off and spoke to the girl, "Tell me what else you know, Jodie, and be quick. We don't have a lot of time," Robbie said to the young girl.

Jodie didn't hesitate, "I saw Marisa the night before she went missing," Jodie began explaining what she knew and looked towards Angela for reassurance.

"Keep going, girl, don't hold back nothing," Angela prodded.

"She was in Ed Carlson's pick-up truck. I know his truck, it's shiny and new and black with flames painted on the sides. She was in the passenger side in front and Ed was driving."

"Ed Carlson is Hank Carlson's nephew. I know Ed and he's not half bad but he is a Carlson and they are all dangerous and they do stick together." Angela informed Robbie not knowing if he knew of Ed's relationship to Hank Carlson.

Robbie asked the girl, "When was this, I mean, what time?"

"It was late, almost midnight, I remember because I was tired and wanted to go to bed but Snake insisted that I should try for one more trick. I was standing by the big tree in the front waiting for someone to drive by so I could flag them down. That's what we are told to do. I saw the headlights and was about to step onto the road when I recognized his truck and stayed where I was. I don't think they saw me because of the shadows."

"Was there anyone else with them?"

"I couldn't see if there was anyone else inside but Jericho

was standing in the back … outside, holding on to the bar on top. Everyone knows Jericho because of his long hair and tattoos. They weren't driving very fast."

"This is serious, Jodie, are you sure it was Ed Carlson?" Robbie asked, his attention focused on the young girl.

"Yes I'm sure. He used to come here a lot. He likes to …" she paused, looked again at Angela for approval before adding, "He likes to tie people up. The girls used to joke about how he couldn't do "it" unless he tied them up but they are scared of him so they keep it hush-hush." She explained.

"Tell him what you saw today morning," the woman said to Jodie.

"I saw you with Tony VanArcen driving by and a few minutes later, Jericho followed in his Jeep. That's all I know."

"How do you know Tony? Does he come here often?" Robbie was curious.

Angela answered, "No, he doesn't come here but this is Chase River and everyone here knows everyone especially when it comes to outsiders. Tony's family is from here but they still think he's an outsider."

"Why it was odd to see Jericho drive by?"

"At first I didn't think nothin' of it. But when we heard what happened at Calico Bluff … the Dorsey cabin burning down, I began thinking. Why would that nice young girl be in the car with Ed? Then she goes missing. A week later, she's found dead and now the cabin, which they used for hunting, burns down. Then Jodie posts a short video of Marisa with some men I never seen and everyone is looking for her. Something ain't right."

"Who's the 'they' that used the cabin?"

"A lot of the local boys use the cabin but mostly it was Ed Carlson, his brother Ray and Jericho."

Robbie stood mulling over what he had just heard and thought, *"Why didn't they come looking for the girl before?"* and almost like Angela read his mind, the woman added, "Jodie didn't tell me this until two days ago and she didn't post the video until today. Monique must have known. She sent Jodie a message. It said *"I know who you are, Taxi Girl!"*."

"Taxi Girl is my Username," Jodie clarified, "Marisa gave it to me. She said it was because people had to pay for the ride. I thought that was neat."

That explains it, he thought. *Ed Carlson, and whoever else was with him, didn't know they had been seen but why the concern over the video? And what was in the video that would make Hank, Ed and the other want to talk to Jodie? What did Marisa see or have that got her killed? Monique must have said something to the other girls or she must have snitched.* And again, like a mind reader, Angela spoke, "Al was trying to beat it out of her when you stopped him. Monique must've ratted and said something to him. That bitch is on drugs and will sell her own mother to get high!"

"As soon as I got Monique's message, I got scared and took my profile down."

"But it's all out there – you can never get rid of it," Robbie mused.

"My Username and ID are fake so unless they trace it to Marisa's laptop, they won't know," Jodie replied but her expression reflected her concern.

"They *can* trace it to your laptop but that would take some doing. What was in the video? Or rather, who was in the video? Can I see it?"

"I promised Marisa … no one. I have to post them and tag the people she listed. I'm supposed to post one every day but now I'm scared because Monique knows."

"The only way Monique could have known is if she recognized the people in the video and somehow tied it back to you. I'm assuming you're not in the video."

"I'm not," Jodie said quickly, "not in that one."

"Then Marisa was," Robbie deduced, "and she knows that Marisa and you were friends. But right now they are not sure. Now I know why they want to talk to you. They have to make sure because if it is not you, then they have another problem; a much bigger problem."

"Yes. Then there is someone out there that has all this stuff on them," Angela surmised.

Robbie thought about it. He needed to know what was on the video but it was pointless to press the girl right now and he was running out of time. He wasn't going to be late again. He studied the woman and the girl; his butt resting against the small table in the corner of the room.

"Why are *you* doing this? This could be dangerous," he said to the woman.

Ronin picked that moment to walk over to Jodie and sniff her hand and clothes before turning to the woman. Angela's eyes went wide with fright.

"I don't like this. I'm scared of dogs!" she exclaimed when Ronin sniffed her face.

"Just sit still, he's checking to make sure you're not a threat to me."

"Oh God, oh God," she murmured while Ronin kept sniffing her face, neck and bandana.

Satisfied that she was okay, the big dog went over to Robbie and lay down by his feet. The relief was evident on Angela's face.

"Okay, now that you've passed the test, where were we? Oh yes, why are *you* doing this? This can be dangerous especially if Ed and

Hank Carlson are as nasty as they say."

"Mister, I've done some bad things in my life. I've cheated, stole, lied and broke my poor mama's heart. I grew up in the French Quarter of New Orleans, in the worst section but I ain't blaming no one. I made bad choices. I got into drugs and when stealing wasn't enough, I sold my body. I had to run away because I stabbed a pimp, not one time but seventeen and God knows he had it coming. I ran and this place was as far from there as I could go, where they ain't gonna find me and that was thirteen years ago. Unlucky thirteen – we say it's bad juju! Every year I tell myself that this is the last year but you can't leave, not when you cross thirty and this is all you know. What I'm doing is the one good thing I done in my life. This little girl has a chance and if they get me, at least Saint Peter will know I ain't all bad!"

Robbie could tell that she was being sincere and truthful. He had once read that angels arrive in different shapes and forms and this woman was surely Jodie's angel.

The girl looked at the woman and said, "You're not bad, Angela, you and Marisa are the only good people here. And now Marisa is gone. I don't know what I would have done without you."

"Shush, child," Angela placed her arm around the girl and spoke to Robbie, "Do it for her, mister, she deserves another chance. I know there is good in you or you wouldn't have done what you did when Snake was beating her. Most would have walked on."

There was an uneasy silence. Robbie knew that time was of essence but he didn't want to lose what he had with Meghan. Angela Mercier was taking a big chance and she wouldn't have come to him if she had other options.

"I'll take you to your brother," Robbie said to Jodie without further discussion. He wanted to make sure he wasn't late for Meghan's dinner, "But you think about this – I can't help you if I don't know what is going on and you don't help anyone by getting yourself killed. Tony is a nice, honest man but he is not cut out for this shit. You need to trust me."

"I'll talk to her, Mr. Olsen, I will convince her but you have to help me," Angela pleaded, "help us, please."

"I can't do it this evening. Tomorrow afternoon would be more like it. Can you keep her safe till then?"

"I don't know. If Seppo comes by here, someone will talk. Most of these girls are not bad people, just misfortunate. But they are all frightened of him. I am too. And they all know that I keep an eye out for Jodie." She left the implication unsaid.

Robbie thought for a second then asked, "Do you know the gas station at the intersection of Route 15 and Route 6?"

"Yes, Maddie Wilkins," the woman nodded in confirmation.

"Can you take her there?"

"Now is too risky. Someone might see us. But later, 8 or 9 o'clock when it's dark, I can do it."

She's right, it is too risky now, he thought and said summarily, "Jodie can stay in my room with Ronin. They are not coming back, not tonight. They will think that *if* Jodie's with me, I wouldn't leave her alone in my room and would take her someplace else. So she'll be safe here. You take her to Maddie's place tonight and I'll take her to her brother tomorrow. How do I reach him?"

The woman fumbled through her purse and fished out a cell phone. She handed it to Robbie.

"This is the phone I used to call him. The calls are listed as 'JB' for Jodie's Brother. It's not my regular phone. Snake and the others don't know about it. They only have this number, my phone," and with that she held up another generic looking cell phone.

Robbie scrolled through the many calls she had made to 'JB', "That was smart, not using your phone. I will give Jim a call and set up a time and place tomorrow."

"Thank you, mister," the relief evident on her face. "I will miss her. She is a sweet, sweet girl who made some bad choices like I did but no one gave me a second chance." She hesitated, looking down at the stained carpet and added, "Everyone deserves a second chance." Her voice quivered, the sudden flood of emotions threatening to overtake her.

Robbie could empathize, "I agree, we can all use second chances."

She got up and hugged the girl tightly and kissed her forehead, "I have to go now. You do as Mister Olsen tells you. I will come back later and knock, remember our code, three quick and then two slow, like we always do. Don't say anything and don't open the door unless it is me. You understand?"

"Yes," the girl nodded.

The woman peeked through the curtains then slipped out of the side door onto the balcony. There was no one around so she quickly scaled the short parapet wall onto the landing and walked down the stairway to the parking lot. She waited near the corner wall making sure she wasn't noticed before proceeding along the corridor towards the front office.

"You're a lucky girl," Robbie motioned to Jodie to sit down, "that woman is risking a lot so you get this chance. Don't let her down."

The tears welled up in the girl's eyes, "I won't let Angela down. I promise."

He got a handkerchief out from his rucksack and handed it to her, "Okay, stop crying. It'll be okay."

"It's my fault," she sobbed; "I'm just no good!" she began to cry, her body racked by sobs then just as quickly she regained her composure, sniffled and blew her nose into the kerchief.

He waited for her to look at him. "It's not your fault, you hear, no twelve-year-old should be taken advantage of."

"Thirteen," she corrected, "I'll be fourteen in two months."

"At fourteen I thought I knew it all and the truth is that I knew nothing," he spoke gently, "You get back to your family and go to school and get on with your life. You have so many wonderful things to experience but whatever happens, don't look back. We can't change the past. We can only make amends and move on."

She studied him before asking, "You have all these scars on your body; did someone hurt you?"

"I was in a war… in Afghanistan. The scars on my body are reminders of the mistakes I made and the soldiers who paid for it with their lives. I have to live with that but I'm learning to move on. Your friend is right, we all deserve second chances."

Robbie added some water to Ronin's water bowl before going into the bathroom for a final appraisal, *'not too bad for a washed-up old Ranger'*, he thought studying his reflection, then returned to where the girl was sitting. "When I leave, you stay low. Lie down on this side of the bed and don't make any sound. Leave the TV off. You don't want anyone getting nosy and don't post anything more until we can figure this out. Okay?"

Jodie nodded, "Okay."

He grabbed two pillows and threw them on the floor on the far side of the bed. He pulled the comforter off and made a makeshift sleeping bag, "Here, you wait here until she comes and stay as quiet as possible. If you have to use the toilet, don't flush. I'll take care of it when I get back."

"I won't make a noise but I have to pee."

"That's fine go ahead, I'll wait. You can flush when I'm here, no one will know the difference."

After a few minutes, he heard the toilet flush and she came out of the bathroom. She had washed her face getting rid of what little makeup she had on and looked even younger than her thirteen years.

"That's much better," Robbie remarked, "you're a pretty girl and you don't need that gunk!"

She smiled and sat on the floor next to Ronin and began petting him.

"Okay, listen up; this is important. Don't open the door unless you are sure it is Angela and you stay with Maddie until I come and get you. Okay?"

"Okay."

"Ronin is going to be with you so you're safe here. We just have to be careful."

He knelt down next to Ronin scratched him on the underside of his neck and jaw, "You stay and be good. You take care of Jodie and I'll come back soon."

On cue, Ronin turned and gave the girl's face a sloppy swish with his tongue.

"Lock the door behind me and when Angela and you leave, make sure the door is locked. Here's the key; you leave it with Maddie. I'll come and see you after I speak to your brother."

The girl nodded, "I'll make sure. Don't worry. Tell Jim, I'm really sorry, please tell him that, okay?"

"Okay, I'll let him know," Robbie assured the young girl. He gave the place a final look and then left closing the door behind him.

Maddie Wilkins

NOSTRADAMUS IN DRAG

He found Maddie Wilkins cleaning the counter top by the register and greeted her, "Hey Maddie, how are things?"

She peered at him over her granny glasses, "Well, things are beginning to happen, Robbie Olsen, just like I said they would. It has started, the Armageddon has started," She replied without missing a beat.

He ignored the Armageddon quip and decided to get straight to the point, "I have a favor to ask."

"You can bring the young girl here; I'll keep her safe until you can take her to her family."

He was in shock and it showed on his face, *how in blazes did she know?*

"Oh, you are wondering how I knew," she said making a soft clucking sound and then laughed at his amazement, "I do see some things but this I knew because Angela Mercier came to see me. That poor woman was worried sick about me and wanted to make sure I wouldn't be in danger if she brought Jodie here." She looked at Robbie cogitating on what she was about to say and then told him,

"Ancient cultures believe in reincarnation and I do too. I feel I have known some people including you in a previous life. Does that sound strange to you?"

"I don't know and I'd be lying if I said I knew anything about reincarnation. I do know that Angela is taking a risk to do something good and that is not always easy. And you, Maddie Wilkins, are a fascinating lady who I admire. I was born too late or we would certainly have gotten to know each other better."

"Oh go on with you, you silver tongued devil! Maybe it's just that I'm old and at the end of my journey and refuse to believe in the finality of it all. Instead, I wish to believe that I will be back and that we will all be back to try our hands at being better people."

"Don't say that. This is not the end of your journey. You're as tough as anyone I know and I have a feeling you will outlive us all," Robbie reassured her.

"You are wrong, dear boy. My time is coming to an end … I feel it here," she replied patting her bony chest and noticing his reaction and the consternation on his face she said, soothingly, "Don't worry, son, I have had a good life and when it happens, I will be ready. But before that, I want you to do something for me. Give me a minute." She got up slowly and walked up the stairs holding on to the banister for support, her gait unsteady and wobbly.

A few minutes later, she returned with a binder in her bent, arthritic fingers. She handed it him. "If you can witness this, it becomes official. The codicil makes you the executor; check the last page."

Robbie scrutinized the papers carefully and was taken aback by what he read. It was a simple will with the usual legal verbiage that left the gas station, the building and a hundred acres that were adjacent to it to Meghan's little boy, Ryan Hollier. The rest of the two thousand acres, across from Route 6, was left to Luke and Allison

Carlson. But it was her final wish that really surprised Robbie; she left a million and a half dollars to a predominantly black church in South Carolina to be used to raise and fund the education of orphaned children.

"I thought you disliked the Carlsons? If memory serves me right, you referred to them as a bunch of vipers," he questioned, looking up from the sheet of paper.

"Ah well, Luke ain't really a Carlson. He's a Henebry. He don't like to talk about it but you can't hide from the truth. Luke and Allison are Jack Henebry's children."

"And who is Jack Henebry?"

"Let it be, son, you don't need to go there. Luke is my Godson and Allison is like my own child. Ryan will have a good man to guide him," she gave him a admonishing look, "and you make sure to do right by him! Now please witness it and let's take some pictures of it with both of us … what do the kids call them, selfies? Yes, let's take some selfies of you me and the will. I don't trust Hank Carlson or the rest of them vultures, they will try to steal what is mine."

"I don't mean to pry, Maddie, but are you affiliated with that church in South Carolina? That is a generous gift."

"The pastor, Teofilo Parker, is a good man and his church runs an orphanage. There are many children who need help. Hopefully, the money will go to make their lives better. Thomas, my dear husband, was an orphan and I do not have kin so this is more for him than it is for me. The money will be overseen by a trust, don't you worry."

"You are special, Maddie, this is a wonderful thing you do."

"Hah!" The old woman retorted, "Money is money and it is easy to give when you have more than you need. I respect those who give of their time, like Pastor Teofilo. He was a successful businessman before he decided to help these children. That is real sacrifice and that is special. Don't be making a saint out of me yet, Robbie Olsen."

Robbie studied her and felt a sense of melancholy wash over him and he had no idea why. From the moment he met her, she had read him like a book and though he didn't know her, he felt connected to her.

She gently touched the side of his face, "It will be okay, son, you trust me. It will all be okay. Now, before Meghan comes looking for you, take those pictures!"

Robbie snapped several shots of the will with Maddie and then, of them both holding the will between them.

"There is a copy machine there in the corner, make a copy for yourself. I will mail the original to my lawyer tomorrow. Please do not say anything to that lovely girl of yours. This is between you, me and the good Lord."

Just then they heard the entrance bell clang and a young couple with a little girl walked in. The girl ran up to the counter delving excitedly through the various items hanging on the display stand by the counter.

Her mother called out, "Don't touch anything, Caroline!" Then walking up to the counter, asked, "Excuse me, I'm sorry to intrude but where are the toilets?"

The woman was obviously very pregnant. Maddie pointed to the back, "Go to the back wall and make a right, you'll see them." She reached over and gave the little girl a lollipop, "Here, child, it is raspberry flavored and my favorite."

Her mother smiled at Maddie and prompted the little girl, "What do you say when someone gives you something?"

"Thank you!" was the cute response as she began undoing the wrapper.

When the family moved towards the back, Maddie said, "Jodie will be safe here. Go on, your woman's waiting for you. She is fire and you, poor boy, a moth ready to singe his wings! But there are

rough waters ahead and you will learn the true meaning of love."
And she laughed a loud cackle shaking her head in glee.

A MOTH TO THE FALME

When Robbie drove up to Meghan's house he noticed a white Ford Crown Victoria with a blue and white light-bar on top. It was parked in front of the small picket fence gate with the trunk facing Hollow Creek Road. When he pulled alongside the cruiser, the escutcheoned script, 'Sheriff' with 'Chase River County', on the side became visible and he wondered what the Sheriff wanted with Meghan. He checked his wristwatch, 7:00 PM on the dot - right on time. He had bought a box of candy at Maddie's store and in lieu of the customary bottle of wine, a six-pack of Bud Light.

The front door swung open even before he had made it up the short driveway and was greeted by a vision in white. Meghan was draped in a strapless, vintage style evening dress that hugged the curves of her voluptuous body. It was fitted on top, showing off her narrow waist before flaring at the hips and falling loosely below her claves. Her hair was coiffed in a silky fishtail braid and rolled into a side-bun accentuating her high cheekbones and long neck. She reminded him of a graceful swan and simply put – he was stunned.

"You're on time!" Meghan called out standing by the door, "I'm assuming there wasn't another damsel in distress that you had to save!"

"Au contraire, mademoiselle, there were several," he shot right back, "but I told them that the prettiest gal this side of the Mississippi was waiting for me. And I wasn't kidding; you look incredible," he complimented and gave her the box of chocolates, kissing her gently on the lips. It was a short kiss because she pulled away, "There's someone here to see you."

"Hello, Mr. Olsen, I'm Sheriff Dolan," the man greeted him with hand extended; "I apologize. I didn't mean to interrupt your evening."

Patrick Dolan was a little shorter than Robbie standing roughly six-two, but that is where any similarity ended. He had hooded blue eyes, salt and pepper hair with a thin, wide mouth but it was the angry red, bulbous nose that was remarkable in an otherwise ordinary face. People often referred to it as a drinker's nose except Dolan didn't drink. His was a bad case of rosacea that had been left untreated for too long. He had an odd looking frame with stooped shoulders and a belly that was a result of his love of ice cream and chocolate. He had a wide, flat posterior with short, inordinately thick legs and a body profile that resembled a caricature of Yogi Bear.

Robbie nodded, shaking the man's hand, "Can't this wait until tomorrow?"

"It will take only a few minutes. I'll be out of your hair before you know it. Can we step outside?" The sheriff assured Robbie, "There's no need to involve the lovely Miss Hollier."

"I'd like to hear what's going on, if you don't mind," Meghan said to Robbie, taking a hold of his hand.

"I don't," was the quick reply.

"Okay then. Let's get started. Have you heard from Jodie, the young girl you rescued from that thug?" Dolan inquired.

"I'm not sure what you mean? Why would I hear from her?" He was back in training, always put the monkey on the other guy's back; deny everything and answer a question with a question.

Dolan hesitated, "She's gone missing without a trace. I'm checking all possibilities because of what happened to Marisa. We don't need another dead girl or worse, the fact that we may have a serial killer on our hands!"

"You should be talking to Hank Carlson; he owns that shithole where the hookers ply their trade," Robbie countered.

"In all fairness, Olsen, you're staying in that 'shithole'."

Robbie gave the Sheriff a hard look, "That's a budgetary consideration. I don't own the place or condone what goes on there. It's common knowledge that Al Goddard works for Carlson and the girls work for him so don't go implying ..."

There was a knock on the door and when Meghan opened it, Deputy Joe Bradley walked in. He flashed her a quick smile, nodded in the direction of Robbie and without preamble addressed Dolan, "He's not at home. I spoke to Paddy Haskell and the last he saw of Tony was right after they replaced the tires on his pick-up. He was heading in the direction of Moose Head Point. That's all Paddy knows."

There was an uncomfortable silence during which Robbie wondered what Tony was doing and debated whether he should tell the Sheriff and his Deputy exactly what had transpired earlier.

"You wouldn't know where Tony was going, would you?" Bradley questioned, breaking the silence.

"Not a clue," Robbie replied, "he was babysitting Ronin while Meghan and I were at the playground with Ryan. He left a note saying he was going to get his truck."

Meghan took hold of Robbie's hand in both of hers. It didn't go unnoticed and Bradley was quick to point out, "Let's go, Chief, they have better things to do than play detective with us."

Dolan looked miserable but it could have been that he was always miserable, "It seems that Marisa kept a diary, a log of things she did. I mentioned the diary to Jacob, that's Marisa's father, and he searched her room but couldn't find it. Some of the girls at the Sleepy Crest said that Jodie and Marisa used to talk quite a bit. That diary could be the key to this whole mess."

"Sorry, I can't help you. I saw a guy assaulting a young girl and I stopped it. That's all I did. This is the first I'm hearing of a diary," was Robbie's terse reply. He was still irritated by the Sheriff's earlier implication.

"Come on, Chief, let's go!" Bradley's impatient tone wasn't lost on Dolan and neither was the disapproving look. He then turned to Meghan, "I'm sorry about all this. It wasn't my idea."

"It's okay, Joe, but dinner *is* getting cold," Meghan replied, hinting that they had overstayed their welcome.

The two lawmen said their goodbyes but as they were leaving Bradley stopped in the doorway and addressed Robbie, "Oh, Gil Dorsey called me this morning. Marisa was killed either the night before or the day you found her. You might have been right – someone was keeping her locked up," he paused, letting the information sink in, then asked, "Any chance we can meet tomorrow, say around 11:00 AM?"

"I'll call you in the morning and we can work out a time," Robbie wanted them to leave so he could be alone with Meghan.

The tall deputy nodded and followed Dolan down the driveway. Meghan waited till she heard the cars start-up then shut the door and turned to Robbie, "Now that I have you all to myself, mister-cool-as-ice, there's nowhere to run and nowhere to hide." She had her arms around his neck, her eyes brimming with the desire.

"Only an idiot would hide from you," he offered in return, bending over so their faces were just inches apart.

The scent of her perfume, a subtle blend of rose petals and lavender, filled his senses stoking the fire that had been building in him. He kissed her gently at first, tasting her lipstick, feeling the whisper of her breath against his face, thrilling in the delicate softness of her lips pressed against his. But as the kiss lingered, she felt his hands on the small of her back, pulling her into him, his knee forcing her thighs apart. She cupped his face in her hands and parted her lips wider, her tongue darting hungrily into the moist warmth of his mouth. Their tongues wrestled, sliding and twisting, exploring and savoring the taste of each other until finally he broke free.

They were both breathing heavily now, "Dinner … I need to heat the food," she gasped, her face flushed, surprised by her own non sequitur.

"It can wait. There's something I've wanted to do from the moment I saw you," he replied and picked her up with ease.

He carried her over to the large couch and placed her down gently then got down on his knees, spreading her legs wide and placing her thighs on his shoulders. It was his show now and she was going to let him do whatever it was that he wanted.

"I promised to make it up to you," he said, looking at her, his voice hoarse with passion, "lie back and close your eyes."

He pushed her dress up and kissed the inside of her thighs, starting at the knees, using the tip of his tongue to lightly trace his way to the V of her crotch. He could feel the heat rising up from her, the moist warmth tinged by the savory aroma of her sex. He ran his thumb along the crease of her slit, pushing the flimsy lace of her panties into her, searching for the little knob crowning the gates of her passion. She let out a soft gasp when he located her clit rubbing it gently before working his tongue in between the fold of her pussy lips. Her excitement, which was evidenced by the slick wetness seeping through the satiny material, titillated him, urging him on. It could have been the newness of her or the fact that it had been a while for him and for her but they were both on edge and now, without pretext, the hunger they felt had taken over.

He worked her panties down and buried his face in between her thighs, his tongue plunging into her, spreading the petals of her slit, slowly licking her up and down, up and down, changing the rhythm from quick little flicks to slower, flatter, longer strokes, again and again until she was writhing with pleasure. Her mewling moans and indiscernible sounds only reinforced the veracity of his actions and added to his heightened concupiscence.

She gasped, "Ohhh! Oh God, baby … don't stop! Mmmm …"

He inserted a finger into her, wiggling it in and out while lapping at the juices like a kitten at a saucer of milk. The myriad flavors of sex had flooded his senses - the balmy redolence, the absinthian taste of her nectar, the sounds of her uneven breathing, the sharp gasps and moans, her hips undulating and grinding against his face, it excited him like he had never been excited before. And as he worked on her, his tongue dancing along the length of her swollen pussy, he could feel her climax building, the tremors rippling through the muscles in her thighs signaling the approach of that moment of nothingness when the body and mind succumb to the sublime explosion; a pleasure filled release into an indescribable transcendence.

He reached up and squeezed her breasts, toying with her nipples, using his thumb and forefinger to pinch and twist them, all the while bathing her clit with his tongue until finally her hips arched upwards, her face contorted in pleasure, "Oh God, I'm cumming, baby, I'm …" and her words faded into a muffled, nonsensical series of gasps, and moans.

He held her hips tightly, trying to control her while her body twisted and torqued, the waves of pleasure washing over her, one wave after another, spreading from her core outwards to her extremities until she was lost in the throes of her orgasm.

He waited, gently running his tongue over her clit, stimulating her just enough to bask in the velvet bliss; the moments of riding the pleasure crest to the warm post-orgasmic glow. She opened her eyes and let out a long sigh of contentment. He picked her up and headed for the bedroom, "That was the repayment of interest. Now it's time for the capital."

She smiled and buried her face in his chest.

THE CARLSON LUMBERYARD

The Carlson lumber business was the major employer in Chase River Town and it was made up of three separate buildings. They were located in close proximity to one another on a twenty-acre plot of land right off of Route 15. It was about ten minutes from Maddie Wilkins gas station. Despite his unrelenting efforts Hank was never able to convince Maddie to sell him the gas station and the hundred acres that it sat on or the two thousand wooded acres that was adjacent to his plot which would have given him access to both timber and fuel. Instead, his trucks had to drive across town to the Shell Station on Main Street which he owned – this was not only inconvenient but expensive. However, Hank was a patient man and Maddie Wilkins was an old woman. Sooner or later, he felt certain, that he would have that land and the Carlson lumber business would grow.

The main building was the newest of the three buildings and was a wood and stone structure with huge glass windows and a large u-shaped parking lot. The steeply pitched roof gave the facade the appearance of an exclusive European ski lodge complete with a stone stairway leading to the entrance. The glass double doors opened to a comfortable seating foyer where people could thumb through catalogs over a cup of coffee and donuts. It was here that they sold custom and prefabricated frames, doors, windows, decks, fencing and the various fittings and hardware that accompanied them. Since most homes and cabins in Chase River and the surrounding towns had nonstandard windows and doors, it was always busy at Carlson's Lumber.

The carpentry department, which occupied the back of the building, had woodworking lathes, mills, drill presses and other sundry machinery required in the manufacture of their custom and off-the-shelf products and was where a lot of the young men in town were apprenticed. Carlson never missed the opportunity to boast that Carlson's woodworkers were in demand all over the tristate, something that was debatable but no one in their right mind questioned Hank Carlson.

The second building was directly behind the showroom. It was a long warehouse that inventoried the various types of lumber. In the back of the warehouse was where the large numerically-controlled Sawmill turned logs into planks of different sizes. The building had a rear entrance to the compound that allowed trucks to circumvent the parking lot and drive right up to the loading docks by the overhead doors. Ray Carlson ran this side of the business and reported directly to his older brother, Ed.

The third building was a little smaller and a lot older than the showroom. It was the metal processing plant located at the right side of the compound and rearward. Here they manufactured or bought metal hardware to support their custom doors and windows. These items were fabricated from metal sheets, forgings or castings. The resurgence of decorative trims and security grills had necessitated increasing their capacity. In order to process the different types of metal, the manufacturing facility was replete with specialized equipment including hydraulic presses, press brakes, turret presses, TIG and MIG welders, buff motors, heat treating furnaces and a spacious cell with two sub-zero freezers which were primarily used subsequent to the solution treating process of aluminum. It was on the second floor of this unassuming building that Edmund Carlson had his office.

There were two men in Ed's office, his brother, Raymond Carlson, and their childhood friend, Jericho Reinhardt. Ray was seated in the chair directly in front of the desk while Jericho was leaning against the back wall facing Ed.

"I asked you to watch them, not try and kill them," Ed Carlson directed his frustration at Jericho, "Why would you have to shoot at them? Now, you've got everyone curious about Gil's cabin and what those two assholes were doing up there. And, this includes Chief Dolan. He calls me this morning and goes on about this being a hornet's nest and getting people all riled up."

The stocky, long-haired man bristled, "Listen Ed, I know they found something. When Marisa went down to the watershed she must have dropped something - a pendant, necklace or something. I don't know because I saw them picking something up and studying it before going into the cabin. And how many times do I have to tell you, I didn't mean to burn the fucking place down! I just wanted to scare them off."

"The cabin burning down was the one good thing to come out of this. Now any evidence of us being there is gone," Ed retorted, his face etched in anger and frustration.

"What about the footprints?" Raymond Carlson asked.

"Hunters use that cabin all the time, so what? Everyone knows that. And, there are so many footprints it will be impossible to determine who was there," Ed replied.

"You seem pretty sure," Jericho replied then added, "I ain't going back to jail, Ed … fuck that! If it means wasting Olsen and that runt, I'll do it but I ain't going back, not ever!"

"No one's going to jail. Whatever happened; happened. If we

stick together…"

The door to the office pushed open slowly and Seppo Heikkinen stepped in. His gigantic presence filled the room and the abrupt change in the ambiance was palpable. All three men had an anxious edge to them now and it was clear that they didn't want anything to do with the big man. Although the three men were big in their own right, they were dwarfed by the Finn.

"So, you fucked up again!" Seppo addressed Ed Carlson without preamble.

"What do you mean?"

"I spoke to Al's bitches and they all said that Jodie saw Marisa with the three of you the night before she disappeared."

"We didn't have anything to do with that," Ed spat out almost as soon as Seppo made the accusation.

"Listen, shithead, I don't give a rat's ass if you three limp dicks gangbanged her and then decided to whack her. It doesn't matter to me. Thousands of girls go missing every day and you think I care? What I don't get is how the three of you dumbasses managed to make sure the body turned up? How, eh? You were born here, you grew-up here, you know these fucking mountains better than most. All this land with caves, fields and rivers and you can't get it right! How fucking dumb can you get?"

The big Finn turned his attention to Jericho. He had the uncanny ability to sense weakness, "Is there something you want to tell me, piss-face?"

"We had nothing to do with Marisa. I swear," Jericho was frightened. He could feel his armpits sweating.

"What about Jodie?" The big man asked.

"I don't know where that little bitch is! She's always hanging out with Angie, the pretty, tall one. Maybe she knows where Jodie went."

"Listen carefully, fat boy, if I find out that you are lying to me or holding something back, you'll wish …"

"Hey, there's no need for that shit!" Ed Carlson interrupted the big Finn, "He's telling you the truth."

"You stay the fuck out of this," Seppo hissed, leaning over the table, "unless you want me to teach you a fuckin' lesson. Hank isn't too happy with you. What did you think? Oh, you thought your uncle will protect you, is that it? I'm going to let you in on a little secret - he wanted me to break your fuckin' legs but you're one lucky motherfucker. Just when I was about to leave, you mother calls and your uncle changes his mind. I've got no luck. First, Olsen then you but my patience is wearing thin so if you interrupt me again, with or without your uncle's permission, I'll bust both your fuckin' kneecaps, get it?"

Ed looked away. He stared out of the window, expressionless, not wanting to provoke the Finn. He knew that his uncle was pissed off and in all probability the bleak scenario that Seppo painted was true. He knew that his mother had been talking to Hank about him and that created a conundrum. He wanted her to stay out of his business but at the same time, it was her interference that had saved his ass.

The big Finn gave Ray Carlson a cold, hard look but Ed's younger brother was quite suddenly intrigued by the metal pencil holder and was unwilling to take his gaze off of it. Seppo then turned once again to Jericho, "Did you hear me, you little cunt? If I find out you're lying, you will regret the day that whore of a mother brought you into this world!"

It was on the tip of Jericho's tongue to respond in anger but the expression on Seppo's face stopped him. The big Finn cocked his head with his hand to his ear, "What? What were you going to say? Give me a fucking reason, asshole. Go on, say something."

There was no response. Jericho looked down at the worn out

carpet, shuffling nervously from one foot to the other, hoping that this interrogation would end. Seppo was unpredictable and he had witnessed some of the big man's handiwork. Not pleasant.

The Finn reached over and grabbed him by the front of his leather jacket and pulled him close, almost lifting him off the ground like he weighed nothing, "So, I'll ask it again: do you know where Jodie is?"

"No. I swear I don't. Try Angie, she'll know… she's either hiding her or knows where she is," Jericho sputtered in fear.

Seppo stared at the biker's tattooed face for a few seconds and then said, "Okay. I'll talk to her."

He let the smaller man go, pushing him back, "In the meantime, you wankers sit here and jack each other off and stay the fuck out of my way. When I call you, you had better answer you fucking phones."

He gave them one last look and much to their collective relief, exited from the office. The men waited listening to the footsteps fading down the corridor. All three were looking at the door almost expecting the Finn to come bursting in like Freddy Kruger.

It was Ed who spoke first, "You shouldn't have mentioned Angela. That sick bastard is likely to do anything."

"I don't think Hank will let him hurt one of the girls," Jericho said then in defense of his position protested, "Hey, I wasn't going to get my legs busted because of her. She's hiding that little bitch; I know that and you know that."

"Angela is the one decent gal in the whole lot. I've known her for close to fifteen years now and I don't want to see her hurt."

"He's a fuckin' asshole! One of these days I'm going to waste that motherfucker!" Jericho spat out, "I'll get him in the parking lot. I've done that before …"

"Sit tight. Our time will come. Don't you worry," Ed said, "Come on, let's get something to eat."

Meghan Hollier

DISCOVERY

When Robbie finally woke up Meghan was gone, she had left for work. He stretched lazily before tumbling out of bed and headed for the bathroom. He found a note on the counter by the sink. It had two hearts on the top with a sketch of a toothbrush and the words "Use mine. There's coffee in the kitchen and eggs in the fridge. Call me when you are up." And more hearts at the bottom of the note. Her handwriting was small and neat and he smiled at the thought of her and their night together.

After his morning shower, he got his trousers on and walked slowly to the kitchen, stopping briefly to look at some of the photographs hanging on the corridor wall. The previous night had revealed nuances in their lovemaking that he had never experienced before. Meghan was the quintessential hybrid of harlot and angel. Her harlequin personality and gentle manner made it easy for him to share his intimate feelings – something he had rarely done. He had never believed in soulmates but he now knew, incontrovertibly, that she had to be his soulmate. He felt surer of this than anything else in his life. He marveled at that fact that he could be so sure of a person in such a short time. He shook his head and smiled: *Soulmates! You're getting soft in your head, Olsen!* But there could be no other explanation.

He poured himself a cup of coffee and was about to call her when there was a knock on the door. It was Tony VanArcen.

"Oh damn, not you!" Robbie groaned, his voice laced with feigned misgiving. In truth, he was happy to see Tony. He was concerned when Bradley wasn't able to locate him.

VanArcen ignored the barb and staring at Robbie's body said, "How do you get muscles like that? Fuckin' ridiculous!" then brushing past Robbie, "You're not easy to find, Valentino. I went to the motel but your car wasn't there. I thought you might be roaming the mountains doing whatever it is you do up there but it struck me – Meghan Hollier or the mountains? That was a no brainer so I assumed you got lucky!"

"Who the heck is Valentino?" Robbie questioned closing the door and following VanArcen into the living room.

"Rudolf Valentino! You've never heard of Rudolf Valentino?" Tony was incredulous, "You must be living in a cocoon. He was only the greatest lover Hollywood has ever known."

"How the heck would you know? I mean, that he was the greatest lover and no, I've never heard of him. Why not Romeo or Casanova or someone we all might know?"

"Romeo was a wimp and Casanova was a French asshole! So, they don't cut it."

"Hey, I served with some French soldiers and they were as tough as they come," Robbie shot back.

"Okay, maybe but they're still French," then mimicking a fake French accent he said, "*Parlez-vous français* and all that shit. They are disqualified forever. You're a Valentino."

"I'm confused. Charlie Bronson, Mister Cool and now Valentino … make up your mind."

"Don't be confused. You're a complex man, Olsen, a little Bronson, a little cool and a lot of the silent, mysterious type and maybe that's what the chick's dig in you. And, those fuckin' muscles must have something to do with it!" VanArcen said with a broad smile. "You hate me, don't you?"

Robbie shook his head, giving up, "You win. Whatever, man, but what did you want to see me about?"

"I have a plan," VanArcen began and at the very mention of that Robbie looked skywards and rolled his eyes but that didn't dissuade Tony, "Tonight is fight night and all the Carlsons will be there. They're going to wonder what we're doing there and just maybe we'll spook them. What do …"

"Hold the thought, Sherlock, I've got some news for you too but I need to make a couple of calls first and then I really need to get back to Ronin," Robbie cut in then added, "We can talk while driving."

VanArcen went into the kitchen and poured himself a cup of coffee and waited for Robbie to finish. He wandered around opening drawers, pulling and rifling through stuff until he dropped a cardboard shoebox, which had been stashed away in one of the drawers, spilling all its contents. The floor was now a mess of old bills and invoices, coupons bundled with rubber bands, a pair of scissors, a stapler, small binder clips, sewing push pins and several photographs. He was kneeling over, picking them up when Robbie came into the kitchen.

"What are you doing?" Robbie was surprised but then saw the photographs, "That's personal stuff, Tony, what's the matter with you?"

"Hey, I was looking for the sugar, that's all and suddenly this box opens up and …"

"Put it back in the box, all of it, and make sure there's nothing under any of the counters," Robbie snapped.

While VanArcen was scrambling trying to collect the papers and the rest of the contents, Robbie quickly gathered up the photographs. There was a stack of them mostly of people at a party. The one on top showed Meghan with another pretty, dark haired girl with several men standing in a group with drinks in their hand. The only man he recognized was the one standing close to Meghan; it was Ed Carlson and he had his arm around her waist. Many of following snapshots were of women, who he didn't recognize, naked or in various stages of undress. There were other more revealing pictures of couples and groups in compromising sexual positions that were explicit and titillating.

He was torn between his voyeuristic curiosity and the respect for her privacy but the inquisitive cat wasn't quite dead and his need to know won out. He continued going through the photographs as quickly as he could – they were random and in no apparent order. There was one particularly explicit photograph of the pretty girl who had posed with Meghan. She was kneeling on the carpet with a man fucking her from behind while she serviced another man with her mouth. He studied it for a while unable to quell the arousal he felt. He kept flicking through the pictures, his mind in a transient state of shock, curiosity and disbelief. He was looking for Meghan and found another one. This was of the same dark-haired girl from the spit roast – she was completely naked except for her panties and was holding Meghan's hand, her head thrown back, laughing. Meghan's blouse had been untucked from her skirt and a few of the buttons on top were undone. Even though Meghan was still fully clothed the implication of the photograph was clear to Robbie: the woman was trying to coax her into taking part.

He was caught in a paradoxical dilemma; the deceitful and unfair prying driven by his understandable need to know versus common decency but it was too late for that – he had already decided.

The next one that he found of Meghan showed her top completely unbuttoned, her bra showing, leaning over a table snorting a line of cocaine. His mind went blank unable to reconcile the person he knew with the images he had just seen. He flipped the picture over hoping to find a date but there was none. The sordid content coupled with the subjective context of her sexual preferences had never crossed his mind until now nor had he ever considered the hypocrisy of dealing with his own fantasies of sex with multiple women.

A myriad of thoughts spiraled out of control, racing through his mind without sequential relevance. What was she doing there? Did she sleep with all those men and how many of these parties did she attend? Was she a sex-addict or a nympho? She did seem overly aggressive with him the first time they met and what if he was just the flavor of the week? And what's with Ed Carlson? What the heck was she doing with him? He wished that he had never seen the photographs.

Just a few moments ago he was convinced that she was his soul-mate, an angel sent from heaven, and now the very foundation of his beliefs had been shaken. She wasn't the responsible, hardworking mother but rather, a party girl who seemingly enjoyed being fucked by many men.

His mood had changed. The euphoric high was gone and he was filled with doubts and an overwhelming sense of disappointment. His mind was now in overdrive; the questions kept repeating themselves: what was Meghan doing with Ed Carlson? And who was the woman with her and who were the other women? And who were the other men? Were they her friends? Lovers?

The pictures were taken inside a home, not Meghan's but a large, well-furnished home. Did she go for these parties often? Why did she make it a point to tell him that she wasn't a party girl? Was she manipulating him? And voyeurism rarely stops at photographs, there must be a video or multiple videos of the whole sleazy affair and where could she have hidden them?

Robbie couldn't mask his irritation and grabbed the box from Tony and put the photographs back under a stack of papers. "Let's go, and put it back wherever you found it."

Either Tony didn't notice the photographs or he pretended not to.

"Yes sir, boss!" VanArcen said, shoving the shoebox unceremoniously into drawer, "Do you want me to follow you in my truck?"

"No. Leave your truck here. We'll stop over at Maddie's place first," Robbie noticed the questioning look on the smaller man's face, "Jodie is with her. I just want to make sure they're okay and get my keys. Then we need to get Ronin."

"Jodie? You mean the young damsel in distress?"

Robbie shook his head, "Damsel in distress? You're not ..." he was about to say *'you're not fucking Meghan, are you'* but he caught himself and instead added with overt sarcasm, "Meghan must have the same scriptwriter as you."

"What's with you, man? A minute ago you were high on love like a teenager and his first crush, and now you're pissed off at everyone and everything," VanArcen parried, "is it that time of the month or what? You're acting as nuts as Liz before her code red."

Robbie was quiet. *What the heck is the matter with me? Tony's right, I need to get a hold of myself. Whatever happened in Meghan's past is none of my business!* But the constriction that he felt in his chest wasn't convinced and the thoughts kept swirling around and around. Finally, he had to admit that he didn't really know her at all – who she really was, what she liked and whether she was right for him. He was so smitten with her that he threw caution to the wind and created an image in his mind that no woman could live up to. He recalled what he had read in some obscure book: *We all have scars and warts. Some of them are visible and some not so much so. They lie buried in our psyche. We are perfect in God's creation and imperfect in man's eye.* Or something like that.

"Sorry. I've got some things I need to sort out," was his lame excuse before explaining what he had learned about Jodie and Marisa.

"Jodie saw Marisa with Ed Carlson on night she went missing and now Hank and Seppo are looking for her. She also saw Jericho following us to Calico Bluff," Robbie looked over at VanArcen. The news had piqued the smaller man's interest.

"I knew it! I knew those bastards were involved!" VanArcen was ebullient. "You can take that freak can't you?"

"Who? Ed Carlson?" Thoughts of Ed Carlson and Meghan were still buzzing in his mind. He couldn't shake the picture of them standing together like old chums.

"No, Ed Carlson's an asshole; I can take him, check that; you can easily take him. I meant that freak Seppo Heikkinen. You can handle him, right? I mean Charlie Bronson can handle anyone!" VanArcen persisted.

"Forget him and let's not jump to conclusions. And, please stop with the Charlie Bronson stuff. I'm not Charles Bronson!"

"Okay, calm down Valentino! For a tough dude, you are one sensitive fella."

He waited to see if Robbie would take the bait to engage him in the silly repartee but he got no response, so VanArcen continued, his demeanor turning serious, "Jericho doesn't do anything without Ed's permission. That means Ed is the one who sent him and if Marisa was with Ed, then it can only mean that Ed was involved in her death. Most probably raped and killed the poor girl himself."

Robbie listened, shutting out the image of Meghan smiling with Ed Carlson's arm around her; he tried to focus. Maybe Marisa was taken to that home he had seen in the photograph. It looked like a big house and definitely not in Chase River Town and that would explain why Bradley and the others couldn't locate Marisa when they had gone looking for her.

"Well, that begs the question: where was Marisa for the following six days?" Robbie said, "And how come no one could find her? Gil Dorsey places the time of death as the day I found her or possibly the night before."

"That's one reason I went to Moose Head Point. No one goes there because it's Luke's place and he can get pretty crazy. About three years back, he chased a bunch of hunters off his land. Injured a few and killed another. After that, except Allison, no one else ventures out there."

"So why would you go there?"

"Because, what better place to hide a body. But now that you tell me she was alive, they would need a cabin to keep her locked up. There are some moonshine stills a little beyond Luke's place. Or maybe Luke was in on this, what do you think?"

"That's a real stretch. I don't think Luke was involved. I think there's something more to this but I can't put my finger on it," Robbie replied unable to shake the images of the photographs he had seen ad trying to decide whether he should tell VanArcen about Jodie and the videos Marisa gave her. " I don't think Jericho was trying to kill us; he was trying to scare us. These boys are all pretty good shots and he would have had to be blind and drunk to have missed us. He had plenty of opportunity to pick us off. Also, let's say they did kill her – it would have been very easy to bury her somewhere in the mountains where no one would ever find her. None of this makes sense."

"And that's why you've got Uncle Tony with you. I'll make sense of it all – let's start by finding that peckerhead Seppo and you kick the shit out of him. He'll sing like a canary, trust me, I know the type."

"You're a lunatic. I'm going to stay as far from him as possible and I suggest you do too unless you have a death wish."

"Death Wish? Hey, that's Charlie Bronson! Remember Death Wish I, II, III … I think they stopped at Death Wish Two Hundred!"

"You're impossible," Robbie acted exasperated but had to smile at Tony's irrepressible nonsense.

"What was that I just saw? Was that a smile? No it can't be; a smile from mister-cool-as-ice!" VanArcen inveigled.

The twenty minute drive to Maddie's place seemed a lot shorter with VanArcen's continual banter and self-deprecating anecdotes. Robbie had always been a listener and though he would never admit it, he enjoyed the diametrically opposite persona that VanArcen presented and it helped to distract him from the disturbing photograph of Ed Carlson with Meghan. *Soulmates be damned!*

When Robbie and Tony VanArcen got to Maddie Wilkins place they were surprised to find Luke Carlson there. He was standing by the register, elbows resting on the counter, talking to Maddie. Jodie was nowhere to be seen. There was a fruit cake in a plastic wrap on the counter with an assortment of fruits in a bag next to it.

"Hey, it if isn't the soldier boy," Luke called out, straightening up. "How have you been, Olsen?"

They shook hands briefly.

"No complaints," Robbie replied, "and you? How's it going?"

"Great! Tonight is fight night so I'm excited," he turned to VanArcen, "Hi Tony, you staying out of trouble?"

"No trouble, Luke, but challenges; life is filled with them especially for guys with short legs but I'm just another of God's creatures trying to stay alive." VanArcen replied with a somber expression on his face.

"You're so full of shit!" Luke laughed but the admonishment was playfully done. "Do you know that Tony's uncle was one of the best damn fighters to ever step into our pit? Danny VanArcen, the name made other fighters piss in their pants."

"I heard," Robbie confirmed and turned to Maddie, "Hi Maddie, I wanted to pick-up my keys. How are things going?" he looked around but couldn't hear or see Jodie.

"Sorry but I have to leave," Luke interjected, "I have to get some stuff for the big event. Hey, why don't you come tonight? Tony, bring him – there are some decent fighters on the card. One fella fought in the World Fighter's League and the UFC. The drinks are on me so come on down. Maddie, if you need anything at all, you let me know."

Luke leaned over and gave the old woman a hug and a kiss on her forehead and with a perfunctory wave he left through the back door.

"You make him nervous, Valentino; Luke never runs off like that," VanArcen noted.

"You heard the man, he had things to do. It had nothing to do with me," Robbie corrected.

"No. Tony is right. You make Luke nervous. He knows that he has to make a choice and that makes him uneasy," Maddie riposted.

Robbie was quiet. Many of the prognostications Maddie had made seemed to come true. Tony, not surprisingly, had a totally different take on the matter, "Luke knows that my brother here can kick his pretty-boy ass! That's what makes him uneasy."

Maddie ignored him and continued speaking to Robbie, "Jodie is sleeping. We stayed up last night talking and I see so much potential in that little girl. You watch, she will do wonderful things with her life. And you don't worry; she can stay with me for as long as it takes."

Before Robbie could respond VanArcen butted in, "Maddie, recidivism among whores is almost as high as criminals. There are plenty of statistics to support this. Most of them like what they are doing so I wouldn't get my hopes up."

"You hush up, Tony. I don't need your statistics, you hear. She'll do just fine." Maddie now addressed Robbie, "Don't judge others by their past and give them a chance. No one is without sin. And, it will do you good to remember that."

Robbie wasn't sure if she was speaking to him about Jodie or if this was something related to Meghan but he didn't respond. Instead, he wanted to make sure that Jodie staying until Saturday was not an issue.

"Are you sure she's not a bother?" he asked wanting to make sure. "Saturday is when Jim, her brother, can meet us."

"She's refreshing and we get along famously. She listens to the mad ranting of an old woman and I am uplifted by her youthful energy. She helps me and I help her. You take your time and get her when you are ready."

He got the keys to his room and they said their goodbye and as hard as he tried, he couldn't shake the images of Meghan with her blouse undone, snorting coke.

"Hey, why don't you leave Ronin with me for the afternoon? You go see your gal. Ronin and I will spend some quality time together; maybe go around scaring the neighbors. What do you say?" VanArcen asked Robbie. Now that the initial fear had abated, he was genuinely getting to like Ronin.

"I don't know if that's such a good idea. The last time I left him with you, you fed him spam and a bunch of other stuff that made him shit like a horse!"

"No more spam I promise and I'll get him steak. Come on, big guy, I'm getting to like the pooch," VanArcen pleaded.

"Okay. No neighborly pranks. I'm not sure you can control him so play in your backyard," Robbie instructed, "no kidding around, Tony, I don't want problems with him attacking someone."

"I swear on my dear Pappy's grave. I'll keep him in the house and play in the backyard. Cross my heart and hope to die!"

Robbie was still undecided when his cell phone rang. It was Meghan.

Robbie looked over at VanArcen and said, "Let me call you back. Tony's taking Ronin for the afternoon. I'll come and get you if you're free for lunch," he tried sounding as normal as possible but it wasn't in his nature and he knew he sounded distant.

VanArcen did a little jig, dancing around like a monkey on drugs until he knocked a heavy ashtray off of the side table. The vintage glass ashtray hit the wall, deflected off the chair and fell with a dull thump.

Meghan's concern was evident, "What was that?"

Robbie shook his head and said to Meghan, "Nothing, just Tony being Tony. I'll call before I leave from the here. Is that okay?"

"Sure, baby, that's fine. I can't wait to see you. I've missed you, I know, that's silly but ..." Meghan's voice trailed off.

Robbie cringed. He wasn't sure what to say. He wanted to tell how much she meant to him but couldn't get past the images that still buzzed in his head. "I'll see you soon," was the best he could muster.

TROUBLE IN PARADISE

The veterinary clinic where Meghan Hollier worked was on Maple Street about five hundred yards down from the Shell gas station on Main. Maple was a short, unpaved gravel road that dead-ended at the gates of Dr. Susan Boswell's Veterinary Hospital and Animal Boarding House. Her office was the converted lower floor of a two-story Colonial home which also served as her residence. The house was painted white with black trim and had a bluish-gray shingled roof.

There was a large sign by the front door that read:

Susan A. Boswell, DVM

General Practitioner

We talk and listen to the animals before treating them

The only other person in the office was Doreen Kiviak, the receptionist. She was a bubbly forty-year old who was constantly playing matchmaker trying to get Meghan hooked-up with any single man she came across. Her mantra that solitude would eventually turn to loneliness and loneliness to sadness made Meghan cringe – it hit too close to home; social creatures need company and Meghan wasn't one who enjoyed solitude.

Dr. Susan Boswell, the vet, was a jovial older woman who left a successful practice in Boston for the quiet blessings of country living.

She had taken to Meghan the moment they first met and had offered her the job as her assistant. Mark Boswell, her husband, was a former Marine who was now the handyman responsible for pretty much all the aspects of the day to day functioning of a hospital. He took care of the computers, the buildings, the landscaping and transport of the animals. He also helped with the husbandry of the many chicken, goats and ducks that provided them with milk, meat and eggs.

The large barn, painted an obscure red, was located about fifty yards to the right of the house. It was where the animals were boarded. The interior of the barn had been redone to include stalls for horses on one side and smaller cubicles for dogs and cats on the other. The stalls and cubicles were positioned back to back with a large aisle in between to avoid unnecessary visual contact between the animals.

There were two weather-beaten pick-up trucks with horse trailers attached that were parked next to the barn along with a relatively new grape colored Ford 150 standing beside them. The hundred or so acres behind the barn had been fenced-in to provide adequate space for the horses to graze and plenty of room for them to exercise. The training circle for yearlings was at the far end of the property with a path that led directly to the barn. There were metal barricades separating the horses from the dog-runs. There was a huge brick silo next to the barn for the storage of feed during the bitter winter months. The animal boarding was an essential and lucrative aspect of Dr. Boswell's business.

Meghan had been on cloud nine the entire morning. She kept humming softly to herself trying to suppress the feeling of unbridled joy that she felt. Everything in Meghan's world basked in the warmth of sunshine. Unable to contain her feelings, she had confided in Doreen telling her just how wonderful Robbie was.

"I can't wait to meet your Prince Charming. When is he supposed to be here?" Doreen asked.

"Anytime now," Meghan answered peeping through the curtains for the umpteenth time, "I've taken the afternoon off. I must be mad but I can't help myself. I feel like a sixteen-year-old on her first date!"

"What did Susan say?" Doreen was curious.

"Considering the state I'm in, and I'm paraphrasing: you're pretty useless and the best thing for you is to get it out of my system! And, her exact words: go get laid!"

Doreen laughed, "Take it from someone who has been married for twenty years; the first few months are the best. The sex is amazing, he's considerate and attentive and... did I say the sex is amazing? After the first year, it's all downhill, girl! So enjoy these moments and yes, go get laid – afternoon sex is almost as good as morning sex."

"Susan pretty much said the same thing. But I know it will be different with him. Here he comes," she ran to the door with Doreen right at her heels.

They watched him stroll up the walkway, head held high, shoulders square, with an aura of self-assuredness. His movements reminded Meghan of a large cat, lazy and smooth until they have to pounce and then it is all grace and power.

"Sally wasn't kidding, he's dreamy!" Doreen gushed.

Meghan smiled and ran to him, hugging him tight and kissing him on the lips. "Hi, cowboy, I've missed you!"

She sensed the tenseness in him but ascribed that to Doreen being there. "This is my friend Doreen," she introduced her to Robbie, "and this is Robbie Olsen."

"I thought I was happily married but if you have a twin, I'll divorce Mike right now!" Doreen said laughing and holding his hand in both hers. "Where's the giant dog that everyone is talking about?"

"You're too kind. My twin would be lucky to get a gal like you!" Robbie shot back and then added, "Ronin is with Tony... Tony VanArcen."

"Oh, we'd love to see him. Susan, that's Dr. Boswell, said she had never seen a Russian Mountain Dog and neither have I."

"I'll bring him over one of these days, unless Tony runs off with him."

"Come on, let's go!" Meghan recaptured Robbie's hand and dragged him towards the car.

He was quiet during the drive to Bucky Johnston's Diner. He kept telling himself that whatever took place before they met was none of his business but the images, especially of the one with Meghan's buttons undone, refused to relinquish their hold on him.

"What's the matter? You seem so distant," she said reaching over and taking his hand off the steering wheel.

"It's nothing. Just thinking about Marisa and stuff," he lied but he had never been good at it. She saw through it immediately.

"Something is bothering you, I know that. Please tell me what it is, Robbie, please?" She pleaded, now worried that it could be something from his past.

"Okay, let's get lunch and then we can talk."

They ordered lunch and during the wait for their meals to arrive, she felt her anxiety growing. She had no idea what this was about but her stomach was in a knot. Once the dishes arrived she asked again, "Tell me what's bothering you. Is it something to do with me?"

He thought about it for a minute staring down at the water glass. There was a part of him, a singularly uneasy part, that didn't want to address his misgivings but deep inside he knew that it was best to settle it once and for all. Either it would work out or it wouldn't and if it wasn't meant to be then they could move on and the sooner the better. It would be difficult because Meghan had affected him like no other woman had.

He put his fork down and looked at her, "This morning Tony came over and ..." he started then he thought about it and decided to rephrase his approach, "While looking for some sugar, a shoebox fell open spilling some photographs."

The shock and transformation was immediate. Her face went ten shades of pale and she looked at him with mouth open.

He waited but she just stared at him. "These were pictures of you at a party. Not a normal party but …"

"You have no right to pry into my personal life! No right at all!" Her face was flushed red now and the anxiety had morphed into defensive anger. She lashed out, her green eyes blazing, "Just because we spent a night together doesn't give you the right to pry into my personal things, you don't own me…"

"That's not how it happened." He cut her off, offended by her assumption, "I wasn't prying. It was …it was …" He wanted to explain how it happened but words failed him. The questions that he had rehearsed so carefully got lost in an emotional labyrinth and he retreated, crawling back into his dark place, where like his father, he shut the world out.

"I don't care what it was! How dare you presume to question my past?" She stared at him, mistaking his silence for some twisted avenue of advantage and prattled on, "I thought you were different. I'm such a fool. I'm so desperate to find the right man that I jump at the first jerk that seems halfway decent. You haven't walked in my shoes, mister, you haven't gone through what I have," she regretted it as soon as she said it realizing that she was talking to a man who served in some of the worst and most dangerous conditions on earth.

Robbie didn't say anything. He was emotionally done. He got up, fished out fifty dollars from his wallet and placed is under the edge of his plate and without another word, he left. As much as he detested the placid and unresponsive nature of his father, he realized then that he dealt with Meghan just the way his father dealt with his mother and it as killing him on the inside.

She sat there staring at his back wanting to run after him, hug him and tell him that those pictures weren't of her but someone else who was lost and lonely. She wanted to apologize but she sat there and cried softly. Her world, which had been perfect a short while ago, was crumbling around her in pieces and there was nothing she could do. A line she had read in a Charlotte Brontë novel played in her mind, over and over again: *"Life is so constructed, that the event does not, cannot, will not, match the expectation."*

Her expectations and dreams had just been dashed and her night in white armor turned out to be the Joker.

Angela didn't argue or protest. She rolled off the bed, got dressed and followed Heikkinen out. She waved to the girls, who were watching from the shadows, and got into the van.

"Should we tell Snake?" Kelly asked.

"No. You didn't see nothing and you know nothing," was the prompt reply.

They watched the van disappear, lit up cigarettes and went back to their conversation.

Tony and Robbie

FIGHT NIGHT

Tony VanArcen was genuinely surprised when he opened the door and saw Robbie standing there.

"That was quick, so what happened?" VanArcen asked when Robbie arrived to pick Ronin up.

"Nothing happened," the reply was brusque.

"You're talking to Uncle Tony – come on, what happened?" VanArcen persisted.

Robbie was quiet for a few moments but realized that VanArcen wouldn't be discouraged, "We had a disagreement … just some stupid stuff!"

"Oh-oh, a lovers' quarrel! And knowing you as well as I do, *you* used monosyllabic replies to probing emotional queries, right? Or did you go with the usual macho bullshit of *'I'm de man, you de woman so shut the fuck-up'*?"

"Let's skip it. I don't want to get into it right now," Robbie was kneeling and petting Ronin "How are you, boy? Did the evil dwarf feed you?"

"Ouch! Et tu Brute! Of course I fed him … two huge steaks! He eats more than Fat Paddy Haskell and that's say something. And from the looks of it, you haven't had lunch either. Sit down, I'll make you one of Mama VanArcen's world famous, grilled cheese and bacon sandwiches and you can tell me all about your problems."

"Thanks, Tony, but you've done enough. I'm going to take Ronin for a run … clear my head," Robbie started but Ronin barked and knocked him over sealing the deal.

"You got no choice, Bronson," VanArcen laughed, "the boss wants to stay."

The sandwich was all that Tony had promised and worthy of being on the menu of any five-star restaurant in New York. It had the look of a Panini with the toasted exterior, the intoxicating scent of grilled bacon fat, and the appetizing visual of the gooey cheese that oozed from between the two slices of crisped bread. The ingredients included sliced tomatoes, sautéed onions, Jalapenos peppers, chopped lettuce, shaved roast beef soaked in a homemade sauce and three different types of cheese, White Cheddar, Parmesan Reggiano and an mild Irish Dubliner.

"Wow, this is good!" Robbie complimented after downing his first bite. "How do you get the bacon to stay so crisp and there's something other than the cheese and the meat… what's in the sauce?"

"I'll have to kill you if I told you – it's a family recipe handed down from generation to generation by mothers to daughters and in my case, sons. I took the VanArcen oath of secrecy; so no can tell. And, why would I give you the recipe? Guys like you don't cook; you get chicks to cook for you! I'll give it to Meghan when you make a decent woman of her."

Robbie ignored the snide remark. "You should get a Food Truck with Liz, that way you could be together and it would be a lot less dangerous. And, you'd make some serious money," Robbie suggested.

"There are a zillion Food Trucks out there and you'll need more than one great sandwich to make it work."

"McDonalds begs to disagree," Robbie quipped back.

Then noticing that Robbie had wolfed down most of his lunch, Tony said, "I'll make you another one if you promise to share with Ronin – he's drooling all over my uncle's precious rug! That rug was the only thing Uncle Danny talked about aside from fighting - he got it from a vagabond hippie in search of a meal."

Robbie had noticed the carpet before. He had a predilection for carpets from the Indo-Persian region.

"That's a very nice carpet. It's from Andkhoy – North Western Afghanistan. I have one that is very similar to this one but not quite as nice. This is a rare piece, Tony; you should take better care of it."

"Okay, let's start by getting your Grizzly to stop drooling on it."

"Then you had better make the second VanArcen special real quick!" Robbie said and tossed Ronin the last bit of his sandwich. It disappeared with a snap and without a trace.

Once lunch was done, they sat on the porch with Tony and Ronin play fighting. Ronin had taken to Tony, something that was unusual for the dog. Robbie, for his part, was still debating whether he should share what he had learned about Marisa and Jodie and the video the young girl had leaked. The fact that Marisa had left a note for Tony was testament to her trust in him but this could get sketchy and the last thing he wanted was to put VanArcen in any danger.

At the same time, he was unable to shake the despondency that he felt; the nagging feeling that he had blown his chance at a normal life with Meghan. The icy fingers of despair clutched at him filling him with an irrational gloom. *What if he had lost her? He needed to figure out a way to reach out to her; to apologize and tell her that it didn't matter. Hell! He's rather face Seppo Heikkinen with an arm tied behind his back than go through this emotional crap!*

He snapped himself out of his bleak reverie. "Tony, I'm going to tell you some things but you need to keep it to yourself," Robbie began and then seeing VanArcen distracted, "Hey, are you listening?"

"Yeah, yeah I'm all ears … just give me a minute," VanArcen replied, "I need to teach this monster just who is boss!"

The roughhousing had shifted gears and moved into full combat mode. Though it was playful, the accompanying snarls and growls would have made most people cringe. Robbie watched them bemused by their antics and surprised that Ronin was being so relatively gentle. After some pushing, dodging and nipping, Ronin knocked Tony to the floor and pinned him down with his enormous bulk. VanArcen tried squirming out from under the huge dog but he couldn't budge a hair. "Fuck! I can't move… he's freakin' heavy! I can't breathe, bro! Help!"

"Ronin! Stop! Let him up. Come on, let him up!" Robbie commanded. The big dog obeyed, reluctantly letting VanArcen free and trotting over to Robbie licked his face before lying down next to him.

VanArcen let out a sigh, "Whew! That was close. For a minute there I thought I would have to use my secret jujutsu move, a very dangerous maneuver that I use only when my life is being threatened. I really didn't want to hurt the big boy," then added, "Now that I have vanquished the mighty dragon I have time to listen and offer advice to you, Mr. Peasant. What is it that you wish to know?"

"Get serious. Did you know that Marisa and Jodie were friends?"

"No. Honestly, I didn't know Marisa that well. She was like the butterflies she loved – here one moment and gone the next. Whenever she stopped by, we talked about her schooling and aspirations. She was beautiful, smart and sweet … an innocent girl who had a passion for butterflies. I'm not sure what the two of them could have had in common but friendship is a strange thing – you never know what makes two people click. Take the two of us, for instance. Me, Butch Cassidy and you, the Sundance Kid though I think Sundance was better looking."

Robbie shook his head but there was truth in what VanArcen said, friendship often defied reason and logic. He had a quick flashback to Calvin and Jaimie but he shook them off, "Marisa shared videos with Jodie asking her to post them on social media should something happen to her, which means she realized she was in danger. I haven't seen the videos but I'm willing to bet they involve two things; drugs and sex. The participants are people who would prefer not to have them in the public domain and would kill to stop it."

"Well, then there's the root of all evil – moolah! Maybe blackmail?" VanArcen noted.

"From everything you've told me, Marisa wouldn't try to blackmail anyone. She was somehow involved with the people who were in the video."

"What do you mean?" Tony asked.

"Marisa witnessed something that involved drugs and/or sex. And possibly, videotaped it or got her hands on the damning evidence."

"No way! Not Marisa," VanArcen protested, "This girl was a straight A student headed for a prestigious Ivy League college. She didn't do drugs and I'll bet my last dollar that she was a virgin until those bastards got their hands on her!"

"So why would the video rock Carlson's boat?" Robbie asked.

"I don't know but I'll tell you this; I'd sooner believe that Mother Theresa was into cocaine and random sex than tarnish the memory of that sweet girl!"

"I'm not implying she was into any of it. I'm just saying that she might have witnessed something and videotaped it. You know kids and their phones, they tape and post everything! How else do you explain this?"

"I don't know. Ever since I heard she was missing, I've lost all faith in mankind," the smaller man lamented. "Why don't we go to the fights tonight and let's see if we can rattle Hank Carlson's cages eh?'

Robbie thought about and nodded in agreement, "Sounds like a plan. I'm going to take Ronin for a run now. What time do you want me to come here? I'd rather leave him here while we are gone if that's okay with you."

"Not a problem. Mi casa su casa, baby!" Tony said to Ronin giving him a kiss on his massive head, "I mean him, not you Olsen. He can come here anytime. You, well you are only welcome if he's with you! Be here at five, the fights usually start at six."

"Okay then. See you at five."

Robbie left with Ronin, his mind riddled with conflicted questions surrounding Meghan, Marisa and Ed Carlson. There had to be a connection but navigating the emotional morass only opened doors that he'd rather keep closed. The very thought of ending up like his father engulfed him like a dark cloud but the dichotomy of emotions, coupled with his intransigent personality, rendered him helpless. His pragmatic answer was to let the chips fall where they may and take things as they come

The drive to the Pit, as it was known, took over an hour. It was located beyond Moose Head Point where Luke Carlson had his cabin and well past the north-western boundary of his property. It was deep in the forest near the base of Mount Katahdin. During the drive, VanArcen kept Robbie entertained with an anecdotal monologue, most of which were exaggerations of several obscure incidents but proved interesting enough to keep him from focusing on Meghan.

"The first time I attended a fight, I was so fuckin' lost it wasn't funny! I had no idea where the heck I was and if it weren't for a bunch of moonshiners, I'd still be trying to find my way out. Like a fuckin' maze, it was."

"But you do know where it is, right?" Robbie asked, concerned by the obscure backroad being taken. The anfractuous route was off of the paved roadway, a mud track, cuddled in shadows and rife with potholes and rocks.

"Relax, tough guy, I've been to a hundred fights since then." Tony assured him and continued, "So, back to my story: I stop when I see these guys and after the customary 'who the fuck are you' routine with a gun in my face, I explained my predicament. They turned out to be a bunch of good old boys and offered to have one of them show me the way in exchange for my wristwatch. A freakin' five-hundred-dollar watch! Well, I really had no choice, they would have snatched it anyway but mama didn't raise no dummies. I agreed to the deal but on one condition, I would hand it over after I get to the Pit."

VanArcen slowed and peered at the narrowing dirt path, "Hmm, this looks different," he mused but seemingly satisfied, continued, "We drank to our deal and I swear that hillbilly hooch can kill a Grizzly! Anyhow, after some coughing and sputtering and backslapping, mainly them slapping my back, this guy named Abe gets into the truck. Now, Abe is a big old boy with hands like sledgehammers and shoulders that King Kong would have been proud of and a head so small, you'd swear it belonged to a five-year-old kid! A real freak of nature, but that's not all, Abe had only one tooth; a single front upper tooth stained brown from years of chewing on tobacco rub. Every few minutes the potato-head would roll down the window and let fly a virulent stream of nasty brown sputum half of which would end on the inside of the window. Fuckin' disgusting but I wasn't going to complain. No siree! Not me. I had flashbacks of the movie 'Deliverance' and just wanted to get the heck out of there."

"And why am I not surprised?" Robbie said, "Appalachian backwoods, moonshine, hillbillies and you … no, not strange at all. Turn your headlights on. It's getting dark. "

VanArcen ignored him and continued, "So we are chatting away, Abe of one tooth and me, becoming real chummy and such so I ask: 'How the heck do you chew with that one tooth, Abe?' Okay, so maybe not the most appropriate or prudent question but the curiosity was killing me and do you know what the fucker does? He smiles, leans over and bites me on my shoulder like a fuckin' chipmunk working on a nut! I almost crashed the damn truck!"

Robbie had to smile trying to picture a one-toothed hillbilly with a tiny head gnawing on VanArcen's shoulder. "That's funny."

"Not funny at all, freakin' painful and scary! Believe me, for a moment there I was sure the pinhead was a Walking Dead zombie all set to feed on my sorry ass!"

VanArcen swerved suddenly, barely missing a large rock. "Turn your headlights on! And, pay attention to the road. You're making me nervous," Robbie told the smaller man, giving him a look of concern, "that was close."

"Okay, okay … sorry, I forgot about that rock!"

"So did he get you there … to the Pit? And did you give him the watch?"

"He got me there alright but I was bleeding like a motherfucker! The potato-head kept looking at me like I was a delicious steak. All that was missing was him asking me to 'squeal like a pig'! You remember that routine from Deliverance? That hillbilly asking Ned Beatty to squeal … anyway, I told him that my Grandma had given me the watch so it had sentimental value and whether twenty bucks would square us up and he agreed, smiling like he had hit the jackpot! The fuckin' inbred retard!"

"You watch too many old movies and are you sure you're not making this shit up?"

"No one believes me! How do you make up shit like this?"

"A vivid imagination and nothing much else to do," Robbie offered.

"That's it. As soon as we get there I'll show you the hole he drilled into my freakin' shoulder! It's never been the same. Liz thinks I was shot."

"I wonder how she ever got that idea," was Robbie's sardonic response.

And so it went until they came to a makeshift post consisting of two rusty 55-gallon metal drums placed on each side of the dirt road. There were two men standing by each drum; big, no-nonsense toughs who flagged the pick-up to a halt. They peered in and recognizing VanArcen waved them through. They drove another five hundred or so yards until the road narrowed even further and led into a large, grassy field where a slew of pick-up trucks, cars and SUVs were parked every which way but orderly; it resembled a gridlock on Fifth Avenue.

"Park in the back, closer to the road," Robbie instructed, "make sure you have a clear exit. You never want to get hemmed in."

"Who are you? James Bond?"

"Just do it. Park there," Robbie asserted, pointing to a spot away from the other vehicles.

"Shit! Now we'll have to walk a mile!" VanArcen protested.

"You need the exercise."

"Oh, you are a nasty man! In my next life I'm coming back as Lew Alcindor," VanArcen complained as they made their way towards the lights of the building.

"Who?"

"Lew Alcindor! Kareem Abdul-Jabbar, the basketball player. He's like seven-foot-ten or so."

"I know who Kareem Abdul-Jabbar is and he's not seven-ten," Robbie corrected.

"He's taller than you, and that's all that matters!" VanArcen quipped back.

Robbie gave up. It was impossible to get the last word with Tony.

THE PIT

The building was an old dilapidated farm house with a large front yard surrounded by a cluster of oak, pine, birch and such. The lighting on the outside was barely sufficient and for good reason: the aphotic aspect of underworld commerce. Standing in the yard, hidden by shadows, there were men and women surreptitiously buying and selling drugs of every kind – from pot to heroin. There was one rule that was strictly enforced - no doing drugs on the property and if you were caught you'd get your ass whipped good and proper. It was Luke Carlson's rule and it had been enforced a few times and proved to be an effective deterrent.

The inside of the building was a little brighter and it was pretty obvious that the place had been remodeled to suit the purpose. The original walls had been demolished to allow for an unhindered view of the combatants. Large beams replaced some of the original joists with overhead lights to keep the Pit encased in a bright, phosphorescent glow. The old, overhead country fans provided some reprieve from the hot, sweaty jam of bodies clambering around the Pit.

There were two counters that were set-up diagonally, in the corners, to enable placing wagers, buying booze and collecting winnings. Carlson had his men monitoring every nook and cranny on a closed circuit network of cameras and despite the illegitimacy of the endeavor; it was run rather efficiently with less trouble than most casinos have.

The Pit itself was similar to a boxing ring except that the floor was made of compressed dirt and sand with a canvas mat drawn tightly over it. It was slightly larger than the average ring, about 20 feet by 20 feet, and the traditional ropes were replaced by urethane coated metal fencing. The blood stains on the mat and the portions of the fencing were testament to the brutal aspects of free-form, bareknuckle fighting.

Most of the men who attended these cage fights were tough, non-nonsense mountain folk and of a prototypical appearance. They were either unshaven or bearded, almost all of them were armed, dressed in T-shirts and dungarees and definitely persons not to be messed with. Interspersed amongst the men were a few women and they were an equally indurate bunch. Some of people came from small towns around Chase River but many were from as far off as Stokes State Forest in New Jersey. The fights were held in Chase River Town once every two months and it was an event that everyone looked forward to mainly because there was no interference from the Law. It was not uncommon to see Chief Dolan and Deputy Bradley at the fights.

There were no weight classes and the combatants were decided on the spur of the moment or by mutual consent. It wasn't uncommon for local toughs to get into the Pit to earn some money or prove just how skilled they were but mostly the fighters were experienced with hard-earned reputations and many of them were on the payroll of mobsters.

There were four entrances, one on each side of the building, and each entrance was manned by two of Carlson's thugs.

"Follow me," VanArcen said and walked through a side door entrance. Robbie had seen one of the men standing by the door before; a tall, lean hard-case who gave him a cold look when they strolled in. The side entrance proved to be less crowded providing them with a decent view of the Pit.

"Let's get a beer," Robbie suggested locating the counter where the booze was being dispensed.

"Good idea. Hey, Luke said the drinks were on him. Let it flow, baby!" VanArcen rejoined enthusiastically.

"Easy, cowboy, we're here to shake the tree not get drunk."

"Can't we do both?"

Before Robbie could reply, he heard his name being called, "Robbie Olsen! Hey Olsen, here, I'm behind you."

It was Luke Carlson. He was making his way through a throng of men, smiling broadly, "Glad you could make it, soldier, you're going to enjoy it!"

They shook hands and he surprised Robbie with a quick hug. Luke was on a high – fight nights excited him and always made him happy.

"What about me? I don't count?" Tony lamented.

Luke turned, laughing, and grabbed VanArcen in a warm embrace, "Tony, it's like the Prodigal Son. You're here all the time; we love you, man. You should know that."

"Well, I have feelings, you know, and would like a fatted calf every now and then."

"A fatted calf, really? I worry about you, boy, but you got it. The drinks are on me. I've told the guys that you can have whatever you want and as much as you want. So go for it. We've got a good crowd tonight and a great card. It's going to be a dandy." He paused scanning the crowd before continuing, "There are some bad-ass fighters here, two from Jersey – Adam Shayk's boys. There's one," Luke indicated to a small clique of tough, no-nonsense men, "the tall one is Don Carnicke. They call him 'La Muerte Oscura', The Dark Death. He is said to have killed a fighter in an underground, bareknuckle fight in Mexico City."

"La Muerte what?" VanArcen asked.

"La Muerte Oscura, The Dark Death." Luke repeated.

"He looks like he's dying! Bronson could take him," VanArcen offered.

"Who?" Luke asked, genuinely confused.

"Don't pay any attention to him." Robbie interjected.

"He's being modest. Olsen is like the legend of Charles Bronson," VanArcen explained, "He could take that guy just go ask Snake."

Luke threw his head back and laughed out loud, "Tony, you're a freakin' riot! I wouldn't doubt it for one minute. Snake is still trying to figure out what happened. But unfortunately, Don is scheduled to fight Syed El Chafic, a three hundred pound wrestler from Abu Dhabi. It should be the best fight of the night, a striker versus wrestler; speed versus strength."

"Well, some things are not meant to be and Bronson here will save his ass-kickery for other more deserving knuckleheads!" VanArcen quipped.

Luke laughed again, shaking his head and said, "Listen, I'd love to chat, I mean it but I have to go – time's winding down." Then in parting, "Have a good time and don't go cracking any heads, Mr. Olsen, or I'll have to put you in the Pit!"

They watched as Luke Carlson made his way towards the Pit, his golden hair shimmering in the incandescent light. He stopped where a group of men were gathering and signaled towards Don Carnicke and his posse of men, waving them down to the Pit.

Robbie turned to VanArcen, "What's with you? I'm not looking to fight anyone. The last thing we need right now is to be distracted."

"You could take him. The fucker looks like a drugged out, old insurance salesman! Just look at the scar tissues around his eyes; he'll bleed like a stuck pig if you breath on him. The guy next to him looks a lot tougher, if you ask me."

The man next to Carnicke had the muscles of a weightlifter - huge biceps, barrel chest that and a neck that was thicker than VanArcen's thighs. He had his sleeves rolled-up and flexed his arms to impress the crowd that was beginning to gather around the Pit.

"Don't ever bet on fights, Tony, you'll lose. Carnicke looks like he can take care of himself. Don't let big muscles fool you – it is more about functional muscles and knowing how to fight. I've never had any trouble taking on a muscle-head. It's the lean guys you worry about. Come on, let's get some beer."

The first contest of the evening resembled a hugging match. The fight went to the mat in the opening seconds and the next four minutes were spent with one man trying to get back to his feet and the other trying to keep him down. After a while, the crowd booed and finally the referee stood them up. There was a short flurry of punches exchanged but then the smaller jujutsu fighter took his opponent down again. He was working for a chokehold and had managed to take the man's back. The crowd cheered hoping to see a choke-out but every attempt to slip his arm around the other man's neck was thwarted. This went on for a few minutes and there was another robust cascade of boos and chants to stand them up. The spectators came to see blood and there was no real blood in the ground game; a lot of skill but not enough blood.

"Not sure why they are booing, the little guy is a pretty skilled fighter," Robbie observed. "He's taking on a guy who outweighs him by at least twenty pounds! His best bet is on the ground."

"No one cares. They want to see knockouts and blood. My uncle was a wrestler but he figured out quickly that this was entertainment. KOs were what excited people so he worked on his stand-up game. He could box, kick, knee and elbow and he could knock you the fuck out. He'd take two to give one ... the crowds loved him."

"And he most probably ended punch drunk and silly," Robbie retorted.

"That he did; but what a life. Like a brilliant shooting star! Fan adulation, women, free meals and with all the other frills and thrills. At his funeral, over five hundred people turned up and every single person said: *that Danny VanArcen was a real man*'. People still talk about him. Damn, I'd switch with him in a New York minute."

Just then Luke walked up, "How's it going? Enjoying the fights?" he paused then continued, "I have some bad news. The Arab is stuck in traffic. He's not going to make it. Carnicke is fuckin' pissed. Fighters get paid only if they fight and they get a cut of the bets. This would have been a big one for him."

"Don't you have someone to take his place?" Robbie asked.

"Hey look, there's Heikkinen," VanArcen pointed out, "maybe he'll fight Doctor Death."

Seppo Heikkinen was hard to miss in any crowd. His size, the blond, frosted Mohawk and his aggressive demeanor demanded attention. He was making his way towards Hank Carlson who was standing in the back. Carlson was with Adam Shayk, the mobster from Jersey and a few of his bodyguards. They were oddly conspicuous in their dark suits. Though Hank was surprised to see the big Finn he kept his curiosity from showing.

Heikkinen approached the men, gave the others a precursory look and whispered in his boss's ear, "I need to talk to you."

"Gentlemen, you'll have to excuse me; business calls. Give me a minute," Hank said as the two men moved away from the others.

"I got the bitch to talk. Jodie is with Maddie Wilkins."

Hank thought for a second, "Go get her. Try not to hurt the old biddy."

"What if she gets in the way?"

"Then do what you have to."

"What about Luke?"

"I'll handle Luke. Take Jodie to the old Bruckman farm and

wait for me. And, take Cat with you."

"I don't need help." The Finn bristled immediately.

"Take him with you. This is not a debate," Hank instructed with a bite in his tone.

The big Finn was irritated but nodded and left, shoving people out of his way. Most of the locals knew the big Finn or was aware of his reputation and those that didn't were intimidated by his sheer size. In room full of tough men, not one seemed eager to confront him as he made his way out of the building.

"That's strange. Seppo never comes to the fights and I do mean, never!" Luke said. "Something's going on. I'll be back. I need to speak to my brother."

When Luke approached the group, it was Adam Shayk who greeted him, "Luke! It's been a while. You are one pretty motherfucker! If I looked like you I'd be in Hollywood humping all those beauties out there," he turned to his men, "just look at him, boys! Is he pretty or what?" And with that, he put his arm around the younger Carlson's shoulder.

"You're not me, Adam," Luke responded, shaking free. There was no mistaking the dislike in his voice, "And, *humping* a bunch of skanks isn't on my bucket list."

"Why the attitude, huh? What did I ever do to you?" Shayk asked, his round face a beacon of wounded pride.

"I don't like you," Luke answered bluntly, "I don't like you or your partner, that asshole, Nikolai. But, I like doing business with you – it's uncomplicated and you don't play games. So let's cut the bullshit and stick to business, okay?"

Looks could be deceiving especially when it came to Adam Shayk. The pudgy face, protruding belly and small beady eyes behind black, horn-rimmed glasses gave him the appearance of an accountant or stockbroker but that was surely misleading as quite a few thugs had the misfortune of finding out. He was a coldblooded killer, a barracuda with no conscience.

The mobster pinned Luke with a cold, hard glare, his face a stone mask. The seconds dragged on as the two men eyed each other, both unblinking, before Shayk burst out laughing, "I like you, Luke. You may not like me but I like you. You say it like it is … no bullshit. So, back to business it is – what are we to do about Carnicke? A lot of people came to see him fight and now that fuckin' Arab finds an excuse to bail. Traffic, my fat, fuckin' ass! We've got to do something. Do you have someone else? Let's give these folk what they came for, huh? Let's put on a show!"

"How about Olsen?" Hank interjected. He knew Luke would be curious about Seppo's appearance and he had to keep Luke here while Seppo was getting Jodie from Maddie's place. If Olsen was fighting, Luke would probably stay put.

"Olsen is a soldier not a fighter. Where is Seppo? I just saw him here. Why not have him fight Carnicke?" Luke countered.

Hank lied, without missing a beat, "Seppo has a personal problem he needs to take care of. The girl he's fucking is pregnant. He'll be gone for a few days."

"Who is Olsen?" Shayk inquired, the suggestion giving him hope.

"He's not going to agree. Just because he can take care of himself doesn't mean he'll fight Carnicke," Luke retorted.

"Who is Olsen?" Shayk asked again, "Is he that tall guy you were with?"

"Yes." Luke responded.

"Money! Offer him enough money and he'll fight. I know the type. He'll fight and unless I've completely misjudged the man, he'll make a fight of it too. Luke, whatever it takes, I'll come in for half."

When Robbie saw Luke and Hank with the short man in a suit

approaching, he knew something was up but it was Tony who had it pegged right from the very beginning.

"I'll bet they want you to fight that ape," he whispered to Robbie.

"You don't know that. Maybe, they are coming here to tell you to stop guzzling all their beer!"

They watched silently as the men walked over to them. It was interesting to see the dynamics and the hierarchal byplay between Shayk and Carlson - two alpha males jostling to establish dominance.

Hank took the lead and addressed Robbie, "Hi Olsen, glad you could make it." They shook hands briefly before Carlson introduced Shayk, "Adam, this is Robbie Olsen. And, this here is a good friend from New Jersey, Adam Shayk."

After the pleasantries were done, it was the short man who broached the subject of fighting, "Hank tells me that you were in the Special Forces. Hey, let me first thank you for your service … you guys are amazing!"

The man sounded sincere but there was something more to this innocuous looking man that made Robbie uneasy. Robbie couldn't quite put his finger on it but his intuition was rarely wrong.

"Army Rangers, and I appreciate the sentiment."

"Listen, I respect you so I'm going to give it to you straight. We need someone to fight Carnicke. His opponent chickened out. Now, this ain't going to be an easy fight so we're willing to make it worth your while. What do you say?"

Robbie studied the man carefully before replying, "Not interested."

"Win or lose you'll get ten thousand dollars and for something you've done in bars for free. That's a lot of dough, soldier," Shayk tried being persuasive.

Robbie looked over at Luke, "Was this your idea?"

"No. I told them you wouldn't do it," Luke replied, denying any culpability, "this was what they cooked up." He nodded at Hank and Adam. "I'd advise you not to fight him. Don is dangerous and has a nasty streak in him."

"I agree," Adam Shayk said, looking at Robbie, "Don is a tough guy and a good fighter but since that incident in Mexico, he hasn't been the same. If there ever was a time to get him, this is it. What's the number that would make you comfortable?"

"Ten grand is chicken shit," Tony countered, "you guys better get real. We're not in the same ballpark, not even the same fuckin' stratosphere!"

His interjection was a surprise to all the men including Robbie. He gave VanArcen a quizzical look but his friend ignored him and continued looking straight at Shayk.

"You stay the fuck out of this, VanArcen!" It was Hank glowering at Tony.

"Hey! There is no need for that. He's with me and you guys came to us so let's keep this civil," Robbie admonished, looking at Hank.

There was an awkward pause, "Come on guys, we're all on the same team. Hank didn't mean nothing by it," Shayk was being conciliatory.

"I'm sorry, Tony, that was out of line," Hank was apologetic, "I was trying to avoid the case of too many cooks."

"Well, when it comes to the dough, I'm the Executive Chef! Talk to me, brother, and if you want this to happen you'd better show us more bread!"

Robbie had to smile. He had always enjoyed competition and despite his claim of not wanting to fight, he had often wondered how he would stack-up against a real professional in a controlled environment. He had had his share of fights and barroom brawls but a fight in the ring was something different and here was a chance to settle the obverse speculation. Add to this his financial dilemma and it might be just what the doctor ordered. He was running out of money and ten grand was certainly tempting. He decided to let Tony play this one out.

"He's my manager and handles my finances," Robbie confirmed, "so I'm going to leave this to him. Not saying I'll fight but I'd like to see how badly you boys would like to see this happen."

It was Luke who spoke next. He smiled at Robbie then said to VanArcen, "Twenty-five grand, Tony, with a five grand bonus if he wins? Now that is a reasonable offer."

"Hey, wait a fuckin' minute ..." Hank started but Luke raised his hand to quiet him.

"I need to discuss this with my man," Tony replied and took Robbie to the side and lowering his voice, "Hey, are you sure you want to do this? I was just fuckin' with those assholes."

"You're the one who said he's a pushover. Remember the 'breathe on him and he'll bleed'?" Robbie feigned surprise.

"I don't have to fight him. I can say anything ... he's beginning to look tougher by the second. He *is* one ugly bastard though!"

"This ain't a beauty contest. The truth is that I could use the money and I've always wondered how all my training would fare against a real pro."

"I knew it! Pacifist my ass! Bronson lives, baby! We're going to kick some ass and take some names!" VanArcen couldn't suppress his enthusiasm.

"Control yourself."

They walked back and rejoined the others, "Thirty grand, win or lose, with a ten grand bonus *when* he wins. That's non-negotiable," Tony said with a deadpan expression.

"That's fucking ridiculous!" Hank exclaimed, "Twenty-five was ridiculous. That's more than all these fighters make together. For thirty thousand, I'll fight him myself!"

"Really?" Tony was genuinely surprised, "You'd fight that …" He was about to say 'ape' but thought better of it, "You'd fight that very dangerous looking man? *I'll* pay you thirty thousand to see that!"

"You don't have thirty thousand!" Carlson snapped back.

"I'll sign my cabin over to you – that's worth at least that!"

"What the fuck is going on here? Cut the shit out. Okay, so both of you have huge fucking cocks! We're all impressed! Hank is not fighting Carnicke. Let's get this deal done!" Shayk intervened, cutting short the irrelevant prating.

"Take it or leave it. Robbie hasn't had a single pro fight and you want him to step into the Pit with a guy named, what was it? La Muerte Oscura or some shit like that? Get real. And all that stuff about him not being dangerous anymore? Save it. He looks plenty dangerous to me!"

Adam Shayk studied VanArcen like he was seeing him for the first time - really seeing him. He looked over at Robbie. This was going to be interesting, he thought. Though he didn't give Robbie a chance, it was a fight and shit happens in fights. Just ask Mike Tyson when he fought Buster Douglas. Thirty-grand would be worth it and he was on the hook for only half of it.

"Okay, we've got ourselves a deal," Shayk said cutting off any further discussion.

"I need to see the dough *before* he steps into the Pit," Tony told the men.

The mobster nodded and said "Not a problem. We'll get you the money before the fight. I'm going to break the news to Don. He's going to be fuckin' thrilled." Then turning to Robbie, "Good luck, soldier, you're going to need it."

Tony couldn't resist a parting dig, "Get your man a banana if you want to see him jump around with joy!"

If looks could kill Tony VanArcen would have been a dead man. Shayk glared at him but said nothing. He turned and left with his men.

MEGHAN AND MADDIE

Meghan Hollier was not an overly emotional person but she had been crying on and off pretty much the entire evening. She was besieged by those imposters, guilt and doubt. They clawed at her insides filling her with apprehension and sadness. When she met Robbie it was as though every prayer, dream and wish she fostered had come true – like hitting the million-dollar jackpot on a scratch-off ticket. She wasn't getting any younger and Ryan was at the age where he needed a man in his life, a father figure so to speak. Unfortunately, Chase River Town wasn't a hotbed for eligible men in her demographic. She couldn't reconcile herself to the fact that she blew her chances by keeping those lewd and incriminating photographs. She didn't really know why she kept them. But why should that matter? It was before she had met Robbie. *We all make mistakes,* she thought, *whatever happened to second chances?*

That one rash decision, made in a moment of desperation and loneliness, was back to haunt her and could jeopardize the relationship she so badly longed for. Marylou Dorsey and that party! Why did she ever agree to go? Her mind was filled with *what ifs* and *whys* and *if only I had done this or that.* It was driving her mad.

She finally decided to visit with Maddie Wilkins. The old lady had a way of putting things in perspective with her straightforward answers and outlandish prognostications.

"Maddie always makes me feel better," she said to herself. She washed her face and noticed the redness in her swollen eyes. "Gosh, I'm a sight! It's a good thing Robbie isn't going to see me like this … *if* he ever agrees to see me again!"

She packed the bowl of Lamb stew she had kept aside for Maddie and got into her old Chevy truck and went to pick-up Ryan from her parent's place. Maddie loved Ryan and though it was getting late, she would certainly get a kick out of seeing him.

Seppo Heikkinen and Maddie Wilkins

THE NIGHTMARE AND THE PROPHECY

Seppo Heikkinen stopped the van at the intersection of Mulberry Lane and Depot Road, the prearranged location for the pick-up. The big man wasn't happy; he disliked working with others and considered Hank's insistence to be an insult to his ability to get the job done. The premise for his preference for working alone was simple – permutations and combinations. His experience had taught him that there was a distinct correlation between the number of guys on a job and the exponentially increased chances for a fuck-up. And adding to his resentment was the animosity he felt towards Cataldo. He considered the Italian to be lazy and worthless. But, Hank had insisted that he take Cat along and he knew better than to argue or circumvent his boss. Not directly anyway.

The lithely built Italian was leaning nonchalantly against a lamppost smoking a cigarette while waiting for Heikkinen. He always dressed sharply – more like a playboy than a hood. He was wearing a brown, suede jacket, a light blue T-shirt and a pair of pleated beige trousers. The crocodile-skin loafers had rubber soles that made little or no noise when he walked. He flicked his half-finished smoke to the gravel sidewalk and got into the passenger's side seat. Cataldo or Cat, as he liked to be called, gave the impression of being easygoing and laidback. He wasn't. He was calculating and wound as tight as a coiled spring. His demeanor was a ploy and had served him well in the past. People were misled by his boyish good looks and friendly manner and would often let their guard down and that was tanta-mount to tickling a cobra.

"Hey Seppo, Buonasera! We work together this evening, unh," he greeted the big man with a smile.

"Shut the fuck up, you little twerp! We don't work together. You keep that faggot mouth zipped up and don't get in my way. Capisce?"

Cat's face was written over with surprise and shock. He didn't understand the big Finn's antagonism. He shrugged his shoulders and gestured with his hands, nonplussed, "Seppo, I just do my job, eh, so why do you talk …"

The blow to the mouth cut him off. It was a hard, backhanded slap delivered with enough force to split the Italian's upper lip. Flashing lights exploded in his brain and the proverbial bells rang in his ears. It felt like he had been hit with a sledgehammer.

"I told you to shut up!" Seppo snarled glancing at Cat.

The smaller man shook his head trying to clear his mind. The high pitched hum in his ears persisted and the metallic taste of his blood triggered his quick temper. Despite his compromised state he reacted and that was a mistake.

"Sei un fottuto stronzo …" he mumbled incoherently, fumbling for the knife tucked in his jacket's inner pocket when a second blow, this time a hammer-fist delivered sideways, slammed his head against the backrest and separated him from his senses. He fell forward, his face bouncing off the dashboard.

"Fuckin' greaseball! Sei tu lo stronzo!" The big man hissed then leaning over, he opened the passenger side door and pushed the little Italian out. Except for Hank, no one knew that the Finn was fluent in several languages, Italian being one of them.

The van was doing over fifty and Seppo glanced at the unconscious body in his rearview mirror. Cat rolled and bounced off the dirt road, his arms and legs flailing disjointedly before trundling unceremoniously into a ditch.

"Ciao, motherfucker!" Seppo hissed and headed towards Maddie Wilkins' place.

When he arrived at the gas station, he drove past the driveway and parked the van alongside a cluster of large oaks. The tall bushes around the trees provided sufficient cover for his van. The element of surprise had always worked in his favor but he hadn't counted on the two security cameras mounted on the building's facade. However, their presence didn't seem to faze him as he carefully surveyed the parking lot before heading for the front door.

Maddie was in the bedroom on the upper floor of the building. She was with Jodie sorting through old skirts and tops that the young girl could take with her when she noticed Seppo on the monitor walking into the driveway.

"Quick into the closet," she instructed the young girl, "it's Carlson's man, the Finn."

Behind the clothes in the closet was a small hidden chamber. It was constructed as a storage space but it was where Maddie kept her safe. And though Jodie had to scrunch up a bit, she had sufficient space to hide without being too uncomfortable. They had practiced her getting in and out, but the reality of the situation frightened the girl and she tripped and stumbled before crouching down.

"Hurry, Jodie, quick, get in there!" Maddie urged the girl glancing at the monitor.

"Seppo is crazy. What's going to happen to you?" Jodi asked looking up at Maddie, her voice trembling ever so slightly.

"Nothing is going to happen, child, as long as you stay quiet. Don't make a sound and don't come out unless I come to get you, understand?"

"Yes," she answered peering past Maddie at the doorway. Her voice and face couldn't hide her anxiety.

"Jodie, you don't come out for any reason until he's gone, is that clear?" Maddie was firm.

The young girl nodded her head as the hatch door closed on her. Maddie moved quickly for a woman her age. She spread the hangers evenly so that her dresses made it impossible to detect the chamber. She gave it a critical look before sliding the closet door home. She then undid her hair and let it loose and put a housecoat on over her dress. To add the finishing touches, she removed her glasses and placed it by the side table and rumpled the pillows and bedspread. She took a quick look in the mirror and was satisfied with the disheveled image she presented; a frail, old woman who had just gotten out of bed.

She heard the clanging of the front door bell and walked slowly down the stairs, holding on to the banister, unafraid and ready to confront her nemesis. She had known all along that it would come to this.

MEGHAN AND RYAN: UNWANTED GUESTS

When Meghan arrived at the Maddie's place, she pulled right up to the front door. She usually parked in the rear but since the place was deserted she opted for the convenience of proximity. The truck's old engine coughed and sputtered in protest when she turned off the ignition. It was badly in need of a tune-up but she kept putting it off trying to decide between buying a new car or spending the money to service the truck. She loved the Chevy and the thought of trading it in or junking it didn't sit well with her.

She said to herself, "It's time to get you serviced, old gal, or maybe just drive you to Zack's Junkyard… what do you say?"

"Is the Chariot sick, Ma?" Ryan asked with childish curiosity. The "Chariot" is what Ryan decided to call the Chevy.

"No. The old girl is …" Meghan began just as Ryan opened the door, "Ryan! Wait! Wait for me!"

The little boy dashed out of the truck and ran into the building accompanied by the rattle of the signum bell. Patience wasn't in the four-year-old's playbook especially when lollipops and chocolates were involved. Maddie always had a container full of lollies just for Ryan. Meghan shook her head and grabbed the stew and quickly followed him in. She was concerned that Ryan's exuberance would get the better of him and he would trip and fall or break something in the store.

"Ryan, don't run! And only one lolly at a ..." she started when she saw Seppo Heikkinen. She froze and the icy fingers of fear squeezed her heart.

The Finn was standing in front of Maddie, towering over her like a blond King Kong and had Ryan by his hand. The little boy looked frightened and even more diminutive next to the giant.

"Let him go!" Meghan told the big Finn, fighting to keep her fear in check.

Seppo laughed, "I'm not going to hurt him. He's Luke's little bastard and I would never hurt a Carlson. You know that!" his voice laced with sarcasm.

"Please let him go, Seppo, you're scaring him!" This time she pleaded, watching Ryan struggle to free his hand.

Seppo ignored her plea and turned to Maddie, "Where's the girl?"

"Do you mean Jodie?" Maddie asked, squinting up at him.

"Don't play with me, you old hag, where's the little bitch?" He snarled, his voice turning menacing.

"She left with that stranger, the soldier ... unh, what's his name? Olsen, yes, that's his name, Robbie Olsen. He came and got her yesterday or was it the day before? I don't remember anymore. My memory ain't what it used to be. Now let the boy go." There was no fear in Maddie Wilkins.

For a moment Seppo looked uncertain. She seemed to be telling the truth. Why would she mention Olsen if it wasn't the truth? But he was a suspicious man by nature and something didn't seem right. Olsen was at the Pit, he had seen him there with VanArcen. The timelines didn't make sense. He let go of the boy's hand and instead held him by the top of his head, the thick, long fingers forming a claw-like crown around the boy's dome.

"You'd better tell me the truth or I'll pop his head like a fucking grape!"

"No!" Meghan screamed and ran towards the Finn but a quick swipe of his hand sent her tumbling.

"You try that again and I *will* hurt the boy," he growled.

Meghan blinked, the blow was a mere tap from the giant but it dazed her. She looked helplessly at her son. She knew the big man wouldn't hesitate to hurt him.

"Please don't, Seppo, I beg of you …" she whimpered, "please let him go. I'll do anything, just don't hurt him."

"Then you had better convince the old bitch. One last time, where is she?" The last part was for Maddie.

The ensuing silence was terrifying as the old woman hesitated; her mind went blank faced with the dilemma of choosing between the little boy and the girl.

"I'm here," the frightened voice came from the top of the stairs. It was Jodie. She had heard enough.

"Get your ass down here! Now!" the Finn barked, looking up at her.

When Jodie got down the stairway, Seppo let the boy go and grabbed Jodie by her hair, shoving her towards the door.

"You got a lot of people hurt because of your stupid antics," he said, his voice angry.

On the way out, Seppo stopped by Meghan. She was on her knees hugging Ryan, stroking his hair. "I know where you live and I know where your parents live. You keep your nose out of this or I'll be paying you a visit. Have you ever seen someone skinned alive?"

The rhetorical question had its effect. He laughed at the fear etched on her face, "I'll make you watch while I skin your parents and then I'll skin the little bastard! You hear me, you bit…"

But that was as far as he got. Maddie drove the scissors into the Finn's back just under the trapezoids and into the shoulder. She used both hands and with as much force as she could muster. She wheezed with the effort, as the tip sank in through the muscle and hit bone. Seppo groaned, a guttural hiss escaping through clenched teeth, and turned around. He still had the girl by her hair.

"You shouldn't have done that," he said softly and then hit the old woman on the side of her head.

Maddie caromed off the balustrade and crumpled in a heap, her head angled oddly to one side, her eyes were open and the body fell limp and lifeless. He hadn't meant to hurt the old woman. He had reacted in anger and to the pain. He let the girl go and leaned over the motionless form.

It was the scream that jogged him back just as Jodie was trying to squeeze by him towards the door. But the Finn was quick, he cut her off and with one huge hand, grabbed her. "You try that again and I'll break your neck." Then, turning to Meghan, "You heard what I said. Don't think I won't do it. You stay the fuck out of this mess if you know what's good for you."

And with that he dragged Jodie to his Van. It was only after he had locked the door that he reached back to pluck the scissors that was still sticking into his shoulder. He ignored the pain and the blood streaming from the wound and started up the van. He knew he would have to come up with an excuse for getting rid of the Italian and the old woman but he was sure that the boss would understand, not that he had a choice.

He dialed Hank's number and waited then hearing the voice on the other end said, "I've got her. I'm headed to the Bruckman farm."

"Okay. Don't do anything until I get there," Hank instructed then asked, "What about Maddie?"

"She's dead."

"Fuck!" Hank hissed and hung up. This was not good. He needed to keep Luke away from Maddie Wilkins' place at least until he could sort things out with Jodie and Seppo.

The Pit

WOLVES, DOGS AND SHEEP

The preliminary fights were over and now it was Robbie's turn. True to his word, Adam Shayk had delivered the thirty thousand dollars to VanArcen who made it a point to count it twice. He did so slowly and carefully.

"Relax, Tony, I trust Luke. I'm sure it will all be there," Robbie tried to assuage his friend's suspicions.

"You can never trust these fuckin' shysters!" Tony muttered while counting the money, "A hundred here, a hundred there and before you know it, they're smoking Cuban cigars and drinking Japanese scotch with your money!"

"I strongly doubt that and what would you know about Japanese scotch?"

"I'm a renaissance man. Yamazaki scotch, baby, it's the best there is. Warren Buffet can kiss my sorry ass! Thirty grand, Bronson! I've never held this much money in my life!"

"Get a hold of yourself. You seem to forget that I still have to fight Mr. Death."

"Don't sweat it. Run around the ring, flick the jab a couple of

times, and let him crack you with a few good ones then take a dive…
who the fuck cares, we have the money, honey!"

"You don't get it, do you? I'm not taking a dive."

"Then go there and play your 'Hard Times' role," VanArcen
quipped.

"The hard timed roll? You mean take the fight to ground?"
Robbie wasn't sure what VanArcen meant.

The shorter man hesitated, confused by the phonetic disconnect. In Jujutsu, taking the fight to the mat was also referred to as
rolling on the mat and meant grappling. It took a few seconds but
VanArcen got it.

"No, no, no! Role as in acting not roll as in rolling around! You
remember Charlie Bronson in Hard Times? He was the bareknuckle
street fighter who kicked ass. Tell me you saw the movie?"

"Nope, not everyone is a big Charles Bronson fan."

"Everyone is except you but don't you worry, just go out there
and do your thing. You'll take this has-been monkey out … I'm sure
of it."

"Don't call him that. It's disrespectful. It takes courage to get
into any ring and face a man who wants to tear your head off! You
should know that, your uncle was a fighter."

"Yeah, but Uncle Danny wasn't ugly. This guy looks like an ape.
He has no front teeth, his forehead protrudes like a Neanderthal's,
eyes are pretty much shut and man, that jaw, it has 'china' written
all over it. And I don't mean the country. A freakin' glass jaw if there
ever was one!"

"I'll say it again, this ain't a beauty contest, brother; I'll leave
it at that."

"It should have been then you'd win hands down!" VanArcen
shot back with a big grin.

Robbie shook his head and smiled. VanArcen was impossible. It was time; he was as ready as he was going to be. He made his way to the Pit with Tony by his side. The adrenalin was pumping and he felt his heart race. It was a good feeling, this nervous uneasiness that stoked the fires of competition. He was eager to match skills with the pro. The thought of getting seriously hurt hadn't crossed his mind but Meghan Hollier had. He wished that she was in crowd – she would have given him an added incentive.

The word that Don Carnicke, La Muerte Oscura, was now fighting Robbie "The Soldier" Olsen sent a buzz through the crowd. Some of the people around Chase Town had heard rumors of Robbie's run-in with Hank's men, Snake and Scarface Jake, and when the story spread, the betting got wild. Gamblers put their money on Robbie, betting against the odds, and the people in the know bet on Carnicke. But either way, it was a good night for the Carlsons.

Carnicke was already in the Pit standing barefoot, shadowboxing to keep himself limber when Robbie got it. The pro was shirtless and wearing faded blue jeans that had a tear on one side. Not the fashionable tears that are marketed to kids but worn through from hard use. He was lean of build and tightly muscled. The scars on his face and the tattoos, an integument running across his body and down his arms, told the story of a rough life lived through tough neighborhoods and even tougher circumstances. This was a hard-bitten, resilient man who had had to fight his entire life. His eyes were unblinking and cold and the confidence he exuded came from years of combat. For someone like him, the Pit was life itself with little or no surprises – he had seen it all and had won a lot more than he had lost. But. there was one aspect of VanArcen's observation that was true and that was the cicatricial tissue over both his eyes. He was what they referred to in the fight game as a bleeder. He was also older, pushing forty and that was old for a fighter especially one with over fifty bareknuckle fights.

As the men stood in their respective corners, Luke Carlson came over to Robbie, "Hey soldier, watch out for his low kicks. He's going to try and take your legs out. He'll go low and then it's the right hand over the top. That's his usual ploy so watch that chin."

Robbie nodded, staring across the Pit at his opponent. They were about the same size in height and build. Robbie was a bit taller but not as heavily muscled as his opponent.

There was no referee in this contest. It was the quintessential bareknuckle, free-form fighting that could only end with a knockout or if one fighter taps-out or is rendered unconscious (as a result of a choke). Luke gave the sign and it was on.

The fighters cautiously circled each other. It wouldn't take much to end a fight like this – a clean shot to the jaw with an ungloved fist and it was over. They were both in the conventional stance, that is, right hand dominant with the left leg forward. However, what Carnicke and the others didn't know was that Robbie was ambidextrous. His left was as strong and effective as his right and the awkwardness of a southpaw often gave the fighter a big advantage. He decided he would leverage this advantage when Carnicke was least expecting it.

Robbie was the first to initiate contact. He flicked out a left jab and checked the hard low kick Carnicke threw in return – Luke had been dead on. He retaliated with a quick left-right combination. These were feeler punches used to gage distance and judge the opponent's reflexes. They didn't seem to faze the older fighter. Carnicke parried the blows, feinted and threw his own probing left following that with another low kick aimed at Robbie's knee but he checked the kick again.

He's kicks like a mule! I have to stop this or it will be a short night.

The way to stop a fighter from kicking was with kicks. He

fired a snapping left jab towards his opponent's head, aimed at the scar tissue, stepped in and dug a right hook to the ribcage forcing Carnicke to cover up and before he could recover, Robbie finished the combination with a hard, low kick; torqueing his hips and digging the shinbone into his opponent's calf muscle.

He noticed Carnicke wince but the pro retaliated immediately with a left-right combination. The left was a probe to set distance and the right glanced off Robbie's shoulder and cuffed him above his ear. His head buzzed from the muted impact of the blow and he was forced to back-up, circling to his right and away from the older fighter's power hand.

Wow, ridiculous! I've never been hit this hard.

"Robbie, stay away from him! Use your reach; stick and move!" VanArcen yelled.

Carnicke's fighting style had evolved over time. It was a slow, plodding style that depended on power rather than skill or finesse. He ambled forward, crouched low, crablike, trying to force his opponent back until he was against the cage. His goal was to turn the fight into a brawl, to exchange strikes in close quarters; willing to take two or three to give one. But, Robbie was too quick and had managed to evade the slower man. He ducked and danced away from wild swinging hooks and haymakers. And each time Carnicke missed, he paid. It didn't take much for the scar tissue above his eyes to open up.

"Come on, soldier-boy, let's fight. Stop being a pussy! Stand and fight," Carnicke snarled, wiping the blood trickling into his eyes and was rewarded with a left jab that snapped his head back.

He blinked and lashed out throwing a left hook followed by a right and ended the combination with a reverse wheel kick that caught Robbie in the chest driving him back. The kick didn't land cleanly and he managed to slide off the cage easily avoiding the rushing Carnicke.

You hit hard but you're too slow. I just have to watch that right hand.

Adam Shayk clapped his hands and called out to his fighter, "Easy, Don, easy … you can get him but don't chase him. Let him come to you." Then turning to the man by his side, Andrei Izhutin, he asked in Russian, "Did you place the bet?"

Izhutin was Shayk's right-hand man and took care of the nasty side of Shayk's business interests.

"Yes. I put the whole lot on Don, like you told me to."

"Yeah, I'm not so sure now … this fucker looks like he can fight."

Izhutin nodded, "Yes, I agree. I had a feeling about him so I placed my money on him!"

"What? Why didn't you say something? I would have hedged my bet!" his boss was livid.

Izhutin laughed, "You never listen! And, I took a chance, boss; the soldier boy may still get his ass kicked. One punch that's all Don needs."

"If you win, you're buying dinner," Shayk snapped at his man.

"If I win I'll buy dinner and pay for the girls!" Izhutin replied with a big grin before both men turned their attention back to the fight.

Each time Carnicke came rushing in, he was met with left-right combinations, not devastating punches, but quick, snapping strikes that opened up the scar tissue over both eyes now. The older fighter pawed at the cuts, wiping the blood that was streaming into his eyes. His mind raced: *This is not working. He's too quick. I need to make him come to me.*

And with that, Carnicke adjusted his style – he waited patiently, circling with hands held high and when the younger fighter came in, he countered with hard lefts and rights not caring where it landed, just so he hit something. Most of his punches were aimed at Robbie's body and they were beginning to have an effect. Robbie's ribs hurt, especially on his left side and he could feel his energy slowly drain. Kill the body and the head will fall was a common refrain in most boxing gyms.

I have to work him over; tire him out. Robbie recalled what his coach and mentor had told him about fighting big, muscular men, *"Keep the pressure on. Those big muscles need more oxygen and will tire and get slow. Make them miss and don't let them rest and soon, they'll be done! Fatigue makes cowards of us all."*

Robbie forced himself to stay light on his feet, circling one way then the other never giving Carnicke the same look or a stationary target. And he never gave him the chance to catch his breath. He darted in and out, bobbing and weaving, throwing left-right combinations mixed in with kicks. The punches were meant to distract; the goal was to attack Carnicke's lead leg and by doing that, neutralize his power. Without his power, Carnicke was a mediocre fighter at best.

"Robbie, his leg is shot! Keep at it … break his fuckin' leg!" VanArcen yelled at the top of his lungs, unable to contain himself.

"That little fart is a pain in the ass!" Shayk said nodding in VanArcen's direction, "But, Don better do something soon or his leg will get broken!"

"This is how Carnicke fights. It looks bad and just when you think he's done, 'bam', one punch and the lights go out!" Izhutin made the observation hoping to keep his boss in good spirits.

"Yeah, I know but this feels different," then changing subjects, Shayk asked, "Did you speak to Hank about Nikolai's laptop?"

"Yes."

"Well, what did he say?"

"He said you worry too much … like an old woman! Those were his words, boss," Izhutin knew better than to insult Shayk. "Say the word and I will show him how old, Russian women take care of things! I'll slice his nuts off and feed it to my dog."

"Not here; this is their world. You never follow a tiger into his cave. You wait until he goes for a drink and when he is busy quenching his thirst, you stick the knife into his heart!" Shayk's face was expressionless but his eyes glittered with anger, "These fuckers have no idea what is at stake. Fuckin' gopniks! We will have to do something."

He stared at the Pit not really watching the fight, his mind preoccupied when he saw Robbie stumble. Finally! Carnicke had managed to land a clean shot, a short right that clipped Robbie's chin and he almost went down. He did the headless chicken dance but steadied himself.

There's a moment in almost every fight where a fighter faces adversity and has to decide whether to cave or fight back. The wannabe tough-guys fold like cheap suits; it is the warrior who clings to the refrain: death before defeat. The absonant ringing in his ears made Robbie dizzy and he watched Carnicke looking through a metaphorical magnifying glass. The old pro was advancing, edging closer in an altered reality; almost in slow motion.

Shayk raised his arms high and screamed, "Finish him. Don't wait, Don, finish it!"

It was easier said than done. Carnicke's left leg was useless. Robbie's repeated kicks had left welts the size of golf balls on the shin and the sides under his calf muscle were badly bruised. He had lost all feeling in that leg and he knew that the window of opportunity was closing and closing fast. *I have to end this now!* Carnicke's mind raced recognizing an opportunity.

He shuffled forward awkwardly, gritting his teeth, willing his leg to work, knowing that this was his one chance but Robbie surprised him; he changed stances to southpaw and the moment of indecision that flashed across Carnicke's face was all that Robbie needed. He faked a kick and when the older fighter dropped his hand to block it, he threw a snapping right jab followed by a straight left that found the point of Carnicke's chin. The punch landed cleanly and old pro dropped like the proverbial sack of potatoes.

"You got him, kick his ass… show him what Rangers are made of!" VanArcen screamed; he was beside himself. He jumped up and down sensing the fight coming to an end.

Carnicke brushed aside the demons of surrender that danced in his head, instead his instincts kicked in and he struggled to his feet. He stood unsteady and woozy when a flurry of punches, none of which he saw, dropped him again. *Quit! You've had enough. Quit!* But old warriors don't quit, they die slow, hard deaths. He struggled to get on all fours, his face a bloody mess; his legs feeling like jelly, his mind, disoriented but the will to keep fighting wouldn't bend - *he couldn't get himself to stay down.* He grabbed the fencing and pulled himself up, staggering drunkenly. He managed to get his arms halfway up to fend off the fuzzy doppelgangers that seemed to surround him. *Fuck! How many soldier-boys are there?*

"Stay down," Robbie told the proud man, "it's not worth it."

But Carnicke refused to submit and came forward waddling like an inebriated duck. It wouldn't take much and Robbie could have hit him at will but chose to push him back instead. A gentle push was all it took. Carnicke stumbled unsteadily and fell again. This time he sat on the canvas shaking his head, trying to clear the cobwebs that were creeping over his consciousness.

"Oh fuck! He's done," Shayk said, "come on, let's stop this."

He climbed into the Pit and stood over his fighter and waved the contest off. It rankled him to see VanArcen leap into the Pit laughing in celebration but like Luke, he had a deep appreciation for fighters and making sure that his ward was okay and lived to fight another day was far more important than his ego. He knelt down and commiserated with the old pro before helping him to his feet.

"We'll get him another time, Don, he got lucky!" He turned to Carnicke's muscle beach sidekick, "Clean him up and take him home and make sure he's okay. Andrei will come by and see you guys tomorrow and settle everything." He handed the man several hundred dollar bills and added, patting Carnicke on the back, "Go grab a good meal. It's okay, Don, it was a good fight and that's what counts."

Meghan

THE PLAN

For several minutes after Seppo had left with Jodie, Meghan remained frozen, clutching Ryan tightly to her. She was staring at Maddie's still body unable to reconcile the sudden violence that had unfolded with the lifeless body lying by the stairway. Time seemed to stall in some amaranthine dimension, a convoluted weaving of the past with the present and creating an altered reality. Images and voices exploded in her mind, some eerily similar to Maddie's, telling her that this was just a bad dream. It was the cruel symphony of shock and fear that distorted her ability to reason.

Ryan's plaintive gasp snapped her out of her dazed stupor. "Let me go, Ma, I can't breathe!" He gasped squirming in Meghan's embrace. It was only then that she realized just how tightly she was squeezing her son.

"Oh baby, sorry …" she reacted, releasing him, "Maddie! Oh no …"

She ran over to Maddie and began to cry when her worst fears were realized. Maddie Wilkins was dead. The blow from Heikkinen had broken her neck killing her instantly. She sat down next to the corpse and placed Maddie's head on her lap, stroking her hair and crying softy, the tears streaming down her face. Maddie had always been there for her – even in the most difficult of times.

She recalled the dark aftermath of her relationship with Luke. She had gotten pregnant and Luke had absolved himself of any responsibility and at his persistent urging she had relented and agreed to have an abortion.

It was Maddie who consoled her and had said, *"God's gifts come to us in different ways, child, and this is His gift to you. Don't do something that you will regret the rest of your life."*

If she had gone through with her decision, she would have lost Ryan and she couldn't imagine a life without him. She began sobbing uncontrollably. *Maddie, Maddie, why did you have to leave us?* It was solely because of Maddie's influence that she changed her mind and the reason she had told the little boy that Maddie was his *real* grandmother.

Ryan wrapped his tiny arms around his mother trying to console her, confused by what was going on. "Don't cry, Ma, everything will be okay." He parroted the words she would say to him when things weren't going that well. "What's wrong with Granny?"

"Granny's gone to heaven to be with the angels, baby, but she'll be watching over you so don't you worry."

After a few minutes Meghan got up, dried her tears and called Deputy Bradley and got his voice mail. She was about to leave him a detailed message explaining what had transpired when she recalled Seppo's threat. Fear constricted her very being and she hung up. She was sure the big man would do exactly what he had promised but there was one person who could handle Seppo and that was Robbie. She had his number on speed-dial and waited while it rang and only then realized that she was trembling. She willed herself to focus and regain control but her hopes were dashed by the annoying recorded message *"The person you are trying to call …"* She hung up and dialed VanArcen's number and got his voice mail.

"What are they doing? Where did they go?" She left a message asking him to call her back.

She then tried Robbie again but with the same result. "Not my lucky day," she mumbled to herself in frustration, "He must be with Tony. Come on Ryan, we're going to find Captain America."

She first drove to the Sleepy Crest Motel but Robbie's room was dark and there was no response when she knocked. All she got were some curious looks from the pavement skanks walking their beat. She hastily bundled Ryan into the truck and decided to try VanArcen's house. Her prime objective now was to keep Ryan safe.

"Where are we going, Ma?" The little boy asked. "Are we going on an adventure?"

The excitement of the unplanned car ride appealed to his young mind. He was rarely allowed out this late and it was hard for him to subdue his enthusiasm. Meghan though was still upset by the fact that Maddie was gone. Try as she might she was unable to suppress the images of Maddie's lifeless body from popping into her mind. The finality of her demise was devastating. Meghan's emotions were beginning to get the better of her.

"You were so brave," she cried silently, "to do what you did, Maddie. I could never have done that… never!"

She began feeling sorry for herself, overcome by a sense of fate's preterition – nothing was going right. First it was the disastrous lunch with Robbie then the mad charade she just witnessed. It was too much, an emotional overload, but she had to focus on Ryan and keeping him safe, "Yes, baby, it's a new adventure."

"Oh goody!" he clapped his small hands together, "Is Robbie coming with us? And what about Robin, is he coming too?"

"His name is Ronin and I hope they are, baby, now be quiet.

We don't want the bad guys to hear us, do we? They have cameras everywhere so we need to be very quiet, okay?"

"They have cameras in the sky?" The boy asked with wide-eyed curiosity.

"Yes. They have cameras everywhere, even in the sky. Keep your eyes open and look out for those evil space monsters so they don't sneak up on us. Can you do that?"

The little boy nodded and stared at the road ahead. She needed to think and figure this out. *What did Seppo want with Jodie? Hank never used Seppo unless it was important. And did any of this have to do with Marisa's death? Should she warn her mother just in case Seppo decided to do something?* She decided against it. *That would only scare Mom. Was there any connection to Marylou Dorsey and her parties? And was Ed Carlson involved? She had to find a place to keep Ryan safe from Seppo.* Thoughts and scenarios kept playing in her mind until she arrived at VanArcen's cabin. She breathed a sigh of relief when she saw Robbie's SUV.

"Thank God!" It was an answer to her silent prayer, "You wait here, Ryan. Stay in the car, okay?"

And with that she ran up the steps and along the porch to the front door. Meghan heard Ronin growl, a deep rumble that sounded ominous in the darkness and it filled her with hope. *Robbie must be here.*

"It's okay, Ronin, it's me…" She wondered if the dog would recognize her. She had been with Robbie when she met him and the huge dog had taken to her. She knocked in anticipation but except for more of Ronin's growling, there was no answer.

She found the key under the doormat. Tony had told them about it in case they wanted to use the cabin when he was away. That quip was accompanied by a conspiratorial wink at Robbie.

She knocked again, "Robbie?"

But there was no answer. She nervously opened the door, just a crack at first. "Good boy, Ronin, you're a good boy!"

She could see him wagging his tail so she opened the door a bit wider not fully confident that the mammoth canine would be friendly. But, Ronin pushed it open with his snout and playfully nudged her backwards, his tail wagging vigorously. There was no hesitation; the dog recognized her and was genuinely happy to see her. *I can only hope that Robbie will be this happy when he sees me,* she thought while looking for a piece of paper to leave a note when she noticed an old photograph of Daniel VanArcen on the kitchen wall. Then it struck her, *It's fight night! I'll bet they are the Pit! Meghan Hollier, you're losing it. Tony must have taken Robbie to the fights.*

Meghan had never been to the Pit. Luke had spoken to her about it a long time ago and the only indication she had of its whereabouts was that it was well past Moose Head Point where he had built his house. Luke would be at the fights too so she decided to visit Luke's sister, Allison. *She can give me directions to the Pit and I can leave Ryan and Ronin with her.*

She quickly scribbled a new note explaining her plan and left with Ronin. She felt safer now that she had the big dog with her. He couldn't fit inside the truck so he sat in the truck's bed, his huge head hanging over the edge. Even Seppo would think twice before trying anything with Ronin present. She felt calm and safe for the first time that evening.

Ed Carlson, Ray and Jericho

THREE STOOGES

Ed Carlson and his brother Ray didn't always come to the Pit but when they had heard that Don Carnicke was fighting a three-hundred-pound wrestler from Saudi Arabia, they couldn't resist. But, when they got the news that the Arab had dropped out, they decided to leave. They were waiting for Jericho, who had gone to get them some beers, when the news that Robbie was replacing the Arab spread through the crowd. Disappointment turned to anticipation and then to excitement.

They had put some money on Carnicke and were caught up in the action when their stocky friend made his way over to them. He gave the fighters a precursory glance and noticing Robbie in the Pit said softly, "Damn, the soldier boy's fighting Carnicke? He's got balls!"

"I hear he's getting a shitload of dough to replace the fuckin' Arab!" Ray answered without looking away from the fight, "El asshole, or whatever he's called, bailed. I guess Carnicke scared the shit out of him."

"Thirty grand, that's what Shayk promised Olsen," Ed Carlson interjected.

"His name's El Chafic and I've seen him fight. He ain't scared; I guarantee that, but thirty grand? Are you kidding me? I'll fight Carnicke for that kind of change," Reinhart was incredulous.

"And you'd get your head kicked in and you ass handed to you," Ed shot back, "This ain't some biker brawl; you can get killed in there." He nodded towards the Pit.

"For that kind of money I'd risk getting my head kicked in!"

"Yeah, but no one wants to watch a fat biker get stomped!" Ed shot back.

"That's for sure," Ray rejoined and laughed, "and you are getting fat, Cochise!"

"I can still kick your sorry ass!" was the only comeback the biker had.

They watched the fighters for a few minutes before Reinhart spoke. "Kelly called. Seppo was at the Sleepy Crest and took Angela with him. He paused, looking at Ed, "Kelly was terrified. She wasn't sure if she should say anything but she's worried about Angela."

"Which Kelly are we talking about, the blonde or the dark-haired one?" Ed asked.

"Why does it matter?" Jericho answered, "But just so you know, blonde Kelly's been gone for a few months now. She was a nasty bitch and Snake got rid of her."

"Really? I had no fuckin' idea," Ed was genuinely surprised, "and it matters because blonde Kelly was a coke-snorting, drugged out whore who'd sell her mother for a teener and I wouldn't believe a word she said! Pretty Kelly is a different matter altogether – I'd more often than not believe her."

"You should know the names of the women that work for you, Ed," Jericho countered, "Blonde Kelly's name is Kelly Obernik and Pretty Kelly is Kelly McMahon. The girls call her Irish or Irish Kelly not Pretty Kelly."

"They don't work for me; they work for Hank." Ed retorted, "And, I can't be bothered with their names. I have enough to worry about."

"And what if something happened to Hank?"

Ed studied Reinhart for a moment and then said, "There's Luke."

"Luke's a dangerous liability and you know that. He's a fuckin' psycho! Anyone who fucks his sister and lives with her like she's his wife is loose in the head. You watch, he'll be the reason Hank gets killed. I wouldn't be surprised if Luke does the killing himself!"

"You're just pissed because he kicked your ass when you made moves on Allison," Ray quipped.

"No, I'm not pissed at him. He's not the first guy to kick my ass, Ray, I'm telling you what you two know but won't admit. Luke is a fuckin' crazy man and should something happen to Hank the two of you better be careful."

"You be careful, Jericho, real careful. He's my uncle, damn it, my blood!" Ed snapped.

Jericho laughed, "If he's your blood then I'm the fuckin' King of England!"

There was an uneasy silence before Reinhart spoke again, "What do we do about Angela?"

"Angela's a fuckin' dyke! Good riddance." Ray offered without thinking. He was constrained about his own lineage and the rumors about who his father was. Luke and Allison certainly didn't look or act like any of them.

"Shut the fuck up, Ray, you know nothing!" Ed snapped at his brother. "Angela's okay. I like her and she's been with us for a long time. She takes care of the younger girls and that's good. They treat her like an older sister and she keeps them in line. And, she's prettier then most of the girls."

"I was only…" Ray began to protest when his brother cuffed him on the back of his head. "Zip it! Let me do the thinking." Ed turned his attention to Jericho, "Did you find out where Jodie is?"

"No but I'm sure Angela knows and Seppo *will* find out," Jericho reiterated, "he'll beat it out of her. If he gets his hands on Jodie she'll squawk louder than a motherfucker with his nuts in a ringer!"

They fell silent again before they heard a whispered rumbling from sections of the crowd and turned towards the Pit in time to see Robbie get clipped and stagger.

"It's over. Don will end this soon," Ed proclaimed then turning his attention to Jericho, "Did Kelly say where he was taking Angela?"

"No, but there's only one place he would take her," Jericho replied. They looked knowingly at each other, smiled, and said in unison, "The Bruckman Farm!"

"Hank's still here," Ray noted, "and, Luke's here too."

"Perfect. Let's go," Ed said.

"What about the money? I bet a hundred on Carnicke?" Reinhardt questioned.

"We'll collect later. I'll talk to Luke."

And with that the three men made their way out through a back entrance ignoring the murmur of the crowd and the shifting fortunes in the Pit.

Robbie Olsen

WARRIOR SPIRIT

Robbie was with VanArcen when Adam Shayk came over.

"You cost us a lot of money, Olsen, but that was impressive. I've watched Don fighting for years and I've seen him lose a few but they were never this one-sided," Shayk said to Robbie. "You should consider fighting – make yourself some serious money."

"Not a chance. This was a one-time deal and I got lucky."

"I doubt that. I've been in this game a long time, brother, and you didn't get lucky, you got lazy when he clipped you," Shayk answered. The mobster was sincere, "If you ever decide to get back in, you let me know."

"Yeah sure," was Robbie's noncommittal reply, "but I think I'll keep my day job."

"Why don't you join us for dinner?" Shayk suggested, "There's a place in Monson – I know the owner and they cook up some fabulous Blini, Russian pancakes… just like mama used to make."

"Thanks but I'm going to soak in a hot tub… he hits like a freakin' mule!" They shook hands before Robbie turned to VanArcen, "Did you see Hank or Luke?"

VanArcen didn't answer immediately but instead grabbed Robbie's arm and pulled him towards the side exit, "Fuck them. We have the money. Forty grand, amigo, you're a rich man. Let's get the heck out of here and celebrate. I'm famished and you're buying!"

Robbie shook his head and smiled before saying, "I wanted to talk to Hank about Jodie and see …"

VanArcen wasn't listening; he was looking at his cell phone. "I got a message from Meghan. She wants me to call her," VanArcen interrupted, "I guess she wants you back, lover-boy."

"You're an idiot. She could be in trouble – give me the phone," Robbie said and reached for the phone, his demeanor changing almost immediately.

He tried Meghan a few times but got no response and was about to give up when she picked up.

"Hi Tony, is Robbie with you?" She sounded concerned.

"It's me," Robbie said, "we were at the fights. I had my phone turned off."

She was quiet and Robbie assumed that she was still mad at him, "Meghan, listen, about this afternoon …"

"Robbie, I was so worried and I do want to talk about that but not now …" she stopped and blurted out, "Maddie's dead!"

"What?"

"Seppo!" she spat the name out. "He came to get Jodie and Maddie tried stopping him."

He was quiet. He recalled his last conversation with Maddie; she knew this was going to happen. It was astounding but she pretty much knew she was going to die. He felt a chill run through him and then anger took hold.

"Where are you?" his voice, edgy. He wanted to make sure Meghan wasn't in danger.

"I'm with Allison… at Luke's place. I have Ronin with me. I

came looking for you at Tony's and saw him there. I felt we would be safer if he was with us. Ryan's here too. You're not mad are you?"

He ignored the question, "Stay there. I'll come and get you after I take care of some things."

"Be careful, Robbie…" Meghan said. She wanted to tell him that she needed him but found herself struggling for the words. She wasn't sure if he was ready to listen and to forgive. She was about to tell him how much she needed him when he spoke.

"Tell Allison to keep a gun handy and keep Ronin with you… I mean don't let him go wandering outside."

"You're scaring me!"

"Nothing's going to happen. It's just a precaution."

There was a short silence. Both of them felt the need to bridge their differences regarding their earlier spat, but neither knew how.

"Robbie, please be careful."

"I will. I will call you later," and he hung up.

A coruscated collage of Maddie filled his thoughts and Robbie felt a rage that he had seldom felt before – a blind anger similar to what he had experienced in Afghanistan. The old woman had affected him in ways he couldn't explain. Seppo would pay and if Hank was involved he would pay too and Maddie's prophecy of the Fourth Horseman will come to pass.

THE MAKING OF THE GANGSTER

Adam Shayk's real name was Andrusha Vasnetsov but he rejected it as soon as he left home – he hated the association. It was his father's name and he intensely disliked his father, who was a drunk and a wife-beater, so he changed it to Adam Shaykhlislamova, taking his mother's maiden name instead. He shortened it to Shayk when he came to the US. It was fate that brought him to America; fate and Alexei Zakirov, one of the most powerful oligarchs in Moscow. Alexei Zakirov had found the young Shayk to be loyal and trustworthy and most importantly, a stone-cold killer – qualities that were assets in their line of work. He had taken the young Shayk under his wing and treated him more like a son than he did his own son.

It was during the bitter turf war in Jersey City between the Italians and the Russians that the opportunity presented itself. Viktor Semyonov, the head of the Zakirov Mob, had been assassinated outside a speakeasy leaving the Russians without a leader. It was then that Alexei Zakirov sent Adam Shayk to the US. His instructions were simple - take over the New Jersey operations and settle matters with the Italians. It didn't take long for the young Shayk to make a name for himself and put an end to the conflict. Jersey City belonged to the Russians and Adam Shayk was a man to be feared.

A year later, Alexei Zakirov sent his son Nikolai to the US hoping a change of scenery would straighten him out. Nikolai was a spoilt playboy whose many proclivities had embarrassed his father. The final straw was when Nikolai got his fourteen-year-old cousin pregnant. He was shipped off to Jersey City and became the responsibility of Adam Shayk.

The mess they found themselves in now was because of Nikolai and his insatiable appetite for young girls. Marisa Gorecki was the latest and if that wasn't enough, he had gotten some very powerful people involved. Those videos could mean a lot more trouble than the Italians had ever presented. And to make matters worse, from Shayk's perspective, Hank Carlson seemed oblivious or unconcerned about the consequences. He needed to be taught a lesson; a reminder of who the real boss was and that the mountains weren't exempt from the tentacles of the Zakirov mob.

After the fights, Adam Shayk, his henchman Andrei Izhutin and three bodyguards had gone to "Katrina's Baltic Kitchen", Shayk's favorite restaurant in Monson. They were seated in the corner, away from the rest of the clientele, and were waited on by Katrina Sysoev herself. After the customary pleasantries, accompanied by the obsequious groveling of the hostess, they placed their orders of Blini topped with caviar and sour cream, the specialty of the house, and Blintzes stuffed with different kinds of meats, fruits and creams. They started their meal off with a complimentary bowl of beetroot borscht soup and duck. It was easy to see why the restaurant was popular – the cooking represented home-style cuisine at its best.

After a few rounds of drinks, Stolichnaya Elit with pickles, they got down to business.

"We have a serious problem. These fucking gopniks need to be taught a lesson. They think because they live in the mountains they can do as they please. Well, I am going to teach them that you do not bite the hand that feeds you - a lesson they will not soon forget." Adam Shayk said in between chews. He was speaking softly and resorting to Russian every now and then. His reference to 'gopniks' wasn't lost on the men; they too saw Hank and the rest of his crew as a bunch of illiterate rednecks.

"You want me to send some men up there?" Andrei Izhutin asked.

"No. I want you to send the Frenchie," Shayk answered.

"Michael McHenry?" asked Izhutin. He wasn't sure he heard his boss correctly.

"Yes."

There was a short break while the men focused on their food and downed some more of the expensive vodka. Curiosity got the better of one of the other bodyguards and he asked Shayk, "Why do they call an Irishman, Frenchie?"

"They call him that because he is said to have an enormous dick… the size of the Eiffel Tower," Shayk replied gesturing crudely. This elicited a round of raucous laughter.

"They also call him Mick the Dick for the same reason," Andrei added.

"Ah, I wish I had a dick like his instead of this little red pepper I was born with. My bitch of a wife wouldn't be complaining then!" lamented one of the others which brought about more laughter and more vodka.

"Maybe I should pay her a visit," Izhutin suggested, "I do not have the Eiffel Tower but I have a very skilled tongue and a carrot for a dick and that is better than a pepper, no?"

There was more laughter and thumping on the table.

"Okay, enough with the dicks already," Shayk said and when his men had settled down, "They call him Frenchie for other reasons – he is fluent in French. Now, without turning this into a war, we need do something, nothing serious, just a little lesson to show them that we mean business."

"Why McHenry? He is a difficult man and expensive. We can send one of our men to show them what can happen…" Izhutin suggested but was cut-off by his boss.

"No, not for this one. For what I have in mind I want McHenry. This one is special," he took a few sips of his drink before continuing, "Did you see the big man? His name is Heikkinen, Seppo Heikkinen. He is a Finn."

"Yes. He is hard to miss … big as fuckin' ox!" Izhutin confirmed.

"He is Hank Carlson's man and from what I hear he would give Abdulrashid a difficult time."

The very comparison to Abdulrashid "The Russian Tank" Sadulaev, one of the world's premier wrestlers, was blasphemy to his men.

"That is impossible!" Izhutin spoke up, "No one can match Sadulaev! No one."

He was the only one close enough to Shayk to be able to contradict his boss. The others muttered their support but did so under their breath in whispers.

"Okay, okay. Maybe he does not beat our man in a wrestling match but on the streets there are no rules and this man is very dangerous. You listen to me and forget about Abdulrashid. He is in Dagestan, somewhere in the hills getting fat. Who the fuck cares? But you may run into Heikkinen and what I tell you is for your own good. This man is not to be taken lightly and that is one reason I want McHenry for this job."

There was an uneasy silence before Shayk spoke again, "I want to neutralize the big man. That will teach Hank a lesson he will not forget. I want Seppo's head delivered to Hank and I mean literally…

like in 'The Godfather'. You remember the horse, eh? So, no screw ups and no mistakes. This thing with the girl and the videos must end now. Hank will learn his lesson."

"What about his brother, the pretty one? He is trouble, Adam, I can sense it," Izhutin said voicing a concern he had felt when he met Luke.

"No, leave the family alone. This is not war. This is only a lesson and that is why I need the best," he took a sip of his drink and belched loudly before addressing Izhutin, "Andrei, you take care of this. Let me know when you have talked to the McHenry and remember, I want Heikkinen's head delivered to Hank. It is not essential but it would be nice if he found it in his bed. Like they say, it will be poetic justice."

The men around the table nodded and raised their glasses as Shayk toasted, "Za tva-jó zda-ró-vye! To your health, boys, drink up."

He motioned the hostess and ordered more vodka, Stolichnaya Elit, only the best for his men. Coming up through the ranks he swore to himself that when he was in power he would treat his men differently and he did and they in turn were fiercely loyal, especially Andrei Izhutin who had a long and colorful history with Shayk.

Family

REVELATION

Fight night was Luke's big moment. It was the only aspect of his job working for his brother that he enjoyed the rest he could do without. He had a particular fondness for the fight game – especially the fighters. These men, for most part, were quiet and unassuming rarely getting into physical confrontations outside the arena. Like him, they were uncomplicated and straightforward men.

Then there was the violence, the purity of it - two men engaged in a primal contest of strength and skill until only one was left standing. This was as close as it came to the gladiators and it sent a thrill through him. He would have been a fighter had Hank not intervened. This was before the Pit when most bareknuckle fights in the local area were unorganized, back-alley affairs with little or no monetary incentive. They were for most part, Friday night rumbles incited by booze and excessive testosterone.

For a paltry twenty dollars and a beer, he had fought a six-foot-four inch, two hundred and fifty pound logger and had disposed of him rather quickly but when Hank heard of it, he was incensed. He dragged the seventeen-year-old Luke to visit with the Northeast's preeminent fighter, Daniel VanArcen. This was a few years before VanArcen had passed away. The sight of the legendry fighter reduced to a wheelchair, blabbering mindlessly with drool running down his chin had a chilling effect on Luke. Growing up, he had idolized VanArcen and the visit had exposed the reality of fighting's lurid aftermath. He didn't say much but heeded Hank's advice. That logger was the last man he fought for money.

Hank, ever the astute businessman, had offered him the opportunity to be engaged in the fight game without risking his health – it involved organizing the underground bareknuckle scene by increasing the purse, changing the rules and providing them protection from the law. This eventually led to the setting up of the Pit and Luke took to it like a bee to honey. Apart from Allison, running the Pit was the one thing that brought him joy. But this morning was different. Instead of the elation that usually accompanied fight night, he woke up with a rebarbative uneasiness in the pit of his stomach. It was when he saw Heikkinen that his earlier apprehension turned dark. For reasons he didn't understand or couldn't explain, he had the premonition that Maddie was in danger.

He had never liked Seppo Heikkinen but they had managed to stay out of each other's way and coexist. Luke understood Hank's need for an enforcer and the big Finn tolerated the younger Carlson because it was something he had no choice in or control over. However, their truce was fragile and neither man hid their dislike for the other.

Early on, Luke sensed that Seppo was nervous around him and like dogs that bite, fear aggression is the most pernicious kind. A frightened tough guy will go to great lengths to mask his fear with false bravado and that usually got people seriously hurt or killed. Hank had sensed it too and was shrewd enough to keep them apart making sure that they rarely met and when they did, it was mostly with him there to mediate. It was one reason Seppo never attended fight night.

Luke had tried to keep the feeling concerning Maddie under control so he could take care of his business and for a while he had succeeded. The El Chafic fiasco with Robbie stepping in had helped to keep him distracted. But once the fight was over, the cloud of uneasiness returned and he needed to resolve it.

He went looking for Hank and saw him hurrying towards the office in the back. Luke quickly followed, navigating through the crowd that was milling around the exits and the betting booths. He wanted to confront his brother about Seppo.

When he got to the office he witnessed his brother rummaging impatiently through the top drawer of the desk. The office was cloaked in partial darkness; the dim light from the table lamp casting arbitary shadows against Hank's pale, gaunt face giving him a vampire-like appearance.

The older Carlson sensing Luke's presence looked up and muttered, "I can't find a fucking thing here anymore! I've told you a hundred times not to mess around with my stuff."

"If you're looking for the Beretta, it's in the bottom drawer. I checked it to make sure it was good to go and put it where you can easily access it – not under all that crap you have in the top drawer," Luke retorted, then questioned, "Why the gun, Hank?"

"We had better find Jodie and soon. Before he left, Adam made it clear – if he sees anymore videos posted, he's going to have to do something and he didn't mean having his lawyer send us a cease and desist letter."

"I don't know what you're talking about but fuck Shayk and his crew. If they come up here, they'll never leave. Now, what was Heikkinen doing here?" Luke questioned.

They studied each other before Hank spoke, "I told you. His

girl's pregnant and..."

Luke interrupted, "Cut the bullshit, Hank, I knew you were lying but I wasn't going to call you out in front of those assholes. Now the truth; where the fuck is Seppo?"

Hank Carlson retrieved the gun and closed the drawer. He straightened up and studied Luke before sitting down. His actions were slow and deliberate. "Take a seat and I'll explain the whole mess to you."

"Just tell me where Seppo is? That's all I want to know," the response was curt and impatient.

"It's not that simple!" Hank snapped back, "Marisa, Jodie, Nikolai Zakirov... they're all connected. If we don't find Jodie and get Marisa's laptop we're going to have to deal with shit like we've never seen before!"

"What does Marisa's laptop have to do with Nikolai or Jodie? And if Shayk tries anything he'll find out this ain't Jersey."

Hank shook his head, "You think they're going to come here with a truck full of men? Wake up! They'll send assassins, hitmen that look like every other Joe around here and those fuckers are professionals, they *will* get the job done." He stopped, his eyes boring into Luke before continuing, "And even if we manage to get a few they'll keep coming and sooner or later..."

"We can play that game too," Luke interrupted his brother.

"They're not going to come after us – you or me; that is not what they do. They'll go after the ones we love. Ma, Emma, Pauline... do you want to find Allison with a bullet in her head? Because that's what will happen." He waited for it to sink in then continued, "And yeah, I know, you'll find them and slit their throats or gut them or whatever but that won't bring Allison back. Use your head, Luke, and keep that temper in check. We can manage this without any hassles."

a sign, anything to indicate that he was lying, but his brother's gaze was steady, unflinching. Luke sat down again gritting his teeth. He was still unclear about the laptop. "Even if all of that is true, what does this have to do with Nikolai and her laptop?"

"Nikolai has a Lolita complex and he particularly enjoyed watching Marisa getting fucked. It turned him on so he videotaped her having sex with a bunch of different men, sometimes several men at the same time. One of the men was Chris Donnelly, Boston's Lieutenant Governor and the other, Sal Castiglioni. Sal is part of Adam Harrison's team. Harrison is the Mayor of Bedford. Both are family men with children older than Marisa. I don't have to tell you that being caught having sex with an underage girl would be a disaster. These are very influential and powerful people who will stop at nothing. They are holding Shayk responsible and have threatened to shut down his 'business' activities if things are not taken care of."

"How did those guys get involved with Marisa or any of this?"

"Matt Hansen." Hank explained, "His father is one of the larger campaign donors and Matt met them at a fund raiser and invited them to one of his parties. Need I say more?"

Luke was in shock. He couldn't imagine Marisa at a swinger's party. "How did she make the videos? I doubt that Hansen or Nikolai would have allowed that."

"I have no idea. She may have accessed Nikolai's laptop and uploaded the videos to her cloud account or maybe copied it on a memory stick, who the fuck knows? These kids grew up with this technology and know a hundred different ways to do stuff. Like us messing around with souped-up cars. You remember the '79 LeMans that Pops bought? That was some summer!"

Luke did remember. It was the one time he had felt close to Hank – they had worked on it day and night until it purred like a big cat. Hank had done most of the 'heavy lifting' while Luke watched and handed him the appropriate tools constantly asking him questions. It was a much simpler time in their lives. He was ten and looked-up to his big brother. Whatever happened to that? And whatever made Hank change?

He shut the memories out and refocused his thoughts. Marisa with these deviants just blew his mind.

"But why would she want to? I mean, why post them?" Luke was still befuddled.

"I don't know; maybe she got a kick out of it! Maybe it got her a million 'likes'… and maybe it is what got her killed," Hank studied Luke hoping his brother wouldn't go berserk when he hears about Maddie, "But if this shit gets posted, it *will* go viral and Shayk will get drawn in even though he had nothing to do with it and that is why he wants the laptop and anything or anyone else that may have access to it. Marisa gave the laptop to Jodie before she turned up dead."

"And how do you know that?"

"Jodie used it to post a video," Hank replied.

It was on the tip of Luke's tongue to ask how he knew about Jodie posting the video but that wasn't important. Now he knew why they were looking for Jodie and the laptop. It wouldn't take Seppo long to find out where the young girl was and that would put Maddie in the crosshairs. Maddie wouldn't give Jodie up and that could only have one outcome.

"So you've got Seppo looking for Jodie, is that it?" Luke asked his brother.

"Yes. I've told him not to hurt her. Come with me, Luke, this is *our* business. We can get this sorted out before it gets out of hand."

Luke was quiet. The more he tried not thinking about that summer of the Pontiac LeMans, the more it kept popping back into his head like pink elephants and blue mice. He was torn between the loyalty he felt for his family and his intense dislike for Hank's machinations, especially where Seppo was concerned. This ambivalence of love and hate tore at his very core and most times, he pushed those feelings aside. But now, it was coming to a head. Maddie has talked to him about the Four Horsemen and Robbie Olsen but he shrugged it off as the ramblings of an old woman. However, now he wasn't so sure. He had a choice to make.

"Where are we going to meet Seppo?" Luke asked.

We? He said 'we'! Hank was relieved and stood up, "The old Bruckman farm. Come, brothers together. Let's go."

"You go on ahead; I'll catch up. I'm going to check on something and then I'll join you." Luke replied and added as an afterthought, "Make sure you take the Beretta, Hank - I have a feeling you're going to need it."

And with that he disappeared through the backdoor, down a short flight of cement stairs and into the night.

A TICKET TO THE DANCE

They were heading for Bucky Johnston's Diner when Robbie finished talking to Meghan and handed the phone back to Tony.

"We need to go to Maddie's place - now!" he paused and added, "Do you know where Luke's cabin is?"

"Yeah, I know where it is but what's going on? You look like your Grandma just died!" VanArcen observed.

Robbie gave Tony a quick look, "Maddie's dead. It was Seppo..." he left the rest unsaid.

For a moment VanArcen was speechless. He slowed down and looked at Robbie in disbelief. "Shit! I knew it! That sick bastard needs to be hanged, drawn and quartered! And then gutted like a feral pig and fed to the wolves."

He stopped the pick-up, his face etched with concern, "Is Meghan okay?"

"Meghan and Ryan are fine. They are with Allison. She's also got Ronin with her so they're safe."

"Depot Road is the shortest way to Maddie's. Luke's cabin is on Moose Head Point and is in the opposite direction."

"Let's go to Maddie's first. Where's my gun?" Robbie asked.

"It's under the mat in the back." VanArcen answered, "Do you want to get it?"

"No, I'll get it when we get to Maddie's."

"What about the money?"

"Leave it in the car. It's not important. Let's go."

The road was dark, lit only by the vehicle's headlights. They were going a bit too fast to accommodate the abrupt twists and turns in the road forcing VanArcen to brake and then speed-up only to brake again.

"Why don't you turn on the floodlights? I can barely see the road." The sudden braking and surges of speed had Robbie grabbing a hold of the dashboard.

"Doesn't work," VanArcen replied, flicking a switch on-and-off on the dash. "It worked for a month after I bought the truck and then it quit."

"Then slow down. You're making me nervous."

"Relax, Bronson, I know what I'm doing."

Just then, they screeched past a sharp curve and caught sight of dark figure crawling along the side of the road. At first Tony thought it was a case of roadkill, a small deer or a dog, but as he swerved to avoid it he realized that it was a person. The decrepit figure raised up and waved a shaky arm hoping to be noticed.

Tony's reaction was immediate. He slammed on the brakes and pulled up, "Fuck! What the heck!"

By the time they stopped they were twenty or so yards past the struggling form. Robbie was the first one out and walked back towards the body. Though it was dark he could tell that it was Hank's man, Cataldo Cascone. The gold chains and crocodile-skin loafers were a sure giveaway.

He knelt next to the man and raised him up, cradling his head, "What happened?"

"Seppo ... Seppo, lo stronzo!" The man whispered, blood trickling down the side of his mouth. And though he was badly hurt, the passion in his voice was unmistakable, "The fucking asshole is crazy, no?"

The very effort of speaking seemed too much; he coughed and groaned as the pain wracked his body.

"Take it easy. Let's get you to a hospital. Can you stand up?"

Robbie could see that the man was in desperate need of medical attention. His boyish face was bloodied and bruised. There were deep gashes near the hairline and around his cheeks and the streaks of dirt mingled with the coagulating blood made him almost unrecognizable.

"I try but… rotto sia gamba…" he struggled, his face contorting in pain, "my leg, it is, how you say, it is busted… broken."

The words were slurred. His upper lip was swollen and split open on one side. His trousers were ripped in places and Robbie could tell by the unnatural angle of his lower leg that it was broken.

"Let's get you into the truck. This is going to hurt so brace yourself; do you understand?" Robbie studied the Italian wanting to make sure he was ready.

Just then VanArcen walked up, "I'll give you a hand. We can put him in the back so he can lie down."

He leaned closer to the injured man and as recognition dawned on him he backed up, "Whoa, hold up cowboy! He's one of Hank's trained monkeys … this one's a bad apple. We should leave the fucker to die!"

"That's not happening. Do you have a blanket or quilt or something we can lay him on?"

"What's the matter with you? This chump is the enemy. He's as bad as Seppo and would sooner slice you open than look at you."

"Listen Tony, we can be like them or we can choose to be different. I refuse to lose my humanity because of a bunch of assholes! I've treated more wounded Taliban than I care to remember and I've never regretted doing that – not once. Now are you in or out?"

VanArcen was silent studying Robbie while cogitating on the choice. Then he smiled, "You know, Bronson, for a hard-ass you're a softie at heart," he moved to the rear of the pick-up, dropped the tailgate and added, "I have a blanket – we can lay him on that."

There was a soft groan from the Italian as Robbie picked him up. He looked up at Robbie, "Grazie, signore, non dimenticherò questo … I'll not forget."

"Save it. I wouldn't leave an injured dog by the roadside," Robbie said then turned to VanArcen, "Where's the nearest hospital or walk-in clinic?"

But before VanArcen could answer Cataldo Cascone clutched Robbie's arm, "Wait! Wait one second… I know where Seppo goes," he gasped and Robbie had to lean down to hear him, "he goes to the farm … it is… it is the old Backmon farm house. We are to meet the boss there. That was the plan. But Seppo…" his voice trailed off.

"The Backmon farm?"

"He means the Bruckman farm. Hank bought it when old man Bruckman passed away. It's in the same direction as Moose Head Point a bit west of Luke's place about twenty to twenty five minutes closer. What do you want to do?"

"Where's the nearest hospital? He needs help now."

"The nearest hospital is in Monson but that's a couple of hours away. The fire station might be our best bet. Dolan has a nurse there. Kathy Mitchel – she's trained to provide urgent care. They could get him patched up before taking him to Monson."

Robbie turned to Cat, "You hang in there. We're going to get you some help."

The Italian seemed almost fragile and much younger, "Grazie, grazie … stai attento. Be careful. Seppo, he is …" his voice trailed off and he closed his eyes.

"We've got to hurry. He's losing consciousness." Robbie said to

VanArcen as they headed towards town.

Tony was driving as fast as the road would let him. The darkness coupled with the unpredictable twists and turns made it challenging but he was able to maintain a steady clip.

"Do you still want to go to Maddie's place or should we go to the Bruckman farm after we drop him off?"

"There's no "we". You stay out of this. It's going to get sketchy and …"

"Screw you, Bronson! You're not leaving me out. My whole fuckin' life I've been treated like the fat kid who was good for nothing. Always the last to be picked for any team, always last in any race, the last to get a date … well, I'm not staying out of this and you need my help so stop acting like James Bond. I'm not totally useless, I have skills, you know, I'm Danny VanArcen's nephew and the apple…"

"Okay, okay, you win. Damn, just stop bellyaching. You're worse than my sister!"

VanArcen grinned and said, "Your sister is most probably the smart one in the family. And, you seem to forget, I'm now Tony 'cold-as-ice' VanArcen! It's ice water running through my veins, brother!"

"Tony, quit playing around; this is not a game. It's going to get dangerous before it's over."

"Listen, I'm not stupid. I'll let you do the Charlie Bronson stuff and in the end, I'll ride off into the sunset with the pretty maiden."

"I thought Liz was the love of your life?"

"She is! And, believe me she a doll. I should have ridden off into the sunset long before I met you! From the moment you barged into my life, things have gone south and I mean really south …" VanArcen prattled on and on.

They dropped the injured man off at the fire station and spoke briefly to Nurse Mitchel before heading for the Bruckman farm. It was a good forty minutes before they came to a turn-off onto a dirt road. Robbie realized that he would have never found this on his own. The dense thicket that fringed the sides of the road coupled with the poor lighting made it impossible to see the turn-off. It was a good thing Tony was with him.

VanArcen stopped the truck, "The driveway to the farm is about five hundred yards from here." He said pointing down a dirt track that seemed to burrow through the congestion of aggregating weeds and bushes. "The farmhouse is fifty yards from the entrance of the driveway but it's in real bad shape. The local kids used to come here to scare each other until the junkies took over. Hank most probably uses the large barn and that's another hundred yards further down. I can see the lights – it must be them. There is no one else around here."

Robbie quickly assed the situation and said, "Turn your headlights off and drive a bit closer. Park somewhere secluded but close to the road. We'll backtrack through the woods. The last thing we want is for them to know we are here."

The road was more of a horse and buggy trail and was similar to the one that led to the Dorsey cabin near Calico Bluff. They drove in silence until they came to a cluster of trees.

"Park there," Robbie instructed, pointing to a spot behind the trees, "That should be good enough."

"What about the money?" VanArcen asked.

"Leave it in the back under the blanket. That's the last place anyone will look for it. Do you have a flashlight?"

"No, but we can use my phone." VanArcen replied.

"I know you're not going to listen to me but it would be smarter for you to stay by the truck. It would give us a head start if we have to get out of here. Also, if the shit hits the ceiling, I won't have to worry about you."

VanArcen surprised him and agreed without hesitation. "That makes sense. I'll stay here. Someone has to feed Ronin if things don't go as planned, right? Hey, Charlie B, what flowers do you like?"

Robbie was relieved and smiled, "Your confidence is reassuring. You're not as dumb as you look, Tony."

VanArcen gave him the finger and said, "I'll wait in the truck."

"No, wait behind those trees. You'll have a jump on anyone who may find the truck. Don't fall asleep and keep your eyes and ears open. Also, if I'm not back in thirty minutes you call Bradley and tell him everything. Okay?"

That's when the cracking sound of a gunshot tore through the stillness of the night. Robbie looked towards the sound, "It's started. I'd better get there."

"Now I'm beginning to wish I had stayed home. Do you want me to come with you – two guns are better than one and all that?"

The memory of Calvin Jones and Jaimie Cranston and that disastrous night in Kunduz came rushing back, "No. this is not for you. You stay here."

"Whew! For a minute there I was sure you were going to agree. I think I just crapped my pants! You won't have a problem finding your way back, that's for sure. Just follow your nose. Bean burritos don't always agree with me."

Robbie shook his head and had to smile, "You stay put." He motioned towards another clump of trees located on higher ground about five or so yards from the truck, "Don't come out until I get back."

With that he headed towards the murky beacon in the distance, his Glock drawn and thoughts of Meghan racing through his mind.

A NEST OF VIPERS

The Bruckman farmhouse was square and symmetrical resembling an old Georgian Colonial. The double hung windows, antique French door and dentils along the roofline gave the building character and an archaic appeal but the years of neglect had ravaged whatever charm the original structure had enjoyed and the dilapidated remains served only as a somber reminder of what once was. The windowpanes were broken and the massive front door hung open balancing precariously on its last remaining hinge. Weeds and brush had overrun the walkway arrogating past the stairs and onto the porch. The left side of the roof had lost most of its slate shingles leaving the weathered rafters and joists exposed. Needles and other drug paraphernalia that carelessly littered the yard were testament that the once proud building was now reduced to a trap house – a place for dealers and junkies to ply their trade.

The barn was a later addition and was in far better condition than the farmhouse. It had a unique metal gambrel roof and two large, double doors – one in the front and the other in the rear. The windows had been boarded shut but light from the lanterns on the inside spilled onto the walkway illuminating the façade. The paint on the white oak siding had faded and peeled but the structure had withstood the elements remarkably well. Inside, most of the horse stalls that lined the right side of the barn had been scavenged – the sliding doors were missing as were the feed-boxes. Stacks of hay were piled high against the wall opposite from the stalls and there was a faint but musty scent of mold and horse that clung stubbornly to the air.

Hank parked his white Range Rover Sport by the side of a meadow, under a canopy of trees and walked the hundred or so yards to the barn. When he arrived at the door he was surprised to see his nephews, Ed and Ray, along with Jericho Reinhardt there. Seppo Heikkinen was seated on an old wooden stool, his back against the barn wall and his feet stretched out in front of him. He was cleaning his finger nails while the Ray and Jericho stood by the entrance. They had shotguns in their hands and though the barrels were pointed towards the floor, they were tense and ready. Ed Carlson was seated on a bale of hay about ten feet from the big Finn – he was unable to take his eyes off of a large gunnysack that covered a body that lay in the corner. Jodie was sitting cross-legged on the floor next to the Finn with her hands tied behind her back. She was crying softly but other than that she seemed unharmed.

"I didn't see your truck, Ed?" Hank said casually as he strolled into the stable past the two men.

"It's in the back," was the reply as Ed Carlson stood up and walked over to the body in the corner and drew back the gunny. "Take a look what he did to Angela."

Angela Mercier's naked body was a gruesome sight. Her breasts and abdomen bore conspicuous signs of cigarette burns. Her face was bloodied and swollen and several of her toes had been crushed and her blood-caked fingers were missing some fingernails. There was a pair of pliers and a large hammer, both covered in blood, lying on the floor next to the big Finn.

"Fuckin' animal! That's what he is!" Jericho spat out staring at Seppo and raising his shotgun.

"Hey peckerhead, she was a tough bitch, a lot tougher than you fuckin' jerkoffs. She wouldn't talk so I had to persuade her. She stuck it out a lot longer than most and I respect her for that. But she's dead so let's move on," Seppo said then stretched his arms and yawned, bored with the charade. He turned to Hank, "Listen, you asked me to find Jodie and I did. You didn't say anything about these three pussy motherfuckers getting involved."

Hank looked at Ed and then at Jericho, "Lower that thing. What are you boys doing here?"

"Angela was a decent person… as decent as they come. There was no need for this," Ed Carlson said the added, "I could have gotten her to tell me where Jodie was without treating her like dirt." He walked over to Angela's body and covered it again.

"You didn't answer the question. What are you boys doing here?"

"We heard he was bringing Angela here and were hoping to stop this from happening but I guess we were too late." He gave his uncle a recriminating look, "She worked for you for what, fifteen years! This ain't right."

"You sound like you're in love with her," The Finn smirked sarcastically then continued, "she was a fucking whore! The bitch is collateral damage and means nothing. Let me have a few minutes with this one and she'll talk – believe me, she'll spill it all!" Seppo said to Hank nudging Jodie with his foot.

"You're a fuckin' psycho!" Jericho snarled back, "I should waste your sorry ass right now!" He pointed the shotgun at the big man and walked towards him, "I'm tired of your fuckin' attitude. You walk around intimidating everyone but I ain't scared of you… I'm not, you big, ugly ape!"

He was working his courage up. Even as he moved forward his legs felt like they were stuck in molasses. Jericho, like most, was terrified of the big Finn.

Seppo Heikkinen was well aware of this and laughed out loud, a bellowing laugh that emanated from deep in his belly. He raised his arms high and smirked sarcastically, "Go on then, shoot me but you'd better make sure I'm dead!" He pointed to his forehead, "Right here... go on, do it!"

Hank quickly stepped in between the two men and reaching over pushed the barrel down. "Stop this shit! All of you! Just stop this juvenile crap. You have no idea what's at stake here. I didn't want Angela to be hurt leave alone dead but if that's what it took then so be it. If we don't get the laptop and squash this nonsense right now, none of this will matter! Shayk will make sure of that ... and that means it affects all of us!"

He went over to Jodie, took a penknife out, leaned over and cut her hands free. The young girl rubbed her wrists and looked up at Hank.

"Listen Jodie, I don't want to hurt you but you have to give me Marisa's laptop and anything else she may have given you. Do you understand? If you don't I will have no other choice but to let that terrible man deal with you ... he will hurt you, I mean really hurt you. You saw Angela's body didn't you? Now where is the laptop?" His deep baritone has softened and had taken on a soothing tone.

The blood drained from Jodie's face at the thought of Seppo doing to her what he did to Angela. Her lips were trembling and tears rolled down her cheeks, "I told him everything!" She pointed to Heikkinen, "Why would I lie? Poor Angela's gone. She was a nice person and he killed Maddie too..." Jodie sobbed then regained control, "I don't have it. I gave the laptop to that nice man," she paused, "to Robbie Olsen, the one who..." she hesitated again trying to collect her thoughts, "punched Snake and Scarface Jake. He has it all, even the diary!"

Hank moved closer and lifted her face up by her chin and looked into her eyes, "How do you know about Jake?"

"I was in Mr. Olsen's room when Fats and the others came there. Angela and I hid in the bathroom but I could hear everything. It was Angela's idea to give everything to Mr. Olsen. She said it would be safe with him."

Hank continued staring into the young girl's eyes. The seconds ticked by but Jodie held his gaze. Finally, Hank said, "You're lying."

"I'm not! I swear I'm not lying!" Jodie pleaded, the desperation evident. She grabbed Hank's arm, "Why don't you ask him… ask Mr. Olsen. He has it."

It was obvious to the men that the girl was petrified. Her hands were trembling and her expression was one of pure terror. Hank studied her and thought, *'There is no way she's making this up.'*

He turned to Ed, "Do you know where Olsen…"

The gunshot was deafening. The men watched in shock as Jericho fell backwards. There was a hole in the center of his forehead and the back of his skull had been blown away by the .44 magnum. Blood, brain and bone fragments splattered the inside of the barn wall creating a gruesome abstract. The eerie silence in the residuum of the sudden violence was shattered by Jodie's high-pitched shriek.

"I don't like people pointing guns at me especially assholes like him," Seppo said calmly and pushed the short muzzle of his Ruger Super Redhawk Alaskan under Ed Carlson's chin and snarled, "Tell that cunt of a brother to drop his gun. Do it now or you'll join your friend. Now! Drop the fuckin' gun!"

Ray Carlson dropped his weapon immediately and moved backwards. His eyes, riveted on Jericho's body, were wide with surprise and fright.

For the first time in his life Hank Carlson was at a loss. The whole sequence of events that had just transpired was something that he hadn't anticipated. He prided himself in preparing for all contingencies but this was one he never could have imagined. Not in his wildest dreams and most worrisome was of all was the thought that Seppo had gone rogue.

"What are you doing?" Hank quizzed Heikkinen, "What the fuck are you doing?"

Seppo smiled, a cold apathetic smile, "You know, Hank, when I first met you I thought to myself, now here is a man who knows how to run things. He's not afraid to make the tough calls, take action and screw them that don't like it. But now I realize that you are just as soft as the other motherfuckers I used to work for – fucking pussies! You want to get things done you have to act, quick and decisive, and with no second thoughts."

Hank didn't say anything. His mind was racing, working the angles, trying to figure out how to get this back on track; back where he could regain control.

Seppo continued, "You should have whacked Adam Shayk and his boys when you had the chance. Do you really think those assholes from Jersey will believe you even if you give them everything? No fucking way! They are going to think you saved a copy to protect your ass or to blackmail them and what do you think they'll do then? One way or the other they are going to make sure that all the loose ends get tied up. And that means you motherfuckers are dead … you just don't know it yet!"

"Shayk will never come up here. Luke and the boys will bury them if they ever try anything and should Adam need some convincing, I'll send Cat to deliver a message!" It was then he realized that the Italian wasn't present. "Where is Cat?" Hank asked.

"Dead. The little cunt had a problem taking orders," Seppo replied, totally unconcerned.

Hank was quiet. The more this played out the more he was convinced that the big Finn had a plan, something he had been working on. He had to stall and buy time. It was Luke who was

Seppo's real Achilles heel. "Guys like Cat are a dime a dozen but you had better think twice, Seppo, if you hurt a Carlson Luke will come looking for you. So far you've …"

The second shot seemed louder than the first, reverberating stridently inside the barn. Ray Carlson was hit in the center of his chest and flung backwards. The hollow-point tore a hole through his thin frame and the gurgling sounds were the last he made while he lay twitching on the ground. A pool of blood spread slowly around his dead body, the old wood floor stained crimson by the sanguinary lacquer.

Ed Carlson tried to get free but Heikkinen shook him like a ragdoll, "Don't even think it!" then turning to Hank, he said in a matter of fact tone, "Well, now I've killed a Carlson. What were you saying?"

Hank was in shock, his usual calm demeanor was gone as he stared at his nephew's dead body in total disbelief and the one thought that raced through his mind was, *'What do I tell Mom and Emma?'*.

The big Finn got animated, "Fuck Luke! If he comes at me, I'll enjoy tearing him apart. That little prick thinks he's some kind of Greek God but I'll fuck up that pretty face before I end his sick, miserable life!"

Hank Carlson tried hard to regain his composure and forced a derisive laugh, "Really? That is going to be interesting. You don't seem too convincing, Seppo. You made a big fucking mistake. You should never have shot Ray."

"Fuck all this. It means nothing. I'll be long gone. Now, we're all going for a ride back to the diner, to your office," Heikkinen instructed, dragging Ed by his neck. "If you try anything, the slightest twitch, I'll waste this little bitch and that will put an end to this stupid game."

"What are you talking about? Let Ed go and we can talk business right now," Hank's breathing quickened and his heart began thumping in his chest as the awareness of Seppo's plan dawned on him. "I've always been fair with you when it comes to money. Just tell me what it is that you want?"

Seppo laughed, "You're so fucking predictable! You still think you can talk your way out of this! You are a persistent asshole, I'll give you that." He paused then smirked and continued, "The safe, Hank, your precious fucking safe – the one behind the Joe Luis painting. That was the give-away. You don't know a single thing about boxing and it got me thinking so I put a small, teeny-weeny camera in your office and boy was I in for a surprise! You certainly have a lot of goodies in that safe; a lot of goodies! What are those diamonds worth, Hank? The ones you caress and play with like they were titties on a juicy whore? What would you say? A million? Two million? Ten?"

He waited, smiling broadly enjoying the look of disbelief and horror on Hank's face, "Now, I could tear it out of the wall and take it to a friend of mine who specializes in cracking safes but this is easier. And I won't have to give him a cut. He is fucking expensive."

The blood drained from Hank Carlson's face. Thoughts swirled in a disjointed array of confused sequences; impromptu plans and actions to thwart this reality but they all led to one definitive and inevitable conclusion. He had no chance even if he pulled the Beretta and surprised the big Finn – he wasn't the soldier. He was the brains, the schemer, the conniver of plans, the old general in the backroom. This was for someone like Robbie Olsen or his brother, Luke, not for the likes of him. He had to be honest with himself or run the risk of being killed and dying here with Ray and Jericho wasn't in his plan.

Seppo interrupted Hank's thoughts, "But you *have* been fair and because of that I'll get this bitch to talk and give you Marisa's laptop, not that it will save you but at least it will buy you some time. That should be an even exchange. Now let's go, leave your cars here, we'll use the van."

Hank felt his heart constrict as a sense of helplessness engulfed him. His expression gave him away and the distress was clearly evident for all to see. He made one last plea, clinging to straws, "Don't do this, Seppo, I'll give …"

"Shut the fuck up and have a little self-respect. Don't demean yourself. Another word and I'll waste these two. Now, get moving!"

Heikkinen pushed Ed in front of him, a rough forceful shove that sent the tall man stumbling. To avoid tripping, he inadvertently stepped into a puddle of his brother's blood. He felt the bile rise up from his belly and the taste of fear sour his palate but there was nothing he could do. His thoughts were of his younger brother and how he would have to break the news to his mother.

The big Finn grabbed Jodie with his left hand and the four of them walked towards the black Chevy Express parked on the left side of the barn.

Sisters in Spirit

THE TIGRESS AND THE DOVE

Allison had made hot chocolate for Ryan before Meghan put him to bed. She fed Ronin a huge Venison steak with some leftover rice and took him out. The two women sat on the porch steps and watched as the big dog surveyed the property in front of the cabin. He wandered past the neatly mowed lawn into thicker brush before disappearing into the woods.

"Ronin! Ronin, come back here! Now!" Meghan yelled out to him. "God, I hope he doesn't run off. Robbie won't forgive me... as it is I doubt he will ever forgive me."

They could hear the crepitating sound of twigs and brush being trampled and just as Meghan was about to chase after him, the big dog was back. He looked at her and wagged his tail before wandering about sniffing until he found the right spot then crouched and defecated, dropping a series of turds the size of bananas. He then walked a short distance and pawed the ground with his hind feet. The territorial gesture made both women laugh.

"Just like a male, he's even proud of his shit!" Allison joked then turning serious, "What did you mean about Robbie forgiving you?"

Meghan buried her face in her hands and sighed. Her silky auburn mane fell around her in a dark veil. "It's a long story. I made such a mess of it … it was years ago," she was quiet, not sure if she should share her feelings, "I made some bad choices."

Ronin came over and lay down by Meghan's feet, his enormous head resting against her ankle. She leaned over to pet him feeling reassured by his proximity. The women sat quietly entertained by nature's symphony – the rasping buzz of the cicada accompanied by the whirr of leaves kissed by the wings of a lingering mountain breeze. The light from the porch lanterns washed golden across the façade, its hue caressing the grass as shadows pranced and pirouetted against the backdrop of the forest. The soothing panacea hid the presentiment building in Meghan's heart. She tried not to think of Robbie or the threats made by Seppo.

It was Allison who spoke first, breaking the comfortable silence, "Bad choices like Luke? Is Robbie mad about Luke?"

Meghan's relationship with Luke was a topic that neither woman had broached before. It was something they had taken great care to avoid. And Allison, for her part, had always been kind and sympathetic without acknowledging the affair. So it was a surprise to Meghan when she asked the question.

"No, no…" Meghan reacted then was silent, collating her thoughts, unsure how she was going to address the subject of incest. "Luke was a mistake but I don't regret it. Ryan is the best thing that has ever happened to me. When I met Luke, I had no idea that you were…" She couldn't find the words to put it gently and without sounding judgmental or repulsed.

"Lovers?" Allison suggested with a smile, cocking her head and looking at Meghan.

"Yes and I'm not judging you. God knows that true love is hard enough to find. You have to hold onto it when and where you can find it."

"Even if that true love is your brother?" The intonation suggested a question.

Meghan seemed at a loss, "I don't have a brother so it's hard for me to imagine but I guess if it is true love then yes, even if it is your brother."

"It doesn't bother you at all?" Allison asked, more out of curiosity than out of any need for Meghan's validation or endorsement.

Meghan was quiet and uncomfortable with the subject. She had never given this much thought so she wasn't really sure about how she felt. "At first I thought it was weird but then I saw the two of you together, you seemed perfect, so beautiful and happy that I never questioned it. I'm sorry but that is the truth."

Allison didn't respond, seemingly lost in thought then looked up and asked, "Who was your first? Who was the first man you made love to?"

"Oh God, it was so long ago and I'm not sure you can call it making love! Alan Drysdale. He was Dad's business associate who was staying with us for the weekend. I was sixteen and he was in his thirties – charming, sophisticated and very good looking and I had a real crush on him. He came into my room when everyone was asleep and…" she paused, "…it wasn't very good. I remember feeling really disappointed and thinking, *Is this it? This is the big deal?*"

Meghan studied the younger woman, '*She is so beautiful, Robbie was right – she's like some picture-book princess, airbrushed to perfection.*' Allison's golden hair, violet-blue eyes and flawless skin looked even more radiant in the lantern's yellow hue.

"How about you? What was it like?"

"It was just the opposite for Luke and me. It was beautiful. I was only fourteen but it was amazing and I remember telling myself that I could never love anyone else. We spent hours making love and exploring each other… I still can't get enough of him."

"Then that is true love and no one has the right to judge you."

Allison smiled, her face glowing auric in the dim light, "I was never angry, Meghan, not at you or Luke. And I think you know that I love Ryan as though he was my own." When Meghan didn't respond she continued, "What Luke and I share is something special and we don't care what others think. When he told me about you, I assured him that it really didn't bother me as long as he came back to me. That's all I've ever wanted."

She raised the hem of her blouse to reveal a small tattoo above her belly button that said "Luke" with a heart on each side. It was done in old English script. "He has one just like this with my name. We got it after your affair had ended. He wanted to reinforce his commitment to me. So you see, it worked out just like it should have. And, now we all have Ryan."

Meghan reached over and took the younger woman's hand in hers, "That means a lot to me. It has been in the back of my mind. I never wanted to hurt you in any way, Allison. I want you to know that."

They sat there holding hands for a short while before Allison stood up and asked, "Some more coffee? I'm going to get a refill."

"Yes, please," Meghan replied handing her the cup.

The younger woman looked down at Ronin and said, "You know, I'm glad he's here. I feel so much safer. Seppo is dangerous and he hates Luke." She could sense Meghan's concern and added, "Don't worry about Robbie; he knows how to take care of himself. I've never met a man who exuded so much inner strength. You are lucky – they don't make them like him anymore."

And with that she went into the cabin while Meghan sat on the porch gently stroking Ronin's head. She was worried about Robbie though she remained ambivalent about their earlier argument. *I don't want to lose him but I think it's unfair to judge me on things that happened before he met me.* Regret and remorse swept through her as she reflected on past decisions. *Why did I let Marylou talk me into attending that party? And why did I keep those photographs? I've never looked at them even though I knew they were there. Maybe on some subconscious level it made me feel desirable … who knows! But, I'm sure we can sort it out and start afresh; at least I think we can.* She was trapped in the melancholic prison of doubt and need.

She was so lost in thought that Ronin's growl startled her. The giant dog raised his head and growled again then got up and walked down the stoop. He stood motionless for a what felt like an eternity, listening intently, before his growls got louder and his shackles raised.

"What's the matter, Ronin? Is someone there?" Meghan's felt her heart begin to pound.

Ronin walked towards the edge of the landing peering down through the trees, towards the flat landing used as a parking terrace. The approaching headlights created a kaleidoscope of flickering patterns as it made its way up the steep, winding driveway towards where Meghan had parked her pick-up. She could now hear the gnarring rumble of a car's engine.

"Who's there?" she called out. Allison had joined her, shotgun in hand.

"Who's there?" She repeated and when there was no answer she added, "You'd better not come up here."

There was still no reply. The chirring of the cicada seemed to get louder and in the distance, the plaintive cry of a coyote echoed through the hills. The staccato visage of light beams streaming through the branches receded to the silver scrim of the woods as the vehicle came to a stop next to Meghan's truck. They could hear the engine sputter and the headlights die out leaving the landing shrouded in darkness.

A sudden gust of wind rallied reckless about them raking up leaves and swirling clouds of dust. There was a loud growl that spooked both women and before they could stop him, the mountain dog was gone, racing down towards the car.

THE SOLDIER, THE KING
RAT AND TROUBLE

Robbie was about fifty yards from the barn when he heard the second gunshot. It shattered the quietness of the night spooking the nocturnal habitués of the woods. He could hear the frenetic scattering of hoofs and paws as they dashed for safety. He was concerned about Jodie. *'Damn! I hope I'm not too late'* he thought to himself. The dense foliage made for slow progress but he crouched low and quickened his pace, cutting through the trees and brush, stepping lightly to avoid betrayal by the crackle of snapping twigs and branches. The darkness along with the heavy thicket that bordered the barn provided ample cover keeping him concealed even though he was now close enough to hear the low muttering of voices.

A few minutes later Hank and Ed Carlson stepped into view followed by Seppo and Jodie - they were making their way towards the van. Hank led the short convoy with his nephew a few steps behind him, followed by the big Finn and Jodie. Seppo had the girl by the back of her neck and held close to his left. Robbie remained crouched until the entourage went by then shifted his position so he could keep Jodie out of the line of fire.

He stepped out from the shadows and addressed Seppo, commanding, "Let her go. Drop the gun and let the girl go!"

They stood frozen; a pantomime of the children's game Red Light-Green Light, then all hell broke loose.

"Fuck you!" The reply was a hiss. Heikkinen swung around using Jodie as a shield, easily lifting her off the ground and holding her in front of his body. He squeezed off two quick shots in the direction of Robbie's voice.

The problem with the Ruger Super Redhawk Alaskan is the short barrel. It was designed for self-defense at close quarters primarily for hikers in Alaska as a last resort in dealing with a charging Grizzly and unless you are really proficient with a handgun, the accuracy at distance leaves a lot to be desired. Seppo's first shot missed but the second ricocheted off a metal post close to where Robbie was standing and struck him on the left side of his abdomen. He grunted and staggered then steadied himself and fired a shot that whistled by the big man's head. He was careful making sure not to hit Jodie. He moved a few steps to the side but was unable to get a clear line of sight.

Clenching his teeth in response to the pain Robbie yelled out, "Stop! Let her go or the next one won't miss! Let her…"

He was cut short by the cracking of gunfire from behind the Finn accompanied by a cry of frustration and anger, "Die you motherfucker!"

It was Ed Carlson. The bullet tore into the Heikkinen's shoulder, the same shoulder where Maddie had stabbed him with the scissors. The big man flinched and instinctively grabbed at his back letting Jodie go and in one quick motion, turned around firing blindly but there was no one there. He stood still, peering into the darkness, trying to get a bead on his assailant. He scanned the area and fired again at an adumbrated movement but this time there was a volley of gunfire in return, it came from both sides of him. A 10mm caliber bullet from Robbie's Glock ripped through the muscles of his thigh missing the femur by a hair and sent him stumbling to his knees. He pivoted towards Robbie and fired again only to hear the loud click of an empty chamber.

"Fuck me!" He hissed and lay flat on the ground, examining his thigh and whispered in disgust as his fingers came up bloody, "Shit!"

The rumble of a car's engine cut through the silent aftermath of gunshots and the red taillights of the SUV glowed in sarcastic retreat as it sped away. It was Hank Carlson and he was hell-bent on getting back to his office and his precious cache of diamonds – the rest be damned.

Though seriously hurt, Seppo was surprisingly quick. He took advantage of the distraction and tumbled into the van slamming the sliding door shut. A short while later the Chevy roared after the Range Rover. The plan he had so carefully conceived was unraveling but he wasn't one to give up. A blind smoldering rage consumed him; the molten scoria of anger that bubbled up from deep within caused him to throw caution to the wind. This was Hank's fault – if he hadn't stopped him from taking care of Olsen at the diner, this would never have happened. Now Jodie was gone. The little bitch had scampered off. She was his ace in the hole. But it didn't matter. None of this mattered. He would get the diamonds one way or the other and finish both Hank and Ed. If Luke got in the way, he'd take care of him too and then he'd find that sister of his – yes, he'd fuck that pretty little thing until she begged for mercy. He had always fancied her.

He was a few yards from the turn onto the main road and had slowed down when he heard the roar of an engine to his left and before he could react, the blinding brilliance of high-beams was heading straight for him. He watched incredulously, frozen, as the black pickup T-boned his van and sent it careening out of control. It slid across a short, grassy patch and rolled down the side of an incline, tumbling wildly until it crashed into a large oak and came to a stop.

The pick-up had pulled up a few yards from the edge of the declivity bathing the ditch and surrounding area in the fluorescence of its headlights. Ed Carlson stepped out and surveyed the wreckage. The van was lying upside down with smoke swirling upwards from the underside of the sputtering, paralytic engine. The distinctive smell of gasoline permeated the air around him as flames spread quickly engulfing the van.

"That's for Ray and Jericho, asshole! I hope you burn in hell!" he shouted into the night as the fire gained in intensity.

He stood motionless, his weapon drawn watching the conflagration, needing to make sure that the big Finn was dead but unwilling to get closer to the flames. He was also terrified that Seppo would somehow survive the carnage and like some flaming monster, rise up and devour him. He waited nervously for a few minutes watching the van burn and satisfied, returned to his truck and checked the bull-bar and grille before driving away. He was beleaguered by the loss of his brother and friend and struggled to keep his emotions in check. But surprisingly, it was Angela Mercier's death that bothered him the most. He had to find Hank and Marylou Dorsey. He had to set things right.

Colder-than-Ice

A FRIEND IN NEED

When Seppo let go of her, Jodie had rushed across the yard to where Robbie was. It was a desperate sprint to safety. On some subconscious level she knew that her chances of survival depended on Robbie.

"Get down and stay down," Robbie instructed pushing the young girl down behind the refuge of a large white pine.

She closed her eyes and cowered in fright as more gunfire erupted around her followed by a short silence before they heard the grinding noise of tires on a dirt path. They watched as first the Range Rover and then the van raced away from the Bruckman farm; the red tracers of their taillights disappearing into the night.

"What happened in there?" Robbie asked the young girl, his left hand pressed against his side.

She ignored the question and almost in disbelief, said, "You're bleeding!"

"Yeah I've been hit. Is anyone alive in there?" He asked, slowly dropping down, sitting on the ground and leaning back against the post that was next to him. He holstered his Glock and closed his eyes. The left side of his shirt and trousers were soaked in blood.

"No they're dead. Angela, Jericho, Ray … they're all dead. Seppo killed them all." She replied and coming over, knelt by Robbie's side, "Mr. Olsen, are you okay? You look pale. You need a doctor … we need to get you to a hospital."

"That is too bad about Angela. She was a decent person and cared for you." He struggled to his feet holding onto the post, "Tony's out there. Let's go, he'll know what to do."

"Can I just say goodbye to Angela? Please, Mr. Olsen, I won't take long, I promise… can I?"

"Okay be quick and here," he handed his cell phone to her, "take some pictures – try and get all of them and don't take too long."

Jodie did as she promised and returned quickly. She handed the phone back to Olsen. "I got several picture of Angela and the other two, Jericho and Ray. We should bury Angela. It's not fair to leave her like that."

"We will but the police need to see this. We will give her a decent burial, you don't worry," he assured the girl, "come on, we need to get back to the truck."

They were about twenty yards from the dirt track where VanArcen's truck was parked when they saw a light filtering through the branches approaching quickly towards them.

"Stop!" Robbie whispered, grimacing in pain and pulling the girl back. He held onto a tree keeping the girl close to him. He was fumbling for his gun when they heard a voice calling out – it was VanArcen.

"Robbie, is that you?" his voice sounding unsure and nervous.

"Yes, Tony, it's me. Can you …"

"He's been shot, Tony, hurry, he's hurt badly!" Jodie called back in desperation.

There was a loud crashing of the underbrush as Tony made a clumsy and incautious dash to get to them. He flashed the light from his cell phone at Robbie's abdomen, "Damn, Bronson, you had to do it, didn't you? You had to go and get shot!"

The forced banter was a cover for his concern. He pushed his glasses back against the bridge of his nose and seeing the expression on Jodie's face, added, "Don't worry, girl, he's indestructible… he'll be fine!"

He threw Robbie's arm awkwardly over his shoulder and heard his friend gasp, "Sorry, cowboy, didn't mean to hurt you. You lean on me, I'll get you home to mama."

"Who's mama?" Jodie asked, then added, "We have to be careful. Seppo may still be out there."

"You don't worry. Go on, you go ahead and push the branches aside."

Jodie led the way through the brush and low hanging branches, cutting a path to make it easier for VanArcen and Robbie. It seemed like an eternity but they eventually made it to the truck and not a moment too soon. Robbie was beginning to lose consciousness, his face was ashen and covered in sweat and he was having trouble getting into the passenger's side but with help from Tony and some Ranger fortitude he finally sat back in the seat, exhausted.

"Jodie, hold him; hold onto his shoulders. The seatbelt may be too tight. Can you do that?"

"Yes. Yes, I can."

The young girl reached around the seat and held tightly onto Robbie's shoulders keeping him pinned to the backrest. He closed his eyes drifting gradually into the dark labyrinth of unconsciousness where amalgamated images of his childhood merged with those from Kunduz; haunting faces blending together in an incongruous collage until they all faded to black. He smiled at the phantasm dancing across the corridors of his subconscious, a sultry goddess whispering things only lovers do.

He murmured her name, "Meghan!"

The Assassin Elite

MICHAEL MCHENRY
AKA FRENCHIE

Michael McHenry sat in the parking lot of a 7-Eleven near Hartford and studied the contents of the manila envelope with interest. The man in the photograph was big, pushing close to three hundred pounds, and from the detailed description of his background would pose a real challenge. Not surprisingly, McHenry enjoyed challenges and the more dangerous it was, the more it piqued his interest. He smiled while reading the man's various associations and the location of the hit. This was perfect; it involved a dangerous predator, remote mountainous area, hillbilly town with little or no law enforcement and most of all, the macabre aspect that appealed to his personal predilections. He laughed out loud when he read the bonus associated with 'head on the bed'.

McHenry was a small, wiry man who could have passed for a college professor or a computer nerd rather than an assassin. But a devious killer he was and one who was very proficient at his chosen avocation. He had a brilliant mind with an eidetic memory and a penchant for the minutest detail. He was skilled in various forms of martial arts and was also an explosives expert. However, it was his fondness for biochemistry and particularly poisons, that set him apart from others of his ilk. He had effectively used them all - from noxious gases and powders to liquids that were pretty much undetectable. Pernicious substances like ricin, aconite, fluoroantimonic acid and succinylcholine left no room for error and the challenges involved in the handling and use outside of a laboratory wasn't for the faint of heart. It took unwavering nerve and skill and made McHenry special even among specialists.

His last victim was the son of a British diplomat vacationing in Bermuda. The hit was sanctioned by his ex-wife and it took the man three long and painful days to die. The woman wanted to make sure he suffered for leaving her for a younger woman and suffer he certainly did. McHenry had used the victim's love of Japanese cuisine to kill him with a combination of arsenic and tetrodotoxin. The latter is the same neurotoxin found in Fugu, also known as Puffer fish, a delicacy among the connoisseurs of sashimi. The clowns who punched the 9 to 5 in the coroner's office ruled it as an accidental death due to some bad sushi; a simple case of extreme food poisoning.

He called the number he was given and when Izhutin answered, he spoke brusquely, "Okay, I'm on it. I'll call in a few days. You know the routine; make sure half gets wired to the account I gave you. The other half when the job is done. Don't try and reach me – I'll get a hold of you if we need to talk."

He hung up without waiting for an answer, removed the prepaid SIM card and destroyed it before driving back to Litchfield County in Northwestern Connecticut. His house was nestled within a hundred and fifty wooded acres which suited his reclusive lifestyle. A long gravel driveway cut a circuitous path to the classic stone patio that overlooked a manicured lawn with Japanese gardens, Koi ponds and waterfalls. He enjoyed the seclusion and anonymity that his home provided while allowing him access to New York and the major airports.

The house itself was an large old Cape that he had restored, converting it to a modern Ranch style contemporary. The interior was just as eclectic. It was remodeled to embrace a rustic, open style that was decorated with a collection of rare Buddhist statues he had shipped from as far away as Bali and Cambodia. This was his haven – the getaway place to unwind and to plan.

He added a large three thousand square feet garage that was connected to the main house through and underground walkway. Here he kept his many vehicles, twelve to be exact. Most of them were souped-up cars that were prerequisites for certain jobs but there were a few like the Bugatti Type 41 Royale and the Jaguar XK-E that were his pride and joy.

He sat in his living room, sipping Yamazaki whiskey listening to strains of Howlin' Wolf's 'Smokestack Lightning' while revisiting the details of the job. This time he made copious notes and created a "to do" list.

The first step was his appearance: he dyed his hair and mustache black and used tinted contacts to change the color of his eyes from light brown to green. And though his eyesight was an astounding 20/10, he picked out a pair of tortoise shell glasses to compliment the change in appearance. He studied himself in the mirror and wasn't fully satisfied so he decided to shave off his mustache. His checked himself again; the transformation was remarkable and he was now ready to play the part of a geologist.

The second step was to select the tools of his trade: he carefully stashed several small bottles of clear fluids along with plastic containers of amorphous powders in the false bottom built into his travel bag. Each item was neatly labeled and encased in several layers of protective wrap. He went through his collection of stilettoes and knives and selected the Buck Pathfinder. This hunter's knife had a high carbon steel blade sharp enough to sever a man's head. He checked the sharpness before sheathing it and closing the compartment shut. He tossed in a few trousers, underwear, shirts and other essential toiletries and zipped up the large leather duffle.

The third step was his accent: he had spent hours listening to tapes he made of himself speaking with a Spanish accent laced with subtle American affectations. He had used this before so it came naturally. He sounded like a Spaniard or Cuban or a confusing mix of both.

He dressed in corduroys and a button down shirt with a loose fitting navy jacket to complete the ensemble. McHenry gave himself a thorough once over in the full length mirror, smiled and said, "Hello Professor Santos". He checked his list carefully for a final time to make sure he had taken care of every detail before flushing it down the toilet.

Finally, he strapped on a .38 caliber Colt under his jacket and was now ready to get the show started. He hummed softly to himself, an off-key rendering of Jimmy Buffet's "Margaritaville", and stood in his large garage trying to decide on which of the cars would suit his purpose. He settled on an beat-up old Toyota Tundra. It would be a lot less conspicuous in mountains and more in line with something a geologist would be driving rather than some of the other sportier vehicles in his collection. He screwed on Arizona plates, placed his attaché case and duffel in the cab, set the alarm and headed out.

Once he got close to Chase River Town, the first place he stopped at was a little shanty called 'The Rancher's Lodge & Drink' off of Route 6. The lodge was long gone and all that remained was the rundown, dinky watering hole frequented by the town's rougher denizens. A few pick-up trucks were scattered out front near the entrance and a Jeep Wrangler sat by itself on the side away from the others. He pulled up next to the Jeep, studied the building and circled around the back before entering. He took mental notes of every detail – the location of the back door, the position of the dumpster, the topography, the closest path to the road and every place he could use for cover. His photographic memory had served him well in the past and experience had taught him that it was the attention to detail that decided every outcome.

The interior did little to change his impression of the place. It was a cramped, smoky room with a beat-up wooden counter that served as the bar. The lighting was dim and he was greeted by the stale redolence of cheap alcohol and the wailing twang of an old Hank Locklin song. A large, frayed Confederate flag was pinned to the back wall with a few faded photographs of rebel soldiers hanging besides it.

He walked up to the bar and in his hybrid accent said, "You have an interesting place!" Then getting no response, asked, "Can I get a Bud Light?"

The barkeep was a burly man with long silver hair tied in a ponytail. His bushy eyebrows accentuated his gray-blue eyes and his pug nose and lipless mouth gave him a hard look. He was a lawless buzzard with a swastika and the number '666' tattooed on the side of his neck and the letters "AB" for Aryan Brotherhood stenciled on his right arm.

He gave McHenry a cold stare and made no attempt to hide his repugnance. "This ain't no place for the likes of you. You ain't welcome here." His voice was deep and gravely.

McHenry raised his hands in a gesture of appeasement before replying, "Sorry. I just wanted a drink and was looking for a place to stay. I'll be going … didn't mean to bother you, sir."

As he turned to leave, a thick, husky man with a huge belly got up and made his way over. "Hey, Chuck, come on now; give our little friend here a break. He looks pretty white to me." He turned to McHenry, "You must forgive Chuck, the man has no manners. Are you lookin' for a place to stay?"

He wiped his mouth with the back of his hand and tugged at his trousers, pulling them up, before continuing, "The Pritchard's place on Elm, that'd be the place for someone like you. Nice and classy and quiet. I'll be heading by there so if you'd like, I can show you where it is. It's kinda hard to find."

"Oh, I would be much obliged, sir, I'm Lorenzo Santos and I'm here from the University of Arizona," McHenry nervously adjusted his glasses and offered the man his hand.

"Tom Bakke," the man said shaking McHenry's hand, "From Arizona, eh? You're a long way from home, Mr. Santos. Now, what would you be doing up here?"

"I'm a geologist. I'm here to study the rock formations in the Northern Appalachian Mountains."

"Rock formations! You hear that, you brainless baboons?" he exclaimed to patrons sitting in the corner, "This here is an educated man." Then turning to McHenry, "That's great. Come on, let's go. You don't want to drink here, the rotgut will kill you. I'll show where the Pritchard's place is. You'll get a decent drink there and you can buy me one, what do you say?"

Before McHenry could answer a female voice cut in, "Go sit down, Tom, go on and leave the man alone. The Pritchard's place has been closed for over ten years. The least you can do is come up with a better line."

She was pretty, really pretty, about five-seven, with dark brown hair cut in a bob skimming her shoulders and large wideset, almond shaped eyes. A strong chin, sensual mouth and perky little nose completed the sultry picture. She had been seated at the corner table with the men. In the adumbral dimness McHenry thought that she resembled his favorite actress, Natalie Wood. He was aficionado of the classics and two of his favorites were "West Side Story" and "Rebel Without A Cause".

"Aw come on, Marylou, I was just funin'!" the man protested but stepped away. He looked at McHenry and said, "Today's your lucky day, Professor, yes indeed, your lucky day."

He retreated to the corner table with a smirk totally oblivious of his brush with death. The men huddled together whispering in hushed tones when the conversation got boisterous and loud enough for McHenry to hear, "… he'd better! She's gonna fuck his brains out!" The table erupted in peals of loud guffaws.

The slightly built assassin looked away, embarrassed. His persona, the professor, had taken over and he stuck instinctively to the script.

The woman took a drag on her cigarette and noticing his uneasiness said, "Ignore them. They're a bunch of redneck hillbillies. He was going to roll you – take you into the parking lot and mug you. Do you understand? Be careful who you trust around here." She studied McHenry before continuing, "There is no Pritchard's place on Elm anymore but my father has a room to rent so if you are looking for a quiet place and don't mind staying with a family, it's a good deal. The other option is the Sleepy Crest Motel… it's a little further away and I wouldn't recommend it but that's about it around here."

"Thank you, Miss…?"

"Marylou Dorsey but you can call me Marylou."

"Thank you, Miss Dorsey, that was kind of you. He seemed like a nice man." He shook his head in mock disbelief and introduced himself with a courtesy, tilting his head and bowing slightly at the waist, "I am Lorenzo Santos and staying with a family would be preferable to a motel. Like a home away from home. I'll be gone most of the day so I won't be in the way and when I'm there, I will try not to intrude."

She squashed the cigarette butt into an ashtray on the counter, "He charges thirty dollars a day or two hundred a week. You will have a large room with a queen bed and an attached bathroom. Breakfast comes with the room and it is whatever my father is having – usually eggs and toast. And, there is a coffee machine in the kitchen that you can use. Is that okay?"

"That is very reasonable and yes, it is okay." He paused studying her then continued, "It has been a long day; shall we go?"

"Give me a minute," the woman replied.

She went back to the table in the corner and engaged in a terse and choleric conversation with one of the men. McHenry heard the man apologize before Marylou gathered her cardigan and purse and walked back towards him.

He was pretending to be preoccupied with his cell phone but had been watching her out of the corner of his eye. He smiled a broad, friendly smile when she got back and put away his phone.

"Ready?" he asked.

"Before we go I have to mention something," she said, "it almost slipped my mind. My brother, Junior, lives at home with dad. He had an accident some years back and it affected his brain. He's a bit slow but he's harmless. If that's a problem, I can tell you how to get to the Sleepy Crest."

"No. That is okay, not a problem at all. I'm truly sorry about your brother."

"Don't be. It was a long time ago and we've all accepted it. Shit happens, you know," she said it in a matter-of-fact manner.

"If I'm not being too presumptuous in asking, do you also stay with you father?"

She looked at him in surprise and laughed, "No, I don't."

"That is too bad. You are a charming lady and speaking with you has been a pleasure."

She found herself blushing at the compliment, "But, I do come over often to check on Dad and Junior. So maybe we'll get to talk some more."

"I look forward to that," and with that, he bowed slightly and followed her to her car.

Killer bod, he thought to himself watching the seductive sway of her hips. She turned and said, "You have a nice accent, where are you from? We don't get too many foreigners here."

"I am originally from Madrid. I came here to study and just stayed on. I have gone back to Spain a few times but America is an addiction and I always come back."

She smiled, getting into the Jeep. "Oh, there are far worse addictions, trust me. Okay, follow me, it's not too far but it's hidden away and not on any GPS."

He smiled more to himself. *This couldn't be more perfect.*

THE VIPER AND
THE NEST EGGS

When Hank arrived at Bucky Johnston's Diner the place was still buzzing with activity and the parking lot was almost full so he decided to use the rear entrance. He parked the Range Rover in the shadows a little away from the building and checked the back lot thoroughly – with the big Finn you could never be too careful. He waited a few minutes, making sure he was alone, before secreting in through the rear door.

His office was pitch-black and he almost tripped over the oak chair, the screeching of the casters testing his already frayed nerves.

"Shit!" He hissed, kicking the chair in frustration, before turning on the table lamp.

He had to act quickly. He took the Joe Luis painting down and tossed it into the corner and in his haste punched in the wrong code. He heard the warning buzz and the red light flash briefly on the keypad – he had one more try before the vault went into lockdown mode and then it would be close to impossible to open. He would have to take a blowtorch to it.

"Calm down!" He said softly, "Calm the fuck down."

He took a deep breath and waited to gather himself. This time, he made certain that the biometric pad was engaged and the six digits were input slowly. He breathed a sigh of relief at the sound of the 'click' as the safe unlocked. He pulled the door wide open and fumbled in the back for the red velvet pouch, took a quick peek inside before stuffing it into his coat pocket. He reached in again and this time he retrieved a folded ditty bag. He shook it out and began stacking the gold bars and Golden Eagles. He was about halfway done when a voice from the dark jolted him out of skin.

"Going somewhere, Hank?"

He grabbed for the Beretta he had placed on the table; a clumsy attempt that knocked the weapon to the floor. He scrambled after it but the stranger was quicker and stepped on it.

"You do have a 21 in the safe; you know that, don't you?" Luke Carlson said with a tinge of derision in his tone.

"Luke! Damn boy, you scared the shit out of me!" Hank exclaimed, the relief obvious in his voice. "What are you doing here?"

"I'm waiting for Seppo. I know he'll be here. You see, he knows about your little nest-egg," Luke answered nonchalantly.

"How did you find out?" Hank said getting up and regaining his composure.

"For a smart guy you make a lot of mistakes. A Joe Luis painting? Really, Hank? It was a dead giveaway. It just isn't you so one day I took it down and there it was - Hank Carlson's secret vault."

Luke was enjoying this; he was amused by his brother's uneasiness. "Once I saw the safe, my curiosity got the better of me and I waited… it was only a matter of time before I caught you playing with the diamonds, rolling them around in your fingers, holding them up to the light. You were lost in your own world."

Hank grit his teeth and asked again, "I meant Seppo. How did you know about Seppo?"

Luke walked to the adjacent wall and took down a large barometric clock and after a few minutes of fussing and fiddling, pulled out a camera the size of an apricot. He tossed it on the table and sat down.

"I saw him come out of your office one day when you were with Ed and Ray at the lumber yard. He didn't see me and I didn't say anything but noticed that the barometer was a bit skewed. So I waited a few days and then when it was dark took it apart and found the camera."

"Why didn't you tell me?"

Luke had never been the diplomat, "I don't know. I thought that the two of your deserved each other. And, I could ask you the same question, Hank, why didn't *you* tell me about the safe and the diamonds? I mean, if something were to happen to you wouldn't you want Mom and the rest of us to share in this?"

Hank didn't reply. They stood there glaring at each other in the uneasy silence. It was Hank who spoke first, "You have Allison and the others all have family. What do I have, Luke? Except for this business I have nothing. I figured one day when things were all settled and all of you were comfortable and when the business didn't need me anymore, I'd go far away and start afresh. Find me a nice gal and maybe even start my own family." He paused, studying his younger brother but Luke didn't react, "Sounds crazy, huh?"

Luke couldn't tell if this was a catharsis for his brother, or whether it was another of his ploys to justify his actions.

"Why didn't you just find a girl here and settle down? Why do you have to go away? Your family is here."

"Because here I am Hank Carlson, the boss, the guy who runs things and I can't take my eye off the ball. Here I have to be who I am because anything else would mean losing it all. Here, everyone depends on me. I'm tired, Luke, this shit with Seppo and Shayk is the last of it. Once this is over, Ed and you can do what you want with the business. I'm out. By the way, Seppo killed Ray and Jericho…

just so you know."

Luke didn't seem perturbed; he had never been close to either of his nephews and he certainly didn't like Jericho. "I'll settle with Seppo, you don't worry about that. I'll make him pay and with interest."

"Listen, there's plenty here so if you want some of the…"

"Relax, Hank, I have no interest in your diamonds or gold," Luke cut him off, "I'm here for one reason and one reason only – Seppo! He murdered Maddie and I aim to exact my vengeance. I will take my time with him. I remember something you said a while ago, something about revenge being a dish best served cold, well, it is cold enough now and by the time I'm done, it will be frozen."

"I don't care anymore. He's gone rogue and the more you make him suffer, the better. But don't underestimate him – he's cunning and dangerous. I did a bit of digging when he first came to us and he's a killer, he's killed more men than anyone I know. He just murdered Angela, Ray and Jericho in cold blood. He could be here any minute. The last I saw of him, he was in a shootout with Olsen."

"What was Olsen doing there?"

"I have no idea but it's a good thing he turned up or both Ed and I would have ended up dead too."

"Where's Ed?"

Hank hesitated before answering. "I don't know. I left… I had to."

Luke was quiet, lost in thought. *It was just like Hank to leave Olsen and Ed holding the bag.* He stepped closer and looked up at his brother, "Did you have anything to do with Maddie's death? Did you tell Seppo to get Jodie from her place?"

Hank didn't answer right away. He finished stuffing the canvas bag before addressing the question. "I told him to find Jodie, that I did but I had nothing to do with Maddie's death. Why would I want that old woman harmed? You may not believe this but I respected her; old as she was, staying alone and running that little gas station. She had strength that I don't have."

Hank could lie with the best of them. All his life he had manipulated others. Lies and half-truths were second nature to him. It was almost impossible to tell when he was telling the truth and when he was lying.

"You're so fucking good at twisting things that I can't tell anymore. I don't think even you know when you're lying! But, if I find out that…"

The loud ringing of Hank's cell phone interrupted their conversation.

"Ed, where the fuck are you? Are you okay?" Hank asked and listened, not saying anything for a while then asked, "Are you sure?"

Luke could hear Ed's animated voice but couldn't make out what as being said. He studied Hank's expression for a clue but was unable to decipher the gist of their conversation.

Hank waited before speaking again, "Are you sure, Ed. Are you absolutely sure?"

Hank listened, nodded, before instructing his nephew, "Okay, you go on home. I'll take care of it. Luke is here and we'll go over to Emma's." He listened some more before he said, "No. don't worry about it. I said I would take care of it. I'll go see your mother right now. Listen, Ray is gone and there's nothing we can do so get some rest and we'll talk tomorrow. And Ed, that was an impressive thing you did. I didn't think you had it in you, son. Good job."

Hank looked across the desk at his brother, "Seppo's dead. Ed took care of him." He waited for a reaction but getting none went on, "It's over. Now all that's left is to deal with Shayk. Come with me to Emma's, she's going to be heartbroken. Ray was her favorite; her baby." Noting the indecision, he added, "She's always had a soft corner for you, Luke, so you being there will help her."

Luke ignored the plea and asked, "Did he actually see Seppo's dead body?"

"He rammed Seppo's van into a ditch and watched it burn. No one came out so unless he's fireproof or the fuckin' Phoenix, he's dead."

"Okay. If he's dead then there is no point in staying here but I feel cheated; I wanted to look into his eyes when I cut his heart out."

"I'm glad you don't have to risk it and being burned alive is punishment enough," Hank said and placed the canvas bag back into the vault but kept the diamonds with him. He locked the vault and hung the painting back on the wall.

"You don't understand. *I* wanted to kill him for Maddie," Luke hissed.

"I don't think Maddie cares how he was killed. And as for me, I just wanted him gone… gone like in dead! Come on; we have to tell Emma about Ray. This is going to be hard."

"You know she's going to want to see Ray's body. How bad is it?"

"It's not good. He's lying in a pool of blood with a hole in his chest surrounded by dried horseshit." Hank replied squeezing his eyes shut, trying to shake the image of Ray's body. "We'll take her to Bruckman's if we have to but I'd rather have Gil clean him up first; make him look presentable before she sees him."

"Okay, I'll talk to Emma," Luke relented and added, "and we can stop at the Dorsey's, it's on the way."

Hank mulled it over before agreeing, "Yeah, you're right. A few minutes isn't going to change anything." He got his wallet out and fished out a piece of paper from behind a flap in the billfold section. He glanced at it before handing it to Luke.

"What's this?" Luke asked.

"It's the combination to the safe. Tomorrow we'll program the biometric pad so you can access it too. I have to look up the procedure on how to do it… the instructions are in my attaché case."

"I don't want your diamonds or gold, Hank, I thought you knew that."

Hank answered softly, "You were right. If something were to happen to me, you make sure that Mom, Emma, Pauline and Allison all get a fair share. I know I can trust you with that. You're the only person I've ever known who doesn't give a rat's ass about money!"

Luke studied his brother, his expression softening, "Careful Hank, or you might turn into someone I actually like! Come on; let's go before I change my mind."

Hank laughed. It was the first time in a long while that he had felt this sense of relief – as though a huge burden had been lifted off of his shoulders. It was also the first time in a long while that they felt like brothers. The last time it felt like this was the summer of the Pontiac. The brothers locked the office and turned off the lights before leaving.

A Wounded Soldier

EVE, THE APPLE
AND A SNAKE

Almost immediately after Ronin had charged off, Meghan and Allison heard a desperate voice clamoring up from the landing below them.

"Help! Meghan! Luke! Help… help me! Robbie's been shot!" The desperation in the voice was unmistakable.

VanArcen moved closer to the flagstone steps leading up to the cabin and was about to call out again when he caught sight of the large Cimmerian form bounding down towards him. In the darkness it resembled a charging bear and he panicked, stumbling backwards on his heels and had to grab the truck for support.

"Oh shit!" then recognition dawned on him, "Ronin, it's me boy… it's me!"

The dog growled brushing by him and pushed his snout through the half-open door. He nudged Robbie's unconscious body and getting no response, began whining softly. He prodded Robbie again and again with his muzzle and then licked his face attempting to revive the unconscious man but except for a soft sigh, there was no response.

"It's okay boy, he's going to be okay," VanArcen cooed, stroking Ronin's massive head and trying to calm the distraught animal. "Daddy's going to be okay, don't worry boy."

Meghan was the first to arrive with Allison close behind. The tightness she felt in her chest was more from concern for Robbie than the exertion of running down the sharp incline. She gave VanArcen a worried look, "What happened?"

"I don't know what happened. He's shot and it was Seppo who shot him; that's all I know. I should've have been there. But Robbie wanted me…"

Meghan cut him off, grabbing Ronin, "Help me with him. Get Ronin out of the way."

Meghan tugged at Ronin's collar, "Move, Ronin, you have to move!"

She tried again but the dog stood resolute. Tony joined her and together they tried moving the big dog but he wouldn't budge; it was like pulling against a giant Redwood. When they tried again, jerking at the collar, Ronin let out a low, guttural growl baring his fangs, a warning to back off and back-off they did, neither wanting to chance any further provocation. But her concern for Robbie overrode any fear she might have had and Meghan grabbed his collar again.

"Ronin! Move!" she hissed, "I need to get by. Move now, damn you!" She tugged in desperation but with no luck.

Finally, it was Allison who got Ronin away from the truck. She grabbed his collar and commanded, "Back boy, come back here."

The big dog looked up at her and reluctantly backed away from the door allowing Meghan to get to Robbie's side.

"Oh God, Robbie!" she gently turned his face towards her, "Robbie wake up, baby, please wake up!" But there was no response. She noticed the blood soaked shirt and turned back to Allison, "It looks bad, Allie. He's lost a lot of blood."

"Let's get him to the cabin. I've got some stuff that will stop the bleeding and help him to heal," Allison said.

Though there were four of them, the awkwardness of hoisting a big man up a steep incline proved to be a bigger challenge than they had anticipated and after a few attempts, the realization sank in.

"This is not going to work," Meghan said in frustration. "Maybe we should take him into town, what do you think?"

"No. We have to stop the bleeding now. I'll run up and…" Allison started to say when she was interrupted.

"Wait, I have an idea," VanArcen quipped. He ran to the back of his truck and got the blanket, "Okay, be careful and let's roll him onto this. I'll take the top; Meghan and Allison, the two of you take the backend. Jodie, you lead and make sure I don't trip."

It wasn't perfect but with coordinated determination and a few minor stumbles they finally managed to get Robbie into the cabin. It was more of a challenge getting him to the bedroom through the corridor. There were several stacks of books by the bed and one, lying face-down on the pillow. It was 'Steppenwolf' by Hermann Hesse.

Allison removed the book on the bed and said to Jodie, "Just move them out of the way. Those are Luke's… he loves to read," she indicated to the back wall, "put them there. I'll deal with them later."

They got Robbie's shoes and shirt off and Meghan began wiping away the blood with a damp towel that Allison had given her. She checked his body to make sure there weren't any other wounds.

"Allison, I think the bullet is still in there. I don't see an exit hole. We need to get it out …"

"Let me take a look. I've done this before." Allison said, kneeling down next to Robbie. Her eyes widened in surprise when she saw the old scars, "And I thought Luke was bad!"

"He got those in Afghanistan fighting the Taliban." Meghan whispered and peering over the younger woman's shoulder, asked,

"Is it still in there?"

Allison wiped away some of the blood and used her fingers to carefully probe around the periwound, "Yes, it still in there. Give me a minute; I need to get the first aid kit."

She left the bedroom and returned a few minutes later with a small black satchel, a brown bottle and some clean cotton swabs. She gave the bottle and swabs to Meghan.

"It's hydrogen peroxide. Use it to clean the wound then put some pressure on it to stop the bleeding." Allison instructed, "I have to disinfect the scalpel and forceps in some boiling water so give me a few minutes. If he wakes up, give him a shot of whiskey or moonshine, he's going to need it."

She pointed to an antique buffet cabinet standing against the wall of the corridor across from the bedroom. It had several bottles of different shapes and sizes stacked neatly on top.

"Okay. Hurry, Allison, please hurry, he doesn't look good. We can't let him die, not like this," Meghan pleaded.

"He's not going to die, Meghan, so stop worrying. We'll get him fixed up and like new again. Trust me. I've done this a few times and no one has died yet. You get him cleaned up and put some pressure on the wound; not too hard." With that Allison left for the kitchen.

There was an awkward silence in the room – each of them lost in their own thoughts. While Meghan was preparing the swabs to clean Robbie's wound, the carousel of questions kept spinning endlessly in her mind. *Why did this have to happen to him? Why did we have to fight? Why didn't I just explain what took place instead of getting defensive? He wouldn't have gone to the fights and none of this would have happened. Why, why, why ...*

And, from the moment Robbie was shot, Jodie blamed herself. *All this is because of me. I got Angela killed and now Mr. Olsen got shot trying to save me. I should never have come here. I should never have run away from home. Just like Molly said, I'm nothing but trouble...* Molly was Jodie's older sister and the one who had taken her in when her parents had thrown her out.

For his part, VanArcen was riddled with guilt and self-doubt for not being there to help. *Why didn't I go? I should have insisted. Where was I when he needed me? Hiding behind some fucking trees scratching my ass! It's the story of my life; the frightened fat kid...* He ambled over to the cabinet and grabbed a bottle of Old Smuggler scotch and took a long swig.

He wiped his mouth with the back of his hand and said, "I needed that. I should've gone with him but you know how he is, stubborn as my Uncle Danny. That's the problem with heroes – they're stubborn! Stay with the truck, he says, it is better for us if you stay with the truck. We can make a quick getaway if need be, he says, but the truth is I was hoping he'd say that! I'm a fuckin' loser!"

He took another gulp before offering the bottle to Meghan, "Here, take a drink. It will help with the nerves."

She shook her head, "No thanks. I need to stay focused. I just want him to come back to me, Tony, that's all I want. And, you're not a loser. If it wasn't for you he'd be dead."

Her endless questions were now scrambled with thoughts of Maddie and filled her with an increasing sense of loss. *I've lost Maddie and I can't lose him. I can't. I won't... I won't lose him!* Her eyes began to fill with tears and she began sobbing softly unable to control the feeling of dread brought on by the sight of Robbie's pallor, he was white as a sheet.

Jodie had been standing back watching silently. She walked over to Meghan and placed an arm around her shoulders and with the optimism of youth, she comforted her.

"Don't worry, Meghan. He's strong. This is not going to kill him. I know because he promised to take me to my brother's place and a marine never breaks his promise."

"Thank you, Jodie, I know, those Army Rangers are a tough bunch and if anyone can come out of this it is him but just look at him... I'm so worried."

Allison returned and was getting ready to begin the extraction when Robbie's eyes fluttered open. He tried sitting up not fully cognizant of his surroundings, "Where..." he struggled, looking at the faces gathered around, confusion etched on his face until he saw Meghan.

"Meghan? God, it's good to see you, girl. I..."

She was so relieved that impulse took over. She gave him a quick kiss, her lips brushing softly against his, "Shhh, baby, you need to lie back. We have to get the bullet out."

He held her hand tightly in his and closed his eyes, "Tony, get me a drink. It looks like I'm going to need it."

He took several small gulps of the whiskey, coughed from the burn of the alcohol and immediately grimaced as the pain wracked his body. He sunk back against the pillow and looked at Allison, "Have you done this before? I can walk you through it if you haven't."

"No need, soldier, I've done this several times. Here bite down on this," she answered pushing a small, rolled-up towel into his mouth. "This is going to hurt."

The bullet had entered at an odd angle which created a challenge but after several tense minutes, Allison wiggled the slug loose and worked it slowly out. Robbie was lucky the .44 caliber hadn't fragmented. The ricochet had caused some of the bullet's kinetic energy to dissipate or else it would have blown a hole the size of a fist on exit and would have certainly killed him.

She held the mangled culprit up so he could see it and smiled, "Here it is, Robbie. You're lucky ... it didn't go too deep." She then dropped it into a tin cup, "You may want to keep it. Luke carries both of his in his wallet.”

“No thank you. I have more than enough of those…” Robbie muttered, then lay back and closed his eyes, squeezed Meghan’s hand and said, “I think I’ll take a nap now.”

“You do that. You’ve earned it. I’m almost done – just need to make sure I didn’t miss anything,” Allison said.

She and checked the wound for fragments and satisfied that there weren’t any, she cleaned it thoroughly and applied a rather pungent, viscid salve before bandaging him up. She looked up and saw that Robbie had passed out again.

“What’s that you put on the wound?” Tony asked, “Damn! It smells something awful!

Allison laughed, “Maddie’s secret ointment. It’s a salve made from a concoction of barberry, St. John’s Wort, bindweed and a few other herbs mixed in with clarified bear-fat. It was something she learned from the native Indians. She used it on Luke when he got shot the first time and it saved his life.” She looked over at Meghan, “We need to clean the wound every few hours and apply Maddie’s ointment and don’t worry, you’ll get used to the smell.”

Meghan nodded, “Maybe I should take him home with me. You think it’s safe to move him now that the bullet is out?”

“No. Let him stay here and once he’s out of the woods, we can move him.” She noticed the concern on Meghan’s face, “I’ll take care of him, Meghan; you don’t have to worry.”

“I’m not leaving him… not until he’s better. I just don’t want to put you out.”

“There a bed in the loft. Luke and I can use that. Ryan and Jodie can share a mattress I have in the shed and if Tony wants to stay, he can use the couch. It’s not a problem.” She looked around at them, “We’ll watch him for the next few days. If he if gets a fever or the wound doesn’t begin to heal, we’ll have to take him to the hospital in Monson but I'm pretty sure he'll be fine."

Meghan stood up and hugged her, "Thank you, Allison, I don't have the words … you are amazing!"

The younger woman smiled and said tongue in cheek, "Practice, practice, practice! Now, he needs to rest. Who wants some coffee and cookies?"

"Maybe later. I'm going to stay with him," Meghan said sitting beside Robbie and holding his hand. "Poor baby's been through a lot. And look at Ronin, he laid there all this time just watching, never taking his eyes off Robbie!"

Ronin was lying near the foot of the bed. He hadn't moved since they brought Robbie in. "He's going to be fine, Ronin, just fine. You are such a good boy… I wish you were mine!" Allison cooed petting the big dog.

"Hey, what about me? I've been through a lot too, you know, it's harder for the people watching. Psychologists all agree…"

"Poor Tony! Mama will make you a nice cup of hot chocolate; how about that?" Allison teased, "Come on, that means you too, Jodie, let Robbie rest."

Tony and Jodie followed Allison into the kitchen but it would take an act of God to get Ronin to leave. He laid there, his eyes focused on his master and let out a long sigh.

BEARS, BULLS AND BANDICOOTS

Gilbert Dorsey's place, like many located on the outskirts of Chase River Town, was hidden away behind hilly terrain and the never-ending cover of trees. His driveway was easy to miss so Dorsey had a large obelisk with a painted white cap placed on one side of the entrance and on the other side was a red mailbox with the number 1067 painted in black.

Hank almost drove past the entrance but caught sight of the obelisk and made a sharp right into the driveway, "Fuck! I almost did it again. The only smart thing Gil did was that huge boulder!"

The driveway twisted and turned, snaking through the pine, birch and oak, up and down, straight one moment only to turn sharply the next.

"Never understood why he didn't just cut a straight road to his place," Hank observed peering at the gravel path, irritated that he was forced to drive slowly. "He could've saved himself a shitload of driving."

"Gil likes to do things his way. I asked him the same question when he first had the driveway done and his answer was 'to maintain harmony with the land'." Luke offered.

"Harmony my ass! He's always been a fucking weirdo!" Hank

snapped. "Martha left him two weeks after they got married. I had to go with him to Boston to fetch her back… she was a saint to put up with his shit. Take his accent; he's never been south of Knox and you'd think he grew up in Alabama! What the fuck is that about?"

Luke smiled but didn't answer and was quiet for a while before making the observation, "He may be asleep now. They go to bed early."

"Well, we'll have to wake him up then." Hank replied.

They drove in silence until they came to a fork in the road. Hank slowed down and said, "I haven't been here in a while not since Martha passed on."

"Go left. The other leads down to the creek," Luke said, indicating to the path veering off towards the right.

"Is that where Junior almost drowned?"

"Yeah, but further down where it leads into the river. It's pretty deep there."

A hundred or so yards past the fork, they could see the lights filtering through the trees; a bright pharos leading them to the house.

"Well, they are not asleep, that's for sure."

They parked in front of the house next to the Jeep and a tired looking old Toyota Tundra. Hank glanced over at the cars and said, "That's Marylou's Jeep. I don't recognize the pick-up… they must have guests. Explains why they're awake."

He knocked and a few moments later the door cracked open. It was Marylou. She smiled, holding the door wide, "Hello Hank… Luke. What brings you here at this hour?"

"I need to talk to Gil. Is he awake? It'll only take a few minutes," Hank was brusque but before the woman could respond, a tall, thin man came up behind her.

"What a pleasant surprise. Come on in … we were just talking to our new house guest," Gil Dorsey said with that peculiar accent and stepped aside to let them in.

"I thought you might have guests. I didn't recognize the pick-up and you usually turn in early. I won't keep you; I need a favor."

"Trouble?" Gil Dorsey asked, knowing fully well that the only reason Hank would visit him was if he needed something.

Hank Carlson nodded and said, "Can we talk in private?"

"Let me grab my coat and we can talk on the patio."

They filed in through the narrow, rectangular mudroom to a large open space with cathedral ceilings and French windows that led to a small patio overlooking the property in the back. The interior was an indiscriminate synthesis of styles. The wood beams, plastered walls and stone floors, reminiscent of a French country home, abutted against wooden floors, windows and walls that seemed more like a modern ranch. It was as though the builder had a change of heart during the construction of the home.

There was a pleasant fragrance, a potpourri of flowers and eggs and bacon, mingled with the redolence of burning wood. The soft crackling of the fire from the black, wood stove accompanied the gentle strains of classical music wafting in the background orchestrated the conflation of sounds and styles.

Gil's son, Junior, was standing near the door leading to the bedrooms and seated on an old leather sofa was a slightly built, dark haired man. The stranger stood up when they entered and placed his cup on the side table.

It was Marylou that made the introductions. "Professor Santos this is Hank and Luke Carlson."

The men went through the perfunctory handshakes. The professor, bowed a bit, and said, "Honored to meet you both. I have seen the sign for Carlson's Lumber when driving here. I am assuming that is yours."

Hank ignored the pleasantry and asked, "Where are you from,

Professor Santos?" He wasn't being polite but rather, intrigued by the stranger's presence.

"I am from Tucson. I teach at the University of Arizona," McHenry replied.

"I meant *where*, which country do you come from? Your accent is not American."

"Oh, I misunderstood. I am from Spain – Madrid to be exact," He answered, nervously adjusted his glasses, "I came here to further my education and stayed on. This is truly a fascinating country."

"That it is. And what brings you to our neck of the woods?" Hank's eyes drilled into the smaller man.

From his expression it was clear the professor was uncomfortable being grilled but he continued to answer Hank's questions politely.

"I am a geologist. I am here to study rock formations in the Northeast."

"Ah, a geologist – just what we need, another damn geologist," Hank said looking around for Dorsey.

"Would you care for some coffee?" Marylou asked hoping to intervene and moderate Hank's brusque and impolite manner.

"Not for me," Hank replied.

"I'll have a cup, if it's not too much trouble." Luke said taking off his coat, "It's been a long day."

"No trouble at all, Luke. How do you take it?"

"Black with lots of sugar or honey; I like it sweet. Thanks." Luke turned to the young man who had been silent, "Hey Junior, how's it going?"

"Hi, Luke! I'm doing okay."

"How's the crossbow coming along?"

"Ed took it away from me. He said I would kill someone," Junior replied with a forlorn expression.

"Ed's an ass…" Luke caught himself and said, "Ed shouldn't have done that. I'll show you how to shoot it safely. Would you like that?"

The young man brightened up, "Yes. I would like to learn and go hunting."

"Okay. Give me a few days… I need to sort some stuff out and then we'll go hunting. I'll get your bow back from Ed."

The boy beamed. "We can go to the cabin…"

Just then Gil Dorsey walked in from the bedroom with a heavy coat on, "Junior, it's time for you to go to bed." He waited, "Now! It's late." Then turning to Hank, "Okay Hank, step this way."

He opened the French window and stepped onto the small patio and shut it after them.

From the living room they could see the men walk to the far end of the patio and light up cigarettes in a conspiratorial huddle before they began talking.

"You heard Dad," Marylou spoke gently to her brother, "it is late. Go to bed. Luke will call you when he's ready to take you hunting. And, I promise, I'll make your favorite cookies tomorrow."

The young man brightened up immediately. She watched him leave and sat down on the sofa next to McHenry, "I've been meaning to ask you something - do they still have bullfighting in Madrid?"

"Yes, yes, very much so… in season on Sundays."

"In season?" She was surprised.

"Yes, from the middle of May, during the San Isidro festival, until October. Every Sunday you can watch the bullfight. It is indeed an experience."

"I would think that they would have banned the sport. It is cruel to the animal, don't you agree?"

He studied her, fascinated by her looks, the large liquid, brown eyes and the slight pout of her mouth. "It is a controversial topic and I do not want to offend anyone."

"You won't be offending anyone. I'm trying to understand the appeal." She said and turning to Luke, "What do you think?"

"Rode a bull once and almost got killed. It takes a lot more courage to fight one." Luke smiled and added, "I guess there are inherent differences. We assume that the rest of the world should think and act like us and use a broad brush to adjudicate issues of conscience. In Spain, they don't see it as being cruel. It is a part of their cultural heritage."

Now it was McHenry who was surprised, He hadn't expected Luke to be insightful. "Well said, Luke, may I call you by your first name?" And without waiting for an answer he continued, "The bull, Toro de Lidia, is truly magnificent. He is bred for courage, aggression and stamina. He is a natural fighter and his sole purpose is to one day fight in the Plaza de Toros. Who are we to take that from him?"

"You could say that about dogs, Pit Bulls in particular. But, if you rear them with kindness and training they are very sweet dogs and despite their fierce reputation, make wonderful family pets." Marylou countered.

"I understand but then the question is whether we have the right to alter their natural propensities, to curtail their true purpose? The relationship between genetics and environment is a gray area and when it comes to tradition versus animal rights, especially when the people screaming loudest are outsiders; it becomes a complex issue and one that involves not just tradition but politics." He paused then pressed the argument, "I could ask the same of boxing or mixed martial arts – why would those sports not be considered cruel?"

As soon as McHenry mentioned mixed martial arts, Luke became fully engaged. Until then he was only curious about the stranger.

"Wait a minute, there is a considerable difference! Two men, or women," Luke gave Marylou a quick smile, "agreeing to fight one another is way different from a bull that really has no choice."

"I concede that. But what about purpose, I mean true purpose. Shouldn't we all be doing what we were born to do?"

"In an ideal world, yes. But in the real world finding our true purpose is influenced by several factors – societal norms, environment, opportunity… I may be the best ballet dancer ever born but if my parents don't have the money or the opportunity to indulge this talent, I will remain a poor farm boy."

"Yes, but a true dancer will dance and the poor farm boy will be the best dancer on the farm. Andrea Bocelli was born into a family of poor farmers in a small village in Tuscany but his voice was so beautiful he became a world famous singer. You cannot repress true talent." The 'professor' countered.

"So to extend this to a different aspect of human nature, are killers born or are they created? And is it possible to suppress the killer's instincts?" Luke asked, a slight smile playing on his lips.

"It is my humble opinion that some men, and women, are genetically predisposed to killing. Does that mean they go round murdering others, certainly not but given the right circumstance they would not hesitate to slit your throat or put a bullet through your head."

"That applies to almost anyone, I mean, under the right circumstance."

"No, not true. I spent several summers in India … now, *there* is a remarkable country. Over seventy percent of the population is pure vegetarian and many of them would not kill another human under any circumstance."

"And that is why they were conquered so often." Luke offered, "The Persians, Greeks, Afghans, Portuguese and British all played a part in destroying arguably the oldest human culture."

McHenry was now concerned. He had made the mistake of taking Luke for a mindless pretty-boy but it was becoming obvious that he was far from that. *Did he bring up the genetics of assassins by chance or did he sense something? I need to be careful.*

"That is a different discussion to be had. The benefits and moral transgressions of human conquest and exploration has been a topic of much discussion. But it is not to be confused with the merits of cultural traditions like bullfighting."

"I disagree. It goes to the heart of the matter. If you bring up purpose then it relates directly to genetics and in the broader sense, to the purpose of all predators and killers." Luke paused but neither McHenry or Marylou said anything so he continued, "Conquerors were intrinsically killers but when it comes to animals, the question of morality does not exist. Male lions kill other male lions to gain breeding rights – natural selection. Those bulls would kill the bullfighter given half the chance and they *have* killed many. The question is does it matter how and why we kill. We kill millions of cattle, chicken, lamb, goats and fish to feed our never ending gluttony. We justify this by telling ourselves that they were bred for that purpose. The moral imperative seems to one of convenience. Take war; we send out soldiers to kill other soldiers, men that they don't know, and justify that by calling it war. Most wars serve a singular purpose and that is financial. I would argue that the war in the arena is purer and more pristine than any fought by men on a battlefield. Ernest Hemmingway was an ardent fan of bullfighting or as it is known in Spain, *corrida de toros*. In his book 'Death in the Afternoon', he describes it as, and I quote, *'the only art in which the artist is in danger of death and in which the degree of brilliance in the performance is left to the fighter's honor.'* I memorized that passage because it is so beautiful, sad and true."

"God! I am impressed, Luke, I had no idea …" Marylou blurted out, her expression revealing her astonishment. McHenry tried hard to hide his surprise too. He realized that his notes and background research on Luke was grossly inadequate.

"Impressed that I can read? Or that I am not as stupid as I look." Luke parried back.

"I didn't mean that!" She could feel her cheeks flush, her tone, instantly apologetic, "I mean, Hemmingway? Come on Luke, not many around here even know who he was! We're talking about Chase River for goodness sake!"

Luke laughed and said to McHenry, "People judge others too quickly, don't you think?"

"I too am guilty, sir, and must agree with Marylou. Your knowledge about bullfighting and Hemmingway is beyond impressive. It is astounding! He is one of my favorite American authors and I would be hard-pressed to quote any of his passages."

Luke smiled and finished by saying, "The bull and the matador are engaged in the purest of contests, a life and death struggle. The bull is simply fulfilling its purpose – to kill or be killed by el Torero, the bullfighter. The fact that we find entertainment in that speaks more about us than the sport."

McHenry threw up his arms and laughed, "Brilliant! Bravo, bravo! I could not have said it more succinctly and it tells me that I should stick to geology. You make a convincing argument, Luke."

"I'm not saying I like the sport because I don't. I appreciate and respect Hemmingway's perspective and his ability to write about in a manner that makes it beautiful. But, I am not going to judge other traditions based on a cultural reference that is so far removed from theirs." Luke answered, making his position clear.

"I am still in shock! However, I think that the right environment and conditions can overcome genetic predispositions. I wish I had something as elegant to quote to support my argument but I don't. It is just how I feel." Marylou said and got up, "More coffee?"

"No, I'm good." Luke answered.

She looked at McHenry raising her eyebrows, "How about you, Lorenzo, coffee?"

"I am tempted but it will keep me awake and I should get to sleep. It was a pleasure speaking with you, Luke, a real pleasure." He turned to leave then stopped and asked Marylou, "Is there a guide I can hire for a couple of days... just to show me around the mountains?"

"Tony VanArcen, wouldn't you say, Luke?

"Yeah, he's a Forest Ranger or something like that. He should be able to help you. Give me your phone number and I'll have him call you."

"I have no cellphone service here. Can I impose on you, Marylou, and have you introduce me to the gentleman? And, only if it is not an inconvenience."

"I'd be happy to." Marylou replied with a smile.

"You are too kind. Thank you." He looked again at Luke, peering at him, and said, "You do not look anything like your brother. Are you really brothers?"

"We *are* brothers and that's none of your business." Luke snapped, his face turning cold.

"Oh, I meant no offense. I am sorry. Truly, I..."

The French window opened and Hank walked in followed by Dorsey. He gave them a cursory look before speaking softly to the undertaker, "I want this kept under wraps. I don't want Bradley or Dolan to know just yet. Is that clear?"

"Yes. I'll go over to the Bruckman place right now and do what I can. Do you want me to take care of all of them or just Ray?"

"All. I'll send some guys over tomorrow to clean up the place." Hank turned to Luke, "Let's go. It's getting late – we don't want to keep them up."

As they said their goodbyes, McHenry took the opportunity to address Luke, "I am truly sorry. I did not mean to pry or insult you in any way."

"Not a problem. No offence taken." Luke replied, he had all but forgotten about the earlier remark.

"What was that about?" Hank asked once they were in the Range Rover.

"It was nothing. He was poking his nose where he shouldn't. There's something strange about that guy. I can't put my finger on it but I'll figure it out."

Hank glanced at Luke, "I thought so too but then we don't get too many foreigners here."

"Yeah, maybe it's just that."

It began raining, a drizzle first and then before they were able to leave Dorsey's driveway, it poured.

WOLVES, WOLVERINES AND VIXENS

When the Carlsons had left Marylou turned to her father, "What did he want?"

"Ray Carlson is dead. As is Jericho and Angela. They were murdered by Seppo," Dorsey replied.

She was shocked. "Oh God, no! Angela? That pretty black girl who works at the Sleepy Crest?"

"Work would be one way to put it. They all work for Hank in some capacity or the other. Seppo works for Hank too but he's gone stark raving mad. He kidnapped Angela and Jodie from the Sleepy Crest and took them to Bruckman's place. He's always had a sadistic streak in him but this is beyond crazy."

Marylou was silent, digesting what she had just heard, "How did Ray and Jericho get involved?"

"Hank had sent them with Ed to check the farm house. He's been thinking of turning that place into a Bed & Breakfast like those in Monson. They saw Seppo in the barn with Angela's dead body and Jodie tied to a chair and all hell broke loose. Ray and Jericho ended up dead and Ed killed Seppo."

"Seppo's dead!" She was incredulous, "Is Ed okay? And, what about the girl?"

"She ran off during the melee. Ed's okay, he's upset about Ray and Jericho but okay. Well, I had better be going."

"Now? At this hour? It's raining, Dad!" Marylou was even more incredulous.

"Yes. I have to take care of it now. And not a word to anyone, Marylou, not one word!" her father glared at her, speaking sternly. "He took care of the bills when your mother was in the hospital; all of it and never asked me to pay him back. He also took care of Junior's bills… I owe him this and you will not breach that trust."

"I won't say anything. Take your raincoat, it's pouring."

It was only then that they noticed McHenry standing quietly, listening to them.

"Sorry, I didn't mean to eavesdrop. I was waiting to ask about breakfast – what time do we have breakfast?" McHenry asked.

"Around six-thirty or seven," Dorsey answered.

"Dad, you're going to be up late. I'll stay over and make breakfast. You can sleep in and get up late." She looked at McHenry, "What time would you like to get up?"

"Breakfast at seven o'clock is fine. Can I make coffee a bit earlier? I like a cup of coffee first but I do not want to disturb the household."

"I'll have a pot on by six and breakfast at seven," Marylou answered. "You won't be disturbing anyone. Your bedroom is in that direction, down that corridor," she pointed to a doorway directly opposite from where Junior had been standing. "Dad and Junior are down this way so you don't have to worry."

"Marylou, you don't have to do this. I can take care of it," her father tried dissuading her.

"I want to do it. And, I have been meaning to bake some cookies for Junior so it's not a problem."

Dorsey studied his daughter and seeing that it was pointless to argue, relented, "Okay then, don't wait up. I'll most probably be gone for a few hours." He hugged his daughter, shook McHenry's hand and left.

The ensuing silence was electric. McHenry and Marylou stood studying each other, basking in the warmth and excitement of mutual attraction.

She smiled and spoke first, "Well, professor, I hadn't planned on staying but it looks like fate has other plans."

"I am glad but I think you know that," he replied, fidgeting nervously with the buttons on his coat, looking awkwardly uncomfortable.

The boundaries of the charade were blurring. Now that Seppo Heikkinen was dead, the clearly defined characteristics separating the assassin from the professor had faded and he was suddenly unsure of his purpose at least until he spoke to Shayk's man, Izhutin. Faced with a woman he was clearly attracted to, he was at a loss and stood there gaping at her.

"The guest room used to be my room. I still have some clothes in there – do you mind if I get something to sleep in?" Marylou interrupted his thoughts.

"You are more than welcome to use the room. I'd be happy to sleep on the couch. Really, it is not a problem," McHenry offered, being chivalrous.

"Thank you but I'll be fine. Junior's room has two beds and I've slept there before and you've had a long day. You will need the rest."

He followed her to the bedroom and stood by the door watching her go through a large armoire. Watching her bend over the drawers, he could feel himself getting aroused. He took off his coat and held it in front of him and waited patiently while she rummaged through the drawers.

His mind was buzzing with fantasies and possibilities when she stood up and held up a tiny lingerie, smiling seductively, "What do you think?"

He didn't say anything; he felt a huge lump in his throat. The only women in McHenry's life were those he paid to have sex with not because he couldn't get a woman but because it was less complicated and suited his need for anonymity. He rarely if ever used the same woman twice. This, however, was different.

"I'm sure you… you, umm, you would look ravishing," he stuttered his Adam's apple bobbing in his neck. His mouth was dry and his pecker harder than a popsicle.

She stood there looking at him, vacillating between desire and reason, then walked over and gave him a quick peck on the cheek. He tried putting his arms around her but she slipped away.

"I think we need to slow it down a bit," her voice was husky. "Play your cards right and you may get to see me in this!"

She smiled seductively before waltzing down the corridor to Junior's bedroom.

"Sleep tight, little angel, and don't let the bedbugs bite!" he whispered watching the door close behind her.

The disappointment did not dampen the incredible thrill he felt, the titillating desire she evoked in him. He was a killer of men and she was no less of a man-killer; though death in each instance was defined a bit differently. The street cliché, *"Sweet as sugar, hard as ice, hurt me once and I'll kill you twice,"* flashed through his mind – a caveat to proceed with caution.

He was wrapped up in the poetic beauty of this development, a magnum opus like another of his favorite movies: 'This Property Is Condemned'. He would take a cold shower and dream of *his* Natalie Wood. She would be Alva Starr to his Owen Legate. And to think he almost turned this assignment down! Fate or karma or whatever it was had other plans for him.

Allison Carlson

KARMIC DISSOLUTIONS

VanArcen woke up to the tantalizing smell of pancakes and fresh coffee. The couch was surprisingly comfortable and he had slept like a baby. He got up and stretched and looked across at the kitchen and smiled. Luke as seated at the small dining table drinking coffee and watching Allison flipping flapjacks. She was wearing a pair of tight jeans and a short, scoop-neck tank top. Her hair, tied in a pouf bun, shimmered golden in the sunshine streaking through the skylights. They did make a stunning pair; transcendental travelers reincarnated from an earlier time.

He greeted them, "'Morning! That smells scrumptious." Then looking towards the bedroom asked, "How is our soldier boy doing?"

"Robbie's fine. A bit of a fever but the wound is healing well," Allison replied and added, "the coffee is fresh and breakfast will be ready in a few minutes."

VanArcen waddled to the bedroom to check in on Robbie. He was asleep with Ronin by the bedside. The big dog raised his head and recognizing VanArcen, wagged his tail. He could find no sign of Meghan, Ryan or Jodie.

He knelt next to Ronin and stroked his head, "And how's my buddy doing?" then speaking softly he spoke to Robbie, "You're going to be fine, Bronson, just fine. You had me worried there for a while, brother."

He came back to the kitchen, "Where's Meghan?"

"When she heard that Seppo was dead, she decided to take Ryan to her mother's. She thought it would be a good idea for Jodie to join him so they wouldn't be in the way here," Allison replied. "She's also going to stop at her place to get some clothes and toiletries."

VanArcen poured himself a cup of coffee and sat across from Luke, "What time did you get in?"

"Late. Allison conveniently forgot to tell me about Ronin. I walk in, soaking wet, and there's a giant beast, eyes glowing in the dark, snarling and frothing at the mouth, ready to tear me apart!"

VanArcen furrowed his brow and said, "I didn't hear a thing."

"How could you? You were snoring so loudly I'm surprised Allie heard me! You sounded like a freakin' freight train!" Luke replied.

"Hey, I had a hard day and I always sleep well when it rains," was VanArcen's excuse.

"I'm sorry baby! Ronin's been such a doll that it didn't occur to me. I have to admit that I sleep better when it rains but I heard him growl and jumped out of bed," Allison said and came over and gave Luke a kiss on top of his head. "I want one ... I want a dog just like him."

VanArcen rolled his eyes and smiled, "Oh-oh! Trouble!"

"She was there in the nick of time or else we'd be having a double funeral in this family!"

"You're so dramatic! He calmed down almost immediately," Allison reproached ruffling his hair and went back to the stovetop. "Luke, I'm not kidding, I want one ... so you better start looking!"

Luke shook his head and smiled, he knew better than to argue,

"We'll get one though I'm not sure where. I'll talk to Robbie when he's better."

He took a sip of coffee before speaking to VanArcen, "Hank and I stopped over at Gil's place before we went to see Emma. We had to let her know that Ray was gone."

"I'm sorry about that, Jodie told us about Ray and about what took place. Do you know what happened to Seppo, I mean, how did he die?"

"I got the story from Hank. Ed rammed Seppo's van and it went up in flames. He watched it burn and according to Ed, no one came out of the van. With Seppo, I would have made damn sure... I mean, I'd want to see his carcass. I'll be going there later to check the site."

"I hope he burns in hell!" VanArcen spat out.

"He deserves worse," Luke growled softly then changed the subject, "Tony, there's a professor staying at Gil's. He's looking for a guide to show him around for a couple of days... mainly in the mountains. He's a geologist. I suggested your name. I hope you don't mind."

"No, not at all! I can use the money. And speaking of money, I have Robbie's winnings with me. It's in the truck. I'd feel a lot better if you kept it for him."

"Sure. Not a problem. Just give it to Allison – she takes care of the money in this house. In fact, she takes care of everything including me."

"And you'd better not forget that, mister!" Allison quipped, smiling and looking back at them.

"How can I? You make it a point to remind me every day!"

She laughed, a sweet, soft tittering laugh, "You're so full of it!"

Luke got up and went over and hugged her from behind, nuzzling his face in the nape of her neck and kissing her cheek.

"Behave! We have guests," Allison playfully admonished.

"You smell good," he said and slapped her behind before returning to his chair.

"It looks like Robbie's in good hands and I need to get back to work. I have a ton of reports to submit. Did the professor say when or what time?" VanArcen asked.

"No. I guess Marylou will call you or bring him to your place."

"Did you notice that ever since Robbie got here, there's hasn't been a dull moment," VanArcen said more to himself than to the others, "and, I could use a zillion dull moments. So while he's on the mend, I'll wrap up some of the must-do stuff."

Allison brought over a stack of pancakes, bacon and sausages and placed them on the table alongside the maple syrup, "Dig in. There's more batter so go to town. I'll get another pot of coffee brewing."

"After breakfast, I'll go over to Maddie's and take her over to the mortuary and speak to Gil. I have to do that first thing today. I locked the place last night and put the 'We're Closed' sign up," Luke's voice was strained.

"I want to see her, Luke, so can you wait till I get there?" Allison asked, adding, "I have to stay here until Meghan gets back."

"Sure, just let me know once you're done. I'll go back later to take her to Gil's." The thought of Maddie damped their mood.

"I can't believe Maddie's gone. But, she's in a better place. I wonder what is going to happen to the gas station and the property behind it?" Allison mused rhetorically.

"I don't know. I don't think she had any kin. I just don't want Hank to get it... he's been after her for years; pressuring her to sell. Anyway, it doesn't matter now."

"Why don't you run it, Luke, you were like a son to her," VanArcen suggested.

"Yes, I loved her like a mother but it was hers to give and

whoever she has left it to will run it; not me."

"Maybe she left it to you," Allison added.

"Maybe but I don't want to think about it. Right now I want to take care of her and make sure she has the best funeral ever. Do you remember when we were kids and Mom was sick?"

The memory of Maddie taking care of them as little children brought memories crashing back, driving home the fact that they would never see her again – not alive.

Allison teared up. "Don't do this. You're going to make me cry."

"Sorry, baby, it's just that I can't seem to get her out of my mind. All the things she did for us. She told me that I would have to make a choice and now it all makes sense," Luke tried to mollify his sister.

The men ate in silence while Allison went into the bedroom. Robbie was still fast asleep. She made a quick assessment of the wound and satisfied, leaned over and kissed him on his lips, a soft lingering kiss, before pulling back. *What are you doing?* She asked herself then smiled, *Naughty Allison!* She straightened up and gave Robbie a long look, *I wonder how it would feel to have you inside me, to taste you and to make love to you? Ah, naughty, naughty Allison. What would Luke say? He's better not say anything. What's good for the goose is good for the gander - he had his fling with Meghan. And since Robbie is Meghan's man, it would be poetic justice!*

From the moment she met him, she had been drawn to him. It wasn't that she was bored with Luke, far from it, but the attraction she felt for Robbie was something new; it invaded her erotic tabula rasa and stoked the fires of desire burning in her. Maddie's death and the sadness she felt only heightened her feelings in ways she couldn't explain. It was Maddie who told her not to worry when she confided in her about Robbie. She took her by the hand and said that things would play out the way they were meant to. *Maddie was always right! Things are destined to happen and there's nothing we can do to change that. We are but puppets manipulated by the master puppeteer.*

She dragged herself away and said to the big dog, "Come on Ronin, I'll feed you. I've got a nice, juicy steak for my boy!"

Ronin got up, gave Robbie a wistful look and followed her. It was a surprise to everyone, the way the monster dog had bonded with Allison. He listened to every word she said. It was as though he realized that his mater's life was in the hands of this blonde tigress.

PLAYING WITH FIRE

VanArcen was working on an overdue report when he heard the grating sound of wheels on gravel. He peeked through the curtains and saw Marylou's Wrangler pulling up to the front. Behind her was a large gray, pick-up with Arizona license plates. *Here comes the professor!* He thought to himself as he strolled out onto the porch. He leaned over, elbows resting on the banister, waiting for them.

"Hey Marylou, it's good to see ya!" he greeted the woman as she walked up the stoop, "It's been too long, eh?"

Following close was a well-dressed man, slender of build and about the same height as VanArcen. He took the steps two at a time; his movements, effortless, reminding him of a gymnast.

The woman hugged VanArcen, "It's good to see you too, Tony. And the reason it's been so long is because you're never up and about! You work far too much."

She turned to McHenry, "This is Professor Lorenzo Santos from the University of Arizona, and this here is the one and only Tony VanArcen." The last part was said with exaggerated flair.

VanArcen laughed, "You flatter me, girl! Good to meet you, Prof. Or would you prefer Lorenzo? I ain't about to call you Professor Santos. So what will it be?"

The diminutive man smiled, "Lorenzo or Enzo would be

perfectly fine, Tony, and yes, we can drop all formalities since we will be spending a lot of time together."

"A lot of time? Luke said a couple of days… is it more than that?"

"I'm not sure. Can we play it by ear?" the professor questioned.

"Well, if it is more than three days, I'll introduce you to my neighbor, Paddy Haskell, he knows this place almost as well as I do and he has more time on his hands. I do have to get back to my regular job. Unlike a lot of people around here, present company excluded, I have to work for a living!"

Marylou laughed at the derogatory reference to the locals, a throaty cachinnate, "Paddy is a good man but I thought he doesn't venture up in the mountains these days or does he?"

"For the right amount of money he'll climb Mount Everest bum knee and all!"

She laughed again.

The man studied VanArcen before speaking, "That won't be necessary. I like you Tony; I like your honesty. We will try and get it done in two days so I can work without putting you out. And as unpleasant as it is, what about the commercial aspect of our relationship?"

"What?" Tony wasn't sure if he heard the man right. Between the man's accent and enunciation, he was having a hard time following him.

"He means the cost; what do you charge for your services?" Marylou explained.

"Oh, it's not unpleasant at all, at least not for me. It is an essential part of any commerce. I charge fifty dollars per person per day for groups of ten or more and a hundred per person per day for groups of five to nine. For a single person, it is three hundred per day and you will have to bring lunch for the two of us. This gets you six hours each day. Anything more than six hours will cost an additional fifty dollars per hour. How does that sound?"

The man thought for a moment before answering, "That is very reasonable. As far as lunch goes, I would be more than happy to reimburse you for your inconvenience. However, it would be almost impossible for me to bring lunch."

"Not a problem. I will bring lunch and we can settle later," VanArcen extended his hand, "Deal?"

"Yes, we have a deal," McHenry smiled, shaking VanArcen's hand. His grip was firm and surprisingly strong.

"One last thing; you will have to come here… any time after six o'clock in the AM is good. I'll be damned if I make that convoluted trip through that maze Gil calls his driveway!"

They all laughed and Marylou said, "That's Dad and his harmony with nature. Growing up, he used to go on about Feng Shui and Wabi Sabi and things that sounded like Greek to me… all about finding beauty in the imperfect and blending with nature. It used to drive Mom nuts!"

"Ah, there is a lot more to it. In India they have a similar aesthetic, they call it Vastu Shastra. Ancient cultures knew the importance of maintaining harmony with nature. It was the West that decided to subjugate our environment and the consequences are evident. Your father was ahead of his time."

"In more ways than one and trust me, it wasn't easy," Marylou replied and added, "I'm late for work so I'll leave you both to it."

"When will I see you again?" McHenry asked her, reluctant to see her go, "I wish you were joining us."

"Like Tony said, some of us have to work… I'll come by this evening and you can explain what you found today. I still have to bake those cookies for Junior." She looked at him, her expression inscrutable, and added with a coquettish smile, "You haven't seen the last of me yet, Lorenzo Santos!"

"That in itself has made my day," he replied bowing slightly, thrilled by her flirtatious banter.

"You're going to have to move your truck so I can get out."

She gave VanArcen a hug and followed McHenry. They stopped by the Jeep and spoke softly before she gave him a quick kiss on the mouth and got into her vehicle.

Wow! A kiss? Things are moving fast around here! Good for her, she deserves better than that Neanderthal, Greg Humphry. She needs a sophisticated man who appreciates and understands her needs. VanArcen smiled to himself. He had liked Marylou from the onset of their first meeting and despite her reputation of promiscuity, he thought of her as a friend. It didn't hurt that she was also one of the prettiest girls in Chase River. *Who exactly was the prettiest? It was a toss-up between Allison, Meghan and her... and maybe Sandra Kedzierski but ever since Sandra got married she's been packing on the pounds. Maybe she's pregnant.* His mind was beginning to wander. *I'll stick to Liz; she is pretty enough for me. Let the wolves fight over the mating rights of these alpha females!*

He had no misgivings at all - under that polished exterior and strange accent, the professor was no lamb but was indeed a wolf.

"Can we leave now or would you like me to come back in a few hours?" McHenry asked after Marylou had left.

"Come on in. Give me a few minutes and we'll leave. Just tell me what you're looking for and I'll lay out some options."

"I'm here to study the rock formation in the Appalachian Trail. So, anything similar to Saddleback or the Sandy River should be fine. I did some research and Moose Head Point would be a good start."

"That's fine as long as we don't wander onto Luke Carlson's property. He's doesn't take kindly to strangers trespassing. The last time hunters wandered onto his property, two of them got shot. I think one died and the other was in the hospital for a pretty long time. "

"Really? He doesn't seem like the type," McHenry feigned genuine surprised.

"And what type is that? Don't let his looks and friendly nature fool you, Prof, Luke is not one to be messed with."

"I don't want any trouble and I certainly don't want to get shot. We can choose another location."

"We can go to Moose Head. We'll stay clear of his land and see how things go. How does that sound?"

"Great, you lead and I'll follow." McHenry said then asked, "I have to make a phone call to my office. May I use your phone?"

"Sorry, Prof, I don't have a landline and there is no cell signal here. But you can make the call at the gas station. I have to fill-up and get us some lunch before we head out. The signal is pretty good there."

During the drive to the gas station, McHenry started by asking questions about Marylou. He made sure that the queries were innocuous and didn't raise any suspicions. He asked about her mother and when she had passed and about Junior's accident and about Gil Dorsey's work; questions that could be easily attributed to the curiosity of an outsider. But the more VanArcen talked the more probing the questions got.

"I guess Marylou takes after her mother though there is some resemblance to Mr. Dorsey. Junior, however, looks a lot like his father."

"Yes, Marylou does look like her mother. Martha Dorsey was a lovely woman. She died of cancer and I wouldn't wish that on my worst enemy," VanArcen elaborated.

"That is too bad. And, speaking of familial resemblance, I must say that there is no resemblance between Luke and Hank. Luke has the looks of a movie star and Hank, well, he doesn't!" McHenry said, giving Tony the opening to expand on the family.

"They are brothers but I have my doubts too. You don't ask too many questions around here, Prof. People get their hackles up and you could end up dead. But Allison, Luke's sister, and he look like their mother. I guess Hank takes after his father's side."

"Interesting. They also have very different personalities. Luke was very friendly not like Hank at all."

"Ah, Hank's the boss. The family has run Chase River for as long as there was a town here. I remember their father - old man Carlson. He was a tough, hard man and now it's Hank. He's used to giving orders, telling people what to do, that is, all except Luke. There are some people who live by their own set of rules and Luke is one of them. No one tells Luke what to do, not even Hank."

"Everyone has a boss - maybe his wife tells him what to do?" McHenry quipped.

"Not Luke, he isn't married," VanArcen was about to mention Allison but thought better of it and added, "But he does have a son. You haven't met Meghan Hollier but Luke used to date her and they have a son, Ryan."

"Are they still dating?"

"No, they broke up a long time ago, just before Ryan was born. I think Ryan is about four now and is the spitting image of his father."

"That's interesting indeed. So, does Ryan stay with his mother or with Luke?"

VanArcen's loquacious personality couldn't contain himself, he had to expound on what he knew about the people of Chase River Town.

"He stays with Meghan. Right now, they are staying at Luke's cabin on Moose Head Point. Well, Meghan is… it's a long story. You should meet my buddy, Robbie. He is convalescing there. He was shot by one of Hank's goons."

"Oh my god, this place is like the wild west. Are you sure I'll be safe here?" He was careful not to overdo the dramatics.

"Don't worry, Prof, you're going to be fine. The lunatic, Seppo, is dead..." he paused then added, "I should write a book on him, you know, like they did with that psychopath, Ted Bundy. I'd rake in millions of dollars. Hey, we're almost there, do you have a preference - tuna fish, ham and cheese, what would you like?."

"Ham and cheese is fine with tomatoes and lettuce and a cup of coffee, please."

While VanArcen was inside the gas station's convenience center, McHenry made the call to Izhutin. "I don't have much time so pay attention. Seppo Heikkinen is dead. Ed Carlson killed him. What would you like me to do?"

"Wait one second."

He could hear the faint exchange in Russian and then, "This is Shayk. Are you sure about that?"

"I heard it from Hank and Luke Carlson," he replied. The details involving Marylou and her father were irrelevant so he wasn't about to mention them, not yet anyway.

"Okay, then we must change the course of action. Luke has a son. His name is Ryan. The boy's mother is Meghan Hollier. Grab the kid and wait for instructions. Do not hurt the boy, just keep him somewhere for a while. You treat him well and wait until I speak to Hank and..."

McHenry heard Izhutin speaking in the background. Shayk said, "Wait a minute."

The animated exchange in Russian continued before Shayk was back on the phone, "My people think Luke will be a problem. You need to make sure that this doesn't escalate so *if* Luke comes after you, release the boy. I am trying to send a message not create an all-out war!"

McHenry was silent giving the new proviso some thought before he answered, "I don't usually take contracts that involve kids. You will pay extra for this. Add twenty percent to the amount to be transferred when the job is done. Is that clear?"

The response was immediate. "I think Seppo was a far more difficult target. Snatching the kid and keeping him safe should be a walk in the park. You are being paid a premium and this... this is taking advantage, like holding me hostage."

"Listen carefully because I'm only going to say it once. *You* changed the terms of the contract. I wouldn't have accepted this if it involved a child," McHenry's voice was a sibilant hiss.

"Really? What about those kids in Nairobi? Or is it only white kids?"

"That was a mistake; a fucking accident!" McHenry bristled, "And, I find your implication that I am a racist distasteful. I am a lot of things but not that." He got himself under control and continued, "I did my homework – the boy is only four. Luke Carlson is a dangerous man and no one, not even me, would want that kind of headache. And it just cost you another ten percent for implying that I am some kind of Nazi asshole. Transfer an additional thirty percent and if you don't like my terms, we can..." McHenry saw VanArcen walking back and said, "I have to go. Are you agreeable to my terms or we can stop this right here and now and call it quits?"

"Okay, agreed but I'm not ha..." The line went dead.

McHenry took the sim card out, chewed it and spat it out before heading back to the pick-up.

"Did you get through to your office?" VanArcen asked.

"Yes, thank you, this stop gave me enough time to go over my schedule. They don't seem to miss me too much so I'm all set."

"I got you roast beef. They were out of ham and cheese and the roast beef smelled outrageous. If you would rather have a slice of pizza we can swap. I'm not fussy as you can see," he tapped his slightly protruding belly, smiled and added, "Here's the coffee, I got you a large."

"Roast beef is fine and thanks, I do like my coffee maybe a little too much," McHenry replied.

The mention of Nairobi and the children brought back the entire fiasco. After years of sleepless nights and nightmares, he had managed to bury the incident, come to terms and forgive himself. It was the one hit he had messed up and now it was back. His mind was suddenly riddled with the smiling faces of the Njoku kids and along with their memory, regret and remorse tore at his heart. The girls, pretty little dolls, dressed in the school uniforms were ten and eight and the youngest was a boy, a mischievous little rascal, only five. How was he to know that the school bus would break down that day? And, that Njoku would be giving them a ride to school? He should have made sure. He was always so careful, he should've, could've... *enough, enough damn it!* He would make Shayk pay, no, not in money but in kind. He would have to figure out a way.

Collateral Damage

JUSTIFICATION

Shayk handed the cell phone back to Izhutin. They were in Shayk's penthouse office located next to the Hyatt House in Jersey City. The office overlooked the Hudson River with a spectacular view of the Manhattan skyline.

"What was that about Nairobi?" Izhutin asked Shayk.

"It was a long time ago. McHenry was hired to take out a candidate running against the President in Kenya. It was a lucrative contract but as you can imagine, very dangerous. McHenry was picked because he had a reputation of taking care of business without creating any waves and he worked alone," Shayk answered.

"And?"

"The man, Francis Njoku, had his kids in the car when the bomb went off – killed every one. Three kids, Njoku and his driver."

"Did McHenry know about the children?" Izhutin was shocked.

"He claims it was an accident but he must have known. You've dealt with this man… he's fuckin' anal about details."

"Shit! That is cold. Children are off limits. We shouldn't have hired this animal."

"You don't send a goldfish to kill a shark – what you need is a bigger shark. Hank is a fucking slippery shark. These gopniks in the mountains are not like us. They are like the fucking Chechens!" Shayk said. He studied his man, lightly tapping his forehead, and asked, "How do you feel about black kids?"

"Why? Is there a difference? Kids are kids, boss, and it is never good to hurt kids."

"I know and I agree. It's just that a lot of our guys are… well, they don't like the blacks."

"They are idiots and most probably jealous because those assholes have big fuckin' dicks!" Izhutin replied.

Shayk shook his head, "There you go again with the dicks!"

"I'm just saying," Izhutin replied with a smile and continued, "I know a few black people and they are just like us… not any different. So what is next, we don't like Spanish people? Why, because their hair is black? Or the Chinese because they're eyes are different? People are fuckin' crazy and waste too much time on this bullshit. We have enough problems without this rubbish."

"You're a good man, Andrei, a fuckin' pussy loving hound but a good man."

"Boss, all men like pussy. I just happen to like all kinds; black, brown, yellow, white… if there was green pussy, I'd fuck it."

"If the woman has a green pussy, you better rush her to the hospital!"

"I'd fuck her first then go to the hospital. You know, get two for one treatment. My father was a Shylock."

Shayk laughed, "You are a bit mad, Andrei, but you are the only one I really trust."

"Thanks, boss, I'm here for you anytime you need me, you know that. Except if a bitch with a green pussy turns up then you're going to have to wait until I take care of business!"

"That will be all of ten seconds!"

They laughed and Izhutin said, "Let's go find some girls to fuck."

"Now you are talking Izhutin language!" Shayk rejoined.

They left for their favorite whorehouse but in the back of his mind, Shayk was already scheming of ways to get even with McHenry. It wasn't about the money, this was chicken shit to him, but he didn't like being taken advantage of and he would square things up if that's the last thing he did.

SURVIVAL OF THE BEAST

Seppo Heikkinen knew he was hurt and hurt badly. He couldn't move his right arm without the shooting pain running up into his shoulder and his head throbbed like a son-of-a-bitch. The skin on his scorched body was excoriated and raw, prickling with every move and parts of his face and blond Mohawk were singed black. His shirt and trousers had all but burnt away in the fiery aftermath of the crash leaving his body exposed to the elements.

He had been jettisoned out of the van as it careened and tumbled out of control and had landed a few feet from where it came to rest. His head had smashed against a large boulder and he was rendered unconscious and as luck would have it, his body was shielded by a dense overgrowth of bushes. But luck was a fickle mistress and though he was concealed, he wasn't far enough away from the blaze to avoid its calefactory wrath. The only thing that had really saved him was Ed Carlson's ineptitude. He was fortunate that Hank's nephew wasn't a thorough man or he would have surely been dead. If it had been Luke or for that matter, Hank, they would have walked down to the bottom of the culvert to make sure and would have discovered his body, badly scorched and unconscious but alive, and would have finished him off. But Ed didn't, and that oversight had saved him.

It started to drizzle, the raindrops stabbing at him like a thousand knives. The pain erupted across the rawness of his face and body in a choreographed symphony of pinpricks. He felt agony like never before; a seething pain which cumulatively ravaged the threshold of his tolerance causing him to bite down and clench his teeth to stop from screaming. Every drop hurt and every move hurt more. He blinked and surveyed the surroundings determined to overcome his current misfortune, this hell he found himself in. He had to find a place to rest, somewhere safe because sooner or later they would come looking for him.

He had always healed quickly, a genetic trait he inherited from his grandfather, a whaler from the Faroe Islands who was also a giant of a man, and he felt certain that if he could rest for a few days he would be well enough to do what he had planned to do.

The vault in Hank's office would be empty, that's for sure, and the only way he could get the diamonds now would be through Hank. That little bitch, Jodie, would be gone, either dead or hidden away. Then there was Olsen; he knew that his bullet had hit the man but it was anybody's guess just how badly hurt he was. Getting to Hank would be a problem but he would figure it out. Right now, the only thing that mattered was finding a place to hide; a sanctuary to heal and recuperate.

The rain was both a curse and a blessing. Every drop was torture but traces of his footprints would be washed away. He had to find shelter and considering his handicapped state, it had to be close by. The only place he could think of was the Bruckman's main house; it should provide shelter and be safe, at least for a while. They would never think of looking for him there. He limped and crawled through the trees and the thicket, wincing in agony each time the brush and leaves scraped against his raw flesh. Alarm bells rang warning when he spotted the van in front of the barn. Hank must have sent his goons to look for him.

"Fuck! You will pay, Hank, you will pay in blood!" He whispered to himself as though speaking it would etch the promise in stone.

Seppo had to backtrack, circling all the way around to avoid them and after what seemed like hours of slow and painful torture, he made it into the Bruckman house through a side door. He literally crawled into the dust-riddled corridor and collapsed.

He stumbled from room to room and after some precautionary inspection, decided that it would be safer on the second floor. He took the dilapidated steps one at a time, pausing to brace himself against the constant pain. The old stairway creaked and groaned under his immense weight but it had held. He limped into a bedroom that was cluttered with ambiguous debris, torn and tattered blankets and sheets and cardboard boxes filled with old newspapers and magazines. There was more garbage and litter tucked under a rickety wooden cot that was pressed against the far wall. The mattress on the cot was stained and torn but it would suit his purpose. He dragged it off the bed and before he lay down, fumbled for his ankle holster. He breathed a sigh of relief, the .22 caliber Walther PPK/s was still there. He crawled onto the mattress and closed his eyes and almost immediately, fell asleep.

THE TIGRESS, SOLDIER AND THE BETRAYAL

The two days following the gunfight at Bruckman's farm proved to be some of the busiest and most taxing in Meghan Hollier's life. She woke up early to take care of Robbie, cleaning his wound and giving him a sponge bath before leaving for her job at Dr. Boswell's clinic. Then after a full and busy day of taking care of the scheduled visits and the animals, she would stop over at her mother's to spend time with Ryan and Jodie before heading back to Luke's cabin on Moose Head Point. She had decided to take a break from her bartending job at Bucky Johnston's Diner. It would cut into her pay but for now she would have to make do.

For his part, Robbie was making progress. It was slow but he was steadily getting better and on the third day, he even managed to walk to the breakfast table with a little help from Meghan. He was still weak but definitely out of the woods.

"Look at you! Pretty soon you'll be beating up bad guys again!" Allison greeted him, tongue in cheek.

"I doubt that but I owe all of you a big thank you," he looked at Meghan, "especially you, Meggie, I don't think I'd have made it without you."

She blushed and quickly corrected him, "Allison did all the heavy lifting. She's the one that got the bullet out and cleaned your wound and used Maddie's magic ointment," Meghan replied.

There was an awkward silence at the mention of Maddie and it was Robbie who was the first to speak, "What's happening with Maddie? Are the funeral arrangements being made?"

"Luke took her body to Dorsey's Funeral Home yesterday and is back at her place today looking for a will or something that may list the next of kin," Allison answered.

"She left a copy of her will with me. It was really strange but it was as though she knew she was going to die," Robbie said.

"What? What do you mean?" Meghan asked, surprised by the fact that Maddie had a premonition of her death and more surprised that she would give Robbie her will.

"I mean that she had this premonition that she was going to die soon and had me witness her will. I have the copy in my duffel." He paused, caught his breath and continued, "It's at the Sleepy Crest. I need to square the bill before they throw my stuff out."

"It's done," Meghan said. "I went there yesterday morning and got all you things and settled the bill. I moved it all to my place. I didn't see your car in the parking lot but assumed it was at Tony's."

"Did you find the gun under the mattress?" There was concern in his voice. Losing a gun meant reporting it to the police and that would open a whole new can of worms.

"I did. I was about to leave but something told me to check under the bed and under the mattress. I gave it to Mark to keep. I had no idea how to unload it and I didn't want Ryan or Jodie to find it."

"Who's Mark?" Robbie asked.

"Mark Boswell. He's Dr. Boswell's husband and is an ex-marine."

"You mean a former marine… there are no ex-marines; once a marine always a marine!"

"Is that the same for Army Rangers?"

"It is absolutely the same - once a Ranger always a Ranger. There's a brotherhood and a bond that is forged in combat that outsiders will never understand."

"I didn't know that about marines. Mark never corrected me. I learned something new today," she smiled and placed his coffee in front of him.

"No, I'm the one who has to thank you. You're something, girl. Where do you find the energy?"

She smiled and said, "Umm, speaking of energy; I was wondering if you were well enough to move to my place. It would give Luke and Allie their home back and I could take Ryan and Jodie off Mom's hands and…"

"He needs to rest," Allison interrupted coming over to the table. "Moving him now would be a risk. If he starts to bleed it would set him back. Give it another day or two and then it would be a lot safer. Don't worry about us, Luke and I have enjoyed having you here."

"Are you sure, Allison?" Meghan asked.

"Yes darling, I'm sure. If you want to spend a bit more time with Ryan don't worry, I'll watch this one and make sure he's not wrestling with bears or baboons!"

Meghan was uncertain but realized that it may be wise to give Robbie a bit more time. Also, having Allison with him while she was at work was a blessing. "I'll take Ronin and leave him at my Mom's or with Tony. That should be one less thing you have to worry about."

"Like hell you will!" Allison shot back, "He's my baby and he's staying!"

Meghan laughed, "Okay, okay, if you insist. I couldn't help but notice how he follows you around. He's taken a liking to you."

"If Robbie's not careful, I'm going to steal him away."

Robbie smirked, ignoring the threat and said, "Can you bring my duffel here? I have Maddie's lawyer's number scribbled on the back of the last page and Luke's shirts are bit small for me. I could use a change of clothes."

"I'll bring it over this evening. I like the tight shirt and unshaven, scruffy look; makes you look like one of those models you see in the magazines," she said, smiling while running her fingers gently along the bristles on his jawline to his chin.

"I think you may need glasses," he quipped back with a smile.

She kissed him on top of his head, "I have to leave. I'm making French toast for Ryan this morning and helping Mom with some stuff for Jodie. Oh, by the way, Ryan's been asking about Captain America."

"Tell him the Captain says 'hi' and will see him soon enough."

She gave him a quick kiss on the mouth and turned to Allison who was watching them, "I hate to leave you with all the work but I promise, I'll make it up to you."

"You don't have to make anything up to me, Meghan. I have no problem taking care of all of you. I love you guys. And Robbie is literally no trouble. He sleeps most of the day and is pretty independent when it comes to the other stuff. The only thing I do for him is clean the wound and bandage him up. Oh, and feed him but looking at him now, I guess he can feed himself."

"You're an angel and Luke is lucky to have you."

She gave Allison a hug and waved goodbye to Robbie, "I'll see you in the evening, baby. You try and get some rest."

After Meghan had left, Allison looked at Robbie, her eyes dancing with mischief, "Well, it's just you and me, kiddo, what would you like to do first? Breakfast or a shower? Maybe fool around a bit? I got it, let's fool around in the shower."

Robbie laughed and said in a jocular manner, "You better watch out, girl. I may just take you up on it."

"So why don't you?" She quipped back. This time her expression had changed, the smile was subtle and she was serious.

They locked eyes and the mood shifted. There was an prolonged silence, tense with sexual overtones, the reciprocity of their attraction sparking like live wires. The innocent flirtation had morphed and the metaphorical cat had slipped out of the bag making them both acutely aware of each other. They were getting precariously close to crossing the line.

Robbie cleared his throat and said softly, "I'd better get to bed. I'll have breakfast later, if that's okay?"

She looked at him; her lips slightly parted, her eyes clouding with desire, then smiled and said, "You can have breakfast anytime. I'll help you to your bed."

"I don't think that's a good idea, Allison, I'll manage. Thanks." The walls of resistance were crumbling and every fiber in his body screamed for him to flee, to get away from this seductress. *Meghan, Meghan... you should never have left me here.*

He stood up but had to grab the table for support. He grit his teeth and was about to take a step when she came over.

"Don't be silly, Robbie, I'm not going to bite! Come on, put your arm around my shoulder and lean on me."

He could feel her body pressing against him, warm and soft, and the strength in her arm wrapped around his waist. There was a fragrance to her, a subtle fragrance of flowers - roses and jasmine, violets and patchouli, it was fresh and enticing, and he felt his blood racing with the thrill of the forbidden. The feelings between them had been building and it was getting harder to resist the temptation and if he wasn't careful, the mess would be more than he would be able to clean up.

"I can feel your heart. I make you nervous, don't I?" Allison whispered easing him onto the bed. Her voice was a murmur, her breath warm and inviting, caressing his ear.

He was quiet, looking from her eyes to her lips, the fullness of her mouth with the slight pout – she titillated his senses with the promise of pleasures unknown.

"You'd make any man nervous… more than nervous. I'd better get some sleep. I feel exhausted." The last bit was an excuse. He wanted her to leave, to break the spell he was under.

She leaned over him and gave him a kiss, it was a sensual kiss. He could feel the warmth rising in his neck to his cheeks when her tongue touched his and for that brief instant it was electric and silky and delicious. He opened his mouth wider to allow her more access but she pulled back and ran her finger along his lips.

"So sweet, my wounded Teddy Bear…" her voice, low and husky, then she straightened up, "you should rest. I'll check on your bandages later."

When she left, she took Ronin with her and closed the door. He lay there unmoving; his head buzzing with conflicted thoughts, his body swirling in a torrent of need and his heart struggling with the hope of love. He was excited by the fantasy and contrite by the betrayal. *How could he say he loved Meghan when he lusted for Allison? Then what he felt couldn't be love or was it possible to love one and want both? He couldn't hurt Meghan no matter how much he desired this seductive Rapunzel.* He drifted off to an uneasy slumber with dreams of unicorns, fairies and the turmoil of Kunduz… the breach of trust and the young men who paid with their lives.

A few hours later he was awakened by a series of inexplicable but amazing sensations shooting through his body. He stifled a groan and looked down and saw a golden head bobbing slowly over his crotch. Allison was fellating him, sucking on his cock like an insatiable vampire.

His first reaction was to tell her to stop, to push her away, but the conscript of pleasure had always been to the detriment of conscience.

"Allison, oh god, please… you mustn't. What about Luke… Meghan…" he whispered, his pleading lacking any real conviction.

She had let her hair down and it fell about her in a golden, shimmering blanket. She licked the knob, running her tongue around the ridge and felt him shiver then stopped and looked up at him, "Shhh, baby, I've locked the door. No one's here… it's only you and me."

Her naked body glowed in the morning sunlight; an ethereal goddess straddling his thighs, her fingers gently toying with him while her violet eyes bored into his very soul. He was about to protest when she leaned over and took him back into the velvet softness of her mouth. She was an expert, knowing exactly what to do and when to do it and how to keep him enslaved; to ensure that his sole raison d'être would be to ride this incredible wave of pleasure until it crested and he lost himself in those mindless, tortured moments of bliss. It excited her; this feeling crusted in power and control, kindling the embers of her arousal.

The room was filled with their groans and moans and whispered ramblings, nonsensical and spontaneous, reverberating with the urgency shared by lovers lost in the rhapsody that preceded the promise of euphoria. They were captive to their solitary needs; trapped in a world of their own and all others, shut out and long forgotten. What mattered, and the only thing that mattered, was the pleasure they shared taking and giving to each other in ways only they were privy to.

She was relentless in her assault and when she sensed his climax nearing, she stroked his shaft with her fingers, feathering up and down, up and down, while she ravaged his dome with her mouth.

She said, in a voice hoarse with desire, "Cum for me baby, cum now … now," and sucked as hard as she could, her cheeks hollowing with the effort, her fingers working furiously until she felt him jerk and writhe.

The bastion of his conscience was destroyed in the swell of their indulgence and any semblance of resistance or doubt was washed away by the undercurrents of lust and desire. His only focus was the need for release. His legs stiffened and his body trembled, "Oh God, baby, I'm cumming, I'm …" he gasped and grabbed her head, flooding her mouth with his seed.

The Monster

RESURRECTION

It was Ronin's growl that stopped the animated buzz of conversation around the dining table. He had sensed the sounds of the approaching car long before it had made its way up to the landing.

"Someone's here," Robbie said and placing his hand on Ronin's head, commanded, "Stay here, stay with me." The big dog had started to get up but lay back down.

He was seated at the table with Meghan and Allison. Ronin was lying next to him and Luke was standing behind his sister, leaning against the pantry door. They had been discussing Maddie's will.

"It must be Tony," Luke said and strolled out onto the porch. A few minutes later he was back, "It is Hank. I wonder what he wants."

"Maybe he knows about the will," Meghan suggested.

"I doubt that. I haven't called the lawyer yet and except for us, no one else knows about it," Robbie said.

Ronin growled again, this time it was deeper and louder.

"I'd better put him in the bedroom; he's likely to get aggressive."

"I'll do it," Allison quipped and came over to Ronin. "Come on, baby, we don't want you hurting poor Hank." And while she was next to Robbie she brushed against him and squeezed his arm and said, "And how're you feeling? Better after your afternoon nap?"

She had been flirting with him all evening, sometimes blatantly, much to his concern. On several occasions he had caught Meghan looking at them and his guilt-ridden conscience had him convinced that she was onto their secret.

He looked up at Allison and controlled his expression, "I'm fine. The nap did me a world of good and I think I'm ready to move to Meghan's."

"Ah, I'll miss you…" she looked into his eyes, "and Meghan. It has been nice; a real change having you here."

She impulsively ruffled Robbie hair before she realized what her actions would convey. The intimacy of the gesture was a familiarity reserved for lovers and couples. She quickly walked away with Ronin following her.

Luke was oblivious to the interactions between them but Meghan was far more perceptive. It might have been a woman's intuition or her own insecurity but her suspicions were beginning to grow. She was about to question Robbie when Hank came in holding a large duffel bag. He was out of breath from the climb up from the landing.

"You need to have an elevator installed! That is like climbing Mount Katahdin!" He paused to catch his breath and handed the bag to Luke, "This is yours. It's everything that was in the safe apart from what I've kept. You can do what you want with it. You can divvy it up any way you choose. I'll add my two cents – Emma needs money and now all she has is Ed, so keep that in mind."

"I'll take this to Mom and between us, we'll come up with the distribution of shares. I don't want any; Allison and I are all set. Before you walked in, we were just discussing Maddie's will. She left most of the land to Allie and me… over four thousand acres." Luke said placing the bag behind the couch.

"It doesn't surprise me," Hank noted, running his fingers through his hair and still breathing hard from the climb. "Damn! I need to get into shape."

"The gas station and adjacent property is for Ryan. The rest of what was hers is to go to a church in South Carolina. That's the gist of it," Luke informed his brother.

Hank was quiet. He had wanted the land for its timber and the gas station for the convenient location. But he could still leverage this to his advantage he just needed a bit of time.

"It's in the family and that's what counts. I didn't expect her to leave me anything. My relationship with her wasn't quite like what Allie and you shared with her. She never liked me and that's okay," Hank said, taking the chair across from Robbie. "How are you doing? I want to thank you for what you did the other night… I don't think I'd be here if it wasn't for you."

"I'm doing fine. And you don't have to thank me. I was there for Jodie."

"All the same, I owe you one," Hank said then turning to Luke, "I came here because I have some unsettling news. Seppo is alive and his usual, loveable self."

"How do you know that?" Luke asked. He had meant to go over to Bruckman's farm but hadn't found the time.

"Fats is dead. I had sent him along with Jake and Arnie to clean up the barn. From what they tell me, Fats stepped out to take a leak and never came back. They found his body lying naked in a ditch with his neck broken."

"And that means Seppo is alive?" Meghan asked, the blood draining from her cheeks.

"The footprints around the body could only belong to Seppo.

Not many people have a a size 14 triple E. And, Fats was strong as an ox. I doubt there are too many men who could break his neck."

Meghan got up off of her chair, suddenly frantic, "Ryan! I have to get to my mom's and get Ryan."

"Don't worry. He's not going to come after Ryan. He's after me," Hank said, trying to calm her down.

"I can't chance that. He threatened me when we were at Maddie's. He threatened to hurt Ryan," Meghan replied. She shivered at the memory and was now almost in a panic, "and what's going to happen to Mom and Dad?"

"Easy girl, nothing is going to happen to them. I'll come with you and we can stay at your parents," Robbie said and got up.

"Hold on a minute! You stay put, Robbie, you need to rest. I'll go with Meghan and get Ryan and Jodie. If Meghan's parents want to come up here, that's fine too but I agree with Hank, I don't think he's after any of you. He'll want to get to Hank. And, there's a good reason for that." He looked over at his brother and said, "Go on, tell them. They have a right to know."

Hank was silent, looking at his hands, then decided to explain, "It's really no one's business but we are all family and friends here so why not? I have some diamonds, well quite a few, and that is what he is after and that's his only motive. He really doesn't care about Jodie or the problems with the Jersey mob. He's after the diamonds."

"Why don't you just give it to him? Nothing is worth getting us killed!" Meghan exclaimed.

"That's not the answer. You don't give in to people who threaten you… what's yours is yours and no one has the right to take it from you," Robbie said, "I'll come with you, Meg. You don't have to worry."

"Listen, hear me out. You're not any good to anyone in your condition. It's safer to be here. He is not going to come here especially with Ronin around. I know just how tough you are, brother, but right now, the best thing you can do is stay here," Luke advised.

Meghan agreed, "I think Luke is right. You stay here, baby, I'll be back as soon as I get Ryan and Jodie. We'll be safer here together."

"Once we bring them back here, Hank and I will go over and take Emma to Mom's for the night. I'll stay there with them and in the morning I'll look for Seppo. I have a score to settle."

Allison was back from sequestering Ronin and gave Hank a warm hug. "You should stay here too," she said knowing fully well that he wouldn't, "if he's after you, then you will be safer here."

"I can't. Luke is right… we need to make sure he doesn't go after Mom or Emma or Pauline to get to me." Hank got up and addressed Robbie, "Jodie has something that doesn't belong to her. It can cause a lot of embarrassment to some very powerful people. I wasn't going to hurt her. I just want the laptop back."

"You weren't going to hurt her?" Robbie scoffed, he was incredulous and then his voice took on an edge, "Did you say the same thing to Angela?"

The two men glared at each other before Hank replied, his voice filled with remorse, "You may not believe me but I didn't want Angela hurt. She had worked for me for many years and I was quite fond of her. I told Seppo to wait until I got there but I think he had decided to implement his plan. He had his own agenda and poor Angela was in the way, collateral damage so to speak."

"You are the boss. You are responsible for the actions of those who work for you and blaming someone else doesn't get you off the hook," Robbie voice was soft but filled with obvious distaste. It reflected his own feeling of culpability in the deaths of his men.

"Listen, we can deal with this later. Right now Seppo's on the loose and we need to make sure innocent people don't get hurt," Luke intervened, adding, "Jodie is safe and no one's going to hurt her unless they want to deal with me. If Adam Shayk and his crew want to turn this into a war, so be it."

Meghan came over to Robbie, leaned over and hugged him, "Jodie is going to be fine. I'll be back as soon as I can. I may take Mom and Dad to Dr. Boswell's place, at least for the night. Are you okay?"

"I'm fine. Get back soon. I don't want to have to worry about you and Ryan. I feel so damn useless…"

"Don't say that! You were shot. Most people would still be in bed!" She lowered her voice, whispering, "I think Allison has a thing for you, she's been flirting with you all evening. Should I be worried?"

"No, you have nothing to worry about … just get back soon." He lied looking away. He couldn't bear to look into her eyes for fear that she would recognize the deception.

He got up and took her hand and walked with her to the door. She gave him a quick kiss and he watched as she walked down the stoop with Luke and Hank. Her movements were graceful and feminine and sexy. She was beautiful, a dark, smoldering beauty that was the counterpoint to her nemesis. She turned around and flashed him a big smile and waved before disappearing down the incline to the landing.

He enjoyed looking at her; she made him feel warm and happy inside but the gnawing tug at his conscience persisted. She was everything he had ever wanted and if fact more. She was too good for him and he had betrayed her and lied about it. *What am I doing? What is wrong with me? Meghan, you need to come back soon… I am lost. Dad was straight as an arrow and had never cheated on anything in his life. Was he like his mother? She was the one who had run off chasing after rainbows. He didn't want to be like either of them. Meghan, come back …*

And just then like a wraithlike sorceress who could read his mind, Allison joined him on the porch, hugging him from behind. Her felt her breasts pressing against his back, her hand roaming salaciously down his abdomen and into his trousers.

"Come on, baby, we don't have a lot of time," she whispered.

He felt helpless, the energy between them sparking, turning intensely sexual. He could hear his inner voice screaming for him to resist, to fight the temptation and to consider his future with Meghan but sadly he realized the futility of it all. She had control over him in a way that no woman ever had. It was something more than just physical; it was a deep, carnal desire rooted in his very soul, a longing that defied all logic. It was something inexplicable, intangible and so overpowering that he was willing to risk everything, even his life, if it came to that. All for a few moments of pleasure shared with this dryad, this golden haired goddess of the woods.

"They'll be back any minute. We shouldn't…" he searched for the words but lost his train of thought as soon as she found his cock, her fingers caressing him, her breath heavy and warm against his neck.

"I need you now! Mmm, you're so hard … my beautiful Teddy Bear," she breathed, enjoying this power she had over him, "I'll make it better. They'll be gone for at least an hour, more likely two so let's not waste another minute." Her voice was a sensual whisper, alluring and seductive. Her violet eyes were bright with desire and her mouth, scarlet and inviting. She took him by his hand and led him towards the bedroom.

They stopped and kissed by the doorway, it was an urgent kiss: his lips pressing rough and hard against her mouth, his tongue probing past her lips to the moist softness within. She pushed back with her hips, her body molded to his, her mouth open, their tongues wrestling fervently while they desperately undressed each other.

He kicked the door shut and carried her to the bed, and as soon as she reached down and guided him into her, any thought of Meghan and the love he felt for her was lost, buried under the weight of his lust.

He began thrusting in and out of her in the primordial dance of lovers, his grunts timed to the rhythm of her moans and lascivious cries. Her legs wrapped tightly around his body, fingers raking his back - both lost in the frenzy of their lovemaking. He was captive to this wanton nymph, a hostage trapped by the promise held within the depths of her thighs. There would be no redemption or escape for this soldier… none.

A MONSTER'S REVENGE

Seppo Heikkinen's residence was located near Bucky Johnston's Diner off the main road on a bylane appropriately named 'Marsh Pit Alley' for the large milkweed-filled wetland that bordered it. The place had belonged to Hank but he had offered it to Seppo when the big Finn had first arrived in Chase River. It was incentive for him to stay on and work for the Carlson enterprises. Now, in the stillness of night, Seppo had managed to make it to the small cottage without being discovered. But, they would know he was alive now and there would be a manhunt soon which made this all the more urgent.

It was imperative that he treat some of his more severe burns and wounds or risk infection setting in – being incapacitated and helpless was something he couldn't accept. His thigh where the bullet had gone through was beginning to throb, the pain so intense that he was unable to put any weight on it. He was running out of time and that is what prompted him to risk coming back to his cabin. He was pretty sure that Hank would have someone on surveillance duty or possibly even waiting for him inside the cabin.

He had waited patiently by the edge of the wetlands, hidden behind trees and the supple crush of weeds, until it was dark and past midnight. The clothes he stole off of Fats were ill fitting and tight and chaffed his burns but it offered him a modicum of protection.

He cut across the shallow end of the bog to the back of the cabin which was blanketed in darkness and entered through the kitchen door in the rear.

He made sure the place was empty before he entered and was careful not to turn on the lights; instead, he used a small flashlight and kept close to the floor so as to remain undetected. He washed and cleaned his wounds then disinfected them using hydrogen peroxide and alcohol from a bottle of Cambridge Gin that he had under the bed and bandaged himself the best he could. Though hurt badly, he was excited by the prospect of danger and the worse the odds the better he liked it.

Finally, he looked in the mirror and he recoiled in shock.

"Fuck!" He gasped at the reflection.

He was a frightening sight! His eyebrows, eyelashes and Mohawk were all but gone and his scalp and face were blistered and raw. His lips were grotesquely swollen and patches of the skin around his cheeks had burned away exposing the blackened and bloody flesh underneath.

He closed his eyes tight and swore to himself: *he would make them pay – all of them. But first, the diamonds.*

Contact

VIPER AND PREY

The days McHenry spent with VanArcen went by uneventfully but not quickly enough for the assassin but he knew he had to convince the locals that he was what he claimed to be. The burden of playing the role of Professor Santos was getting tiresome and cumbrously taxing especially with the newfound comradery between the men. Tony VanArcen had a knack for putting others at ease. The formality, usually reserved for strangers, was giving way to familiarity and in between the jocular banter he had to fend off questions about his past which had him in a conundrum. Some of the bits and pieces didn't add up but VanArcen wasn't the type to track the details.

Even the best occasionally let their guard down and he was sure that sooner or later he would slip-up and even Tony would catch on that something wasn't quite right. So he devised a different strategy. He decided to bore the heck out of VanArcen with longwinded explanations of the various rock formations and their relevance pertaining to the different archeological time-periods. He spared no detail in describing the differences between igneous, sedimentary and metamorphic rocks and their development during the Paleolithic, Epipaleolithic, and Neolithic ages and by the time he got to the Byzantine era, he could see that his guide had reached the breaking point.

VanArcen had given him a petulant look, scratched his head and said, "Prof, my mind's gonna explode! This Neolithic bullshit might rock your boat but brother, it's killing me! Let's talk about women, sports or food, what do you say?"

"Okay, okay, Tony, I will stop boring you. It is a passion of mine, this history of our home, our mother, our earth. I think I have enough for now," He pointed to the varied lot of rocks samples they had collected. "I will keep quiet, or like you Americans say, zip it, and you can tell me about your passion, what is it?"

"That's easy, Prof, food and women! Isn't that every man's passion? " VanArcen quipped, "Let me tell you about my gal, Liz; she's fuckin' beautiful maybe not in the traditional sense like Meghan or Marylou but she's sure as heck gets me hot and bothered. And the things she does in bed, my friend, things that would blow your freakin' mind! She so darn flexible…" and so it went. VanArcen did the talking and McHenry did the listening.

Though McHenry had grown to like VanArcen, he was relieved when they parted ways on the third day.

"Thank you for everything, Tony, you are the best. I enjoyed our time together and I'm pretty sure I can manage from here on."

"If you need anything, Prof, just give me a holler. You're a good man and I hope it works out with Marylou. You didn't say anything but Uncle Tony knows shit like this. She deserves a sophisticated man like you. Just be careful, my friend, you are in the mountains and these inbred assholes can get crazy!"

He wasn't sure how much Marylou would have told the professor but Greg Humphry was a shit-kicking knucklehead and would most probably stomp the poor professor to death.

"That means a lot to me, Tony, it really does. I'm sure Miss Dorsey has her share of admirers and that some of them could be overly possessive," McHenry paused then added, "but love is irrational and leads us all down strange and interesting pathways. Don't worry, I have learned to take care of myself; I have the gift of the silver tongue and can talk my way out of any jam."

"Okay, but should you run into a problem you call me. Not that I'm Charlie Bronson but I know some head-knockers who'd be happy to step in."

"I'll keep that in mind. Hey, why don't we have dinner one of these nights?"

"You got it. Just give me a call," VanArcen replied and with that they said their goodbyes.

He didn't give VanArcen's cautionary advise another thought. He knew how to take care of himself and his size usually gave him an advantage. Men tended to underestimate him. After the car bomb has killed Njoku and his kids, there was a massive manhunt and at one point, before he crossed the border into Tanzania, he was accosted by a 6'4", two hundred and fifty pound mercenary who was part of team hired to track him down. It was a no-contest: in seconds, the big man had his trachea crushed and his neck broken.

McHenry needed to plan Ryan's abduction carefully and being fully aware of the unpredictable nature of children he wanted to make sure that there would be no mistakes this time around. He couldn't afford another fiasco like Nairobi. It had taken him years to get over those kids but their faces continued to haunt him in his nightmares.

He would never have agreed to the abduction of a child but he wanted to pursue this "thing" he had with Marylou. And, of course, there was the question of the money. He was being compensated rather handsomely and it would be a nice retirement bonus. He had decided to quit the killing business. Over the years he had made more than enough to escape to his chalet in the Swiss Alps and meeting Marylou had precipitated his decision. It was time to lead a quiet and inconsequential life and to pursue some of his other artistic interests but it wouldn't be complete without a partner and Marylou seemed to have everything he desired. First he had to take care of the job at hand.

He started by gathering information and that involved reconnoitering the general area around the two homes where Ryan spent most of his time. He needed to study the habits and schedules of the adults who supervised him before implementing the actual abduction. He had scoped the property around Meghan's little cabin and even managed to pry open a bedroom window to enter the house. After a hasty check of all the rooms he had left without disturbing a thing.

He was in the process of surveying Meghan's parent's home when he noticed the SUV pull outside the front gate. He watched with interest as Meghan Hollier followed by Luke and then Hank Carlson got out and went into the house. Even from a distance he recognized Meghan from the photographs hanging on her corridor wall. *Damn! These mountain gals are pretty. I wonder what's going on with Luke and Hank. It would be virtually impossible to grab the kid if they were going to stay with him.*

There was only one way to find out. He put the binoculars away and crossed Main Street to Hollow Creek Road. He waited a few minutes to compose himself before sauntering casually up the gravel walkway. He stood in front of the door and listened to the low, muffled conversation and eschewing the doorbell, knocked instead.

"Professor Santos! What the heck are you doing here?" Luke asked, surprised by the smaller man's presence. "I thought you'd be up in the mountains digging up rocks!"

"Ah, I am taking a break, Luke. Three days of wandering around, burrowing for rocks like a ground squirrel would drive any petrologist to drink." He answered in his accent. "I was on my way to the diner and saw Hank's SUV. I wanted to stop by and thank you for introducing me to Tony. He was the perfect guide."

"No thanks needed. But, this is not a good…" Luke was about to dismiss him when Meghan came to the door.

She gave McHenry a quick look and said, "Hi! You must be Professor Santos. Please, please come in."

"I don't want to intrude," he bowed and asked, "and who do I have the pleasure of talking to?"

"Meghan Hollier," he extended her hand, "now come in. You're not intruding."

"Miss Hollier, your reputation doesn't do you justice. You are even more beautiful than Tony had described," McHenry said and kissed the back of Meghan's hand with exaggerated flourish.

Meghan laughed and said with a big smile, "Tony is a friend and he's too kind and you sir, should come by more often. Women never tire of compliments!"

The professor glanced at Luke and said, "I can see that you are all busy and I have overstayed my welcome. Also, I am to meet Miss. Dorsey for lunch at the diner so maybe another time."

It was Meghan's turn to be surprised, "Marylou?"

"Yes, the very same Marylou Dorsey."

Just then Ryan poked his head past the folds of his mother's dress and with a shy smile said, "Hi."

McHenry returned the boys smile, "Well, who do we have here? Do we have a little elf?"

"This is Ryan, my son," Meghan introduced, with a gentle hand on her son's head ushering him forward.

McHenry took note of the fact that she called Ryan her son and not *our* son though Luke was standing there. The boy was the spitting image of his father.

He fumbled in his coat pocket and fished out a piece of candy and kneeling down, offered it to Ryan, "Here, this is for you."

"Thank you," the boy said shyly. He took the candy and with unwavering attention, began unwrapping it.

"It is butterscotch, my favorite," the man said to the boy.

"You've just made a friend for life," Meghan said, shaking her head.

"Well, it was a real pleasure meeting all of you," McHenry tousled the boy's hair, "especially you, Ryan. You have a wonderful day and I'll see you soon."

Luke and Meghan watched McHenry walk down Hollow Creek Road until he disappeared at the intersection of Main Street.

"He seems like a really nice man," Meghan said closing the door.

"Of course you'd say that," was Luke's sardonic reply.

"What do you mean? You mean he's not a nice person?"

"I mean the guy compliments you and you are ready to anoint him pope!" Luke said with a chuckle.

Meghan shook her head, "That's just like you! I said he seems like a nice person. And, men often compliment women when they first meet simply out of politeness. It has nothing to do with what he really feels or thinks."

"You'd have to be deaf, dumb and blind to miss the fact that he was fawning over you. A few more minutes and he would have gotten down on all fours and kissed your feet!" was Luke's phlegmatic reply.

"You know, Luke, you can be such an ass! You are judgmental and a xenophobe! He was a cultured, educated man and that doesn't count because unless you grow up in the mountains you are not to be trusted. That's essentially your take on anyone who's not from here!"

"That's not true. I like Robbie Olsen and he's not from here," Luke countered.

She was quiet at the mention of Robbie's name, seemingly preoccupied, and then asked, "Do you think there's something going on between Robbie and Allison?"

The question caught Luke by surprise, he responded emphatically, "No! I think she finds him intriguing and attractive. He is a good looking guy and an Army Ranger… there aren't too many like him around. I don't think it's anything else. I trust Allison."

He said that but deep down he didn't believe it. He was experiencing the same misgivings but he didn't want Meghan to know that. Allison had been acting aloof and disinterested in him and that was a first. And, when he noticed the way she looked at Robbie, he was sure there was more to their flirting. He was concerned but he didn't know what to do.

Meghan looked at him and smiled, "Forget what I said… it's my insecurity. I'm always looking for something to go wrong."

"Robbie's crazy about you. It is obvious in the way he looks at you so don't mess this up, Meghan."

She sighed and replied "I know… we don't get too many chances at happiness and I had almost given up hope. You are right about Robbie being special but you are wrong about Professor Santos."

Luke didn't say anything. There was something about the professor that made him uneasy but he couldn't put his finger on it. He wondered what Greg Humphrey would do when he found out about Marylou and Santos. Humphrey had the reputation for having a volatile temper with a penchant for violence. But, that was none of his business.

"Hank and I need to get to Emma's… what do you want to do?" Luke asked.

"You can leave. I'm taking Mom and Dad to Susan's place. She said there was no problem and she offered to take Jodie too.”

“That’s a good idea. I think Jodie can benefit by staying there. Dogs are good with kids and that’s the last place Hank’s goons will look for her.”

“Thanks for being here. I mean that… I felt safe.”

Luke smiled and gave her a peck on the forehead, “You take care of the soldier boy and don’t worry, I’m going to find Seppo and I’ll put an end to this.”

When Meghan arrived at the Boswell’s place, Dr. Boswell’s husband, Mark, was waiting to greet them at the front door. He was about five feet-ten and thickly built with a mop of curly gray hair with a hooked beak of a nose, a Sundance Kid mustache and a square jaw. Though he had retired from the Marines a while back, he was exceptionally fit and would be a handful for anyone including Seppo. He had a large Rottweiler sitting next to him. The dog got up when the pick-up pulled up and the doors opened.

“Don’t worry, he looks fierce but he won’t bite,” he paused and added, “Unless I tell him to! His name’s Zack. Let me get the bags.”

Once Hank and Luke had left, Meghan gathered her parents, Jodie and Ryan and left for Dr. Boswell’s place. When they made it to the upper level they were met by Dr. Susan Boswell and three more dogs, all Rottweilers and all of them large. Susan Boswell took Jodie’s hand and said, “Don’t worry dear, they are sweethearts. You’ve met Zack. This one here is Zillow; she’s the smallest but she’s the boss. The one with the white patch is Freddie and the big boy is Kruger.”

Jodie laughed, “You mean like Freddie Kruger from Friday the 13th?”

“Yes. Mark thought it would be funny. We were going to call these two Jack and Jill but that was too obvious for Mark,” she gave her husband a smirk before continuing, “he wanted to name them Zack and Zill. I thought Zill sounded too odd. I had wanted to name her, Willow so we compromised and agreed on Zillow."

Jodie bent down and hugged Zillow then sat Indian style on the carpet and began playing with the dogs. Meghan spoke to her parents and assured them she would be back as soon as it was safe, thanked the Boswells and left with Ryan.

The next stop for Meghan was her cabin to pick up a few more clothes, toiletries and sundry items. While she was searching for one of Ryan's favorite toys she came across the photographs that were the root of all her troubles. It had been a while since she had looked at them so she sat down and went through them carefully reliving those moments – most of which she regretted. Finally, after some thought, she decided to take them with her. She was going to settle this issue that had come between them so they could move on with their relationship. She was determined not to lose Robbie and if it meant facing her past then so be it. She wasn't going to let Allison or anyone else derail her chance at happiness.

STRAYING FROM THE PATH

They were exhausted. Robbie and Allison had made love several times and finally lay basking languidly in the afterglow.

"What are we doing?" Robbie asked the woman lying in his arms, her head cradled against his neck.

"What do you mean? We just spent the last hour making love… is that so bad?" Allison replied, tracing his profile with her fingertip and placed a gentle kiss on his cheek then noting his somber expression, she postured up on her elbow and looked into his eyes, "It was amazing for me, everything I'd hoped it would be and more and someday when I'm old and gray, I'll think back on these moments we shared and relive the thrill in my mind. I won't ever have to wonder how it would have been with the only man I desired other than Luke."

She leaned over him, her hair falling about them in a golden veil, and placed a kiss on his lips. It was a soft, tender kiss, the kind shared in the intimacy following intercourse.

"What about Luke? Aren't you feeling even a little bit guilty?" Robbie persisted.

"No, and you need to stop beating yourself up. You did nothing wrong. You're not married to Meghan and my relationship with Luke is not what you'd call normal, not by any stretch of the imagination. But I love him and there no one, not even you, that I would trade him for."

They lay quietly together, bodies intertwined, meshing together almost perfectly like they were made for each other. She was tracing lazy patterns on his chest when he spoke.

"I was disappointed in Meghan because I thought she may have been indiscreet," he paused, his mind racing back to his reaction on seeing the photographs of her at the swinger's party. "I had no right to be. I'm just a hypocrite!"

He was pensive and a bit remorseful now that the edge of his lust had been dulled.

"You're not a hypocrite. You're just a man," she laughed, "I know you are a good man, Robbie Olsen, and Meghan should be happy to have someone like you."

"So you think it's okay for men and women to indulge their fantasies or desires irrespective of a commitment?"

"No, I didn't say that. But there are exceptions in life and if you are honest with yourself, you'll recognize them and not use it as an excuse to cheat on the person you love. I don't love Luke any less because I made love to you."

He looked at her and felt an overwhelming sense of affection, "I don't want you to think I regret this because I don't. I'm happy we've shared these times together. You stir something in me that I can't explain. I don't know if I could have resisted you even if I was married to Meghan. I want to spend the rest of my life with her and the fact that I want you..." he struggled for the words, "it even sounds ludicrous!"

She raised up on her elbow and looked into his eyes.

"Listen, baby, you need to accept things for what they are. Some things are meant to be; they happen and you live in those moments. Don't look back and don't look forward – just live in the now. I never wanted anyone except Luke until I met you. And then when I saw you with Meghan and the way you looked at her, you became a fantasy, the secret lover who lived in my mind." She paused, then continued, "I live in two worlds; one that is steeped in reality and the other in my mind and sometimes, if I'm lucky, the one in my mind merges with my real life. You are one of the rare crossovers, from fantasy to reality!"

He squeezed her tightly touched by her uncomplicated and accepting nature, "I wish I could be as pragmatic but I can't. I think if you love someone, I mean really love someone; you need to be faithful to that person irrespective of how much you want someone else. That is the entire premise of a marriage or a commitment."

"We're different then. I don't confuse love and desire. I'm not promiscuous. I don't jump into bed with every man I think is attractive. You are the exception and this is a once in a lifetime thing for me. I am hoping that we get to spend a few more afternoons together before you ride off into the sunset with Meghan. A few more..." she thought for a moment and then said, "what are they called - trysts, right?"

"Yes, trysts. But these are more than trysts for me. If I had met..."

She placed a finger on his lips, "Shhh, don't say it! There are no ifs only what is. I learned that from Maddie. My life is with Luke and yours is with Meghan. I know that and I accept it. But, in my fantasy world you will always be my Teddy Bear!"

He smiled, "What's with the Teddy Bear?"

"Oh, because you are so cuddly!" she replied, playfully biting the tip of his nose.

"Cuddly...? Okay. I guess there are worse names a guy could be called."

"When I was a little girl my dad got me a teddy bear for my birthday. I'd go to bed hugging him and as long as he was with me, I wasn't frightened of the dark."

"I guess it's a mountain thing, these nicknames. Tony has a hundred different names for me and believe me some are downright strange!"

"Tony may be creative with the names but can he do this?" And with that she kissed his neck and slowly nibbled her way down until she had engulfed his cock in her mouth.

"Oh God!" He closed his eyes lost in the satin softness of her mouth. "You'll be the death of me, girl."

They were fast asleep and didn't hear Ronin's growls but the sounds of roughhousing along with the noisy ruckus from the corridor woke them up. At first Robbie thought it was all a dream but then he heard the playful snarling and he sat up, waking Allison.

"You missed me, didn't you, boy? I know you did! Come here you monster puppy, where's your pops at?" And before they knew it, VanArcen was standing by the bedroom doorway staring at them in disbelief and shock.

Time seemed to stretch endlessly in the awkward silence that followed. Tony stood motionless, gaping at the naked couple in bed with eyes wide open and mouth agape. Then in a panicked scramble that was almost comical, Robbie and Allison grabbed for the comforter and pulled it over them.

"What are you doing here?" Robbie snapped, angry and embarrassed.

"I'm sorry! I … I just wanted to make sure you were okay. I hadn't heard anything … oh, shit! I'm really sorry, I should've called or knocked or whatever!" VanArcen stammered his face flushed with confused embarrassment. He quickly turned away, heading back into the living room.

They heard the footsteps fading and the soft squeal of the front door being opened followed by the rattle of the doorknob as it slammed shut. VanArcen, his mind reeling with what he had just witnessed, retreated to the sanctuary of the porch.

"Oops!" Allison smiled and noticing the expression on Robbie's face, laughed, "You should see yourself! Like your dog just died!"

"It's not funny, Allison, I don't want to hurt Meghan. I really don't …"

"Stop. No one's going to say anything to Meghan unless it is you. Tony may have a big mouth but he understands the meaning of discretion. Everybody in Chase River has skeletons in their closets, things that are private and sometimes even disturbing. We've learned not to interfere or gossip about personal matters. Trust me; he's not going to say a thing."

Robbie wasn't concerned about Allison or Tony saying anything to Meghan. He was trying to reconcile the need for secrecy with the guilt that was gnawing at his insides. "I'd better get dressed. I'm going to shower unless you want to first?"

"No, you go ahead. I need to change the sheets and light some incense. There's that unmistakable scent in the air." Allison replied rolling of the bed then added with a playful smile, "Unless you want to fool around in the shower!"

He grinned at her not-so-subtle offer, "You're something else, girl! You're beautiful and I'm tempted but sex in the shower is out of the question for now. You've plumb worn me out." He gave her a smack on her ass, "You'd better put something on before he comes back wanting to get another look at you! I think his eyes nearly popped out of his skull!"

"Ouch! That hurt… " she rubbed her behind feigning pain and added, "I'd better take a shower first. You're leaking out of me. Be a doll and strip the bed. Leave the sheets on the floor. I'll take care of it once I'm done."

It was a while before Robbie strolled out onto the porch. He had showered and changed his clothes and helped Allison remake the bed.

He found VanArcen seated on the stoop playing fetch with Ronin tossing an old rubber ball. His friend was studiedly ignoring him.

"Well, are you going to say something or pretend that playing with Ronin is the only thing on your mind?" Robbie said.

"I was worried about you, man, I mean really worried because I didn't hear a thing the last few days but I can see that you are just fine, more than fine, you're like a bee pollenating every flower you come across." He looked over at Robbie, the disappointment plainly etched on his face, "Do you know what you are doing?"

"I appreciate the concern, Tony, but this is none of your business."

VanArcen was quiet for a while, watching Ronin who was lying down with the ball in his mouth. The big dog was playing by himself. He would drop the ball and dribble it back and forth between his front paws before snatching it up again. He would look up at Robbie and then do it all over again.

Finally, VanArcen spoke, his voice reflecting his hurt, "You're wrong there. You're my friend, Robbie, and that makes it my business. This is not going to end well no matter how you look at it. Meghan is one of the sweetest people I know and Luke, one of the most dangerous. Don't let breakfast over pancakes and a cup of coffee fool you… a pissed-off Luke makes Seppo and the rest of the Cossacks from Jersey look like a bunch of choirboys! Now, if you still want me to stick my nose out of it, I will but don't insult our friendship by brushing me off."

Robbie squeezed his eyes shut tight and rubbed his temples with his fingertips, a habit he had developed after returning from Afghanistan. He knew that everything VanArcen had just said made sense. *This thing with Allison wasn't going to end well.*

"You're right. I don't know what I'm doing and I'm sorry for being an asshole. You are my friend and if you were doing something that was detrimental to your wellbeing, I would be the first to step up and caution you. I am really sorry, Tony."

"Apology accepted. I don't know how you're going to manage this…" he struggled for the right words, "this three ring circus but you can't hurt Meghan; you just can't. She has been through a lot in her life and doesn't deserve this."

VanArcen waited knowing that his motive was colored by twinges of envy. For as long as he could remember, he had to deal with rejection from women. Even with Liz it had taken a year of dogged persistence before she relented and went out with him. It was hard not to feel some resentment seeing how easy it was for Robbie. It seemed unfair. But he did feel a sense of concern though it was mostly for Meghan.

"She will be devastated, Robbie, but it's not just her, there's Ryan, I see how he looks at you. You're the role model he needs… you know, Captain America and all that."

"It's a mess. I'm the last person to be role model for anyone. Damn, I can hardly look at myself in the mirror! I care deeply for Meghan and don't want to hurt her in any way. I know how it looks but I do love her. I'll deal with Luke if he decides to…"

"Luke won't decide to do anything," Allison said breezing onto the porch. She was dressed in an oversized, white, woolen jumper and a pair of tight blue jeans. Her hair was done in a casual upside down braid that accentuated her long neck and with the slightest hint of makeup, she looked breathtaking. She added, "You let me handle Luke."

Robbie could feel the embers of passion flaming-up again. There was a peculiar tightness in his chest knowing that this thing he had with her was time-restricted. It was going to end very soon and like she said, it would be relegated to memory for a cold night when he was old and gray. His eyes were glued to her as she traipsed down the steps and got the ball from Ronin. The big dog's reaction was immediate; he leaped up wagging his tail and was ready to play. She ran a few feet down the front lawn with Ronin close at her heels, then threw the ball and yelled, "Go, baby, go get it!"

There was a natural grace to her movements, a feline grace laced with sensuality. She wasn't trying to be sexy or cute; it was an intrinsic part of her. And while Ronin chased after the ball she turned to Robbie, her eyes dancing with mischief and a smile on her lips, said, "I'm going to steal him from you. He won't want to leave."

"We'll see," Robbie was distracted, struggling with his feelings which had nothing to do with Ronin; he was smitten with this creature, but no one, not even she would ever take his dog. "Ronin may like you but he's *my* baby and you'll have to kill me first!"

"Now that's a thought! But, there's more than one way to skin a cat," she answered smiling sweetly, the innuendo not lost on Robbie.

After a few minutes of tossing the ball, she said, "I'm going to take him for a walk. Do you want to come?"

"Me?" VanArcen asked, surprised.

"I was talking to Robbie but you can come too if you'd like," she replied.

"Yeah, sure, I could use the exercise," VanArcen answered, getting up off the stoop and dusting off the back of his trousers.

"I'll pass. I need to sort some stuff out. You two go ahead and don't let him go wandering off. I mean Tony ... Ronin can take care of himself!" Robbie said and disappeared into the house.

"With friends like you ..." Tony shouted after him.

DEMONS AND DEATH

The rain had persisted all night and continued through the morning and into the late afternoon. The light drizzle had given way to the occasional heavy downpour but for most part it was a misty shower that accompanied Ray Carlson's funeral service. It had been a private affair with only the immediate family present. They had eschewed the customary post-burial reception and decided instead to have a simple dinner together at their mother's place. Lisa Carlson was an excellent cook and her house was big enough to accommodate the Carlson clan.

Hank was sprawled out on a large sofa with Ed Carlson near his feet, straddling the armrest. Luke was seated on a leather Ottoman skimming through an old photo album and Pauline's husband, Nate, was at the wet bar pouring drinks for everyone. Emma Carlson, the oldest sibling and Ray's mother, had retired to one of the bedrooms upstairs and was resting while Pauline and Allison were in the kitchen helping their mother with dinner. The somber mood in the house matched the dark and overcast skies.

It was Ed Carlson who spoke first. He addressed Hank, "Any word on Seppo?"

"Nope, there's no sign of him. My men have looked pretty much everywhere. We even got Scully's hounds to help find the son-of-a-bitch. Those dogs can track a flea up a bear's ass! He's long gone from here or hiding somewhere high in the mountains," Hank replied.

He sat up and glared at his nephew and reprimanded, "Fats would still be alive and we wouldn't have to deal with conjecture if you had been more thorough. You had him and you let him get away."

"I was sure he was done. The whole fucking place was lit up like a wild fire! How could I..." Ed began protesting when his grandmother came in from the kitchen. Her attractive face was contorted in anger and she cut him off.

"I'll have none of this. Not tonight. You can figure out what needs to be done later but tonight we will all show some respect and help Emma through her pain. Is that clear? She lost her son and I, my grandson; doesn't that count for anything?"

Lisa Carlson rarely got angry but when she did, they all knew better than to argue. There was a muttering of apologies before she turned to Allison, "Play some music, dear, something soft and soothing."

"I'll do it, Ma. I know exactly what to play," Pauline interjected. She was a softer version of Hank, tall and lean, with long dark hair that reached the small of her back. The dark, deep-set eyes, thick eyebrows, long, gaunt face along with the loose black dress that fell to her ankles gave her a witch-like appearance.

"Ray liked Crosby, Stills and Nash. I used to play 'Teach Your Children' when he was a kid and it would calm him down and put him right to sleep. Do you remember that, Ed?"

"Yeah, he liked the old hippie stuff. We were all listening to hard rock and he'd be humming 'Homeward Bound' or 'Seven Spanish Angels'! Ray had an offbeat taste in music."

"Not just music - his spider collection was the worst. He insisted on showing me that tarantula he bought while feeding it a live snake! It made my skin crawl," Allison shivered at the memory.

Pauline riffled through the CDs and found the album 'Déjà

Vu'. They listened for a while, reminiscing on the many humorous anecdotes that involved Ray when Lisa Carlson called out from the kitchen doorway.

"Hank, go and check on Emma. Make sure she's okay and see if she'd like to join us for dinner. The rest of you wash-up, dinner is almost ready."

"Okay Ma," Hank replied and got off the couch. He stretched and made his way up the stairs.

As he walked down the corridor leading to the bedrooms he noticed that the door to Emma's room was open but none of the lights were on. *She must have gone to the bathroom.* It was the only explanation he could come up with.

"Hey Emma, 'you up?"

He turned on the light and had to suppress the panic that welled up in him like a giant wave. Shock, fear, disbelief and anguish flooded his mind creating a synaptic overload. His stomach churned and the taste of bile soured his mouth. He grabbed the bedpost to steady himself, fighting the urge to gag; he was unable to reconcile the ghastly spectacle on the bed to any rational expectation he had harbored. Hank Carlson struggled to regain control and was about to call out for help when a huge hand clamped over his mouth.

The voice was an eerie, whispered growl, "Make a sound and I'll slit you from ear to ear."

Hank felt the sharp edge of the knife against his throat and stopped struggling immediately. His eyes were fixed on his sister. Her throat had been slashed and the pillow and sheets around her head and shoulders were soaked in the viscid velvet of blood. The contrast of the glistening reddish stain against the white of the cotton sheets lent a surrealistic appearance to the backdrop much like a gory scene from a B-rated movie. His sister was dead, brutally murdered by the demon he feared most.

"I have the house rigged with explosives. You make a sound and I'll blow the fucking place up. Do you understand?" Seppo said, releasing Hank. "All I want is the diamonds and that's it. Give them to me and I'll be on my way. You'll never see me again."

Hank was still staring at Emma, "You didn't have to kill her."

"I had to. She saw me and she was about to scream. Look at me, look what you assholes did," the giant shook Hank to emphasize his point. "Do you think I'll ever look normal again? None of this was necessary if you had given me what I wanted. So, it's on you, you stupid cunt. You are responsible for her death. Now come on, I don't have all day."

"I don't have the diamonds. After what happened at Bruckman's I moved it all to a safe deposit box at my bank."

"Which bank? I know of at least three that you use."

"Greystone Savings and Loan in Dexter. They're closed until Tuesday. Monday is a bank holiday. You picked a bad time, Seppo."

The big man wasn't convinced. He grabbed Hank by his shirt and hissed, "You're lying!"

"I'm not. You can kill me and blow this place up but that isn't going to change anything."

"Well then we're just going to have to kiss and makeup and spend the weekend together. Come on, move!" the big man snarled, his tinny voice echoing in Hank's ear.

"I need to bury my sister. Meet me at the bank and I'll give you the diamonds. There's no need to…" Hank began to reason but was silenced by a cuffing blow to the head.

"Shut the fuck up. You're coming with me," and with that he shoved Hank towards the doorway.

They left through the door located at the far end of the corridor that exited onto a wraparound deck.

"We'll take your car; mine is *borrowed* from the parking lot at the diner. We wouldn't want Bradley or that fat idiot, Dolan, stopping us. Just remember, if anything goes wrong your fucking family goes *'boom'*, get it?"

As they walked down the deck stairs onto the back lawn, Seppo jerked Hank back and pointed to a package strapped to the underside of the deck, "You see that? There are plenty more like that in case you think I'm kidding."

Hank didn't say anything. He was kicking himself for parking his SUV so far down the driveway. It was unlikely that Luke or the others would hear the engine start up. He knew that Seppo wasn't bluffing about the explosives. Several years back, he had blown up a warehouse in the Adirondacks belonging to a wannabe gangster who had tried muscling in on Hank's business and when questioned, he confided that his brief stint in the Finnish Army included training as an explosives technician. The narrative was shared not just to offer his unique services but to convey a subtle threat. This giant Philistine was certifiably insane and Hank's only hope of survival was to stall, to give Luke enough time to track them down. He would come looking for him as soon as they discovered Emma. Luke would know and his younger brother would save him. That was his prayer.

SAVING THE CARLSONS

Allison and Luke had left for Ray's funeral and the cabin was quiet. Meghan had her suspicions about Allison and Robbie but said nothing. She was happy that they were together again and it gave them the opportunity to talk about their relationship. She had just put Ryan to bed and was getting coffee and an after-dinner snack ready when her phone rang. Before she could say anything, the voice on the other end cut in.

"Hi, this is Luke. Is Robbie there? I have to speak to him now… it's urgent!"

"Just a minute," Meghan replied. She quickly crossed the kitchen and handed the phone to Robbie, "It's Luke, he said it's urgent."

"For me?" Robbie mouthed the words, eyebrows raised, surprised.

His first thought was that Luke had found out about his affair with Allison. Guilt is a strange companion. She can create remorse and regret which is often accompanied by suspicion bordering on paranoia – every shadow becomes the foil, the justifier of actions and the police of conscience.

He took the phone, "Hi, this is Robbie."

"I didn't want to alarm Meghan," he paused, trying to control his emotion, "Seppo just killed Emma and took Hank with him. When I was outside checking for signs I discovered explosives under the deck and around the periphery of the house... do you know anything about diffusing bombs?"

"Don't touch anything! Get everyone out of the house now and get them to a safe distance. That is step one." Robbie's demeanor changed immediately, he took charge and commanded, "Get everyone out of the house, *now!* I'm on my way."

He hung up and got up, handing the phone back to Meghan.

"What's happening? Tell me what's going on?" She knew something terrible had happened. The snippets of the conversation she just heard were disturbing.

"Seppo killed Emma and has wired the house with explosives. I'm going to see if I can disarm the damn thing. I'd tell you to stay here with Ryan but I don't know where the place is and in the dark..." he paused, grabbing his coat, "I could most probably find it but it would take me time and that is the one thing we don't have. You need to come with me."

"What about Ryan?" Meghan didn't question him. She understood the urgency of the situation.

"Bring him along but we need to hurry."

When they got to Lisa Carlson's place, Luke had the family outside, standing at the bottom of the driveway about five or six hundred yards from the house. Luke walked up to meet the pick-up truck and opened the door for Meghan.

"I'm so sorry, Luke," she said and hugged him. It was an awkward hug, both of them uncomfortable with it. She had never seen Luke cry but Emma was like a second mother to him, she had always treated Luke like her own child, more so than she did Allison.

"No one deserves this. I will make sure he pays, if that's the last thing I do. First it was Maddie now this. He's taking the people I love most."

"You stay here with them and keep Ronin with you," Robbie

said to Meghan before speaking to Luke, "I'm sorry, Luke, really sorry about your sister but we need to hurry so let's go. Do you have a wire cutter?"

"I have a toolbox. It has everything you'll need."

Just as they were getting ready to leave an older woman came over and even before she introduced herself Robbie knew who she was. The resemblance was unmistakable.

"I'm Lisa Carlson," she said, "you take care of my boy, do you hear? I've lost a grandson and now a daughter and I don't want to see Luke hurt."

There was a regal air about her. Her once blond hair was more silver than gold and the crow's feet and wrinkles on her face lent character to her presence but it was the air of subdued authority that caught Robbie attention.

"Your son's going to be safe, ma'am, he's going to show me where the explosives are and then he's going to move back out of harm's way. I am sorry for your loss."

The woman studied him closely before speaking, "Then *you* need to be careful. If the place blows up I'll be sad but if you were to get hurt, I wouldn't forgive myself. We don't need to lose more lives."

She was about to go back to the rest of her family when she turned and said to him, "I can now see what my children and others say about you. I guess you know what you've doing but I will pray for you, Robbie Olsen."

Robbie nodded and motioned for Luke to lead the way.

"He's got it in three places," Luke said, pointing to the odd looking package strapped to one of the support beams of the deck. There was a cell phone attached to it with duct tape. "What's with the cell phone?"

Luke walked over and looked at the contraption carefully. "This is a pretty basic IED, an Improvised Explosive Device. He needs to communicate with the initiator to set off the explosive and is using the cell phone to do that. The phone acts like a switch. This was pretty common in Afghanistan."

He stepped back, "Okay, give me the cutters and get the heck back. I should be able to snip the detonator cord and if all goes well, that should do the trick."

"And if it doesn't?" Luke asked.

"Well then, make sure Ronin has a good home. Now move back… go join the others."

"That's not happening. I want to learn how you do this and I am not letting you take all the glory by yourself. No risk, no glory!"

"You *are* moving back and I mean now. Don't give me any bull-shit. I need to concentrate – it has been a while since I did this."

They locked eyes in a battle of wills before Luke reluctantly acquiesced. "Okay," then without the slightest hint of anger he added, "now before you go and get yourself killed, I want to say something to you face to face. I'm not sure what's going on between Allie and you but something is going on. I know my sister better than she knows herself," he paused, again, waiting for a reaction but got none. Robbie was stone-faced so he continued, "I don't care. I'm glad it's you and not some asshole… after all the shit I've put her through, she's entitled to her little fling and that's all this is. She's mine, she'll always be mine so don't go getting any fuckin' ideas."

He smiled with his mouth but the smile didn't reach his eyes - they were cold, icy blue cold, "Now you can go blow yourself up!"

Robbie's mind went blank. *How did he know? There's no way Allison told him anything. No way.* But he didn't address the non sequitur instead he instructed, "Go on, get back."

Luke took a few steps backwards. Robbie waved him back, "Further back. You need to be about five hundred yards to be safe."

He waited until Luke had backed up about two hundred or so

yards. "Okay, that's good but it would be better if you joined the rest of the family."

He studied Seppo's handiwork carefully before cutting the detonator cord at both ends and that was it, as simple as that. He did the same for the other two IEDs and conducted a thorough reconnaissance of the deck and house before calling out to Luke. "Looks like those were the only ones. I think we got them all."

"I checked the underside and the periphery and also tracked his footprints, those were the only three," Luke answered, walking towards Robbie.

"That was more than enough. It would have blown up the house and killed everyone in it."

"Two can play that game. I don't need explosives; I'll get the son-of-a-bitch!"

Robbie was still hyped from the adrenalin dump and when they got to where the others had been standing, most of the family had started back to the house. Allison was by herself waiting for them. It was obvious that she had been crying. She looked vulnerable and helpless and when they got close, she ran by Luke and into Robbie's arms hugging him in a tight embrace. It was an awkward moment.

"I'll be in the house," Luke said, his tone terse and angry but he turned away, following the others into the house.

"I'm really sorry about your sister, baby, I don't have the words..." Robbie was holding her now, stroking her hair gently.

She began crying again, sobbing uncontrollably and letting her emotions run the course. He soothed her whispering sweet nothings and kissing the top of her head. Finally, she sniffled and said, "I was so worried, Robbie, I thought this might be the last time I see you. I couldn't live with that!"

She was pressing herself against him and he found himself falling under her spell again. The desultory struggle between rationale and caprice favored his impulse and a part of him screamed: *To hell with them all… she is all that matters.*

Her mouth searched for his and they kissed, it was a desperate kiss prompted by grief and adrenalin. She tasted of honey and spice, the freshness of her mouth mingled with the hint of her tears. He wanted to carry her off to someplace secluded and make wild and passionate love to her and to forget – to forget everyone and everything. And it was like she read his mind.

"Make love to me, Teddy Bear, I need you. I need to feel you inside me," she moaned, her hand snaking between them, cupping the hardness she could feel pressing into her.

There was a moment of uncertainty while he vacillated, torn between his lust and his love. And when she began unbuttoning his jeans, reason returned.

"No, Allison," he pushed her back gently, "not now, baby… Meghan, Luke… I can't. We can't." He held her at arms-length. "I want you more than I've ever wanted you but we can't hurt them. Luke is upset and I cannot do this to him and especially while Meghan is here."

His mind was buzzing with the urgency of her need and the promise of pleasures she would provide, but taking this any further tonight would mean the end of his relationship with Meghan and he wasn't willing to do that.

She wasn't sure if he meant it was over between them or whether this moment wasn't right. They stood looking at each other oblivious of the world outside; it was as though no one else existed.

"Promise me you'll come and see me, promise me that."

"I promise, baby, I don't know if I could stay away even if I tried."

She was about to throw herself into his arms when they heard Luke's voice calling down to them. "Allison! Allie, Mom needs help with Emma… you need to get back."

At the sound of Luke's voice, the spell between them was broken. She squeezed his cock and smiled seductively at him then quickly headed back to the house.

Luke stood a few feet above him and warned, "Remember what I told you, soldier boy, she's mine and don't you forget that."

They walked back to the house with Robbie following Luke, his mind preoccupied with emotions that defied logic. *How could he love Meghan and want Allison with such passion? Was he taking advantage of both women - Meghan with her dreams and need for a man in her life and Allison, young and naïve, looking for adventure and romance?*

What he didn't know was that fate had other plans for him that would set him on a course he could never have seen coming. Maddie Wilkins had been right all along.

ANGELS AND PROFLIGATES

The day after they laid Ray Carlson to rest there was another funeral in Chase River Town but unlike the Carlsons, this was for one of society's forgotten denizen. It was the service for Angela Mercier. She had no family or friends and rather than let the State decide her fate, Dr. Susan Boswell and her husband, Mark, stepped in. They had learned about Angela through Jodie. The young girl explained, in detail, her relationship with the dead woman and what Angela had meant to her. So without any hesitation they took care of all the funeral arrangements.

When Angela's body arrived at the mortuary she was naked and unrecognizable. She had been severely beaten and disfigured so they spoke to Gil Dorsey and had him work his magic to make her presentable. They bought a white silk dress and shoes and selected a special white casket. They wanted to make sure that Angela Mercier was treated like a family member without the stigma of her profession. The headstone, a pedestal design in white granite, with a beautiful carved angel on top was what Jodie picked out and they had it engraved with the following words:

Angela Mercier
1984-2019
Fly, Beautiful Angel, You Are Finally Free

Sadly, only one other person attended the funeral. It was Kelly Borden, the one they called pretty Kelly, who worked at Sleepy Crest. But just as they were about to leave, Ed Carlson showed up surprising them all. He looked disheveled and tired and distraught.

The moment Jodie spotted him fear shot through her like the devil's dagger and she moved closer to Susan and clutched her hand. Mark Boswell stepped alongside her, "Don't worry, Jo, no one's going to hurt you."

Carlson came over, stumbling and almost falling but managed to catch himself. It was obvious that he had been drinking.

"I just wanted to pay my respects. Angela was a decent person and didn't deserve this. It was really, umm…" he paused, trying to find the right words, before mumbling, "It was really nice of you to do this for her, really nice."

Susan smiled at Jodie and explained, "It was Jodie. She told us all about her – Angela was a remarkable woman considering the cards she was dealt. It's too bad there are people like Seppo Heikkinen around. No one should have to be buried without family or friends being present so when we heard about what had transpired, we felt it was the only decent thing to do."

Ed nodded and then looked away. He wanted to speak to Jodie but he could see that the young girl was frightened of him.

"We heard about last night, about Emma and Hank. We're really sorry, Ed… you must have liked Angela a lot for you to be here. Have you heard anything from Hank?"

"No, but Luke is out looking for him. If there is one thing I know it is that Luke will find him and when he does, Seppo will get what he deserves. And about Angela, I think at another time and another place, things would have been different for us. She…"

He couldn't finish his thoughts. He looked at the ground, his emotions getting the better of him. Losing Ray and Jericho and now his mother all in close order, and being alone for the first time, had frayed his nerves and he had spent the night examining his life. As far back as he could remember, he had been attracted to Angela but he lacked the courage to pursue it outside the boundaries of her profession. She was the one person who accepted him for who he was - warts and all. He decided then that he was going to set things right and it would start with Jodie.

"Listen Jodie, you don't need to be frightened anymore. Luke has taken over the business and he's called Hank's men off. No one is looking for you. The Sleepy Crest is going to be bulldozed and I'm trying to convince Luke to set set-up a Bowling Alley in its place so families can go and spend the evening doing something fun. You're safe now."

"What about Marisa and her laptop? She made me promise to post those videos," Jodie wasn't convinced.

Ed hesitated and then said, "That's up to you. You do whatever you think is right but you may want to talk to Luke or Robbie first. Posting those videos could hurt a lot of people including some very nice ladies who live here."

Jodie was quiet. She didn't quite trust the tall man. "I will talk to Mr. Olsen and see what he says."

Ed stood there vacillating, unsure of what he should do or say until finally he announced, "I'd better go. I promised Grandma that I'd be there to help. You take care. I know that Angela thought the world of you, Jodie. She wanted you to go back to school. She was going to pay for your..."

And again, words failed him. The tears welled up in his eyes. He turned and walked away, shoulders stooped and staring at the ground. That's when Susan elbowed her husband and nodded, "Go on, Mark, ask him... ask him to join us. The poor man is suffering!"

Her husband raised his eyebrows but knew better than argue.

He took a few steps towards the receding figure and called out, "Hey Ed, wait up!"

Ed Carlson stopped and turned around, unsure of what the former marine wanted.

"We're going to Bucky Johnston's for ice cream. Would you like to join us?" Mark Boswell asked.

The tall man hesitated then smiled, "Thank you, I think I will. I've could use the company and I promised Luke I'd speak to the staff. The timing couldn't be better."

When they got to the diner, there was a crowd gathered outside in the front parking lot near the entrance. Deputy Joe Bradley's car was parked right up near the door and there was an excited buzz rippling through the crowd.

"You'd better stay here. I'll go in and see what's going on. It could be Seppo," Ed Carlson said and pushed his way through small mob of people and disappeared into the restaurant.

Mark asked one of the men next to him, "What's going on?"

"Some guy beat up Greg Humphry. Beat him up real bad."

"Who... do you know who?" Mark thought it might have been Robbie.

"Naw, I don't know for sure but I heard someone say it was a little foreign guy who done it."

One of the other bystanders, a tall, broad shouldered youngster, who was standing nearby said, "He was a fuckin' Ninja. I was at the counter waiting to get my sandwich when it happened. Saw the whole damn thing, like in slow motion. Greg came in all angry and mad and grabbed Marylou and that's when the shit broke loose. The next thing you know he's lying on the floor staring up at ceiling. Then this little guy does a freakin' pirouette, jumps in the air and stomps down on his face. I heard Greg's jaw snap and his teeth go flying out like fuckin' chicklets! Just like that, it was done! Over! That's why

I mind my own business and don't mess with guys I don't fuckin' know 'coz, brother, you just don't know!"

The people in Chase River were a close-knit bunch and if one got into it with an outsider the chances were that others would intervene.

"So why didn't you step in and help Greg?"

"Not me, bro, I ain't getting into it with some foo fighting fool. And, Greg was an asshole!" the man replied and walked away.

Mark Boswell was shocked. It couldn't be Professor Santos! The man was too polite and dignified to be violent and Greg Humphry was a hulking brute of a man. Something wasn't right about the story but it wasn't until the ambulance had taken Greg away that the crowd gradually began to trickle back in.

Susan Boswell turned to Jodie and Kelly, "You girls go find us a table and we'll join you in a minute. I need to talk to Marylou."

Marylou Dorsey and Professor Santos were seated at a table in the corner being questioned by Deputy Bradley. The officer was taking notes on a small pocket pad.

"Hello Joe!" Susan greeted the deputy, "Chase River is certainly getting its share of excitement!"

"Hi, Doc, you can say that again. It was a nice peaceful place until… well I guess nothing remains the same for long," the tall deputy muttered.

"Are you okay, Marylou?" Susan asked the pretty woman seated next to the professor.

"Can I go or do you need me to stay?" Marylou asked the deputy.

"No, you can leave. I did have some questions about Marisa but I'll come by your Dad's place later. I'm almost done here just a few more minor details."

Deputy Bradley continued with the professor while the women stepped to one side. As soon as they were alone Marylou couldn't contain herself, she took hold of Susan Boswell's arm and leaning close whispered, "Greg was the one who started the whole thing. I told him a week back that we were through but last night he calls me and goes off - I mean ranting like a madman. He was yelling about killing Lorenzo and killing me and teaching me a lesson. I hung up on him and turned off my phone."

"Good God! That must have been frightening!" The doctor exclaimed, "I could never figure out what you saw in that oaf!"

"He was sweet in the beginning and I'm… oh, what's the use?" It was rhetorical and then she continued, "I *was* terrified because he can be violent but I was staying at Dad's so I knew Greg would dare to come there."

"What happened here?"

"He's gone crazy before but never like this. He barged in here and created a real fuss. When I told him to leave, he slapped me and grabbed my hair. That's when Lorenzo stepped in and stopped him. It was amazing, Susan, he was like a ballet dancer!" She looked over at the professor and smiled, "It happened so quickly, one minute I'm being dragged by my hair and the next, Greg's on the floor!"

Dr. Boswell smiled, "My, my, my! Who would have thought that the bully would get his just deserts and that too at the hands of one so charming? God does work in mysterious ways."

"I think I'm in love!" Marylou blurted out.

"Girl, I think I'm in love too!" Dr. Boswell joked. The women tittered softly, coconspirators enjoying the moment.

"For the first time in my life I've found a man who makes me happy and satisfies me. He treats me like a princess and who wouldn't want that? I know it sounds like infatuation but it's not. I think about him all the time now…"

"You deserve it, dear, and I know exactly how you feel. It was the same when I met Mark. I knew right away that I had found the man

I'd marry. So go and find happiness and don't let anyone stop you."

Mark Boswell came over to where the women were chatting and smiled, "Looks like we have the reincarnation of Bruce Lee here. Did you know he was a martial artist, Marylou? Aikido, Jujitsu, Karate, you name it he's got a black-belt in it!"

"He never mentioned a thing about martial arts or fighting. He's so dignified and gentle that I never thought of him as anything but a geologist. In fact he told me that he abhorred physical violence."

"The real martial artists seldom talk about it. Humility is part of their code. If and when you do find out, it's most probably too late, like Humphry just learned."

Susan Boswell was a strong, opinionated woman and she had no problem letting others know how she felt.

"Well, I for one am not shedding any tears for that bum! I hope he rots in hell!"

Her husband corrected her, "He's not dead, Sue, just badly hurt."

"Well, maybe the professor should have killed him!" Susan Boswell snapped and then turned to Marylou, "I'm glad you decided to move on Marylou and I'm hoping that the professor helps you settle down. It's time for you to stop with the partying and other nonsense."

The last bit was an overt hint at Marylou's propensity for partying, sometimes a bit too much and with too many men.

"What's Ed doing here? I heard the terrible news about his mother… is Hank okay?" Marylou asked when she saw Ed Carlson behind the counter. He was speaking with some of the waiters and waitresses.

"Ed came for Angela's funeral, to pay his respects and say good-bye. Did you know that he liked her? I mean he *really* liked her?" Susan Boswell asked.

"It was common knowledge at the lumberyard. I work for him and he would constantly talk about her… wanting to get her out of the business, buy her a house, you know, sentimental stuff, but he never did and now it's too late." Marylou answered with a doleful look on her face, "You have to act when the opportunity presents itself, that's the lesson here and I plan to."

"Just make sure of him before you go running off," Mark advised, "men, even cultured ones, can change once they…" he was unceremoniously interrupted by his wife.

"Oh shush! You are the least romantic person I know but I do love you. Now be a dear and make sure those girls order what they like, go on, I'll join you in a minute."

After Mark Boswell departed, heading for the table where Jodie and Kelly were seated, Marylou let her guard down, "Do you think someone like me can find happiness with one man?"

"Yes, you certainly can. We are all afforded the freedom to experiment. I think society has progressed and more and more women are testing the boundaries of their sexuality and that's a good thing. But at some point you have to decide on the type of life you want. If you are looking for a traditional relationship you will need to change a bit but don't let the past stop you from finding happiness and a future. Chalk it up to experience."

Marylou smiled, "Experience I've got. I'm not sure how it will turn out but I'm going to try and give it my best. I know I haven't been happy until now."

"Don't listen to the noise. He seems like a charming man and so well educated. I love his accent," Susan said then added, "I'd better get back before Mark orders everything on the menu. Good luck, Marylou and you should bring the professor over one evening; we'll have some wine and catch up. And it will give me the opportunity to flirt with a beautiful man!"

They laughed and hugged before Marylou went back to where the professor was seated. He was waiting patiently for her while Bradley gathered his things. The deputy was done with his investigation.

"I do need to talk to you about Marisa. Can I come by later this evening?" Bradley asked though it was more of a statement than a request.

"Sure. We should be home," Marylou replied. The officer nodded and left, stopping to talk to some of the other patrons that he knew.

The watched in silence before Marylou asked, "What else did he want?"

"Nothing really," McHenry answered nonchalantly, "he wanted to know if he should be concerned about me and my propensity for violence." He paused with a big smile, "I'm joking of course! He wanted to know how long I was planning to stay in Chase River."

She tried to hide her anxiety. She had wondered about this herself, "And what did you tell him?"

"I said not until Marylou says I can leave," he said it deadpan.

"You're such a liar!" she smiled and reaching across the table took his hand in hers. "Well, in that case, you are doomed to a life in this boring place!"

"Boring? More has happened here in the last few days than in Tucson in a year!"

"Lorenzo, you never told me you were a martial artist. You were beautiful… you reminded me of a dancer, a ballet dancer!"

"I think I told you this before but I don't like violence. I was bullied in school and my father wanted me to be able to defend myself and that is how it began. But I loved the code of the warrior, the peaceful warrior. My mentor, an old Japanese man, told me once that true peace can only be achieved through strength. So, I persevered and found that I had a natural aptitude for the various different forms of martial arts. That's it in a nutshell; I'm not proud of what

I did but I will never let anyone harm you… never!"

She squeezed his hand and in a voice that was soft and tantalizing, said, "I think you're going to see me in that skimpy nightie tonight."

He looked at her in amazement. There was a part of him that still couldn't believe that she was interested in him. He would have to tell her the truth but not yet, no, not just yet. He needed her to fall deeply in love, so deep that even his past wouldn't matter. She was his Natalie Wood, and he wasn't going to let this opportunity slip through his fingers.

When Susan Boswell got to the table she asked her husband, "What is Ed doing with Joe?"

"He's most probably going over last night's events. Hank hasn't been gone long enough to warrant being a missing person but Emma's death was murder. Joe's job is to catch the person who did it. Chasing poachers is not his primary responsibility."

"There's nothing much else going on here!" his wife scoffed recalling the incident with hunters on their property and Deputy Bradley wearing the Game Warden's hat. It was a standing joke that his job was relegated to chasing poachers and moonlighters and stopping hunters from trespassing.

But Bradley wasn't interested in Emma's death. There was no question that Seppo was the one who committed the murder and he was sure that Luke would exact the appropriate justice. He was okay with that – it was mountain justice. He was, however, interested in the professor and getting as much information on the man as he could.

He had called the university and they confirmed that Professor Lorenzo Santos was on their staff and that he was a geologist but there was one problem, the man was sixty years old and he was currently on campus teaching several courses. So unless he is incredibly well preserved and had figured out how to exist in two places simultaneously, the Professor Santos in Chase River was an imposter. The question begs: why was he really here and what was his true identity?

This incident with Greg Humphry was self-defense something that was corroborated by several eyewitnesses but no man weighing hundred and forty five pounds, unless he was a pro, could take out a hulk like Greg Humphry, especially as easily as he did. There was a lot more to this than meets the eye and he was determined to get to the bottom of it but he wasn't about to spook the professor. He would set the bait and let the man walk into the trap.

TIGERS, WOLVES
AND A KILLER

Adam Shayk wasn't happy. It had been over a week since he heard from McHenry and the pressure from certain political offices was mounting. The videos implicating Chris Donnelly and Sal Castiglioni with underage girls needed to disappear and that required Hank Carlson's cooperation. However, Hank wasn't treating this with the urgency it demanded but he was reluctant to lean on Hank; he had to be careful. A war up in the mountains wouldn't be easy, not like Jersey City; they could lose a lot of men. As far as he knew, Seppo Heikkinen was dead and that was a positive but the other thugs he had met up there weren't exactly the kind of people you wanted to mess with, especially Luke; it would be like poking a sleeping tiger.

He called his right hand man, Andrei Izhutin, on the phone, "Andrei, where are you?"

"I'm at the bistro, boss, with Milo and Sergei. Can you believe this? This fucking guy wants to change his name from Miloslav to Mark! Mark, of all the fucking names he could choose from!"

"Fuck him and listen up. I need to do something about those hillbillies up in Chase River. McHenry didn't call, did he?" Shayk asked knowing the answer.

"No. No news. He told me not to call him but maybe we should, what do you think?"

There was a brief pause while Shayk considered his options, "No, don't call him but we need to do something. I need to give those sewer rats in Boston a progress report soon or we will have a million cops crawling up our assholes!"

"Let me go there. I'll take these two lazy bastards with me and we will find McHenry and talk to him."

"Do you know what he looks like?"

"No, but how hard is it to find a little guy with a wheelbarrow?"

"A wheelbarrow?" Shayk was confused.

"If his dick is like the Eiffel Tower then he must have a wheelbarrow with him to push that thing around!" Izhutin answered straight-faced.

"You know, Andrei, I'm beginning to worry about your obsession with dicks. It is troubling but yes, you take a couple of guys and drive up there and shake the tree - let's see what falls out."

"Okay, boss, you got it. We'll go up there now."

"And Andrei," Shayk said before hanging up.

"Yes, boss?"

"Don't pull down the pants of every little guy you see. They will think we Russians are a bunch of gomiks!"

"These two lazy assholes with me *are* faggots, boss, but I got it, no pulling down pants. We just look around, observe and get some news. You leave it to me."

The line went dead and Izhutin looked at his companions, "You bums get ready. We're heading up into the mountains ..."

Before he could finish he was interrupted.

"What is wrong with Mark, eh? I am in America now and I don't want to be like some fuckin' hillbilly from Moscow with a stupid name like Miloslav," Milo lamented.

Izhutin smirked at the young man, "Fuck your name. You heard the boss. We are going up in the mountains for a few days. It's like going to Chechnya except the food is bad and the fucking women are uglier than your mothers!"

"Those Chechens in the mountains are like wolves, Andrei; you do not mess with them. I have never been to the mountains here, what are the people like?" Sergei asked.

"Like fucking tigers. Wolves run in packs. Tigers walk alone. These people are independent and tough. They eat Chechens for breakfast so you two fuckers better stop clowning around and worrying about your names and keep your fucking eyes open. You hear me, Milo?"

"Yes, boss, I hear you. If you don't like the name Mark, what do you think about Bill? Like Wild Bill Hickok. They will call me Wild Bill Pozdnyakov!" he pretended to draw his gun from the hip, squinting his eyes and going, "Bang, bang!"

The younger men laughed while Izhutin just shook his head, "You faggots are no use. I don't know why I keep you around."

DEMONS, DESIRE
AND DANGER

The relationship between Meghan and Allison remained cordial though there was an undercurrent of tension that both women tried to ignore. Nothing had really changed except that with Ryan and Meghan there, Allison couldn't find the opportunity to weave her spell. However, with the long weekend being over and Meghan having to get back to work, Allison was sure that Robbie and she would find time to resume where they had left off.

Ever since Hank went missing, Luke would leave early and come back late - he had taken over the responsibility of running the business and was discovering that it was a lot more difficult than he had imagined. He also had a new found respect for what Hank did – it was a lot of work handling the men, women, the many complaints and the worst part, working with the accountant. Sitting in John Pruitt's office was torture but the accountant was intransigent when it came to going over the numbers: "Hank insisted on doing it and I'll be damned if I let you skip off! It's your responsibility, young man, so buckle down and pay attention."

He had tried tracking Seppo and Hank but it as though they had vanished into thin air. There were a few decisions to be made regarding the Sleepy Crest and the personnel at the Lumberyard and once those were taken care of he would resume his hunt for Seppo. Secretly he was happy that Meghan and Ryan were at the cabin but his emotions were in turmoil – Allison had changed and he knew it was because of Robbie and that created an emotional conundrum. He liked Robbie, even looked up to him, but this thing with Allison had him on edge. He was hoping that Robbie and Meghan would move on and his relationship with Allison would revert back to what it had been. He wasn't used to this lack of control and was happy that work provided him with the necessary distraction or else he would have lost his mind.

Allison, on the other hand, was in her own world. For as long as she could recall, Luke had been in control of their relationship and she had willingly followed. But now, it was different. She was calling the shots and it felt good. She was infatuated with Robbie and couldn't wait for Meghan to leave for Dr. Boswell's office. She found herself humming to herself while getting breakfast ready and fantasizing about her next tryst with Robbie. Life was good.

Meghan and Robbie were on the porch watching Ryan and Ronin playing in the front yard. It was as though Ronin knew that Ryan was still a little boy and was extremely gentle with him. He would run after Ryan and nudge him playfully and when Ryan fell, he would lick his face making the boy laugh hysterically. The sequence turned into a game they co-invented – Ryan would run, Ronin would chase and then nudge him so he fell. The boy would laugh, get up and tag Ronin before running as fast as his little legs could carry him. They didn't seem to tire of the game they invented.

"Why don't we move to your cabin and let Luke and Allison have their space back? I'm okay now so there's really no need for us to stay on here," Robbie suggested.

He knew that if he stayed here at Moose Head Point, the affair with Allison would continue. They had to move on and he didn't want to lose Meghan.

"I thought you'd never ask! Let's do it now, after breakfast." Meghan responded, excited that Robbie was the one to suggest it. She had wanted to give him enough space to decide on what he really wanted and not influence or pressure him in any way.

"Tony and I are going to the bank in Dexter this morning. I think it's called Greystone Savings. He knows the manager and I'd like to open an account. Why don't we move after I get back?"

"Okay. Call me when you're finished and I'll meet you here. I've told Susan I need some time off to get things organized at home so it won't be a problem if I leave early. I'll get my parents moved back to their home while you are at the bank."

Robbie looked at her, "I know things have been crazy but if your heart is still in it, we can make it work. I wouldn't blame you if you are undecided and want to reconsider our relationship."

She moved closer to him and put her arms around his neck, "I'm not rushing you into anything. When you're ready I'll be here. Just know that I love you, Robbie Olsen."

He kissed her on the mouth, a sweet, tender kiss and held her close to him for a moment, savoring the feel of her against his body. When they parted he said, "I don't deserve you. But I love you too. I will spend the rest of my life making you…"

"Hey, you two lovebirds should get a room! You're embarrassing the wildlife here." The booming voice cut into their intimate moment. It was VanArcen, "Hi there, Miss. Hollier, you're certainly a sight for sore eyes!"

She laughed, "Hello Tony, you seem to be in fine spirits! Is Liz in town?"

"No, but she's coming up this weekend – made my day. Come on, Bronson, we've got a forty minute drive. Move your lazy ass!"

Robbie looked at Meghan and said, "He's a pushy little bastard, ain't he?" then turning to VanArcen, "Allison's making breakfast.

Let's leave after we eat."

"There's a real nice place on the way. We'll get breakfast there and I promise the food won't give you a heart attack! Come on, we have to hit the road."

VanArcen was determined to keep Robbie away from Allison. It wasn't that he didn't like the younger woman but he was convinced that Meghan and Robbie were meant for each other *and* because of Luke, Allison posed a real threat.

"I think I've eaten there once. Is it the small ranch style building on Eagle Creek just before you get to Route 23? It's run by that old lady… I forget her name but if it is, the food is fabulous." Meghan corroborated.

"The very same and her name is Grandma Jo."

Meghan turned to Robbie, "He's right this time, the food is very good. Go on. Have fun and call me."

The Greystone Savings and Loan was located in a rectangular brick building just off Mill Street. It had a large well maintained lawn in front with a walkway that was paved and fringed by short, neatly trimmed hedges on each side. A flight of stone steps led up to the landing of an ostentatious façade boasting large entry glass doors and a huge gold and black sign with the bank's name and emblem – a shield with a pair of swords crossed in an 'X'. There was a drive through window on the left side of the building with the customer parking lot in the back. The property was bordered by landscaped hedgerows of shrubbery and trees.

Behind the bank, hidden from view, was an old, rectangular, two-story brick building that had once been a warehouse for lumber. One of the two overhead doors at the loading dock was off the vertical track leaving a gap at the bottom and the windows had all been boarded up. Other than that, the building was in decent condition without too much disrepair.

Across the street from the bank was a gas station and next to it, at the intersection, was a McDonalds. There were a few other buildings clustered around that housed small businesses and offices and yet others that were vacant with 'For Sale' or 'To Rent' signs in front of them. It was typical of most small towns in northern Maine.

Robbie and Tony had arrived a little before the bank officially opened so they decided to get some coffee and kill time at the McDonalds.

"See, you didn't have to drive like a NASCAR driver," Robbie said sipping his coffee.

"I hate to be late and it gave us time to do some method reconnaissance. I thought a Ranger would appreciate that."

"Method recon? What the heck is that?"

"It's like passive recon except we focus on foods. It's the 'method' to the recon!" VanArcen replied, taking a big bite out of a large Cinnamon Roll.

"We just had breakfast! How can the heck can you eat so soon?" Robbie was truly amazed.

"I'm like a cow. I have four compartments in my stomach - breakfast, lunch, dinner and the most important one, snacks! Breakfast is full but the snacks section is empty!" he answered between chews and a self-satisfied smile.

Robbie just shook his head and studied the neighborhood through the large glass window.

When the bank finally opened one of the girls recognized VanArcen and quickly ushered them into the manager's office.

Murray Garlow was a nerdy looking, middle-aged redhead. He had a long stork-like neck with a prominent Adam's apple and a small, narrow face that wore a perpetual scowl. His pale skin was covered in freckles and the glasses he wore were wraparounds that were tinted to help him cope with his photophobia – a painful condition that made him overly sensitive to light. The shades of his office were drawn and the fluorescent lights were all turned off. He had the peculiar habit of peering over his glasses when he spoke.

"Good to meet you, Mr. Olsen. Please do sit down," the manager greeted Robbie after the introduction. "And I apologize for rather dim environs. It's my eyes. I have a genetic disorder, an issue with bright lights."

"It's not a problem," Robbie assured the manager.

"Tony and I go way back. I was a friend of his uncle's and a big fan. Everybody knew and loved Danny VanArcen… he was what legends are made of!" Murray Garlow gushed peering at VanArcen, "How long has it been, Tony? I think the last time we met was at Dylan's daughter's wedding reception and that was five years ago. Her husband and she were just in the other day. They're expecting their third child. Can you believe that? Little Nancy Molnar going to be a mother of three!"

"Was it that long? Wow, time flies. What are you gonna do? I heard Dylan retired and moved to Boston," VanArcen replied.

"Yes he did. All the older folk are moving out. It used to be the other way – the kids were running off and leaving the old folk behind but now, it's the baby-boomers. They want to be close to hospitals and the convenience of city life. It's the way of things now. Can I offer you some coffee?"

"Sure, I can use a cup," VanArcen said.

"No thanks. We just finished breakfast," Robbie said giving VanArcen a disapproving look, hoping to end the reminiscing and get on with the purpose of their visit.

"Okay, I'll pass too. Like I mentioned on the phone, Robbie needs to open an account. He's brought cash that he will deposit. We are in a bit of a hurry so if you can help get this wrapped up, that would be great."

"Not a problem. I'll get Mary to help you with it. She's the assistant manager and smart as a whip. She will explain the various options to you." He dialed the extension, "Hi Mary, could you…"

There was a knock on Garlow's office door before it opened and a young, fresh faced girl poked her head in. "I'm sorry Mr. Garlow but Hank Carlson is here. He needs to get into his Safe Deposit Box and he said it was urgent. I told him you were busy but he insisted. I'm really sorry."

"It's okay, Gail, I'll take care of him."

Robbie and VanArcen looked at each other then stood up.

"Hank Carlson? Was there anyone with him?" Robbie asked the young girl.

"No sir. He's alone."

"Ask him to come in here. Tell him it's Robbie Olsen."

No sooner had the girl left when Hank Carlson burst into the office. He looked like a prisoner of war. He was gaunt, unshaven and his clothes reeked. It was pretty evident that he was stressed to the point of being manic. He closed the door after him and turned on the lights, much to Garlow's chagrin, and sat down.

"Seppo is at the warehouse, in the back. He's waiting in the parking lot. He's got explosives strapped to my chest and under mother's house. I don't have a lot of time. He has threatened to detonate the bombs if I talk to anyone. He said he's watching me," Carlson said to Robbie with a helpless look on his face.

He undid the buttons on his shirt to expose his chest. Robbie took a close look and said. "Not sure I can help with this one. Let me take a look again." He moved the wires around gingerly, studying them, "The wires run through the strap and they seem to be cross-wired to the detonator cord. There's also a wire that runs directly from the initiator to the switch, tricky stuff. I've never seen something like this."

Robbie stepped back and said, "I diffused the bombs under the house so your mother is safe. I'm not sure I can do anything with this."

A look of fright and panic was etched on the gaunt man's face. Robbie wanted to ask him where he had been but instead got straight to the point, "What are you doing here?"

"Seppo wants the diamonds. I have them stored in my deposit box. He's promised to let me go once he gets them but I don't trust him – I know he plans to kill me one way or the other."

There was a part of Robbie that gnawed at his rationale: *Stay out of this. It's none of your business. Meghan's waiting for you.* But he couldn't. All his life he had fought on behalf of the underdog and there was the debt to be settled on account of Maddie so once again, he took charge.

"Okay, listen up. You do as I tell you and there's a chance we can save you or you can call the cops but either way, I wouldn't trust Seppo. He's going to kill you as soon as he gets what he wants. It's up to you."

"No cops. Let's go with whatever you have in mind," Hank answered without hesitation.

Garlow couldn't contain himself. He had been listening to the conversation with growing trepidation, piecing together what he could. His face had lost all color, almost white, "I think we should call the police. This is crazy."

Hank Carlson finally cracked. The stress of the last few days was too much and leaning over the manager's desk he snarled, "Listen you redheaded freak, you are where you are because of me. *I* made you the bank manager. This is my life we are talking about so you shut the fuck up and do as you are told. Is that clear?"

Garlow recoiled in shock. He was appalled and aghast at the intensity of the retort, but he wasn't about to say anything. Hank was his largest investor and the most powerful man on the Board of Directors.

"I just thought…" He stuttered.

"Don't fucking think. Just do as you are told," Carlson hissed.

While this was going on, Robbie peered through the slats of the window blinds at the parking lot in the back. He could barely see the top level of the warehouse but it was sufficient enough to give him the relative location to the bank.

"Hank, you need to calm down. If this is going to work, it is imperative that you stay under control. I think I have a plan that might work. It's a bit risky but it gives us a chance." He turned to the manager, "Is there a way for me to get to the back of the warehouse without being seen?"

The man thought for a minute and then answered, "You would have to go around two buildings on the left and climb up a steep slope that will take you to the side of the warehouse but it would depend on where they are in the parking lot… I think I have a better solution."

He paused and looked at Carlson when Robbie said, "Go on, I'm listening."

"The bank was considering acquiring the place. I have the keys to the front, sides and back doors. If you go through the side entrance on the far side, they won't be able to see you at all."

"Excellent. Give me the keys and show me the one to the right side door."

The manager opened a drawer in his desk and fished out a set of keys, "They're stamped with F for Front, R for Rear, and RS and LS for Right Side and Left Side. From where we are the right side of the building gives you the best cover."

Robbie gave the keys a quick look before slipping them into his pocket. "Thanks. Now, here's what we are going to do."

Robbie cleared the manager's desk, pushing the files and papers aside. He took a pad and a red sharpie to make a quick sketch then explained exactly what he had in mind.

They huddled around the desk while Robbie went through the steps and timing and the position of each person. When he had finished he asked, "Any questions?"

The men shook their heads and VanArcen said, "No, it's pretty clear."

Robbie turned to Carlson and said, "Hank, remember, stick to the plan. Don't get creative no matter what happens. Give me a ten-minute start and then go back to Seppo and do exactly as I explained. Tony, you know what to do and Mr. Garlow, if you hear an explosion you call the ambulance. Is that clear? "

"Yes."

"Are you ready, Hank?" Robbie studied the man carefully. The only way this was going to work is if Carlson held his nerve.

"As ready as I'll ever be," he stopped and extended his hand, "If things should go bad, I want to thank you now, you didn't have to do this."

"Thank me when it's over," Robbie said and headed for the exit on the side of the building.

VanArcen caught up with Robbie and exclaimed, "You call that a plan? That's a fucking suicide mission!"

"Do you have something better in mind?"

"No."

"Then clam up and remember to keep your eyes open when you pull the trigger!" Robbie chided with a hint of sarcasm and walked out.

"You know, Bronson, one of these days I'm going to have to save your ass and…" VanArcen reacted to the barb but Robbie was already beyond earshot.

AN ASSASSIN'S SECOND THOUGHTS

McHenry watched Meghan leaving in her truck and refocused on Allison, Ryan and Ronin who were engaged in their own version of tag in the front yard. They seemed to be having a whale of a time, laughing and running from each other while the huge dog snarled and growled playfully chasing after them. He used his front paws to trip them up and once he had them down he would pin them with his huge body, licking their faces making them squirm and giggle. McHenry was transfixed; there was something about the woman that he found intriguing. She exuded an aura of innocence and sensuality – it was in the way she moved and her face and a remarkable face it was. She reminded him of the mythological Aphrodite or at least his take on what the goddess of eroticism should look like. The boy could have been her son – the resemblance was striking.

Then there was the dog. He had never come across a dog this frightening. He had accosted Dobermans, German Shepherds, Rottweilers and Great Danes and once ran into an Irish Wolfhound that was over forty inches at the shoulders but none of them were as intimidating as Ronin. He would have to neutralize the dog, maybe even kill it before he could abduct the boy. Killing animals didn't bother him but the consequences needed to be considered. He may have to deal with Robbie Olsen. People, especially men like Olsen, get unreasonable and crazy if you hurt their dogs. He could never understand that: *it's a fucking dog!*

He would also have to account for Allison; what would he do with her? If anything happened to her, there was no doubt in his mind that Luke would come looking for him and wouldn't rest until he had exacted his pound of flesh. This was getting far more complicated than he had anticipated mainly because of Marylou. He had planned to retire from the killing business soon but since he met her, he was developing a conscience and that didn't bode well in his profession.

He adjusted his binoculars to get a closer look and it was when Allison knelt down and hugged the little boy that he made up his mind; he was done. He would return the money to the Russians and retire with Marylou to the little town in the Swiss Alps. Zermatt had always fascinated him and he knew that Marylou would be happy there. It was a place where he could reinvent himself and forget his murky past.

He put down the field glasses and called the number he had for Izhutin. He waited while it rang and felt a sense of relief like a huge weight being lifted off his chest. He chuckled to himself, happy that he could now focus on the woman he desired and their future together.

There were no pleasantries exchanged when his call was answered.

"Listen carefully. I'm done. I'll wire the money back and you assholes can take care of this yourselves," he said, his voice brusque.

"What do you mean, done? We had a deal. You cannot just walk away. We have wasted time because you took the job. You will…"

"Listen, shithead, your boss changed the assignment. I have no problems killing some asshole who resembles King Kong but I'll be damned if I hurt some kid!" he paused but when he got no response he continued, "You find someone else. I will wire your money back. And if you ever call me again you tell your boss he'll have more trouble than you can imagine. Your cars, homes, women, children, businesses and whores will all becomes targets. Poison gas, garrotes, car bombs, even that shit you call food… you will never know when but it will happen so get your fuckin' head out of your ass and find someone else!"

And with that, he hung up. He sat back on his haunches relishing the sense of freedom coursing through him. He was so caught up in this new found liberation combined with the anticipation of seeing Marylou that he didn't pay attention to the faint rustle of leaves that sounded like an animal cutting through the trees and brush. It was only when the soft, hushed sound of footsteps got close that he broke out of his reverie. He turned and got up, startled, his hand snaking inside his pocket for his gun but relaxed when he saw who it was.

"Luke! You surprised me," He feigned laughter to hide his uneasiness at being caught off-guard, "I am delighted to see you. Ah, this place you have is beautiful, no? The air, so clean…"

"Drop the act. I heard you speaking on the phone. Who are you and what are you doing here?" Luke bent over and picked up the binoculars. He looked casually towards his cabin then tossed the binoculars aside, "You're not Lorenzo Santos, so who *are* you?"

"Who I am doesn't matter and is of no consequence. I have my reasons for the charade," McHenry replied without the accent.

"Fair enough but when you are trespassing on my property and ogling my woman it is of consequence to me."

McHenry studied Luke before answering and decided that some form of the truth would prevent this from escalating, "I came here for Seppo, to kill him. I was hired by the Russians."

The man's demeanor had changed. There was something about him that reminded Luke of a rattlesnake. McHenry slithered casually to his right making sure he was safe, out of striking distance.

"An assassin; never met one before," Luke smiled, a sardonic smile.

"If you have a mirror, than you have. We are not that different, Luke. I heard about the hunters… killing a couple of poor slobs for trespassing? What does that make you?"

"I don't know what you heard but there's more to that story so don't go making assumptions."

"Killing is killing, my friend, it doesn't make a difference."

"You are wrong. There's killing and then there is killing. I don't kill for money. I confronted four men, armed and close to my home and advised them to leave. One took objection and pointed his rifle at me and told me to fuck off. You don't point a gun at a man in this part of the woods so I shot him."

Luke's manner was nonchalant but there was an edge to his voice. "His friends didn't take too kindly to that and decided to even the score. At that point I was simply defending myself. I was better with the gun than they were or it would have ended differently."

"Listen to yourself. Four armed men deep in the woods and you don't hesitate, not one bit. You confront them and take care of business. That is rare and not many men would dare to try that? Trust me, brother, you are a killer and I mean that in the best way."

Luke hadn't taken his eyes of McHenry, "You believe what you want. What are you doing here?"

"I just told you, I was hired by the Russians to kill Seppo and that's the truth. Once he died, I stuck around for personal reasons which had nothing to do with my contract. Why would I make up a story like this?"

Luke wasn't going to tell him about Seppo. He wanted to take care of the big man himself.

"I don't know. That stuff about Spain and bullfighting and India, was all that just conversational bullshit?" he paused, "I guess it was. You're nothing but a conman, a hired killer playing a role you created."

"No, it wasn't all an act. I dropped out of college and made my way through Asia and Europe. I loved Spain and lived in Madrid for two years. I learned to appreciate their culture. That part was true."

"I don't know what to believe but it doesn't matter anymore. Don't come trespassing around here again. You've been warned. And if you think that chop-suey crap will work on me, you'd better think again," Luke's voice was cold and threatening.

McHenry rarely used physical force and only did so when it was unavoidable. It was not only avoidable in this instance but judicious. Taking on Luke served no purpose and the odds were certainly not in his favor.

"I got no problem with you, Luke. I actually like you. I was passing some time exploring while Marylou worked. I heard a dog bark and took a look. I wasn't prying... just curious. That dog is something. I've never seen one like him – pretty intimidating. And your woman is exceptionally beautiful... I mean that as a compliment and with no disrespect." He didn't see any purpose in sharing the bit about abducting Ryan especially since he had decided to abort his mission.

There was a short silence while the men continued to size each other up.

"I have an uneasy feeling about you and I don't like that. Don't come around anymore, Lorenzo, or whatever your name is," Luke asserted, accepting the assassin's plausible explanation. He was about to leave but decided to delve into something that was personal.

"Marylou is a kind and decent soul. She deserves the truth. We grew up together so I have an interest in making sure she's doesn't get hurt by some phony character you cooked up. You can tell her the truth or I will."

McHenry was caught off-guard; he hadn't expected this. "I give you my word that I will tell her the truth. My name is Michael McHenry. That is my real name… some people call me Frenchie for reasons I don't care to discuss."

Luke didn't respond. He waited studying the smaller man then nodded and slipped back into the forest as quickly and silently as he had appeared. McHenry watched him blend into the surroundings like a chameleon and realized that in this environment he had no chance. Luke had the upper hand and could have easily killed him.

He sat still contemplating what had transpired and knew he had to let Marylou know the truth and he had to do it soon. But he had no idea how he was going to tell her about his past without the risk of losing her.

NEW GAME, NEW RULES

Andrei Izhutin had known his boss, Adam Shayk for a long time. He was in his early thirties and Shayk was almost forty. They had fought the wars with the Italians, the Mexicans and the Albanians to claim sovereign over Jersey City and in fact all of Jersey and much of the tristate area. It would be a mistake to judge Shayk by his appearance. The rotund, jolly persona hid the killer very effectively. Izhutin loved and respected his boss but he also knew that Shayk had a temper so it was with some reservation that he called him to report McHenry's decision.

"Did you find McHenry?" Shayk asked after the pleasantries were done.

"No, but he called me."

"And?"

"Not good news, boss. He said he would return the money and to find someone else. He had no problem when it came to the big man but children are off limits for him."

The phone went silent. For a moment, Izhutin thought that Shayk had hung up.

"Boss, it will be easy to find him here. Ask a few questions, pay a few of these hillbillies and they will tell me all I need to know. This is a small place, everyone knows everyone else and word gets around quickly. I found out that he is involved with a woman here. He calls himself Professor Santos… she is a pretty woman. Her name is Marylou Dorsey. I thought he was fucking her to pass the time but maybe it's more than that. Maybe he is in love and wants to settle down and spawn a bunch of little assassins! You say the word and I will slit this motherfucker's throat and bring his head to you."

"You will end up dead, my friend, and I will spend the rest of my life worrying about every bite I take, every place I go, every person I love. No, I am not going to risk that or risk your life. Forget about him. We will have to deal with this ourselves," Shayk replied, his voice reflecting the concern he felt.

"What do you want me to do?"

"Find the kid. Don't hurt him but keep him safe and happy. Then talk to Carlson and get the laptop and if anyone interferes, deal with them. I'm losing my patience."

"What about the brother, the boy's father and that soldier, Olsen? I did some poking around and he likes the boy's mother…" Izhutin left the obvious unsaid. He also wanted to make sure if Luke and Robbie were off limits before he whacked them.

"Luke? Hmmm, good question." Shayk thought about it and then said, "It will be a pity to hurt him; he is a rare one. It would be like killing a white tiger."

"A tiger is dangerous," Izhutin noted, "whether they are white or not."

"You are right. If he gets in the way, waste him and throw him in a the middle of the road where everyone can see him. It is time we taught these assholes a lesson! Olsen will be a bigger problem but the same goes for him. Cut him up and feed him to the dogs but be careful, Andrei, I do not want to lose you. Are those two morons with you enough or should I send more people up there, maybe Viktor, Dimitri and Old Sergei?"

"No need, boss. These two assholes should be enough. They are young but they are good men and this will be a good experience for them. I will call you soon."

Izhutin hung up and turned to Milo and Sergei, "We have a job to do so stop playing with those little pickles you call dicks and concentrate."

"Finally, we will see some action," Milo said.

"This is not action, this is like shooting fish in a barrel! The fucking Italians in Jersey City… now, that was action." Sergei commented, reminiscing, "Do you remember, boss, every corner, every coffee shop… blood on the streets! Even the fucking whorehouses weren't safe."

"Yeah, that was something. I remember one time we were in that Chinese massage parlor in Edison, the bitch was giving me a blowjob and just as I was about to feed her some premium Russian cream, bang, bang, bang… gunshots in the next room! She got so frightened she bit half my cock off! It was Adam; he shot some Italian baker who was in the wrong place at the wrong time. Scared the fucking piss out of me."

"What did the Chinese bitch say after biting off your cock?" Sergei asked tongue in cheek.

"You taste vely, vely goood!" Izhutin quipped trying to mimic an Asian accent.

The men laughed and Milo asked, "Hey, boss, who was your first, eh?"

"She was an old bitch in Moskva. I was fifteen and hornier than a rutting bull. She let me fuck her for a couple of rubles and half a bottle of samogon! It was the fastest fuck in history, two strokes and …"

"I mean, who was the first man you killed?" Milo interrupted.

"Oh, my first kill… hey, you never forget your first fuck or your first kill. He was a fucking Ukrainian thug who tried muscling in on our action. We were young, like you two assholes, Adam and me, and we thought we owned the streets of the city! I stuck that fucker a hundred times with a knife but he refused to die. He begged for his life, kissing my feet and showing me pictures of his children… finally, I shot him in the head to end the madness! Fucking blood, brains and shit all over the place. I had nightmares for a month. I could see his face everywhere and in everything. Ruined my vodka, it was like drinking piss! But after that, it got easier and soon it was easy-peasy. Why do you ask? Are you shitting in your pants or what?"

"No. I'm not afraid. I'm a killer, boss, like Wild Bill…"

Izhutin cut the young man off, "You're a fucking idiot. I should send you home and get a real man. Don't mistake these motherfuckers for fish. They are dangerous. So, keep your eyes open and your gun ready and I don't mean that little thing between your legs!"

THE WOLF AND
THE SERPENT

Seppo Heikkinen waited in the shadows but not by the SUV where Hank had assumed he was. No, he wasn't a dumbass hillbilly like the locals he despised. He had moved across to the narrow alleyway between the warehouse and the adjacent building on his left which was also unoccupied. Standing on top of the landing provided him with a clear view of the parking lot through the labyrinthine tracts in between the trees and it gave him the advantage of surprise.

He was getting impatient – Hank should have been out by now and was about to call him on his phone when a tall, gaunt figure appeared from around the side of the building. Finally, the diamonds! Once he got his hands on them he'd get the heck out of this godforsaken place and start afresh somewhere far away from here. He watched as the figure slowly approached the parking lot.

Hank was moving unsteadily, almost like he was drunk or heavily sedated. When he got past the cars that were parked against the rear of the building, he held up a small bag in front of him then to the Seppo's surprise, Carlson stumbled, steadied himself and slowly got down to his knees. He was still for a moment before pitching forward, face first onto the blacktop.

Heikkinen's brain screamed: *It's a trick.* But after a few minutes of closely observing the body and the bag of diamonds that had escaped Hank's grasp, he couldn't contain himself. He sprung out from the shadows, gun drawn, and made his way up the incline and cautiously approached the prone body. He looked around checking to see if there were any passerby but the parking lot was deserted. He bent down and picked up the bag and when he looked in, he was shocked beyond belief. He shook the contents from the bag and out fell paperclips, small pencils, crayons and marbles. *It was a fucking trick! He should have known, Hank was up to no good!*

"You shouldn't play games with me, Hank, you know better. Now, I'm going to have to blow you and your fucking family to pieces!" the big man snarled.

There was no reaction from the body lying on the macadamized blacktop. He nudged the body with his foot but there still was no response.

"Are you looking for these?"

The voice cut through the parking lot and made the big man pivot. Robbie stood on the edge of the incline, in front of the trees, with the velvet bag of diamonds in one hand and his Glock in the other.

Seppo tried hard to control his emotions. His mind, cunning as ever, quickly assessed the situation. He was in a tough spot with very little room to maneuver. If he blew Hank up, he would be shot. If he put down the trigger, he would be shot – he had no doubt in his mind that Olsen wouldn't let him go.

He had one desperate move left.

"Put down your gun and throw the bag to me, now! Do it now or I'll blow his ass to hell!" He instructed Robbie in a voice that sounded both desperate and intransigent.

He showed Robbie what looked like a garage opener. "I press

this and he goes boom!" The big man assured him. He smiled, an eerie, frightening smile on his scarred and fire-ravaged face but, it failed to elicit the reaction he had hoped for.

"Ah, what we've got here is a Mexican Standoff. Hank goes boom and you get a bullet through your skull and I most probably will get one through mine," Robbie said, his voice taking on a hard edge. "You give me the trigger and I'll give you the diamonds. You have my word."

Seppo considered the suggestion for a moment, "I don't trust you, Olsen. If I give you this then I'd lose my bargaining chip. You could shoot me and I'd be one dead asshole. Don't play me for a fool."

Hank still hadn't moved. "What's with him? Did you drug him so he doesn't feel anything?" Seppo asked.

"I guess the stress was too much. Forget him for now. What if we both put our guns away and you give me the trigger in exchange for the diamonds? Now, that makes sense and everyone goes home happy," Robbie offered sounding propitiatory.

"Look at me! Look at my fucking face… do you think I'll ever be happy?" Seppo spat out softly, "The Carlsons owe me. They fucking owe me more than just the diamonds."

"You killed Ray and Emma; I think they would disagree."

"Fuck them!" The big Finn snarled, "Fuck them and fuck what they think. Give me the diamonds or I'll blow the motherfucker up and we'll let the chips fall where they may. I don't give a shit anymore!"

Robbie realized that Seppo was at his breaking point. He wasn't immune to the stress of being hunted and if he wasn't careful, Hank and he could end up dead.

"Okay, calm down. You look bad but there are options especially when you have money. There's reconstructive surgery and you'll be good as new. I had a friend whose face was blown away in

Afghanistan… what they did for him was remarkable, really amazing. Listen, I appreciate your need for the diamonds. It's the way to get your life back," Robbie's voice had taken on a softer tone, "It's not a problem – I don't care about the diamonds. You can have them and you can leave. So before you do something we both will regret, let's put the guns away. What do you say?"

The big Finn's mind was in overdrive. What Olsen suggested made sense and it gave him a way out. Hank and the Carlsons didn't mean anything to him so why not? He'd get the diamonds in exchange for Hank.

"How do I know those are the diamonds? He tricked me once."

Robbie pulled the drawstring on the velvet bag and shook a few of the sparkling stones into his palm. "Here, take a look."

The big Finn squinted making a quick appraisal and satisfied that those were indeed the diamonds asked, "How do I know you won't follow me? You tracked me here."

"I didn't track you," Robbie quickly countered, "It was a coincidence. I was here opening an account when Hank showed up and explained what his situation. Luke did try to track you but lost the trail once you headed out of Chase River. You can leave and no one will know. Like I said, you have my word that I won't try and stop you. I can't speak for Luke or the others."

"Fuck Luke! He doesn't scare me!" Seppo spat back. He was quiet, cogitating Robbie's offer, and finally acquiesced, "Okay, I'll put the gun away then what?"

"I will place the diamonds on the ground and you do the same with the trigger and at the count of three we'll walk towards what we each want. If you decide to pull your gun, I'll do the same and it won't end well – for you or me. If you don't, I won't either. You can leave and then I'll get the bomb off Hank."

The big Finn eyed Robbie suspiciously but realized that there was no other way to get the diamonds and without them, he might as well be dead.

"Oh, I looked at the bomb and it looks tricky. How do I diffuse it? There are several additional wires that seem to be interconnected with the igniter, what are they for?"

"They are dummy wires to confuse anyone trying to disarm it. They don't do anything. The one going through the strap is also a dummy. Cut the red and black wires that go in or out of the initiator and it's done; no boom!" Seppo explained and put his gun away, "Okay. Let's do it and no tricks."

Robbie holstered his weapon and dropped the bag of diamonds next to his feet. Seppo waited then tossed the garage opener close to where he was standing but it hit the back clasp and rolled a few feet away. For a moment he was tempted to go after it but decided not to and remained still.

"You've got a set of balls, Olsen, I'll give you that. Risking your life for this piece of shit… he's not worth it," Heikkinen mused and added, "I'll do the counting and we go at three."

He counted slowly, "One-two-three!"

The first thing Heikkinen did was to examine the contents of the bag. He took a quick look and spoke to Robbie, his tone accusatory, "Where's the rest? These are only half of what was there."

"That's everything that was in the bag. I was there when he got it from his safe deposit box… he didn't take anything. He just handed it to me," Robbie assured the big Finn.

"Fucking Hank! You can never trust… shit!" Seppo exclaimed, as the bag slipped from his hand and hit the ground. He knelt down, facing away from Robbie, looking for any diamonds that may have fallen out and scattered then without warning the big man drew a .38 from his ankle holster, pivoted and shot at Robbie while laughing.

"You're a sucker, Olsen!"

The first bullet whizzed by Robbie's head and the second came precariously close to his ear. In an instant, surprise was replaced by instinct. He threw himself behind one the cars parked nearest to him and was in the process of getting his gun out when gunshots from the far side of the bank erupted creating an immediate and incendiary distraction. It was VanArcen and he walking towards Heikkinen, blasting away like some old time gunslinger.

"Tony, get down! What are...." Robbie screamed but his friend couldn't hear him. He was in a trance-like state oblivious of all danger. The only objective in his mind was stopping Heikkinen.

The new threat surprised the big Finn and in the chaos he took the only option he had. He scrambled back towards the warehouse firing wildly as he retreated. A single bullet from the barrage of shots hit VanArcen; he jerked and dropped to the pavement.

"Fucking hell!" The small man groaned in pain, grabbing at his shoulder.

"Damn! Tony..." Robbie ran towards VanArcen, firing a few rounds in the general direction of Heikkinen.

"Are you okay?" He asked his friend who was now sitting up.

"I'm fine... it's just a scratch. Don't let him get away, Robbie! Go... go get the motherfucker!"

"I'll take care of him. You go on..." It was Hank. He had finally worked up the nerve to get involved and had come over to where they were. "Here take this. I had it in the safe."

In his hand was a .50 caliber handgun, the Desert Eagle, and one of the most powerful handguns available. It was capable of stopping a grizzly in its tracks. "I had a feeling that someday I would need it to stop Seppo."

Robbie gave it a quick once over then returned it to Hank.

"Thanks, but I'll stick to what I have. This isn't the time to experiment. You make sure he's okay," Robbie said, indicating towards VanArcen, and took off after the big Finn.

He heard a loud crashing sound as he scampered down the incline and caught sight of Seppo kicking in the overhead door and disappearing into the warehouse. Robbie waited then ran up onto the loading dock and peeked in to make sure the big Finn wasn't waiting to ambush him. He heard the heavy thudding of hustling footsteps and of boxes being kicked aside and followed the commotion into the building.

Maddie was right all along. It was the time for the reckoning and the fourth horseman.

FOXES ON THE TRAIL

Izhutin was a tough and dangerous man with an astute mind. He had to be to survive the bitter cold of Yakutsk as a young boy and the mean streets of Moscow as a teen. Yakutsk was the coldest city in Siberia and one of the coldest places on earth. His family was originally from Saint Petersburg but had moved to Yakutsk to work in the diamond mines. After several years of coping with the bitter cold, his father finally relented and moved them to Moscow hoping to provide a better life for his children. It was in Moscow that the young and impressionable Andrei Izhutin met Adam Shayk and forged a friendship with the street thug. The rest, as they say, is history.

Izhutin figured that Ryan would have to be in one of four places – with his mother, his grandparents on his mother's side, his father, Luke, or with his grandmother, Lisa Carlson.

They tried Meghan's place first but there was no one at her cabin so the logical next stop was her parents' cottage since it was just a stone's throw away. As tough and hard a man as Izhutin was, he abhorred inflicting pain especially on people not in the business. He had no problem putting a bullet in someone's head or sticking them with a knife but the thought of torture made him squeamish. He had decided to let Sergei take the lead on this one.

Of the two young men that were with him, Sergei Volkin was older and a lot tougher. He had been in and out of Russian prisons before Alexei Zakirov recruited him and sent him to Jersey. He was about six feet tall and built like a fighter with prison tats covering his neck and arms. His dark eyes and darker hair betrayed his mixed Slavic-Asian ancestry something he was proud of. Milo Pozdnyakov was younger and was a lot less intimidating with impish good looks and a perpetual smile on his face. He was related to one of Alexei Zakirov's henchman and was originally sent to be a companion and to watch over the big boss's son but Nikolai Zakirov wanted nothing to do with the charming Miloslav hanging around his women so instead of sending him back to Russia, Adam Shayk decide to keep him as part of his mob.

Izhutin dropped the men off at the corner of Main and Hollow Creek Road with some final instructions, "Sergei, you take Milo and go to the parent's house. If the boy is there you get him and wait for me. If the boy is not there you talk to them so they will tell you where he is. And, Milo, you will listen to Sergei and do exactly what you are told, is that clear?"

"Yes, boss!" the young man answered, "You can count on me."

"Sergei, don't go crazy; grab the boy if he's there or get them to talk. If you scare them they will talk. We are not animals. We do not make war on the innocent. Now, I am going to fill gas and will be back soon. Don't let me down."

They waited while the car drove away and made their way to the house and walked down the gravel walkway to the front door.

"Nice garden," Milo commented, looking directly at the small waterfall and the artistic mosaic of flower beds with rocks interspersed.

"I'll do the talking. Don't speak unless you are asked a question and if that happens don't say too much. Understand?" Sergei instructed the younger man ignoring his horticultural observation.

Milo nodded and tapped the wind catcher on a large wind chime hanging by the door creating a high-pitched, tuneless melody. Pleased by the pleasant strains, the young man tapped the wind catcher again, this time, harder.

"What the fuck are you doing? Stop this shit! You're like a fuckin' five-year-old!" Sergei hissed, irritated, and rang the doorbell. Milo immediately stepped away and stood beside his partner with his hands in his pockets and a remorseful look on his face.

There was a imperceptible movement of the shades and a few seconds later the front door cracked opened just enough for them to see an attractive, older woman.

"Hello. How can I help you?" Beth Hollier greeted the two men, through the narrow opening in the doorway.

"I am sorry to bother you, madam, but we are strangers here and looking for place to eat. Is there restaurant nearby?" Sergei asked with a disarming smile displaying small, even teeth.

Though he seemed friendly, his appearance was unnerving but the woman looked over at Milo and her initial concern was allayed. The boy was slim and good looking with large blue eyes, straight blond hair and a friendly smile. His congenial demeanor put Beth Hollier at ease.

"Oh! There are two or three places where the food is really good," she said, removing the safety latch and opening the door wide, "but the easiest to find is Bucky Johnston's Diner… it's just down the road on Main Street. You go that way."

She pointed in the direction of the restaurant.

"Thank you, madam, we are in appreciation. So I go to intersection and make left, is correct, huh?" Sergei's manner remained unsure but friendly as he peered inside past the door.

"Yes. You can literally walk from…" She began when the door was pushed open with such force that it sent her tumbling backwards.

"Close the door!" Sergei commanded and in one quick stride,

grabbed the woman and hissed into her ear, "Don't make noise. You make noise and I slit your throat. You understand?"

The short blade pressing against her jugular was all the convincing she needed and she acquiesced with a nod. Beth Hollier had never been so frightened in her life. She was trying to come to terms with the sudden metamorphosis of the placid, friendly man to the menacing monster that had her from behind, knife at her throat. She was in what could be best described as confused psychological shock, a form of Acute Stress Disorder.

Sergei reverted to Russian and said to his partner, "Go check the rooms and see if the boy is here and find the old man. Hurry, we don't have too much time."

After a few minutes, Milo returned with a frail, older man whose hands were trembling uncontrollably.

"He was in the dining room. He is not well… look at his hands," Milo said then added, "The boy is not here."

"Please don't hurt him. He's sick, he has Parkinson's!" Beth Hollier pleaded, "Take whatever you want but please don't hurt us."

Sergei laughed, "She thinks we are here to rob her! For an old bitch, she is beautiful, no? I would fuck her."

"Please let him go. Please! Take what you want… the jewelry is in the bedroom. You can have it, just don't hurt him," Beth Hollier continued to plead with her captors.

Sergei ignored her and spoke to the younger man, "You are sure the boy is not here?"

"I'm sure."

"Put him in the chair and tie him up. Use the electrical cord. Tie him nice and tight," Sergei instructed.

Beth Hollier's inability to understand the dialog only added to her confusion and terror. She pleaded again, "Please leave him alone. Don't hurt him!"

"He a sick, old man, he's not going anywhere," Milo protested looking at the old man's trembling hands.

"You ever question me again and I will cut your cock off and feed it to the goats, you hear me?" Sergei snarled, his voice was soft but the tone so menacing that it made the younger man flinch, "Now tie the old fucker up!"

Milo acted swiftly. He walked over to the floor lamp in the corner and pulled the plug out from the socket and using his knife, cut the wire from the base of the lamp. He then halved the cord and split it once more and tied Mark Hollier's arms to the armrest of the sofa and stood back.

Sergei turned to Beth Hollier and said in English, "Now, you tell me what I need to know or I will break his fingers one by one. You understand me?"

Beth Hollier began crying. At first, she tried choking back the sobs but when she realized that this wasn't a robbery, she began crying uncontrollably.

The Russian stepped around and slapped her, not hard but with just enough force to get her attention, "Stop the crying! You stop now," he shook her by the shoulders before stepping back. "If you want to save your man you better tell me what I need to know. Where is your grandson?"

"I don't know! I really don't know..." she stuttered through the tears.

She was trying to understand why they would want Ryan. Were they trying to kidnap him? Meghan had no real money and neither did she so what could they possibly gain? Her mind raced uncontrollably filled with wild notions and then it struck her: child pornography! She had heard horror stories of children being abducted and made to perform sexual acts while being filmed... horrific stuff. Her mind went blank.

"Break his finger," Sergei instructed Milo in English.

"No! Please, I don't know where he is. He could be with Allison..." Beth whimpered.

Milo grabbed a hold of the old man's forefinger and slowly pulled it backwards but stopped when Mark Hollier groaned.

"The bitch is lying. Break his finger, do it now!" This time he spoke in Russian.

The younger man started again but he couldn't get himself to hurt the old man. He stepped back and shook his head, "I can't... you do it."

Sergei pushed him aside and without a thought, wrenched the finger back until it snapped. There was a loud scream and Beth Hollier knew that the nightmare had just begun. It didn't take long before the Russians were convinced that the boy was at Luke's cabin up on Moose Head Point.

When they left, the cabin was eerily quiet.

AN ASSASSIN'S ABNEGATION

When Marylou Dorsey got home she found McHenry in the garden at the back of her father's home. He was reading a book and making notes on a small pad. He looked up and smiled and put the book down.

"Hey, what are you reading?" She asked and leaned over and kissed him on the mouth, a quick 'hello' kiss but he held her by the back of her head and kissed her again, this time it was a long, sensual kiss that made her heart flutter.

She broke away and standing back asked, "Wow! What's that for?"

"For being who you are and for how I feel about you," McHenry answered placing the book over his obvious erection. Though the man was rather well endowed, the rumors describing the size of his cock were overly exaggerated.

"Mmm, I can't wait for tonight!" She murmured and pushing the book to the side, plopped herself on his lap and wriggled her ass on his erection.

"You're going to have to stop doing that if you want me to answer the question."

"Mmm, I couldn't resist but I'll behave. Dad and Junior will be home any minute. So what are you reading?" She asked again.

"Being and Nothingness." He replied, "It's a book by Jean Paul Sartre."

Marylou took the book from McHenry and was astonished, "It's in French! Do you speak French?"

"Yes as well as Spanish, German, Italian, Russian and a bit of English," was the man's quiet response.

"A bit of English?"

"I was being facetious."

"What's it about?" she asked toying with his earlobes.

"Existentialism… how we relate to the world around us; the fundamental dilemma we face as humans. It challenges the ideas of freedom, of our ability to choose, our actions and our responsibility to others. It deals with what we deem as reality and the predictive processing of our perceptual consciousness."

She was fascinated though she did not fully comprehend what he had just said.

"I feel so inadequate… so ignorant! What are you doing with me? Is it just about sex?" she asked, overwhelmed by his obvious education and cerebral perspicuity.

He hugged her to him and held her tightly before answering, "You are smarter than most of the people I know and have known. Just because you haven't read Sartre doesn't mean you are not smart. I love you for your mind, your body and who you are. You are a decent and kind person and that means more to me than some pseudo-intellectual garbage."

She kissed him on his forehead. "You're being kind but I won't argue the point. You can explain things to me so I won't be so uninformed or… hmmm, sound like a pseudo-intellectual!" She laughed after the last bit.

He loved her cute laugh and her naiveté. There was a comfortable pause before he said, "Get up. There is something I have to tell you that is very important."

She studied his face and his expression and got the feeling that whatever it was that he was about to tell her would affect them in a manner that would change their lives forever. She struggled awkwardly trying to get up off his lap and finally managed with some help from him. She straightened her dress before sitting down on the chair next to his.

"What is it?" her heart was now pounding with anticipation and dread.

"My name is not Lorenzo Santos. My name is Michael McHenry."

The accent was gone and the shock on Marylou's face told him that he was on a slippery slope but he was determined to tell her everything. "I came here to kill Seppo Heikkinen. I am, what they call, a contract killer."

For a moment she thought he was joking but his expression was dead serious. He waited for some sort of response but she sat looking at him dazed, wide-eyed in disbelief so he continued, "Now, before you go hating me and despising me, let me assure you that I only accepted contracts on those who were in the business - mobsters, gangbangers, politicians, corporate thieves and such. I'm not justifying what I did. It wasn't a moral issue for me; it was simply what I was skilled at and it afforded me a very good living."

She remained silent but couldn't hold back the tears welling up in her eyes.

"I love you more than I can explain. I loved you the moment I saw you, no, even before I saw you. You were a thought, a figment of my imagination who suddenly manifested and appeared in my life." He was speaking softly now, his voice reflecting the earnestness of his confession, "I wouldn't blame you if you didn't want to see me again… if you hated me. I deserve nothing less but knowing you, even for this brief period, has made me a better person."

He reached over to hold her hand but she moved away. She got up off the chair, the tears streaming down her face and began walking back towards the house.

"Wait! Marylou, please say something… anything!"

He got up and chased after her but he was too late. She had rushed down the corridor and locked herself in the bedroom.

"Marylou?" he was speaking softly, his face pressed against the door, "Marylou, please talk to me."

He could hear her sobbing and then through the tears, "Leave me alone. Please go away!"

He waited a few minutes before returning to the patio. He looked over the pretty landscape and picked up the pad and book and walked down the narrow pathway to a pond at the base of a slight incline. He sat down on the grass by the edge of the water and noticed a pair of wood ducks swimming at the far end of the pond. The drake with his iridescent green plumage and red eyes and the hen in her camouflage speckled brown were hard to miss. The male postured for the hen, turning his head, preening his feathers and flapping his wings in an obvious display of courtship. They swam in small circles together, dabbling bottoms up before preening and grooming each other.

McHenry was beginning to think that Kant, the German philosopher, was right and that he had no way of understanding the external world around him; only his perception of what he thought was real. He watched the ducks for a while wondering if what he assumed was their courtship was actually something less romantic and far more primal; a need to propagate and nothing else. Maybe *his* feelings had less to do with love and romance and like these ducks, more to do with the opportunity to mate with a desirable female. He smiled a self-effacing smile: *I'm losing it! Ducks in love and Immanuel Kant's concepts of noumena?*

He needed to make a decision one way or the other – to stay and try and win Marylou back or to leave. The thought of leaving her was unbearable but it was obvious that she needed time.

He wandered around the vast property lost in thought before heading back to his room. He decided that best course of action would be to leave and give her some space. If she loved him as much as he loved her, she would call if not, he would sell his property in Connecticut and move to the Swiss Alps. The chalet in Zermatt was old and needed work and he would immerse himself in the repair and renovations. He would also pursue his interest in art and antiquarian books. Staying busy would help him get over her.

He was folding his clothes putting them neatly away in his travel bag when she came to his room. She was standing by the doorway in her bare feet and had changed into a casual chemise-like dress. Her hair fell loosely against her shoulders and her eyes were red from crying. His back was to the door so he didn't see her.

"What are you doing?" she asked in a voice that was soft and strained with emotion.

He turned around slowly, surprised but secretly relieved that she was speaking to him.

"I'm packing. I didn't think you'd want anything to do with me," he answered while appraising her. He had taken off the glasses and removed the tinted contacts but she didn't seem to notice or to care.

She looked so much like Natalie Wood right then that he had to use every fiber of his self-restraint to stop from going over to her.

"Well, you can stop. I can't un-love you even though you lied and were deceptive," she said, watching as he put down the shirt he was folding. His expression reminded her of a boy who had just been told that detention was over.

"I want you to tell me everything and I mean everything. How you got into the business, how many people you've killed... everything! And then I never want to discuss it or refer to your past ever again. Can you do that?"

"Yes, I swear to you I will tell you everything and never mention it again unless you bring it up. I will never lie to you again, Marylou."

The relief he felt was overwhelming. The waters of his life had been turbulent and lonely and he felt he was drowning in a morass of violence and negativity. He was a man going under for the final time when she threw him a lifeline – it was his only chance at redemption.

"One more thing; you will never, ever go back to that way of life... *never!*" her face was set and uncompromising.

"I promise. I'm done."

He spent the next hour and a half telling her everything about his past, sparing no detail. When he got to Francis Njoku and his children, he literally choked up but he didn't leave out any of the gory details. He explained the mistake and the nightmares that followed, the children's faces that haunted him to this day.

When he was finished, she sat silently studying him, her eyes boring into his soul, and after a few moments she got up and locked the door. He was seated on the edge of the bed unsure of what was happening and was about to stand up when she pushed him back onto the duvet.

"Make love to me... no, just fuck me!" she whispered while slowly unbuttoning his trousers.

In some inexplicable way the confessions and his vulnerability had aroused her and the deal between them was consummated when he buried his cock deep inside her. When he felt her tremble and heard the soft moan, he knew with absolute certainty that he could never live without her. Kant was wrong, what he saw was a pair of ducks in the primordial game that males and females play and that the drake was in love or he wasn't the Frenchie, Michael McHenry.

THE WOLF AND THE MONSTER: KISMET

Once inside the warehouse, Robbie crouched behind one of the many pallet racks that ran halfway down the length of the building. The boarded windows and closed doors made for a dim interior and though he had identified the breakers and the switches on the wall, the nebulous shadows offered him a certain refuge. His training had taught him to stay as quiet and still as possible and observe before taking any action. If he had learned anything from his stint in Afghanistan it was that impulsive moves and kneejerk reactions often led to disaster. He remained still using the dust covered boxes and products that were stacked on pallets as cover.

The seconds dragged on turning into achingly long minutes but Robbie remained unmoving, eyes peeled, listening intently, and confident that sooner or later, Seppo would crack. The initial commotion of cans and boxes being booted and trampled had been replaced by the whirring of a neighboring generator and except for the occasional sound of a truck driving by, the warehouse was eerily quiet. He edged closer to the end-post of the rack, gun in hand, chasing the slightest whisper that would help him to zero in on the big Finn. It was reminiscent of his childhood hunting elk and deer in Montana.

And just when he thought that Seppo might have exited the building, there was a loud rattle of a falling metal chair and an accompanying expletive, "Fuck!"

Robbie scooted towards the sound staying low, maneuvering around a rolling ladder that was in the adjacent aisle. He got to the rack nearest the sound and quickly scanned the factory floor for the chair.

There were three forklifts parked against the side wall blocking the exit and just past them was a metal stairwell leading to the second level. He saw the chair lying on its side near the bottom of the stairs but was immediately on alert. This had to be a ploy to throw him off – he would have heard footsteps going up the stairs especially with someone as large as the Finn.

A little past the forklifts, back towards the rear of the building, were three rows of pallets with boxes piled over six feet high which could provide enough cover for Seppo. *That had to be it.* Robbie thought to himself, *Seppo was somewhere in that maze.*

He stood up, gun pointing in the direction of the boxes, and made his way cautiously towards the cluster of pallets. He was in hyper-sensory mode as he inched forward. His eyes had adjusted to the dim light and his hearing was tuned to pick-up the slightest incongruous sound. He could feel his heart thudding in his chest and the adrenalin coursing through him. Images of Kunduz flashed briefly through his mind but he shook them off and focused on the rows of boxes half-expecting Seppo to leap out shooting.

Robbie was an arms-length from the nearest pallet when the piercing blare of the factory shift-horn knifed through the quiet jarring his senses and startling him. He took a quick step to the side, gun ready in anticipation when a black, 55-gallon steel drum, half-filled with hydraulic oil, rammed him in the back. He was propelled forward; crashing into the boxes and instinctively threw up his arms to brace for impact. In the frantic moments that followed, he lost the Glock and was fumbling for it when he heard Seppo.

"Drop it and back away or you die."

The big man was standing at an oblique angle to the side with the .38 pointed straight at his head. At this range there was little chance he would miss. "Stand up, come on, get up!"

While Robbie was getting to his feet, the giant kicked the Glock away. "Don't want you trying something that'll get you killed… not just yet."

"Now what?" Robbie said dusting himself off.

"Now you die. Pretty damn simple, soldier."

Robbie smirked. If Seppo was going to kill him he would have been dead already. The big man had other plans for him.

"Why do I get the feeling that you have something else in mind, huh?"

The big man smiled, "You're right. I do have something else in mind, something that is a lot more painful than a .38 through your thick skull. You are a fucking bulldog, I'll give you that."

He studied Robbie for a few moments then instructed, "Take off your shirt."

"What?"

"Take off your fucking shirt… now! We're going to fight; hand to hand combat, no weapons. I want to make sure you're not hiding something."

Robbie was incredulous, "You want to fight here, in this place?"

"Sure, why not. It's as good as any. There's some space there," he pointed to an open space behind the front lobby. "That's about the size of a ring… should work fine."

Robbie peeled off his shirt and the Finn quickly patted him down. Seppo noticed the scars on Robbie's body, "Looks like you've been in a few wars but it's not going to help."

Seppo followed suit and took off his shirt revealing a huge, heavily muscled body without an ounce of fat on it. He flexed either out of habit or to posture with intent to intimidate. He was severely burned in places but it didn't seem to bother the big man. He then proceeded to unload the .38, a Wesson Guardian, and tossed the bullets and the gun to the side.

"There. Now it's just you and me. You represent the Land of the fucked-up and the Home of the fat-asses and I represent the Finnish Special Forces."

Robbie bristled and took umbrage at the snide reference. "If you hate this country so much why did you come here?"

"Au contraire, my soon-to-be-dead friend. I love America… I hate fucking Americans. You are a bunch of lazy, self-indulgent, spoiled children who have no idea what's going on in the rest of the world and as long as you can get your pizza, burgers, MTV and tweets, you could care less!"

Robbie shook his head and smirked, "Whatever, dude. Let's cut the chatter and get on with it."

"One more thing, asshole, I want you to know that I enjoyed killing that old bitch, she was a fucking waste of oxygen. And when I fucked that black slut, Angela, she moaned like the whore she was!" Seppo studied Robbie and realizing he had hit a nerve, continued, "Before I killed her, I took my time and enjoyed every minute. She kept saying that you would be coming for me; so, heeeere's Johnny! Come and get it." And the Finn laughed a taunting, other-worldly cackle.

Rage, in burst of hot lava, washed over Robbie. The thought of Maddie and Angela made him want to destroy the giant, to make him suffer and to prolong the pain. He started to walk towards the designated space when the big Finn charged. Seppo's shoulder hit him squarely in the chest lifting him off the ground and the two men crashed into the boxes, busting open several and spilling their contents.

They fell together entangled in a mess of arms and legs and ended up on their sides buried among loose balusters, posts, fittings and other accouterment for staircases. There was a brief and awkward struggle before Robbie broke free, taking advantage of the clutter through which Seppo was trying to free himself. The big man's foot was stuck in between the slats of a pallet and when he leaned over to jerk free, Robbie hit him, a quick one-two to the lower back, but it was like hitting stone. It did nothing to the big Finn.

"You hit like a little girl!" The giant snarled.

A side swipe from Seppo's huge hand sent Robbie stumbling back. He regained his balance and took his stance on the balls of his feet. Robbie wasn't a small man by any standard but the difference in size made him look like a Chihuahua taking on a Saint Bernard. Seppo was in spectacular shape unlike some belly-over-the-balls big man. His incredible physique could only be attributed to a freakish genetic manifestation. However, fighting is not always about size; skill plays a large role in it, skill and mindset, and that's where Robbie had an advantage.

Robbie bobbed and weaved and feinted, darting in and out, striking with quick combinations, left-right-left mixed in with the occasional right crosses and left hooks to keep the big man guessing. The punches weren't causing any consequential damage but it was an irritant and created a distraction.

"Come on, let's fight, asshole... dancing is for faggots!" Seppo hissed, swatting aside another left and charged in, unconcerned about the repercussions. He was hoping to pin the smaller man against the rack.

Robbie sidestepped the big man like a matador evading a charging bull and using Seppo's momentum pushed him into the steel rack as he went by. Some boxes on the upper shelves came crashing to the factory floor but the impact had little effect on the giant. He smiled, a grotesque distortion of his torrefied face, and closed in again. In a grappling contest, Robbie stood no chance; Seppo was just too powerful and would overpower him so he had to keep this fight on the feet.

A low kick to Seppo's leg felt like his shin had slammed into a fire hydrant. The big man chuckled; he had checked the kick, shin on shin, and the pain shot through Robbie's making him wince. *That was a bad idea!* He faked a jab to Seppo's head to distract him and followed it with another kick but this was aimed at the knee. He torqued his hips and snapped the kick to generate maximum force but once again, the big man just smiled. *This is ridiculous! That should have buckled this monster!*

"Is that all you got?" Heikkinen bellowed, "Then you're in some serious trouble, motherfucker!"

Robbie recalled his sensei's mantra when fighting bigger men: *"Don't give up. Keep kicking the knee joint and sooner or later it will give. The human knee wasn't designed to take repeated high-impact trauma."*

But Seppo seemed immune to the kicks and kept pressing the action, coming forward, inexorable; and at times rushing in forcing Robbie to give ground. Robbie spun and turned, dodged and ducked, slipping one way then the other to effortlessly avoid the huge fists thrown with no skill but with enough force to break bones. To stand and engage in a brawl with this monster was out of the question. Every blow that Robbie parried, whether it was using his forearm or his shoulder, felt like he was being hit with a sledgehammer. And each time he landed something it was like hitting a brick wall.

Robbie had retreated past the racks to the adjacent woodworking department littered with chairs and workbenches. The back wall of the cell was lined with lathes, drill-presses, sanders and other auxiliary machinery all of which were covered in layers of dust. He had to navigate around the clutter, leaping over tables, dancing lightly between crates and benches, while Seppo chased after him, relentless in pursuit, until he had Robbie cornered against the tool crib.

"Now I've got you, you fucking cunt!"

Robbie threw a quick left-right combination hoping to create space but the big man ducked and grabbed his arm and in one quick motion, lifted him over his head and flung him across the floor. Robbie landed on top of a workbench, rolled off of it and fell onto a chair before hitting the ground. The impact sent hammers, screws and an assortment of tools scattering along the concrete floor. He had the wind knocked out of him and struggled to get back up. A myriad of thoughts raced through his mind echoing an underlying sentiment: *damn, he's strong as an ox!*

"You didn't think you had a chance, did you?" Seppo mocked and came towards him kicking and tossing chairs and benches out of his way. "I thought you Rangers were a tough bunch but you're just a fucking pussy!"

Robbie ignored the barb and changed stances, turning southpaw. He faked again sliding left then darting in threw a kick to the big man's liver. A blow to the liver was debilitating but it had to land just right. It didn't. Seppo trapped the leg against the side of his body and with surprising agility did a half-pirouette and flung Robbie against the tool crib. He bounced off the expanded metal mesh landing on his back gasping for air.

The giant was enjoying this. He felt totally in control now, overcome with confidence that Robbie posed no real threat. The anger, hatred, paranoia and emotional alienation had come to a boil. He was going exact his frustrations on this good-looking man who seemed to have everything. The Finn pushed a chair out of the way and as Robbie was getting up, he aimed a kick at the smaller man's ribcage and had it landed would have certainly ended the fight. But Robbie saw it coming and instinctively brought his arms up, fading sideways, off center and lessening the impact. But despite the quick move, the force of the kick was enough to lift him off the ground sending him airborne.

This was fun. Seppo thought to himself. *If Hank hadn't stopped him that first night at the diner, none of this would have happened. It was time for the soldier-boy to pay the piper.*

A feeling of helplessness threatened the fringes of Robbie mind. He experienced a flashback to a muggy, sweltering night in Bermuda. A disagreement with three sailors over a woman led to a back alley brawl. That was a rough night but he had worn them down by sheer doggedness. There was a pertinacious aspect to his personality, a stick-to-itiveness that farm life had hammered into him. He just needed to keep it going and the big man would fatigue. It was impossible for those huge muscles to sustain in a long fight but he had never felt power and strength like this. He needed an edge and saw an opportunity and grabbed it.

"Don't quit on me now, asshole. We're just getting started. You're in for…" Seppo began when the steel bar smacked him on the side of the head. This time it did have an effect; the giant stumbled sideways knocking over a small table.

"Doesn't feel so good, does it?" Robbie asked twirling the gooseneck crowbar, moving in, and when Seppo turned he swung again. The blow caught the Finn on the arm and high on the shoulder making the giant grimace.

A blind, scarlet rage consumed Seppo. This was hand-to-hand combat and Robbie had broken the unwritten rule by using a weapon.

"You slimy, shit-eating cunt! You can't fight fair can you, motherfucker? I'm going to tear you apart, limb from limb! I'll tear your head…"

The crowbar slammed into his thigh, midway to the hip, numbing the muscles on the outside of the femur. The big man groaned, feeling the impact but he shook off the pain. He dipped his head and charged in low and just as his shoulder was about to strike Robbie he felt the straight end of the crowbar sink into his back. He let out a deafening scream as Robbie drove the chiseled tip deep using both hands and all the strength he could muster. He felt the bar rip through muscle and flesh until it struck bone before the giant's forward momentum bowled him over forcing him to relinquish his grip. Seppo stumbled drunkenly forward, tripped on a box and fell clutching at his back. Blood seeped out of his mouth and his breathing came in labored, heaving grunts. The harbingers of death, pain and suffering, had arrived but it was his hated nemesis that would deal the final blow.

Robbie walked over and straddled the giant and before jerking the crowbar out, snarled, "This for Maddie and Angela. Do you remember what she said? Well, I did come for you and this is for them, asshole!"

He raised the crowbar high over his head and hacked down chopping at the back of Seppo's skull, once, then again and again and again until the giant lay motionless, his head crushed into a mangled, gory pulp. This time the monster wasn't coming back. This time the rabid colossus was deader than a dead pig on barbeque day.

Robbie stood over the lifeless form, his breath rasping heavy from the effort, his body splattered with blood. He felt numb before a variegated spectrum of emotions flooded through him – satisfaction, joy, anger, regret but most of all vindication. The abacus of accountability had settled the balance owed for the lives of Maddie, Angela, Emma, Ray and the many others Seppo had killed. There could be no appropriate recompense for the innocent lives taken but their deaths had been avenged. There was closure, at least for him.

THE TIGRESS AND
THE FOXES

The Russians had arrived at Moose Head Point at the bottom of the hill where Luke's cabin was located. They had parked the black sedan behind an agglomeration of trees and bushes about five hundred or so yards past the entrance of the driveway that lead up to the landing where Allison's truck was parked.

"Do you want me to stay with the car?" Sergei asked his boss.

"No. Leave it here. No one can see it," Izhutin replied. "If the pretty boy is here I will need both of you."

They circumscribed past the driveway choosing instead to navigate the steeper gradient of the hill hoping to remain undetected. They labored up the incline making slow but steady progress and had to stop a few times to rest and catch their breath. The scree slopes made the climb hazardous and the steep ascent was far more of a struggle for Izhutin than his younger associates.

"Fuck! This is harder than chasing after a pretty Chechen bitch!" Izhutin hissed between gasps.

"You're getting too old for this, boss; leave it to Milo and me, we'll take care of it. You can sit here and rest and think of all the old women you have fucked," Sergei suggested.

"Remind me when we get home to slice off your cock and send it to that bitch you call your mother!" Izhutin wheezed between gasps.

"You will have to pay double. My dick is like a club!" Sergei quipped back.

"Then I will roast it and feed it to my dog! He likes sausages."

The men laughed and continued up the hill. The going was painful but they finally made it to the edge of the front lawn and huddled close behind a thicket of Canadian thistle and morning glory among other wild brush. The herbaceous perennials were in bloom and the pretty rose and lavender flowers caught Milo's attention. He reached to pick one and was pricked by the thorny stem.

"Ouch! Fuck, it's just like a pretty woman. Looks good but comes with…"

Izhutin slapped the back of Milo's head, "What's the matter with you? You're like a fucking child. This is serious, you dumb bastard. These mountain assholes will kill you sooner than look at you!"

"Sorry, boss, I was…" he started then with an apologetic look said, "I will pay attention."

They stayed still, breathing hard, recovering from the strenuous climb and studied the cabin and the surrounding compound.

The smoke from the fireplace was a positive sign but it was imperative for Izhutin to know whether Luke was there or not. The Russian's strategy was predicated on this criterion. If Luke was there, he would have to be taken out before they could abduct the boy and that would call for patience and an ambush. If he wasn't, he would resort to his charm like he did with strangers in the past. His seemingly innocuous appearance had fooled many and he could be charming when he chose to be. He smiled to himself recalling the look of surprise on people's faces when he reverted back to the killer he was.

A visual reconnaissance of the surroundings revealed very little except that the cabin was small and sturdy but provided no clues of the occupants. The windows had curtains that were drawn tight and as far as they could tell, the front door provided the only access to the house. There were no doors on the sides but there had to be a backdoor for convenience – they could see the corner of a shed located in the rear of the building.

"You go around to the back, Sergei," Izhutin motioned with his hand, "don't do anything just observe. If you see anyone, especially Luke, you come back here."

Sergei nodded silently acknowledging the kinesics and staying low, made off circling to the rear. Milo moved closer to Izhutin and whispered, "What do you want me to do?"

Milo was much younger than Izhutin and several years younger than Sergei. He had no real combat experience but was a pretty decent shot with the pistol and was keen to make his bones and prove to his boss that he could be counted on, the incident with the Canadian thistle notwithstanding.

"You stay here. I'm going to knock on the door and if things go badly don't hesitate. Except for the boy you kill anything that is a threat. But make sure you don't hit me! I will slice your…" He stopped and smiled, "just don't put a bullet in me! I don't want to be your first."

"Boss, you worry too much. They don't call me Wild Bill Pozdnyakov for nothing!" the young man chuckled at the odd sounding moniker.

"You're a fucking clown! Now get serious, this could be trouble," the older Russian growled and made his way tentatively across the lawn.

The Russian moved slowly, his eyes darting left then right, scanning the surroundings, expecting the unexpected, and sure enough before he reached the porch steps, a golden haired tigress stepped through the front door.

"Stop right there!" she commanded.

The shotgun was aimed right at Izhutin's chest. He raised his arms and said in English, "Sorry to bother, madam, but we are lost. We are no trouble. We are looking for gas station."

Like many mountain folk, Allison was wary of strangers but the mistrust bordered on xenophobic antipathy when it came to foreigners. The boyish charm that had worked on others was ineffective with Allison.

"Step back. Go on, move back," she commanded, motioning with the gun.

Izhutin complied immediately taking a few backward steps keeping his hands clearly visible and hoping that Milo wouldn't do anything stupid. His cold, calculating mind assessed the situation quickly: *this blond beauty was unafraid and a killer*. He was certain of that. A wrong move and he would be dead. He would prefer to die fucking her but right now, he didn't want to do anything to piss her off.

Allison walked casually to the edge of the porch and stood at the top of the steps with the gun still pointed at the Russian's chest. A gentle gust tousled strands of golden locks across her pretty face, a cynosure mesmerizing Izhutin. He wasn't immune to the spell of this beautiful creature.

"Which direction did you come from?" she questioned brusquely.

For a moment he didn't answer, staring at her, riveted by her presence.

"Where did you come from?" Her voice had an edge now, cold and hard.

Izhutin snapped out of his trance and pointed westwards away from town, "From there."

"Why didn't you use the driveway?" She persisted.

Izhutin's mind was immediately on alert. *How did she know*

that they had climbed up the hill eschewing the driveway? Did she see them? And did she see Sergei or Milo? He had to assume that she had not or her concerns would have been focused elsewhere.

"We did not see driveway. We park on that side and I saw smoke from chimney so I take the nearest way up. Not easy for old man like me!" he gestured with his arms and shrugged his shoulders. He used broken English to add to the credibility of his story.

Her eyes were unblinking but she did have the fireplace going and admittedly the driveway was not the easiest to locate. However, there was something about the man and his story that didn't sit well with her. Maybe it was just her ethnocentric bias but she was still unconvinced.

"You are not alone so how many men do you have with you?" her eyes remained focused on the Russian, unwavering.

"Only me and driver. He is with car," Izhutin lied, flashing a broad friendly smile and began lowering his hands.

"Keep them up! Keep your hands where I can see them."

He raised them quickly and said, "I will go now. I do not mean to frighten you. Just need direction to gas station, please."

She laughed, a derisive soft laugh, and asserted, "You don't scare me. You do anything, a twitch, a sudden move; anything! And, you'll be dead. Do you understand?"

Izhutin was cunning, a fox playing a game, circling the tigress. "Tweetch? I do not understand, madam. My English is not so good."

"Your English is just fine. Don't make any sudden..." Allison started when a gut-wrenching scream tore through the air. It came from behind the cabin.

A few seconds later Sergei burst into view screaming like a banshee and running for his life, "Help! Help me! Ovcharka! Fucking devil dog! Milo, do something..."

Chasing close behind him was a huge and ferocious dog. Ronin was a sight! He had his head low, ears flattened and his mouth in a vicious snarl. The rumbling growls emanating from deep in his chest would have frightened off a grizzly. He leapt and before any of the others could react, had Sergei pinned under him on the grass and was tearing at his neck. The hysterical screams were the catalyst for the hell that broke loose.

Miloslav Pozdnyakov was terrified. He had heard rumors about the devil dog, the Ovcharka that guarded prisons, but had never seen one in real life. The stories of these monstrous animals chasing down prisoners who tried to escape and ripping them apart seemed so very real now. He stood up from behind the bushes and lumbered tentatively towards Ronin totally oblivious of Allison and the threat she presented. His hands were trembling when he fired a shot at the huge beast. His only objective now was to save Sergei. The screaming had stopped and the massive dog was turning towards him when he fired again just as Allison pulled the trigger. The blast lifted the young Russian off the ground and flung him several feet back. She pumped the shotgun spinning towards Izhutin and was about to fire when the 9 mm caliber bullets ripped through her. There was a look of shock on her face; her eyes glazed over and the long-gun fell from her hand clattering on the wooden planks. She staggered back against the doorframe, her hands groping blindly and slid gracefully to the floor. It was the final act of the show, the reverence of the beautiful ballerina.

Allison lay motionless listening to the strident calls of a Northern Mockingbird. She felt no pain, her mind filled with thoughts of plush meadows, mountains and crystal blue lakes and of Luke and Robbie and she smiled to herself. It wasn't so bad, this dying. A metallic saltiness slowly spread from the back of her throat into her mouth and the bird's plaintive requiem began to fade as she slowly drifted into unconsciousness.

When the proverbial smoke had cleared, Izhutin was the only one standing. He checked on Allison's lifeless form first. He kicked the shotgun away and bent over the young woman. Her eyes were partially closed and she wasn't breathing. He felt for a pulse on the side of her neck then stood back up: w*hat a fucking waste, she was a real beauty!* He quickly rushed over to the gurgling sounds coming from Milo and knew at once that there was no saving the young man. *A pity*, he thought, *a nice looking bastard just starting out and Mark wasn't such a bad name after all.* He put a bullet through Milo's head, a mercy kill, and walked over to Sergei. He was dead too. Parts of his jugular had been ripped out of his neck and he lay in a bloody pool. The expression on Sergei's face reflected the panic, terror and helpless impotence of his final moments.

He would miss Sergei. They were a lot alike and he had groomed the young lad into the loyal soldier he was. *Life is a mysterious and fickle mistress,* he thought, *she deals the cards and you play the hand.* He said a silent prayer for the souls of both his men, made the sign of the cross twice while reciting the blessing, "Gospodi spasi e sohrani." ("God bless and protect").

The huge dog was lying unmoving on top of his victim but was alive, barely so. He was about to shoot the animal but stopped and lowered the gun to his side: *a fucking Russian Bear Dog in America, in the mountains in Maine, killing Russians! Life is not just a fickle mistress but one strange and funny bitch!* He had a particular fondness for dogs and thought this one was special; *if you survive then that's your fate, great Ovcharka,* he mused, *I'm not going to be the one who takes your life but sooner or later death comes for us all and even you cannot escape that.*

Izhutin knew he had to act fast and find the boy before Luke or someone else turned up in response to the gunshots. He was certain that apart from the boy there was no one else in the cabin or they would have come out during the melee. He stepped over Allison's body and went into the cabin and in his haste missed the slight twitch of her fingers. He checked the living room and the kitchen before heading down the corridor to the bedroom. At first glance there was no sign of Ryan. The lambskin throw was rumpled and the shallow depression of the pillows disclosed all he needed to know. He glanced around the room but there was no place to hide so he checked under the bed and there he was; Ryan, eyes squeezed shut, lying curled in a fetal position.

A TIGER'S DILEMMA

By the time Luke left Bucky Johnston's Diner, it was during the dinner rush hour, a bit past 7 PM. He had been there since 5 AM working with staff to keep the place running smoothly. Luke had taken over the leadership responsibilities in Hank's absence and his appreciation for what his brother did grew with each passing day. But, his free spirit longed to be outdoors or at the Pit not in a restaurant dealing with malfunctioning equipment, disgruntled employees and worst of all, the balancing of the cash register. He had spoken to his nephew, Ed about taking over the diner but the younger Carlson wasn't ready. He was still mourning the loss of his mother and Angela. The last time they spoke Ed was in a drunken stupor babbling on about Ray and Jericho and how much he loved Angela. He realized that his nephew was in no state to return to work and it was up to him to carry the load.

He wasn't sure why he didn't feel the loss as deeply – Emma was his elder sister and Ray was his nephew but apart from the initial shock and sadness, he hadn't really given it much thought. He did worry about Hank, more so now, than before.

Luke had tried to find them, Hank and Seppo, but they seemed to have disappeared into thin air. Seppo might even have killed Hank and disposed of the body; there was no telling what that maniac was capable of. He would try and track Seppo again but not today, he would do that first thing in the morning, for now he was done. He wanted to get back to Allison before Robbie returned. This thing between Allison and Robbie had him confused and hurt and though he didn't blame either one of them he wished it would end. Be over.

If it had been any other man he would have gutted him like a pig and fed him to the crows but Robbie was different. Maddie had said that they were brothers in spirit and that he would have to choose. Robbie did feel more like the brother he wished he had instead of Hank and maybe that wasn't fair but that's how he felt. On some level he understood Allison's attraction and her infatuation with Robbie. He was sure it was infatuation and not to be confused with love. What Allison and he shared was love, it had withstood the test of time and societal norms. He closed his eyes thinking about his beautiful sister and was overcome with emotion. He could smell her, feel her, taste her... she would come to her senses once the soldier boy had moved on. In the meantime he was going to run interference as much as he could to disrupt their relationship.

Luke walked down Main towards the Hollier residence to drop off a container of the much vaunted lamb stew. He needed the exercise and a brisk walk always helped to clear his mind. He would come back to get his truck before heading up to Moose Head Point. He missed Maddie, missed her terribly. She had been like a second mother, no, even more than that, she was like a doting grandmother and her death had left an empty space in his heart, a space he was hoping that would soon be filled by the Holliers.

Beth and Mark Hollier had always been fond of him even after the break-up with their daughter. They didn't understand his reasons for ignoring Ryan or relinquishing his parental responsibilities but they accepted that as part of his wild and untamed spirit. In many ways, he was the son they never had. And in return, he liked them just as much and would stop by regularly to make sure they were okay especially after Mayor Mark took ill.

Walking up Hollow Creek Road, Luke noticed that the cottage was dark and that the landscape lighting in the garden hadn't been turned on. Beth Hollier was proud of her green thumb and usually had the lights on early.

He rang the doorbell and getting no response, knocked on the door. At first, it was a polite knock but when there was no answer, he banged on it with a hammer-fist. He placed his ear to the panel listening for any sign of life and heard a muffled, scraping sound. He then tried the latch and was surprised that the door was unlocked. This could only mean trouble. What he saw when he turned on the lights spurred him into action.

Both Beth and Mark Hollier were bound to chairs. Mark Hollier seemed to be unconscious, stooped over, head down against his chest, and Beth had been gagged and bound and sported a bruise on the side of her face. She was struggling to speak, making guttural sounds, so he freed her first, tearing off the duct tape and removing the small rag that had been stuffed into her mouth.

She swallowed to wet her throat and squawked, "Ryan... they've gone to your place to get Ryan! The Russians... hurry!"

"What Russians?"

"Luke, just go... you need to get to Allison and Ryan. They are in trouble and these men are ruthless!" Her voice was hoarse and raspy.

He got her a glass of water and carried Mark Hollier to the bedroom and before he left he called Dr. Boswell's office to get a hold of Meghan. He was lucky, it was Meghan who answered.

"Dr. Boswell's office, can I help you?" She sounded perky and sweet. She always did.

"This is Luke. I'm at your parent's place and you'd better get here quick. I don't have time to explain. Just get here... right now!"

Her voice reflected the anxiety that overtook her, "Is it dad?

Luke, is he okay? Is Mom…"

"They are okay but your father needs some help. Just get here as quickly as you can," and with that he hung up. He didn't want to mention the bit about Ryan for fear of sending her over the edge.

"Go on, Luke, don't worry about us, I've called Dr. Hannah and he's on his way. We'll be fine. You have to hurry… go on, son, they are your only hope," Beth Hollier urged.

"I've left the lamb stew on the kitchen table. I know Mark likes it. I'll call once I get there and figure out what's going on." He gave her a hug, "Tell Meghan to be calm and not to come up there no matter what. Okay? I'll make sure Ryan is alright and I'll bring him back to her."

Beth Hollier nodded, "Hurry, Luke, please, don't worry about us… they are after Ryan and they will kill Allison to get him."

The front door slammed close and Luke ran towards the diner's parking lot. *He should have brought his truck but how could he have known?* He kept telling himself that Allison knew how to take care of herself and with Ronin there, they were safe. But the nagging uneasiness kept gnawing at his belly. He could have kicked himself… *he should have brought his truck instead of walking here.*

The sight that greeted Luke when he arrived at Moose Head Point was worse than his worst nightmare. There were two dead men, he assumed were Russians, in the front yard and Ronin lay unmoving by the front porch steps. There was a bloody trail from one of the dead men to where the big dog was lying. Luke curbed the instinctive urge to check on the animal and ran up the steps and was met by more blood on the porch. His heart sank when he entered the cabin: Allison was lying on her back in a pool of blood, deathly white with her right hand over her left shoulder.

He knelt down and raised her up, holding her against him and that's when her eyes fluttered open. "Luke, Luke…" she sighed a softly, "I love you so much." She stopped, trying to focus, "Ryan; they got Ryan…"

"Shhh," he shushed her, "Don't speak. Oh baby girl, what have they done to you? Let me take a look at you."

He cut the shoulder strap of her blouse and gently pulled it down over her breast revealing two bullet holes. She had lost a lot of blood and he needed to act quickly to stem the bleeding. He was crying silently when he carried her to the bedroom. His life meant nothing if he lost her and nothing meant more than saving her.

A SOLDIER'S ANGER

Robbie and VanArcen were driving back after having stopped for dinner when Tony's phone rang. Robbie was at the wheel and they had been celebrating an end to Seppo's madness.

"Hi Tony, is… can I speak to Robbie?"

VanArcen could hear the soft sobbing on the other end.

"He's driving. What's the matter, Meghan?"

"They took Ryan…" she broke down and was crying uncontrollably now, her voice broken and unclear.

"Who? Who took Ryan? Meghan, who took Ryan?" he repeated, speaking over her sobs.

Robbie reached across and wrangled the phone away, "Meghan, this is Robbie. Who took Ryan?"

"Oh God, Robbie… the Russians. The Russians took Ryan. Please get him back. Get my baby back." Now she was bordering on hysteria.

"Meghan, you need to calm down and tell me exactly when they took Ryan and who it was that took him? Do you know?"

"Mom doesn't know who it was but they were Russians, she is pretty sure of that. They broke Dad's fingers and slapped Mom around. Mom thinks it was around 4 or 5 in the evening. She's not sure. There were two of them, both young. One had tattoos and a the other was a good looking, younger man."

"How do you know they got Ryan? Wasn't he with Allison?" Robbie asked, his concern growing. This must have to do with Jodie and the laptop and they were planning to use Ryan is a pawn.

"Mom had to tell them. It was that or they would have broken all his fingers and then killed him. I just spoke to Luke. They shot Allison and Ryan's gone. I don't know what to do… Robbie, you have to bring my boy back to me. Poor Allie…"

The news about Allison stunned him. He was quiet for a moment before asking, "Is she okay?"

"Luke's not sure. She lost a lot of blood and is sleeping now. He's using Maddie's salve," she paused and was contemplating whether she should tell him about Ronin when he cut through her thoughts.

"What about Ronin?" his voice was tense.

"Robbie, I'm sorry but they shot him too and Luke doesn't think he'll make it… he's bandaged up… there's nothing you can do. Please, get Ryan back… I'm sorry about Ronin but get my baby back!" She was rambling in non sequitur, sobbing, trying hard to control herself.

"Meghan, you need to stay calm. I'll get Ryan back, I promise. You take care of your parents. I will call you as soon as I find them even if I have to go to Jersey City. Okay?"

"Thank you, Robbie. I don't know what I'd do if something were to happen …" her voice was a whisper.

"Just stay calm and don't say anything to anyone. They are not going to hurt him. They are going to use him to negotiate. This may have to do with Jodie and the laptop so just remain clam."

"I love you, Robbie, and I know you'll bring him back to me."

He hung up and gave the phone to VanArcen.

"I'm going to drop you off and then head for Moose Head Point. You need to rest that shoulder. I'll speak to Luke and Allison if she's up to it. And then go and find Ryan," his voice was cold and indifferent. "I need to take a look at Ronin first… I may not get another chance."

VanArcen was about to respond with a smart aleck quip but realized that this wasn't the time for frivolous or friendly banter. He would do whatever it took to help his friend. "Robbie, we have to pass Luke's place to get to mine so go straight to Luke's. I'm fine, really, no pain… those painkillers kicked in a while back. I'll stay with Ronin while you are gone."

"That makes sense," Robbie was distracted and heartbroken. He felt sadness that he thought he was incapable of feeling and the sadness gave way to anger and the anger bubbled into a cauldron of seething hatred.

He found sanctuary in this anger and hate; a smoldering hate that took him back to Afghanistan, to that apocalyptic night in Kunduz. He would exact the worst kind of revenge from those who did Ronin harm. Memories came flooding back and he reflected on the early days with Ronin. That first night filled with moments of uncertainty after Rachel and Derek, her husband, had dropped him off. He was hopped up on opioids and Ronin was unsure of him and the new surroundings. He sat staring at Robbie with his sad eyes, barking tentatively to get his attention. Finally he came over and tried scrambling up onto the sofa but it was too high for him. He kept trying and failing but he refused to give up until Robbie scooped him up. The puppy curled up on his lap and went to sleep.

It took Robbie a few days to realize that Ronin was there to stay and it took the puppy less than a day to make his presence known. Robbie woke up in the morning to a pile of poop near the bed and a rambunctious little devil gnawing at his feet. He couldn't but smile at that memory. As a puppy, Ronin was a mischievous little rascal, hiding behind couches and doors to ambush him. He would nip at Robbie's heels with those sharp little milk teeth and then run for cover until he could surprise him again. At night, he would lie curled up against Robbie, sweet as can be, and like an alarm clock, would wake him up at 6 every morning by licking his face, ready to play.

He had matured into a loyal friend who would give his life for Robbie like the time in Montana when a grizzly had charged them. Ronin didn't hesitate, without a second thought he went straight for the bear ready to protect his master with his own life. Luckily for both of them, the eight-hundred pound animal turned on his heels and ran and an unbreakable bond had been forged and if loyalty could be measured then Ronin would top the class.

The thought of his friend fighting for his life sent him spiraling into an emotional quagmire and the hatred resurfaced. Robbie clenched his teeth and tried not to get too far ahead of himself. *One thing at a time*, he told himself, *plan before you act.*

When they arrived at Moose Head Point, the two dead Russians had been moved to one side of the stairs leading up to the porch. Both men were on their backs, face-up. Robbie didn't recognize either one - they were young men, too young to die in this manner but they had made their choices. It was pretty easy to spot Ronin's handiwork, the man's neck was a mess.

"This guys is a kid. I don't recognize him. I don't think he was at the Pit with Adam Shayk." VanArcen commented, "This guy with the tattoos might have been there but I'mm not sure."

"These boys weren't at the fights. I'm pretty sure."

Robbie took the steps two at a time and went into the cabin with VanArcen following behind. The blood and signs of Allison's struggle screamed at them from the stains on the floor. The sanguinary smudges painting a grotesque, crimson picture of her crawling into the house. They stood shocked by the amount of blood when Luke emerged from the bedroom to greet them.

"Ronin heard the truck before you made the turn. He's amazing.

He tried to get up but I held him down. He's hurt bad. I didn't think he'd make it but that dog has a spirit like nothing I've seen. If he hadn't been here Allie would have been dead or worse."

"Can I see him?" He asked then seeing the sadness in Luke's eyes, commiserated, "I'm sorry this happened, Luke, how is Allison?"

"She's sleeping," he struggled with his emotions before getting a hold of himself, "and, Ronin is resting. I cleaned their wounds and used Maddie's ointment on both of them. Hopefully it will work like it did for us. I know Maddie is watching over her. I don't know what I'll do if…"

He couldn't bring himself to verbalize his worst fear and sensing Robbie's impatience to see his dog and Allison, said, "Go on in, I put him on a mattress next to the bed. Allison would have wanted that. She loves him almost as much as you do. You can see them both but don't wake her. She needs to rest."

The bedroom was cast in shadows, lit only by the slivery beams of moonlight streaking in through the curtains. He waited until his eyes had adjusted to the dim flickering light and caught the adumbrate outline of Ronin trying to sit and quickly went over, squatting down on the mattress next to the big dog. The wounded animal wagged his tail and growled, a protesting gnarr, before placing his massive head on Robbie's lap. Ronin had always seemed indestructible, never sick , never hurt and blessed with an abundance of energy. This improbable vulnerability broke his heart.

"I'm sorry, bud, I should never have left you. You have to get well… it's you and me, Ronin, it will always be you and me, buddy."

He felt his heart sink at the thought of losing his friend. He stroked the big dog's head whispering encouragement, making promises and praying for divine intervention and felt the anger return boiling slowly over until all he wanted was retribution.

THE FOX AND HIS MASTER

Andrei Izhutin was sitting at the corner table in a small truck-stop diner in Brighton about forty five minutes south of Chase River Town. He had ordered an ice cream soda for Ryan and a coffee for himself and while waiting decided to call Adam Shayk on his private cell phone. As a member of Shayk's inner sanctum, he was one of the few trusted with the number.

"I have the boy but it was not easy. Luke's cabin is like a fortress. Sergei and Milo are dead and I had to kill the blonde girl… Luke's sister. She was as fearless as any man I have known. In any case, she is dead."

There was protracted silence and Izhutin knew that his boss was angry. Over the years he had learned to read Shayk. He spoke in Russian; they always conversed in their mother tongue unless they were dealing with outsiders.

"I'm sorry, boss, I should have listened. It would have been different with Old Sergei and Viktor or Dimitri instead of the two boys. I did not think the woman would be so much trouble and then there was the Ovcharka. The devil dog was…"

"I don't fucking care! You were in charge of this and it is up to you to make the right decisions! You head's getting too big, Andrei, you don't listen anymore."

"You are right, boss. I deserve to be sent back to Siberia with my dick sliced off!"

"That doesn't solve anything. Is the boy with you?"

"Yes."

"Slit his throat and throw him in the parking lot of Carlson's diner!" Shayk hissed, "They killed two of our men, now we kill ten of theirs. Killing Luke's boy is like killing ten of those fuckers! That will teach them a lesson. You do not kill Russians without paying a price."

Izhutin was quiet. He looked over at the boy noting his smile and the innocent expression and thought: *this kid is like an angel. I cannot harm him. My soul will be damned to perdition…*

Sensing reluctance, Shayk asked. "Did you hear me, Andrei?"

"I cannot do that, boss, we are not animals. We do not kill children."

"You will do what I order you to. Slit his fucking throat and throw him where they can see him! Do you hear me?" Shayk screamed into the phone, "Did you hear what I said, Andrei?"

"I heard you, boss, I will come home and you can put a bullet in my head. I deserve that but I cannot kill this child. And if you send Dimitri and Old Sergei to do the job then I will have to stay here and protect the boy."

Izhutin realized that this was blasphemy and a breach of every code that the mob lived by. But killing or hurting a child was beyond the ties that bound him to his Russian brotherhood and encroached on his deeply religious beliefs. It was something he could never do or condone despite the dire consequence he would certainly face.

"Are you mad? You turn against your own for an outsider?" Shayk's voice sounded incredulous.

"I will follow you into hell and gladly give my life to save yours but I cannot kill a child or stand by and watch my people make war on children. We have to draw the line somewhere," he paused before pleading, "Boss, listen to me, we do not kill children or the innocents! That is a sin against God."

"We sin against God almost every day. We kill, maim and brutalize men as part of our daily lives! I don't remember how many men I've killed. Do you?" Shayk retorted.

"Men have been killing men before Cain murdered Able. God forgave Cain for killing his brother. But there is no forgiveness or redemption for killing a child. I beg you not to kill this boy," Izhutin countered, obdurate in his belief and obstinate in his refusal to hurt the child.

There was a protracted silence. Izhutin could hear Shayk's breathing. His boss was trying to calm down and to get a hold of himself. Finally, Shayk spoke, his voice more even.

"You are a fucking contradiction! For a coldhearted, horny bastard you are blessed with a conscience and that is something I have always admired about you. I lack that and I depend on your conscience to keep me from burning in hell."

There was a sense of relief on both sides. Shayk would have been hard-pressed to replace a loyal soldier and more importantly, a dear friend and for Izhutin, he knew he had just dodged a bullet.

Izhutin chuckled and said, "We are both going to purgatory, boss, that's for sure but maybe some of our kinder acts will get us out of there, eh? The boy is a sweet child. He looks like his father and who knows, maybe one day he will do great things in life and we can look back and remember your kindness."

"Or maybe he grows up like his father and makes war on us!" Shayk was quick to point out.

"That is for God to decide, not us."

"Ah, Andrei, you are right again. Take him to the diner and drop him off. Make sure he is safe and come back as quickly as you can. Luke will want to avenge his sister. It is better if you get back here."

"What about the laptop and the videos?"

"We'll deal with it when you get back. We are getting more heat from Boston but now it is Luke and these fucking hillbillies we need to worry about. Those bastards in the mayor's office can go fuck themselves!" Shayk snapped and added as an afterthought, "Oh, one more thing, where are the bodies? I mean Sergei and Milo?"

"I left them there, at Luke's place. I said a prayer for their souls and got the boy. There was nothing more I could do for them."

"They were too young to die but life is unpredictable. Maybe that blond bastard will bury them and say a prayer for their souls too. You come back as soon as you can. Don't stop at any of those whorehouses on the way… they are full of disease and your little pecker will fall off!"

Izhutin laughed, "You are like my wife, reading my mind. The other day she said the same thing to me but she doesn't know that my dick is Teflon coated! I will keep my joystick hidden in my pants for now and will be home soon."

Shayk enjoyed Izhutin's nonsensical anecdotes and odd take on things. They had been together for so long it would be hard for him to imagine a life without his friend.

"Andrei, we have been through a lot together. I didn't mean to be angry with you… you're a good man; a better man than me."

The phone went dead. It wasn't like Shayk to get sentimental but he could tell that his boss was overcome with emotions. Izhutin looked over at the boy, smiled and said in English, "Are you ready to go home, Ryan? Uncle Andrei is going to take you back."

"Can I finish my ice cream?" Ryan asked.

"Of course, my myshka, you take all the time you need. Uncle Andrei is going to have another cup of this horrible coffee."

Ryan looked at him and after scooping some whipped cream into his mouth, asked, "What is mushka?"

The Russian laughed, "It means little mouse but in nice way. You are my golden-haired myshka!"

The boy giggled and refocused his attention on the remaining ice cream floating in his soda.

REDEMPTION AND RETRIBUTION

After some discussion, Marylou Dorsey and Michael McHenry decided that it was best that they maintain the charade and that revealing the true identity of Professor Lorenzo Santos would be risky at best especially when it came to the law and Deputy Joe Bradley. Other than Luke no one in Chase River Town knew who McHenry really was.

"We'll go see Luke and explain our plans. I'm sure he'll understand," Marylou said.

"Maybe, but he wasn't too thrilled when I told him who I was. He warned me to never come back."

"Let me handle it. He will listen to me. We need a bit of time before we can leave and I really don't want to upset Dad. If he found out what you did for a living he would be beside himself." She paused before adding, "And, we definitely don't want Joe asking too many questions. He seemed suspicious after what you did to Greg."

She was in front of the full-length mirror getting ready. She had a red and white, tea-length dress that clung to her body accentuating her curves.

She looked at McHenry's reflection in the mirror and said, "Zip me up."

He whistled appreciatively, "Wow! You are so damn beautiful." He stood behind her and hugged her tight, burying his face in her hair and kissing her neck, "I don't deserve you and I promise you, I will do everything I can to make you happy. Once you see the place in Zermatt you will fall in love with it."

She leaned back in his arms, "I've never been out of Chase River Town let alone the country. I'm excited and a little scared but I feel safe with you. My heart is racing just thinking about it!"

He ran his hand under her breast, feeling for her heart, then caressed her breasts, squeezing gently, wanting to make love to her again. She titillated and excited him like no other woman ever had.

"You leave everything to me and don't you worry. Once we get the chalet renovated we can travel and see the world. There is so much to explore, my darling, so many wonderful places and cultures to experience that you will never want to come back here again."

He kissed the curve of her neck and nibbled at her earlobes, intoxicated by her perfume, a delicate fragrance of lavender and muguet. His voice was hoarse with desire, "Let's make love before we go…"

She could feel his cock throbbing against her ass and had to fight the urge to reach behind her. She loved the way he filled her up when he was inside her but they needed to speak to Luke and prolonging the anticipation of their lovemaking made it all the more intense. It could wait till after dinner.

"I'd love to but we have to talk to Luke. We have to, baby, we don't want him saying anything to anyone. We will have all the time in the world later."

"Mmm, promises, promises, promises… but I guess you're right." He stood back and looked her, drinking in every detail. "You can't blame me for trying, you look exquisite, simply ravishing!"

She smiled, "You're sweet for saying that. It makes me feel good about myself." Her expression turned somber "I'm worried about my father and Junior… it's not like moving to Connecticut. Switzerland is so far away and if there was an emergency I wouldn't be able to just hop on a plane and be here the same day. My father is getting older and if something were to happen to him, there would be no one to care for Junior. I don't want the State putting him in a home."

It had been on her mind. Leaving them behind would be difficult and worrisome.

"Once we are settled, we will bring them to Zermatt. We will have enough room," he said to assuage her fears.

"My father would never leave. And what would Junior do there?"

He could sense the conversation taking a direction he wanted to avoid. "Listen, baby, we'll do whatever it takes and if it means we live in Connecticut, then so be it as long as we are together. But, let's go to Switzerland and see the place and then decide, what do you say?"

She smiled, "I'm sorry, Michael, I'm not being a wet blanket. Ever since Ma died I've always been here for them. But what you suggested makes sense and I do want us to be happy so if it is Zermatt, then that's where we'll stay and we'll deal with the logistics and the travel if and when it happens."

He kissed her again and smiled, "There's my gal. One step at a time and I'm sure we'll come up with the right solution. And God forbid should something happen to your father, we'll take Junior and I'll make sure he is actively engaged in some productive endeavor. Your family is my family now."

She turned in his arms so she was facing him now. She looked into his eyes and the earnest love she saw put her at ease.

"That makes me feel so much better. Come on, let's go and put your contacts and glasses back on," she reminded him, "and you are getting awfully lazy with the accent."

"I am sorry, Ma!" He playfully slapped her on her behind and reverting back to the accent he used for Santos, "A lovely woman like you makes me forget I'm from Madrid."

He parodied a matador's molinete, twirling to let the imaginary bull pass by and said "Olé!"

She laughed, "You can be quite the funny man when you want to be. Come on, before the place gets too crowded."

While driving to Bucky Johnston's, Marylou rested her head on McHenry's shoulder and decided to probe her lover and to reveal more about her needs and desires especially in the bedroom. It was an important aspect of who she was.

"I love you so much Michael, that I don't want anything to affect how we feel about each other. But I don't want you to get bored with me or me with you." She paused then said, "I want to be able to challenge your brilliant mind, to discuss matters without feeling like an idiot; I want be a true partner. And when it comes to sex… I need a lot of it. I've always been this way."

"I know that. I've been around the block a few times so I know just what you need and trust me, it's not going to be a problem, baby. I'll make you happy and will keep you satisfied. And that's why I'm so sure that we are perfect for each other."

She closed her eyes lost in thought, "I'm going to start reading more, you'll see, then I won't be a self-absorbed, pseudo-intellectual!"

"I'll love you either way, darling, and I love you more for wanting to try," he assured her.

She sighed contently and slowly ran her fingers along his thigh before straying onto his crotch, feeling for his manhood. She began rubbing McHenry's huge cock through his trousers and could feel him respond immediately.

"Push your seat back a bit," she whispered softly, her breath a susurrate tickle against his ear.

He didn't argue, and moved his seat back, giving her more room to maneuver. She undid his fly releasing the throbbing erection, an engorged pillar of flesh with a red, bulbous head, and though she had held it and sucked on it before, the sheer size of it never ceased to amaze her. She began stroking it, up and down, up and down, feathering her fingers around the dome, teasing, tickling and arousing him until drops of pre-ejaculate leaked out from the tip. She used her tongue to whisk away the sticky, clear liquid, probing around the ridge, before sucking him into her mouth.

He groaned, "Oh God! I'd better pull over."

He leaned back and closed his eyes, losing himself to the waves of pleasure coursing through him and it wasn't long before he let out a strangled cry and climaxed, holding her head and pumping his muculent seed into her mouth.

She was insatiable, sucking and swallowing as quickly as she could until she had drained him of every last drop. She kept him in her mouth, nursing on him tenderly until the sensations exceeded his pleasure threshold and he gasped, "Stop, baby, I can't; it's too much…" and gently urged her off his cock.

She opened her mouth and looked at him, smiling and murmured, "All gone! Mmm, that was the best appetizer ever, baby!"

She wiggled back into her seat and closed her eyes with a smile of a satisfied Cheshire cat. He studied her profile, fascinated by the curve of her lips, then leaned over and kissed her on the mouth, a deep, lingering kiss and thought: *I'm the luckiest man alive. I'll never let her go. Never!*

"I'll return the favor tonight. I'll take you to the moon and back and to places you've never been," he said his eyes darkening with desire and then got the truck back on the road.

"I'll be holding you to that, cowboy," she quipped while adjusting the mirror to reapply her lipstick.

When they finally did arrive at the diner, the parking lot was almost full and they were so preoccupied looking for a parking space that they didn't notice the black sedan driving away. At first, the little, blond boy standing at the side of the steps didn't catch her attention and it was only when McHenry was backing up to an open spot that Marylou realized that it was Ryan. The boy looked disheveled and lost and seemed to be by himself.

"Stop the car," she said and got out of the truck and hurried over to where the child was standing.

"Hey Ryan, what are you doing here?" Marylou asked, kneeling down next to him.

"I'm waiting for Mom," he replied.

"Where is your mom? Is she inside?"

"I don't know. Uncle Andrew dropped me here," the boy answered looking up at McHenry who had joined them.

"Uncle Andrew?" Marylou asked, giving McHenry a quick questioning glance.

Ryan nodded, "Yes."

She picked the boy up, "It's alright honey, we'll take you back to your mom, okay?"

McHenry's face hardened, "Andrei not Andrew. It was Andrei Izhutin."

"Do you know him?" Marylou felt a caliginous foreboding at the pit of her belly.

"Yes. He works for Adam Shayk and was the one who wanted me to kidnap Ryan but when I refused he must have come up here to do the job himself. I don't get it; why would they let him go?" The last bit was rhetorical, he was thinking out loud.

"I don't know," she answered absently, fussing over Ryan.

"Either they got what they wanted or they have something else planned," he didn't trust the Russians.

McHenry watched as Marylou gently wiped away smudges of chocolate around the boy's mouth comforting the child using her baby voice. He knew right then that she would make an excellent mother and felt something he had never felt before. The certainty struck him like a bolt of lightning – she was the one he would marry, have children and spend the rest of his life with. He was sure before but now he was an absolute certainty.

They bundled into McHenry's Tundra with Ryan sitting on Marylou's lap. She hadn't said a word; the fact that Ryan had been abducted and that it was indirectly linked to McHenry had hit too close to home. Maybe Zermatt was the only real place for them. It was far enough away from here and they could start afresh – leave their questionable pasts behind.

"This is never going to end, is it?" She asked.

"It will end. Let me take care of some unfinished business and I promise this madness will end."

"No!" She was emphatic, "I'm not losing you now. You promised never to go back and we are sticking to our plans. You promised, Michael!" she was intransigent.

"And I will never break my promise to you. We will drop Ryan off and go home and stick to our plans. We can have dinner at home."

"Good. Meghan should still be at Dr. Boswell's… let's go there. We can also tell Mark and Sue about our plans to leave. Remember your accent."

"I've never been to Dr. Boswell's place. You'll have to give me directions."

"It's easy, make a left out of the driveway and go past the Shell station and make the first right onto Maple. Her place is at the end of the street."

When they got to the Boswell's place both Dr. Boswell and her husband were in her office. Mark was on the phone and hung up as soon as they walked in. Both Mark and Sue Boswell were delighted and relieved to see Ryan safe.

"Hi there, little man, heard you've been wandering around with some strange people. You had us all worried sick!" Sue Boswell said pinching his cheek gently.

Ryan gave her a big smile and said, "I was with Uncle Andrew. He said I was a…" he struggled to remember the word and finally quit, sputtering, "a mouse."

"Well then, a little mouse you are!" she smiled and tousled his hair.

Susan Boswell briefed McHenry and Marylou about what had happened to Meghan's parents and what she knew about Allison. The secondhand version of the story was a bit confusing but though McHenry held his tongue, he was able to fill in the gaps. They spent a few minutes explaining how and where they had found Ryan and the sheer providence of it all.

"We came to the clinic because we were sure Meghan would still be here but I'm glad we got to see you both at least for a short while," Marylou said.

"Talk about timing being everything. It's fortunate that you arrived at the diner when you did. These days you never know – there are way too many perverts out there. But, he's okay and that's all that matters. My Mark here was all set to get a search party together. He's such an Action Jackson!" Dr. Boswell put her arm around her husband's waist and gave him a hug, "Well, you'd better take Ryan to Beth's. I'll call Meghan so she can stop fretting. She's been worried sick."

Turning onto Hollow Creek Road they noticed Meghan standing by the gate. She ran to the truck even before it had come to a stop and it was only when she saw Ryan, face pressed against the window, smiling and waving at her that a surge of irrepressible relief and joy flooded through her.

Almost as soon as Marylou opened the door, Meghan grabbed

her son, "Oh, baby! I was so worried about you. Did they hurt you? Let me look at you."

She pushed his hair back and examined her child like only mothers can. There were tears of relief rolling down her cheeks while she fussed over her little boy.

"Don't cry, Ma, I'm okay. Uncle Andrew was nice… he gave me ice cream and sweets! See," the boy fished out some peppermint candy from his pocket and held it up to his mother.

Meghan looked at McHenry and Marylou, "Thank you both. Thank you so much! I can't begin to explain what I've been going through. You start imagining…"

"It's over, Miss. Hollier, he is safe and that's all that really matters," McHenry comforted Meghan in his hybrid accent. The professor was back.

"What happened, Meghan? Was Ryan here or with Allison? And are you parents okay?" Marylou asked.

"Mom and Dad will be fine. They broke two of Dad's fingers but he'll be okay. Dr. Hannah has them in splints and said it would take about six weeks to heal. He's prescribed some painkillers so right now Dad's not feeling a thing." She paused and pushed her hair back, before continuing, "Ryan was with Allison. Robbie and I were supposed to go over this evening to collect all our stuff and move back to my cabin with Ronin. That was the plan."

She kissed her son's cheek, "I'll never let you out of my sight again! Now go and see how Grandma is doing and don't wake Pappy, let him sleep. Okay?"

They watched the boy trot down the gravel pathway and disappear into the house before Meghan resumed, "They shot Allison and Ronin, Robbie's dog. I just spoke to Robbie. Luke and he are going to go after the Russians as soon as Allison stabilizes and is out of the woods. Robbie didn't say much but I can tell, he's really angry.

I really don't want him to go but Robbie…"

Marylou and McHenry exchanged looks. Marylou said, "We'd better get there. Lorenzo knows somethings that might help them."

Meghan was surprised, "Like what? What do you know?"

"It is better you know as little as possible, Miss. Hollier, these are indeed dangerous men and you are very lucky that Ryan was unharmed," McHenry said not wanting her to dig any further.

"Well okay. Do you want to come in and have some coffee? I have freshly baked chocolate chip cookies that my mother made… she makes the best; they're really yummy!"

"Very tempting but I think the sooner we speak to Robbie and Luke the better. We will visit again and sample those cookies." McHenry replied.

Meghan gave Marylou a warm hug and then hesitated before hugging McHenry.

"Thank you again," she said as the couple got back into the truck.

"There's no need for any thanks, Meghan, we were lucky to have been there. Ryan is such a precious boy; always smiling… he deserves nothing but a safe and happy life. I don't know what I would have done if it had been my child! You are so incredibly strong," Marylou said, reassuring her friend. She hesitated then added, "In a few days I'll be leaving with Lorenzo. We haven't quite decided where but I wanted you to be the first to know."

"That's such wonderful news, Marylou! Now, you must come over before you leave."

"We will, especially since you mentioned those cookies. Lorenzo loves chocolate chip cookies. I have so much to tell you so I'll call when all this settles down."

"Can I talk to you for a minute?" Meghan asked Marylou, "Privately? I'm sorry Lorenzo; this is something personal."

"No problem, Miss. Hollier, I'll wait in the truck and you take your time," McHenry replied politely recusing himself and getting into the Tundra.

Marylou was curious, "What is it, Meghan?"

"This is awkward but I need to know. Do you remember that night at Matt Hansen's party? He had rented the Waterford mansion for the weekend and you convinced me to go with you – do you remember that?"

"I'd rather forget that part of my life," Marylou answered, her expression changing.

Meghan looked away and then said, "Okay, I understand."

"I didn't mean it that way. It's just that… never mind, ask away, what about that night? I remember you telling me how lonely you were and that there were no men in Chase River worth dating. So I asked you if you wanted to come to his party and that there would be a lot of men there. I don't remember you needing much convincing, Meghan."

"You're right. I had broken up with Luke and…" she paused, "and I did want to see that mansion! Growing up that was all we thought of. The Waterford mansion and what it would be like. Do you remember Jake Horneck trying to break in and being hogtied by that private security company?"

"How can I forget Horny Jake Horneck… that's what the boys called him except that boy was more crazy than horny!"

"That's for sure. I ran into him a few years after graduation and he had become a social worker and was leaving for Africa…"

"I'd love to chat, honestly, Meghan but we need to speak to Luke so let's reminisce when we come over some other time." Then seeing the look on Meghan's face, she added, "I've always respected you and envied you - beautiful Meghan Hollier who was nice to everyone; every girl's envy and the girl every boy wanted to ask out to the Prom!"

"Oh please!" Meghan protested.

"No seriously, that's who you were and still are. I was actually flattered that you would agree to go with me to the Hansen party. I know what people said about me and I deserved it. I was the town slut, the wild, party girl so when the epitome of the perfect woman wanted to come to party with me, I was surprised and genuinely flattered. You wouldn't understand. It was like, *I'm not the only one even Miss Goody Two Shoes likes to get fucked*!"

Meghan blushed and her voice turned cold, "That is rude, Marylou, and if that is what this is about then you can leave!"

Marylou was surprised by her own words and how it sounded. The years of the whispered innuendos and not-so-subtle tittering behind her back had taken its toll.

"I'm sorry, I really am," she reached out and put her hand on Meghan's shoulder, "I guess there's some hidden resentment along with the envy. Nothing happened that night. You wanted to leave when things began to get a bit wild so I told you to relax and try some coke. I remember Matt Hansen hovering over you and I was a bit jealous. I liked Matt despite his reputation. He too encouraged you to try some coke to get you to loosen up. It was obvious he was taken with you. Anyway, after a bit of cajoling you did one line and had a bad reaction. You had seizure of some kind and passed out."

"I remember Matt trying to unbutton my top and being very scared. I mean I saw people having sex right next to us and that's something I had never seen before. I looked over at you and you were so cool that I thought it was just me and the coke *would* help me to calm down," Meghan added, the events becoming clearer in her mind.

"Matt carried you to one of the bedrooms and that's when Ed took me by the arm and we followed him and a good thing we did. That sick perv and one of his cronies were undressing you. I've never seen Ed so pissed off – he chased them out of the room while I got your clothes back on and we drove you to my place. You slept in my bedroom and Dad dropped you off at your mother's the next day. That's what happened."

"Thank you for doing that. I'm not judging you or any of the other girls who were there but I'm not cut out for that," Meghan said.

"Honestly, I don't know if I would have done anything. It was Ed Carlson you need to thank."

"I will thank him. Someone sent me photographs, nothing too bawdy but in one I looked like I had my top almost off. Do you know who sent…"

"It was me. I got them from Nikolai, Nikolai Zakirov. He's another creep who's a regular and as usual he had cameras everywhere videotaping and taking photographs. I wanted you to have them for posterity. I'm not really sure why I sent them. It could be the resentment… I don't know but I wanted you to have them to remind you that we weren't that different. Or so I thought."

"We aren't that different. I'd be lying if I said I didn't think about what I might have missed that evening. I've thought about having sex with multiple partners but I would never act on it. Maybe I just don't have the courage to. So you see, Miss Goody Two Shoes is a lot more like you than you think," Meghan told the woman.

"Thank you for saying that but we are not the same. And, I'm glad that Ed was there and nothing happened to you that night. Having a fantasy is not the same thing. Trust me, I know. I'm just hoping that my life with Michael will be different and that I will remain true to him and that we can be happy. That's all I want now."

"I know you will make it work and that you will be happy, Marylou. I just know that. Thank you again for being honest. And, if there's anything I can do for you, just ask," Meghan said and gave the woman a warm hug before walking back to the house.

For the first time since Robbie found the photographs, Meghan Hollier felt vindicated.

Marisa Gorecki

REVELATION

Ed Carlson took a final drag on his evening smoke and flicked the butt out of the truck's window. He was in the parking lot of the Sheriff's office and the only other car there was Joe Bradley's Suburban. Carlson waited, seemingly undecided, but after a while he got out of the truck and made his way slowly up the front steps.

When Carlson walked in Deputy Bradley looked up, surprised, "Hey Ed, what are you doing here?"

The deputy studied the young man and thought Carlson looked troubled and like he hadn't been sleeping.

"Do you have a few minutes?" Carlson asked.

Bradley closed the folder he had been perusing, leaned back in his chair and said, "For a Carlson, I've always got time."

"Yeah, right! You've been busting Hank's chops for years!"

"If I followed the letter of the law, I should have busted Hank! But enough of that, sit down... what can I do for you?"

"It's about..."

"Hold that thought. I'm going to get a cup of coffee. Something tells me I'm going to need it. Do you want a cup?" The big deputy asked getting up from behind the desk.

"No thanks, too much caffeine gives me the shakes."

A few minutes later Bradley returned with a large mug of steaming hot coffee, "Okay, where were we?"

Ed Carlson fidgeted with the phone in his hand before looking up and replying, "I'm here to tell you about Marisa... about what actually happened."

Bradley was quiet. He took a sip of his coffee and placed the mug down on his desk. Then very deliberately, pulled out a small pad from his pocket, "Are you going to incriminate yourself, Ed, and if so, are you sure you don't want a lawyer present? I don't think Hank is going to be around much longer to protect you."

"I'm not sure if I'm going to incriminate myself or not but in either case, no, I don't need a lawyer present."

"You realize you are giving up your right to counsel."

"Yes." Carlson confirmed, looking directly at the deputy.

"Do you mind if I record this?" Bradley asked.

"No, go ahead." Carlson acquiesced without hesitation.

The deputy got up and walked over to a storage cabinet. After rummaging through the shelves, he returned with an old fashioned tape recorder and a mike.

"They don't like us using digital recorders, something to do with manipulating the zeros and ones to alter stuff! Who the fuck knows but here we go. Let me make sure this contraption works and we can get the show on the road."

He placed the mike pointing in Ed Carlson's direction and said, "Go on say something. Here's your chance to be a rock star!"

Carlson ignored the deputy's remark and obliged, "Testing one-two-three, one-two-three."

Bradley played it back, smiled and after recording the time and date, said, "Okay Elvis, we're ready to roll!"

Carlson took a deep breath, "Well, here goes. It was Friday night, about three weeks ago, we were at Donoghue's Bar…"

"Who's the 'we' and what was the date?" The deputy interrupted.

"It was Friday, June 21st, I remember because it was Junior's birthday. It was Ray, Jericho, Junior and me."

"What was Junior doing with the three of you?"

"Like I said, it was his birthday and we were celebrating. He turned eighteen."

The deputy stopped the recorder and asked, "Why Donoghue's? That place is a fucking cesspool."

"They usually have pretty girls there, topless dancers, and since it was Junior's big day we thought it was time for him to get a look at some titties, maybe even get laid. What was your eighteenth birthday like? You weren't sitting in your room with your old man, were you? We took him there for some beer and some laughs. You should understand."

"It's not the same and you know it. Junior is not a normal eighteen-year-old. Did Gil know you were taking him to Donoghue's?"

"No. We just said we were going to celebrate and would bring him back late and he didn't seem to mind. He said he'd leave the door unlocked."

Bradley did understand. There were certain things that young men learn from friends that most parents would be hard pressed to address especially when it came to sex.

"Okay, let's get back to Marisa and your story," the deputy said, hitting the record button again.

"It's not a story – this is what happened," Ed Carlson paused and gave the deputy a cold look before continuing. "Well, that night there wasn't much of a crowd so the girls left early and we decided to call it a night but Ray and Jericho wanted to go up to Calico Bluff to smoke some weed and just hang out."

"Is this something you guys do regularly?"

"Not regularly but we use Gil's cabin to hang out, you know, like a man cave. It was Friday and I really didn't have any other plans and since I had some weed and several cases of beer in the truck, I…" Ed Carlson paused, staring at the tabletop, his mind lost in thought.

"So you decided to go up to the cabin. Go on," the deputy coaxed.

"When we turned onto Stapleton I saw Marisa and stopped to offer her a ride," he continued then stopped and asked, "Do you mind if I smoke?"

"Go ahead. I don't usually let people smoke in here but I'll make the exception," Bradley replied and opened a drawer in his desk. He slid a glass ashtray over to Carlson, "Use this. What was she doing out so late and by herself?"

"Thanks." Ed lit a cigarette, a Marlboro, and took a deep drag before blowing the smoke out away from the deputy, "I asked her the same question. She had just finished babysitting for the Sarah Mobley."

Carlson toyed with the cell phone, taking his time, "Damn, this is harder than I thought but let's get on with it. I've known Marisa for a while so she didn't hesitate. Jericho was riding shotgun. He jumped out and Marisa got in. She asked us what we were doing and when I told her it was Junior's eighteenth birthday and we were going up to Calico Bluff to celebrate, she said she wanted to join us."

"What did she say? I mean her words."

"I think it was Ray who asked her if she wanted to come with us or maybe it was Jericho, I'm not sure." He closed his eyes trying to recall the incident, "But Rico had jumped onto the bed of the truck… it must have been Ray."

"So let me get this straight; Ray asks her if she wanted to join the four of you and she said 'yes', is that right? Or, did she ask you if she could join the four of you when she heard you were heading to Calico Bluff?"

"No, she didn't ask. I remember someone asking her if she wanted to join us. I'm pretty sure it was Ray who asked her and she said 'yes'. Why is it so important?"

"I'm trying to picture this and I've got to tell you, it seems highly improbable that a sixteen-year-old girl, who is an A-student, would jump into a pick-up with four grown men at 11:30 at night. It seems highly improbable."

"I know but then you don't know Marisa like I do… that's why I want you to watch the video. You can spare me this bullshit!"

The deputy glared at Carlson, "Keep going. I'll take a look at the video later."

"So we all went up there. We were enjoying the cool night air, drinking beer and smoking weed when Rico pulls out a bag of coke. Honestly I didn't know he had it. I don't usually snort the stuff but we did a few lines of each, that is, all of us except Junior. He was just drinking beer."

"You do realize that's illegal? Both Junior and Marisa are under twenty-one. Did Marisa also snort coke?" Bradley asked.

"Yeah, she did several lines and even rubbed some on her gums."

The deputy raised his eyebrows and shook his head, "Okay. I just wanted to make sure I'm getting it straight."

"I didn't think about it. Honestly, I didn't think of her as being underage. In any case, she played some ZZ Top on her iPhone and began dancing. I think it was 'Sharp Dressed Man'… I mean it was like dirty dancing on steroids! The girl could move. We were all watching her, sort of mesmerized, when she came over to me and told me to join her." He took a deep drag, holding the smoke in his lungs before blowing several smoke rings up towards the ceiling, "It gets pretty raunchy from here. I have the video that shows everything.

It would be better if you just looked at the video."

"I'll look at the video later," Bradley snapped impatiently. "Finish your story."

"Well we danced for a while, she got Rico to join us and soon one thing led to another and to cut the story short, we all took turns fucking her."

"You mean she was intoxicated or high and you took advantage of her... in effect, you guys essentially raped her," Bradley said.

"No she was sixteen and it was consensual. She'd been to several of Matt Hansen's parties... why do you think everyone wants her laptop? Chris Donnelly and some other dude from the Mayor's office in Boston were there and they had fucked her *and* some of the other younger girls. They had no idea that Nikolai was making porno movies with them as the stars!"

The deputy studied Carlson before saying, "Matt Hansen is a fucking lowlife and if it weren't for his father, he'd be in jail. But we are digressing. Finish your story."

"Okay but don't go making us out to be a bunch of rapists. Your boss, that fat pig Dolan, attended some of Hansen's 'soirée for swingers'. He knew there were underage girls there and did nothing," Ed riposted before adding, "I've never raped anyone in my life! I stayed away from the young gals Nikolai would bring to the parties. You'd better be careful making accusations or I'm gone... a ghost, you hear!"

Bradley backed off, turning conciliatory, "Fair enough and Chief Dolan will have to answer for this someday soon. But go on."

"When I say we took turns fucking her, it was Ray, Jericho and me but we made sure that one of us was with Junior outside the cabin at all times. We didn't want him wandering off or falling over the ledge. Hey, why don't you just look at the video, man, it's not easy talking about this stuff."

"You're doing fine. Keep going."

"After a while, we took a break and smoked some more weed. Marisa had put her dress back on and wanted to freshen up so she went down to the pond. I told Junior to go with her just to be safe. I mean it was late and there are fucking bears and coyotes around all the time," Carlson paused and fished out another cigarette. He took a couple of puffs before continuing, "When they were gone, Rico said what we were all thinking, 'Do you think she'll agree to fuck him? I mean it's his birthday and it would sure beat fucking a whore.' But Ray didn't think she would agree. In any case, we were talking about it when they returned. The only difference now was Junior was carrying Marisa."

"Was she hurt?"

"No. She had tripped and fallen into some thorny bushes... she wasn't really hurt, some scratches but he decided to carry her. And when he put her down she gave him a peck on his cheek and complimented him on how strong he was. Made Junior blush. I thought that was encouraging so when she went into the cabin to get her shoes, I followed her in and asked if she would fuck him, take his cherry, you know, make a man out of him. She hesitated for a minute before smiling, 'why not, sure'..." he stopped, looking distressed. "It was my fucking fault. I should never have..."

"So what happened?" the deputy interrupted.

"That's it, I'm done. You watch this," Ed Carlson said and tossed the phone towards the deputy.

Bradley picked the phone up and studied the screen, "Which one?"

"The one titled 'Marisa'... that's the only one," Carlson answered.

Bradley watched for a while, the sounds of sex filling his office. His expression slowly changed to disgust, "I don't need to watch this shit!"

Carlson took the phone back and fast forwarded the video until he came to the appropriate spot, "Here… just hit play."

Deputy Bradley resumed watching the video but this time it was with growing disbelief and horror. He would never be able to un-see what he had just witnessed.

KILLERS, MUSKETEERS AND STOOGES

The silence in the truck was unusual for them. The soothing strains of a piano playing over McHenry's stereo system accompanied the monotonous whirring of the engine.

"That's nice. Do you mind if I make it a bit louder?" Marylou asked and before he could answer she increased the volume a bit. "Is that okay?"

"Sure, that's fine," he replied and they both drifted back into the morass of their thoughts.

Usually, they'd be talking about their plans or Marylou would ask him about all the places he had been to and would listen with rapt attention while he elaborated on his experiences in India, China, Indonesia and other exotic places that she had only read about. But right then, the only thing on her mind was Ryan and what could have happened and wondered how she would have reacted if he had been her son. For his part, the picture of Marylou holding Ryan in her arms and fussing over him kept playing over and over in his mind. *What if Ryan was ours? I know what I would do; I'd go after those motherfuckers and kill each and every one of them! That's what I'd do.*

It was Marylou who spoke first, breaching the silence. It was almost as though she had read his thoughts.

"If Ryan had been our son I'd want you to go after them and punish them for putting us through the nightmare. I can't begin to imagine the pain and worry. Meghan is incredibly strong. I'm not sure I could have held it together."

"I wouldn't hesitate a second. They would pay with their lives for hurting you and for the pain stress they inflicted on our child," he responded immediately. "You say the word and I'll end this madness."

"Can you promise me that you'll come back to me? I couldn't bear the thought of losing you, Michael."

"This is what I've done pretty much my whole adult life. I give you my word that if it looks even remotely dangerous or if I feel compromised in any way, I'll back off."

She was quiet still not wanting to test fate. "Why do you want to do this? I mean we could just go away and forget about it. We have so much to live for now."

"There are two reasons; first, they will not stop until they get what they want. I mean the Russians and the politicians who are really behind this. And more importantly, it is a bit of redemption for me, especially for my actions in Kenya and the Njoku children. I feel I owe it to them."

She looked at him, "You are hard to figure out, Michael. There's this gentle, sweet side to you and then there's the…" she couldn't bring herself to say it.

"You mean the psychopath; the coldhearted assassin?" He completed her thoughts then explained, "People are multifaceted. The good are rarely all good and the bad are never all bad. I'm a sinner with some redeeming qualities but, baby, you are my true redemption. I was lost until I met you."

"I saw what you did to Greg so I have no doubt you are what you say you are. It's the very divergent personalities that I am having a

hard time coming to terms with. I worry about you and about us...
but there's a part of me that feels safe and protected when I'm with
you and I've never felt that way before. And, if I'm your redemption
then you are mine too. We are a pair, aren't we?"

He smiled and touched her cheek in a gentle caress, "That we
are. Just know that I would never let anyone hurt you or our family.
It's my job to keep us protected and safe."

They were turning onto the driveway when Marylou relented,
she took his hand on hers, "I'll support whatever you think is best.
Just make sure you come back to me, Michael McHenry. If you don't
I'll kill you myself!"

When Marylou and McHenry arrived at Luke's cabin, Robbie
and VanArcen were finishing with the clean-up of the porch and the
living room. They had moved the dead Russians to the back of the
building near the storage shed with the intention of burying them
later. Luke had wanted to dump their bodies near Bear Ridge, a small
forested hill that was home to a large population of black bears, but
Robbie had convinced him otherwise. The men were young and were
most probably from impoverished families without too many options
and irrespective of their actions, they deserved a decent burial. Luke
had reluctantly agreed primarily because he didn't want to leave
Allison's side.

"That's some climb. Only Luke would pick a hilltop to build a
cabin on!" Marylou commented.

"The view is spectacular and if you don't like a lot of people
around you, I guess it makes sense," VanArcen replied. "Good seeing
you again, Marylou, you look fabulous as always."

"I'll bet you say that to all the women you meet!" She teased.

"I do except in your case it happens to be true!" he quipped back.
He was happy to see the professor again, "Hey Prof, how goes it? Do
you need any more help with your rock collection?"

But before McHenry could answer, Marylou asked, "Is Allison okay? And, is Luke here?"

"She's resting," Robbie answered, "Luke is with her."

Marylou smiled at the tall stranger, "You must be *the* Robbie Olsen. Sally wasn't exaggerating. How is your dog doing?"

"He'll make it. How did you know about Ronin?" Robbie was surprised that the news had spread so quickly.

"Word travels fast here. So you know, we found Ryan and he's fine. He's back with Meghan. Apparently, the man who kidnapped him must have brought him to the diner and let him go. I guess he figured that..."

McHenry placed a hand on Marylou's arm to gently interrupt and spoke without the accent. "Mr. Olsen, if I may. There is something I need to discuss with Luke and you. It is about the dead Russians and the very serious consequences."

"I thought I told you not to come here, McHenry," Luke said, walking into the living room, "You've caused enough trouble already."

"Who is Mc..." VanArcen started, looking from Luke to McHenry, but they ignored him.

"I had nothing to do with this. I would never harm a child," the assassin refuted.

"I don't care. What are you doing in my house? You need to..." Luke began when Marylou interjected.

"Please Luke, just listen to him. He didn't want to come here. I asked him to because it could save lives."

"Give me a chance to explain. If you still want me to butt out, I will but hear me out." McHenry said to Luke then addressed Robbie, "I was hired by the Russian mob to kill Seppo Heikkinen but when they found out that the Finn was already dead, they wanted me to abduct Ryan. Of course, I refused so the head of the mob, Adam Shayk, sent one of his men to do the job. His name is Andrei Izhutin and trust me this man is dangerous. Don't go after him - that would be a mistake. Let me handle this. It is a different jungle out there, one I'm very familiar with. I give you my word that I will end this insanity and we can all get on with our lives."

"You mean you can go back to being a paid assassin?" Luke riposted, scowling at the smaller man.

McHenry didn't react to the barb. He remained even tempered and cool, "No. I'm not going back to that. Marylou and I are going to leave and find a place far away where we can begin a new life and put my past behind us."

The three men studied McHenry with varied degrees of interest and skepticism.

"So let me get this; you're not Professor Santos?" VanArcen asked, "And all that rock collecting was some kind of twisted joke?"

"Regrettably, the truth is yes, Tony," McHenry confirmed. "I am sorry. I was using it as a cover."

"Marylou, did you know about this?" VanArcen was incredulous. The thought that Marylou would go along with the farce was beyond him.

"No I didn't, not until a few days back. But Michael confessed everything including his meeting with you, Luke. We were planning to leave here in a few days but when he told me about the kind of men that were involved, I thought it was best that he handle this… he knows how to deal with men like them. We don't, Luke, and yes, I know you're capable of taking care of things up here but it's different in the city."

"What are you planning to do?" Robbie asked.

"Leave that to me. This goes back to the Mayor's office in Boston. It needs to stop at the source."

"What do you mean?" VanArcen inquired, feeling at a loss. He had been so sure that McHenry was a Spanish geologist and was still adjusting to the transmogrification of the professor to McHenry.

"The less you know the better. I will clean up this mess but I need you to keep my cover intact. There can be no leaks about the Professor and his identity. I need your assurances concerning this and that as far as you know, I am Professor Santos."

"I don't know," Robbie said, "I'm not a stranger to dangerous places and people. I did two stints in Afghanistan and the last one was in Kunduz. That's about as dangerous as it gets. And, I'm used to taking care of my business."

"I think that Robbie and I can handle this. Nobody comes up here and attacks my woman without paying the price. I'm going to make them regret they ever came up here," Luke added, "so thanks but no thanks."

"Luke, I know how you feel but Allison needs you and your mother needs you. What good would it do if something were to happen to you?" Marylou reasoned.

"Hank is back so it's not like..." Luke started to explain but she cut him off.

"He's been telling everyone that he's done and is leaving. He's put his house on the market, the one on River Road. I know the agent, Ann Womack... you remember Annie? She went to school with us. He's also selling his apartment in Portland."

Luke knew this was true. Hank had spoken to him about his decision to leave. He studied the assassin and the man seemed to be sincere but he was still undecided.

McHenry sensed the indecision and decided to press the point.

"This isn't Afghanistan and I don't mean any disrespect. I doubt I could have survived a day there but this is different. These men will not stop. You can kill Adam Shayk and Izhutin but that means nothing. There will ten more and each one will make it their priority to kill all of you. They will start with your loved ones; that's how they operate. They won't fight you in ways you are familiar with. They will send assassins like me, men who masquerade as innocuous visitors or tourists and who are impossible to identify. And, they will keep at it until all of you and your loved ones are dead. The only reason Ryan is not dead is because they have an alternate plan, one that is pragmatic and makes more sense to them. Let me take care of this. I know how to play their game," McHenry implored the men.

There was a lot of truth to what McHenry said. Robbie knew that once they went after Shayk, he would live the rest of his life looking over his shoulder. He was willing to risk his life but not the lives of Meghan, Ryan and his sister's family… that he wasn't going to do.

"Why are you willing to do this?" Robbie asked the diminutive killer.

"I don't think you'll understand. It is redemption for past sins… mistakes I've made that cost the lives of innocent children. That's the best reason I can give you. But this evening, when I saw Marylou with Ryan it struck home. If he were my son, they would be dead already irrespective of any consequence."

Marylou took his hand and smiled. "We can all use second chances. I certainly can and believe me; I didn't want Michael to get involved. But, he convinced me. Robbie, you need to let Michael handle this. He knows what he is doing."

Robbie understood the need for redemption perfectly well. The lives of Calvin Jones and Jaimie Cranston were the crosses he bore and the atonement and eventual expiation *he* so desperately sought. "What do you want us to do?"

"Keep the charade going and go about your daily lives. Don't do or say anything to the contrary. As far as you know Professor Santos and Marylou went back to Arizona and make sure no more videos get posted at least till you hear from me."

Robbie wondered how the man knew about Jodie and the videos but he refrained from pursuing it. "Meghan and I are moving to Montana with Ryan and Ronin. We are hoping that Jodie will join us. I think a change of scenery and some discipline is what she needs. Farm life with a family who loves and cares for her will help her get over her past and be a child again. And no, there will be no more videos."

McHenry turned his attention to Luke waiting for his consent.

"You are a curious man, professor, a contradiction in many ways. Most men would have left and moved on. But redemption, at its core, is a selfish gesture."

"That was Philipp Mainlander's perspective and though I agree that there is some truth to it, guilt and reparation have roles to play in the scope of one's redemption," McHenry replied. He enjoyed the cerebral fencing with Luke.

"Actually, Philipp Mainlander gleaned some of his ideas from the writings of Indian sages who spoke about eternal recurrence and the concept of being reborn to atone for past sins. It was imbedded in eastern philosophies long before the west existed," Luke argued.

"You're right but eastern philosophies were a mystery to the west. It was Nietzsche who postulated on those philosophies and spoke about Eternal Recurrence... the same sequence of events repeating through eternity. It provided the basis for our understanding of karma in the west."

"Will somebody please speak English? What the fuck are you guys talking about? Who is this asshole from the main land and what in blazes is eternal recurrence? I thought we were going to kill us some fucking Russians!" VanArcen quipped.

They all laughed, taking the edge of the seriousness of the moment.

"I'm with you, Tony. I have no idea what these two are talking about," Marylou sympathized with VanArcen.

McHenry addressed Luke again, "You are also a contradiction, Luke… I have yet to meet anyone who defies first impressions quite like you."

"You give me way too much credit, Professor. I'm just a hillbilly, mountain boy who likes to read. In any case, I can empathize with your reasons - we all look for redemption in some form or the other so I'll wait to hear from you. If I don't then all bets are off. Adam Shayk will pay for what he did to Allison and Ronin and I could give a shit about the consequence," Luke said.

"Fair enough; all I ask is a bit of patience. I will leave in a week or so and Marylou will stay back to wrap things up. I will take care of business and you *will* hear from me," McHenry assured the men.

"Can I see Allison?" Marylou asked.

"I'll tell her you were here and wanted to see her. Ronin is in there with her," Luke motioned to the bedroom, "and he's going to get riled up. He needs to rest just as much as she does."

"I understand. Just tell her that I asked about her and hopefully we'll get to see her soon," Marylou replied.

Before leaving, the assassin stopped alongside VanArcen, "Tony, the three days we spent together were some of the most enjoyable I've had in a long time. Your quick wit and the lighthearted repartee made the time fly. You're a decent man and a very funny one. I hope you can find it in your heart to forgive me for the charade."

"I miss the damn accent, Prof. I was beginning to feel like a renaissance man with international friends who are actually educated and not just these two clowns! All they can do is drink, fart and kick ass and not necessarily in that order – they often fart while drinking and that's so, so damn undignified!" VanArcen replied with shake of his head.

"Hey now… I resent that! I don't just fart and drink; I track and hunt pretty darn good too!" Luke interjected using an exaggerated intonation of the local accent.

"And don't forget, you also sleep with your sister!" Robbie couldn't resist the dig but softened it with a smile.

There was a moment when Luke's expression changed, getting deadly serious. He gave Robbie a look but then laughed, "How could I forget? You keep reminding me, brother!"

"See what I mean… please Prof, you've gotta keep the accent for my sake. But for the record, I am kind of blown away by the fact that I actually know an assassin."

"A reformed assassin," Marylou corrected. She then turned to Robbie and asked with a smile, "How do you cope with these two?"

"It's not easy, Marylou, but friends, I mean real friends, are hard to come by so I had to scrape the bottom of the barrel here," Robbie answered staying with the spirit of the conversation.

"And the bottom of the barrel is right," Luke added, "We do make a strange threesome - somewhere between the Three Musketeers and the Three Stooges. A hillbilly redneck, a soldier boy and whatever that runt is," He nodded towards VanArcen who protested immediately.

"Hey, now *I* resent that! They call me 'Tony 'Colder-Than-Ice' VanArcen' so you can shove that…"

"That's not all they call you, Tony!" Luke cut in.

"I don't know why I tolerate this," VanArcen said with a sad expression and commiserated with McHenry, "One day when we smaller men rule the world, you can share some of your experiences and we can laugh about those damn rocks we collected. Almost broke my freakin' back!" VanArcen said and gave McHenry an affable back-slap.

"Ah yes, small men shall indeed rule someday," was the quick rejoinder.

Robbie and VanArcen walked the couple to the top of the steps that led down to the landing where the cars were parked. They said their goodbyes before strolling back to the cabin.

"What do you think?" VanArcen asked.

"I think Adam Shayk and his cronies are in for a surprise," Robbie mused, "a real nasty surprise."

"You can say that again, brother, that fucker is cold and anyone who can morph seamlessly from one character to another frightens the crap out of me! That's why I hate chameleons… those cold-blooded freaks give me the creeps."

"Hmmm, and I thought you were Tony 'Colder-Than-Ice' VanArcen."

"Oh, shut the fuck up, Bronson! Don't forget who saved your sorry ass!"

"How can I? You haven't stopped reminding me," was Robbie's sardonic reply.

And so it went.

The Fox and His Master

SURPRISES

It had been just over a month since Izhutin had dropped Ryan off at Bucky Johnston's Diner and things had quietened down a bit. Adam Shayk was in his office perusing the morning newspapers. He enjoyed the routine preferring to read the hardcopy rather than watching the news on the television.

He came across something that caught his attention and took a sip of his coffee, shaking his head, "Interesting!"

He adjusted his glasses and read the article carefully going over the details several times before putting the news rag down. He looked out of the window and mulled over what he had just read before calling his adjutant, "What are you doing?"

"We are about to go and check the warehouse in Brooklyn. The one you wanted me to look at," Izhutin answered.

"Get Dimitri and Sergei and come to my office. Forget the warehouse. We can do it together later."

"Okay, boss, give me ten minutes to find those lazy bastards and I'll be there. Should I get some syrniki? The bakery has made some fresh."

"Yes. Bring me a dozen. My wife has me on a fucking diet. She tells me my belly is getting bigger… a man my age should have a belly, no?"

"Don't worry, boss, I'll bring two dozen. Maybe you'll have a stroke then I can run this shitty outfit," Izhutin replied with a laugh.

"Ah, you joke about it but that could happen. How the fuck do you stay so thin? I see what you eat… you eat garbage all day!"

"I fuck a lot. That is the secret. You fuck two or three times a day and you'll never put on weight."

"That is just rubbish," Shayk said.

"Boss, it is science. When you fuck there is a transfer of energy especially if you fuck a fat girl. Put her on top and it is a fucking workout. You know, she bounces up, she bounces down, things jiggle this way then they jiggle the other way… she's pounding on you like a freight train on a trampoline. And finally, when the train is reaching the station, you go, woo-woo-woo and then your whistle blows." He made a salacious groaning sound and continued, "You unload your package and lose the weight and she takes the load and becomes fatter. I think it was Einstein who came up with this theory. I remember studying it in school, the theory of the energy transfer during sex. It explained why horny women are fat or was it why fat women are horny? I forget but I know it was Einstein."

"Einstein?" Shayk asked with a chuckle, enjoying Izhutin's preposterous ideas.

"Yes, boss, everyone knows Einstein was a horny bastard. Why do you think his hair was like that? He was so horny he once shoved his dick into an electrical outlet!"

"He must have had a very tiny dick!"

"He was a white Jew, what do you expect. His cock was smaller than mine and everyone knows we Russians have the smallest cocks in the world!"

"Next to the white Jews I presume. And dare I ask, why do Russians have tiny cocks?"

"It's the fucking winters, boss. It makes our pricks shrivel up," Izhutin answered without missing a beat.

"And you personally conducted a survey of all the cocks in the world?"

"You don't have to measure the temperature of a fire to know that it is hot!" Izhutin replied, "It is just common knowledge. Call it universal consciousness or some shit like that. I made the mistake of naming my first dog Einstein. That mutt used to hump everything even my grandfather's bald…"

"Andrei, one day they are going commit you to a mental asylum. The only thing you are losing when you fuck is your damn brain cells! Now get the syrniki and hurry up. I'm tired of the bran cereal every morning."

When Izhutin got to Shayk's office he saw Nikolai Zakirov seated in the lobby outside Shayk's office. The young man had a boyish face accentuated by large brown eyes, a full mouth that was set in a perpetual pout and soft auburn hair that he kept long. His father, Alexei Zakirov, was the powerful head of the Russian mob in Moscow with ties to Putin himself.

Nikolai offered Izhutin a friendly smile and said, "Hi Andrei, how're you doing? Hey, do you know why I'm here?"

It wasn't just that Nikolai Zakirov insisted on speaking English that bothered Izhutin; he had always despised the young man and made no bones about it. Izhutin had spent time in prison and child molesters were among the most hated.

"Maybe he wants to slice off your dick and stick it up your ass," He riposted with a glare.

The pretty girl sitting behind the reception desk tittered and said, "He's waiting for you. Did you bring jam with the syrniki? He has been asking every minute."

"Yes, yes, I know what he likes," Izhutin said stopping by the girl's desk. "You are getting prettier every day, Stephanie, you should let me buy you dinner… we go to a real fancy place."

"My boyfriend will kill me!" Stephanie protested.

"Don't worry about your boyfriend. I'll take care of him. One dinner is not going to hurt, unh?" Izhutin flirted, "We drink a little, dance a little and make love like never before. It will be the best…"

"Your wife will kill us both," she interjected with a smile.

"Ah, that may be true, she is a jealous bitch, but they will write a story about us. We will be like Romeo…"

The jarring ring of the phone interrupted Izhutin and he listened to the girl, "Yes, he's here. He was waiting… right away, I'll tell him."

The receptionist placed the phone back in the cradle, "You'd better go in. Now!"

"Ah, malyshka, we will continue this sometime later."

"Hey, you're an old fart. You're too old for your baby girl," Nikolai scoffed looking at Izhutin with a sullen glare.

"You mean she's too old for you, right? You sick bastard. Everybody knows that the only way you can get that sorry little pickle up is with little girls. And watch your mouth. Your father told me to smack you if you got out of line. So sit quietly and don't poke your fucking nose in my business!"

The young man looked away. He was intimidated. Izhutin had a reputation and Nikolai knew better than to push his luck. *His father most probably did instruct his men to smack him. His father was an asshole and had always despised him.* Nikolai felt sorry for himself, looking out at the skyscrapers across the river and thought: *one day, I'll teach all these bastards a lesson. Papa won't live forever.*

Izhutin winked at Stephanie and waltzed into Shayk's office. He could feel he was making progress with the pretty young woman and it was only a matter of time before he tapped that sweet little pussy.

He placed the cardboard box of cottage cheese filled dumplings on the desk. "Here, boss, the best damn syrniki in the whole fucking world… even better than those shitholes in Moscow."

Shayk's face lit, his fat fingers struggling with the string tied around the box. Finally in frustration he ripped it off, opened the box and held it up to his nose and inhaled deeply.

"Mmm, like heaven, no? It takes me back to my grandmother's kitchen," Shayk murmured.

He grabbed a flaky, deep-fried dumpling from the box, smeared an ample portion of the thick strawberry jam on top and took a a big bite. He chewed with his eyes closed savoring every morsel and snacking his lips said, "Oh, this is so fucking good… if I die tomorrow, it will be worth the heart attack!"

Izhutin sat watching Shayk with a look of amusement, "Boss, I swear you like syrniki more than sex!"

"Right now, the answer is yes. But after I finish the box, who knows? I could change my mind. Where are Dimitri and Sergei?"

"They are coming. They're parking the car - finding a parking spot here is like finding a virgin in Chechnya. They do not exist."

A few minutes later while Shayk was on his third dumpling and Izhutin had poured himself a cup of tea, the men walked in. Dimitri was tall and lean with a lantern jaw that made him look like Herman Munster. While Sergei, or Old Sergei, was a smaller version of the young Sergei who was killed by Ronin at Moose Head Point. He was slim and light on his feet and had a serious demeanor.

They stood patiently in front of the desk until Shayk nodded and said, "Sit, sit. Do you want coffee or tea?"

"No, boss. We just had breakfast at the bakery," Dimitri answered for both. The offer was a courtesy and the men knew better than to accept it.

"Okay, let's get to it. Three weeks ago, you all know that Matt Hansen was found dead. He had hung himself. When I read the news I thought good, that's one less pervert in the world. His father, Patrick Hansen, was screaming in the papers that it was murder and that there was a cover up blah, blah, blah but they could find nothing. So I didn't think much about it."

Shayk picked up another dumpling and meticulously spread a thick layer of jam on it. He took a large bite and chewed the pastry slowly. Dimitri and Sergei waited patiently for their boss to finish and studiedly looked away. Izhutin, on the other hand, found humor in the spectacle. He sat with a grin on his face watching Shayk devour dumpling after dumpling.

"Then a week later, I get a call from my contact, a captain in the Boston Police Department, and he says the assistant mayor, Chris Donnelly, had a car accident and is dead. Now, I was beginning to think that there might be something, a connection but the cop said Donnelly had a history of DUIs and his blood alcohol level was four times the legal limit. Maybe a coincidence, I think, and karma has a way of setting things right. He was fucking young girls one moment and the next; he's lying in a morgue. Life can be a fucking bitch!"

He polished off the remainder of the dumpling, licked the jam off of his fingers and washed it down with a sip of coffee.

"What are really thinking, boss, you think someone is killing these bastards?" Izhutin asked.

Shayk raised his hand, smiled and continued, "Yesterday, Sal Castiglioni was found dead in his home. They think it was a heart attack but they are investigating the cause of death. I bet they don't find anything."

The men stared at their boss silently unsure of where this was leading. Finally Izhutin asked, "What do you think, boss?"

"Connect the dots. Matt Hansen, then Donnelly and now

Castiglioni… these are the three bastards in the videos. Who do you think will be next? Who was the fourth?"

There as a moment's silence before Izhutin burst out, "Nikolai! Next will be Nikolai. Someone is killing the fucking perverts at Hansen's parties and Nikolai was at every one of them. He and that Hansen boy were close… maybe too close!"

His boss picked up another dumpling and spread the remaining jam on it, "You never bring enough jam, Andrei, what? Is there a shortage of fucking strawberry jam?" He used the speakerphone and buzzed the receptionist, "Stephanie, go get me some jam. It's the strawberry jam at the bakery and make sure you get enough, maybe three of four bottles. You tell Aldo it is for me."

"You're not eating the syrniki with a little jam… you're eating jam with a little syrniki," Izhutin countered, "There was enough jam for ten dozen, boss!"

"Next time you bring more jam!" He snapped at Izhutin then continued, "Yes, Nikolai is in danger and maybe we are too. From now on, Sergei you will stay with me. You sleep in my place and Dmitri, you will stay with Andrei." Shayk noticed Izhutin about to protest, "This is not a choice. I am telling you that this is how it will be. If you are fucking some fat whore, Dmitri will be in the room watching you. And I don't give a shit about your choo-choo train and trampoline or whatever other shit you're into. He will be with you. Is that clear?"

Izhutin knew when to back off. "Sure, boss, maybe the stupid bastard will learn something from the master fucker of all time!"

The men laughed and then caught themselves seeing Shayk's reaction.

"This is not a joke. I have a feeling that McHenry is involved. His modus operandi is all over this. Now the two of you can leave and wait outside," Shayk motioned to Dmitri and Sergei. "I have some business with Andrei," he paused, then added, "and Dimitri, you make sure you are attached to him like a shadow, is that clear?"

"Yes, boss, I will stay with him until you tell me not to," the tall man answered with a solemn look then gave Izhutin a glance and shrugged.

After the men had left Izhutin couldn't contain himself, "That fucking retard will kill my sex life! Adam, I don't need him…"

"Enough. He will stay with you for a while. Don't argue. This time you listen, it is for your own good. McHenry is not what you think. He is the most dangerous man I know."

"But why would McHenry do this? He returned the money and…"

"Exactly! He returned the money so now he feels no obligation to us. Maybe someone else has hired him for more money… to end this nonsense once and for all. I don't know anyone else who can whack a politician and make it look like an accident. If it is him, along with Nikolai we will be next."

"That does not make sense. Why would he kill the people that hire him… it is about money for these bastards and we can be potential clients in the future."

"Not always. He's not being hired by the people in Boston, that's for sure or he wouldn't be killing them. Matt Hansen's father has no idea who he is so by default it's Hank or Luke. Hank is a cunning bastard but his brother, that pretty blond boy is dangerous. You killed his sister, and you snatched the boy, his son. Add to this the fact that McHenry is involved with a woman there, what's her name? The pretty girl who likes to party…"

"Marylou Dorsey."

"Yes, yes, her. If I had to put money down, I'd bet that the Frenchie is doing this for them. Maybe Luke was fucking her too and blackmailed her to get him to go after everyone in the video.

Who the fuck knows? "

"So what do we do? We can hire another assassin to take out this one."

"No, we will handle this ourselves. But first we have to make sure Nikolai is safe," Shayk said and belched loudly. He took a sip of his coffee. "We need to speak with Alexei and explain what is going on. I am going to suggest sending Nikolai back to Moscow. If he gets killed here I will get the blame."

"Good idea, boss, the boy is a pain in the ass. Everywhere he goes he finds these young girls and…"

"Yeah, I know but what are we going to do? He's Zakirov's son. You sit quietly and listen, I will do the talking."

Izhutin looked at his watch, "He will be having dinner now. It is 6:00 PM in Moscow. Maybe we should call later?"

Shayk dialed his boss' private number, put the phone on the desk and sat back, "I know Alexei; he has dinner around 9:00 PM. Now be quiet."

The man who answered spoke slowly and with a deep, gravelly voice, "Adam, is everything alright?"

"Hello Alexei, yes, yes, everything is alright… but you know, there is always the usual nonsense. I would not bother you unless it was important."

There was a short silence before the Zakirov spoke, "You are calling about Nikolai, no? He is a pain in the ass but what am I to do? His mother loves him or I would have smothered him with his own pillow when he was a boy."

"It is more than that, boss, I think his life is in danger here. The father of one of the young girl's or someone close must have hired an assassin and he is going after everyone that was at Nikolai's parties. So far he has killed Nikolai's friend, Hansen, and some other very powerful people."

"I read the papers, Adam, what are you suggesting? That we go after some ghost… a phantom killer?"

"No, boss, I think it might be a good idea for Nikolai to visit Moscow for a short time, at least until this settles down. He will be under your protection and will be safe."

"Are you forgetting my brother? He got Iryna pregnant and she was only fifteen! He cannot come back here, Rolan will kill him and then I will have to avenge… no, he cannot come here," Zakirov spoke slowly but had raised his voice. The thought that he might have to kill his own brother was too much for the elderly Russian.

There was a prolonged silence before Zakirov spoke again, "I have a place in Belize near the lighthouse… the Baron Bliss Lighthouse. It is a fucking fortress and I have my people there. I will call and let you know. You can make arrangements to send him there for a while."

"Okay, boss," Shayk said relieved that the monkey was off of his back.

"I don't know how a son of mine can be like this. If he didn't look like me I would swear he was a bastard spawned by one of my wife's many lovers but he is a carbon copy of me so what can I say? I am stuck with the boy. Keep him safe and make sure nothing happens to him. And Adam, one more thing, I have treated you like a son and have trusted you without much interference but don't let me hear that you involve children in our business. We lost two young men, one was a boy really, because of your misguided plans involving that child in the mountains. You are lucky, it seems this nonsense with the videos is being taken care of without your help." He paused before continuing, "Don't ever involve children. We are not animals. I am glad you came to your senses. Okay, enough. Make sure my boy is safe."

"Yes, boss. I will keep him safe and wait for your call. We were not going to hurt the boy…"

"I said enough!" Zakirov was suddenly furious, "Even criminals like us have a code of conduct and that does not involve children or innocent women."

"Yes, sir, I will make sure…"

The phone went dead.

"Who the fuck told him about the boy?" Shayk exploded. He demanded uncompromising loyalty from his mean and this breach could only mean that someone within his ranks was reporting back to Zakirov. "You find out who it is and you bring the bastard to me. I will skin him alive!"

"That is a bad idea. We will find out who it is and watch him carefully. If you do something to him the big boss is going to be more suspicious and there will be more shit to pay," Izhutin cautioned.

Shayk studied his friend before speaking, "Sometimes I think you should be sitting in this chair. Do you know that in a wolf pack it is not the alpha male who does the fighting, there is a warrior wolf who leads the fight when there is conflict between packs. I am that wolf. I do my best in war."

"You are also my boss and my friend, Adam. I will never forget that you saved me from the streets of hell. So, the day you go is the day I go as well. Now, let's go fuck some pretty girls. You need to work off the syrniki!" Izhutin said with the last part tongue in cheek.

Shayk sat still for a while contemplating what Alexei Zakirov had said. His mood had turned sour and the syrniki that were roiling over in his belly didn't help. He belched loudly a few times regretting his gluttony and wished he hadn't eaten so many. He reached into his desk drawer to retrieve a bottle of antacids and tapped a few chewable tablets into his mouth hoping it would provide him with some relief. It was true that the big boss had treated him like a son but even fathers don't forgive their sons for all their sins. He also knew that he was lucky to have Andrei Izhutin by his side.

"I'm not sure who saved who but I am glad you are my friend, Andrei," he said in between chews. "We will fuck the girls later, now we need to make arrangements for Nikolai. Call the little bastard in."

FROM THE APPALACHIANS TO MONTANA: GOODBYE

It was late evening at Moose Head Point and the sky was emblazoned in twilight's iridescent hue. For the past three weeks Meghan and Robbie had stayed on in Luke's cabin to help with Allison's convalescence. It was much needed especially during the day when Luke had to attend to business. They were now getting ready to move back to Meghan's place before making the long trip to Montana.

Luke had taken over the Carlson enterprise and his first order of business was the demolition of the Sleepy Crest Motel. The construction of the planned bowling alley with an adjacent movie theatre was underway. His focus was to legitimize all aspects of their various verticals and get out of the drug and prostitution businesses. He had applied for a permit to convert the Pit into a casino which would provide the platform for future fights. His free spirited persona had undergone subtle changes – he was a lot more serious about running the business and showed a keen interest in the wellbeing of the people that worked for him.

Robbie and Luke were sitting on the porch watching Ronin romping in the yard. Unlike Allison, Ronin had made a remarkable recovery and apart from a slight limp he was as boisterous as ever.

The two men had gotten a lot closer over the past weeks and had spent a considerable amount of time talking, learning about their pasts and came to the realization that they were very similar in personality.

Robbie was impressed with how well read and knowledgeable Luke was and Luke was beginning to treat Robbie like an older brother. The more he got to know Robbie the more he respected him.

"How's the bowling alley coming along? Is Ed going to run it or do you have someone else in mind?" Robbie asked.

"I don't know… haven't decided. Ed is still working through his problems. Losing Emma and Ray has been traumatic and like Hank, he is reconsidering his path in life. I wish you were staying, I could use your help but I understand about moving to Montana, sometimes change is good for us. "

"I guess we have all changed a bit. You've changed, that's for sure," Robbie commented.

"Maybe this version of me is really who I was and everything before was just a rebellious façade, an apparition waiting to manifest."

Robbie smiled, "I will quote our brother Tony, speak English."

"I think what happened to Allison, almost losing her, and…" he paused, glancing at Robbie, "and what happened between the two of you made me realize what she means to me. I had always taken her for granted. Not anymore."

"I'm not being judgmental here. I had heard rumors, I mean she *is* your sister and I never really thought that I was infringing in anyway," Robbie noted, trying to provide some amnesty for both of them.

"I believe in karma, in the concept of eternal recurrence and for Allison and you, it was meant to be… maybe lovers from a past life reincarnated to wrap up some unfinished business. There are no coincidences, just cases of synchronicity. Carl Jung called it meaningful coincidence."

"You know what scares me? I'm beginning to understand you," the taller man muttered.

Luke laughed, got up and stretched, "Forget it, it's something I read." He paused as though lost in thought then spoke again, "I'm not suggesting incest is for everyone or that the laws are misguided; far from it. But Allie and I are meant to be together, that much I'm certain of."

"There are exceptions to every rule," Robbie added knowing that what Luke said was true. This brother and sister were meant to be together.

They were quiet for a while comfortable in each other's company. The smaller man sat down next to Robbie, "It doesn't matter anymore. I think all the pieces fell exactly where they were meant to. You will make a great father and husband. I know Ryan and Meghan deserve that. And, I will be the here for Allison for the rest of our lives."

"You make a beautiful couple and in many ways, a perfect one. I never thought I'd make friends when I first arrived in Chase River but Maddie had the foresight that a lot of this would come to pass. It's strange but I feel her around me when I'm alone, especially up here," Robbie wasn't used to confiding his feelings to anyone let alone another man. He struggled with verbalizing what he felt and finally said, "If you ever need a friend, I'll be there… all you need to do is to let me know."

"I appreciate that." Luke replied, "If I could chose a brother it would be you. Maddie kept talking about kindred spirits and the arrival of the fourth horseman and I always assumed it was you. But now I know, the one who rides the pale horse is McHenry."

"I think the pale horse represents a figurative state. Some

choices we make lead us to circumstances that deal in life and death. Warriors get to ride the pale horse at one time or the other. Damn! I'm beginning to sound like you…" Robbie got up trying to suppress the memories of Kunduz. He noticed a rustle in the bushes and rushed onto the lawn and called out, "Ronin get back here. Now! Back here, boy."

The big dog had spotted a deer and was about to give chase. He stopped and trotted back to his master wagging his tail. "That's a good boy. You stay here, stay with me."

"I never thought about getting a dog before but I'm going to get one just like him. Allie is going to be heartbroken when he goes." Luke paused and looked fondly at Ronin before asking, "Why don't you leave him with us for a while?"

"Not a chance, brother, but hang on, I've got a surprise for both of you. Give it a week or so," Robbie revealed petting his dog.

For a moment Luke was speechless then exclaimed, "No! A dog! A puppy! Come on, don't kid me, brother! Are you seriously getting us a puppy?" the astonishment on his face made Robbie smile.

"I spoke to Rachel, my sister, and you're one lucky hombre. The breeder she got Ronin from had a litter two months ago and there's puppy, a male, the same coloring as Ronin on its way to you."

Luke was quiet, touched by the gesture. He shook his head in disbelief before making a request, "Please don't say anything to Allie. I would love to surprise her."

Robbie smiled and gave him the thumbs up and went back to roughhousing Ronin. "I'm hoping the puppy arrives before we leave for Montana. I'd like Ronin to meet him."

Luke looked around and asked lowering his voice, "Does Meghan know?"

"Yes. But I've asked her to keep it a secret. I wasn't going to tell you either but when you brought up Allison and how much she'll miss Ronin, I couldn't help myself."

"Are you sure Meghan won't tell Allison?" Luke persisted.

"Relax, she won't. She's like the freakin' CIA!"

Meghan was with Allison taking care of the last-minute details before Robbie and she left. She made sure that the bathroom was clean with fresh towels and soap and the loft, where they had slept, was spotless. She had stocked the fridge with enough food to last Luke and Allison a week or more.

"I don't know how to thank you, Meghan, you've been like a sister," Allison said to her while Meghan fussed around the bed making sure everything Allison needed was within arms-reach.

"Are you sure you'll be okay? We can stay on for a few more days; it's not a problem, Allie. Montana will still be there."

"No, I'm fine. Mom said she'll come by to make sure I'm okay. I don't need help in the bathroom any longer and that was my biggest concern. You were God sent. It's time for Robbie and you to begin your life together…" she paused, "Do you want to talk about us, I mean Robbie and me?" Allison reached out and took Meghan's hand, "We don't have to but we can if you want to."

'No. Like Maddie would have said, it is what it is and we have to move on."

"God, I miss her so much! She was my rock… I used to turn to her every time I needed someone to talk to."

"You can call me. I will listen. I don't have Maddie's knowledge or experience but I'll listen and offer my perspective," Meghan stopped and stroked the younger woman's lustrous hair, looking into her eyes, "You *are* my little sister, a sister I never had."

Allison squeezed Meghan's hand. "I will call you. I may call every day so don't get cross with me."

"I won't ever be angry with you. You can call as much as you like and if Luke and you want to visit us you will find a warm bed and a loving home," Meghan assured her.

The women hugged and Meghan left walking out to the porch joining Robbie and Luke. She found them chatting and watching Ronin run around the front yard.

"Allie's fine. I gave her a bath… well, she bathed herself I just watched to make sure she didn't slip and fall. I think she'll be as good as new in a few days." She said to the men then addressed Robbie, "We need go, baby, I need to get Ryan from Mom's."

"Okay. Let me have a few minutes with Allie. I'll be out in a minute."

When Robbie walked into the bedroom, Allison was resting, propped up on pillows, eyes closed, listening to music. He sat beside her on the bed and gently removed her headphones. She opened her eyes and looked at him. For a while they sat silently, basking in each-others warmth before she smiled and reached for his hand.

"I was just thinking about you. So my baby is leaving. I will miss you Robbie Olsen and I will think of you often," she said and pulled him towards her. They kissed, a gentle, lingering kiss that neither one wanted to end.

It was Robbie who ended it. He leaned back and ran his fingers along her lips, "Do you remember what you once said to me? When I'm old and memories are all I have, the moments we shared will keep me warm. I don't regret anything we've done but I know that you belong with Luke and I, with Meghan."

She nodded, her eyes welling up, the tears threatening to break loose, "Don't forget to visit. You promised…"

"I will… we will come back, I promise. Don't cry, baby, what we have shared is forever."

He got up, leaned over and kissed her on top of her head and left without looking back. He could hear her crying softly and knew that if he went back to her, he would never leave and that wouldn't be fair to any of them. He loved Meghan, he was sure of that. This thing with Allison was something he couldn't define. It wasn't just physical but an obfuscation of several impalpable feelings. Maybe Luke and Maddie were right and there was more to this eternal recurrence than he had considered or could have imagined.

When he joined Meghan and Luke they were discussing the property that Maddie had left for Ryan.

"Luke has agreed to run the gas station until Ryan is old enough to decide what he wants to do with it. And, he's also promised to look in on Mom and Dad," Meghan said looking relieved. "It would have been too much for Mom to look after and I don't want to sell it. Maddie wanted Ryan to have it and it's for him to decide."

"I don't know what Ryan will decide to do… kids will grow up and become young men with minds of their own. He may end up in the Army Rangers, who knows! However, I have a feeling that the two of you will be back here and when you do come back, the gas station and the property behind it will be waiting for you. Maddie would be tickled pink to see you running it," Luke said with a smile. "And, don't worry about your Mom and Dad, I will check on them every day. Now that Maddie's gone, I'll need them more than they need me."

They were walking towards the steps when Luke reached out and stopped Meghan, "Can I speak to you for a minute?"

She was surprised but stepped to one side, "Sure. What is it?"

Robbie walked on and waited by the top of the stone steps and watched Ronin scuttle down to where the trucks were parked. The big dog ran to Meghan's truck and looked back up at Robbie.

"Stay. I'm coming." Robbie called out.

Luke glanced at Robbie then spoke softly, "It's about Ryan, I would have made a lousy father. There is no excusing my behavior but in hindsight, Robbie is the kind of man he needs in his life. If I can impose and ask a favor, I would like to hear about Ryan and how he is doing. You don't owe me this but it would mean a lot to me."

Meghan smiled and gave him a hug, "Of course. I will email you photographs and we will be coming to visit Mom and Dad so you won't be a stranger to him. We can also facetime if you want to. When the time is right Robbie and I will explain what happened and your relationship to him. We both think that is the right thing to do."

He smiled, a warm smile that reached his eyes, "Thank you."

As they drove off they could see Luke standing on top of Moose Head Point watching the taillights receding into the night. His silhouette conveyed the iconic image of a Mountain Man - independent, indomitable and free.

A REQUIEM FOR MARISA

Deputy Bradley handed the phone back to Ed Carlson and said, "That is disturbing, very disturbing. I see what happened but you need to fill in the blanks. You're not leaving here until you tell me exactly what happened between Marisa and Junior and how it was that Olsen found the body near Devil's Ridge almost a week later."

Ed Carlson sat still and stared at the floor before continuing with his account of the events of that fateful night. "When she agreed to fuck... when she agreed to make a man out of Junior, I waited to make sure he knew what to do but Marisa seemed to have it under control. When they began fucking I saw her place his hands around her neck. That's when I left."

"You mean she liked to be choked during sex?" Bradley asked.

"Yeah, she did. Autoerotic Asphyxiation... she was the one who showed me how. I had never heard the term before nor indulged in it before her."

"Why would you let Junior do that? He's is not a normal kid and this was his first sexual experience with a woman!"

"I just assumed that she would guide him and he would do what she told him. How the heck was I to know he would choke her to death? Junior is the gentlest guy I know. He wouldn't hurt a fly."

"He is also strong as a fucking ox and doesn't know his own

strength. You guys were outside. Didn't you hear her struggle?" the deputy was mystified.

"No. We heard her moaning and heard him making some very strange sounds. We were smoking weed and it sounded funny. We couldn't stop laughing so we moved away to give them some privacy. When we didn't see them for a while, Jericho went to check on them. He came out screaming and that's when I went back in. Junior was sitting with his back against the wall, a blank look in his face, and kept saying her name over and over. And, Marisa was dead."

"Why didn't you report it… why didn't you come and see me? You had the whole town looking for her. You were looking for her when you knew all along that she was dead."

Carlson was quiet then got up and asked, "Can I use the john? I need to take a leak."

"Sure. Go down the corridor to the back," Bradley pointed to the door on the side of the office leading to the corridor, "the men's room is on the right."

He got up and got himself another cup of coffee and sat making notes on his pad until Carlson returned. The deputy turned the tape recorder back on.

"You wanted to know why we didn't report it and honestly I don't know. We were scared and confused. I guess for one, we didn't want anyone to know about Marisa. Everybody thought of her as this sweet, innocent girl. If people were to find out it would kill her father… and damn, that just ain't fair. He's suffered enough already. Also, we weren't sure what the consequences would be for Junior and for us."

"So why come forward now?" Bradley asked.

"Ray and Rico are dead. Marisa is dead and I don't think Junior has a clue as to what happened. That leaves me. If something were to happen to me then the truth would never be known. Marisa deserves better than that. I just lost my mother, brother and friend and a woman who I liked so I don't care what happens to me. Junior is innocent so if there is blame to be doled out, I deserve the brunt of it. I gave her the ride, it was me that she trusted and I should have known better than to leave Junior alone with her. Lock me up if you want to – I don't care anymore, just leave Junior out of this and keep the sordid shit from getting to old man Gorecki."

"We'll get to that. Right now there are some questions unanswered. According to Gil, she had been dead only a day but according to the date you gave me, she was dead for six or seven days. That doesn't make sense unless Gil is lying. And he claimed that there was no DNA found on her body. How do you explain that?"

"I saw a program on the Iceman, Richard Kuklinski… he was a serial killer. He was called the Iceman because he would murder his victims and then freeze them to screw up the time of death. We have two, large sub-zero freezers at the lumber yard. We use them to store our aluminum fittings in between operations. We stored Marisa in the bigger one. We were planning to store her for a couple of months but Hank sent a rush order to the yard and both freezers were needed."

"So you threw her in the river?" Bradley asked.

"No. I was going to take her up to Bear Ridge. She was dead anyway and the bears would dispose of her but in case someone did stumble onto the body, the time of death would throw off any real leads." Carlson paused, he scratched his head struggling with what he was about to say. "Jericho shot her in the head to make it seem like the cause of death was the gunshot. That was hard to watch even though she had been dead for about a week."

"So what happened? How did she end up in the river?"

"It was a coincidence. That morning Gil comes into my office and goes on about Junior and how he keeps repeating: *nice Marisa, pretty Marisa and dead Marisa…* this was before anyone knew for sure that she was dead. Jericho was in the office and after a while he just showed Gil the video. It freaked him out and he started to cry. I've never seen anything like it. It was like Marisa was his kid."

"We all liked Marisa. This isn't easy to listen to… she needed help, that's obvious and instead you guys took advantage of her."

Carlson covered his face with his hands taking several deep breaths, "What a fucking mess! I swear, I haven't slept at all ever since this happened. I wish I had never… oh, fuck it, whatever happens, I just don't give a damn anymore!"

"Keep going, so what happened after Gil saw the video?"

"After he calmed down, I told him what we had planned to do with the body but he got agitated and threatened to come to you. He wanted to bury her. His exact words were: *I knew that girl since she was a child. I aim to give her a decent burial.* We offered to help but he refused. There was no way to dissuade him so we helped him get the body into his van and he left. He was going to bury her near that giant rock, the one the kids call Big Boulder. I didn't know it but it was Marisa's favorite place because of the butterflies."

"How did she end up in the river?"

"While he was digging the grave some hikers passed by and waved, they were too far to notice anything but he panicked and pushed the body into the water. The current took her downstream and that's where Olsen found her."

"Okay, that explains it but Gil didn't carry the body so where was his van?"

"Once the hikers had disappeared, Gil ran after the body along the bank hoping to drag it back to Big Boulder but by then Olsen and his dog had discovered the body so he kept walking. He spoke to Olsen briefly hoping to try and scare him off but that didn't work. After Olsen had gone to get help he circled back to where the body was but the dog was there and one look at that monster sent Gil scurrying back to his van. He had parked near Big Boulder behind some trees. He drove back to my office and when he told us what had happened, Jericho wanted to go shoot the dog and retrieve the body. I talked him out of it."

"And that's when VanArcen brought Olsen here," the big deputy sat back and sighed. "If Olsen hadn't found her none of this would have happened. Makes you wonder."

"What now?" Carlson asked.

"I don't know. I need to think about it. Leave Jericho's phone here. That is evidence. I'll go over everything in detail when I can think clearly. I have two little girls and this hits too close to home." Bradley stood up, "I'm going to go home now and I'm going to hug them and pray that they never run into the likes of you."

Ed Carlson didn't respond. He sat quietly twirling the phone in his hand. He got up and pushed the phone across the deputy's desk, "Can I go?"

"Yeah, you can go for now. Don't take any trips out of town, you hear? And don't say a word to anyone and I mean, *anyone*!"

Ed Carlson nodded and walked out of the police station. He stopped at the top of the steps and took a deep breath, a sense of relief coursing through him, then got into his truck and drove up to Calico Bluff. It was getting dark and except for the nocturnal sounds of insects and the bristling rustle of leaves, the place was eerily quiet.

He sat by the charred remains of Dorsey's cabin where Marisa had died and smoked the last of the Marlboros. He took a final drag and flicked the cigarette butt into the night. He remained still for a while looking out at the dark silhouette of the mountains then got his gun out, put the muzzle into his mouth and pulled the trigger.

**"And I looked, and behold a pale horse: and his name that
sat on him was Death, and Hell followed with him."**
— Revelation 6:8

Adam Shayk was a creature of habit. He woke up at 4:30 AM sharp
each morning, took the family's three-year-old beagle for a walk,
had breakfast with his wife, showered, got ready and was at work
by 6:30 AM. The laxative he took the previous night had worked and
the good bowel movement did wonders for his mood.

He had eaten way too much the previous night. He had gone out
for dinner with Izhutin, Sergei and Dimitri to a Greek restaurant
and had overindulged once again. It was becoming a habit with him
but he seemed unable to control his gastronomical cravings. The
desert of warm baklava served a la mode after the decadently rich
moussaka was a mistake. The apéritif didn't help either. They had
done several shots of ouzo toasting every Russian they knew. By
night's end the heartburn and acid reflux that followed would have
killed a buffalo. He swore he would never repeat that again. He
would control himself and indulge in moderation. *Yes, moderation,
that was the key,* he said to himself.

He liked being the first to get to the office. He enjoyed the
mundane act of unlocking the doors, switching on the lights and
getting the coffee brewing all the while looking across the Hudson
River at the Manhattan skyline. It reminded him of just how far he
had come from those bitter cold streets of Moscow.

So when he got to the office he was surprised to find the lights
in the lobby and his office turned on. He walked by the reception
desk and noticed a pink and purple coat hanging on Stephanie's
chair but there was no sign of the young woman. *She must be in the
bathroom;* he thought to himself, *I will give her a bonus. Not only
is she easy on the eyes but she is also very efficient. And now, she's
in here earlier than me? He would have a talk with her and tell her*

that it wasn't necessary to come in this early.

He went into his office and was greeted by the distinctive aroma of brewing coffee mingled with the hint of fresh-baked pastry. There on his desk, in front of his chair, was a box of syrniki with two bottles of strawberry jam next to it. A note on the box, written in a neat feminine handwriting, read: *It was freshly baked and I couldn't resist. I hope you don't mind my getting it. The coffee is fresh. I forgot my phone. I'll be back in a few minutes. Enjoy. Steffi* There was a smiley face next to her name.

He smiled: *she's definitely getting a bonus.* He got the newspapers out from his leather attaché case, poured himself a cup of coffee and spread the jam over the warm dumpling. He sat back and took a bite, sipped his coffee and began reading the papers. His earlier resolution was long forgotten lost to his pathological compulsion, his polyphagia, and all he could think of was the box full of tasty pastry. He placed the papers down forgetting the upset stomach of the previous night and focused on the task at hand. He polished off the dumpling washing it down with the coffee and was about to work on his second when he heard a shuffling sound in the lobby. He assumed it had to be Steffi, who else could it be this early?

He was about to get up but decide to buzz her extension. "Good morning, Steffi! Can you come in?" He got no answer so he tried again, "Stephanie?" There was still no answer. *I'm hearing things,* he thought.

He got up to refill his cup and felt a bit woozy but didn't think much of it. He stood by the coffee machine and filled his mug with an unsteady hand spilling some of the hot beverage over the counter top. He put the pot back and was reaching for the paper towels when he stumbled forward and fell face-first in a heap. The nitrazepam in the coffee had done its job and Shayk was fully sedated.

When Shayk came to he found himself gagged and bound to a

chair. For the first time in his life, he felt fear, a real and unmitigated terror that hit him like a runaway train. His mind raced in every which way and the premonition of death hung about him like a bad odor. There was no help in sight. Sergei was either dead or incapacitated. The subject of his fear was standing in front of him, studying him like a snake eying its prey. Even though he had never met the man, he knew immediately that it was McHenry and the terror magnified exponentially.

"Your gluttony is what is going to kill you," McHenry said in a voice that was emotionless. "Your mind lost track of all the irregularities that should have warned you that something wasn't right but your sybaritic obsession with food shut your brain down. Her car wasn't in her parking spot and that wasn't her coat. It was way too big for her and she has never come in early or brought you syrniki before. But I knew that once you got a whiff of the pastry you would be like a fish that is hooked. You are a cold, calculating killer and now it's time to pay the piper."

Shayk struggled against the restraints, making guttural sounds attempting to speak but his mouth was taped shut and stuffed full of rags and his arms and legs were bound tightly to the chair. His eyes were wide and bulging out of his head and the veins on the sides of his temple were throbbing from fright. He watched helplessly as the assassin removed several vials from a small black case and studied each one carefully. Not knowing what was in store for him only heightened Shayk's fear.

McHenry had a hypodermic syringe in his hand and bending over he injected the liquid intravenously in Shayk's arm. Within seconds of administering the shot paralysis began setting in. Though McHenry had used a variety of drugs in the past, drugs like Ricin, Aconite and Abrin, Succinylcholine remained his favorite. It was a muscle relaxant and depolarizing agent used by anesthesiologists in very controlled environments. Without the proper intubation and respiratory support, death was certain to follow. And what made it the near perfect poison was that it was almost impossible to detect.

The assassin placed the syringe on the desk, took the rags out of Shayk's mouth and cut him free. His victim tried getting up but his arms and legs refused to cooperate. His attempts to cry for help were futile – he thought he was screaming but no sounds came from his mouth. With supreme effort he leaned forward and would have fallen but for McHenry. The assassin caught him and eased him onto the carpeted floor.

Uncontrolled panic set in when Shayk realized that his body was shutting down. He was having trouble swallowing and breathing as he went into pulmonary failure. He stared blindly, unable to blink, unable to move and unable to breathe and began sinking into the dark morass of unconsciousness. The last thought Shayk ever had was: *I'm dying. No more syrniki.*

THE THREADS THAT BIND...

Luke was at Bucky Johnston's Diner when he received a frantic call from his mother. She was worried sick about her grandson. She knew Ed was still in grieving having lost his mother, brother and friend within days of each other. He had also confided in her about his feelings for Angela Mercier, the dead prostitute who used to work for Hank. Though it had shocked her, she was supportive and nonjudgmental. She adored her grandchildren and wanted them to be happy. He had taken to staying at her home to get away from the ghosts that haunted him. The cottage he had shared with Ray and Jericho held too many memories and he couldn't bear to be there alone. Lisa Carlson was hoping that her emotional support would help him to get over his grief and get back to living again. She had told him several times: *The dead don't want us to mourn; they want us to celebrate their lives by living ours to the fullest.*

"Ed didn't come home last night. He usually has dinner with me and sleeps in the guest bedroom near the garage but he didn't show. I made his favorite meatball and spaghetti with chocolate pudding for desert. I must have called him a hundred times but he doesn't answer. I went over to his cottage but there was no one there. I'm worried, Luke. Please find him and make sure he is okay."

"Ma, he's most probably trying to figure out what he wants to do. He'll show up, don't worry," Luke said trying to placate his mother and to calm her down.

"Please Luke; I haven't been able to sleep. Ray is dead and Meghan is taking Ryan to Montana." She stopped; the thought of Ryan moving across the country was too much for her. She steeled herself and continued, "Ed is the only grandchild I have left. I have a bad feeling about this."

"Okay, Ma, I'll find him. You stop worrying," Luke assured his mother. He knew that she must be really concerned or she wouldn't have bothered him. It was unusual for Lisa Carlson to call anyone without good reason.

The first stop he made was at the lumberyard. He checked Ed's office but found nothing of significance and decided to speak to a few of the employees. No one had seen Ed since Angela Mercier's funeral and that was a while ago. It wasn't like Ed to just take off and disappear. Luke's next stop was at the shop foreman's office that was next to the tool-room. Ed had left Randall Mosby, the foreman, in charge until he returned.

Mosby was one of the few African Americans living in Chase River. He was a tall man, dignified and quiet. He had worked at the lumberyard since he was a teen and knew everything there was about the business. It was Mosby who trained Ed Carlson when Hank brought his nephew in to take charge of the yard. The job should have rightfully been his and though he had felt hurt and disrespected, he had taken the young Carlson under his wing and had taught him as much as he could. Life for a black man in Chase River had never been easy and he accepted his lot without complaint.

Mosby had also helped Luke when he was building his cabin so the men knew each other well. Luke was unlike the other Carlsons – he was an anomaly. He read a lot, cared little for what people thought and was as wild as the bears that roamed the mountains. But, he had always treated Mosby with respect and kindness.

"Hi Randall," Luke greeted and walked into the foreman's office. "It's been a while."

They shook hands and Mosby said, "You stopped coming by but I hear things and they tell me you're taking over the Carlson business. Good for you."

"I never thought I would. Chalk it up to karma," Luke said and sat down.

"What can I do for you, boss?"

"You can start by not calling me boss. We're friends or have you forgotten. I've eaten more meals at your place than at my mother's and I would never have finished my cabin without your help. I learned more in those three months than any book could teach me."

"You were a quick study," the foreman replied with a smile recalling the difficult construction on top of a hill.

"Have you heard from Ed?" Luke asked, "My Mom is worried sick and I need to track him down or I'm not going to hear the end of it."

"He called two days ago. Said he needed more time off and told me to keep a handle on things. I don't mind. Hank gave my father a job when no one in this town would. And Hank made it clear that if anyone messed with my old man, they would have to deal with him. My father reminded us of that at every turn so I'll never forget. I'll manage this place as long as Ed is out or as long as you want me to."

Luke was a kid but he recalled the problems Jerimiah Mosby, Randall's father, had with some of the town's folk, "Hank had his good side and your father was a good man. I know it hasn't been easy for you but things are going to change. You'll see. Did Ed say where he was?"

"No but he did say he was going to speak to Joe… Deputy Bradley. He said it was important but didn't say what and I didn't push it." He waited, distracted, and rubbed his chin before adding,

"There was something going on with him. I try and stay in my lane and mind my own business but I was worried for him."

"He took his mother's death badly and who can blame him," Luke said, "and losing Ray…"

"He liked Angela," the foreman interjected, "he would come home to see her. Angela spent a lot of time with Dora and the boys. We were the only family she had."

"Yeah, Ma mentioned that… then why didn't' he do something about it? I don't get it."

"He's not like you, Luke. Like most of us, he needed approval and he was worried what Hank and the others would think."

"That he loved a pretty girl?"

"Who was black and a whore," Randall reminded him.

"We're all whores in some way or the other and no one has a right to judge her unless they have walked in her shoes. People are such fucking hypocrites!" Luke riposted.

"I'll second that, brother."

Luke was quiet. He knew that without Randall, Ed would never have managed the place. It was Randall Mosby who really ran the lumberyard. The only reason Ed got the job was because he was Hank Carlson's nephew and the only reason Randall Mosby didn't was because he was black.

Luke decided that it was time for a change, "You're doing a fine job, Randall – you've always done an exemplary job. This position is yours if you want it and we'll discuss the adjustments to your salary next week. I have a new accountant, Bill Denis. He and I will stop by to go over some stuff. He will help you with the financials. I will make the announcement to the employees and make sure everyone is on board or they can find employment elsewhere."

"What about Ed?"

"I think running the bowling alley is something Ed would be

more suited for."

Though he kept a straight face, Randall Mosby was ecstatic. Finally, he would be able to show everyone and especially his family that the hard work and loyalty had paid off. "Thanks, Luke, this means a lot. I only wish that my old man was around to see it… would've made him proud."

"Oh, he sees it alright and he was always proud of you. How's the family?"

"All doing well. The boys are growing faster than I'd like. Dora asks about you all the time, the wild-eyed, golden boy, that's what she calls you."

Luke smiled, "I'll drop by. Her chicken with gravy is the best I've had… don't tell my mom but damn, you wife can cook better than anyone I know."

Randall Jones patted his belly and said, "She sure can. This is a testament to her cooking."

"One of these days I'll take your boys hunting if you don't mind. It's time to learn to hunt and to fight."

"Fight they know, I'm tired of pulling them apart but hunting, I'd surely appreciate that. I can't shoot worth a damn!"

They shook hands and Luke left to see if Bradley could shed light on Ed's disappearance. A few hours after speaking to the deputy, Luke found Ed Carlson' body next to the burned down Dorsey cabin with the back of his head blown away. He hadn't been scavenged by animals as yet but he was in no condition to be viewed by his grandmother. There had been too many deaths and Luke was emotionally numb. They had never been close – Ed was more like Hank and didn't really care for the mountains. Luke now wished he had done more with his nephew to try and better their relationship, especially for Emma's sake, but it was too late now. *All this killing and it's not over yet. McHenry and the Russians… I wonder what it's all for.*

His nephew was a big man but Luke carried him like he was a child. He decided to bury him near the Dorsey cabin and gently break the news to his mother. It was, in many ways, a poetic end because Calico Bluff was the only place where Ed Carlson had felt at home.

A WOLF AMONG FOXES

Stephanie Prokup was getting ready for work, humming to herself and thinking about Izhutin. Yes, he was older but there was something of the rogue about him and his reputation as a dangerous man only added to the mystery and intrigue. A friend of hers had once told her that older men made the best lovers and really knew how to please a woman.

A smile crossed her face at the recollection of what she had said, "They have experienced tongues, Steffi, and that beats the heck out of a big cock!"

Her job as Shayk's receptionist and girl Friday was nice but the pay was not nearly enough. Her family back in Russia needed money and was constantly pressing her for more. She didn't resent them; she understood their need. Life in Saratov was difficult especially for her parents. Her father had worked at one of the largest ports along the Volga river until his emphysema confined him to his bed. Her two brothers and younger sister were too young to work so her mother worked two jobs to make ends meet. The only way they could afford the medication her father needed was if she sent money home.

Her boyfriend, Gavin Holstein, was of no help. He was always broke and to make matters worse, he was cheating on her with her best friend Alanna and though they both denied it, her intuition was rarely wrong. And as if this wasn't enough, he had to be the worst lover in the world. All he ever wanted was a blowjob. The last time they were in bed he couldn't maintain an erection and had asked her to suck him off. She had refused and had laughed and taunted him.

"You're pathetic. You can never get it up! Maybe you're gay or impotent. Yeah, that's it... you're fucking impotent!" She hissed and tumbled out of bed.

That had sent him into a rage and they had fought; it was a bad fight that came close to getting physical. Gavin had backed away only because he knew who Adam Shayk was and that scared the piss out of him.

The memory of that day and the fact that she had clung to their toxic relationship made her angry. The timing was perfect. She would break up with Gavin and see where this thing with Izhutin would lead. She was sure he could get her more money and make her life a bit more comfortable. He could be her *papik*, her sugar daddy. The ringing of the doorbell startled her out of her reverie.

She lived on the top floor of an old three-story building with a buzzer at the front door - she hadn't buzzed anyone in and wondered who it could be. She looked through the peephole and saw a man holding a large bouquet of red roses. He was wearing a beige jacket that had the company insignia: Grand Flowers & Candy.

"Who is it?" She asked without opening the door.

"Flowers for Stephanie Prokup, ma'am," the man answered in a friendly voice.

"I'm getting dressed. Can you leave it by the door?"

"I'm sorry, ma'am, but you will have to sign for it. Do you want me to come back later?"

"No, no... give me a minute," she said and ran back into the bedroom. She was excited; she rarely got flowers. *It must be from Andrei!*

She picked up her bathrobe that was lying on the bed and made sure it was wrapped tightly about her before she opened the door.

"Good morning, ma'am, these are for you," the man said with a smile. "Beautiful flowers for a beautiful lady."

He handed the flowers to her and watched as she did what most women do. She instinctively raised them to her face and closed her eyes, losing herself in the intoxicating fragrance of the roses and was about to read the card when he shoved her into the apartment. It happened quickly, before she had time to think. The next thing she was aware of was the muzzle of the gun pressed against her forehead. The man closed the door behind them and the roses fell from her hand. Fear and confusion paralyzed her replacing the joy she had experienced a moment ago.

"Don't make a sound if you want to live," the man said. His voice sounded cold and menacing and frightened her to the point of near hysteria. Her eyes were wide and she could hardly breathe. She was struggling to stay calm.

"Don't hurt me; please… please don't hurt me. I don't have any money. I…" she squeaked.

"If you do exactly as you are told, you won't get hurt. Do you understand?"

Her throat felt parched. She nodded and swallowed. Her breathing was becoming more labored and her heart was pounding. The man was small but he was strong. He grabbed her by the robe and dragged her with him to the bedroom. At that point she was sure he was going to rape her and panic began setting in. She was too frightened to fight him.

"Please, please don't hurt me…" she pleaded.

He didn't answer her but made a quick reconnaissance of the apartment before going back to the living room. He pushed her onto a sofa and relief washed over her: *he's not going to rape me. But what does he want?*

"You are going to call Andrei Izhutin and invite him over," the man instructed adding to her confusion.

"What?" She wasn't sure she understood him clearly.

"Don't play games with me or you *will* get hurt. I'm not going to rape you so stop imagining shit. I will cut your face up so badly a stray dog wouldn't fuck you. Take a look," he said and pulled a photograph from his pocket and shoved it in her face. "Take a good look. That was the last girl who refused to do what she was told."

It was a picture of a pretty young woman with her faced horribly disfigured by acid. There was a before and an after that made Stephanie shiver. She went pale. The man was not lying – she was sure he would do exactly as he promised.

"Call Andrei Izhutin now and invite him over. Make up a story. Tell him you took the day off and was thinking about him and what he had said. Go on, call him."

He took off the baseball cap he was wearing revealing a shock of curly blond hair. The Van Dyke goatee and long, dark sideburns gave him a strange look and made him seem all the more sinister.

She was shocked – *how did he know about Izhutin? Did Shayk have a spy in the office? Maybe Nikolai had hired someone. Yes, it had to be Nikolai. That little rat!*

"How did you know?" She asked, feeling safer now. "How did you know about Andrei and me?"

He grabbed her hair and shook her, not hard but it was enough to get her attention.

"Do you want me to hurt you, is that it? It doesn't matter how I know – I know. Now call him!" His face was expressionless and his eyes were like chips of ice. It sent a shiver down her spine.

"Sorry, I'm sorry… my phone is over there," she pointed to the coin tray on top of a small dresser by the door and added, "My boss is going to wonder where I am. He will call and if I don't answer, he will send someone here to check on me."

The man smirked then got his phone out from his jacket and after a few moments found what he was looking for. He handed the phone to her. She stared at the screen and what she saw made her sick to her stomach. There lying on the floor of his office was Adam Shayk, his mouth and eyes were frozen in a grotesque, lifeless scream. The picture resembled a still shot of a fish gasping for air.

"Go back and hit camera 3," He instructed, his voice soft and cold.

When she pulled up camera 3, she saw Sergei. He was also obviously dead. He had been shot and the blood trail indicated that he had been dragged into the lobby of the office. It became clear to her then that the offices had been bugged.

"Your boss and his bodyguard are dead," he said without missing a beat and took his phone back. "Now get your phone and call him," he then surprised her even further by reverting to Russian, "I speak your language so be careful what you say and how you say it. Call him."

Her legs felt like jelly and the sick feeling in the pit of her belly only got worse. She had been hoping to mention Shayk's name to scare the man off but now that was pointless. Her ace in the hole was gone and she knew in her heart that there was no way out of this predicament.

When Izhutin got the call from Stephanie he was on his way to the Shayk's office. To say he was surprised would be an understatement. He was sure he had a lot more work to put in before she relented and went out with him.

"My malyshka, I couldn't sleep thinking about you and all the things I will do to you," he said flirtatiously.

She giggled, playing the coy ingénue, "Me too. I was awake until late thinking about what you said. I called Adam and told him I was sick. Can you come over? I have some pancakes and coffee ready. We can spend the day together."

Izhutin almost feinted! He couldn't believe his luck: *The horny bitch wants to get laid!* And then reality hit home: *Shit! I have to go to Brooklyn with Adam to look at that stupid warehouse that he bought. Of all the cursed days in the week, why today? But it was important and Adam would not be happy if he bailed.*

"Malyshka, you know I want to be with you more than life itself but I have work to do. I will come by there in the afternoon, I promise, baby, and I will make you the happiest woman who walks this earth!"

There was a short silence before she was back on the phone.

"I know you have to work. What was I thinking?" Her voice laced with disappointment, "I am just a silly, romantic girl. It is okay, Andrei, maybe some other time."

"Why don't you go to work and tell Adam that you are feeling better. In the afternoon you can tell him you are not feeling that…"

She interrupted, "That's okay. I will call my stupid boyfriend and tell him to come over. I have the day off so I'm not going to waste it."

No fucking way! This peach was too ripe to leave on the tree. The thoughts flashed through his mind in a series of lascivious sequences. *I will fuck her and then fuck her again before I go to the warehouse. Then I'll come back and fuck her some more.*

"No, no, my beautiful flower, I am the stupid one. Who cares about work? Love is the most important thing in life." He paused for effect, "What are you wearing, malyshka? It is important to whet the appetite, no?"

She giggled then morphing seamlessly into a vamp, her voice sounding breathless, said, "I'm wearing only a nightie… nothing under it. Hurry up, I don't like waiting."

"My heart just stopped and my cock has ripped through my trousers, it is stiffer than a steel rod! I will be there before you can blink," Izhutin said and hung up.

He dialed Shayk's office phone number but there was no response. He tried his private cellphone but got his voice mail. He must be speaking to Zakirov now that Nikolai was on his way to Belize. He would call him after he had fucked this beautiful peach.

McHenry was quite impressed with Stephanie's role playing. He continued to speak in Russian, "Very good, you did well. Now remember, I will be in the bedroom and will leave the front door unlocked. You stand by the bedroom door and invite him in. Take off the bathrobe. Take it off now!"

"I'm not wearing anything… I mean I only have my panties on," Stephanie protested.

"I've seen titties before, all kinds, so you don't need to be coy with me. Go on take it off," he commanded the young woman.

The man frightened her. She obeyed and turning away from McHenry, stood in her panties by the bedroom door.

"Toss me the bathrobe," the man commanded.

She did as she was told. She bent over to pick up the robe knowing that he was watching her. Her face was flushed and hot and she felt a strange tingling between her thighs. She was shocked: *Am I getting excited by this?*

The diminutive man continued, "If you make any sign to warn him, not only will I mess-up your face but I will cut your tongue out. If his man, Dimitri, follows him in you will tell Izhutin to send him out. You will insist that you want to be alone with him. Is that clear?"

Though she knew that he had the office bugged, the man's detailed knowledge of their every move was baffling: *How did he know all this? It was like he was in the room with Andrei, Dimitri and Serge.*

"How do you know about Dimitri? Are you working for Nikolai?" She asked with a slight quaver in her voice. She was frightened and self-conscious, standing topless in front of him.

McHenry studied her before answering. She was a pretty girl and young enough to be his daughter. He felt remorseful using her as bait but Izhutin would be the dangerous one among the Russians and he wanted to get this over with. In his mind Marylou and their life in Switzerland justified the means.

He lied with a straight face, "No, it was his father, Alexei Zakirov. He sent me to handle this. They made a mess of things up in the mountains and now they have to pay. That's just the way it is."

"But Andrei was only doing what Adam told him to do. Why are you going to kill him?" She blurted out.

"Careful little girl, or I will have to kill you too. Don't ask too many questions and do as you are told and maybe you will live to have a family someday."

She clammed up and waited, her heart thumping in her chest. The fear in her was building but strangely enough she found herself excited by the absurd situation she found herself in.

On the Wings of an Angel

JODIE GRASSHOFF

D r. Susan Boswell and her husband Mark were in the office discussing Jodie. Her easy smile, affectionate nature and youthful energy had reinvigorated both of them. Mark loved having her with him when he fed the animals and took the horses out to the pastures and Dr. Boswell enjoyed her company in the office while she examined and treated a variety of animals. Over the years, they had considered adoption or fostering but the timing was never right. Having Jodie stay with them for over a month now had brought the focus back on their plans to include a child or young person in their lives.

"Why don't we just adopt her?" Mark asked, "She's a sweet gal and with some love and guidance, she would get over her past. She's great with animals and loves the horses. We just need to keep an eye on her. Everyone is entitled to a second chance."

"Oh, I couldn't agree more, dear, but Robbie and Meghan are planning to take her with them. Meghan said that Montana would give her a fresh start and get her away from the bad memories associated with Chase River. And, she would be living on a farm which would instill a sound work ethic, " Dr. Boswell replied.

"I understand but Jodie gets a say doesn't she? She may not want to move so far away from everything she knows. And, irrespective of her decision we will have to contact her brother. He may want her with him," Mark added.

Just then Doreen, the secretary, knocked and poked her head in, "Meghan and…" she rolled her eyes, "Mr. Gorgeous are here. Should I tell them you're busy or do you want to see them?"

Dr. Boswell laughed, "You're a trip, Doreen. Of course we'll see them. I'm never too busy to see Meghan and as for Robbie, I wish I was younger," she patted her heart before adding, "Please have them come in. We were just discussing Jodie and the timing couldn't be better."

When Meghan and Robbie walked in, Dr. Boswell greeted them, "So you're leaving poor Mark and me to deal with these crazy locals. What will I do without you, Meggie? You are my rock."

"Don't make me cry, Sue. You've been so great. You've stood by me…" Meghan left it unsaid, fighting her emotions.

The women hugged and the men shook hands. Mark Boswell said, "Hey, we're going to step outside and talk shop for a while… military stuff. We'll leave you gals to decide about Jodie."

When the men stepped outside Meghan, with eyebrows raised, asked, "What about Jodie?"

"We have been thinking of adopting a child for a while and having her with us this past month got us thinking; why not her?" Dr. Boswell answered, sitting back down behind her desk.

"That would be so fantastic except staying here, so close to everything that was wrong in her life? I don't know if that's good for her," Meghan argued.

"I agree but with some discipline and love I think it can be managed. She loves animals and is eager to learn. She has a small notebook and writes everything down… I watch her and it strikes me that all she ever needed was some attention, love and guidance. In any case, I think it's premature, we will have to talk to her brother, it's possible he'll want her to stay with him."

"We thought of that. Robbie spoke to him a few days ago and though he would be happy to have her stay with him and his family, Boston isn't the best place for her. He liked the idea of her moving to Montana, away from the influences that got her in trouble. He was fine with the move as long as he could check in on her and come and visit."

The older woman was quiet. She had moved to Chase River from Boston and was well aware of all the distractions and possible traps that big city life presented, especially for young teens. Though she had gotten really fond of Jodie she needed to do what was best for the young girl. If it came to it, they could adopt another child.

"Why don't we ask Jodie and see how she feels about all this?" Dr. Boswell ventured.

"I agree, she needs to be happy with whoever she's going to stay with. She's with Ryan at my parents right now. We came here to ask you to have dinner with us before we left. How about tomorrow evening at my place? Nothing fancy, just a thank you for being so good to me all these years."

"That's interesting. We were planning to take you both out for a goodbye meal. I'm a lousy cook so Mark suggested driving to Monson to one of the nicer places there."

"We still have time. We aren't leaving just yet so how about it, dinner tomorrow evening?"

"That sounds lovely. And about Jodie, it doesn't matter either way. I think she will have a wonderful home so it's not an issue with me," The older woman added wanting to make sure that Jodie's welfare was what was important.

"We'll bring this up tomorrow when we are all together. I feel the same way - Mark and you would make excellent parents so if she chooses to stay, I'm really okay with that too." Meghan said, "I want what's best for her."

Meghan got up and was about to leave when the door to the office opened and Marylou came in with Robbie and Mark following close behind.

She looked distraught, tears welling up in her eyes, "I knew it. It was just too good to last."

DANCING WITH KILLERS AND FOXES

The apartment that Stephanie Prokup rented was in a building owned by Adam Shayk. It was one of his many real estate holdings. This building, unlike the others, was reserved for friends and family acquaintances most of whom were from the 'old country'. She was fortunate that he had subsidized her rent or she would have been forced to live in a far less desirable neighborhood.

Dimitri parked in a spot that was reserved for Shayk and was about to get out when Izhutin stopped him. "You stay down here. She is on the top floor… there is nowhere to go. I don't want you fucking this up for me!"

"Sorry, boss, I have to come up with you. That is straight from the big boss. You were there, you heard him so please don't put me in the middle," Dimitri pleaded, his long face taking on a solemn expression. He rarely questioned his boss but he was between a rock and a hard place.

"He didn't mean you have to hold my dick when I'm fucking a pretty girl. Use your head, you fucking moron!" Izhutin spat back.

"Boss, he actually said to stand in the room *even* if you were fucking some fat whore! Those were his words. He also mentioned something about a choo-choo train and a trampoline but I did not really understand that. What did he mean about…"

"Forget that. Okay listen, I'm not an unreasonable man. You can come up with me but you stand outside the apartment door. That's it. Don't make me shoot you, you big, ugly bastard, I like you but I like fucking a lot more. And if I have to choose between a pretty girl and your ugly ass, you'll lose."

Dimitri thought about it and decided that it was a good compromise. He'd stand outside and wait until Izhutin had finished with the girl and no one would be the wiser. Izhutin had a reputation and his men, though they liked him, also feared him.

"Sure, boss. That's fine. I'll wait outside the door."

The men took the elevator to the third floor. Stephanie was in apartment 3A which was a few yards down a narrow corridor. Apartment 3B was further down at the very end of the corridor and was the only other apartment on the top floor. It was occupied by an older Russian couple related to Shayk. All the occupants in the building were of Russian or Ukrainian descent and most of them were known to each other.

Izhutin rang the doorbell and could hear the chime-like ringing inside.

"It's open! Come on in," Stephanie called out in a forced, upbeat voice.

Izhutin winked at Dimitri and placed a finger to his lips. He spoke in a hushed tone, almost a whisper, "You stay here. It won't be too long."

He stepped inside the apartment and closed the door behind him but as soon as he saw the half-naked girl and the frightened expression on her face, his uncanny intuition kicked in and he became suspicious. Something wasn't quite right. His felt the hairs on the back of his neck bristle. If nothing else, he was a realist – this had been too easy. He was no rock star; women weren't throwing themselves at him and the last thing he expected was a young beauty waiting to fuck him.

"Malyshka, why are you standing there?" He asked, his eyes scanning the room quickly, "Come here. Come to papa!"

She smiled, nervously, "Let's go in the bedroom, Andrei… it's nicer there."

"I was hoping to eat some breakfast before eating the peach," he replied, his eyes looking past her into the bedroom, "but I don't see any slapjack. What is going on, baby? You look worried but those tits are…"

Stephanie stood frozen by the door; arms crossed trying to cover her chest, unable to speak and had the sudden clairvoyance that she was going to die. Her legs turned to jelly, the overt tension in the apartment proved too much for her. She turned to find sanctuary in her bedroom when her worst nightmare manifested in a volley of gunfire.

McHenry's line of sight was hindered by the girl, he would have preferred to wait but Izhutin wasn't fooled and Stephanie was close to panicking, he had to take the shot. He shifted to avoid the girl and fired twice in quick succession. The sound of the gunshots, despite the silencer, resonated loudly within the small apartment. The first bullet grazed Izhutin's ear and the second missed his face by a whisker. He felt the feathery hiss of the bullet as it whizzed past his face and he reacted – he dove for cover behind the sofa. *Fuck! It was a trap… a fucking trap!*

He fumbled for the Beretta tucked into his waistband just as the front door crashed open and Dimitri burst in, gun drawn. It took the tall Russian a second to get his bearings as he scanned the room, his boss, the girl and then a fleeting shadow that was McHenry. It was a second too long. There was another muffled crack of gunfire, this time McHenry didn't miss. The bullet struck Dimitri in the middle of his forehead and he fell. He was dead before he hit the ground.

Izhutin was quick to seize the opportunity created by the distraction and with Stephanie blocking McHenry's line of sight, he reared up from behind the sofa and began firing. He squeezed off five shots in the direction of the assassin: two rapid shots, a short pause no longer than a millisecond, followed by three more in quick succession. The first bullet hit the girl in the back, near the upper shoulder, and knocked her forward onto the bedroom floor. Two of the other shots hit McHenry - one in the chest and the other through his upper thigh of his right leg. He stumbled, corrected himself and fired a shot at Izhutin before dropping down alongside the girl. The Russian didn't wait instead he leapt over Dimitri's body sprawled across the open doorway and ran. He took the stairs, quick as a cat, and made a mad dash for the exit.

A few seconds later McHenry got up. The ballistic vest under his jacket had saved his life but the impact of the 9 millimeter had knocked the wind out of him. He grimaced and shed his jacket and took the bulletproof vest off and saw where the slug was embedded – it had his number stamped on it and was heading straight for his heart.

His leg was bleeding but he was lucky, the bullet has gone clean through missing the large bone. A bit to the left and it would have shattered his femur. He found some vodka and cleaned around the wound and checked for any fragmentation before wrapping it in makeshift bandages that he ripped from his shirt. He applied pressure on the wound using the heel of his hand hoping to stem the bleeding and then bent over the girl to assess the damage. She was holding her shoulder under the clavicle, wincing and in obvious pain but she didn't make a sound.

"You're lucky, it's a flesh wound and you will heal. Do you have bandages or cotton swabs?" McHenry asked the girl.

"In the bathroom," she motioned with her head, "there are cotton balls for removing make-up. Also some gauze bandages."

He retrieved the items and carefully cleaned around the wound with the alcohol. He bandaged her up the best he could, making every attempt not to touch her breasts, but the back of his hand brushed against her nipple and she felt a thrill shoot through her. *What is wrong with me*, she thought to herself, *why does he excite me?* She was surprised by how gentle he was and by his chivalry. He had found an oversized, button-front shirt in her closest and helped her put it on.

"You are bleeding," the girl said on noticing the blood soaking through his trousers.

"I'm fine. Don't worry about me," he said and instructed, "You have to apply pressure on it to stop the bleeding. Press hard and keep the pressure on it."

He helped her sit up and then inquired, "Do you know where he would go?"

She was quiet and sensing her reluctance reminded her, "He didn't care about you. He took the shot even though he knew you were in the way. These people don't care about anything but themselves. You should find some other line of work or move somewhere else, away from this place."

Stephanie studied his face; her fear and anxiety were long gone, smoked out by the violence and suddenness of what had just transpired. She had been shot and had survived and with that came a certain cavalier attitude.

"You know nothing about our lives. We are slaves to these people. If we don't do as they say, they will do things to us that you cannot imagine *and* they will murder our families back home. Our lives are mortgaged forever and controlled through fear. It is a curse to born a pretty girl," she retorted.

She was wrong about him. He was familiar with 'debt slavery' or the palatable term for it: bonded labor. Many of his clients were from Eastern European countries and several from Russia so he was well aware of the practice. A few years back a very powerful Albanian had placed a hit on a young Ukrainian girl who had run away from one of his brothels in the UK. McHenry had turned the contract down but a few months later the girl was found in Amsterdam, floating on the river Amstel, her throat slit and her body burned. She had been raped and tortured before being killed. It was a clear message to the other girls reminding them of the consequences of breaking their unwritten indenture.

He understood Stephanie's predicament, "I understand. You don't have to say anything."

She looked away unable now to meet his eyes. She was torn between her sense of loyalty and the sad reality of his words. She was luckier than most of the pretty girls brought to the US. Her family was known to Shayk and he had taken her under his wing so she wasn't working off the never ending debt lying on her back with her legs spread.

It was also clear to her now that all Izhutin wanted was a quick fuck and had no real feelings for her. The morbid reality of the continued exploitation stung but now, with Shayk's death, she knew better than to trust any of them. And in the aftermath of the violence, she had developed inexplicable feelings for McHenry; psychologists refer to this as the Stockholm syndrome where captives form emotional bonds with their captors.

She looked up at him and said, "He will run to his boss, to Adam, you will find him in the office. Alexi Zakirov is not going to be pleased."

"I lied. I do not work for Zakirov," he didn't know why he decided to tell her the truth but her courage and vulnerability had touched him. If he had a daughter he'd want her to be as brave as this girl.

"Then your friends in the mountain are in danger. Once he sees his boss's body he will go mad. They were closer than brothers."

"They didn't hire me either."

"That won't matter. He will blame them," she replied matter-of-factly.

He had a feeling that Izhutin would run to warn Shayk and having her corroboration set the course for his immediate actions. He was looking for her phone when an elderly couple came into the apartment.

The man was thin and stooped; his spirit broken by the weight of a life lived in debt and hard labor. The woman stood tall and proud, her silver streaked hair along with the stern expression added to her austere appearance. They were both terrified and went pale when they saw Dimitri's lifeless body but despite the potential danger they inched forward to check on the girl.

"Steffi, are you okay?" the woman called out hesitantly and seeing McHenry asked, "Who are you?"

They knew who Dimitri was and that he had worked for Shayk but neither one asked the obvious question - they knew better than to get involved. They also knew that McHenry wasn't Russian and were immediately suspicious. "What are you doing?"

"Never mind who I am or what I'm doing. You stay with her. I'm calling an ambulance. She will be alright," he answered in Russian.

He used the girl's phone to dial 911 and spoke briefly to the dispatcher then tossed the phone towards the couple and reverted back to speaking Russian. "They are coming, Stephanie. You hold on and you'll be fine. You're a brave girl and I'm sorry this happened to you. You listen to what I said. There are no slaves in this country – you can find a new life. I have to go now."

The couple stepped aside, backs pressed against the wall, to let

McHenry through. He ignored them and the pain emanating from his thigh, his mind preoccupied with intercepting the Russian. *Izhutin will try and get a hold of Shayk like a dog running to his master. And finding him dead, he will go after Marylou, Hank and Luke and maybe others.* He pulled up the camera he had set-up outside the office and watched as he waited for the elevator to make its way up.

He knew that Izhutin had a jump start and his chase to catch the Russian would be hampered by his wounded leg. He had to call Marylou to warn her about the danger before he did anything else. While waiting for her to answer, he realized that his love for her had altered his perceptiveness and with that, his decision making. He was incapable of acting with the same calculated indifference that had made him a very effective assassin. The fact that he was concerned about Stephanie Prokup was evidence that he had changed, that Marylou had changed him. In the past, there was a good probability that he would have used the girl as a shield and shot Izhutin before he had a chance to get away. His concern for Stephanie's safety had now put others at risk.

This was it – he wasn't very good at this anymore and if he wasn't convinced before, he was convinced now. Izhutin would be his last hit but first he had to take care of his leg.

Andrei Izhutin's only thought was Adam Shayk. He had to warn his boss about McHenry. He ran his finger over the nick above his earlobe – *it is nothing, a scratch*, he thought to himself. His life had been filled with violent skirmishes and he had always survived unscathed - he was born lucky. Shayk and the men would joke about Izhutin being indestructible and that there was an angel who watched over him. It had become a standing joke so much so that he began believing the myth.

He was sure he had hit McHenry but just how badly the assassin was hurt was anybody's guess. *The Frenchie had used the girl to set me up! You can never trust these bitches! She was most probably fucking him but they don't know that I have something a lot better than a huge cock - I have an angel who watches over me.*

The moment he saw Sergei's body in the lobby, his heart fell. He screamed profanities as he rushed into Shayk's office and knelt down, leaning over his friend. He was struck by the grotesque expression of terror etched on Shayk's face. Raw emotions, the likes of which he had never experienced, flooded through him. Tears streamed down his cheeks and his body was wracked by sobs.

"No, no, no! This can't be. We were meant to die together, brother, together…"

He sat by Shayk's body holding his hand, distraught and torn by an unbearable sadness. After a while, denial and grief gave way to acceptance and anger. Retribution was now his salve and vengeance his sole objective.

"You said kill ten of them for one of ours. You were right. You were always right. I should have listened but I think with my dick. You rest in peace, my friend, I will kill a hundred of them for you. McHenry, Luke, the soldier, Hank… they are all dead, all of them, dead, dead, dead! I will kill their women, especially McHenry's woman, that bitch will pay. I will take my time with her and I will make sure that McHenry knows… if he is still alive."

He moved Sergei's body next to Shayk's and covered them with a blanket that was stored in the coat closet. He found the keys to Shayk's SUV and took the stairs down to the parking garage located adjacent to the building. The metallic blue G-Class Mercedes Benz was parked in Shayk's reserved spot – he knew Shayk had a veritable cache of arms under the mat in the trunk and would need them for what he had in mind. Shayk was a borderline diabetic and a man who believed in planning for every contingency. He kept chocolates and nut-bars in the glove compartment and had blankets and pillows packed into a sleeping bag. Though he didn't smoke he had cigarette lighters in the console. Izhutin smiled thinking back on their many conversations. He could hear Shayk's voice: *'You never know when you need to light a fire!'*

The 8-hour drive gave him plenty of time to reminisce and the memory of his auspicious meeting with Shayk came rushing back as clear as it was the day it happened. It was a Sunday, the 10th of December, 1995. Izhutin had been living in the streets of Moscow for several months. He was a frightened seventeen-year-old with no money, no skills and no place to turn to. He had considered selling his body to the many chicken-hawks cruising the streets looking for sex but he couldn't bring himself to do it. *I'd rather starve to death!*

That evening while he was scrounging through a garbage bin hoping to find something that was edible, a well-dressed, chubby man in glasses spotted him and had walked over and without any preamble said to the emaciated boy, "Come with me."

At first he had though that Shayk was another gay man looking for sex but that notion was quickly dispelled.

"Come on, I'm not going to hurt you. I like women; I'm not into boys. I'm going for dinner so if you want a meal, you come with me."

He took the young Izhutin to an upscale restaurant, bought him dinner over the objections of the maître d' who had protested Izhutin's filthy, ragamuffin appearance and the decaying, repulsive odor that clung to the boy. Shayk had bribed the man into giving them a corner table away from the other patrons. Over dinner he had explained exactly what he did and how he made a living. He talked about his small chop-shop that processed stolen cars, moved drugs and anything else that he could sell to make a buck but he stayed out of the way of the big boys. His mantra was: *small fish must live in the small pond or get eaten by the bigger fish.* That was before Alexi Zakirov and their accession to power.

He also invited Izhutin to sleep on his couch until he could afford a place of his own. That chance meeting had changed Izhutin's life and had saved him. Not many kids survive the streets of Moscow – most succumbed to drugs and violence or the bitter cold of winter. He had taken an oath that he would remain loyal to Shayk no matter what and now his mentor, friend and boss was dead, poisoned like some lab rat and denied the dignity of a bullet.

The loss filled him with a sense of hopelessness and the anger resurfaced and he swore over his dead mother that he, Andrei Ivanovich Izhutin, would avenge his boss. He would find McHenry's woman first and he would make her wish she had never met the assassin and then he would kill Luke and the others or he would die trying.

IN A CIRCLE OF FRIENDS

"Michael was shot. He said it's not serious but I think he's just saying that so I won't freak out," Marylou said. "He thinks the Russian, Andrei Izoo-something-or-the other, is coming here to kill Hank, Luke, you and me. Michael will try and intercept him if he can, that's all I know. He didn't want to say much." She paused and struggled to gain control of her emotions, "Michael is all by himself… I don't want him to die alone."

"He's not going to die; he knows what he's doing. Did he say whether the Russian was acting alone or with a crew?" Robbie asked.

Marylou didn't answer; she squeezed her eyes shut and took a deep breath. Her thoughts were about her lover and their conversation. It had filled her with a pessimistic dissonance that she was unable to shake.

"Did he say if Izhutin was alone?" Robbie repeated.

"He didn't know but he thinks he might be acting alone. I went home to warn Dad but he refused to leave. I've tried to get Junior to come with me but he won't leave Dad. I don't know what to do. Michael suggested that I should stay with Luke or with you," she answered, looking at Robbie.

Meghan took the woman's hand and said, "Of course you can stay with us. Robbie will take care of this man if he shows up. And Ronin…"

"Wait! Wait a minute," Mark Boswell interjected, "he doesn't know who we are… all of you should stay here. Get Ryan and Jodie and your parents and bring them here. We have plenty of room and we have cameras all over the place to monitor the animals. It will be impossible for him to break in. What do you think, Robbie?"

"That makes sense. It is easier to protect one location than a bunch of fragmented places, especially with limited resources. Did you call Luke?" Robbie asked.

"I tried several times but either he doesn't have a signal or he's off somewhere and isn't answering his phone."

"What about Allison? Did you try her?" Meghan asked.

"She isn't answering either. I left her a message to call me."

"Do you think Tony's at risk?" Dr. Boswell asked.

"He's not here. He's gone to get Liz. He wanted her to meet us before we left for Montana," Robbie answered, then turned and addressed Meghan. "Let's go and get your parents and the kids. We'll need more than one car so we'll go get my car first. With Ronin in the car there won't be enough room for everyone."

"I'll come with you. We should be able to fit everyone," Marylou offered. She was still holding Meghan's hand, finding comfort in the proximity of a friend.

Robbie said to Dr. Boswell and Mark, "Are you sure you want in on this? He's not coming for you so this is trouble you don't need."

"These are our friends. If he wants one he has to take us all!" Mark Boswell answered.

Susan Boswell scoffed, "You heard Mark, bring them here. Meghan is family so her trouble is our trouble." She turned to Marylou, "We'll deal with your father later though I understand how he feels, wanting to stay in his house. Now go on, we'll get the place ready for everyone."

Assassins and Killers

THE FOX ON THE TRAIL

It was late evening by the time Izhutin drew close to Chase River Town. He got off of Route 6 and pulled into the parking lot of a dimly lit, ramshackle tavern. It was The Rancher's Lodge & Drink. There was a pickup parked on the far side, closer to the rear in the shadow of the building, but he didn't pay any attention to it. He parked near the entrance, got out and stretched and headed straight for the front door. He was hungry and craved a drink. It had been a long drive made longer by the memories that now haunted him and demanded recompense.

When he walked in, the two men seated at a corner table gave him a quick look before returning to their muted conversation. The big man behind the bar had his back to Izhutin; his attention was focused on a small TV screen mounted on the wall under a Confederate flag. He was watching a movie, an old western with Gregory Peck and Jean Simmons. Other than the three men, the place was empty.

Izhutin waited a few seconds then tapped the countertop and said, "Vodka, neat."

The man turned around and eyed Izhutin with suspicion and growled, "I've got Smirnoff, that's it."

"That is fine. Do you have any food?"

The bartender poured Izhutin his drink and said in a deep, raspy voice, "Chips, pretzels and nuts… you want a meal you go into town." He reached under the counter and fetched a small bowl of peanuts and placed it in front of Izhutin and asked, "Where are you from?"

"Minnesota," Izhutin answered before knocking back his drink. He tapped the bar and said, "One more."

"I meant which country do you come from?" The big man persisted pouring Izhutin another shot, intrigued by the Russian's accent.

The smaller man grabbed a few nuts, rolled them in his palm before tossing them into his mouth. He took his time relishing the salty crunch of the nuts before answering, "Russia."

He reached for another handful of nuts but the big man snatched the bowl away and said in a voice that had turned cold, "Finish you drink and leave. We don't like your kind here… motherfuckin' commie bastards!"

This was Izhutin's first experience with overt prejudice in the US. He was surprised and offended by the xenophobic hostility but said nothing. The swastika and 666 tattooed on the big man's neck did not escape his attention. *A fucking racist pig!* He thought.

He tossed back the drink in one gulp and queried, "How much?"

"It's on the house now fuck off!" the man's slit of a mouth was set in a snarl.

"Thank you but I do not want anything for free, especially from you."

The Russian reached behind him as though fumbling for his wallet but instead drew his Beretta and without hesitation shot the bartender, pointblank, in the face. The loud resonating crack of the gunshot startled the two men in the corner.

"Hey, what the fuck…" It was the bigger man seated facing the bar.

Both leapt to their feet knocking the table over. The husky dude with a big belly pulled out a revolver and fired almost at the same time that Izhutin did, their shots blending together sounding like one. The man missed, Izhutin didn't; he hit the burly fellow in the throat. The second man saw his friend grab at his neck and fall.

"You motherfucker!" he screamed and without hesitation came charging at Izhutin, head lowered like a bull ready to gore the matador.

The Russian stood still, the gun extended in front of him, his manner, unwavering, until the man was a few feet from him and then fired two shots – both struck the target. The first shot hit the man on top his head, through the crown, killing his instantly and the second caught him in the shoulder throwing him askew. His momentum sent him crashing into a table and he fell motionless, a foot from Izhutin.

The Russian walked calmly over to the corner where the first man had fallen and put a bullet through his brain ending his miserable existence. *Ninety seven to go*, Izhutin thought and was about to re-holster his weapon when a sound from the bar caught his attention.

The bartender was leaning over the counter, his face a bloody mess, with a shotgun in his hands. He struggled to raise himself and tried aiming his weapon but seemed unable to focus. It took all the strength he had to point the gun at Izhutin but he was too slow, the Russian was on him and pushing the barrel aside said, "I am not a motherfucking commie bastard. I am a motherfucking capitalist bastard and here is your last payment!"

He shot the barkeep in the center of his forehead, the impact causing the man's ponytail to bounce like a jackrabbit's tail. This time the bullet did its job and the man folded, sliding to the floor behind the bar as dead as his friends. Blood, brain, clumps of the man's scalp splattered across the rear countertop in a dark, vulgar mosaic.

Izhutin walked around the counter, stepping over the dead barkeep, and got another shot glass and placed it next to his. He filled both glasses with vodka and took a sip, admiring his handiwork, and then said out loud, "Vashe zdorovie!" He raised his glass in a toast, "To your health, Adam."

He downed the rest of the beverage in a single swill, grit his teeth and shut his eyes tight, relishing the searing burn of the alcohol as it scorched its way down his throat to the pit of his belly.

"Ninety seven to go, my friend," he whispered looking skywards at the ceiling and poured the second drink on the floor.

He turned off the TV and the lights and flipped the sign that said "Open" to "Closed. Gone Fishing" and drove towards town. Twenty minutes later he pulled up at the Shell gas station on Main Street and filled the tank before stopping at Bucky Johnston's Diner. His appetite was stoked by the thrill of the recent kills and the aroma of burgers and fries wafting into the parking lot.

He picked a corner table, ordered dinner and studied the local map on his iPhone. He was ravenous and wolfed down a huge 16 ounce prime rib with mashed potatoes, a serving of Apple Pie and washed it all down with several cups of black coffee.

Once he was done, he felt rejuvenated and stepped out into the cool evening chill, belched loudly and said, "It is good! Now I'm ready for war and ready to die."

It took him a while to locate Gilbert Dorsey's house. The GPS in the Mercedes was pretty much useless in the mountains and he was about to stop and head back into town when his headlights caught a flash of the large obelisk with the white cap. When he slowed down and backed up he saw the mailbox with the number 1067 on it.

"Fortune is with me," he said humming to himself, "and that is good because she is a fickle bitch!"

He drove up the driveway winding through the trees until he came to the fork in the road. He could see the lights from the house flickering through the labyrinth of branches and leaves and took the right towards the creek and away from the house. He parked near a culvert behind a large boulder and retrieved a blanket from the sleeping bag. He put his seat back and with the Beretta in his lap fell asleep almost immediately.

BLOOD TIES

Marylou had been worrying about McHenry and her father the entire evening. At dinner, she was distracted and had stepped outside several times to try and reach them but neither one answered their phones. She sent the obligatory text messages to appease her concerns before returning to the dining table.

She tossed and turned all through the night, her uneasiness compounded by the novelty of an unfamiliar bed. The Boswells had gone way beyond customary courtesy to make sure all their guests were comfortable and safe but anxiety and fear are thieves that steal rationale and puissance. Marylou's concerns couldn't be placated by cameras and guns or the giant dog. Her tormentors were emotional and there was very little Mark or Robbie could do to assuage that.

She was sharing a room with Jodie and did her best not to wake the young girl during her morning ablutions and got dressed as quietly as she possibly could. She had no idea where McHenry was – it was not like him to ignore her and that only went to exacerbate her worry. Finally, she decided she was going to check-up on her father and Junior and try to convince them to join her at the Boswells place.

She tiptoed down the stairs, stopping each time the wooden boards creaked, and was almost to the front door when she caught a whiff of freshly brewed coffee. She stood still, eyes closed, debating whether or not to leave but the enticing aroma was seductive and she made her way into kitchen. *One quick cup and I'll be off.*

"Hey, Marylou, you're up early. Did you sleep well?" It was Mark Boswell. He placed the magazine down, and took off his reading glasses.

She smiled, "As well as can be expected. I've been worried sick about Michael and Junior and my dad. I have no idea where Michael is but I'm going to make a quick run to check on Dad and Junior."

"Have a cup of coffee and let's talk about it," the man said, "that is, if you want to. Worry leads to stress and stress is a heart attack waiting to happen. How do you take it – cream, sugar?"

"With a dash of cream and no sugar. Thank you."

He handed her a cup, "Come on, take a load of your feet. Sit and let's talk."

She took a sip and was impressed. "This is good coffee! I mean really good coffee."

"Yup, I consider myself a bit of a connoisseur. I worked as a barista at a local Starbucks when I got back from Iraq. I was wounded in the war and decided it was time to do something else. And that's how I met the lovely Dr. Susan Cross."

She sipped her coffee studying him carefully. He had a rugged, masculine appeal – the square jaw, long nose askew at the bridge, a result of a barroom fight, curly mop of hair peppered with gray and the crow's feet around soft hazel eyes that added to the mature mystique.

"And you were sure she was the one?" She asked.

"I was sure the moment she came back to the counter and insisted on speaking to the 'idiot' who made the coffee. She was this feisty little thing who tolerated no bullshit. And she was pretty as a picture; how could a guy resist that? I mean, I was the idiot who made her coffee, so, after she spent five minutes telling me how incompetent I was and that a baboon could have made a better cup of coffee, I smiled and asked her out and that was it."

Marylou laughed, "You're lucky… being certain of something as serious as a mate."

"Whoa! I'm sensing some doubts here. Are you having second thoughts about Mike?"

"No! I'm sure about him. It's me… I keep wondering why he's so interested in me. My reputation around here is no secret. Can a man really love someone like me?" She asked, almost rhetorically and looked away.

"Hey, stop selling yourself short. So you've had some wild experiences and that's not all bad. You are not going to go through life asking the 'what ifs'. Some of us take circuitous routes to happiness… I certainly did. The marines and Sue found the lost soul and gave me hope and a second chance."

"So you wouldn't hold it against Sue if she had…" Marylou paused searching for the appropriate words, then finished lamely, "a colorful past?"

"For all I know she might have. We don't talk about that and I really don't give a shit. Pardon my Portuguese. What she did before we met is none of my business as long as she's committed to me now; that's all that matters."

"Really? You never wonder if she's had multiple partners and…" Now Marylou was lost unable to verbalize her innermost thoughts.

"And whether I'd be able to satisfy her and make her happy?" Mark completed her thoughts, "No never. After the initial intensity of our relationship had morphed to a more comfortable one, we learned how and what it took to make each other happy and I don't mean just physically. It takes work but we are best friends who happen to be lovers so it wasn't that difficult for us."

"I know that sex is only a part of a relationship but what I don't know is whether he will tire of me and get bored after the *initial intensity*, as you put it, is over. He has a brilliant mind and is cultured and sophisticated and I'm… I'm a girl who's never been out of Chase River!"

"You don't control that aspect of your relationship. If he loves you, he obviously sees more in you than just a girl from Chase River. I'm not nearly as smart as Sue but there are things I bring to the table that she doesn't. Can you believe that despite her brilliant mind she still doesn't know how to hookup a wireless printer? But I do. We fill the blank spaces in each other and that make us incomplete." He smiled, poured himself more coffee and said, "We complete each other."

"And you knew this when you met?"

"I did, it took Sue a bit more time but once we began dating and talking to each other, the deal was done. The months I spent convalescing gave me time to think, to put things in perspective. There was a period of self-pity, the 'why-me' syndrome, but then I realized that many of my friends had died in Iraq… young men who would never experience another Christmas or share a drink with friends or make love, have a family…" he paused looking down, lost in the moment, "I was lucky to be alive. I promised myself I would never again worry over stuff that I can't or don't control and focus on the things that I do. So enjoy what you have now and I know it is a cliché but live in the moment and if you truly love each other, the rest will fall in place. It will take work but believe me, it's worth it. "

"And if it doesn't work out?"

"Then you move on and chalk it up to experience. But, I see the way he looks at you, the man is deeply in love and will be devoted to you."

She sat quietly staring out through the window, lost in thought, and finally said, "Thank you, Mark. I feel better about myself and it gives me hope. I'd better go. I'm going to try and convince Dad to join us here. Is that okay?"

"Of course it's okay. I'll add one last thought and we'll leave it at that. We are all multi-faceted, Marylou, and no single trait defines who we are. It is the collective aspects of our character, the various shades taken as a whole that creates the rainbow. I've gotten to know you over the years and you are a kind, gentle person who cares for others and a beautiful lady to boot. If I had a son, I'd be delighted if he brought you home to meet the parents."

"Watch out! He's a silver tongued devil but he's too old for you, girl," came the jocular quip. Susan Boswell trundled in wearing her bathrobe over her nightgown.

Both Marylou and Mark laughed.

"Hey, don't go selling us OGs short. We have our own brand of charm and there's nothing like experience. And what, my dear, are you doing up so early?" Mark asked his wife.

"I could hear bits of the conversation and wondered who you could be talking to at this ungodly hour," she stood beside her husband with an arm around his shoulders. She sighed and pushed back strands of her hair before adding, "And I've been thinking about Jodie and what's best for her. As much as I want her to stay with us I think she needs to get away from here. Meghan and Robbie will give her everything she needs and having Ryan as a younger brother will help her revert to being a child again."

Mark pulled her onto his lap, "We'll adopt some other kid. God knows there are plenty who need a good home."

"I know. I just feel so down about it. She's such a sweet girl and I've grown really fond…"

"Come on now; don't get Debbie Downer on me!" Mark chastised, "We want what is best for the gal and there are plenty of needy kids looking for homes. Don't worry, mama, we will find another

Jodie or maybe a Jack."

"I know you will find the right child. For what it's worth, I also think Jodie needs to get away from here and a farm in Montana with Meghan and Robbie would be the best thing for her." Marylou said and getting up drained the rest of her cup, "That is simply the best coffee I've ever had. I would stay for seconds but I better go. Dad leaves early for work and I do want to catch him before he heads out."

"Where are you going?" Susan Boswell asked getting up off of her husband's lap.

"I want to make sure Junior and Dad are okay. I'll be back soon."

"Oh no, you don't! Marylou Dorsey, have you totally lost your mind? There is a madman out there looking to kill you. You will wait until Robbie or Mark can accompany you. And, don't even think of arguing with me!" Susan reprimanded, shaking her finger at the younger woman.

"I'm really worried about them, Sue, I tried calling Dad but he's not answering," Marylou replied then turning to Mark, "Can we go now? Please?"

Mark looked at his wife who said, "Of course you can leave now. I overheard Beth and Meghan talking so I guess everyone's up. I'll need to get breakfast going and Jodie can help me."

Mark got up and put the cups in the sink, "Let me change and get my jacket and we can head out. We'll take my truck."

"I'm sorry for being such a pain but..." Marylou

"Don't say another word," the older women interrupted, "have a cup of coffee with me while we wait for the marine. Do you know when I first met Mark I thought he's not my type. I was attracted to slim, blond men with boyish faces and here was this dark-haired, husky man, very masculine, who made the worst coffee so go figure. Now, all these years later, I don't even notice that; I see the wonderful person who still treats me like I am special and is kind and gentle with a strength of character that very few men have and he is beautiful to me."

"You are both so lucky. Your love is obvious. I'm hoping things will be the same for Michael and me. That he won't tire of me. He has a brilliant mind and I'm…"

"You're a lovely girl," the older woman cut in, "and one who has a kind heart and a fearless spirit. People judge others without empathy or knowing all the facts. Well, screw all of them. We learn from our past and experience is the best teacher. Don't try and be something you are not; just be yourself and I know you will be happy."

DECEPTION AND A FOX
AT THE DOOR

The grating sound of tires on gravel along with the sunshine streaming through the car window woke Izhutin up. He got out of the SUV in time to catch a glimpse of the grape colored Ford 150 as it swerved left at the fork and headed towards the house. He had slept like a baby, snoring loudly to the soft pitter patter of rainfall during the night. He watched the pick-up disappear, yawned, stretched and walked through a forested area making his way down towards the creek.

He stopped by a large oak, unzipped his fly and relieved himself. He sighed, enjoying the amelioration of emptying his bladder as the seemingly endless stream of piss splashed noisily against the tree.

"Too much fucking coffee last night," he mused, squeezing the last few drops out from his cock.

He knelt at the edge of the water and used his fingers to brush the night-scum out of his mouth and gargled loudly unconcerned about the noise. He undressed quickly and splashed his face and body with the frigid water. The intense jolt gave him goosebumps, eliciting a loud gasp but he felt revitalized and alive.

"I'm awake now, like living on the streets again," he quipped through chattering teeth. He was, by nature, a meticulously clean man, a habit he had developed after joining Shayk.

Using his shirt, he dabbed his body perfunctorily before putting it back on and walked back towards the car.

"Now, it's time for the killing. A hundred lives for yours, Adam," he said looking skywards, "and even a hundred will not suffice!"

He circled around the house behind the ubiquitous maple, beech and yellow birch, the dense cluster of trees providing him with cover until he was able to scuttle across the yard. He crouched, kneeling under the window on the patio flagstones that abutted the wall, and peeked in.

The first person he saw was Marylou Dorsey and was immediately struck by her looks. She was standing over the stove top making what looked like pancakes.

"Fuck! These mountain bitches are beautiful," he whispered to himself and only then did he notice the others.

The man seated at the kitchen table would be a problem. He had the look of a military man. The skinny old man standing next to the woman would be less of an issue. Izhutin was studying the layout of the living room adjacent to the kitchen when a husky young man, or maybe a boy, came into sight.

"Hi Junior, I made your favorite chocolate chip pancakes for you," he heard the woman say to the boy.

Izhutin couldn't hear the muffled reply but watched as the husky lad hugged the woman. *Sister and brother*, he thought to himself, *must be, she's too young to be his mother. McHenry doesn't deserve a woman this beautiful.* He was filled with remorse about what he was about to do but the memory of Shayk's face contorted in death quelled any misgivings and buttressed his resolve. *It's time to make them pay, all of them, they must pay.*

He heard the woman speak again, "There are only two eggs left. I need more eggs. Junior can you get me some eggs from the garage?

Get the bacon too."

Izhutin couldn't believe his luck. He could take the boy out and wait in the garage until someone came looking for him and take them out one at a time without really exposing himself to any real risk. He would deal with the woman last and had special plans for her.

He ducked low and made his way towards the detached garage located about fifty yards to the left of the house. He moved quietly, placing his steps with care making sure to remain hidden from view – stealth was of essence and was his only chance at success. He waited until the boy had gone into the garage and after a quick look around, followed him in.

Marylou placed the stack of pancakes on the table and spoke to the men, "The eggs and bacon are coming up but start with these while they are hot." She got the maple syrup and butter dish and sat them next to the pancakes, "Where's Junior? What's taking him so long?"

"He gets distracted easily. He's most probably going through the old magazines stacked in the corner. I'll go get him," Dorsey chimed in, starting to get up.

"No, Gil, you sit and start with breakfast. You're the one that has to leave for work. I'll fetch him," Mark Boswell said.

When Mark walked into the garage the lights were on and the door to the fridge was open but he didn't see Junior and called out, "Hey Junior! Where are you boy? We need to get the eggs…"

The first blow struck him on the back and knocked him down. The second rendered him unconscious. Izhutin dropped the wooden baseball bat and dragged the limp body behind a large tractor parked to the side of the garage and hogtied him. He stuffed some rags into

Mark's mouth and taped it shut using duct tape. His movements were quick and efficient. He checked on the boy he had tied to an old chair and once satisfied, picked up the bat and stood behind the door. This was easier than he had anticipated and he was sure the old man would be next.

But the old man wasn't next. When Mark didn't return, Gil Dorsey sensed that something wasn't quite right. He put down his fork, hurried to his bedroom and retrieved a shotgun and came back to the kitchen. He motioned to his daughter to get low, to crouch behind the table.

"What's the matter, Dad?"

"Shhh," Dorsey placed a finger to his lips, "do have the keys to Mark's truck?" He spoke softly.

"Oh God, he's here, isn't he?" The awareness of what might have transpired dawned on her and fear shot through her like flames running along a gasoline trail.

"Do you have the keys?" her father repeated, his voice a low hiss.

"It must be in his coat," she said flustered but a quick check of the living room revealed the keys lying on the coffee table in front of a large sofa, "No, it's here. I've got it."

"Okay, go get Luke." Dorsey was looking out the kitchen window but his view was hindered by the shrubs and trees that bordered the side walls of the guest bedroom. "Come on, I'll distract them while you get into the truck."

"I'm not leaving you here," Marylou replied and picked up her phone. Her hands were trembling while she dialed Luke's number.

"What are you doing?"

"I'm calling Luke," Marylou waited but couldn't get through. She checked her phone and realized that she had no signal.

"We don't have time for this. You need to get out of here and get help. I can hold them off," Dorsey urged his daughter.

"Come with me. We can both go…"

"And leave Junior and Mark behind? That's not happening. Marylou, please leave. I'll be fine. Get help and come back. The signal is pretty decent once you're near the railroad tracks – call Luke and Olsen from there. But you have to go like now!"

She knew it was pointless arguing and though the railroad tracks were in the opposite direction from Luke's place, it was the spot where the signal magically reappeared. Her father was right, she needed to get away and get help. Robbie would be the surer bet. He was farther away but at least she knew where he was. On the other hand, Luke could be anywhere.

Father and daughter stood by the front door scanning the yard. The garage door was open but there was no sign of Mark Boswell or Junior. She had had her share of disagreements with her father primarily over her lifestyle but after her mother had passed away they had gotten closer. Junior and the help he required was the glue that bonded them. She felt sorry for her father and was overcome by a melancholic sadness. *He's had such a difficult life and never once complained. It must have been hard for him with people talking about her and those parties. He deserved better.*

"I love you, Dad," she whispered moving closer to him.

"I love you too, baby."

"I'm sorry for…" she began but he cut her off.

"Don't worry about it. When I say go, you make a run for it and get into the truck as soon as you can."

"Okay. I'm scared, Dad," Marylou said standing close to her father.

"Don't be scared. I'll blast them if they try and stop you. Go, now, run." He looked at her, holding her gaze and added, "I never judged you. The only thing I ever wanted was for you to be happy."

She felt the tears beginning to well up and gave Dorsey a hug then made a mad dash for Mark's truck. Urged on by her fear, she covered the five or so yards quickly and got in on the passenger side which was closer to her. She scooted over center console and settled into the driver's seat fumbling with the keys.

"Come on, come on, Marylou!" She whispered to herself, the panic building, but managed to calm herself and get the truck started and put it in reverse.

The noise of the footsteps and the slamming of the car door was enough to draw Izhutin out. He stuck his head from behind the garage door and saw the pick-up backing up.

"Fuck! No escape... you will stay," he snarled and fired at the pick-up. His first shot rattled loudly, ricocheting off the tailgate and the second, shattered the rear window of the cab.

Marylou slammed on the brakes just as her father fired the shotgun at the Russian. He got off two more shots walking deliberately towards the garage oblivious of the danger to his own safety. Though neither shot did any real damage it forced Izhutin to take cover and bought Marylou some time. She spun the truck around and floored the pedal, racing down the driveway, wheels spitting gravel and disappearing in a cloud of dust.

In her panic she cornered the first bend going way too fast and skidded off the driveway into a ditch and slammed against the embankment. Her head bounced off the steering wheel and the last thing she remembered was the sound of gunfire being exchanged.

LAW DOG

About an hour or so after Mark Boswell and Marylou had left for her father's house, Deputy Joe Bradley pulled up outside the front door to Dr. Boswell's office. He was familiar with her practice having been there on several occasions with his young daughters, their two Maine Coons and little Terrier mix. However, this time it was on official business.

The office was still closed so he rang the bell to the residence and waited. After a short delay he heard footsteps tracking down the stairway before the door swung open. It was Meghan Hollier.

"Joe! What a nice surprise," she greeted the deputy with a broad smile.

"Hi Meghan, it's a bit early for work isn't it?"

"We're just finishing up with breakfast," she answered unsure of how much she should divulge.

"I wanted to speak to Marylou. When I called the lumberyard, Randall said that she had quit and was staying with the Boswells."

"I didn't know she had quit but she just left to see her father. How did Randall know she was staying here?" Meghan curiosity piqued.

"He needed help with some stuff in the office so he called her. I guess she must have told him. Luke's put him charge of the lumber-yard now," the tall man explained.

"It's about time. Randall is a decent man and works harder than anyone I know."

"That's for sure. You say she's gone to Gil's place? I need to talk to her about Professor Santos."

Meghan was immediately on alert and deflected the topic, "Why don't you come up and have a cup of coffee. We're just finishing up and Robbie will be much more of a help."

They walked up the stairs to the Boswell residence with the tall deputy following Meghan. When they got to the kitchen, Bradley was surprised to see the number of people seated around the table including Meghan's parents but the deputy knew better than to pry. As soon as he saw Ronin he stopped, his expression changing to one that reflected his sudden anxiety.

Ronin growled and with raised hackles got up but was immediately restrained by Robbie, "Down boy! Stay down."

"That dog doesn't like me," Bradley said moving away from where Robbie was seated.

"It's your badge," Robbie kidded, "but relax he's okay now."

"Yeah, that's easy for you to say. I swear that dog has gotten bigger in the last month!" Bradley retorted finding safety and comfort on the other side of the table.

Once the greetings were summarily over, Dr. Boswell got up and said, "Robbie be a dear and get a chair for our deputy. There are chairs down the hallway, all the way back and to your left."

"He can have my chair, I'm done but I'd be happy to bring in another chair and put Ronin out," Robbie replied.

"No, please… I've been sitting at my desk the last few days and standing is actually a relief. I'll try and make this brief," Bradley looked over at Jodie and Ryan and then addressed Meghan, "it would be better if the kids went out and played."

"Jodie, take Ryan and go outside and play. Take Ronin with you and don't go too far," Meghan said to the young girl.

"Can we go see the horses?" Jodie asked.

"Yes, of course you can just hold on to Ryan."

"Okay. Come on, Ryan, we'll go see the horses," the young girl took the boy's hand and called out to the dog, "Ronin! Ronin, come here, come, come with us!"

The young girl waited at the doorway for Ronin but the big dog remained motionless looking up at his master.

"It's okay, boy, go on, go with them," Robbie said to Ronin and the massive animal got up, gave the deputy a final unnerving look and tramped after the children wagging his tail.

Bradley waited until he heard the door close then picked up where he had left off. "Yesterday, we're not sure exactly when, someone shot and killed Chuck Mayfield, Tom Bakke and Burt Helsing at the Rancher's Lodge. The stippling around the wounds suggests that they were all shot at close range and with a 9 millimeter."

There were several gasps followed by a shocked silence. Though the men who had been murdered weren't necessarily the most liked in town, they were a part of the Chase River community. Many of the town's residents were either related by blood or by marriage and they stuck together bonded by years of generational history. However Dr. Boswell was from Boston and was considered an outsider. She had never liked Mayfield or his friends.

"Good riddance!" She blurted out.

"I didn't like them either but murder is murder. Tom has three little kids. Burt's wife is suffering from depression and schizophrenia and Chuck's mother depends on him for almost everything so this is not just about a bunch of white supremacists but all the people their deaths will impact." Bradley said, looking at the vet, "I need to know where Lorenzo Santos is. Do any of you know?"

Robbie shrugged, "No. He said he was leaving for Arizona to

wrap things up and would return to get Marylou. If I recall, they had plans to move to one of the islands."

"His name might be Santos but he isn't *the* Professor Santos from the University of Arizona. I called the University and there is indeed a Professor Lorenzo Santos but the man is over sixty, balding and is about six feet tall. And not surprisingly, he was lecturing at the university while *our* Professor Santos was demonstrating the finer points of the martial arts to Greg Humphry!"

Robbie controlled the urge to smile and kept a straight face, "There must be an explanation. Why would he impersonate a professor? I mean, he could have picked something less demanding - he spent days with Tony, collecting rocks for his study. It doesn't make sense."

"Maybe he likes rocks or maybe he was casing the territory; I don't know but what I do know is that he isn't the Professor. Here are the facts – Marylou was dating Greg Humphry and she had dated Burt Helsing on and off before that. Along comes 'Professor' Santos and now Greg is in the hospital and Burt is dead. I'm not sure what happened at the Rancher's Lodge but my guess is that Mr. Santos stopped for a drink and knowing Chuck he must had said something or done something - next thing you know you have three dead men."

"You said a 9mm, right? I can vouch for Lorenzo – he has a .38 Colt so unless he stole a 9mm, he's not the shooter," Robbie refuted.

"He could have more than one gun," the deputy argued.

"That's a stretch, Joe. Beating up someone for being abusive to your date is a far cry from committing multiple murders." Beth Hollier chimed in, "Greg Humphry was a bully and was abusive to Marylou. I've witnessed it personally and though I do not condone violence, I'll make an exception in this case. I'm with Sue – you reap what you sow."

There was a short silence before the deputy spoke.

"Fred Mayfield, Chuck's father ran The Rancher's Lodge & Drink before him and he was far more of a racist than Chuck. Do you recall the incident with Jeremiah Mosby? He shot and killed Mosby's white bulldog because he said a white dog should never be a slave to a black man!"

Robbie was shocked and asked, "What did Mosby do?"

"Mosby let the law handle the case and Mayfield had to pay him for his dog and for pain and suffering."

"I don't know who Mosby is but he is a better man than me. I would've reacted very differently if someone had harmed Ronin." Robbie paused and then asked, "What does this have to do with Lorenzo?"

"Just because someone is a racist doesn't mean we shoot and kill them. Fred ran the place for years without any problems even after the incident with Mosby's dog. When Fred passed, Chuck took over and we've had no problems until a few strangers blew into town." He looked at Robbie, "I know you didn't do it and the Russians who assaulted Beth and Mark and shot Allison are long gone. That leaves Santos."

"People were frightened of Fred Mayfield and when Chuck returned from prison, they were more frightened of him. The tattoos on his arms and neck and the stickers on his car didn't win him any friends or engender affection," Beth Hollier noted, "There were plenty of folk around here who didn't like him so to assume it was a stranger is being a bit xenophobic."

"People may have been wary of Chuck but no one was looking to kill him. Chuck and Tom were no choirboys; both spent time in prison and could take care of themselves so whoever did this was a either a pro or was used to extreme violence."

"For goodness sakes, it could be anyone!" Dr. Boswell exclaimed, "I didn't know Fred Mayfield but he sounds like a real loser. However,

I did know his son and he was a no good scoundrel filled with hate. His place was fraternized by crooks and bums who couldn't spell dog if you spotted them the 'd' and the 'g'. One of them most probably did it. You should be looking into them instead of bothering with an cultured man like the Professor."

The deputy bristled, it had been a long few days and he was tired, "With due respect, ma'am, I don't need you to tell me how to conduct my business!"

"Then you had better leave my house. You weren't invited…" the fiery doctor retorted but was interrupted by Robbie.

"Hey, hey hold on a second! We're on the same side here." He spoke to Bradley, "It might be best if you were to speak to Marylou directly. Meghan and I are planning to leave for Montana in a few days and I need to speak to you about Marisa's computer. I'll come with you and we can talk on the way."

"Okay. I'll wait for you in the car," the tall lawman turned to leave.

"Wait. I'm sorry, Joe," Dr. Boswell said, her tone conciliatory, "I was out of line. It is your responsibility and you have every right to pursue this any way you deem fit. Sit and have a cup of coffee. My Mark makes the best coffee in the world."

The deputy stopped and studied the older woman and graciously accepted the olive branch, "No apology needed, Sue. But I think Burt could have spelled dog especially if you spotted him the 'd' and the 'g'."

Everyone laughed and the tension evaporated.

"Cream and sugar?" Meghan asked the deputy.

"Black, thanks," Bradley said, "I make a pretty mean brew myself so I'll have to try it and see if we need to have a coffee runoff."

"I hate to say it but you'll lose, Joe. Mark makes the best coffee, trust me, I've tried but he's got some special recipe that he refuses to share," Meghan smiled and handed the lawman his cup.

"It's all in the roasting of the beans," Dr. Boswell offered with a smile.

Bradley took a sip and with raised eyebrows said, "Damn, this *is* good coffee! It's a no contest, I concede."

After Robbie and the deputy had left, Meghan turned to Dr. Boswell, "My God, Sue, I've never seen you so angry!"

Dr. Boswell was quiet, she sighed deeply and explained, "My father taught law at Harvard Law School. In 1965, during the height of the civil rights movement, he drove our old Volkswagen Bug from Boston to Selma to march with Dr. Martin Luther King. He was spit on, beaten and called names that were far worse that what they called African Americans all because he saw a grave injustice that needed to be set right and stood up for what he believed in."

She paused trying to find the right words, "When he came home, he had three broken ribs, a broken nose and his glasses had be trampled and ruined. A professor didn't make much money those days and he had a wife and three young children to take care of. I was only six and saw this gentle, soft-spoken man who never raised his hand against anyone, bloodied and hurt and I was so angry I could barely speak. I cried every time I saw him walk, bent from the pain, nursing his ribs and dabbing the blood trickling from a broken nose. It was awful but he never once complained." She sighed again, "He led by example and what I learned was that you don't back down from bullies and you must stand up to hate and injustice no matter what the consequence. If you let it grow then indecency triumphs over decency and what happened in Germany can happen again."

"It took brave men like him to initiate change. I know a lot of people who didn't agree with segregation and racism but they never spoke up." Beth Hollier said, "Your father was special man."

"He was and I was fortunate to have had him guide me. It bothers me to know that people like Charles Mayfield are still around," Dr. Boswell said, "but, I shouldn't have been rude to Joe; he's doing his job. Unlike my father, I haven't learned to hold my tongue."

"And I'm glad you don't. Women need to stand up and speak for themselves. We are too timid or conscious of hurting other people's feelings!" Meghan responded.

"I can't get past the fact that he thinks Professor Santos had something to do with these murders. The professor isn't even here," Dr. Boswell said.

Meghan was about to reveal the truth about McHenry but thought better of it. She hugged the older woman and said, "I've always admired you and your ability to say what's on your mind. I will really miss you, Sue."

"And, I will miss you, dear," came the somber reply. "Doreen will be here soon. We'd better get ready."

"Yes, we have to hurry. We have several appointments and a sick bull that is due in this morning," Meghan said beginning to clear the table, "I'd better get the kids in and make sure Ronin stays in the bedroom."

"What will I do without you, Meggie?" Susan Boswell said, the realization that Meghan would soon be gone sinking in.

"You'll do just fine. Doreen is capable of a lot more and you will find someone else," Meghan replied, smiling at the vet.

Susan Boswell didn't reply but instead got up and trudged towards her bedroom. She felt old and tired and knew that things wouldn't be the same once Meghan was gone. And the thought that Jodie would also be leaving filled her with gloom. *Why did things have to change?*

THE FOX AND THE BUTTERFLY

When Marylou Dorsey regained consciousness she found herself in a strange and unfamiliar place. Her hands and legs were bound tight and she was lying on a bed on top of an embroidered quilt. She looked around trying to get a bearing on her surroundings, her mind, foggy and dazed, was struggling to rationalize her predicament. She caught glimpses of trees through slits in the curtains of a small window to the left of the bed and she could hear the sounds of birds chirping in symphony to the soothing strains of a nearby babbling brook. She found the cacophonous propinquity weirdly comforting.

A barrage of thoughts, some random and others sequential, flooded her mind. *Where am I? What are they going to do to me? What happened to Dad and Junior? What happened to Mark? My head hurts and my arms ache. I am thirsty. Michael, where are you? My throat and mouth are so dry...*

She had to assume that 'they', the frightening 'they', had brought her here to rape and kill her as retribution for McHenry's actions and accepting the inevitable, filled her with an equanimous intransigence, 'a fight until I die' mentality. And as her mind cleared, nascent contrivances of escape and self-preservation began to emerge but first she would have to assess her captors - who they were and what exactly they wanted and how, if at all, she could manipulate them. She would weaponize her skillsets and use her charm and if necessary, sex, to barter her release. She wasn't going down without a fight.

The nondescript room was typical of rental log cabins in Northern Maine. There were two small bedside tables with lamps on top, a closet with moose heads for knobs and on the floor next to the bed was an old rustic carpet, faded and frayed at the edges. The large oak door leading to the living room was left half-open through which she had a partial view of sofas and tables lit by overhead lights and covered in muted shadows. It was still bright outside so they, the terrible 'they', must have drawn the curtains and shades for all the pernicious and barbarous deeds they were about to commit. Her mind raced with fear and excitement, the adrenalin causing her heart to pound against her ribcage, drums thumping to some primordial beat, stirring in her undefined emotions and concocting monsters in her rampant imagination.

Just then the door to the bedroom was pushed fully open and in walked a slim, blond haired man. He was of medium height, had light blue eyes and a boyish face that belied the streaks of gray at the temples. He moved silently like a thief in the night; athletic and balanced. The sleeves of his shirt were rolled up revealing muscular forearms covered in tattoos. The two that caught her eye were of the Virgin Mary holding the baby Jesus on one arm and a wooden cross on the other. *A religious monster!*

"You are awake. That is good," the man said with a heavy accent.

"My throat is dry," she mumbled, "Can I have some water?"

"Yes, yes… of course," he replied and promptly turned and left the room. She heard the tap running and a few minutes later, he returned with a paper cup filled with water.

He helped her sit up and held her head forward placing the tumbler against her lips and watched closely as and she quenched her thirst. There was something intrinsically sensuous and sexual about her lips and mouth and the fact that she was bound and his to do whatever he wished filled him with excitement. When she leaned forward to relieve the awkwardness of her position, her cheek bumped against the glass spilling some of the water down her chin and onto her blouse. The wet top, now translucent in places, clung to her body and he had to force himself to look away.

"Wait," he said and fished out a pocketknife, "I will free you if you promise not to give trouble."

She nodded and looked at him in surprise, "You're going to let me go?"

"No! But I am going to cut the ropes. You must promise, no running or escape. There is nowhere to go here. We are far from everything."

She nodded at the monster that he was proving not to be.

He freed her from the tethering cords, "If you give me trouble I will have to hurt you, do you understand?"

Maybe the monster was back.

"What are you going to do with me? And what happened to my father and brother? And what did you do to Mark?" She asked rubbing her wrists and clenching her fists, squeezing tightly, trying to get the circulation back.

He didn't answer instead he left the room and returned with a second glass of water.

"Here. You can drink properly," he said handing the glass to her. She took a few sips of the water, placed the glass on the side table, and looked at him expectantly waiting for an answer.

"What? What do you want?" He asked.

"My father, brother and Mark, what did you do to them?"

"They are all safe. The man you call Mark has a bump on is head and was not very happy. Your father and brother are unharmed. I was going to kill them but…" he stopped, looked away, before ending lamely, "I could not do it."

"I don't get it; you came here to kill us so why didn't you kill them when you had the chance?"

He didn't answer instead he asked, "Mark is a popular name, is it not? A young man I knew wanted to change his name from Miloslav to Mark."

She was puzzled by the non sequitur but was curious, "Miloslav sounds nice. Did he change his name?"

"No. He was shot and killed in the mountains by a golden haired tigress. It was not her fault; we came to take her nephew… how to say it… to kidnap the boy. She was only protecting what was hers."

It dawned on her then that this was the Russian who shot Allison and kidnapped Ryan. He had let the boy go at Bucky Johnston's Diner, unharmed, and that's where they had found Ryan. It began making sense to her now. *A golden haired tigress! That was indeed an apt description of Allison.*

"I know who you are!" She exclaimed, "You are Andrei Izoo…"

"Yes, I am Andrei Izhutin friend and brother to the dead Adam Shayk who was murdered by your man!" his outrage and fury returned.

She caught a flash in his eyes and a fleeting glimpse of the monster within. She was quiet before asking, "So what now?"

"I don't know. Everything is confused in my mind. I was going to…" his voice trailed off.

"You were going to do what with me? Hold me hostage, kill me, what? What were you planning to do with me?" Her curiosity and excitement were growing. This was becoming a game to her.

"My plan was to rape you and take video. I wanted to post it on internet, you know, Facebook, Instagram, Tweeter and all the others so McHenry could see it and know that it was payment for killing my friend. I was going to kill a hundred of your people for taking Adam's life but I am too soft, I could not do it."

At the thought of him raping her she felt a thrill, fear comingled with an inexplicable sensual excitement. It emanated at her core, from between her legs, racing in electric pulses to her extremities. Her cheeks flushed with sudden effulgence.

He mistook her blushing for embarrassment, "I'm sorry; I do not know how to say this in nicer way."

She had not anticipated this… this repentant reprobate. *He's a strange monster, a very strange but childlike man.*

"You are not a killer, I can see that. You seem like a nice…"

"I have killed many people. Many!" He interrupted, "But they were all people like me. Not nice people, they were gangsters and criminals," he paused before adding, "I do not make war on children or women. I have never molested or raped anyone and when I saw you lying on the bed, so beautiful and helpless… I wanted to but could not." He looked skyward and added, "I'm sorry, Adam, I let you down. I cannot do it."

"So you think I'm beautiful?" She wanted to hear him say it again.

"You are very beautiful. I think you know this," he said a bit confused.

Marylou felt strangely affected by the Russian's sincerity.

"So now what?" She asked again.

"I don't know. I don't know what I'll do now. Without Adam this business means nothing and my big boss is not going to be happy. He will blame me for the fuckup." He paused, looked at her and continued, "My home is empty. It is like a box with nothing inside. My bitch wife do not love me or even respect me. She thinks I'm uneducated, ignorant peasant. There is nothing there for me."

"Do you have children?"

"No. My wife she don't want kids."

"Then why do you stay with her?"

He thought for a while and then said, "She is pretty and was kind at one time. That was before. Now we are comfortable. She does her thing and I do mine – two strangers sharing the same space. She likes theatre and artsy type people, eating cheese and drinking French wine and talking bullshit. She has a hundred lovers who look like boys and talk like faggots. I like vodka and people who are real. But she is right about one thing - I am uneducated. I dropped from high school after fighting with my papa. I was living on the streets in Moscow and that is when Adam found me. He take pity on me and saved me."

She felt sorry for the man, "I'm sorry. What do you do for love? We all need to be loved. Do you have a woman, a mistress?"

"No, no mistress or special woman. But I like fucking. I fuck as many women who will agree to be with me. I don't care if she is fat or thin, black or white; it does not matter as long as she is a woman. I love all women, they are interesting to me," he said it so simply and honestly that it didn't sound crude to her. "I am sorry for the rough words but I do not know any fancy English. You see, I do not drink wine and eat cheese and talk all that fake bullshit."

They were alike, she thought to herself. She finished high school without learning anything worth knowing and she too enjoyed sex - the more of it the better. Ever since she was fourteen and an older cousin had taken into the barn and performed cunnilingus on her and then fucked her until she had screamed with pleasure, she couldn't get enough. She didn't know exactly when it was that she enjoyed having multiple partners but at some point, it had morphed into an obsession.

It was the one thought that nagged at her - could she be happy with one man? So she pretended that the reason for her uncertainty had to do with McHenry and whether he would be intellectually bored with her. It was easier that way.

"How about you, are you happy with the Frenchie… sorry, McHenry?" he asked like he had read her mind.

She ignored the 'Frenchie' part assuming he had made a mistake with McHenry's pseudonym. Santos was a Spanish name but it was possible that the Russian thought that it was French.

"Yes, he makes me happy for now but that doesn't guarantee happiness for life," she answered honestly.

"No guarantee. Life is not like Amazon – no free returns! Divorce is expensive and break-ups are difficult, no? We must do the best we can. Come on, I will take you back to your family," the Russian said, getting up.

"I am hungry. Can we get something to eat?" Marylou asked.

"Yes of course, I am not thinking properly. I am hungry too. There is a small restaurant in town we can go there if you like or there is McDonalds on way back but they have shit for food except the fries; I like the fries and the coffee."

"I like the fries too," she smiled, "but we can go to the restaurant if that's what you prefer." She looked across at the bathroom door and got up off the bed, "I need to use the little girl's room before we go."

When she returned she saw the Russian seated at the foot of the bed, bent over, his face in his hands, sobbing silently. At first she wasn't sure if he was crying or laughing and stood watching him with curious astonishment. But then his body was wracked by sobs and she knew that he was weeping like a little boy and her heart went out to him.

"Why are you crying?" She walked over and sat next to him,

placing her arm around his shoulders, trying to comfort him. "It will be okay. You'll see… things will work out."

"I am nothing… like babushka doll; nothing inside just more and more of the same bullshit!" he muttered.

The reference to the nesting Russian dolls was lost on her but she felt his pain and her motherly instincts wanted to shield and comfort him.

"We all have many sides to us, we are not one thing," she told him trying to paraphrase what Mark Boswell had said to her. "You are more than just Adam's friend. You will be able to find yourself now, out from under his shadow. Do you understand?"

He looked at her surprised by the tenderness of her gesture and nodded but wasn't convinced.

"I cannot do anything in right way. I feel sad and useless. I had promised my friend that I would avenge his death and now, I realize that…"

"You can find happiness. You have to believe that."

His soul was filled with helpless anguish, a child lost and needing reassurance. And that did it for her. At that instant their roles were reversed. The captive was the captor and the prey, the predator. The energy sparked between them, filling them both with desire – he could see it in her eyes.

"How do you know…"

"Shhh, you will get over this, trust me, you will soon discover who you really are," Marylou whispered, leaning closer.

He caressed her face, fingers trembling, pushing her hair back unsure of what was taking place. He could never have imagined that this beautiful woman would consider someone like him, not even in his wildest dreams. It was then, at the moment of his insecurity, that she kissed him, her lips brushing lightly against his, a probing, tentative kiss at first before opening her mouth to let him in. That act of submission was all it took and Izhutin, the greatest fucker of women, was back in control.

Their tongues danced and fought, twisting, sliding, exploring and savoring the essence of the other, unable to breathe and unable to stop, suffocating in that unbearable prelude, the aching anticipation of the act that was to come when their bodies would merge and drown in a liquid sea of pleasure.

He helped her up and pulled her to him, burying his face in her hair, kissing the curve of her neck, nibbling at her ears, intoxicated by the fragrance of her, titillated beyond belief by the very newness of this delicious creature who was giving herself to him. He had never felt like this before.

She felt his cock, hard and throbbing against her and was filled with the need to have him buried inside her, deep inside her, thrusting in and out with that peculiar urgency fed by nature's primordial concupiscence. She wanted to taste him, to suck him into her mouth and hear him groan, to wield the power she had over him. It was a balance between submission and control – the giving and taking that thrilled her the most.

Her fingers wandered down unbuttoning his trousers with practiced ease. She was expert at this intimate act having done it a hundred times if not more, while he took off his shirt and began undressing her. His fingers lacked her dexterity and fumbled with nervous excitement, tugging impatiently at the buttons that stood between him and sexual nirvana. He cursed under his breath, anxious at the possibility that she would change her mind, until she took pity and helped him. Finally, they stood naked amongst the carnage of strewn haberdashery basking in the transparence and spontaneity of the moment.

"You are more beautiful than Aphrodite herself, malyshka, so beautiful," he said in Russian.

She smiled reaching for him, "What does that mean?"

"It means you are more beautiful than the goddess Aphrodite," his answer was hoarse and urgent. Passion raced through him and though the voice in his mind screamed, *slow, go slow, make it last forever*, lust and desire overtook him. He pushed her back on the bed and knelt between her thighs, drinking in her nakedness and readied himself for the feast.

And when he spread the petals of her cunt with his tongue, she gasped and grabbed his hair, hips thrusting upwards, grating her pussy against his mouth. Her mind was filled with nothing but the awareness of the intense pleasure shooting through her and any thought of McHenry was gone. For now, all that mattered was the ache between her thighs and the craving in her soul.

LADY BUTTERFLY

During the drive from Jersey City to Chase River Town, McHenry was forced to make a decision. There was no way he could make the eight hour trip in his condition. He would have to attend to the wound and the sooner he did it, the better. He suffered from a mild form of Von Willebrand disease, a genetic disorder that prevented his blood from clotting normally. The detour to his home in Connecticut would cost him about two hours but he needed the fibrin glue in his medicine cabinet to help with coagulation.

Once inside the house, he called Marylou and told her to stay with Robbie or with Luke until he could get there. He could sense her anxiety and avoided mentioning the extent of his wound not wanting her to worry any further. He was pretty certain that Izhutin would go after Hank Carlson or Luke before he attempted to hurt Marylou. It was anybody's guess as to where the Russian really was. He may have decided to lay low for a while until things settled down before taking any action – there just was no way of knowing but McHenry's immediate concern was the blood soaking through his trousers. He had to stem the bleeding.

After attending to his wound, he downed a few tablets of ibuprofen, made a sandwich, drank a cup of green tea and promptly fell asleep on the couch. He was exhausted and slept through the night. When he woke up the next morning, he felt reinvigorated and alive.

The bleeding had stopped and apart from the inflammation around the wound, he was good to go. The first thing he did was to try and get a hold of Marylou but got her voicemail and left her a message telling her he was on his way. He then took a shower, made some oatmeal with maple syrup, redressed the wound and got back on the highway prepared for the long trip ahead - it was roughly a seven hour drive to Chase River Town and could take him longer if he had to stop frequently to accommodate the soreness in his leg.

As he drove, McHenry's mind was preoccupied with plans for the future. The first item on his checklist was to get new identity for Marylou. He had discussed this with her and they decided on the name Annamarie Du Bellay. He was already in possession of a passport under the identity of Rene Du Bellay but would have to get one for Marylou before they left for Zermatt. The man he dealt with had his people working in the State and Immigration departments and the documents they produced were ironclad. He was expensive, prohibitive perhaps, but foolproof documents were priceless and he wanted to be sure that there were no footprints leading the wrong people to his villa in the mountains.

He made a call and spoke briefly to his contact before calling Marylou. He had tried several times to reach her but each time it went into voicemail and he was beginning to get concerned. It was unlike her to be unresponsive for so long. When he was about an hour from his destination he got a call and much to his relief, it was Marylou.

"Hi baby, I tried calling but kept getting your voicemail," he said, "I was beginning to worry. Is everything okay?"

"Everything's fine. I'm back at home with Dad and Junior... you are not going to believe what happened. Where are you?" Marylou asked.

"I'm about an hour or so from Chase River... just outside Dexter right now. I had to stop at home and take care of some stuff," he replied.

"Come straight here. I'll tell you all about it," she quipped happy that he was close by.

"You can tell me now, I mean, I've got nothing to do. Do you know if the Russian turned up there?"

"Yes he did."

"And?"

"I'd rather tell you in person. I need to take a shower and Deputy Bradley is here. He's been asking questions about you and…" she hesitated not knowing whether she should to tell him about Izhutin and the killing that took place at the Rancher's Lodge, "just come home. I'll tell you about it." She paused then said, "I miss you."

"Not as much as I've missed you," he said adding, "I love you Marylou and that has changed things. I cannot do this anymore. We need to leave for Switzerland as soon as we can… it will be a new beginning but I promise you won't be disappointed. You will love it there."

"Yes, baby, I feel the same way now. We can leave whenever you want. Come home, I'll have dinner ready. Love you," she said and hung up.

When she returned to the living room she found Deputy Bradley, Robbie, Mark and her father discussing Izhutin and the possible reasons for his bizarre actions.

"I was sure the dumb fuck was going to kill us," Mark Boswell said, "especially when he put the gun to my head! Damn! I think I pissed my pants!"

Dorsey nodded his head, commiserating, "I was pretty sure too, Mark. He looked demented, you know, he had that look, that crazy-man look!"

"The asshole left a knot the size of baseball on the back of my head," Mark added, rubbing the his head, "I'd like to get my hands on the mother…" he noticed Marylou walking in and caught himself, "Hey Marylou, are you okay?

Marylou smiled, "Just tired but I'm fine." She looked at Bradley, "I'm going to take a shower. It's been a long day… do you need me for anything?"

"No, you've told me everything I need to know. I was wrong about Santos. From the timing of things, it must have been Izhutin who shot Chuck, Matt and Burt. I've got an APB out for him so hopefully, we'll catch him soon. I am still not sure why he spared all of you."

"If you recall he had spared Ryan too. I guess he's really not a killer," Marylou replied.

"What about Chuck and the others? You knew Burt, he didn't deserve to be shot," Deputy Bradley countered.

"I don't know. All I know is that he was nice to me and dropped me off without hurting me. He could have done anything he wanted but he didn't." Marylou took a deep breath before adding, "I had dated Burt and he could get nasty and mean. He might have said or done something to the Russian that was offensive. He was almost as bad as Chuck when it came to foreigners and people of color."

"I guess we'll never know for sure."

"I guess so. I'm tired so I'll say goodnight," she said.

"You will have dinner won't you, Marylou?" Gil Dorsey asked his daughter.

"Yes, Dad, I'll have dinner a bit later," she answered, "right now, I need a glass of wine and a hot bath."

Marylou had lied and told Bradley that Izhutin was driving a black sedan, a Lincoln Continental, and gave a description of the Russian that could have fit almost anyone. She noticed Robbie giving her a questioning look but he said nothing. No one had gotten a good look at Izhutin and despite his protestations she had him drop her off in Monson instead of Chase River Town. It would be too risky for him to be seen in town. A friend of hers in Monson had driven her home.

She recalled the last conversation she had with the Russian, "Get away from here, Andrei, go somewhere new and start over. You will find the right woman and you will be happy. Michael and I are going to Switzerland, far away from here. You should do the same… find a place where you can be yourself, not what people expect you to be."

"Why don't you run off with me, malyshka? We go far away to some beautiful island with sunshine and blue skies. I know I can make you happy," he had asked in earnest, clinging to the threads of hope spun by their afternoon together.

"No. What we shared was beautiful but my life is with Michael. Our time together was special but you need to move on and find a new life." She had been emphatic, leaving no room for ambiguity or hope.

It wasn't what Izhutin wanted to hear and had looked sad and disconsolate. As she was getting out of the car, he had pressed a slip of paper into her hand, "Here you keep this. It is my private cell phone. You call me anytime… anytime you need *anything!* I come running, malyshka. I swear to you, I will be there."

She had smiled at him touched by his sincerity and looked at the number scribbled on a small piece of paper before saying, "Thank you, Andrei, I will keep it to remind me of our time together but you must move on. I know you will find a nice woman who will make you happy."

She gave him a peck on his cheek and got out of the car and walked away. He waited watching her in the rearview mirror hoping she would turn back but she didn't and after she disappeared into a building he drove away.

She knew exactly what he was going through. She had been there many times in her life – alone and unsure. That was until she met Michael, he had changed that. She felt safe and anchored with him; the most secure she had ever felt with any man. The fact that she was able to separate love from sex didn't change that. In her mind, she justified her liaison with Izhutin as her need for physical fulfillment and it had nothing to do with love.

She drew a hot bath, lit the candles in the corner, undressed and threw her clothes into the hamper making sure that her panties, stained with the juices of her earlier dalliance, were hidden at the bottom. She nursed a glass of red Bordeaux while soaking in the bathtub languidly recalling the details of her strange and exciting day. It had been an incredible afternoon but it was over and now she had to get ready for McHenry and their life together. For her it was easy, a butterfly flitting from one flower to the next. She felt no remorse or guilt and would do it again if the opportunity presented itself. She smiled thinking about the new life she would embark on. The doubts she had harbored about leaving Chase River Town were gone – this incident had filled her with new found confidence; a realization that she was stronger and more resilient than she had ever imagined.

She couldn't wait for McHenry to get back to her. The thought of his big cock pumping in and out of her sent a shiver down her spine. She laid her head back and closed her eyes, enjoying the warmth of the water with images of the afternoon scrolling through her brain like a sleazy X-rated movie. She sipped the wine and without thinking slipped two fingers into her cunt imagining that both McHenry and Izhutin were there with her. She placed the wine glass on the ledge conterminous to the bathtub so she could pleasure herself unencumbered - kneading, squeezing and rubbing, soaring higher and higher, wings fluttering wildly, until she crested over the peak in a brilliant flash, writhing mindlessly, falling into that indescribable abyss of pleasure. She had to bite down on her lip to stop from screaming… the insatiable lady butterfly was alive and well and her world was full of flowers.

THE PRODIGAL SON

When Nikolai Zakirov heard that Adam Shayk was dead he could barely contain his joy – he had never liked Shayk or his overbearing attitude and saw him as an impediment to his end goals. He was standing on the terrace of his father's mansion in Belize, looking out over the turquoise-blue waters of the Caribbean Sea, and shouted out as loud as he could.

"Yes! Yes, yes, yes!"

He had hated the isolation and the overly protective attitude of his chaperone, Viktor Kozlov, and had on more than one occasion tried to shake free. The first time he had slipped away was after a week of being cloistered behind the walls of the mansion's estate. He had slipped into town on the pretext of sightseeing but before he could locate a brothel that offered the services he was looking for, his bodyguards had found him and no amount of cajoling, threats or bribes could dissuade his father's men. They had physically dragged him back to the villa.

When he heard that along with Shayk's death, Izhutin had disappeared and may have been killed, he was ecstatic, no beyond ecstatic – he was euphoric. He found Shayk to be an irritant but he intensely disliked Izhutin and had complained several times about him to his father to no avail.

His father's response was a surly, "Take it to Adam. He will deal with it. He is the boss there."

And now, they were both gone! This was the break he was looking for. Finally, he could approach his father about taking over the US side of the business. He was sure his father would laugh at him but the request was a Trojan Horse, his real goal was to get back to America and back to his lavish, playboy lifestyle and at some point, worm his way into the organization.

The void that Shayk and Izhutin left gave him the perfect opening to approach his father so after going over his strategy in his mind, he worked up the courage and called his old man.

"What do you want?" His father never liked hearing from him.

"Hi Papa, I just heard. Poor Adam; it was very unfortunate and a terrible way to die. And where is Andrei? I heard he is missing, maybe dead or maybe the coward killed Adam and ran off."

"Speak Russian!" the command was curt and without preamble.

"Sorry, Papa, I am so used to speaking like the Americans," Nikolai answered in Russian.

"What do you want?" Alexei Zakirov repeated, "No more money, you are spending way too much for a lazy bastard who has not worked a day in his life!"

"Well, that is why I'm calling. I have changed, Papa, I really have. Staying here has given me time to think about things. I want more responsibility and now that Adam is gone, let me take over his job. I can do it, Papa; I swear I will not let you down."

The older Zakirov laughed and asked, his tone, contemptuous, "You? You will run the business in America?"

"Yes! Why not? I am your son – your *only* son! I have your blood running through my veins. Why do you laugh? I can do it. Let me prove to you that I can do it!"

"Do you have any idea how much business Adam was responsible for? Do you really think I will risk it by putting you in charge?"

His father's voice was derisive, "What do you take me for, boy?" He paused, taking a sip of his schnapps, a ginger-lemon digestive, "You are a spoiled child. I don't blame you, I blame your mother. She sheltered you and treated you like a girl. Adam Shayk was a killer. Andrei Izhutin is a killer and I do not believe he is dead. There is something going on with the Italians and Albanians and I will find out what that is. I need a killer to run things there not some spoilt child who is still sucking on his mother's tits."

"The apple does not fall far from the tree, Papa. I am a killer in a different way. I am clever and cunning. Adam did not do it alone. He had the accountants, henchmen, soldiers and the organization to help him. The same will be for me. Why do you doubt me? Why won't you give me the same chance you gave Adam?"

"Why you ask? Because you run around drinking, snorting coke and fucking young girls. And you make videos of those insidious acts to share with other sick bastards on the internet. You do this to mock me instead of looking into the business! That is why."

"I have changed. A lot of what I did was because I was bored and no one not even you, my father, would take me seriously. Mother keeps asking me when I will follow in your footsteps and I have nothing to tell her. Nothing! Is that fair? You give Anya everything she wants. She wants a pony, you get her a pony. She wants a Ferrari, you buy her a Ferrari. She wanted to go to Rio for the carnival and you send her to Rio with her friends. I don't blame you for loving her more than me, we do not control who we love but I am your son! She cannot be your heir."

There was a long silence and for a moment Nikolai thought he had gone a bit too far and his father had hung up on him. Anya was his younger sister and the apple of their father's eye. She was beautiful, smart and talented and she had their father wrapped around her little finger. Nikolai hated her even more than he hated Izhutin.

"Father? Are you there?"

"Quiet! I am thinking," Alexei Zakirov barked at his son. After what seemed like an eternity to Nikolai, he said, "Okay, here is what we will do. Listen carefully, this is not a negotiation and I am doing this for your mother. I will send one of my men to be by your side, to help you, and we will try this out for six months. If you do a good job we will try it for another six months and if all goes well then we do it for another six months and on and on and on until I am convinced and satisfied that you can handle the responsibility. Then and only then will I let you run the business without interference. If you fail me, I will cut your stipend in half and you will never talk about running the business again. Do you understand, Nikolai?"

"Yes, Papa, it is clear. I will not disappoint you. Who are you sending to help me?" Nikolai couldn't believe his luck and had to fight to control his enthusiasm.

"Never mind who I'm sending. Talk to Viktor and make arrangements to get back to New Jersey. I will let you know who is coming to help you. Listen to him and learn and just maybe you will become a real Zakirov instead of being a fucking moron! One more thing – if you fuck up, Anya *will* take over the business!" And, with that his father hung up the phone.

The young Zakirov was stunned. It wasn't the bit about his sister, he could deal with her, but this opportunity to take over as Shayk's replacement was way more than he had expected. He was going to be the head of one of the largest crime syndicates in the country. The days of being the brunt of inside jokes were over. And for the next six months he would focus and make sure the business thrived or he would have his men castrated and thrown to the wolves! *They were wrong, all of them, he was a killer just like his father but far more vicious.* Nikolai Zakirov smiled – this was perfect.

He called Viktor Kozlov and following a brief conversation with the older man, packed and got ready. That afternoon he left Belize, changed flights in Miami and arrived at JFK Airport with his two bodyguards. The stretch limo that was waiting took them straight to the Waldorf Astoria located in midtown on Park Avenue. Nikolai loved New York City. It was the city that never slept where he could get anything, anytime he desired. And he knew just the right people to help him indulge his dark fantasies.

The concierge, a thin pleasant looking man, dressed immaculately in a black suit, white shirt and a contrasting yellow tie, wearing patent leather oxfords was waiting at the door to greet Nikolai and his men. He knew every single one of the hotel's most valued guests and the Zakirovs were on top of that list. Nikolai was dressed casually in a faded polo shirt, jeans and flip-flops in violation of the hotel's dress code but the concierge ignored the breach and after a few minutes of obsequious pandering, escorted Nikolai to his penthouse suite circumventing the checking-in formalities.

The suite was a spacious two bedroom pied-à-terre that the young Zakirov used whenever he was in New York and he was there often, so often that many of the staff knew him by name. He would occupy the master bedroom and his two bodyguards would share the other. One of them would be by the door at all times so it had never been a problem. Both men were aware of the Nikolai's predilections and knew that there would be young girls arriving shortly. They had been instructed to look the other way and focus on protecting Zakirov's only son.

No sooner had the concierge left than Nikolai called his contact, "I need girls, maybe two or three."

"I have the perfect pair for you. Twins from Norway with blond hair and blue eyes and…" the female voice answered.

"How old?" Nikolai cut her off.

"Eighteen but they look…" she began but was interrupted again.

"Fuck you. If I was looking for some used up old bitches I would call Felix. He is cheaper and faster and I don't have to listen to his bullshit. Can you help me or are you wasting my time?"

"I will have what you want there in thirty minutes. They will be accompanied by two chaperones. The ladies don't fuck; they are there to make sure that the girls are safe. They will call your room from the lobby and if they spend the night that will cost you extra. Is that…"

"Send them," Nikolai snapped and hung up the phone. Finally, he could stop staring at his computer screen and jerking off. The videos of Marisa and Jodie had gotten old and jaded and he needed something fresh to get him going. It was time for some serious fucking.

He was getting ready for what was to come by setting-up the cameras around the bed. He checked the computer's monitor to make sure he had all the angles covered. This was a new laptop and he wasn't quite familiar with the upgraded software. His mind wandered back to the old one, the laptop that Marisa had taken: *That little bitch was a good fuck but she was a thief. Well, she might have gotten away with my computer but she's dead!* His friends, Matt Hansen and Chris Donnelly, were the ones who pressured Shayk insisting on getting the laptop back. *I warned Donnelly to let it go… no one cares about some fucking videos but he had to press the issue and now he's dead and Matt is dead too. And, Castiglioni! Fuck! All his friends were dead!*

The realization had a sobering effect on Nikolai. He stopped with what he was doing and sat down on the edge of the bed overcome by a feeling of loss and despite his best efforts, fear, the great subterfuge, began creeping in. From the moment he heard about Matt Hansen's death he was sure he was the killer's next target and had lived in fear of every shadow imagined or real. Now, the thought of his friends had dulled his desire. His mood had shifted to a dark place.

He called his contact back, "Send them tomorrow, not tonight. I am tired and want to sleep now. I will call you tomorrow to arrange the time."

He hung up without waiting for an answer. He rummaged through his suitcase and found the prescription bottles and tossed several pills into his mouth and swallowed them with a swig of vermouth that he drank straight from the bottle. He needed to sleep and these pills helped him relax and to control his fear. He then found the "special" container in a secret compartment at the bottom of his suitcase and snorted a few lines of coke. He sat back, eyes closed, and waited for the magic to happen.

He would show them. He would show them all... *Nikolai Zakirov, the killer nonpareil, had finally arrived.*

THE DANCING FOX

Izhutin was asleep when his cellphone rang. It was his old phone not the new one that he recently purchased. He had been hoping that Marylou would call but through his sleep addled stupor he knew it wasn't her. He had given her the new number. *Who the fuck is calling me at this hour?*

"Who's this?" His voice was brusque.

"He's here. The brat is staying in the same place, in his usual penthouse suite," the husky female voice informed him. "He cancelled his order so tonight he'll be alone."

"Okay," Izhutin said and hung up and went back to sleep.

It was Adam Shayk who had traced Nikolai's contacts and found Wicked Velvett – that was the name she chose for herself. She had been a model at one time and was now the facilitator for the depraved and those seeking thrills outside the law. She provided them with whatever they needed to satisfy their increasingly sick appetites but at a price, a very steep price, and of course, her services usually came with total anonymity. Her clients included movie stars, politicians, jetsetters, the very wealthy and to her great regret, Nikolai Zakirov.

It was fun at the beginning. He was good looking, playful and paid without question or hesitation and hobnobbing with the son of a Russian mobster seemed so avant-garde. It wasn't long before his demands became increasingly sordid but that didn't surprise her, it was what typically happened. Then one day, a few months back, four men turned up at her luxury apartment in SoHo. One of the men was Andrei Izhutin. They had roughed her up and when her partner had protested, threatening them with dire consequences, they sliced off her ear. The dyke had an attitude and a mouth and that didn't sit well with the men – they were about to cut her tongue out when Wicked Velvett begged for her lover's life. She was terrified of Izhutin and had agreed to let him know whenever Nikolai was in town. She kept her side of the bargain and her lover kept her tongue.

Izhutin had chosen a small, nondescript motel in the Bowery. He woke up around six the next morning, went for a walk, and had breakfast at a café across the street before returning to his room. He checked his watch and called Alexei Zakirov. It was around 3 PM in Moscow; *the big boss will be having his afternoon apéritif.*

"Andrei, I knew you weren't dead. Where were you?" The gravelly voice answered the phone without preamble.

"Hello boss, I had to take care of some business. The man who killed Adam had to be found and dealt with."

"And you do this without permission and without saying a word to anyone?" The tone had turned cold with an underlying threat that was unmistakable.

"Adam was my brother. I would fight the Angel of Death himself to avenge him," Izhutin hissed, "McHenry is a clever man and a very dangerous killer. I could not risk his finding out that I was after him." He paused then added, "Boss, it was a good thing I did this; I found him in Miami. He was on his way to Belize to kill Nikolai."

There was a short silence before his boss answered, "And what happened in Miami?"

"I killed the motherfucker! I am here and Nikolai is alive, yes?" Izhutin replied.

"How did you know he was in Miami? The man is very hard to

track, no?"

Answer a question with a question – it was an old game Zakirov played. But, Izhutin was a master at these games.

"The fox dances in the rain but never gets wet. He has learned to dodge the raindrops and others wonder how. I am that fox. I have my ways of finding out things and weeding out people. Now, I am calling to ask you what it is you want me to do. If you want me to come back to Moscow, I will be on the next flight. If you want me to eat a bullet, I will do so without question. I have avenged my brother and that is all that matters to me." There was an edge to his voice now that hadn't been there before.

The old man was quiet. He demanded unquestioning loyalty but he knew that Andrei Izhutin was a bit of an anomaly. He had his quirks but had been a loyal soldier and would be hard to replace at least until the new man had a chance to get familiar with the business.

Finally Zakirov spoke, "Don't ever do this again. You will speak to me before you decide to embark on any personal vendetta, is that clear?"

"Yes."

"Adam loved you and trusted you. He was like a son to me. I am sparing your life because of his trust in you," Zakirov said. "I have asked Nikolai to take over. I know he needs help and will send Andriy to assist him."

"Andriy?" Izhutin hadn't heard of him before.

"Andriy Dovzhenko. You do not know him but he is a trusted man. He will call you when he is ready. You will support him in the same way you supported Adam. The two of you will work together to turn my son into the leader that Adam was."

"It is not possible to turn a poodle into a tiger," Izhutin replied without thinking.

"I will feed you to my dogs if you ever question me again!" The old man growled, "Adam may have tolerated your tongue but remember who you are talking to."

"I am sorry, boss, I am here at your disposal and will do as you have instructed," Izhutin was contrite knowing that he was flirting with death. Zakirov had men killed for far less.

"Let Nikolai know that you are alive. He thinks you are dead," and with that Zakirov hung up.

The name Andriy Dovzhenko was Ukrainian and it was strange that the old man would trust an outsider but Izhutin knew that stranger things had happened in the past. It didn't change anything. His plans would proceed as before.

By the time he had showered and dressed it was a little past 9 AM – perfect timing. He glanced in the mirror and liked the new look – the beard and mustache moderated his boyish appearance and gave him a more arresting look. *I look like a fucking Viking! I could scare the shit out of constipated monkey! Now, I have to turn the poodle into a wolf.*

He picked up the rental car and drove the twenty odd minutes to the Waldorf Astoria cursing the morning traffic as he swerved in and out of the lanes. He drove around for a few minutes and parked the rental in a garage a few blocks from the hotel.

He called the room from the lobby and a few minutes later, he was asked to come up to the suite by one of the bodyguards.

"Andrei! Damn, brother, it's been a long time!" The bodyguard who opened the door exclaimed. He was a punk kid Izhutin had known many years back in Moscow.

"Taras the asshole! The last time I saw you, I think you were fucking a cow!"

"The cow was you mother," Taras replied, tongue in cheek.

"I could swear that she was *your* grandmother but then you're a horny bastard and will fuck almost anything!"

The men laughed and hugged.

"What is with the beard? You look like Robin Hood," the bodyguard asked, "I would never have recognized you."

"I am robbing hoods, right? The new look makes me handsome, no?"

"Like putting lipstick on a fucking pig! But it looks okay and…"

"Enough! Where the fuck were you?" Nikolai Zakirov snapped walking into the living room of the suite and standing arms akimbo. He was determined to let Izhutin know who was boss.

"I had to take care of business. Now I am here. I spoke to your father and he…"

"Bullshit! My father thinks you are dead," the young man retorted.

"I just spoke to him. You can call him. Here, check my phone," he tossed the phone to Taras.

The bodyguard studied the phone and offered it to Nikolai, "Yes, he spoke to your father… they talked for a long time."

Nikolai took the phone and looked at the call list but wasn't really paying attention. He had always felt insecure around Izhutin and now he felt the insecurity returning. "Well, if you spoke to my father you know that I am now in charge. You will do as I order you to."

"Easy, little boy, your father is sending Andriy Dovzhenko to train you. I am to help him and just so you know, your father said I should kick your ass and do whatever it took to make a man out of you," Izhutin replied insolently and plopped himself on the couch.

Nikolai hadn't known about Andriy Dovzhenko and felt betrayed.

He whined, "Who told you about this… this Andriy Dovzhenko?"

"Your father did. You mean he did not tell you?"

Now the young Zakirov felt even more insecure. He ignored the question and asked, "Do you know who he is? And did Papa say when he is coming?"

"He will be here in the next few days," Izhutin lied, "and he is not an easy person like me. He is a ballbuster. They call him the Barbarian from Kyiv because he has eaten the hearts of many little dickheads who opposed your father." Izhutin scratched his crotch and smiled at the young man, "You look pale, are you okay?"

"What am I supposed to do now?" Nikolai was unable to control his insecurity.

"I have heard of him, this Andriy Dovzhenko. He is indeed a killer. I did not know that he was from Kyiv or that he was the Barbarian but that does not surprise me. He has a reputation of being a hard man with no mercy." Taras was either playing along or Izhutin had guessed correctly.

"Okay, enough about this Ukrainian asshole. We will worry about him when he is here. Right now, we have a special shipment coming to our warehouse near the port. These are the fucking Turks. They know Adam is dead and now they want to meet the new boss. So, you have to stop shitting in your pants and act like a man. In about one hour we have to meet these fuckers so go put on some nice threads and show them that you have some balls, a set of big, fucking Russian balls! Come on, move! We must hurry."

Nikolai turned and left for his room. He was deflated. The euphoria from the previous day was gone, dissipated like piss flushed down a toilet. He was back to feeling inadequate and like a boy. But, he would make this work. He had to make it work. He would use Izhutin to help him with the Barbarian from Kyiv. *Why didn't his father tell him about Dovzhenko? It was because his father hated him; he had always hated him even as a little boy because he was like his mother and loved her more. Why else would a father hate his only son?*

He showered and donned an off-white silk-blend suit. He was a handsome man and looked more like a teenage heartthrob than the head of the Zakirov mob.

When he walked into the living room, Izhutin smirked and said, "You look like a fucking gigolo. Do you have anything else?" He glanced at his watch and shook his head, "Never mind, we will have to leave now. We will go shopping later for some good clothes. Do you have a gun?"

"No."

Izhutin turned to the second bodyguard, a big hairy gorilla, with dark brooding looks, "What is your name?"

"Demyan," the man replied, "Demyan Abdulov."

"Okay, Demyan Abdulov, go get this man a gun. Go on, get him a gun. Make sure the safety is on. I don't want to be shot by some fucking gigolo cunt!"

"What about us?" Taras asked, "Do you want us to come along?"

"Yes, of course you are coming along. What did you think? You think I'm meeting the Turks with this fucking gigolo holding my cock, is that what you think? Stop asking stupid questions. You two fuckers are coming along in case there is trouble. I have a big car, a rental, so it is no problem. We will all fit, even this big monkey," Izhutin said, gesturing towards the second bodyguard.

Izhutin had taken the lead and the others followed. Adam Shayk had once told him that men will tell you that they would like to be leaders when in reality most want to follow. Only a select few are born to lead because the burden of leadership comes with great responsibility and with that responsibility is the knowledge that there is always someone gunning to take the leader's place. And in their business it meant a bullet to the back of the head.

Adam Shayk was right. He had always been right.

BYE-BYE QUEEN BUTTERFLY

McHenry and Marylou were the first to leave Chase River Town. A week after the incident with Izhutin, with the briefest of goodbyes and promises of staying in touch, they left for his house in Connecticut. He wanted Marylou to experience the home in Litchfield before putting it on the market. The only items he was having shipped to Switzerland were his artifacts – the statues, paintings and carvings he had spent a lifetime collecting and were invaluable. The rest was to be disposed or sold with the house.

The seven hour drive was uneventful but that changed when they arrived at the entrance to the driveway. McHenry couldn't help but smile at the expression on Marylou's face; she watched awestruck as they made their way, winding through manicured emerald expanses interspersed with waterfalls and koi ponds, pollarded trees and intricate topiary until finally they arrived at the horseshoe roundabout in front of the large ranch-style house. She sat still for a moment taking it all in.

"My God! Is all this really yours?" she asked when he opened the door and helped her out of the truck.

"Ours, darling, this is ours," he replied, smiling at her and holding her to him by her waist.

She turned in his arms to face him, "Why would you want to leave this? It is so beautiful and exquisite and…"

He laughed, pinching the tip of her nose playfully, "Wait until we get to Zermatt and you will have your answer."

Within a week she had assumed the responsibilities of the house and took over dealing with the cleaning service, the maids and the landscaping crew. She was now undoubtedly the mistress of his mansion and there was a subtle but definite power-shift in their relationship. They both realized that she was becoming the dominant partner and for his part, he was relieved and happy to relinquish that role to her. Her blossoming into a strong and self-confident woman only strengthened their bonds as a couple.

They got married in a quiet secular ceremony conducted by the town clerk and left for Switzerland as husband and wife, Rene and Annamarie Du Bellay. They flew into Geneva and stayed a few days there to experience the culture and take in the nightlife before catching a train to Zermatt. It was during the four hour train ride, over a glass of champagne, that she told him that she was pregnant. He was astounded and overjoyed.

He stood up and raised his glass and announced to everyone in their compartment, "I'm going to be a father! How about that? I'm going to be a freakin' dad!"

The usually unemotional and subdued Swiss, cheered and the passengers nearby congratulated him. He insisted on pulling Marylou up to her feet so everyone could see her, "This is my beautiful wife! Have you seen anything prettier?"

The Swiss cheered some more, this time more enthusiastically, making her blush. A group of English tourists that were seated close to them came over to shake hands and share hugs and complimented her to the point of embarrassment.

She was happy but her happiness was tinged with a bit of concern. She wasn't sure if the baby was his or Izhutin's. Both McHenry and she had brown eyes – his were a bit lighter but they were brown. Izhutin's eyes were large and strikingly blue. She knew enough about dominant and recessive genes to know that there was a small chance, a very small chance that a baby born to a brown-eyed couple could inherit blue eyes from an ancestor but the parents would have to carry the recessive gene. She put aside her worry and decided she would deal with it when the baby was born. She felt certain that McHenry would believe anything she told him, not because he was gullible but because he desperately wanted to believe in her.

Zermatt turned out to be everything he had promised her. The huge stone chalet style house built high on a cliff dwarfed the house in Litchfield. It looked more like a castle or fortress than a house and offered magnificent views of the Matterhorn Mountain. If she had been astonished before she was in shock now. She stood by the massive iron gates staring at the building, a veritable alcazar made of stone, before walking slowly into the cobblestone compound.

"How are we going to take care of this?" she asked in curious amazement.

"Don't worry; we have several people hired to keep the place functional and clean."

"Isn't that expensive?"

"We can afford it, baby, you don't ever have to worry about money," he assured her then took her hand and led her through the portico and into the house, "Come on, you have to see the place and meet the staff." He turned to the chauffeur who had picked them up from the train station, "Bring the bags in, Antonio."

Antonio Falzone was an older gentleman and as his name suggested, was originally from Italy. His dark skin and black hair peppered with gray were vestiges of his Sicilian ancestry. He had worked as the head gardener for the previous owners but now drove McHenry's Mercedes, ran errands and helped the staff with odd jobs. He had slowly but surely become McHenry's fidus Achates and as such, the person who was in charge of the place and the staff in McHenry's absence. McHenry had made it clear to Antonio that it was imperative that his wife takes a liking to the place or he would have to sell it and move back to America.

The staff consisted of six women and three men and every single one of them liked McHenry. Though he was aloof and valued his privacy he was kind and generous and always polite when he interacted with them. He was also determined to restore the old building back to its much heralded past. This meant work for many in the small town of Zermatt. Antonio and his wife both worked at the chalet and they wanted their oldest daughter to join them so they had a vested interest in making sure that the Americans would remain in Zermatt.

The staff stood patiently in a single row in the large foyer waiting for the new mistress to greet them but Marylou dallied by the entrance, hat in hand, uncertain of what was expected of her. McHenry did not rush her. He wanted her to take her time and get used to the new surroundings and more importantly, her new position.

Seeing the hesitation on her face Antonio said, "It will be okay, madam, the people here are nice and they will take good care of you. We are here to make sure that you are happy. Where would you like me to put the bags?"

She felt reassured by the old man's words. She liked his lined and leathery face, finding comfort in his warm smile, "Place them by the stairs, Antonio, and it's late, you can all go home. We will deal with everything tomorrow."

"As you wish, madam. I will be here early in the morning and if there is anything you need, you let me know. Some of the staff do not speak English so my wife or I can translate for you. My wife is the big one. Her name is Elena and she runs the kitchen and she understands English but does not speak it too well. We stay here in the quarters at the back so we are here at your call anytime you need something. When would you like to have your supper?"

The plump woman dressed in a loose fitting long dress and a clean, crisp white apron smiled and came forward. Marylou smiled back at her, a nervous smile, and suddenly felt tired and overwhelmed. She looked helplessly at McHenry so he stepped in, "It has been a long day and the madam is tired and wishes to go to bed early. Elena, we have eaten and will not have supper today. You can put the food away and if madam is hungry later, I will warm it up for her. We will have coffee at 7 o'clock and breakfast at 8." He turned to Marylou, "Is that okay, dear?"

"That is fine. This will take some getting used to but we will deal with things one day at a time," she said smiling as she walked by them and entered the large living room. She felt her breath catch in her throat, struck by the immense splendor of the architecture.

The spacious room was dominated by a beautiful crystal chandelier that hung low from the high cathedral ceiling over a large, stunning Persian rug. She stood under the lights in the center of the carpet, Alice in Wonderland, tumbling down the rabbit-hole. She had lost all semblance of control and felt the thrill of freefalling head first into this new reality. She made her way slowly up the marble stairway stopping to admire the statues in the alcoves and the faded fresco covering the ceilings. *God, this is so freakin' amazing. What am I doing here? Me, Marylou Dorsey, a poor, naïve mountain girl! Except now I am Annamarie Du Bellay and this will be my new beginning, my Swiss fairytale...*

"Wait!" McHenry called up to her and took the marble stairs two at a time and without warning swept her up in his arms and carried her down a long corridor and over the threshold of the master bedroom, "My darling, everything I have is yours. I know it seems like too much right now but in the morning, when you meet the staff again and get to know them and when we walk around the property, you will see that you were meant for this."

He wasn't sure whether it was the fact that she was pregnant or whether it was the brisk mountain air but there was an alluring radiance to her that made her irresistible to him. It hadn't gone unnoticed to his experienced eye, how the staff had reacted to her presence - they were fascinated by their new American mistress, the lady with the movie star looks, and would do their part to make sure she was happy here.

He laid her down on the bed and looked at her adoringly knowing that he had hit the jackpot and that finally he would make his forever home here with her. They christened their house by making love late into the night. It was Alice and the Mad Hatter fucking like, yes, rabbits and tumbling farther and farther down the rabbit-hole.

The Dancing Fox

DANGEROUS MOVES

The drive to the warehouse was slow and tedious. The lane closures due to the never ending roadwork on I-478 and I-278 only added to the misery brought on by the congested traffic but Izhutin was cheerful and kept the men entertained with his many self-deprecating anecdotes. When they finally arrived in Bensonhurst where the warehouse was located, the men got out stretched their legs while Izhutin unlocked the padlock that secured the gigantic overhead door then opened the side entryway and disappeared inside the building. A few minutes later there was a noisy, grating sound as the metal door scrolled slowly upwards.

"Why the fuck would anyone want a warehouse here? It looks and smells like shit!" Demyan Abdulov noted looking around the rundown and graffiti ridden neighborhood.

"It's near the port, dumbass, that's why," Taras informed his partner, "There must be a fucking garbage dump nearby… smells like rotting fish!"

"It's the dead bodies that Zakirov has stashed inside," Izhutin joked and the men laughed, all except Nikolai. He found the odor inherently unpleasant and the humor to be disrespectful but he wasn't sure if he should say something so he held his tongue.

They men strolled casually into the warehouse and Nikolai said, "We live in the twenty first century, we must upgrade and use new digital technology to secure the place. Replace this old bullshit with cameras and electronic locks." He wanted to let them know that despite Izhutin's impertinence, he was still in charge and looking at Izhutin added, "You will replace..."

"That will be your next job," Izhutin cut him off, "since you are the digital guru, you can take care of that as soon as we get to your new office. You can make the arrangements to have cameras installed and the locks replaced. The cameras are a good idea and I hear you make some very interesting videos. So now you are in charge of the security system. That is a good job for a fucking gigolo!"

Nikolai turned red wishing now that he had kept his mouth shut. He noticed Taras trying to suppress a smile and Demyan grinning openly. His men were losing respect for him. His hatred for Izhutin was reaching a boiling point and he stood glum-faced and angry and overcome with a feeling of impotence as he watched Izhutin pull into the warehouse and park the car close to the rear wall. The hundred thousand square foot, rectangular space was vacant except for the racks that lined one of the side walls. Izhutin got out of the car and walked up to the men.

"Demyan, you go up," he pointed to the metal stairway leading to the upper level, "and stand by the window that looks over the road. When they get here you stay at the top of the stairs and keep your gun ready and aimed at the bald bastard with a mustache and beard that is black like coal. He is their boss. If they try anything, you shoot that baldheaded motherfucker, do you understand?"

The big man nodded, "Yes."

The bodyguard stood still, hesitating, "What are you waiting for? Get your hairy ass up the stairs and wait by the window. They will be coming any minute now!" Izhutin barked.

As the big man turned and hurried up the stairway, Izhutin said to Taras, "You go to the end of the street, to the left – most probably they will be coming from there. When they make the turn onto this road, you call me. They may come from the other direction but in either case you will able to see the van so let me know as soon as you spot them. Make sure they do not see you. Then you come back here so you will be behind them and that will give us the advantage."

"You think there will be trouble?" Taras asked.

"I don't know but I don't trust these bastards. When drugs and money are involved, I would not trust Mother Theresa," he said. He looked around the warehouse, adding, "Let me know when you get in place. We need to make sure there are no surprises."

The young bodyguard nodded and left the warehouse hurrying towards the intersection at the end of the street. He looked for a secure place, crossed the road and picked a spot in the shade of an awning. His position was well concealed and it would be difficult, if not impossible, for the Turks to pick him out.

Taras called Izhutin, "Okay, I'm in position."

"Good. Call me as soon as you see them so we can be prepared. The bald bastard will be in the front so you can't miss him," Izhutin reiterated and hung up.

"What do you want me to do?" Nikolai asked. They were standing by the overhead door.

"You must act like the boss - that is what they want to see. You cannot show any fear or we will all be dead," and noticing the expression on Nikolai's face, Izhutin added, "Don't worry, little man, I am here. Now, close the door."

Nikolai was frightened. He had never been in a dangerous situation before and wished that he had stayed back in the comfort and safety of his suite. The mention of Turks with their black hair and blacker eyes conjured up images of marauding warriors on wild stallions slicing people's heads off and it sent a wave of fear through his slender body.

Maybe being the boss wasn't such a good idea. His father was right – you had to be a killer and he was faced with the irrefutable fact that despite the assurances he made to his father and the lies he told himself, he wasn't a killer. It was obvious to him now that Izhutin was just that - a coldblooded killer with no fear. *How could he have been so blind?* It was his ego that indulged the self-deception and filled his head with the fantasy of taking over from Adam Shayk.

The truth shall set you free, he thought, and the candid acceptance that he was not like his father or Shayk or Izhutin lifted a huge burden off of his shoulders. His sister, Anya, could have the business. She *was* the killer in the family and he would be happy to live in her shadow, snort coke and fuck young girls until he died.

As soon as this was over he would let his father know...

"Close the fucking door," he heard Izhutin snarl snapping him out of his reverie.

Nikolai hit the garage door opener and watched the huge steel door as it rattled noisily shut. It made such a racket that he didn't hear Izhutin stepping behind him and it was too late when the hand clamped tightly over his mouth. He struggled briefly before the knife slashed his throat from ear to ear. The blood spurted out, a horrific, viscid geyser splattering the wall, streaming down his chest turning the beautiful ivory suit crimson. The last thought he had was of those rapacious Turks with black hair and crazy black eyes lopping off heads.

Izhutin waited a few seconds then slowly lowered the young man's body to the floor and disdainfully stood by, studying Nikolai twitch and jerk as the life bled out of him.

"You can never sit in Adam's chair you sick little motherfucker. Now you can say hello to the devil and for all the sins you have committed, may you burn in hell!" Izhutin cursed and spat at the body, his voice barely a whisper. He wiped the blade clean on Nikolai's trousers and headed for the stairs.

When he got to the second level, the big bodyguard turned towards him, "Nothing! I see only a few cars. Are you sure they are coming?"

"They will be here," Izhutin assured him and walked towards the window where Demyan was stationed, "Do you see Taras?"

The bodyguard leaned forward craning his neck to get a better look, "No I cannot…"

Izhutin put a bullet through the back of Demyan Abdulov's head killing him instantly. He put two more bullets through the man's heart to make sure that he was dead and though he used a silencer, the gunshots were a staccato requiem echoing like drumbeats in the empty building.

Izhutin walked nonchalantly down the stairs back to where Nikolai's body lay and moved it to one side and then called Taras, "Come back. I just got a call, they are not coming today."

"I was beginning to fall asleep here… like counting sheep, looking at the cars going by."

"These fucking Turks! What are you going to do? Come on, I know a good place where we can get some lunch."

"I hope you brought your wallet because I'm starving and that fucker, Demyan, can eat," Taras said, "Last night he…"

"He can eat all he wants now. Come on, hurry back, we are all hungry."

Izhutin walked back to the stairwell and stood with his back leaning against the railing. He had his pistol strategically positioned on the step nearest him. He would prefer not to kill the young man but there was no telling how Taras was going to react.

Izhutin made a few practice grabs at the pistol adjusting the orientation of the grip and just as he was about to try it again, the side door opened and Taras walked in. The first thing the bodyguard saw was Nikolai's body lying in a pool blood and for a moment his mind went blank. He looked from the body to Izhutin and back several times, his face contorted in disbelief and fear.

"I killed the sick motherfucker and the hairy ape upstairs," Izhutin informed the bodyguard, a smile playing at the corners of his mouth, "I hope you weren't best buddies or lovers or something because he is fucking dead!"

The bodyguard was in shock. His mind was unable to fathom the implication of the scene before him. It screamed treason.

"Why? Why would you…? Have you gone mad?" Taras stuttered.

"I've never felt saner in my life. He was a sick little bastard and I wasn't going to watch him sit in Adam's chair and take Adam's place and act like he was the boss. That would be a fucking sacrilege and it wasn't going to happen."

Taras felt his chest constrict; a giant vise tightening around his heart and squeezing the very breath out from him.

"Oh, God! Oh, Mother of God, we are dead for sure. Zakirov will hunt us down like rabid dogs and make us pay! You know that, don't you? You're a fucking dead man!"

"We all die it's just a question of when, where and how. If you were looking for longevity you should have become a gardener or a fucking cook. This life we have chosen guarantees only one thing and that is a violent death!"

When Taras didn't respond, Izhutin felt sorry for the young man and in a gentler voice said, "It is done now. Go somewhere far and change your name. Do not make friends and do not talk to anyone and be ready for anything. Sleep with one eye open and get yourself some dogs, attack dogs, and then hope for the best. That is all you can do."

"No! No, no, no!" the young bodyguard spat out, "I had nothing to do with this. I will explain to the boss after I kill you… I will tell him exactly what you did! You have lost your fucking mind."

"*You* are going to kill me?" Izhutin asked incredulous with eyebrows raised.

Taras drew his gun and pointed it at the older man, "I have to kill you. You leave me no choice, Andrei. It is the only chance I have."

Izhutin pulled the placket of his shirt to one side exposing his chest and pointed to his heart, "Go on, shoot me… shoot me here! You think I give a fuck? I don't give a shit! I have lived ten lives in this one and if today is the day and this is the place and you are my passage to the other side, then so be it."

Taras didn't know what to do, his mind was spinning and his hands were trembling – in his young and violent life he had always known who the enemy was but this situation was new and unfathomable. This whole thing was like a fucking nightmare and he was hoping he would wake up and realize that it was all a bad dream. He squeezed his eyes shut tight and opened them again but nothing had changed: Nikolai's body remained in the pool of blood, his throat a gaping red gash smiling at him, taunting him, his face pale and ashen like the winter's breath.

He took a couple of tentative steps towards the stairway and that's when Izhutin reacted – he spun, grabbed for his weapon but in his haste knocked the pistol down the stairway and out of his reach. It bounced noisily from step to step until it landed, with a soft thud, on the warehouse floor.

Both men stared at the gun, hypnotized for a moment before Taras fired, a loud deafening shot that whistled past his target's head. In a split second and without hesitation Izhutin hurdled over the bottom newel post just as the second shot ricocheted off the handrail a few inches from his shoulder.

"Fuck me!" Taras exclaimed in frustration, "I am going to kill you, you crazy bastard!"

He couldn't believe he had missed both shots. The young bodyguard crouched and shifted to his right to gain a clear line of sight but the stairwell was in his way and as he circled around the lower fascia he caught a quick glimpse of a shadow and saw Izhutin dive to the floor, rolling catlike towards the weapon. He fired again and missed again.

"You are a lucky motherfucker, Andrei, but I will..." that's as far as he got.

Izhutin had recovered his gun and in one quick motion aimed and pulled the trigger - he didn't miss. The first bullet tore into Taras, hitting him in the chest, knocking him backwards and as he staggered trying to right himself, a second bullet blew parts of his skull away. He looked surprised, his mouth moving, struggling for words, before falling to the floor in the center of the warehouse.

Izhutin stood over the young man's body and made the sign of the cross twice, "It didn't have to be like this, Taras. You could have lived somewhere far away but fate is fucking whore. She must get paid and this time the payment was your life. God will bless your soul, my friend."

He quickly moved the two bodies to the back of the warehouse away from the road. The rear of the building bordered a small garbage dump so the stench of rotting bodies would go unnoticed and wouldn't raise suspicions. He left the big bodyguard upstairs and after a final check, opened the garage door. He made sure that there was no one in sight before driving out. He secured the place and drove away.

He stopped briefly at a gas station to fill the tank and to get something to eat. He was ravenous. He went inside to use the toilet and got a cup of coffee and a Hershey's bar and stood by the rental enjoying the chocolate and coffee, watching the cars scurrying by like ants.

"I thank you Adam; I thank you for giving me a life that is different. I have done what I could and now I will see to the next chapter. It will be interesting and that is all you can ask of this life. I will join you soon, my friend."

While crossing the Verrazzano Bridge, he tossed his gun and old cell phone into the Narrows and saluted the Statue of Liberty – this was indeed the land of the free and the home of the brave. It was not meant to be polluted by the sick sniveling cunts like Nikolai Zakirov. *God Bless America!*

He knew that it would be a year or more before they discovered the bodies. The warehouse was owned by an offshore LLC located in Nevis that would be impossible to trace. It was Shayk's idea and was being set-up for a side-business importing electronic goods from Hong Kong. All the bills were paid through an accounting firm in the Seychelles and as far as anyone knew, the business was owned by the head of a Chinese Triad.

Alexei Zakirov had no inkling of the warehouse or that it was being set-up as a separate venture - the only ones that knew about it were Shayk and Izhutin. No one, not even their wives had a clue. He smiled: *Adam Shayk was a fucking genius!*

Now, he was going to escape to Alaska to a small place called Chignik and find a cabin located on high ground. He would get himself four or five dogs, big dogs, fierce like the Ovcharka belonging to the golden haired tigress. He would make no friends and would sleep with one eye open with a pistol for a pillow and be ready for them. He was sure that within a week or a month when Andriy Dovzhenko couldn't get a hold of Nikolai, the assassins would be on his trail, hounds sniffing for blood. But he was the fox that dances in the rain and knows how to dodge the raindrops. He would wait for the hounds and show them just how wet it can get and he would wait for the call from Marylou.

A MIRACLE AT THE
BIG BOULDER

And finally the day had come for Meghan and Robbie to leave for Montana. The dinners, lunches, visitors and tearful farewells were all done and they were standing by the RV making sure all the boxes, suitcases and must-have items were accounted for when a pickup truck pulled up – it was Luke Carlson.

"I almost forgot," he said walking up to them with a big smile, "Hank had left this for you. I was to give it to you before you left."

He handed a brown envelope to Robbie.

"Open it later. I was planning to be here a bit earlier but I stopped by Maddie's place. Tony and Liz are getting the gas station ready for the reopening. He wanted to be here but he said you'd understand," Luke informed them.

"We had dinner with them last night. Maddie would be really happy," Meghan said, "Liz reminds me of her – no nonsense and tough."

"That's funny, I thought so too. It made perfect sense when Liz decided to move here and Tony quit his job," Luke explained. "He said after meeting you, *Bronson*, his words, he needed a break from the excitement and managing a gas station made for a welcome change."

"I will miss Tony," Meghan was filled with the nostalgia of leaving. "He was always there if you needed something."

"He also said that you're leaving Chase River would make it a more dreary place, Meghan. And, whenever Ryan is ready, he'd hand over the reins to him but he had the feeling that the two of you would be back before too long and that Ryan would end up being a Navy Seal or an Army Ranger… his money was on the Rangers."

"Or a Mountain Man like his father," Robbie added.

They laughed and then fell into an awkward silence not knowing what to say and yet having so much to talk about.

"How's the bowling alley coming along?" Robbie asked.

"It's coming along. You know how it is here, we march to our own beat and urgency isn't part of our DNA. But, it will get done and Tony will manage that too."

That's when Ronin came up to Luke and sniffed him thoroughly, going around his legs a few times before walking back to Robbie.

"For a moment there I though he was going to have me for a snack," Luke uttered in relief.

"He smells your puppy." Robbie noted and asked, "What have you decided to call him?"

"You're not going to believe this," Luke said with a shake of his head. "I wanted to name him Kody with a K for the Kodiak grizzlies but Allison wouldn't hear of it. I even suggested Rocky for the Rock, her favorite action hero, but she said I would be sleeping on the couch for the rest of my life if I did that."

"So? What did you name him?"

"Not me, brother, she did… she named him," Luke paused, "Allie's gone and named him Ronin!"

"What?" Robbie was genuinely surprised, "That's going to be interesting when you come up for our wedding."

"She said that we have shared almost everything else so why

not the name of our dogs. And the strangest of things is that the little mutt listens when you call him Ronin! His head perks up and he comes waddling over."

That brought a smile to all their faces and Meghan said, "We can call them Big Ronin and Little Ronin at least for a year and then it will be Old Ronin and just Ronin."

"Or something... we'll work it out," Robbie said, "We'd better get going, I'd like to make it to Montreal by this evening. We will have to take it a bit slow with the fifth wheel."

He had traded in his SUV for a 2018, Ford F250 so they could accommodate the Alpine RV. It weighed almost fourteen thousand pounds and there was no way Robbie's old Ford Expedition EL could have hauled that across the country. The RV and the truck had cost them a tidy sum, almost all the money he had won fighting Carnicke, but it gave them enough room and they didn't have to worry about bathroom stops and booking hotel rooms.

"I didn't think I'd miss Hank but with Ed and Ray gone..." Luke hesitated then said to Robbie, "I'm going to miss you, brother."

"Hey, we're going to see you soon. I will call as soon we set the date. Meghan and I want a small wedding – just family. So you had better make it or I'll fly back here and drag your sorry ass up to Montana!"

"We'll be there," Luke reassured him, "Allie and I discussed it and decided we are going to drive there with Tony and Liz."

"Five days of listening to Tony... good luck!" Robbie sniped.

"It'll be more like ten days. We're planning to do Route 66 and see some of the country."

"Invest in some earplugs! That's all I have to say."

"Don't be mean," Meghan chided but she knew that the jibes were a way of covering up how he really felt about VanArcen. Robbie had sat on the porch for a long time after they had said their goodbyes the previous night. When he finally came in he had confessed, "I'm going to miss him and his craziness."

They had gone to the cemetery the day before so Jodie could say her farewell to Angela Mercier. The young girl had spent quite a bit of time weeding and clearing the graveside of debris and making sure that it was neat and clean. They placed flowers by the headstone and said a short prayer but when it came time to leave, she burst into tears and sobbed until Ryan went over and hugged her and said in his innocent little voice, "Don't cry, Jodie, angels don't die they live forever!"

The obligatory visits were done and the goodbyes said and over with and it was time to leave. Luke helped Ryan into the RV and held the door open for Ronin and Jodie but the young girl hesitated before asking Meghan, "Can we please stop at the Big Boulder? I have to say goodbye to one more person. I have to say goodbye to Marisa. Please?"

Luke noticed the earnestness in her expression said, "It's not much of a detour. Depot will take you to Guilford and that will put you on Route 7 and get you to I-95."

They knew how much Marisa had meant to the young girl so Meghan put her arm around Jodie, "Of course we can, dear, we'll stop. Devil's Ridge is on the way."

They parked on the side of the road under the shade of a large oak and had to cross a small patch of rocky terrain and walk down a slight incline to get to the riverbank. When they arrived near the Big Boulder, Jodie unzipped her backpack and retrieved a laptop, a bundle of photographs and some letters.

She held them against her chest, "I want to bury them here. I want to leave all these bad memories behind and remember only the good times we shared. I want Marisa to be set free… to join Angela."

"I think that's a splendid idea," Robbie said to her and took her hand. They walked around together looking for a suitable place.

"Can we bury them here?" she stopped by the side of a tall pine, high enough off the river's edge.

"Sure, that's a really nice spot."

It was not far from where Robbie had found Marisa's body. It seemed like an eternity since that fateful day and incredibly, they had returned to the place where it had all begun. He dug a hole and they buried the laptop, the photographs and letters along with a jumper that was Marisa's – it symbolized a metaphorical break with Jodie's past and the dawn of a new beginning for her.

They selected a rock, a smooth, rather large rock, and placed it on top to mark the site. And as a final tribute to her friend, Jodie waded through the shallow waters and climbed onto the Big Boulder. She lay back, closing her eyes and whispered, "I'm going away, Marisa. Far away but I will never forget you. I know you are free now."

"Can I go on the rock with Jodie?" Ryan asked, tugging at his mother's arm.

"No, baby, we have to go now. Come on, Jodie, we have to get going," Meghan called out to her.

And as Jodie was about to get off of the boulder a remarkable thing happened. A passing cloud cast a long shadow over her and a sudden gust of wind rustled the leaves, stirring up dust and debris. And when it had settled, a butterfly with striking blue wings appeared skimming playfully along the water before landing on the boulder inches from the young girl's legs. Jodie sat perfectly still, her eyes wider than the headlights on an eighteen wheeler, mesmerized by the brilliance of the butterfly, sitting so close to her, flexing its wings.

The moments seemed to stretch interminably in this strange tableau of the girl and the butterfly and just then the sunshine broke free from the shackles of the cloud and surrounded them in an eerie, haloed radiance. The butterfly took its cue and rose circling around Jodie's head, inches from her face; its fluttering wings brushing her cheeks in whispered kisses before it skittered away, vanishing into the forest almost as quickly as it had appeared.

"Did you see that?" The young girl squealed in delight, "Robbie, did you see that?"

"I did. I wouldn't have believed it but… damn, I think she came to say goodbye," he couldn't conceal the amazement in his voice.

"No one is going to believe this!" Meghan was just as astonished, "That butterfly was identical to the tattoo on Marisa's ankle."

"I *know* that was Marisa coming to say goodbye! Did you see her circle my face? I know it was her!" Jodie exclaimed.

"It probably was," Robbie hesitantly agreed, "Maddie once talked about reincarnation and who knows? I'd like to believe it was Marisa."

"She came to say goodbye to all of us and to thank you, Robbie, because you found her," Jodie said before standing up on the Big Boulder. She looked around hoping to get another glimpse of the butterfly and called out to the forest, "I love you, Marisa, thank you for being my friend and for everything… goodbye, Marisa, goodbye!"

They were all caught up in the moment, in a feeling of childlike wonder in the aftermath of the miracle, for it was indeed a miracle. The incident strengthened the bonds that held this family together. If there had been any doubts about Jodie, they were gone. They knew that things were as they should be and that Jodie belonged with them and though they were different and fragmented, together they were whole.

Children are resilient and have the uncanny knack of living in the now. Jodie had Ryan by his hand and was busy planning the next phase of their lives, picking names for the horses they would get for

Rachael's farm. The past was history and her circle was complete.

For Meghan, the years of searching and disappointment were over. She had crossed the bridges of frustration and loneliness and had what she had always wanted - Robbie was hers, unequivocally hers. There were no doubt or second thoughts; he had made his choice and they were moving forward to create a family of their own. As much as she had wanted to be near her parents, Montana was the road to a new beginning.

For Robbie, the experience was more profound. He felt the presence of the spirits of those who had gone before him; his father, Maddie Wilkins, his brothers in the Army Rangers and especially those of the Renegade Brigade, of Calvin Jones and Jamie Cranston, the young men who had lost their lives in Kunduz. The guilt he carried with him had been inexplicably cleansed by the phenomenon of the butterfly. He felt liberated, something he hadn't felt in years. It took the death of a young girl to break the chains that had bound him to his past. The pieces of his shattered soul had been put back together and the glue that held them in place was the redemption he had found in Meghan Hollier.

When they got back on the road, they were quiet for a while, each lost in their own thoughts until finally Meghan broke the silence, "I wonder what Hank gave you? I could never figure that man out. There were two sides to him, two very distinct sides. I hope he finds what he's looking for."

Robbie smiled, "Go on, I know it is killing you. Open the envelope. It must be a note of some sorts saying goodbye."

"No, I can feel something else in there," Meghan said and carefully slit open the envelope.

She emptied the contents into her palm and studied them in disbelief – four sparkling stones; diamonds of the clearest and most pristine quality and each one a different size.

"They are beautiful!" she said softly, "Are they real?"

"Yeah, I think they are. Read the note," Robbie replied, "maybe there's an explanation."

She unfolded the enclosed letter and read it out loud.

"Robbie, I can never repay you for saving my life but this is a small token of my appreciation.

One is for saving a miserable person not worthy of a second chance.

Two is for my nephew, Ryan. He deserves a man he can look up to and emulate.

Three is for Meghan – you have in her the perfect mate.

And four is for the new beginning and the family you now have.

I will reinvent myself and make a life that is worthy of the second chance you gave me.

With gratitude,
Hank Carlson"

Robbie was quiet. Meghan looked at him and said, "That's a far cry from the first meeting you had with him. Do you remember?"

"Yes, I do… it was Bucky Johnston's Diner with Seppo Heikkinen and of course you, Meghan Hollier. It seems like a lifetime ago."

"You certainly had an effect on him, Robbie. Do you think that someone like him can change?"

"That's what second chances are all about – the opportunity to change. He is a man who had lost his way. We all get lost and it takes someone to give us a second chance." He thought for a moment and then continued, "You are my redemption, my love, and if you hadn't come along, I would be just as lost as Hank."

She leaned over and kissed him on his cheek, "And *you* are *my* redemption and I wouldn't trade you for all the diamonds in the world. I remember what Maddie once said when someone made a derogatory remark about Allison and her relationship with Luke. She quoted the bible: He that is without sin among you, let him first cast a stone at her."

"Amen to that," Robbie added, "Maddie was special and so much of what she prophesied has come to pass."

Meghan moved the diamonds around in her palm, rolling each one between her fingers before holding them up to the light. Even to her untrained eye the clarity of the stones were spectacular, "God, they are simply exquisite!"

"Seppo died for this. They are some of the highest quality diamonds I've seen. We can put them aside for the kids; for their education. College is expensive and I want a big family so get ready, girl!" Robbie said and smiled.

"I've been ready for a while, cowboy, I want a big family too. I was an only child and grew up being jealous of all the kids who had brothers and sisters," Meghan replied and took his hand in hers.

They had never felt closer and Robbie confided, "I came here a lost soul and found you. I'm sorry if I hurt you in any way, Meghan, with…" he paused, trying to find the right words, "with Allison but it made me realize how much I really loved and needed you."

She squeezed his hand, "I don't care, I've got you and that's all that matters to me. From the moment I saw you I was sure you were the one but if there had been any doubts on the way, they were gone when I saw how Ryan looks at you and how Jodie… she thinks the world of you. I hope your sister knows what she's in for."

"Rachael and Derek are the sweetest people you will meet. She said that the farm was growing and they could use the help and having you there would give her the sister she never had. I know we'll be happy."

"To new beginnings then," Meghan said filled with anticipation for the adventure ahead of them.

"Yes, to new beginnings and to family!" Robbie Olsen echoed. His journey back from the nightmare of Kunduz was now complete.

Six months later in Zermatt, Switzerland

Elysian Dreams

The 'Two Bells Café' was a success from the day it opened. The etymon was a play on the name Du Bellay. It was McHenry's idea when they bought a struggling pâtisserie and the souvenir shop next to it. They broke down the partitioning walls and converted it into a modern, spacious internet café with an art gallery on one side. A month later, they acquired the travel agency had been adjacent to the pâtisserie and converted that into a bookstore. The three coextensive businesses worked in conjunction to create a collaborative ambience that made for a very distinctive experience.

The business enjoyed a core base of habitués made up of young men and women in their twenties and thirties and an older demographic that came in to wander through the gallery and the bookstore. Augmenting this was the never-ending stream of tourists enticed by the free wifi, beverages and addictive pastries. It was also a comfortable space to relax and communicate with their friends and family back home.

The café was always bustling with customers and often had people queueing outside which had McHenry considering a second Two Bells Café in a different part of town.

"We will soon send Starbucks packing out of Switzerland," McHenry boasted to his wife.

"And who will run that?" Marylou asked.

"We will train some smart person," he quipped back, "maybe turn this into franchises and offer it to young entrepreneurs."

"You are a dreamer but I love that about you," she said, "I would never have thought of this. When you first brought it up, I thought the pâtisserie might work but the gallery and bookstore? I wasn't so sure."

"And that's why we make a perfect team. I have a flair for business and you, my dear, are the facilitator. Do you recall when I told you that you were a lot smarter than you give yourself credit for?"

"Yes, I do," she walked over to him and plopped herself on his lap, "but I think you know that without you, I would never have done any of this. You *are* the wind beneath my wings."

Marylou had blossomed into a charming and gracious hostess and her friendly demeanor made her a favorite among the locals. It seemed like everyone knew Annamarie Du Bellay, the pretty American lady, who ran the new pâtisserie.

It was not so with McHenry. He was a private person who rarely spoke to their neighbors or the people in town. He would, on occasion, come to the bookstore to immerse himself in his beloved antiquarian books. His favorites were those that delved into various philosophies or ones that had historical significance but other than that, he kept busy with the restoration work at the chalet. They couldn't have been more different – she was a bubbly, extrovert who loved people and enjoyed company and he, an introvert who lived in quiet solitude except for her; he was passionately in love with his wife and would do anything to keep her happy.

A few months after the grand opening, Elena Falzone, Antonio's wife, who initially helped at the café, suggested serving soups, salads and sandwiches for lunch and that too met with immediate success. It seemed that the Du Bellays had found their Shangri-La and everything they touched turned to gold.

Marylou's evolution into this version of herself was McHenry's pride and joy. He basked in his wife's achievements, encouraging her at every turn to fulfil her potential which he thought had yet to fully manifest.

"One day soon, you will run for office and win," he said, "I can see you running this entire town. We could use a pretty face instead of the dour, ugly bastards in charge now!"

"Stop dreaming. Once our baby is born, I want to be a good mother and make sure that the café is doing well. I will have no time for politics."

"You will soon find out that you can be both, a good mother and an astute business woman and when the time is right, you can also be a voice for a better Zermatt. And I mean to be a very involved father. Not like my father who was hands-off and uninterested."

"Okay, King Rene, for now, let's make sure the work in the house is done soon… I am tired of all the banging and hammering!"

"Your wish is my command. I am on top of it, my lady!"

Most of the remediation of the interior had been completed and all that was left was a large chamber located in a separate wing of the building. Once that was finished the restoration of the exterior could begin. He spent hours going over the exordial designs with the architects and the landscapers making sure that the every detail had been considered. He was meticulous and brilliant and had caught several flaws in the work that surprised even the expert masons contracted from the Zermatt Historical Register. It didn't take long for them to develop a deep respect for the diminutive American.

McHenry was a creature of habit. He would rise before the crack of dawn to go for a run and train his martial arts in the gym he had installed in the lower level of the chalet. By the time he showered and got ready for the day, Elena had his coffee waiting for him at his desk. He would spend the next hour listening to the financial news and checking on his various investments before greeting his wife with coffee in bed.

Marylou enjoyed being woken up by her husband and especially enjoyed the luxury of having her coffee in bed. She had been the caregiver at home from the time she was a young girl so this aspect of her life was one that she cherished. Once she got ready, they would have breakfast together before she left for the café.

Elena and the rest of the help had gotten familiar with their itinerary and though they respected the man of the house, with Marylou it was different; they genuinely liked her and would do anything for her. For his part, McHenry was happy that Marylou had embraced Zermatt and her position as the mistress of the house. It was everything he had hoped for.

"I'm leaving, baby," Marylou called out to her husband, "I'll be back for lunch."

"Hold on!" McHenry called back from his office, "You shouldn't be driving anymore. Let Antonio take you to work and he can hang around until you are ready to get back here."

"Yes, madam, it is better that I drive you," Antonio chimed in. He liked the new electric cars that McHenry had bought and would use any excuse to drive them into town. His favorite was the Tesla Model 3, Marylou's car, mainly because no one else had one.

Marylou scoffed, "Antonio, you're such a ham! You just want to drive the Tesla."

"That is true, I cannot deny that but I think it is getting time, madam, to let me do the driving for you," Antonio replied.

"Let him drive! He is no good for anything else now and you have to be careful as the baby grows," Elena scolded, "You do too much, madam. You need to rest."

Marylou smiled knowing that this day was coming and resigned herself to her fate. She walked into his office and leaning over her husband kissed him on top of his head, "Okay, he can drive me if it will make you feel better. But just so you know, I can still drive."

"I'm sure you can. Humor me and stop pushing yourself. Emilia can handle the café in the afternoons and that will give you a break and give us more time together."

Emilia was the daughter that Antonio and Elena had hoped could join them at the chalet and when they had approached Marylou with the request, she welcomed the young woman. Their daughter spoke perfect English and turned out to be a happy and fun-loving companion and it didn't take long before she became Marylou's favorite.

"Okay, boss-man, whatever you say. I'll see you at lunch," she kissed him again and said to the chauffeur, "Come on, Antonio, we should go."

McHenry finished his coffee and while Elena was clearing the table, said to her, "Elena, the architect will be here today so I will be going out to the cottage with them. Do you know if there is anything that needs to be done on the inside?"

The caretakers cottage was a big brick and wood building located behind the chalet and that was where Elena and Antonio resided. Unlike most caretaker cottages, it was a large house that the original owners had stayed in while the chalet was being constructed.

"No, sir, inside is very good but I am not…" she replied in English and struggled for the words before resorting to German, "I haven't looked that carefully. The door is open and you can go in."

"Are you sure you don't mind? I don't want to intrude. I can wait until Antonio comes back and have him join us." McHenry liked the couple and didn't want to impose on their privacy.

"You can go in whenever you like, Mr. Du Bellay, we do not mind," she reiterated.

"Okay then," he said and left.

He was standing by the pillars of the huge portico, when a young man who was working as the head mason's assistant came up to him and said in German and with a pronounced lisp, "Pardon me, sir, I just noticed a big crack in the back wall of the cottage."

McHenry studied the lad carefully. He had seen him work with Lukas Leuenberger, the head mason, and was impressed with his attention to detail and the level of skill he showed. He was a thin, tall lad with long brown hair and light blue eyes and very pale skin. His face was unremarkable except for the scar on the side of his chin and the slightly protruding front teeth. He literally towered over McHenry.

"What were you doing behind the cottage?" McHenry questioned.

"I had to use the toilet and it was occupied. I needed to…" he hesitated, his cheeks flushed, "I had to take a piss very badly so I went in the bushes far away from the house. I am sorry, sir, it will not happen again."

The young man seemed genuinely distressed by having to confess this.

"It's okay. In the future, come and see me and you can use one of the other toilets. You do not have to go in the bushes," McHenry said putting the young man at ease.

"Thank you, sir," the assistant replied sounding relieved, then after hesitating for a moment added, "I better get back, Master Leuenberger does not like anyone taking too much time away from the work."

He turned to go when McHenry stopped him, "I will speak to Lukas. Show me where the crack is. I am expecting the architect and his engineers shortly. I will need to show this to them."

The assistant seemed nervous and unsure, looking behind him towards the far end of the building where the stonemasons were busy at work.

"I will inform the master before we go," he answered not too happy about being caught in the middle. Though this was the owner, his boss could make his life miserable – really miserable.

The young man's insecurity irritated McHenry. His tone turned impatient and brusque, "I said I would speak to Lukas. Now, let's go. Show me where the crack is."

The assistant acquiesced immediately, "Okay, sir, as you wish."

"What is your name, boy?"

"Lars Steiner, sir."

"Okay Lars, stop worrying about Lukas and let's go and take a look."

The caretaker's cottage was about a hundred and fifty yards from the main building so they made small talk while walking there.

"Where are you from, Lars?"

"From Dusseldorf originally. My parents moved to Zermatt when I was five."

"Interesting. What does your father do?"

"He's a teacher and my mother cleans houses. I wanted to play basketball but I was not good enough for the professional league."

"Masonry, especially the kind that you are learning from Lukas, will last you a lifetime. Basketball, or any sport for that matter, is not very dependable and there is no job security. You could hurt your knee and then you would be flipping burgers!"

"Flipping burgers?" Lars questioned, puzzled by the analogy.

"Working at McDonalds for peanuts," McHenry explained.

Lars smiled, "That is also what my father said."

"Listen to you father. Life experience is invaluable."

They arrived at the cottage and Lars took the lead to the back of the building. He walked to the center, a bit to the right of the fireplace, and moved some creepers aside and pointed to a crack that ran all the way up to the top of the wall.

"Here," he said, "here it is."

McHenry came closer and examined the fault studying the jagged propagation, checking the concrete for micro-cracks and other indications of fracture. The aggregates used in older cements were mostly responsible for the age-related cracking and he wanted to make sure that the wall wasn't, in any way, compromised.

"Let's look on the inside," he mused more to himself, "this could have gone right through to the other side."

The young man walked ahead of McHenry and opened the door for him and asked, "Can I go back, sir?"

McHenry chuckled, "You are really nervous about Lukas aren't you? Calm down, let's look at the crack and you tell me what you think and let me worry about the master. Okay?"

"Okay sir," the assistant answered and followed McHenry into the house, closing the door behind him.

The interior was immaculate. The granite floors were scrubbed clean and the wooden tables and chairs in the living room, though old, were polished and well maintained. The worn leather sofas sat on a large vintage wool rug and a medium sized television set hung on the wall across from the sofas. The living room was still warm from the glowing embers in the fireplace.

McHenry walked towards the wall, "I can see a small…"

He heard a rustling sound that instantly triggered warning bells in his head. *A trap! It's a trap.* But it was too late. *Marylou, my love…*

she was his last thought. The .22 caliber bullet fired at point blank range from behind ended McHenry's life.

Lars Steiner exited the cottage and closed the door behind him. He looked casually around and satisfied that no one had heard the gunshot, quickly cut through the endemic brush of Edelweiss, Alpine Roses and Lupines and down the hillside with the ease of a mountain climber. His lanky frame was deceptive. The man was fit and nimble and moved like a large cat. When he got to the bottom, he took off his overalls, his false teeth and the wig and put them in a cloth bag he had left there. He made his way through the ubiquitous fir and pine to a car parked about half a mile away. He changed into a custom tailored suit, put on his glasses and ruffled his short hair completing the physical transformation and drove away.

He stopped near a densely wooded area about five miles from the chalet and using lighter fluid to drench the cloth bag, he set fire to his overalls and disguise. He waited a few minutes watching the flames eradicate the traces of his assumed identity before leaving. He stopped again at a small stone bridge and threw his gun with the silencer into the deeper end of the stream, then took off his latex gloves, shoved them into his pockets and drove into town.

After returning the car, he walked to the Two Bells Café, ordered a scone with coffee, found a secluded spot in the corner and dialed a number. He waited a few seconds and said, "It is done. What about the woman? I'm here and can take care of it now."

The gravelly voice answered, "I told you before. We do not make war on the innocents. You leave her alone."

"Okay."

The phone went dead.

People in town were shocked by the murder and conspiracy theories and half-baked stories ran wild. Some wondered if the killing was a random robbery gone wrong or whether a neighbor, jealous of the Du Bellay's rapid ascent to the top of the social ladder, was somehow involved. Others were convinced that the mysterious Mr. Du Bellay had crossed the wrong people in his "nefarious" business dealings and had paid for it with his life. The police, however, were taking no chances. They were looking into all the possible suspects including the beautiful Annamarie Du Bellay. But their investigations revealed no wrong doing, no huge life insurance policy or jealous lover and after interrogating the staff, crossed her off the list.

Four days later, Marylou buried her husband. She was surprised by the number of people who turned up to pay their respects and offer their condolence. Most of them were strangers but she had greeted them with the same affection and warmth reserved for family. But what surprised her most was the impact McHenry's death had on the staff – they were devastated especially Antonio Falzone. He was inconsolable and cried openly for days following the murder.

"Why? Why would anyone kill him?" Antonio lamented, "He was a quiet man who never made trouble. I should have been here. I am useless. If I had been here, none of this would have happened."

"He would have killed both of you and I would have lost my husband and the man I count on for every little thing. What good would that have done?" Marylou had tried consoling the distraught caretaker.

"I should not have left him alone. I would have seen to it that nothing happened. Mr. Du Bellay saved our lives. Who else would keep an old man like me? I don't know what to do, madam, I see his face everywhere... in the shadows, in my sleep... everywhere. I will pray for him and light candles for his soul."

She had done her best to console him and the others ignoring her own pain. The house had to function so her bereavement had to be done in private, in the hours she lay alone in bed.

After the post funeral reception, Marylou called the staff together and addressed them.

"Nothing changes. I will stay home now and supervise the renovations. I intend to fulfill my husband's wishes. Emilia, you will run the café. Take Julia or Nora to help you and report back to me. Antonio, I will need your help more than before so you need to be strong. Elena, you will manage the kitchen and the rest of you will work with Antonio and Elena to make sure that things run smoothly." She paused noticing some concern on the faces of the men, "Do any of you want to leave? I will understand if you do."

"No, madam, we have discussed this and we all want to stay with you." The sentiment was unanimous.

"I am happy to hear that. Now go about your work and finish cleaning up. Elena, I will have something very light for supper, maybe a salad."

"Leave it to me, madam, I will take care of it," Elena turned to the rest of the help, "What are you waiting for? You heard the Madam, go finish cleaning up."

Having settled matters with the staff, Marylou ventured into McHenry's office and retrieved the key to his desk. It was hidden under the arm of a life-sized statue of the Indian goddess, Parvathi. He had shown her where it was in case something unforeseen was to happen to him. The statue was one of his favorites, "She represents strength, nourishment and spirituality," he had said to her, "all the aspects necessary for a full life."

Why did you leave me, Michael? I have so much to learn and our child will now grow up without a father. Without you, I feel insecure and useless...

She unlocked the desk and opened the middle drawer under the mount and saw a large manila folder with her name on it.

"For Annamarie Du Bellay"

She smiled to herself running her fingers lightly over his neat handwriting. *It was just like him to be so organized.* She felt the tears beginning to well up but controlled her emotions and opened the folder. She carefully slid the sheets of paper out and began to read the cover page.

'If you are reading this, my darling, it means that I am no longer alive. I either died of natural causes or was killed – most probably the latter. Don't mourn for me. The time I have shared with you was more than I deserved. The bible says, and I paraphrase, the way you live is the way you will die. I have lived by the sword and can expect nothing more than to die by the same. I have no regrets and that is only because of you.

I want you to live life to the fullest. Don't waste a single day crying over me. Tell our daughter that I love her more than life itself (pretty amusing considering I am dead). I know it will be a girl and I pray that she takes after you, my love, that she is as beautiful and smart and loving. And that she is nothing like me.

Everything we own is now yours and what you need to know is in the following pages.

1. Page 1 is the contact information of Andrew Monaghan, our lawyer. He has the Will and details of our estate.
2. Page 2, 3 and 4 lists all our assets, the banks with the account numbers, the real estate holdings, the investment accounts and the contact information for Josef Steiger, our accountant. He knows everything concerning our finances and has been instructed to work with you. He is handling

the sale of the property in Litchfield. The user name and passwords for all the account are in Appendix A.

3. Page 5 is the information for Roshan Mehta. He is our accountant in the Seychelles. On page 3 you will notice that a certain amount of our assets are in gold and that is to hedge against the devaluation of the US Dollar. In that case, you will have access to a tangible form of currency. Roshan is the person to contact should you need to access the gold. The user name and password for that account is in the appendix B.

4. Page 6 lists the contact information of our brokers and their companies. Josef Steiger will work with you to manage these investments. Heed his advice - he is a shrewd and trustworthy man.

5. Page 7 is a listing of all the charities I have supported and this is the only thing I will ask of you. Please continue with the donations I have set-up. They support orphanages in Kenya, India, Thailand and Indonesia. The contact names of the people running these orphanages are listed by country. India and Kenya are close to my heart and I would advise you to visit them if you can. Before I met you, I had considered adopting a child from one of these orphanages and maybe you can find it your heart to do the same.

The rest of it will be explained to you by Andrew and Josef. If you need to meet with them, they will come to the chalet so just let them know. Remember, you are in charge. And more importantly, you have a practical and sharp mind – do not doubt yourself.

This next part is so you have some closure and is not for any act of vengeance. The people I name are very dangerous and the farther you stay away from them, the better.

The person responsible for my death is Alexei Zakirov. He is an oligarch and the head of the most powerful mob in Russia. And there is only one man who could have reached me, an assassin by the name of Henry Baker. He is English but like me, speaks several languages. I have never met him but I know of him and that Zakirov uses him for difficult assignments. Forget them and forgive me for my past indiscretions. It is that life that had resulted in my death.

Finally, I have loved you with all my heart and will continue to do so from the other side for there is life after death. Why else would a beautiful lady intervene on the behalf of Lorenzo Santos? And why else would she allow a disenfranchised and broken soul like me into her heart if not preordained by the mystical force we call God? Life is an eternal circle and we will meet again in a different life.

With love and kisses, many hundreds of them,
Your husband,
Rene Du Bellay (Michael McHenry)'

When she rifled through the pages she was astounded by the amounts in the various accounts. Her assets totaled over $50 Million dollars and that didn't account for the real estate holdings in Holland and the Seychelles. It was no wonder that they could afford to keep the chalet and the staff. She would call the lawyer and the accountant and have them come to Zermatt and she would take over where her husband left off.

Marylou placed the papers back and locked the desk. She placed the key in its secret place and touched the face of the goddess. *Why didn't you intervene?* And then it struck her: *It was meant to be, that's why.* She looked out at the imposing view of the Matterhorn and sighed. *You are wrong, my love, our child, son or daughter, will avenge you. I will make sure of that. If Zakirov is still alive and if Baker is still alive, they will pay for your death.*

That night her dreams weren't of her dead husband or Izhutin or the many men she had bedded but of Marisa. She dreamed of the butterfly on the dead girl's ankle. It had come to life floating high above the forest dancing between the words *L'amant des Papillons* and then just as strangely, a kaleidoscope of thousands, no, millions of dazzling butterflies appeared besides it, their iridescent wings lighting up the night sky, flowing between the mountain peaks like a raging river... a butterfly river.

The End

9 781737 769101